ହାତ ମୁଠାରେ ଜୀବନ

ହାତ ମୁଠାରେ ଜୀବନ

ଲଳିତ ଦାସ

BLACK EAGLE BOOKS

2021

BLACK EAGLE BOOKS

USA address:
7464 Wisdom Lane
Dublin, OH 43016

India address:
E/312, Trident Galaxy, Kalinga Nagar,
Bhubaneswar-751003, Odisha, India

E-mail: info@blackeaglebooks.org
Website: www.blackeaglebooks.org

First International Edition Published by
BLACK EAGLE BOOKS, 2021

HATAMUTHARE JEEBAN
by **Lalit Das**

Copyright © **Lalit Das**

Cover & Interior Design: Ezy's Publication

ISBN- 978-1-64560-152-4 (Paperback)

Printed in United States of America

ଉସର୍ଗ

'ଇଶାନୀ'କୁ ଆମ ପୂର୍ଣ୍ଣତାର ସୂର୍ଯ୍ୟୋଦୟକୁ।

— ପାପା

ମୋ କାହାଣୀ ପଛର କାହାଣୀ

ଭାରତୀୟ ସଂସ୍କୃତିରେ ବିବାହର ଏକ ଗୁରୁତ୍ୱପୂର୍ଣ୍ଣ ଭୂମିକା ଅଛି। ଜୀବନ ଏଠି ମୋଡ଼ ବଦଳାଏ। ପ୍ରତ୍ୟେକ ଯୁବକଯୁବତୀଙ୍କ ମନରେ ବିବାହକୁ ନେଇ ଅନେକ ସମ୍ଭାବନା ଓ ସ୍ୱପ୍ନ ଥାଏ। ମୋର ବି ଥିଲା। ମୋ ସହ ଆଦ୍ୟାଶାଙ୍କ ବିବାହ ହୁଏ ୧୯୯୪ରେ। ସେ ଇଞ୍ଜିନିୟର ଅକ୍ଷୟ ଚନ୍ଦ୍ର ରାୟ ଓ ଡ. ପ୍ରତିଭା ରାୟଙ୍କ ଥଲିଥଲୀ ଝିଅ। କିନ୍ତୁ ବିବାହରେ ଦୁଇ ମା' ଆମ ବିବାହର ନିର୍ଣ୍ଣାୟକ ଥିଲେ। ମୋ ମା' ଅନ୍ନପୂର୍ଣ୍ଣା ସାହିତ୍ୟପ୍ରେମୀ ଥିଲେ। ଶାଶୂ ପ୍ରଖ୍ୟାତ ଲେଖିକା ଏବେ ଜ୍ଞାନପୀଠ ବିଜୟିନୀ ପ୍ରତିଭା ରାୟଙ୍କର ବହି ପଢ଼ି କୋଟେବଲ କୋଟ୍‌ଗୁଡ଼ିକ ନିଜ ଡାୟରୀରେ ଟିପି ରଖୁଥିଲେ। ତେଣୁ ସେ ଏ ପ୍ରସ୍ତାବରେ ଅତ୍ୟନ୍ତ ଖୁସି ହୋଇଥିଲେ। ମୋ ପିତା ଶିକ୍ଷକ ଥିବାରୁ ମୋ ଶାଶୂ ଏ ପ୍ରସ୍ତାବଟି ପଠାଇଥିଲେ। ତାଙ୍କର ପିତା ମଧ୍ୟ ଜଣେ ପ୍ରଖ୍ୟାତ ପ୍ରଧାନଶିକ୍ଷକ ଥିଲେ। ତାଙ୍କ ମତରେ ଶିକ୍ଷକଙ୍କ ପିଲାମାନେ ଭଲ ପିଲା ହୁଅନ୍ତି। ବିବାହ ପରେ ଶ୍ୱଶୁରଘର ମୋତେ ନିଜ ଘର ଭଲି ଲାଗେ। ଶ୍ୱଶୁରଘରେ ସବୁବେଳେ ସାହିତ୍ୟ, ସଂଗୀତର ଚର୍ଚ୍ଚା ହୁଏ। ଆଦ୍ୟାଶା ସେତେବେଳକୁ ଜଣେ ଜଣାଶୁଣା ଗାୟିକା। ଆଦ୍ୟାଶାଙ୍କ ଘରର ପରିବେଶରୁ ଅନୁପ୍ରାଣିତ ହୋଇ ୧୯୯୧ ମସିହାରେ ନିଜ ପୋଲିସ ଅଭିଜ୍ଞତାରୁ ଗଞ୍ଜଟିଏ ଲେଖିଥିଲି। 'ଜୀବନରଙ୍ଗ' ପତ୍ରିକାରେ ମୋର ପ୍ରଥମ ଗଞ୍ଜ ପ୍ରକାଶ ପାଇଥିଲା ପୂଜାସଂଖ୍ୟାରେ। ଆଜି ମୁଁ ଜୀବନରଙ୍ଗର ସଂପାଦକ ସ୍ୱର୍ଗୀୟ ରଣଧୀର ଦାସଙ୍କୁ ଭକ୍ତିସହକାରେ ସ୍ମରଣ କରୁଛି। ବିଜୟିନୀ ମାଉସୀଙ୍କୁ ପ୍ରଣାମ କରୁଛି। ସେହି ଗଞ୍ଜଟି ମା' ପ୍ରତିଭା ରାୟଙ୍କ ଦ୍ୱାରା ଆଦୃତ ହୋଇଥିଲା। ପତ୍ନୀ ମଧ୍ୟ ସାବାସି ଦେଇଥିଲେ। ଶ୍ୱଶୁର ଅକ୍ଷୟ ଚନ୍ଦ୍ର ରାୟ ଇଞ୍ଜିନିୟର ଥିଲେ ମଧ୍ୟ ସାହିତ୍ୟର ଆଦର କରୁଥିଲେ। ତାଙ୍କଠାରୁ ବି ଉତ୍ସାହ ମିଳିଲା। ମୋର ବଡ଼ ଭଉଣୀ ବାଗେଶ୍ୱରୀ, ବଡ଼ ଭାଇ-ଭାଉଜ, କଲ୍ୟାଣ, ଶୁଭ୍ରା, ସାନଭଉଣୀ ଗୀତିକା ଏବଂ ରାଗେଶ୍ୱରୀ ମୋର ଗଞ୍ଜଗୁଡ଼ିକ ପଢ଼ି ଆନନ୍ଦିତ ହୁଅନ୍ତି ଓ ସେମାନେ ନିଜେ ଗଞ୍ଜର ପସରା ପାଲଟି ଯାଆନ୍ତି। ସବୁ ମିଶି

ମୋତେ ପ୍ରେରଣା ମିଳିଥିଲା ଆଗକୁ ଗଳ୍ପ ଲେଖିବା ପାଇଁ। କିନ୍ତୁ ବ୍ୟସ୍ତ ପୋଲିସ ଜୀବନ ଭିତରେ ଲେଖାଲେଖି ହୋଇପାରିଲା ନାହିଁ। ୨୦୧୪ରେ ମାନାଲିରୁ ଲେହ ଏବଂ ୨୦୧୫ରେ ଭୁବନେଶ୍ୱରରୁ ଭୁଟାନ୍ ପର୍ଯ୍ୟନ୍ତ ଆମ ସାଇକେଲ ଗ୍ରୁପ୍‌ର ସାଇକେଲ ଯାତ୍ରା ହୋଇଥିଲା। ସେତିକିବେଳେ ହିମାଳୟର ଅସୀମତା ଓ ସୌନ୍ଦର୍ଯ୍ୟ ଭିତରେ ଆମେ ସବୁ ଆମ୍ବିଭୋର ହୋଇଯାଇଥିଲୁ। ମୋ ମନରେ ଅନେକ ଭାବନା ଉଦୟ ହୋଇଥିଲା। ସେହି ଯାତ୍ରାରୁ ଫେରି କେତୋଟି ଗଳ୍ପ ଲେଖା ହୁଏ। 'ନୀଳକଣ୍ଠ' ପତ୍ରିକାରେ ସୁସ୍ମିତା ଦାସ ପୂଜାସଂଖ୍ୟାରେ ବର୍ଷକୁ ଗୋଟିଏ ଗଳ୍ପ ଛାପନ୍ତି। ତେଣୁ ବର୍ଷକୁ ଅନ୍ତତଃ ଗୋଟିଏ ଗପ ଲେଖିବାକୁ ହୁଏ। ଶାଶୁ ପ୍ରତିଭା ରାୟ ସବୁବେଳେ ଗପଗୁଡ଼ିକୁ ଆପ୍ରିସିଏଟ୍ କରନ୍ତି। ସେଥିରେ ମୋର ମନୋବଳ ବଢ଼ିଯାଏ। ଆଦ୍ୟାଶା ମଧ୍ୟ ଗପ ପଢ଼ି ଖୁସି ହୁଅନ୍ତି। ତେଣୁ ଏହି କ୍ଷୁଦ୍ରଗଳ୍ପ ସଂକଳନ ପଛରେ ପ୍ରତିଭା ରାୟ ଏବଂ ଆଦ୍ୟାଶା ଦାସଙ୍କ ଅନେକ ପ୍ରେରଣା ଓ ଅବଦାନ ରହିଛି। ମୋ ମା' ଓ ବାପା ଛୋଟବେଳୁ ଓଡ଼ିଆ ଗପ ଓ କାହାଣୀ ପଢ଼ୁଥିଲେ ଓ ଆମକୁ ପଢ଼ିବାକୁ କହି ଲେଖକ ହେବାର ବୀଜ ବୁଣୁଥିଲେ ଆମ ଭାଇଭଉଣୀଙ୍କ ମନରେ। ପୋଲିସ ଚାକିରି ଭିତରେ ଗାଢ଼ିକ ଭାବରେ ଶାଶୁଙ୍କ ସାଙ୍ଗରେ ପ୍ରତିଯୋଗିତାରେ ପାରିଲି ନାହିଁ। ତାହା ବି ଏକପ୍ରକାର ଆନନ୍ଦ। ଆନନ୍ଦ ନ ମିଳିଲେ କେହି ଗଳ୍ପ ଲେଖେ ନାହିଁ। ମୋ ଭିତରେ ଭାବନାର ଯେତେ ଉଦ୍ବେଳନ ହୁଏ, ସେତେ ପ୍ରକାଶ କରିବା ସମ୍ଭବ ହୁଏ ନାହିଁ। ପ୍ରାୟ ସବୁ ଲେଖକଙ୍କର ସେହି ଅବସ୍ଥା ହେଉଥିବ। ମୋ ବାପା ମୋ ଗଳ୍ପ ପଢ଼ି ଆନନ୍ଦିତ ହୋଇଛନ୍ତି। ମାତ୍ର ମୋ ମା' ମୋ ଗଳ୍ପ ପଢ଼ିବାର ସୁଯୋଗ ପାଇନାହାନ୍ତି। ଟିକିଏ ଆଗରୁ ଲେଖିଥିଲେ ବୋଧେ ଭଲ ହୋଇଥାଆନ୍ତା। ଆଜି ଏହି ଗଳ୍ପ ସଂକଳନଟି ପ୍ରକାଶପାଇବା ବେଳକୁ ସେମାନେ କେହି ନାହାନ୍ତି।

ଆମର ଏକମାତ୍ର କନ୍ୟା '**ଇଶାନୀ**' ହେଉଛି ଆମ ପୂର୍ଣ୍ଣତାର ସୂର୍ଯ୍ୟୋଦୟ। ସେ ମୋର ଗେହ୍ଲା ଝିଅ। ତେଣୁ ତା' ହାତରେ ଏହି ଗଳ୍ପଗୁଚ୍ଛକୁ ଉତ୍ସର୍ଗ କରିଛି। ଏହା ମୋର ଚରମ ଆନନ୍ଦ। ସୁଦୂର ଆମେରିକାରୁ ସତ୍ୟବାବୁ ଉତ୍ସାହ ପ୍ରଦାନ କରିଆସିଛନ୍ତି। କହିବାକୁ ଗଲେ ସଂକଳନଟି ପଠାଇବା ପାଇଁ ମୋ ଉପରେ ରୂପ ପକାଇଛନ୍ତି। ବହିଟିକୁ ସେ ଛାପିବାକୁ ଆଗ୍ରହ ପ୍ରକାଶ କରିଥିବାରୁ ମୁଁ ତାଙ୍କ ପାଖରେ ଚିରଋଣୀ। ଶେଷରେ ଯେଉଁ ସାଙ୍ଗସାଥୀ, ସାଇପଡ଼ିଶା, ସାଇକେଲଗସ୍ତରେ ଭେଟିଥିବା ଅନେକ ବ୍ୟକ୍ତି, ଯେଉଁମାନେ ମୋ ଗଳ୍ପର ଚରିତ୍ର ହୋଇଯାଇଛନ୍ତି ସେମାନଙ୍କ ପାଖରେ ମୁଁ କୃତଜ୍ଞ।

ଲଳିତ ଦାସ

ତା.୨୪.୦୭.୨୦୨୧ରିଖ

ସୂଚିପତ୍ର

ହାତ ମୁଠାରେ ଜୀବନ

ମନାଲିରୁ ସୁଦୂର ଲେହ ସହରକୁ ଦୀର୍ଘ ସାଇକେଲ ଯାତ୍ରାର ଅଦମ୍ୟ ସାହସ ଧରି ବାହାରିଛି ଆଶୀର୍ବାଦ ପଟ୍ଟନାୟକ, ଦଳର ସର୍ବକନିଷ୍ଠ ସଦସ୍ୟ। ନିଜର ବ୍ୟବସାୟରୁ ପନ୍ଦରଦିନର ଅବ୍ୟାହତି ନେଇ ଘରସଂସାର ଝଞ୍ଜାଳରୁ ମୁକ୍ତ ହୋଇ ନିଜ ସହିତ ଟିକିଏ ଏକାନ୍ତ ମୁହୂର୍ତ୍ତ କଟାଇବେ ବୋଲି ଆଶା କରିଛି। ଭୁବନେଶ୍ୱର ଏୟାର୍‌ପୋର୍ଟ‌ରେ ଶ୍ରୀମତୀମାନେ ହାତ ହଲାଇ ବିଦାୟ ଜଣାଇଲେ। ସୁଟ୍‌କେଶ୍‌ରେ ସାଇକେଲ୍ ଚଲାଇବାର ସମସ୍ତ ସରଞ୍ଜାମ ସହ ଗରମ ପୋଷାକ ଓ ରେନ୍‌କୋଟ୍ ମଧ ଭର୍ତ୍ତି କରାଯାଇଛି। ତା' ସହ ମୋବାଇଲ ଫୋନ, ପାୱ୍ଵାର ବ୍ୟାଙ୍କ, ଏଲ୍‌ଇଡି ଟର୍ଚ୍ଚ, ସାଇକ୍ଲିଂ ସର୍ଟସ୍ ଓ ଜର୍ସି ଓ ଜରୁରୀ ଔଷଧପତ୍ର, ଚକୋଲେଟ୍ ମଧ ଭର୍ତ୍ତି କରିଦେଇଛନ୍ତି ସହଧର୍ମିଣୀ ଶାନ୍ତି। ଆଶୀର୍ବାଦ ଯେତିକି ଅସ୍ଥିର, ଶାନ୍ତି ସେହିମାତ୍ରାରେ ସ୍ଥିର ଓ ଶାନ୍ତ। ହିମାଳୟର ଅନିଷ୍ଠିତ ଜଳବାୟୁରେ ଯେକୌଣସି ମୁହୂର୍ତ୍ତରେ ବର୍ଷା କିମ୍ବା ତୁଷାରପାତ ହେବାର ସମ୍ଭାବନା ଥାଏ। ଆଶୀର୍ବାଦଙ୍କର ଗୋଟିଏ ନରୱେଜିଆନ୍ କୋଟେସନ୍ ମନେ ପଡ଼ିଲା – 'ନୋ ଓ୍ଵେଦର୍ ଇଜ୍ ବ୍ୟାଡ, ଓନ୍‌ଲି ୟୋର୍ କ୍ଲୋଦିନ୍

ଇଜ୍ ବ୍ୟାଡ୍ ।' ତେଣୁ ଥାଟର ଗ୍ଲୋବ୍, ଥର୍ମାଲ୍ ଗ୍ଲୋବ୍, କଳାଚଷମା, ରବରଜୋତା, ସ୍ପୋର୍ଟ୍ ଜୋତା, କାନବନ୍ଧା ମଫ୍ଲର୍, ଶୁଖିଲା ଓଠ ପାଇଁ କ୍ରିମ୍ ଇତ୍ୟାଦି ଗୋଟି ଗୋଟିକରି ସୁଟ୍‌କେଶରେ ରଖିଛନ୍ତି ଶାନ୍ତି ।

ଭୁବନେଶ୍ୱରରୁ ଦିଲ୍ଲୀ ଯିବେ ଉଡ଼ାଜାହାଜରେ । ପୁଣି ଦିଲ୍ଲୀରୁ ମନାଲି ଯିବେ ହିମାଚଳ ଟୁରିଜିମ୍ ବସରେ । ଏୟାରପୋର୍ଟ କାଉଣ୍ଟରରେ ଚେକ୍‌ଇନ୍ ଓ ସିକ୍ୟୁରିଟି ଚେକ୍ ପରେ ନିଜ ହାତରେ ସାକ୍ସାଫୋନ୍ ବ୍ୟାଗ୍‌ଟିକୁ ଧରିଲେ । ସାକ୍ସାଫୋନ୍ ବଜାଇବାରେ ଆଶୀର୍ବାଦଙ୍କର ବହୁତ ସଉକ । ତେଣୁ ଯୁଆଡ଼େ ଯାଆନ୍ତୁ ସାକ୍ସାଫୋନ୍ ସାଙ୍ଗରେ ନେଇଥାନ୍ତି । ବିମାନର ପାଖ ସିଟ୍‌ରେ ବସିଥିବା ଝିଅଟି ଅଙ୍କଲ ବୋଲି ସମ୍ବୋଧନ କଲା । ଆଶୀର୍ବାଦଙ୍କୁ ଆଦୌ ଭଲ ଲାଗିଲା ନାହିଁ । ବୟସଟା ଏବେ ଟିକେ ଜଣାପଡ଼ିଲାଣି କି ? ତାଙ୍କ ଭିତରେ ସବୁବେଳେ ଚଳଚଞ୍ଚଳ ଯୁବକଟିଏ ଥାଏ । ବୟସ ଗୋଟାଏ କ'ଣ ? ଡାହାଣ ହାତରେ ଦୁଇଟି ଧଳା ଲୋମକୁ ଦେଖି ମନକୁ ମନ ହସିଲେ । ଟୋକିଟା ତାଙ୍କୁ ଅଙ୍କଲ ଡାକିଲେ ଡାକୁ । କିଛି ଯାଏ ଆସେ ନାହିଁ । ସେ ତ ଜାଣିନାହିଁ ଯେ ଆଶୀର୍ବାଦ ଏ ବୟସରେ ୧୭୦୦୦ଫୁଟ୍ ଉଚ୍ଚ ହିମାଳୟରେ ସାଇକେଲ୍ ଚଳାଇବେ । ଅନେକ ଗଭ୍ଡ଼ା ଟୋକା ମଧ୍ୟ ଏ କାମକୁ ପାରିବେ ନାହିଁ । ମନକୁ ମନ ସାନ୍ତ୍ୱନା ଦେଲେ ଏବଂ ଏୟାର ହୋଷ୍ଟେସ୍‌ଙ୍କ ଗୋଟିଏ କପ୍ ବ୍ଲାକ୍ କଫି ମାଗିଲେ । ଆଖିବନ୍ଦ କରି ହିମାଳୟ କଥା ଭାବିଲେ । ୨୦୧୪ ମସିହାରେ ମନାଲିରୁ ଲେହ ପର୍ଯ୍ୟନ୍ତ ପ୍ରଥମଥର ସାଇକେଲ୍ ଯାତ୍ରା ଆରମ୍ଭ କରିଥିଲେ । ମାତ୍ର ଲେହ ପହଞ୍ଚିବାର ୧୫୦କିଲୋମିଟର ପୂର୍ବରୁ ତାଙ୍କର ବ୍ଲଡ୍‌ପ୍ରେସର ପାଙ୍ଗଠାରୁ ବଢ଼ିଗଲା ଏବଂ ରକ୍ତରେ ଅକ୍ସିଜେନ୍ ୭୦କୁ କମିଗଲା । ତେଣୁ ଆର୍ମୀ ଡକ୍ତରଙ୍କ ପରାମର୍ଶକ୍ରମେ ଆଗକୁ ସାଇକେଲ୍ ଚଳାଇବା ବନ୍ଦ ରହିଲା । ସେଥିର ସେ ତାଙ୍କର ଯାତ୍ରା ସମାପ୍ତ କରିପାରି ନଥିଲେ । ମନରେ ଅବସୋସ ରହିଯାଇଥିଲା । ଏଥର କିନ୍ତୁ ସେ ରୀତିମତ ପ୍ରାକ୍ଟିସ୍ କରିଛନ୍ତି । ଜିମ୍‌ରେ ବହୁତ ସମୟ ଏକ୍‌ରସାଇଜ୍ କରି କୋର୍ ଷ୍ଟ୍ରେନ୍ଥ ବଢ଼ାଇଛନ୍ତି । କହିବାକୁ ଗଲେ ସେ ଏଥର ଜଣେ ଭେଟେରାନ୍ ସାଇକ୍ଲିଷ୍ଟ ଭାବେ ଯାଉଛନ୍ତି । ମାତ୍ର ବୟସ ଯେ ଏ ଭିତରେ ଋଚିବର୍ଷ ବଢ଼ି ଯାଇଛି ! ଦେଖାଯାଉ ହିମାଳୟ ଏଥର କି ପ୍ରକାର ଆହ୍ୱାନ ଦେଉଛି ! ଆଖିବୁଜି ସବୁ ଭାବୁଥିଲେ ଆଶୀର୍ବାଦ । ଏ ଭିତରେ ସେ ଝିଅଟି ତାଙ୍କ କାନ୍ଧକୁ ଆଉଜି ନିଶ୍ଚିନ୍ତ ନିଦରେ ଶୋଇପଡ଼ିଛି । ଆଶୀର୍ବାଦ ଭାବିଲେ ଝିଅଟି ନିଶ୍ଚୟ ତାଙ୍କ ଭିତରେ ଅଙ୍କଲ ହେବାର ସବୁ ଗୁଣକୁ ବାରିପାରିଛି ।

ଦିଲ୍ଲୀରେ ଓହ୍ଲାଇ କନ୍‌ନଟ୍ ସର୍କଲ ପାଖରେ ମଣ୍ଡିହାଉସରୁ ଭାଲ୍‌ଭୋ ବସରେ ବସି ମନାଲିକୁ ଋଲିଲେ । ବସରେ ଗୋଟିଏ ଝିଅ ଭାଇ ବୋଲି ଡାକି ୫ର୍କ ପାଖ

ସିଟ୍ ମାଗିଲା। ଆଶୀର୍ବାଦ ଖୁସୀ ହୋଇ ତାକୁ ନିଜ ସିଟ୍ ଦେଇଦେଲେ। ହିମାଳୟ ଯେତେ ନିକଟତର ହେଉଛି ତାଙ୍କୁ ସେତେସେତେ ଯୁବକ ଭଳି ଲାଗୁଛି। କଥାରେ କହନ୍ତି– ହିମାଳୟରେ ଯିଏ ରହେ, ତା'ର ବୟସ ଦଶବର୍ଷ କମିଯାଏ। ଉଡ଼ାଜାହାଜରୁ ଓହ୍ଲାଇ ବସ୍‌ରେ ବସିବା ଭିତରେ ସେ ଅଙ୍କଲ୍‌ରୁ ଭାଇ ହୋଇସାରିଲାଣି। ହିମାଳୟରେ ପହଞ୍ଚିଲେ ଆଉ ଯେ କ'ଣ ନହେବ ଭାବି ଆଶୀର୍ବାଦ ନିଜ ଭିତରେ ଚଞ୍ଚଳତା ଅନୁଭବ କଲେ। ହିମାଳୟରେ ହୋଟେଲ୍ ହିଲ୍‌କ୍ୱିନ୍‌ରେ ରହିବା ବେଳେ ସେ ନିଜକୁ ଯୁବରାଜ ବୋଲି ମନେକଲେ। ପୁନେରୁ ଆସିଥିବା ଆଉଜଣେ ସର୍ବକନିଷ୍ଠ ସାଇକ୍ଲିଷ୍ଟଙ୍କ ସହିତ ତାଙ୍କର ପରିଚୟ ହେଲା। ସମୁଦାୟ ୧୧ଜଣ ସାଇକ୍ଲିଷ୍ଟ ଏହି ସାଇକେଲ ଯାତ୍ରାରେ ସାମିଲ୍ ହୋଇଥିଲେ। ଦଳର ଲିଡର ଅଭିଜିତ୍ ସମସ୍ତଙ୍କୁ ଗୋଟିଏ ପ୍ରାରମ୍ଭିକ ଭାଷଣ ଦେଲା। ପାହାଡ଼, ପର୍ବତରେ ନିଜର ନିରାପଭା ପ୍ରତି କିପରି ଧ୍ୟାନ ଦେବ ତାହା ବୁଝାଇଲା। ରାସ୍ତାରେ ଉପରୁ ପଥର ଖସିପାରେ, ମାଟି ଅଥଡ଼ା ଓ ବରଫ ଅଥଡ଼ା ବି ଖସିପାରେ। ସମସ୍ତେ ନିଜ ବ୍ୟାଗରେ ଟର୍ଚଲାଇଟ୍ ଓ ରେନ୍‌କୋଟ୍ ସହିତ ଦୁଇଦିନର ସରଞ୍ଜାମପତ୍ର ଧରିବା ପାଇଁ ପରାମର୍ଶ ଦେଲେ। ତା' ସହିତ ଗୋଟିଏ ଇଣ୍ଡେମ୍‌ନିଟି ବଣ୍ଡ ମଧ୍ୟ ସାଇନ୍ କରାଇନେଲେ। ଅର୍ଥାତ୍ କୌଣସି କାରଣବଶତଃ ଅଭିଯାନ ସମୟରେ ମୃତ୍ୟୁ ହେଲେ ଏକ୍‌ପେଡିସନ୍ ଲିଡର ଦାୟୀ ନୁହନ୍ତି। ସବୁ ଆଉଭେନ୍‌ଚର୍ ଟ୍ରିପ୍‌ରେ ଏହା ଏକ ଫର୍ମାଲିଟି। ଆଶୀର୍ବାଦ ମନେ ମନେ ଭାବିଲେ ଶାନ୍ତି ଏ ସବୁ କଥା ଜାଣିଥିଲେ ଆଦୌ ସାଇକେଲ ଯାତ୍ରା ପାଇଁ ଅନୁମତି ଦେଇ ନଥାନ୍ତେ। ଆଶୀର୍ବାଦଙ୍କୁ ଗୋଟିଏ ମିଡିୟମ୍ ଫ୍ରେମ୍‌ର ମାଉଣ୍ଟେନ୍ ବାଇକ୍ ମିଳିଲା। ସ୍କଟ୍ କମ୍ପାନୀର ସାଇକେଲ – ଦାମ୍ ନିଶ୍ଚୟ ୬୦ହଜାର ଟଙ୍କା ହୋଇଥିବ। ଆଶୀର୍ବାଦ ସିଟ୍‌ର ଉଚ୍ଚତା ଇତ୍ୟାଦି ଆଉଜଷ୍ଟ କରିନେଲେ। ଆଗରେ ତିନୋଟି ଓ ପଛରେ ନଅଟି ଗିଅରବାଲା ସାଇକେଲ। ସାଇକେଲଟି ବେଶ୍ ଗଡ଼ିଲା। ଆଶୀର୍ବାଦ ସାଇକେଲରୁ ଓହ୍ଲାଇ ସାଇକେଲକୁ କିସ୍ କଲେ ଓ ଆଉଁଶିଲେ। ଆଗାମୀ ଦଶଦିନ ପାଇଁ ଏହି ବାହନଟି ହେଉଛି ତାଙ୍କର ସାଥୀ। ଜୀବନ ମୃତ୍ୟୁ ତା'ରି ଉପରେ ନିର୍ଭର କରେ। ଆଶୀର୍ବାଦ ବିଶ୍ୱାସ କରନ୍ତି ଯେ ନିର୍ଜୀବ ପଦାର୍ଥର ମଧ୍ୟ ଜୀବନ ଅଛି। ସେମାନେ ସମସ୍ତଙ୍କର ମନକଥା ବୁଝନ୍ତି, ଦୁର୍ଘଟଣାରୁ ରକ୍ଷା କରନ୍ତି। ବାଟରେ ପଞ୍ଚର ନ ହୋଇ ଘରକୁ ଫେରିଆସି ପଞ୍ଚର ହୁଅନ୍ତି। ଏହିପରି ଅନେକ ଅଜେନିଭା ଅନୁଭୂତି ଆଶୀର୍ବାଦଙ୍କର ରହିଛି।

ଅଗଷ୍ଟ ଦୁଇ ତାରିଖରୁ ଯାତ୍ରା ଆରମ୍ଭ ହେବ ଏବଂ ଅଗଷ୍ଟ ୧୧ରେ ଲେହ ସହରରେ ପହଞ୍ଚିବାକୁ ହେବ। ମନାଲୀ ସହର ସମୁଦ୍ରପତନଠାରୁ ଛଅହଜାର ଫୁଟ ଉଚ୍ଚରେ ଅବସ୍ଥିତ। ପ୍ରଥମଦିନ ସେମାନେ ମନାଲୀରୁ ଯାତ୍ରା ଆରମ୍ଭ କରି ବାରହଜାର

ଫୁଟ ଉଚ୍ଚରେ ଥିବା ରୋହତଙ୍ଗ ପାସ୍ ପାଖରେ ରହିବେ। ଦ୍ୱିତୀୟ ଦିନ ରୋହତଙ୍ଗ ପାସ୍ ଦେଇ ଏକ ସୁନ୍ଦର ଗାଁରେ ରହିବେ। ତୃତୀୟ ଦିନ ଚଉଦହଜାର ଫୁଟ ଉପରେ ଥିବା ବିଶ୍ୱପ୍ରା ଗାଁରେ ରହିବେ। ଚତୁର୍ଥ ଦିନ ଜିଙ୍ଗ୍‌ଜିଙ୍ଗ୍‌ ବାରରେ ରହିବେ। ପଞ୍ଚମଦିନ ଆହୁରି ପନ୍ଦରହଜାର ଫୁଟ ଉଚ୍ଚରେ ଥିବା ବାର୍ଲାଚଲା ପାସ୍ ଅତିକ୍ରମ କରି ସାରଚୁଠାରେ ରହିବେ। ଷଷ୍ଠଦିନ ସାରଚୁରୁ ଗୋଟିଏ ବଡ଼ ପର୍ବତ ଉପରେ ଥିବା ୧୬ହଜାର ଫୁଟ ଉଚ୍ଚରେ ନଟିଲା ପାସ୍ ପାରିହେଲେ ପାଙ୍ଗଠାରେ ପହଞ୍ଚିବେ। ଗତଥର ପାଙ୍ଗଠାରେ ଆଶୀର୍ବାଦଙ୍କର ଯାତ୍ରା ସମାପ୍ତ ହୋଇଥିଲା। ଏଥର କିନ୍ତୁ ସେ ଆଖୁ ଭିଡ଼ିଛନ୍ତି ଯାତ୍ରା ସମାପ୍ତ କରିବେ ଲକ୍ଷ୍ୟସ୍ଥଳରେ। ସପ୍ତମଦିନ ପାଙ୍ଗଠାରୁ ଯାଇ ଏକ ଲମ୍ୟ ଉପତ୍ୟକାଠାରେ ସମତଲରେ ଥିବା ଦବରିଂଠାରେ ରହିବେ। ଅଷ୍ଟମଦିନ ସବୁଠୁ ଉଚ୍ଚା ଟାଙ୍ଗଲାଙ୍ଗରା ପାସ୍ ୧୭ହଜାର ୫ଶହ ଫୁଟ ଅତିକ୍ରମ କରି ରୁସେସୋରୁ ଯାଇ ରହିବେ। ନବମ ଦିନ ରୁସେସୋରୁ ବାହାରି ଲେହରେ ପହଞ୍ଚିବେ। ଦଶମଦିନ ଲେହରୁ ଯାଇଥିବା ପୃଥିବୀର ସବୁଠୁ ବିପଜନକ ରାସ୍ତା ଖାରୁହବାଲାରେ ପହଞ୍ଚିବେ ଯାହା ୧୮ହଜାର ଫୁଟ ଉଚ୍ଚରେ ଅବସ୍ଥିତ। ସେଠାରେ ସାଇକେଲ ଧରି ପହଞ୍ଚିବା ପରେ ସମସ୍ତ ଅଭିଯାତ୍ରୀଙ୍କୁ ଗୋଟିଏ ଲେଖାଏଁ ପଦକ ମିଳିବ ବୋଲି ଅଭିଜିତ୍ କହିଲେ। ସମସ୍ତେ ପେଟପୂରା ଖାଦ୍ୟ ଖାଇବେ ଏବଂ ଖାଇବା ସହ ପ୍ରଚୁର ପାଣି ପିଇବାକୁ ଅଭିଜିତ୍ ଉପଦେଶ ଦେଲେ। କାରଣ ଯେତେ ଉପରକୁ ଉଠିବ, ବାୟୁମଣ୍ଡଳରେ ଅମ୍ଳଜାନର ମାତ୍ରା ସେତେ କମିବ। ଫଳରେ ସାଇକ୍ଲିଂ କରିବା ପାଇଁ କଷ୍ଟ ହେବ ଓ ଶ୍ୱାସପ୍ରଶ୍ୱାସ ବାଧାପ୍ରାପ୍ତ ହୋଇପାରେ। ସମସ୍ତେ ମନଖୁସିରେ ଉତ୍ସାହର ସହ ଯାତ୍ରା କରିବା ପାଇଁ ଉପଦେଶ ଦେଲେ। ପ୍ରଥମରୁ ଏ ସବୁ ବିପଦକଥା ଭାବି ଭୟଭୀତ ହେଲେ ଯାତ୍ରା ବ୍ୟାହତ ହୋଇପାରେ। କାରଣ ଖୁସି ମନରେ ପାହାଡ଼, ପର୍ବତର ସୌନ୍ଦର୍ଯ୍ୟ ଉପଭୋଗ କରି, ସେମାନଙ୍କୁ ସମ୍ମାନ ଦେଇ ଯାତ୍ରା କଲେ ଯାତ୍ରା ସଫଳ ହୁଏ। ମୁଁ ଯାହା କରୁଛି ବା କହୁଛି ସେଇଟା ଠିକ୍ ବୋଲି ଭାବି ଯାତ୍ରାପଥରେ ଯୁକ୍ତିତର୍କ କରିବା ଉଚିତ୍ ନୁହେଁ। ବହୁତ ସ୍ଥାନରେ ଟେଣ୍ଟରେ ଶୋଇବାକୁ ପଡ଼ିବ ଏବଂ ଶୀତରୁ ରକ୍ଷା ପାଇବା ପାଇଁ ସ୍ଲିପିଂ ବ୍ୟାଗ୍ ଭିତରେ ଶୋଇବାକୁ ପଡ଼ିବ। ପ୍ରତିଦିନ ସକାଳ ୭ଟାରେ ପ୍ରସ୍ତୁତ ହୋଇ ବାହାରିବାକୁ ପଡ଼ିବ। ସବୁବେଳେ ଦୁଇଜଣ ମିଶିକରି ରହିବେ। ପାହାଡ଼, ପର୍ବତରେ ଏକା ଏକା ସାଇକେଲ ଚଲାଇବା ମନା। କାରଣ ପାହାଡ଼ରୁ ଖସିପଡ଼ିଲେ ଉଦ୍ଧାର ପାଇଁ ପାଖରେ କେହି ନଥିବେ। କାହାକୁ ଖବର ମଧ ମିଳିବ ନାହିଁ। ଏକମାତ୍ର ମହିଳା ସାଇକ୍ଲିଷ୍ଟ ଆଶୀର୍ବାଦଙ୍କ ଯୋଡ଼ି ଭାବରେ ମୂଳରୁ ରହିଛି। ଦୁଇଜଣଙ୍କ ମଧ୍ୟରେ ତାଳମେଳ ଖୁବ ଭଲ। ଦୁଇଜଣଙ୍କର ସାଇକେଲ ଚାଳନାର

ବେଗ ପ୍ରାୟ ସମାନ। ଆଉ ଦୁହିଁଙ୍କର ବ୍ୟକ୍ତିତ୍ୱରେ ମଧ ବେଶ୍ ସାମ୍ୟ ଅଛି। ଦୁହେଁ ଚୁପ୍‌ଚାପ୍‌। ମାତ୍ର ଗୋଟିଏ ତାରତମ୍ୟ ଅଛି – ବୟସର। ଆଶୀର୍ବାଦଙ୍କଠାରୁ ପଲ୍ଲବୀ ପ୍ରାୟ ପନ୍ଦରବର୍ଷ ସାନ। ସେ ଆଶୀର୍ବାଦଙ୍କୁ ଦାଦାଭାଇ ବୋଲି ଡାକନ୍ତି। ପ୍ରଥମ ତିନିଦିନ ଖୁବ୍‌ ଭଲରେ ସାଇକ୍ଲିଂ ହେଲା। ପାଗ ଖୁବ୍ ଅନୁକୂଳ ରହିଲା। ରୁପା ରଙ୍ଗର ଖରା, ନୀଳ ଆକାଶ, ଖଣ୍ଡି ଖଣ୍ଡି ଧଳା ବଉଦ ତା'ସାଙ୍ଗକୁ ବରାଫାବୃତ ପର୍ବତଶିଖର ଏବଂ ତୁଷାର ନଦୀରୁ ଝରିଆସୁଥିବା ଶୁଭ୍ର ଝରଣା। ବାଇଗଣୀ ଓ ହଳଦିଆ ରଙ୍ଗର ପାହାଡ଼ୀ ଫୁଲରେ ମନଲୋଭା ଉପତ୍ୟକା ଉସ୍ନାହ ବଢ଼ାଇଦେଲା। ପ୍ରକୃତିପ୍ରିୟ ଆଶୀର୍ବାଦ ଏ ସବୁ ଉପଭୋଗ କରି ସାଇକେଲ ଚଲାଉଥାନ୍ତି ଓ ମଝିରେ ମଝିରେ ଓହ୍ଲାଇପଡ଼ି ଫଟୋ ଉଠାଉଥାନ୍ତି। ବେଳେବେଳେ ପଲ୍ଲବୀ ଆସି ପାଖରେ ଠିଆ ହୋଇଯାଏ। ଆଶୀର୍ବାଦ ଭାବୁଥାନ୍ତି ଯଦି ପର୍ବତ ତା' ଛାତିରେ ରାସ୍ତା କରିବା ପାଇଁ ଅନୁମତି ଦେଇ ନଥାନ୍ତା, ତେବେ ଏପରି ପର୍ବତକୁ ଅତିକ୍ରମ କରିବାଟା ଅସମ୍ଭବ ହୋଇଥାନ୍ତା। ପର୍ବତ ମା' ଭଳି ଛତି ଚିରି ପିଲାମାନଙ୍କୁ ବାଟଚଲା ଶିଖାଇଛି ଏବଂ ସ୍ନେହମୟ ସୌନ୍ଦର୍ଯ୍ୟରେ ସେମାନଙ୍କ ମନ ଭୁଲାଇ ନେଉଛି। ଆଶୀର୍ବାଦ ଲକ୍ଷ୍ୟକଲେ ଯେ ତାଙ୍କର ସାଙ୍ଗମାନେ ବହୁତ ଉପରକୁ ଉଠିଗଲେଣି ଏବଂ ତଳୁ ବେଶ୍ ଖର୍ବ ଦିଶୁଛନ୍ତି। ତାଙ୍କର ଟିକିଏ ଈର୍ଷା ହେଲା। ସେ ପଛେଇ ଯାଇଛନ୍ତି କି? ତାଙ୍କ ଗୋଡ଼ରେ କ'ଣ ଶକ୍ତି କମ୍? ପୁଣି ଭାବିଲେ ଦିନ ଶେଷରେ ସମସ୍ତେ ସେହି ଗୋଟିଏ ଜାଗାରେ ପହଞ୍ଚିବେ ଓ ସେହି ଗୋଟିଏ ଟେଣ୍ଟରେ ଶୋଇବେ। ଏହି ପଦଯାତ୍ରା ଠିକ୍ ଜୀବନଭଳି। ଆଗପଛ ହୋଇ ପହଞ୍ଚି ସମସ୍ତେ ଗୋଟିଏ ସ୍ଥାନରେ ଶୋଇପଡ଼ିବେ। ଗୋଟିଏ ଟ୍ରକ୍ ପଛରେ ଲେଖା ହୋଇଥିଲା– ନିର୍ଦ୍ଦିଷ୍ଟ ସମୟ ପୂର୍ବରୁ ଏବଂ ଭାଗ୍ୟରେ ଲେଖା ହୋଇଥିବା କଥାଠାରୁ ଅଧିକ କିଛି ମିଳେ ନାହିଁ। କିଏ ଟିକେ ଆଗ ତ କିଏ ଟିକେ ପଛ। ଆଉ ପଛଲୋକ ପଛରେ ବି ଆହୁରି କିଛି ଲୋକ ଅଛନ୍ତି। କାହା ଉପରେ ଈର୍ଷା କଲେ ନିଜର କ୍ଷତି। ଭଗବାନ୍ କାହାର ଉଚିତ୍ ପ୍ରାପ୍ୟରୁ କାଣିଚାଏ ଊଣା କରନ୍ତି ନାହିଁ। କେବଳ ଧୈର୍ଯ୍ୟର ଆବଶ୍ୟକତା ଅଛି। ଆଶୀର୍ବାଦ ପ୍ୟାଡେଲ ମାରିବାରେ ମନ ଦେଲେ। ଉଦ୍ୟମ ବା ଧୈର୍ଯ୍ୟ ହରାଇବା ତାଙ୍କ ଜାତକରେ ନାହିଁ। ପ୍ରତିଟି ପେଡାଲରେ ଛାତି ଧଡ଼ଧଡ଼ ହେଉଥିଲା। ଜଙ୍ଘର ମାଂସପେଶୀରେ ଓ ନିଶ୍ୱାସ ନେବାରେ କଷ୍ଟ ମଧ ହେଉଥିଲା। ମାତ୍ର ଅଧାରାସ୍ତାରେ ଅଟିକଗଲେ ଯିବେ କୁଆଡ଼େ? ତାଙ୍କୁ ତ ଘରକୁ ଫେରିବାର ଅଛି! ରାସ୍ତାକଡ଼ରେ ଲେଖାଯାଇଥିଲା, 'ଆଜି ଯଦି ଚେଷ୍ଟା କରିବ ତେବେ କାଲିକୁ ତୁମେ ଶକ୍ତିଶାଳୀ ହେବ।'

'ସଂସାରରେ କୌଣସି ପରିଶ୍ରମ ବୃଥା ଯାଏନାହିଁ।' ଏଥର ସେ ଯଥେଷ୍ଟ ପରିଶ୍ରମ

କରି ଅଭ୍ୟାସ କରିଛନ୍ତି। ତାଙ୍କର ଗୀତାର ସେହି ଶ୍ଳୋକ ମନେପଡ଼ିଲା। - କର୍ମଣ୍ୟେ ବାଧିକାରସ୍ତୁ, ମା' ଫଳେଷୁ କଦାଚନ। ଯେମିତି ହେଲେ ଲକ୍ଷ୍ୟସ୍ଥଳରେ ପହଞ୍ଚିବାକୁ ହେବ। ହିମାଳୟରେ ରହି ସେ ମଧ୍ୟ ସାଧୁସନ୍ତଙ୍କ ଭଳି ଭାବିବା ଆରମ୍ଭ କରିଦେଲେ। ହିମାଳୟ ପ୍ରକୃତରେ ଦେବଭୂମି ଓ ସନ୍ତଭୂମି। ଏତିକିବେଳେ ସାଇକେଲ୍ ଆଗକୁ ଶଅଁବାଲୁଆଟିଏ ମାଡ଼ିଆସିଲା। ଆଶୀର୍ବାଦ ବ୍ରେକ୍ ମାରି ହ୍ୟାଣ୍ଡେଲକୁ ମୋଡ଼ି ବିଚରାକୁ ବଞ୍ଚାଇଦେଲେ। ସେ ତା' ବାଟରେ ଯାଉଛି, ତମେ ତାକୁ ମାରିବା ଅଧିକାର ନାହିଁ। ନିଜ ଅଜାଣତରେ ଆମେ କେତେ ପାପ କରିଥାଉ! ହଜାର ହଜାର କୀଟପତଙ୍ଗ ଆମ ଗାଡ଼ିଚକା ତଳେ ପ୍ରାଣ ହରାଉଥିବେ। ମାତ୍ର ଜାଣତରେ ଏପରି ପାପ କରିବା କଥା ନୁହେଁ। ସମସ୍ତଙ୍କର ବଞ୍ଚିବାର ଅଧିକାର ଅଛି।

ହଠାତ୍ ଯାଉ ଯାଉ ପାହାଡ଼ ଉପରୁ ଗୋଟାଏ ପଥର ଖସିଆସିଲା। ସେ ହଠାତ୍ ବ୍ରେକ୍ ମାରିଲେ। ପ୍ରଥମ ଓ ଦ୍ୱିତୀୟ ପଥର ଖସିବାର ଫାଙ୍କରେ ବାହାରି ପଳାଇଲେ। ହିମାଳୟ ପର୍ବତ ଆଜି ମଧ୍ୟ ବଢ଼ି ଚାଲିଛି। ଏଠାରେ ପଥର ଖସିବା ଓ ଅତଡ଼ା ଖସିବା ଗୋଟାଏ ସାଧାରଣ କଥା। ଈଶ୍ୱର ମାରନ୍ତି ଏବଂ ରକ୍ଷା ବି କରନ୍ତି। ନଚେତ୍ ଆଜି ଗୋଟାଏ ପଥରମାଡ଼ରେ ପ୍ରାଣ ଯାଇଥାନ୍ତା? ଆଶୀର୍ବାଦ ପଛକୁ ଋହିଁଲେ, ପଲ୍ଲବୀ ବଡ଼ ଆରାମରେ ସାଇକେଲ ଚଲାଉଥାଏ। ତା' ଉପରେ ପଥର ଖସୁନାହିଁ। ହୋଇପାରେ ଯେ ସେ ପାର୍ବତୀଙ୍କ ଅଂଶରୁ ଯାତ ଏବଂ ତା' ଭିତରେ ଶକ୍ତି ବିରାଜିତ। ଆଶୀର୍ବାଦ ଭାବିଲେ ବୋଧହୁଏ ଶଅଁବାଲୁଆଟାକୁ ବଞ୍ଚାଇଥିଲେ ବୋଲି ଈଶ୍ୱର ତାଙ୍କ ଜୀବନ ବଞ୍ଚାଇଦେଲେ। ବାଟରେ କିଛି ମେଣ୍ଢା ଚରାଲି ତାଙ୍କୁ ଅତିକ୍ରମ କଲେ। ମେଣ୍ଢା ଦଳରେ କିଛି କୁକୁର ମଧ୍ୟ ଥାଆନ୍ତି। ସେମାନେ ମେଣ୍ଢାମାନଙ୍କୁ ଏପଟସେପଟ୍ ଯିବାକୁ ଦିଅନ୍ତି ନାହିଁ। ଘଉଡ଼ାଇ ଆଣି ଦଳରେ ମିଶାଇ ରଖନ୍ତି। ଆଶୀର୍ବାଦ ବେତାଳ ଭଳି ଭାବିଲେ ଆମ ମନ ସବୁବେଳେ ଚଳଚଞ୍ଚଳ। ମାତ୍ର ବିବେକ ମେଣ୍ଢାଦଳର କୁକୁର ଭଳି। ମନକୁ ଟାଣିଆଣି ଠିକ୍ ବାଟରେ ଚଲାଇଥାଏ। ମେଣ୍ଢାଚରାଲି ପିକା ଟାଣି ଟାଣି ଆରାମରେ ଋହିଥାଏ। କାନ୍ଧରେ ଗୋଟିଏ ବନ୍ଧୁକ। ଆଦିତ୍ୟ ତାଙ୍କୁ ପଚରିଲେ "ବନ୍ଧୁକ କାହିଁକି ରଖିଛ?"

ବ୍ୟକ୍ତିଜଣକ କହିଲେ "ପାହାଡ଼ି ଚିତାକୁ ଘଉଡ଼ାଇବା ପାଇଁ ଏହା ଦରକାର।" ଆଶୀର୍ବାଦ ମେଣ୍ଢା ଚରାଲିକୁ ପ୍ରଣାମ କଲେ। ଏତେ କଷ୍ଟସାଧ୍ୟ ପରିବେଶରେ ବିନା ଦ୍ୱିଧାରେ ବାଟ ଅବାଟରେ କାମ କରିଚାଲୁଛନ୍ତି, ମାତ୍ର ଆମେମାନେ ଟିକିଏ ଅଧିକ ଥଣ୍ଡା କିମ୍ୱା ବର୍ଷା ହେଲେ ମନ କଷ୍ଟ କରୁଛୁ। ଏମାନଙ୍କୁ ଦେଖିଲେ ଜୀବନର କୌଣସି ଅଭିଯୋଗ ଯଥାର୍ଥ ନୁହେଁ ବୋଲି ମନେ ହୁଏ।

ଆଗରେ ପାହାଡ଼ୀ ଝରଣାଟିଏ ରାସ୍ତା ଉପରେ ବହିଯାଉଥାଏ। ଦିନରେ ବରଫ ତରଳି ଅଧିକ ସ୍ରୋତ ଥାଏ। ଆଦିତ୍ୟ ସାଇକେଲରୁ ଓହ୍ଲାଇଲେ। ଜୋତା ମୋଜା କାଢ଼ିଲେ। ସାଇକେଲକୁ ଧରି ପାଣିରେ ପଶିଲେ। ବରଫ ପରି ଥଣ୍ଡା ପାଣି। ଗୋଡ଼ ବଧିର ହୋଇଯାଉଥାଏ। ପାଣି ତଳ ପଥରରେ ଗୋଡ଼ ଖସିଯାଉଥାଏ। ସର୍କସର ଦଉଡ଼ି ଉପରେ ଚାଲିବା ଭଳି ଭାରସାମ୍ୟ ରକ୍ଷାକରି ସେ ଚାଲୁଥିଲେ। ଆଗରେ ଗୋଟିଏ ବଡ଼ ଗାତ, ସେ ପଡ଼ି ଯାଉ ଯାଉ ସମ୍ଭାଳି ନେଲେ। ସାଇକେଲ ଭାସି ଯାଉଥାନ୍ତା। ତେଣୁ ସାଇକେଲକୁ କାନ୍ଧରେ ଧରିଲେ। ଜୀବନ ସହ ଅବିରତ ସଂଗ୍ରାମ। ଗୋଡ଼ ବଧିର, କାନ୍ଧ ଉପରେ ଭାର, ଶ୍ୱାସପ୍ରଶ୍ୱାସ ପ୍ରଖର। ଛାତି ଧଡ଼ଧଡ଼। ପାହାଡ଼ୀ ସ୍ରୋତ ତାଙ୍କ ଗୋଡ଼କୁ ଖୁବ୍ ଜୋରରେ ଠେଲି ଦେଉଥାଏ। ସାଇକେଲଟି କାନ୍ଧରେ ଥାଇ ହସୁଥାଏ। କାରଣ ଚଢ଼ାଳିଙ୍କ କାନ୍ଧରେ ସେ ଏବେ ଚଢ଼ୁଛି। ଜୀବନଟା ଏମିତି। ଆଶୀର୍ବାଦ ସାଇକେଲରେ ବସିବାକୁ ମନକଲେ। ତାଙ୍କର ମନକଥା ବୁଝିପାରି ବେତାଳ ଭଳି ସାଇକେଲ କାନ୍ଧରେ ଥାଇ କହିଲା, "କେବେ କେବେ ନିଜ ଶ୍ରୀମତୀଙ୍କୁ ଏମିତି କାନ୍ଧରେ ବୋହିବାର କଥା। ତେବେ ଯାଇ ଜୀବନର ଶ୍ରମ ଲାଘବ ହେବ।" ଝରଣା ପାରି ହେବା ପରେ ଶୁଷ୍କିଲା ପଥରରେ ଆଶୀର୍ବାଦ ଛିଡ଼ା ହେଲେ। ଗୋଡ଼ ପୂରା ନାଲି ଓ ନିର୍ଜୀବ। କେମିତି ଯେ ଟାଇଟାନିକ୍ ବୁଡ଼ିଲା ବେଳେ ସେ ଥଣ୍ଡାପାଣିରେ ଲୋକେ ବଞ୍ଚିଲେ ତାହା ସେ ଭାବିପାରିଲେ ନାହିଁ। ଆମେ ଗ୍ରୀଷ୍ମତାପରେ ଜନ୍ମ ହୋଇଥିବା ଲୋକେ ହିମ ଅଞ୍ଚଳରେ ଠକ୍‌ଠକ୍‌ ମରିଯିବା। ଧନ୍ୟ ସେ ବ୍ରିଟିଶ ଓ କାନାଡ଼ାର ଲୋକ। ବରଫରେ କେମିତି ବଞ୍ଚୁଛନ୍ତି ଈଶ୍ୱରଙ୍କୁ ଜଣା। ଆମେ ଲୁଙ୍ଗି ଗାମୁଛା ପିନ୍ଧା ଲୋକଙ୍କୁ ବରଫାଞ୍ଚଳ ପ୍ରାଣାନ୍ତକ କଷ୍ଟ। ଆଖିରୁ ଦି'ଟୋପା ଲୁହ ଗଡ଼ିପଡ଼ିଲା। ଲୁହକୁ ପୋଛି ନେବା ପାଇଁ ପାଖରେ ପଲ୍ଲବୀ ମଧ୍ୟ ନଥିଲା। ଆର୍ମିର ଦୁଇଟା ବଡ଼ଚକାବାଲା ଗାଡ଼ି ଆରାମରେ ପାଣିରେ ପଶି ବାହାରିଗଲା। ବାରାଲାବାଲା ପାସ୍ ପରେ ଗୋଟିଏ ବଡ଼ ଗଡ଼ାଣି। ସମସ୍ତେ ଆଗପଛ ହୋଇ ଗଡ଼ାଣି ଗଡ଼ୁଥାନ୍ତି। ସାଇକେଲର ବେଗ ପାଖାପାଖି ଘଣ୍ଟାକୁ ୪୦ରୁ ୫୦କିଲୋମିଟର। ହଠାତ୍ ଆଗରେ ଦୁଇଟା ସାଇକେଲ ଭାରସାମ୍ୟ ହରାଇ ବ୍ରେକ୍ ମାରିଲେ। ଆଶୀର୍ବାଦଙ୍କ ଆଗଚକ ଯାଇ ଲାଗିଲା ପଛଚକ ସହ। ସେ ପାରୁ ପର୍ଯ୍ୟନ୍ତ ଚେଷ୍ଟା କଲେ ଭାରସାମ୍ୟ ରକ୍ଷା ପାଇଁ। ସାଇକେଲ ଦୋହଲିଗଲା। ରାସ୍ତାକଡ଼ରେ ପ୍ରଚଣ୍ଡ ଖାଇ। ପଡ଼ିଗଲେ ହାତଗୋଡ଼ ଚୁନା। ସେ ଜୋରରେ ଚିକ୍କାର କଲେ। ଭାଗ୍ୟବଶତଃ ସାଇକେଲଗୁଡ଼ିକ ଦୂରକୁ ଗଡ଼ିଗଲା ଏବଂ ପଛରୁ ତିନିଜଣ ପଡ଼ିଯିବାରୁ ବଞ୍ଚିଗଲେ। ସେ ଭାବିଲେ– ଜୀବନରେ ଅନ୍ୟର ଭୁଲ୍ ପାଇଁ ଆମକୁ କ୍ଷତି ସହିବାକୁ

ପଡ଼େ। ନିଜର ଭୁଲ୍ ପାଇଁ କ୍ଷତି ସହିବାରେ କିଛି ଯଥାର୍ଥତା ଅଛି। କିନ୍ତୁ ଅନ୍ୟର ଭୁଲ୍ ପାଇଁ କାହିଁକି କ୍ଷତି ସହିବ? ସେ ବୁଝିପାରିଲେ ଯେ ସମସ୍ତେ ସାବଧାନତାର ସହ ସାଇକ୍ଲିଂ କଲେ କାହାକୁ କିଛି ବିପଦ ପଡ଼ିବ ନାହିଁ। ମାତ୍ର ତାଙ୍କ ଦଳର ଜଣେ ବରିଷ ସଦସ୍ୟ କହିଲେ, "ଜଣେ ଭୁଲ୍ କଲେ ସମସ୍ତଙ୍କୁ ବିପଦର ସମ୍ମୁଖୀନ ହେବାକୁ ପଡ଼ିବ। କାରଣ ଆମେ ଗୋଟିଏ ପରିବାରର। 'ବସୁଧୈବ କୁଟୁମ୍ବକମ୍' ଆମ ସଂସ୍କୃତିର ଆବଶ୍ୟକ। ଆଶୀର୍ବାଦ ସାଇକେଲକୁ ସ୍ୱାଣ୍ଟ ମାରିଲେ ଏବଂ ଟିକିଏ ପାହାଡ଼ ଆଡ଼କୁ ଢ଼ଳିଗଲେ ସକାଳର ନିତ୍ୟକର୍ମ ସାରିବା ପାଇଁ। ତଳିପେଟର କଷ୍ଟକୁ ଅଧା ଉଶ୍ୱାସ କରିଛନ୍ତି କି ନାହିଁ, ଉପରୁ ମାଟି ଅଠା ଖସିବାକୁ ଲାଗିଲା। ଆଶୀର୍ବାଦ ସେହି ଅବସ୍ଥାରେ ଦୂରକୁ ଦଉଡ଼ି ପଳାଇଲେ। ଜୀବନଟା ତ ବଞ୍ଚିଗଲା, ମାତ୍ର ତାଙ୍କ ସାଇକେଲ ଓ ତାଙ୍କ ଭିତରେ ଗୋଟିଏ ଭୂସ୍ଖଳନ ହୋଇଯାଇଛି। ଦୁହେଁ ବଞ୍ଚିଯାଇଛନ୍ତି। ମାତ୍ର ସାଇକେଲ ପାଖରେ ପହଞ୍ଚିବାକୁ ଗଲେ ତାଙ୍କୁ ପାହାଡ଼ ଉପରକୁ ଚଢ଼ି ଗଡ଼ାଣିରେ ଗଡ଼ିବାକୁ ପଡ଼ିବ। ଭାଗ୍ୟକୁ ବ୍ୟାଗ୍‌ଟି କାନ୍ଧରେ ଅଛି ଏବଂ ଗୋଟିଏ ରାତି ବଞ୍ଚିଯିବା ପାଇଁ ଅତ୍ୟାବଶ୍ୟକ ସାମଗ୍ରୀ ଅଛି। ସେ ଟିକେ ବିଚଳିତ ହେଲେ, କିନ୍ତୁ ନିଜକୁ ସମ୍ଭାଳିନେଲେ। ଭାବିଲେ – ବିପଦ ସମୟରେ ବିବ୍ରତ ହେଲେ ବିପଦ ବଢ଼ିଯାଏ। ଢୋକେ ପାଣି ପିଅ ସେ ପାହାଡ଼ ଚଢ଼ିଲେ। ମାତ୍ର ସେତେବେଳକୁ ସନ୍ଧ୍ୟା ନଈଁଲାଣି। ଗୋଟିଏ ପଥର ଖୋପରେ ବସି ବିଶ୍ରାମ ନେଲେ। ବ୍ୟାଗରୁ ପଲିଥିନ୍ କାଢ଼ି ତଳେ ପାରିଲେ। ବ୍ୟାଗରୁ ସର୍ଭାଇଭାଲ୍ କିଟ୍ କାଢ଼ି ସେଥିରୁ ଗୋଟିଏ ମହମବତି ଓ ସିଗାରେଟ୍ ଲାଇଟର କାଢ଼ିଲେ। ରାତିଟା ଏହିଠାରେ ହିଁ କଟାଇବାକୁ ପଡ଼ିବ। ମହମବତିକୁ ପଥରସନ୍ଧିରେ ଖୋସିଲେ। ଲାଇଟର୍ ଜଳାଇ ମହମବତି ଲଗାଇଲେ। ମହମବତିର ଆଲୋକ ପାହାଡ଼ୀ ଅନ୍ଧାରକୁ ତାଙ୍କ ପାଖରୁ ଦୂରେଇ ଦେବାରୁ ମନରେ ସାହସ ଆସିଲା। ବ୍ୟାଗରୁ ଗ୍ଲୋବ୍‌ସ ଓ ଜ୍ୟାକେଟ୍ କାଢ଼ି ପିନ୍ଧିଲେ। ଏୟାର ପିଲୋକୁ ଫୁଙ୍କି ମୁଣ୍ଡତଳେ ଦେଇ ଶୋଇଲେ। ଆପାଦମସ୍ତକ ଗୋଟିଏ ଲୟ। ପଲିଥିନ ଘୋଡ଼ିହୋଇ ଶୋଇବାକୁ ଚେଷ୍ଟା କଲେ। ଖାଇବାକୁ ଇଚ୍ଛା ନଥିଲା। ଅଛ କିଛି କାଜୁବାଦାମ୍ ଅଛି, ଅଧା ବୋତଲ ପାଣି ଅଛି। ଆକାଶକୁ ଋହିଁଲେ। ତାରାମାନେ ପାହାଡ଼କୁ ଖାତିର ନ କରି ଚରାଚରିତ ଢଙ୍ଗରେ ମିଟ୍ ମିଟ୍ ହସୁଥିଲେ। ଘଡ଼ି ଦେଖିଲେ। ସମୟ ସନ୍ଧ୍ୟା ୭ଟା ବାଜିଥାଏ। ଦଶଘଣ୍ଟା ପରେ ସୂର୍ଯ୍ୟ ଉଠିବ, ସେ ପର୍ଯ୍ୟନ୍ତ ଏହିଠାରେ ହିଁ କଟାଇବାକୁ ପଡ଼ିବ। ସମ୍ପୂର୍ଣ୍ଣ ଏକା। ଗୋଟିଏ ପର୍ବତ ଶିଖର ହିଁ ସାଥୀ। ଘରକଥା ମନେପଡ଼ିଲା। ଚନ୍ଦ୍ର ନଥିବା ଆକାଶରେ ଶାନ୍ତିକ୍ ମୁହାଁଟା ଦିଶିଗଲା। ଶାନ୍ତିକ୍ ମୁହଁ ଦିଶିବାରୁ ସେ କାନ୍ଦି ପକାଇଲେ। କିଏ କହୁଥିଲା ଏ ସବୁ

କରିବା ପାଇଁ। ଅସ୍ଥିର ମନ ଘରେ ବସିବାର ଅଭ୍ୟାସ ନାହିଁ। କେତେବେଳେ ସ୍ତ୍ରୀ ପିଲାଙ୍କ କଥା ଭାବିବାକୁ ବେଳ କାହିଁ? ସବୁବେଳେ ଖାଲି ଆଡ୍‌ଭେନ୍‌ଚର। ଘରକୁ ଫେରିଲେ ଶାନ୍ତିକୁ ବହୁତ ଗେଲ କରିବେ ବୋଲି ସ୍ଥିର କଲୋ। ମାତ୍ର ଯେତେ ଯାହା କଲେ ବି ସମୟ କଟୁ ନଥାଏ। ଘଡ଼ି ଦେଖି ଦେଖି ୮ଟା, ୯ଟା, ୧୦ଟା ବାଜିଲା। ଅଧରାତିରେ ଟୋପାଏ ଟୋପାଏ ବରଫ ପଡ଼ୁଥାଏ। ଆଶୀର୍ବାଦ ମୁହଁ ଘୋଡ଼ାଇ ପକାଇଲେ ପଲିଥ୍‌ନ୍‌ରେ। ନାକ ପାଖରେ ବରଫ ତରଳି ଗୋଟିଏ ଛିଦ୍ର ଦେଇ ଟିପ୍ ଟିପ୍ ନାକ ଉପରେ ଖସିଲା। ସେ ତାଙ୍କର ଭାରତୀୟ ପୋଲିସ ସେବାର ଟ୍ରେନିଂ ସମୟ କଥା ଭାବିଲେ – **When going gets tough - tough gets going** ବାକ୍ୟଟି ସେ ମନେ ରଖିଥିଲେ। ପୁନି ଭାବିଲେ ଏ କଷ୍ଟ ଦୂର ହୋଇଯିବ। ପ୍ରତ୍ୟେକ କଥା ସମୟକ୍ରମେ ଦୂର ହୋଇଯାଏ। ଧୈର୍ଯ୍ୟ ଧରିଲେ ଓ ଆଖି ବନ୍ଦ କରିଲେ ଏବଂ ଜୋର୍‌ରେ ନିଶ୍ୱାସ ନେଲେ ବାୟୁମଣ୍ଡଳରେ ଅମ୍ଳଜାନର ପରିମାଣ କମ୍। ଜୋର ଜୋର ଶ୍ୱାସପ୍ରଶ୍ୱାସ ଟ‍୍ଲିଲେ ବଞ୍ଚିବ ନ ହେଲେ ଉଠିପାରିବ ନାହିଁ। ଭାବିଲେ ସବୁ କଷ୍ଟକାମ ଏକା ହିଁ କରିବାକୁ ପଡ଼େ। ଯେତେବେଳେ ଆରାମ ଏବଂ ସୁବିଧାର ସମୟ ଥାଏ ସମସ୍ତେ ଟ‍୍ରିକଡ଼େ ମେଳ କରୁଥାନ୍ତି। କିନ୍ତୁ ନିଜର ଦୁଃଖ ପଡ଼ିଲେ ନିଜକୁ ହିଁ ସହିବାକୁ ପଡ଼େ। ଟିକିଏ ଛାଇ ନିଦ ଲାଗିଗଲା। ଭୟ, ଦୁଃଖ ଓ ବିଷାଦ ଦୂର କରିବା ପାଇଁ ନିଦଠାରୁ ବଡ଼ ସାଥୀ କେହି ନାହିଁ। ଆଖି ଖୋଲିଲା ବେଳକୁ ଆକାଶ ଟିକିଏ ଫର୍ଚ୍ଚ ହୋଇଯାଇଛି। ସେ ଉଠିବସିଲେ। ଦେଖିଲେ କୋଟା ହଲକ ବାହାରେ ପଡ଼ି ବରଫ ପାଲଟିଯାଇଛି। ତାକୁ ପିଟି ପିଟି ଭାଙ୍ଗିଲେ। ଟ‍୍ରିଆଡ଼େ ବରଫ। ପାଣି ବୋତଲଟା ମଧ୍ୟ ବରଫ ପାଲଟିଯାଇଛି। ଟିକିଏ ଦୂରକୁ ଯାଇ ନିତ୍ୟକର୍ମ କଲେ। ହାତ ସଫା କରିବାକୁ କେବଳ ବରଫ ହିଁ ଅଛି। ଦୂରରେ ପର୍ବତରେ ସୂର୍ଯ୍ୟକିରଣ ପଡ଼ିଲା। ଆଶୀର୍ବାଦ ଟିକିଏ ଟ‍୍ଲିଲେ। ସେ ଦେଖିଲେ ଯେ ବରଫ ଉପରେ ଗୋଟିଏ ପଶୁର ପାଦଚିହ୍ନ ପଡ଼ିଛି। ସେ ପଦଚିହ୍ନକୁ ଅନୁସରଣ କଲେ। ଦେଖିଲେ ତାଙ୍କ ଶୋଇବା ଜାଗାର ଟ‍୍ରିପଟେ ସେହି ପଦଚିହ୍ନ ପଡ଼ିଛି। ତାଙ୍କୁ ଭୟ ଲାଗିଲା। ଗୋଟିଏ ପଶୁ କ'ଣ ତାଙ୍କ ସହ ଟ‍୍ଲୁଛି କି? ଦେଖିଲେ ପଦଚିହ୍ନଟି ତାଙ୍କ ଆଡ଼କୁ ଯାଇଛି। ସେହି ପଦଚିହ୍ନକୁ ଅନୁସରଣ କରି ଟ‍୍ଲିବାରୁ ଏକ ଗୁମ୍ଫା ପାଖରେ ପହଞ୍ଚିଲେ। ଭାବିଲେ ପଶୁଟି ବୋଧହୁଏ ରାତିରେ ତାଙ୍କୁ ପ୍ରଦକ୍ଷିଣ କରି ଫେରିଆସି ଗୁମ୍ଫା ଭିତରେ ଶୋଇଛି। ସେ ଗୁମ୍ଫା ଭିତରକୁ ଚାହିଁଲେ। କୌଣସି ଜନ୍ତୁ ନଥିଲା। ମାତ୍ର ଟର୍ଚ୍ଚ ଆଲୁଅରେ କିଛି ଗୋଟାଏ ଜିନିଷ ଚକ୍ ଚକ୍ ମାରିଲା। ଆଶୀର୍ବାଦ ଶୂନ୍ୟ ଗୁମ୍ଫା ଭିତରେ ପଶି ସେହି ଉଜ୍ଜ୍ୱଳ ପଦାର୍ଥଟିକୁ

ଉଠାଇଆଣିବେ ବୋଲି ଭାବିଲେ। ତାହା ଥିଲା ଗୋଟିଏ ହାତଘଣ୍ଟା। ଘଣ୍ଟାଟିକୁ ଟାଣିବା ବେଳେ ମାଟି ତଳୁ ଗୋଟିଏ କଙ୍କାଳର ହାତଟିଏ ବାହାରିଆସିଲା। ଆଶୀର୍ବାଦ ପଛକୁ ପଛକୁ ଡିଆଁଟାଏ ମାରିଲେ। ପୁଣି ଦେଖିଲେ ଯେ କଙ୍କାଳ ହାତରେ ଅଛି ଗୋଟିଏ ପାଣି ବୋତଲ। ପାଣି ବୋତଲକୁ କାଢ଼ି ଦେଖିଲେ ଯେ ତା' ଭିତରେ ଗୋଟିଏ କାଗଜ। ଆଦିତ୍ୟ ଘଣ୍ଟାଟିକୁ ମଧ କାଢ଼ି ଆଣିଥିଲେ। କମ୍ପିତ ହାତରୁ ଘଣ୍ଟାଟି ପଡ଼ିଯାଇ ଟିକ୍ ଟିକ୍ ରୁଳିବାକୁ ଲାଗିଲା ଏବଂ ଗୁମ୍ଫା ଭିତରେ କମ୍ପନ ସୃଷ୍ଟି ହେଲା। ଆଶୀର୍ବାଦ ଘଣ୍ଟା ଓ ପାଣିବୋତଲ ନେଇ ଗୁମ୍ଫାରୁ ବାହାରିଆସିଲେ। ବାହାରେ ଫର୍ଚା ହୋଇଯାଇଥିଲା। ଆଶୀର୍ବାଦ ପଥରକୁ ଆଉଜି ବସିପଡ଼ିଲେ ଓ ଘଣ୍ଟାକୁ ଦେଖିଲେ – ସ୍ୱିସ୍ ମିଲିଟାରୀ ଘଣ୍ଟା। ୨୦୦୬ ମସିହା ଜାନୁଆରୀ ୧୧ଟା ୩୦ ମିନିଟ୍ ସମୟ ଦେଖାଉଥିଲା। ତେବେ ସେହି ବ୍ୟକ୍ତିଟି ସେହି ନିର୍ଦ୍ଦିଷ୍ଟ ତାରିଖରେ ଗୁମ୍ଫାରେ ପଡ଼ି ଶେଷ ନିଃଶ୍ୱାସ ତ୍ୟାଗ କରିଛନ୍ତି। ବୋଧହୁଏ ବରଫ ଅତଡ଼ା ଖସିଥିବ। ତେଣୁ ଗୁମ୍ଫାରେ ଫସିଯାଇଥିବ। ହୁଏତ ବରଫ ଗୁମ୍ଫା ଉପରେ ବହଳ ଆସ୍ତରଣଟିଏ ସୃଷ୍ଟି କରିଥିବ ଓ ବରଫ ତରଳିବା ପାଇଁ ସମୟ ଲାଗିଥିବ। ବ୍ୟକ୍ତିଜଣକ ସେହି ସମୟ ଭିତରେ ଗୁମ୍ଫାରେ ଶ୍ୱାସରୁଦ୍ଧ ହୋଇ ପ୍ରାଣ ହରାଇଥିବେ। ଆଶୀର୍ବାଦ ବୋତଲ ଭିତରୁ କାଗଜଟି କାଢ଼ିବା ପାଇଁ ଚେଷ୍ଟା କଲେ। କାଗଜଟି ଯନ୍ତ୍ରରେ ରୁରି/ପାଞ୍ଚ ପରସ୍ତ ଭାଙ୍ଗହୋଇ ବୋତଲରେ ରଖାଯାଇ ଠିପି ଦିଆଯାଇଥିଲା। ପୂର୍ବେ ଏମିତି ବୋତଲ ମଧରେ ସମ୍ବାଦ ରଖି ସମୁଦ୍ରରେ ଭସାଇ ଦିଆଯାଉଥିଲା। କେବେ କାହା ହାତରେ ବୋତଲ ପଡ଼ିଲେ ଲୋକେ ସମ୍ବାଦଟି ପଢ଼ି କେଉଁ ନିର୍ଜନ ସ୍ଥାନରେ ଥିବା ଲୋକର ଘର, ଅକୁହା କଥା ଜାଣିପାରୁ ଥିଲେ। ତେବେ ଏହି ବ୍ୟକ୍ତିଜଣକ କ'ଣ ଲେଖିଛନ୍ତି ? ଆଶୀର୍ବାଦ କାଗଜଟିକୁ କାଢ଼ି ଖୋଲିଲେ। ଚିଠିଟିଏ, ଲେଖାଅଛି ଇଂରାଜୀ ଭାଷାରେ –

ଓଡ଼ିଆରେ ଚିଠିଟି ଏମିତି –

ଲିସା ! ମୋ ହନି।

ମୁଁ ମୋର ଶେଷପତ୍ର ଲେଖୁଛି, କାରଣ ଏଠାରେ ମୋବାଇଲ୍ କାମ କରୁନି। ବରଫ ଅତଡ଼ା ଖସିବା ଦେଖି ମୁଁ ଗୁମ୍ଫାରେ ପଶିଗଲି। ବରଫ ଏବେ ଗୁମ୍ଫା ଉପରେ ମାଡ଼ିବସିଛି। ଗୁମ୍ଫା ଭିତରେ କିଟ୍ କିଟ୍ ଅନ୍ଧାର ଓ ଅସହ୍ୟ ଥଣ୍ଡା। ମୋବାଇଲ ଲାଇଟରେ ତୁମକୁ ଲେଖୁଛି। ଅକ୍ସିଜେନ୍ ଅଭାବରୁ ଆଉ କିଛି ଘଣ୍ଟା ପରେ ମୁଁ ମରିଯିବାଟା ନିଶ୍ଚିତ। ବୋଧହୁଏ ତୋର ଭଲ ପାଇବା ମୋତେ ଆଉ କିଛି ସମୟ ବଞ୍ଚାଇ ରଖିବ। ଜୀବନର ଶେଷ ମୁହୂର୍ତ୍ତରେ ତୁମ ସାଙ୍ଗରେ ମୁଁ ରହିପାରିଲି ନାହିଁ। ମତେ କ୍ଷମା କରିବ। କିନ୍ତୁ

ତୁମେ ଆଉଥରେ ତୁମ ମନ ପସନ୍ଦର ଯୁବକୁ ବିବାହ କଲେ ମୋ ଆତ୍ମା ଶାନ୍ତି ପାଇବ । ମୋ ଘଡ଼ି ପଛର ସ୍ୱିସ୍ ବ୍ୟାଙ୍କ ଆଲମେଟା କୋଡ୍ ଅଛି । ତୁମ ପାଇଁ ଅଶୀ ମିଲିୟନ୍ ଡଲାର୍ ଅଛି । କିଛି ଅର୍ଥ ବରଫ ଅତଡ଼ା ଖସିବା ରିସର୍ଚ ଉପରେ ଖର୍ଚ୍ଚ କରିଲେ ମୁଁ ଖୁସୀ ହେବି । କେବେ ଯଦି କୌଣସି ସହୃଦୟ ବ୍ୟକ୍ତି ଏହି କାଗଜଖଣ୍ଡକ ପାଇ ଲିସା ସହ ମୋବାଇଲରେ ଯୋଗାଯୋଗ କରିବେ ତେବେ ମୋର ଆତ୍ମା ତାଙ୍କୁ ଆଶୀର୍ବାଦ କରିବ । ଲିସାର ନମ୍ବର +୧୭୨୯୭୨୪୫୧୬ । ଲିସାକୁ ନ ପାଇଲେ ସେହି ବ୍ୟକ୍ତି ଏହି ଅର୍ଥର ଅଧିକାରୀ । ଭବିଷ୍ୟତର ପର୍ବତ ଚଢ଼ାଳିଙ୍କ ପାଇଁ କହି ରଖିଛି "ମୁଁ ଯଦି ଗୁମ୍ଫାରେ ପଶି ନଯାଇ ବାମପଟ ଝରକାକୁ ଡେଇଁ ପଡ଼ିଥାନ୍ତି ତେବେ ଜୀବନଟା ବଞ୍ଚିଯାଇଥାନ୍ତ । ଅନେକ ସମୟରେ ଆମେ ଯାହାକୁ ଜୀବନ ପାଇଁ ଆଶ୍ରା କରିଥାଉ ତାହା ହିଁ ମୃତ୍ୟୁ ହୋଇ ମାଡ଼ିବସେ । ମୋର ବିଶ୍ୱାସ ମୁକ୍ତାକାଶ ହିଁ ସବୁଠାରୁ ବିଶ୍ୱସ୍ତ ସାଥୀ ।

ପୁଣି ଆରଜନ୍ମରେ ଆମେ ଭେଟିବା ।

ଇତି

ଆଲ୍ଫ୍ରେଡ୍ ସୁଙ୍କି

ଆଶୀର୍ବାଦ ଚିଠିଟି ପଢ଼ିଲେ ଏବଂ ଘଡ଼ିଟି ହାତରେ ବାନ୍ଧିଲେ । ସେ ମୁକ୍ତାକାଶକୁ ଭକ୍ତି ସହକାରେ ରୁହେଁଲେ । ଠିକ୍ ସେତିକିବେଳେ ପାହାଡ଼ ଉପରୁ ଏପରି ଏକ ଶବ୍ଦ ହେଲା ଯେଉଁଥିରେ ଆଶୀର୍ବାଦଙ୍କ ହଁସା ଉଡ଼ିଗଲା । ପାହାଡ଼ ଉପରୁ ବରଫ ଅତଡ଼ା ଖସିବା ଆରମ୍ଭ ହେଲା । ଆଶୀର୍ବାଦ ଆଗପଛ ନ ଭାବି ଗୁମ୍ଫା ଆଡ଼କୁ ଦଉଡ଼ି ଯାଉଥିଲେ । ମାତ୍ର ରୁହେଁ ରୁହେଁ ଗୋଟିଏ ପଥରରେ ଝୁଣ୍ଟିଲେ ଏବଂ ପଛରୁ କିଏ ଯେମିତି ତାଙ୍କୁ ଶକ୍ତ ଧକ୍କା ଦେଇ ଗୁମ୍ଫାର ବାମପଟରେ ଥିବା ଝରଣା ଦିଗକୁ ଠେଲିଦେଲା । ଶହେଫୁଟ ତଳକୁ ସେ ଗଡ଼ି ଗଡ଼ି ଖସିପଡ଼ିଲେ ଝରଣାର ନରମ କୋଳରେ । ବରଫ ଅତଡ଼ା ଧୁଁଆ ହୋଇ ଗୁମ୍ଫା ଉପରଦେଇ ରୁଲିଗଲା । ନିଶ୍ଚୟ ଗୁମ୍ଫାର ମୁହଁ ବନ୍ଦ କରିଦେଇଥିବ । ଆଶୀର୍ବାଦଙ୍କ ମୁଣ୍ଡରୁ ରକ୍ତ ବାହାରୁଥାଏ । ଗୋଡ଼ ହାତ ଉଠାଇଲେ ସବୁ ଠିକ୍ ଅଛି । ଆକାଶକୁ ରୁହେଁଲେ – ନିର୍ବିକାର । ଜୀବନଟା ବଞ୍ଚିଯାଇଛି । ହାତରେ ଘଣ୍ଟା ଥିଲା । ମାତ୍ର ଚିଠିଲେଖା ଯାଇଥିବା କାଗଜଟି ହାତରୁ ଖସିଯାଇଛି । ଘଟଣାଗୁଡ଼ିକ ଏତେ ଶୀଘ୍ର ଘଟିଗଲା ଯେ ସବୁକିଛି ସ୍ୱପ୍ନ ଭଲି ଲାଗୁଥିଲା । ମାତ୍ର ସେହି ପଦଚିହ୍ନ, ହାତରେ ବନ୍ଧା ଯାଇଥିବା ଘଣ୍ଟାଟି, ଗୁମ୍ଫାରେ ପଡ଼ିଥିବା କଙ୍କାଲ ଏବଂ ହଜିଯାଇଥିବା ଚିଠିରେ ଲେଖା ହୋଇଥିବା ସନ୍ଦେଶ କେମିତି ମିଥ୍ୟା ହେବ ? ପୁଣି ଗୁମ୍ଫା ଭିତରେ ପଶି ଯାଉ ଯାଉ କିଏ ତାଙ୍କୁ ପେଲିଦେଲା ଝରଣା ଗର୍ଭକୁ – କ'ଣ ସେହି ପବିତ୍ର ଆତ୍ମା ? ଆଶୀର୍ବାଦ

ପୁନର୍ଜନ୍ମ ପାଇ ଉଠି ଛିଡ଼ାହେଲେ। ଆଉ ଗୋଟିଏ ବିସ୍ମୟ ତାଙ୍କୁ ଅପେକ୍ଷା କରିଥିଲା। ତାଙ୍କଠାରୁ ଅନତି ଦୂରରେ ପଡ଼ିଥିଲା ତାଙ୍କର ପ୍ରିୟ ସାଇକେଲ। ଅର୍ଥାତ୍ ତାଙ୍କୁ କିଏ ଯେମିତି ସାଇକେଲ ପାଖକୁ ପଠାଇ ଦେଇଥିଲା। ସେ ସେହି ଆତ୍ମାକୁ ଭକ୍ତି ଓ କୃତଜ୍ଞତା ଜଣାଇ ପ୍ରଣାମ କଲେ। ଏବେ ହାତମୁଠାରେ ଜୀବନ, ପାଖରେ ସାଇକେଲ ଏବଂ ଆଗରେ ରାସ୍ତା। ପ୍ରକୃତରେ ତାଙ୍କ ଜୀବନଟା ତାଙ୍କ ହାତମୁଠାରେ ନଥିଲା। ଥିଲା ଈଶ୍ୱରରୂପୀ ସେହି ଆତ୍ମିକ ହାତରେ। ବିଚିତ୍ର ଜୀବନ। ନିଜ ଦେହରେ ଶକ୍ତି, ସାମର୍ଥ୍ୟ ଓ ଯୌବନ ଥିଲେ ମଣିଷ ଭାବେ ତା' ଜୀବନଟା ଏବଂ ଭାଗ୍ୟ ତା'ର ହାତମୁଠାରେ ଅଛି। କିନ୍ତୁ ମଣିଷ ତା' ଜୀବନର ମାଲିକ ନୁହେଁ କି ଭାଗ୍ୟର ମଧ୍ୟ ନିୟନ୍ତା ନୁହେଁ। ଏକ ଅଦୃଶ୍ୟ ଶକ୍ତି ହିଁ ସବୁ କରି କରାଉଥାଏ।

ଆଶୀର୍ବାଦ ସାଇକେଲକୁ ଆଦର କଲେ। ଏବେ ଏହି ନିର୍ଜୀବ ବସ୍ତୁଟି ହିଁ ତାଙ୍କ ଜୀବନର ନିୟନ୍ତା। ଯେମିତି ସାଇକେଲ କହୁଥିଲା - ମଣିଷ ନିଜେ ହିଁ ରଥୀ, ନିଜେ ସାରଥି ଏବଂ ନିଜେ ଯୋଦ୍ଧା। ଜନ୍ମ ମୃତ୍ୟୁ ସତ୍ୟ। ମାତ୍ର ଆମେ ତାକୁ ଏକାଭଳି କାହିଁକି ଗ୍ରହଣ କରୁନାହିଁ? ଏକଥା କ'ଣ ସାଇକେଲ କହୁଥିଲା ନା ହିମାଳୟ କହୁଥିଲା ନା ପବନର ସ୍ୱରରେ ସେହି ଆତ୍ମା ଜୀବନମୃତ୍ୟୁର ଗୀତ ଗାଉଥିଲା!

ଲଜ୍‌ରୁ ଫ୍ଲାଇଟ୍‌ରେ ଫେରୁଥିଲେ ଆଶୀର୍ବାଦ। ଦିଲ୍ଲୀରେ ସମସ୍ତଙ୍କର ବ୍ୟାଗ୍ ଫ୍ଲାଇଟ୍‌ରୁ ଆସିଲା। ତାଙ୍କ ବ୍ୟାଗ୍‌ଟି ନାହିଁ। ସମସ୍ତେ ନିଜ ବ୍ୟାଗ୍ ନେଇ ଚାଲିଗଲେଣି। କେବଳ ଗୋଟିଏ ବାଇଗଣୀ ରଙ୍ଗର ବ୍ୟାଗ୍ ଏକାକୀ ଚୁଲୁଥିଲା। ତାଙ୍କ ବ୍ୟାଗ୍‌ର ରଙ୍ଗ ମଧ୍ୟ ବାଇଗଣୀ ଥିଲା। କେହି ଜଣେ ଭୁଲରେ ତାଙ୍କ ବ୍ୟାଗ୍‌ଟି ନେଇଯାଇଛି। ଆଶୀର୍ବାଦ ବ୍ୟାଗ୍‌ଟି ତଳକୁ ଆଣିଲେ। ବ୍ୟାଗ୍‌ର ଟ୍ୟାଗରେ ଲେଖା ଥିଲା - ମିସ୍ ଲିସା। ଏ କ'ଣ ଆଲଫ୍ରେଡ୍ ସ୍ୱିଙ୍କିର ଗାର୍ଲଫ୍ରେଣ୍ଡ ମିସ୍ ସ୍ୱିଙ୍କି? ବ୍ୟାଗରେ ତ ମିସ୍ ସ୍ୱିଙ୍କି ହିଁ ଲେଖାଥିଲା। ଆଶୀର୍ବାଦ ଦଉଡ଼ିଯାଇ ଏୟାରପୋର୍ଟ ଅଥରିଟିକୁ ଜଣାଇଲେ ଯେ ତାଙ୍କର ବ୍ୟାଗ୍ କେହି ଜଣେ ମିସ୍ ଲିସା ଭୁଲରେ ନେଇଯାଇଛନ୍ତି। ଏୟାରପୋର୍ଟ ଅଥରିଟି ସଙ୍ଗେ ସଙ୍ଗେ ମିସ୍ ଲିସାଙ୍କୁ ଫୋନ୍ କଲେ ଏବଂ କହିଲେ - "ମିସ୍ ଲିସା କ୍ଷମା ମାଗି କହିଲେ ଯେ ସେ ଭୁଲରେ ଆଉ କାହାର ବ୍ୟାଗ୍‌ଟି ନେଇଯାଇଛନ୍ତି।" ସେ ସଙ୍ଗେ ସଙ୍ଗେ ଏୟାରପୋର୍ଟ ଫେରୁଛନ୍ତି। ଦଶ/ପନ୍ଦର ମିନିଟ୍‌ରେ ପହଞ୍ଚିବେ। ଆଶୀର୍ବାଦ କର୍ତ୍ତୃପକ୍ଷଙ୍କ ସହ ଆରାଇଭାଲ୍ ଗେଟ୍‌ରେ ଅପେକ୍ଷା କଲେ। ନିଜର ବିରକ୍ତିକୁ ପ୍ରଶମିତ କରିବା ପାଇଁ ଭାବିଲେ - ଏହି ଅଘଟଣ ପଛରେ କିଛି ଉଦ୍ଦେଶ୍ୟ ଅଛି। ଏତିକିବେଳେ ଜଣେ ବିଦେଶିନୀ ମହିଳା ଆସି ପହଞ୍ଚିଲେ ଏବଂ କ୍ଷମା ମାଗିଲେ। ବ୍ୟାଗ୍‌ଟି ଆଶୀର୍ବାଦଙ୍କ ହାତକୁ ବଢ଼ାଇଦେବା ବେଳେ କହିଲେ "ଆପଣଙ୍କ ହାତଘଡ଼ିଟି ବହୁତ ସୁନ୍ଦର। ମୋ

ବୟୋଫ୍ରେଣ୍ଡଙ୍କର ଏହିପରି ଘଡ଼ି ଥିଲା। ଆଶୀର୍ବାଦ ପଚାରିଲେ "ଆପଣଙ୍କ ବୟୋଫ୍ରେଣ୍ଡଙ୍କ ନାମ କ'ଣ ଆଲ୍ଫ୍ରେଡ୍ ସୁକି ?"

ଲିସା କହିଲେ "ହଁ, କିନ୍ତୁ ଆପଣ ତାଙ୍କୁ କେମିତି ଜାଣିଲେ ?"

ଆଶୀର୍ବାଦ ଘଡ଼ିଟି ହାତରୁ ଖୋଲି ଲିସାଙ୍କୁ ଧରାଇଦେଲେ ଏବଂ ପୁରା କାହାଣୀଟି ଗୋଟିଏ ନିଶ୍ୱାସରେ କହିଦେଲେ। ଶେଷରେ କହିଲେ, "ଘଡ଼ି ପଛରେ ସୁଇସ୍ ଆକାଉଣ୍ଟ ଓ କୋଡ୍ ଅଛି। ଚିଠିରେ ଲେଖାଥିଲା ଅଶୀ ମିଲିୟନ୍ ଡଲାର୍ ଅଛି। ଆପଣ ତାକୁ ଉଠାଇନେବେ ଓ ଖର୍ଚ୍ଚ କରିବେ ଏବଂ କିଛି ବରଫ ଅତଡ଼ା ରିସର୍ଚ୍ଚରେ ଖର୍ଚ୍ଚ କରିବେ। ଚିଠିରେ ଆପଣଙ୍କୁ ଆଲ୍ଫ୍ରେଡ୍ ଅନୁରୋଧ କରିଥିଲେ ଆଉ ଏକ ମନପସନ୍ଦର ଯୁବକକୁ ବିବାହ କରିନେଲେ ତାଙ୍କ ଆତ୍ମା ଶାନ୍ତି ପାଇବ। ଆଶୀର୍ବାଦ ଏତିକି କହି ଲିସାଙ୍କଠାରୁ ବିଦାୟ ନେବାବେଳେ ଲିସା ତାଙ୍କ ହାତ ଧରିପକାଇଲେ ଏବଂ କହିଲେ "ମତେ ସେହି ଗୁଣ୍ଟା ପାଖକୁ ନେଇଯାଇପାରିବ ?"

ଆଶୀର୍ବାଦ କହିଲେ "ଲାଭ କ'ଣ ? ଆଲ୍ଫ୍ରେଡ୍ଙ୍କ କଙ୍କାଳକୁ ଦେଖି ତୁମେ କ'ଣ ଖୁସୀ ହୋଇପାରିବ ? ବରଂ ଆଲ୍ଫ୍ରେଡ୍ଙ୍କ ଭଳି ଜଣେ ଉଦାର ବ୍ୟକ୍ତିକ ଇଚ୍ଛାକୁ ସମ୍ମାନ ଦେଇ ଆଉଥରେ ଜୀବନ ଆରମ୍ଭ କଲେ ତାଙ୍କର ଆତ୍ମା ଶାନ୍ତିଲାଭ କରିବ। ଆଲ୍ଫ୍ରେଡ୍ ଚିରଦିନ ତୁମ ପାଖରେ ଯେଉଁ ରୂପରେ ଥିଲେ ସେହି ରୂପରେ ରୁହନ୍ତି। ତାଙ୍କ କଙ୍କାଳ ଦେଖାଇ ତୁମ ମନରେ ଅଯଥା ଦୁଃସ୍ୱପ୍ନ ଆଣିବାକୁ ମୁଁ ଚାହେଁନାହିଁ। ତୁମେ ଜଣେ ବିଶ୍ୱସ୍ତ ପ୍ରେମିକା। ମୋ ଦ୍ୱାରା ଆଲ୍ଫ୍ରେଡ୍ ତାଙ୍କର ଇଚ୍ଛାକୁ ତୁମ ପାଖରେ ପହଞ୍ଚାଇଥିବାରୁ ମୁଁ ଭାଗ୍ୟବାନ ମଣୁଛି। ଆଲ୍ଲା, ବିଦାୟ। ତୁମର ଫୋନ୍ ନମ୍ବରଟି ମତେ ଦିଅ। ଆମେ ପରସ୍ପରକୁ ସାହାଯ୍ୟ କରିପାରିବା। ଏକଥା ଶୁଣିଲେ ମୋର ସ୍ତ୍ରୀ ଶାନ୍ତି ନିଶ୍ଚୟ ତୁମକୁ ଦେଖା କରିବାକୁ ଚାହିଁବ।"

ଲିସାର ହସ ହସ ମୁହଁ ମଉଳିଗଲା। ସେ ଅନୁଚ୍ଚ ସ୍ୱରରେ କହିଲେ "ଓଃ, ତୁମେ ତେବେ ବିବାହିତା। ଈଶ୍ୱର ତୁମକୁ ଖୁସୀରେ ରଖନ୍ତୁ।" ପରସ୍ପରଠୁ ବିଦାୟ ନେଲେ ଲିସା ଓ ଆଶୀର୍ବାଦ। ଦୁହିଁଙ୍କ ହାତମୁଠାର ମୋବାଇଲରେ ଦୁହିଁଙ୍କ ନମ୍ବର। କେଜାଣି ଲିସାଙ୍କ ଚାହାଣିରେ କ'ଣ ଏକ ସନ୍ଦେଶ ଥିଲା ଯେ ଆଶୀର୍ବାଦଙ୍କ ଛାତିରେ ଗୋଟିଏ ଅବୁଝ। ଯନ୍ତ୍ରଣା ସୃଷ୍ଟି ହୋଇଥିଲା, ଯାହା ସେ ଶାନ୍ତିଙ୍କୁ ବା ଲିସାଙ୍କୁ କହିପାରିବେ ନାହିଁ।

ଏବେ ନିଜ ହାତମୁଠାରେ ତାଙ୍କ ଜୀବନର ଶାନ୍ତି।

ପକ୍ଷୀ ଭାଷା

ବ୍ରାହ୍ମଣୀ ନଦୀ କୂଳରେ ସାନ ଗାଁଟିଏ। ଗାଁ ପାଖରେ ଛୋଟ ଜଙ୍ଗଲଟିଏ। ଜଙ୍ଗଲରେ ରହୁଥାନ୍ତି ଦିଇଟି ଚଢ଼େଇ- ଭାରି ସାଙ୍ଗ। ଦୁଇଟି ପାଖାପାଖି ଗଛରେ ବସା ବାନ୍ଧି ପିଲାଛୁଆ ନେଇ ରହନ୍ତି। ଛୁଆଏ ପର ଲାଗିଲେ ଉଡ଼ିଯାଆନ୍ତି। ଦୁଇଜଣ ମିଶି ପରସ୍ପର ବସା ତିଆରି କରନ୍ତି ଓ ମିଳିମିଶି ଖାଇବା ଖୋଜନ୍ତି। ଦିହିଁକର ସାଥୀ ମଧ୍ୟ ଏକାଠି ମିଶି ଆହାର ଖୋଜି ବୁଲନ୍ତି। କେଜାଣି ଦିନେ କ'ଣ ହେଲା ଆଉ ଫେରିଲେନି। କୋଉ ଜନ୍ତୁ ହାବୁଡ଼ରେ ପଡ଼ିଲେ କି ବଣୁଆ ଶର ବିନ୍ଧିଦେଲା। ସେଦିନଠାରୁ ପକ୍ଷୀ ଦୁହେଁ ଆଉରି ଘନିଷ୍ଠ ସାଙ୍ଗ ହେଲେ। ସେମାନଙ୍କର ନିୟସଙ୍ଗତା ଦୂର ହୋଇଗଲା।

ସେ ଗାଁର ଲୋକମାନେ ବିପଦ ଭୋଗନ୍ତି ନାହିଁ ଏପରି ନୁହେଁ। ବିପଦ ତ ଜୀବନ ସାଥୀ। ତେବେ ବି ସେମାନେ ଶାନ୍ତିରେ ମିଳିମିଶି ରହନ୍ତି, ହସଖୁସିରେ ବଞ୍ଚନ୍ତି। ଦିନରେ ଖଟନ୍ତି, ସଞ୍ଜ ବୁଡ଼ିଲେ ଟୁଲି ନିଆଁର ଧାସରେ ଚଉତରା ଉପରେ ବସି ସଂସାରଯାକର ଗପ କରନ୍ତି। ରାତି ହେଲେ ସଅଳ ଶୋଇପଡ଼ନ୍ତି। ଦୁଃଖ ସୁଖ ବାନ୍ଧିକୁନ୍ଦି ଭୋଗନ୍ତି। ଦିନେ ସେହି ଗାଁ ଆକାଶରେ ଗୋଟେ ବଡ଼ ଚଢ଼େଇ ଘୁଁ ଘୁଁ ଉଡ଼ିଲା। ଏଡ଼େ ବଡ଼ ଚଢ଼େଇ ଗାଁ ଲୋକେ ବା ସେହି ପକ୍ଷୀ ଦୁଇଜଣ ଆଗରୁ ଦେଖ୍ନଥିଲେ। ପ୍ରକୃତରେ ସେଇଟା ଚଢ଼େଇ ନଥିଲା, ଥିଲା ଗୋଟେ

ହେଲିକପ୍ଟର-ଜଙ୍ଗଲ ଦରୋଗା କହିଲେ। ସେହି ବଡ଼ ଚଢ଼େଇଟା କିଛି ସମୟ ଚକ୍କର କାଟି ଉଡ଼ିଗଲା। ତା'ପରେ ଗାଁରେ ଜରୁରୀ ଗ୍ରାମସଭା ହେଲା। ସେ ସଭାରେ ଲୋକେ ଦୁଇଦଳ ହୋଇଗଲେ। ପ୍ରବଳ ପାଟିତୁଣ୍ଡ ଆଉ ଗଣ୍ଡଗୋଳ ହେଲା। ଏପରି ଗଣ୍ଡଗୋଳ ଏଇ ଗାଁରେ କେବେ ହୋଇନଥିଲା। ଚଢ଼େଇ ଦି'ଜଣ ସେମାନଙ୍କ କଥାରୁ ଜାଣିବାକୁ ପାଇଲେ ଯେ, ସେଠାରେ ଗୋଟାଏ କାରଖାନା ବସିବ। ଚଢ଼େଇମାନେ କିଛି ବୁଝିପାରିଲେ ନାହିଁ। କାରଖାନା ବସିଲେ ତାଙ୍କର କ'ଣ ଯାଏ ଆସେ? ତେଣୁ ସେମାନେ ପୂର୍ବପରି କିଚିରି ମିଚିରି ଗୀତ ଗାଇଲେ। ମାତ୍ର ଗାଁଲୋକମାନଙ୍କର ପାଟିଗୋଲ ସେଇଦିନଠାରୁ ଆରମ୍ଭ ହେଲା– ଚଢ଼େଇ ଦିଇଟି ମନ ବ୍ୟସ୍ତରେ ରହିଲେ। ଏଇ ଶାନ୍ତିପ୍ରିୟ ଲୋକମାନଙ୍କର ହେଲା କ'ଣ?

ଦିନକର କଥା। ଗୋଟେ ବଡ଼ ମେସିନ ଆସିଲା। ତା' ସାଙ୍ଗ ଚଢ଼େଇର ବସା ଥିବା ଗଛଟିକୁ ଓପାଡ଼ି ପକାଇଲା। ସାଙ୍ଗଟି ଉଡ଼ିଯାଇ ପ୍ରାଣ ବଞ୍ଚାଇଲା। ଆର ସାଙ୍ଗଟି ତା' ସାଙ୍ଗ ପାଇଁ ନିଜ ଗଛରେ ଗୋଟିଏ ବସା ତିଆରି କରିଦେଲା। ଦୁହେଁ ଗୋଟିଏ ଗଛରେ ମନ ଖୁସିରେ ରହିଲେ। ଦିନେ ଟିକେ ଦୂରକୁ ଆହାର ଖୋଜି ଯାଇଥିଲେ। ସଞ୍ଜକୁ ଫେରି ଦେଖିଲେ ଯେ, ତାଙ୍କର ଗଛଟି ମଧ ଉପୁଡ଼ି ମାଟିରେ ଶୋଇଛି। ବଡ଼ ମେସିନଟା ନିର୍ଦୟ ପରି ଜଙ୍ଗଲର ଅଧାଅଧି ଗଛ ଓପାଡ଼ି ଶୁଆଇ ଦେଇଛି। ଦୁହେଁ ଉଡ଼ିଯାଇ ରାସ୍ତାପାଖ ଗଛଡ଼ାଳରେ ରାତିଟି କଟାଇଲେ। ସକାଳୁ ଦି'ଗୁଣା କାମ– ବସା ବାନ୍ଧିବା ଓ ତା' ସହ ଆହାର ଖୋଜିବା। ଗାଁର ଲୋକମାନେ ନିଜ ଗାଁ ଛାଡ଼ି ଦୂରକୁ ଉଠିଗଲେ। ସେମାନଙ୍କୁ ପକ୍କାଘର କରି କଲୋନୀରେ ରଖାଗଲା। କେତେ ଲୋକ ଘର ନକରି ଟଙ୍କା ନେଲେ, ସେଇ ଟଙ୍କାରେ ମୋଟରସାଇକେଲ୍ କିଣିଲେ, ନୂଆ ତିଆରି ହୋଇଥିବା ଢାବାରେ ଖାଇଲେ ଆଉ ଚଢ଼େଇ ଛାପ ବୋତଲରୁ ନାଲି ନେଲି ପାଣି ପିଇଲେ। ପିଇସାରି ଧସ୍ତାଧସ୍ତି ହେଲେ। ହଠାତ୍ ପଇସାପତ୍ର କାରବାର ଗରିବ ଲୋକଙ୍କ ହାତରେ ହେଲା। ମତ୍ ସେଇ ସରଳ ଗାଁର ଶାନ୍ତି ଭଙ୍ଗ ହେଲା। ଖାକି ପୋଷାକପିନ୍ଧା ବାବୁମାନେ ଆସି ଚକ୍କର କାଟିଲେ। କର୍କଶ ସ୍ୱରରେ ସାଇରନ୍ ବଜାଇ ବଡ଼ବାବୁମାନେ ଗାଡ଼ିରେ ମାଡ଼ିଆସିଲେ। ରାସ୍ତା ପାଖର ଗଛଟା ଧୂଳିରେ ପୋତି ହୋଇଗଲା। ଜଙ୍ଗଲ ସଫା ହେଇ ଖାଁ ଖାଁ ଲାଗିଲା। ଟାଙ୍ଗ ଟାଙ୍ଗ ଖରା ନିଆଁ ଭଳି କାଟିଲା। ଚଢ଼େଇ ଦିଇଟିକୁ ପାଣି ଖୋଜିବାକୁ କଷ୍ଟ ହେଲା। ଧୂଳିରେ ତାଙ୍କର ଆଖି ଅନ୍ଧ ହୋଇଯିବ ଓ କର୍କଶ ଶବ୍ଦରେ ତାଙ୍କର କାନ କାଲ ହୋଇଯିବ ବୋଲି ଭୟ ହେଲା। ଆହାର ବି ମିଳିଲା ନାହିଁ। ଜଙ୍ଗଲ ନଥିବାରୁ ଫଳମୂଳ, ପୋକଜୋକ କମିଲା। ଯୁଆଡ଼େ ଦେଖିବ ଖାଲି ଧୂଳି ଆଉ ଧୂଳି। ଖାଲି ଚଢ଼େଇମାନେ ନୁହେଁ, ଗଛ ବି

ନିଶ୍ୱାସପ୍ରଶ୍ୱାସରେ କଷ୍ଟ ପାଇଲା। ଚଢ଼େଇ ଦୁହିଁଙ୍କର ଶ୍ୱାସରୋଗ ବାହାରିପଡ଼ିଲା। ଏଣେ ପେଟରେ ଭୋକ। ଚିନ୍ତାରେ ପଡ଼ିଲେ କୁଆଡ଼େ ଯିବେ ?

ଚାହୁଁ ଚାହୁଁ କାରଖାନା ବସିଲା। ନୂଆ କଲୋନୀ ହେଲା। କଲୋନୀ ଭିତରେ ଘାସ ବଗିଚ୍ଛ ହେଲା। ଧାଡ଼ି ଧାଡ଼ି ହୋଇ ଅଫଳନ୍ତି ଗଛ ଲାଗିଲା। ଗଛଗୁଡ଼ା ଖାଲି ଦେଖା ସୁନ୍ଦର। ଚଢ଼େଇ ଦିଓଟି ବୁଝିପାରିଲେ ନାହିଁ ଯେ, ଫଳନ୍ତି ଗଛଗୁଡ଼ା କାଟି ପକାଇ ଅଫଳନ୍ତି ଗଛଗୁଡ଼ା କାହିଁକି ଲଗା ହେଲା। ଚଢ଼େଇ ଦିଓଟି ରାସ୍ତାପାଖ ଗଛରେ ଶାନ୍ତିରେ ଘୁମେଇ ବି ପାରିଲେ ନାହିଁ। ରାତିରେ ଗାଡ଼ିମୋଟର ପେଁ ପାଁ ଶବଦ, ଦିନରେ ରାସ୍ତାରୋକ, ହୋହଲ୍ଲା, ବାଡ଼ିଆ ବାଡ଼ି, ଲୋକଙ୍କ ଗଣ୍ଡଗୋଳ।

ତା'ପରେ ରାସ୍ତା ଚଉଡ଼ା ହେଲା। ଦିନେ ସଞ୍ଜକୁ ଫେରି ଦେଖିଲେ– ତାଙ୍କର ଶେଷ ଆଶ୍ରୟ ରାସ୍ତାକଡ଼ ଗଛଟି ବି ଲମ୍ୱଜାଲ ହୋଇ ପଡ଼ିଛି। ଚଢ଼େଇ ଦିଓଟି କଲୋନୀ ଭିତରେ ଗୋଟିଏ ଗଛରେ ରହିଲେ। ମାତ୍ର କଲୋନୀର ଲୋକମାନଙ୍କର ସେହି ସରଳ ଜୀବନ ଆଉ ନଥିଲା। ଘାସ ପଡ଼ିଆରେ ପିଲାମାନେ ଆଉ ଖେଳୁନଥିଲେ। ସକାଳ ହେଲେ ନାଲି ନେଲି କପଡ଼ାର ଏକା ପରି ପୋଷାକ ପିନ୍ଧି ରାସ୍ତାରେ ଚୁଲୁଥିଲେ। ସାନ ପିଲାମାନେ ସ୍କୁଲକୁ ଯାଉଥିଲେ, ବଡ଼ ପିଲାମାନେ ଯାଉଥିଲେ କାରଖାନାକୁ। ଚଢ଼େଇ ଭାବିଲେ ଭଲ ହେଲା। ଏଥର ଗାଁ ପିଲାମାନେ ବାବୁ ହେବେ, କାରଖାନାରୁ କଞ୍ଚା ପଇସା ରୋଜଗାର କରି ଗାଡ଼ି ଚଢ଼ିବେ। ମାତ୍ର ସେମାନଙ୍କ କାନ ତ ପୁରା କାଲା ହୋଇଯିବ। ବଡ଼ ବଡ଼ କୋଠାଘରର ବାବୁଆଣୀମାନେ ଚଢ଼େଇଙ୍କ ପାଇଁ ଛାତ ଉପରେ ଦାନା ପକାନ୍ତି। ଚଢ଼େଇମାନେ ଖୁସ୍ତି ଖୁସ୍ତି ଖାଇଲେ ଖୁସି ହୁଅନ୍ତି। କଷ୍ଟେମଷ୍ଟେ ଜୀବନ କଟୁଥାଏ। ଚଢ଼େଇମାନଙ୍କର ଖାଦ୍ୟକଷ୍ଟ, କଂକ୍ରିଟ ଜଙ୍ଗଲର ଦାଢ଼ି, କାରଖାନାର ଧୂଆଁ, ଗାଡ଼ିମୋଟରର ଧୂଳି, ଘର୍ ଘର୍ ଶବ୍ଦ, ଗଛପତ୍ରର ଅଭାବ, ଲୋକମାନଙ୍କ ଭିତରେ ଝଗଡ଼ାଝାଟି ଶାନ୍ତିପ୍ରିୟ ଚଢ଼େଇ ଦିଓଟିଙ୍କୁ ବିଚଳିତ କଲା। ଦୁଇବର୍ଷ ତଳର ଜୀବନ ସେମାନଙ୍କ ସ୍ୱପ୍ନ ଭଳି ଲାଗୁଥିଲା। ନିଜକୁ ବୁଦ୍ଧିମାନ ଭାବୁଥିବା ଚଢ଼େଇଟି ସାଙ୍ଗ ଚଢ଼େଇକୁ ବହୁତ ଦୂରକୁ ଉଡ଼ିଯାଇ ଆଉ ଏକ ଜଙ୍ଗଲରେ ବସା ବାନ୍ଧି ରହିବା ପାଇଁ ପ୍ରସ୍ତାବ ଦେଲା। ମାତ୍ର ସେତେବେଳକୁ ସାଙ୍ଗର କାନ, ଆଖି, ଡେଣା ଆଉ ମନ ଦୁର୍ବଲ ହୋଇଗଲାଣି। ତେଣୁ ସେ ନୂଆ ଜଙ୍ଗଲର ସନ୍ଧାନରେ ଉଡ଼ିଯିବା ପାଇଁ ସାହସ କଲା ନାହିଁ। ଭାଗ୍ୟକୁ ଆଦରି ସେଇଠି ପଡ଼ିରହିଲା। ଆର ଚଢ଼େଇଟି ସକାଳୁ ସକାଳୁ ଆଖିରେ ଆଖିଏ ଲୁହ ଭର୍ତ୍ତି କରି ସାଙ୍ଗ ଚଢ଼େଇଠାରୁ ବିଦାୟ ନେଇ ଦୂରକୁ ଉଡ଼ିଗଲା, ପୁଣି ଆଉ ଏକ ଜଙ୍ଗଲର ଗହଳିଆ ଗଛରେ ବସା ବାନ୍ଧି ରହିଲା। ସାଙ୍ଗ ଚଢ଼େଇ କଥା ମନେପଡ଼ି

ଆଖିରୁ ଲୁହ ଗଡ଼ିପଡ଼ିଲା। ସେତିକିବେଳେ ତାକୁ ନୂଆ ସଙ୍ଗିନୀଟିଏ ମିଳିଗଲା। ସେ ପକ୍ଷୀଶାଟି ବି ଦୁଃଖରେ ଥିଲା। ସେମାନେ ଏକାଠି ବସା ବାନ୍ଧି ରହିଲେ। ସେ ମଧ୍ୟ ଦୂରରୁ ଉଡ଼ି ଆସିଥିଲା। ମାତ୍ର ସ୍ଥାନୀୟ ଚଟେଇମାନେ ସେମାନଙ୍କୁ ବିଦେଶୀ ଭାବି ସାଙ୍ଗରେ ମିଶାଇଲେ ନାହିଁ। କଥା କଥାକେ କଳି କଲେ। କହିଲେ- "ତୁମେ କିଏ ହୋ! ଆମ ଖାଇବାରେ ଭାଗ ବସାଇବାକୁ ଆସିଲ?" ଚଟେଇ ଦିହିଁଙ୍କ ମନକୁ ବଡ଼ ବାଧିଲା। ଭାବିଲେ "ଏଥର ବଂଶ ବଢ଼ାଇବା ଉଚିତ ହେବ। ପକ୍ଷୀଶାଟି ଅଣ୍ଡା ଦେଲା। ସେମାନଙ୍କ ମନର ଦୁଃଖ ଦୂର ହୋଇଗଲା। ଏଣିକି ତାଙ୍କ ବସାରେ କିଚିରି ମିଚିରି ଶବଦ ଶୁଭିବ ତାଙ୍କର ନିଃସଙ୍ଗତା ଦୂର ହେବ। ମାତ୍ର ଭାଗ୍ୟ ତ ପ୍ରତିକୂଳ ଥିଲା। ସେହି ଗଛର କୋରଡ଼ରେ ଗୋଟିଏ ଭୟଙ୍କର ସାପ ଥିଲା। ସାପ ଆସି ପ୍ରତିଦିନ ଅଣ୍ଡା ଖାଇ ଦେଉଥିଲା। ଚଟେଇ ଦିହେଁ ଦୁଃଖରେ ଭ ଙ୍ଗିପଡ଼ିଲେ। ସେମାନଙ୍କର ଛୁଆପିଲା ହେବାର ଆଶା ମଉଳିଗଲା। ତଥାପି ବି ପକ୍ଷୀଶାଟି ଆଉ ଥରେ ଅଣ୍ଡା ଦେଲା। ଅଣ୍ଡାକୁ ଛାଡ଼ି ଯିବନାହିଁ ବୋଲି ପର ଘୋଡ଼େଇ ବସି ରହିଲା। ପୁରୁଷ ଚଟେଇଟି ଆହାର ଖୋଜିବାକୁ ଗଲା। ସଞ୍ଜକୁ ଫେରି ଦେଖିଲା- ଅଣ୍ଡା ନାହିଁ, ସାଙ୍ଗ ଚଟେଇଟି କାନ୍ଦି କାନ୍ଦି ଆଖି ଫୁଲାଇ ଦେଇଛି। ଚଟେଇଟି ଭାବିଲା ଯେମିତି ହେଲେ ସେ କୋରଡ଼ରୁ ସାପଟିକୁ ଲୋକଙ୍କ ଦ୍ୱାରା ମାରିବ। ଉପାୟ ଚିନ୍ତା କଲା। ସେ ଦେଖୁଥିଲା ଯେ ଲୋକମାନେ ଗୋଟିଏ ସାନ ଘରୁ ଗୋଟାଏ ମେସିନରେ କାର୍ଡ ଗେଞ୍ଜି ଦେଇ ଟଙ୍କା କାଢ଼ି ଆଣୁଛନ୍ତି। ସେଇ ମ୍ୟାଜିକ୍ କାର୍ଡର କରାମତି ଦେଖି ଚଟେଇଟି ଆଶ୍ଚର୍ଯ୍ୟ ହୋଇଗଲା। କିନ୍ତୁ ତାକୁ ଉପାୟ ଦିଶିଗଲା। ସେ ଭାବିଲା କାହା ହାତରୁ କାର୍ଡଟିକୁ ଝିଙ୍କିଆଣି କୋରଡ଼ରେ ପକାଇ ପାରନ୍ତା ତେବେ ଲୋକଟି ତା' ପଛରେ ଗୋଡ଼ାଇ ଗୋଡ଼ାଇ କୋରଡ଼ରୁ ସାପଟିକୁ ମାରନ୍ତା ଆଉ କାର୍ଡଟିକୁ ନିଅନ୍ତା। ଦିନେ ଦେଖିଲା, ଜଣେ ଲୋକ ଆଉ ଜଣେ ଲୋକର ମୁଣ୍ଡରେ ପିସ୍ତଲ ଲଗାଇ ଟଙ୍କାତକ ଛଡ଼ାଉଛନ୍ତି। ଲୋକଟିର ହାତରୁ ସେତିକିବେଳେ କାର୍ଡଟି ଖସିପଡ଼ିଲା। ଚଟେଇଟି କାର୍ଡଟିକୁ ଧରି ଚଟ୍ କରି ଉଡ଼ିଗଲା ଆଉ ଲୋକଟି ତାକୁ ଅନୁସରଣ କରୁଛି କି ନାହିଁ ଅପେକ୍ଷା କରି ପାଖ ଘରର ଛାତ ଉପରେ ବସି ରହିଲା। ମାତ୍ର ଫଳ ହେଲା ଓଲଟା। ବନ୍ଧୁକବାଲା ଲୋକ କାର୍ଡ ଲୋଭରେ ଚଟେଇକୁ ଲକ୍ଷ୍ୟ କରି ଗୁଲି ଫୁଟାଇଲା। ଭାଗ୍ୟ ବଳରୁ ଗୁଲି ତା'ଠାରେ ଲାଗିଲାନି। ବନ୍ଧୁକବାଲା ଏଥର ମୋଟରସାଇକେଲରେ ପଳାଇଲା। ଚଟେଇ ଭାବିଲା କାର୍ଡର ମାଲିକ ତା' ପଛେ ପଛେ ଆସିବ। ମାତ୍ର ସେ ଲୋକଟି ପକେଟରୁ ସାନ ଫୋନଟିଏ କାଢ଼ି ତା' କାର୍ଡର କାରବାର ବନ୍ଦ କରିବା ପାଇଁ କାହା ସହ କଥାଭାଷା ହେଲା କି କ'ଣ କାର୍ଡ

ନେବାପାଇଁ ଚଢ଼େଇ ପଛରେ ଦୌଡ଼ିଲା । ନାହିଁ । ଚଢ଼େଇଟି ମନ ଦୁଃଖରେ ସେହି ବିପଜନକ କାର୍ଡଟିକୁ ଫୋପାଡ଼ି ଦେଇ ନିଜ ବସାକୁ ଫେରିଲା । ମାତ୍ର ଫେରିଆସି ଦେଖିଲା ସାପ ତା'ର ସଙ୍ଗିନୀଟିକୁ ମାରିଦେଇଛି । ଚଢ଼େଇଟି ଏଥର ଆଉରି ନିଃସଙ୍ଗ ହୋଇଗଲା ।

କିଛିଦିନ ପରେ ସେ ଜଙ୍ଗଲ ପାଖ ନଦୀ ଉପରେ ଗୋଟିଏ ବନ୍ଧ ତିଆରି ହେଲା । ପାଣି ଭର୍ତ୍ତି ହୋଇ ପାଖ ବଣ ବୁଡ଼ିଗଲା । କେନାଲ ଖୋଲା ହୋଇ ଜମିରେ ପାଣି ମାଡ଼ିଲା । ସେତିକିବେଳେ ଗୋଟିଏ ନେଉଲର ଗାତ ପାଣିରେ ବୁଡ଼ିଗଲା । ଗୋଟିଏ ହାତୀର ରାସ୍ତା କେନାଲ ଦ୍ୱାରା ପୋତି ହୋଇଗଲା । ସମସ୍ତେ ଏଥର ଅଘରି ହେଲେ । ମିଳିମିଶି ଚିନ୍ତା କଲେ ଏ ସମସ୍ୟାର ସମାଧାନ କ'ଣ ?

ନେଉଲ କହିଲା– "ପାଖ ସହରର କଲେକ୍ଟରଙ୍କ ପାଖକୁ ଚାଲ । ଆମ ଦୁଃଖ ଜଣାଇ ଦରଖାସ୍ତ କରିବା । ସେ ଆମକୁ ନ୍ୟାୟ ଦେବେ । ଆମକୁ ଥଇଥାନ କରିବା ଦାୟିତ୍ୱ ତାଙ୍କର ।"

ହାତୀ ଶୁଣ୍ଢ ହଲାଇ କହିଲା– "କିଛି ଲାଭ ନାହିଁ । ଯୋଉଠି ଜଙ୍ଗଲ ନାହିଁ, ମଣିଷଙ୍କ ଘରଦ୍ୱାର ପାଣିରେ ବୁଡ଼ିଗଲା ସେଠି ଆମକୁ ନ୍ୟାୟ କୋଉଠି ମିଳିବ ? ଆମେ ସହଜେ ପଶୁପକ୍ଷୀ ।"

"ଚଢ଼େଇଟି ଦୁଃଖରେ ରହିଲା । ସବୁବେଳେ ମନମରା । ଗୀତ ଗାଇବାକୁ ବେଲେବେଲେ ଇଚ୍ଛା ହେଲେ ଦୁଃଖର ସ୍ୱର ବାହାରିଯାଏ । ଭାବିଲା– ଯାହାହେଲେ ବି ବଞ୍ଚିବାକୁ ତ ହବ । କୁଆଡ଼େ ଆଉ ପଳେଇବ ? ଦିନେ ଆଉ ଗୋଟିଏ ହେଲିକପ୍ଟର ସେଇ ଜଙ୍ଗଲ ଉପରେ ଉଡ଼ିଲା । ଚଢ଼େଇର ହଂସା ଉଡ଼ିଗଲା । ପୁଣି କଠୋର ଦିନ ଆସିଲା ବୋଲି ଦୁଃଖରେ ଭାଙ୍ଗିପଡ଼ିଲା । ଭାବିଲା– ସାଙ୍ଗ ଗଲା, ସଙ୍ଗିନୀ ଗଲା, ଛୁଆପିଲା ଗଲେ । ଭବିଷ୍ୟତର ଅଣ୍ଡାଟିଏ ବି ରହିଲା ନାହିଁ । ଘରଦ୍ୱାର ସବୁଗଲା, ଆଉ ବାସ ଖଣ୍ଡେ ମିଳିବାର ଆଶା ନାହିଁ । ଏମିତି ବଞ୍ଚ ଲାଭ କ'ଣ ? ପାଖ ପାହାଡ଼ର ଶିଖରରୁ ଡେଇଁ ପ୍ରାଣ ହାରିଦେବ କି ? ସମସ୍ତେ ବୁଝନ୍ତେ ଯେ, ଏଡ଼ିକି ଟିକେ ଚଢ଼େଇକୁ ବି ମୁଣ୍ଡ ଗୁଞ୍ଜିବାକୁ ଥାନ ଟିକେ ଦେଲେନାହିଁ । ଚଢ଼େଇଟି ସକାଳୁ ସକାଳୁ ପାହାଡ଼ ଉପରକୁ ଉଡ଼ିଗଲା । ମରଣ ପୂର୍ବରୁ ପାହାଡ଼ ଛାତିରେ ଥଣ୍ଟରେ ଉଖାରି ଉଖାରି ମରଣ ପୂର୍ବର ଶେଷପତ୍ର ଲେଖିଲା । ନୈଲେ ଆତ୍ମହତ୍ୟାକୁ ହତ୍ୟା ରୂପ ଦେଇ କୋଉ ନିର୍ଦୋଷକୁ ବାନ୍ଧିବେ, ରାସ୍ତାରୋକ ହେବ, ଗଣ୍ଡଗୋଲ, ଫାୟାରିଂରେ ଆଉରି ଜଣେ ଦି'ଜଣ ମରିବେ । ଲାଭ କ'ଣ ? ଚଢ଼େଇକୁ କ'ଣ ଏଥରେ ନ୍ୟାୟ ମିଳିବ ? କାହିଁକି ଯେ ଲୋକମାନେ ବେଲେବେଲେ ଏମିତି ପାଗଲ ହୁଅନ୍ତି ଚଢ଼େଇଟି ବୁଝିପାରିଲା

ନାହିଁ। ମରଣ ପତ୍ର ଲେଖିସାରି ଚଢ଼େଇଟି ଶେଷଥର ପାଇଁ ତା'ର ପ୍ରିୟ ପୃଥିବୀକୁ ରୁହିଁଲା। ତା'ପରେ ମୁଣ୍ଡ ଟେକି ନୀଳ ଆକାଶକୁ ରୁହିଁଲା। ଭାବିଲା, ଛି! ସେ ଆତ୍ମହତ୍ୟା କରିବା ପାଇଁ କେମିତି ଭାବିପାରିଲା। ସମସ୍ତଙ୍କ ଜୀବନରେ କେତେ କେତେ ଦୁଃଖ ଆସେ। ସମସ୍ତେ ଯଦି ଜୀବନ ହାରିଦେବେ ତାହାହେଲେ ଏଡ଼େ ସୁନ୍ଦର ପୃଥିବୀ ଲୁହରେ ସମୁଦ୍ର ପାଲଟି ଯିବନି କି? ସେ କେତେ କେତେ ଝଡ଼ର ସାମ୍ନା କରି ବଞ୍ଚିବା ପାଇଁ ଲଢ଼ିଆସିଛି। କେତେଥର ବସା ଭାଙ୍ଗିଛି, ପୁଣି ବସା ଗଢ଼ିଛି। ଜୀବନକୁ ଭଲପାଏ ବୋଲି ଦୁଃଖ ଦିନରେ ବି ଗୀତ ଗାଇ ରୁଲିଛି। ସେ ପୁଣି ମୂର୍ଖ ମଣିଷଙ୍କ ପରି କଥା କଥାରେ ଆତ୍ମହତ୍ୟା କରିବ? ତା'ରି ଆଖି ଆଗରେ କେତେ କେତେ ଆତ୍ମହତ୍ୟା ଘଟିଯାଉଛି। ସେଥିରେ ଦୁଃଖ କାହାର ଉଣା ହଉଛି? ଯିଏ ମଲା ତା'ର ନା ଯିଏ ବଞ୍ଚିଲା ତା'ର? ଯିଏ ଦୁଃଖ ଦେଲା ତା'ର ବା କି କ୍ଷତି ହଉଛି? କ୍ଷତି ତ ଯିଏ ଗଲା ତା'ରି। ନା, ଏ ସୁନ୍ଦର ପୃଥିବୀରେ ସେ ବଞ୍ଚିବ, ସେ ଜୀବନକୁ ଖୋଜିବ। କୋଉଠି ନା କୋଉଠି ଗଛର ଶାଖାଟିଏ କ'ଣ ମିଳିଯିବ ନାହିଁ?"

ମୃତ୍ୟୁକାଳୀନ ସ୍ୱୀକାରୋକ୍ତିକୁ ଗାର ଟାଣି ଲିଭାଇଦେଲା, ସେଠି ଜୀବନ କବିତା ଲେଖିଲା। ପୁଣି ନୂଆ ଗୀତଟିଏ ଗାଇଚାଲିଲା। ଏତିକିବେଳେ ଦି'ଜଣ ଖାକିବାଲା କୋଉଠି ଥିଲେ, ତା' ବେକମୁଣ୍ଡକୁ ମାଡ଼ିବସିଲେ। କହିଲେ- "ତୁ ଆତ୍ମହତ୍ୟା କରୁଥିଲୁ? ସେଇଟା ତ ଦଣ୍ଡନୀୟ। ଆଉରି ଦୁଃଖ ପାଇବୁ? ତୋ ଦୁଃଖ ଆମେ ସହିପାରୁନୁ! ତୋତେ ଆମେ ମାରି ଆଜି ଭୋଜି କରିବୁ। ତୋତେ ଦୁଃଖରୁ ମୁକ୍ତି ଦେବୁ। ଏଥରେ ଆତ୍ମହତ୍ୟା ମହାପାପ ଦୋଷ ତୋଟି ଲାଗିବନି।" ଚଢ଼େଇଟି ନ୍ୟୁନ ହେଇ ତାକୁ ଛାଡ଼ିଦେବା ପାଇଁ ଗୁହାରି କଲା। ସେ ଆତ୍ମହତ୍ୟା କରିବାକୁ ଯାଉନଥିଲା ବୋଲି ଜୀବନ କବିତା ପଢ଼ି ଶୁଣାଇଲା। ପ୍ରମାଣ ପାଇ ଖାକିବାଲାମାନେ ପ୍ରଭାବିତ ହେଲେ। କହିଲେ- "ତୋ ଜୀବନ ଦର୍ଶନରେ ଆମେ ପ୍ରଭାବିତ ହେଲୁ। ତୁ ଆମର ଗୁରୁ। ତୋତେ ଆମେ ସୁରକ୍ଷିତ ବସାଟିଏ ଦେବୁ।"

ଚଢ଼େଇକୁ ଆଣି ଖାକିବାଲା ତାଙ୍କ ବଡ଼ବାବୁଙ୍କୁ ଭେଟିଦେଲେ। ବଡ଼ବାବୁଙ୍କର ଆନନ୍ଦ କହିଲେ ନ ସରେ। ସମସ୍ତଙ୍କୁ ଜାଲିଘରେ ପୁରାଇ ଦେବାରେ ତାଙ୍କର ସୁନାମ ଅଛି। ସେଥିରେ ତାଙ୍କର ବଢ଼ତି ହୁଏ। ଚଢ଼େଇଟା ବି ପାର ପାଇଲା ନାହିଁ। ବଡ଼ବାବୁ ତାକୁ ପଞ୍ଜୁରିରେ ରଖିଲେ, ସକାଳ ସଞ୍ଜ ଦାନାପାଣି ଦେଲେ। ଚଢ଼େଇ ତ ଏମିତି ଜୀବନ ରୁହିଁନଥିଲା। ଜୀବନଟା ବଡ଼ କାଉଆ, ନିରାଶ, ବିରକ୍ତିକର ଆଉ ନିଃସଙ୍ଗ ଲାଗିନାଲା। ଭାବିଲା- ଏପରି ଜୀବନର ମୂଲ୍ୟ କ'ଣ? ଦିନରାତି ପଞ୍ଜୁରି ଭିତରେ ମନମରା ହେଇ ବସି ଗୀତ ଗାଇବା ଭୁଲିଗଲା।

ଦିନେ ବଡ଼ବାବୁଙ୍କ ପ୍ରିୟ ବାନ୍ଧବୀ(?) ଖରାବେଳିଆ ଆସିଲେ। ସେ ଜାଣିଥିଲେ ଯେ, ଘରେ ମାଲିକାଣୀ ନଥିବେ। ବଡ଼ବାବୁ ତାଙ୍କୁ କୋଳେଇନେଲେ। ମାଲିକାଣୀକୁ ଏମିତି କୋଳେଇନେବା ଚଢ଼େଇ କେବେ ଦେଖ୍‌ନଥିଲା। ବଡ଼ବାବୁ କହିଲେ - "ଦେଖ୍‌ଲ ମୁଁ ତମ ପାଇଁ କେଡ଼େ ସୁନ୍ଦର ଉପହାର ରଖ୍‌ଛି। ଏ ଚଢ଼େଇଟିର ସ୍ତ୍ରୀ ନାହିଁ ବୋଲି କେଡ଼େ ଶାନ୍ତିରେ ସେ ଅଛି। ଆଉ ଆମର ସ୍ତ୍ରୀ ଅଛି ଯେ, ଡରି ଡରି ମରିବାକୁ ପଡ଼ିଛି।"

ପ୍ରିୟତମା କହିଲେ- "ଏମିତି ଉପହାର ମୋତେ ଦୁଃଖ ଦେଉଛି। ମୋ ସାନ କଥାଟି ମାନ। ନିଃସଙ୍ଗ ଚଢ଼େଇଟିକୁ ବନ୍ଧନରୁ ମୁକ୍ତ କର। ତାକୁ ଖୋଲା ଆକାଶରେ ଉଡ଼ିବାକୁ ଦିଅ। ଆମେ ଦୁହେଁ ପରା ସମାଜର କେତେ କେତେ ବନ୍ଧନରୁ ମୁକୁଳି ଯିବାକୁ ରୁହୁଁଛେ। ସମାଜର ସବୁ ପ୍ରଥା ଓ ନିୟମ କ'ଣ ସୁଖ ଦିଏ? ମଣିଷ ଭିତରେ ପରା ମୁକ୍ତିକାମୀ ପକ୍ଷୀଟିଏ ସର୍ବଦା ପଞ୍ଜୁରି ଭାଙ୍ଗି ଉଡ଼ିଯିବାକୁ ରୁହୁଁଥାଏ। ଏଇ ନିରୀହ ସାନ ଚଢ଼େଇଟି ତ ମୁକ୍ତାକାଶର ପକ୍ଷୀ। ମୁଁ ଜାଣେ ତମର ନିର୍ଦୋଷକୁ ଜାଲି ଘରେ ପୂରାଇବାର ଅଭ୍ୟାସ ଅଛି। କିନ୍ତୁ ଆକାଶର ପକ୍ଷୀଟିର ବି ତ୍ରାହି ନାହିଁ! ଏଇଟା ମାହାପାପ ନୁହେଁ କି? ଚାଲୁନ, ଆମେ ଦୁହେଁ ଅଗ୍ନଅଗ୍ନି ବନସ୍ତକୁ ପଲାଇବା। ସେଠି ଅନେକ ପକ୍ଷୀ ଚଞ୍ଚୁରେ ଚଞ୍ଚୁ ରଖ୍ ମିଳନ ଗୀତ ଗାଉଥିବେ। ଆମେ ବି ସେମିତି ମିଳନ ଗୀତ ଗାଇବା। ଏ ମନମରା ଚଢ଼େଇଟା କି ସୁଖ ଦଉଛି।"

"ଆଉ ଅଗ୍ନଅଗ୍ନି ବନସ୍ତ କାହିଁ ଯେ" - ବଡ଼ବାବୁ ହତାଶିଆ ସ୍ଵରରେ କହିଲେ। ପ୍ରିୟତମା କହିଲେ- "ଚଢ଼େଇଟି ଯୋଉ ଦିଗରେ ଉଡ଼ିଯିବ ସେଇ ଦିଗରେ ଆମେ ଛୁଟିବା। ଚଢ଼େଇମାନେ ଅଗ୍ନଅଗ୍ନି ବନସ୍ତର ବାସ୍ନା ବାରି ପରନ୍ତି। ନିଶ୍ଚୟ ଅଗ୍ନଅଗ୍ନି ବନସ୍ତ ଆମେ ପାଇଯିବା।"

"ବାଃ, ତମେ କେଡ଼େ ବୁଦ୍ଧିମତୀ। ମୋ ସ୍ତ୍ରୀଟା ଭଲା ଏମିତି ହୋଇଥାନ୍ତା, ଏକବାର ଉଲ୍! ଛାଡ଼, ଆପଣା ଭାଗ୍ୟକୁ ନିନ୍ଦିବା ଛଡ଼ା ଆଉ କ'ଣ କରିବି? ତମେ ବି ତମ ମନକଥାଟି କହିଦେଲ। ଏ ଘରର ରୁଚିକାନ୍ତୁ ଭିତରେ ମଣିଷର ଶ୍ଵାସରୁଦ୍ଧ ହେଇଯାଏ। ବେଳେବେଳେ ମନ ହୁଏ- ଜଙ୍ଗଲକୁ ଭଲା ପଲାନ୍ତି"। ଏତିକି କହି ବଡ଼ବାବୁ ପ୍ରିୟତମାର କଥା ମାନି ପଞ୍ଜୁରିର ଦ୍ଵାର ଖୋଲିଦେଲେ। ମାତ୍ର ଚଢ଼େଇଟି ପଞ୍ଜୁରିରୁ ନବାହାରେ, ଚଢ଼େଇଟିକୁ ଧରିଆଣି ଅଗଣାରେ ରଖ୍‌ଲେ। ଭୁସ୍ ଭୁସ୍ କରି ହୁରୁଡ଼େଇଲେ, ଚଙ୍କିଲା ନାହିଁ- ଯେମିତି କଳ ବିଗିଡ଼ିଯାଇଥିବା ଖେଳଣା ଚଢ଼େଇଟିଏ। ଚଢ଼େଇଟି ପୁଣି ଠୁକୁ ଠୁକୁ ପାଦ ପକାଇ ପଞ୍ଜୁରି ଭିତରକୁ ଉଠିଗଲା। ଚଢ଼େଇର ପର ଥାଇ ମଥ ଉଠିବାର ଉତ୍ସାହ ଆଉ ନଥିଲା। କୁଆଡ଼େ ଯିବ? ବଣ କାହିଁ? ନିର୍ମଳ ଆକାଶ କାହିଁ? ସବୁ ତ ଶୂନ୍ୟ- ବିଷାକ୍ତ!

ଏତିକିବେଳେ ଘର ଭିତରକୁ ମାଲିକାଣୀ ପଶିଲେ। ପ୍ରିୟତମା ବାରି କବାଟ ଖୋଲି ପଳାଇଲେ। ବଡ଼ବାବୁ ଖବରକାଗଜରେ ମୁହଁ ଲୁଚାଇଲେ। ଚଢ଼େଇ ଦେଖିଲା ଖବରକାଗଜରେ ଆଉ ଏକ ବଣର ଗଛମାନ କଟା ହୋଇ ପଡ଼ିବାର ଫଟୋ ବାହାରିଛି। ବଡ଼ବାବୁ ବଡ଼ ପାଟିରେ ପଢ଼ୁଥିଲେ– "ଶିଳ୍ପାଞ୍ଚଳ ପାଇଁ ବଡ଼ ବଡ଼ କମ୍ପାନୀଙ୍କ ସହ ଚୁକ୍ତିନାମା ସ୍ୱାକ୍ଷରିତ ହୋଇଯାଇଛି। ବଣ ଉଜୁଡ଼ିଲେ ମଧ୍ୟ ନୂଆ ଜଙ୍ଗଲ ସୃଷ୍ଟି ହେବ। ବଡ଼ ବଡ଼ ଆପାର୍ଟମେଣ୍ଟ ଚତୁରିକଡ଼ ସୌନ୍ଦର୍ଯ୍ୟ ବୃଦ୍ଧିକାରୀ ବୃକ୍ଷ ରୋପଣ ହେବ।"

"– ଆଉ ଅଗାଅଗ୍ନି ବନସ୍ତ ?" ଚଢ଼େଇଟି ଚିଁ ଚିଁ ହୋଇ ପଚରିଲା। ମାତ୍ର ଚଢ଼େଇର ଭାଷା କ'ଣ ମଣିଷ ବୁଝେ ଯେ ତା' ପ୍ରଶ୍ନର ଉତ୍ତର ମିଳନ୍ତା ?

ବିପନ୍ନ ଅରଣ୍ୟ

"କଂଗ୍ରାଚୁଲେସନ୍ସ !"

" କ'ଣ ପାଇଁ ?"

"ଠିକ୍ ସମୟରେ ଖସିଗଲେ" ଅପରପକ୍ଷରୁ ବ୍ୟଙ୍ଗାତ୍ମକ ସ୍ୱର ।

"ହଁ, ମାତ୍ର ଅଳ୍ପ ସମୟ ପୂର୍ବରୁ" ସ୍ମିତ ହସି କବୀର କହିଲେ ।

"ଆପଣଙ୍କ ପରମାୟୁ ବାକି ଅଛି । କିନ୍ତୁ ଜାଣିଲେ କିପରି ?
ପ୍ୟାକେଟ୍ ମଧ୍ୟ ଖୋଲିଲେ ନାହିଁ ।" ଅପରପକ୍ଷରୁ ଅଜଣା ବ୍ୟକ୍ତିର
ସ୍ୱର ।

"ପୋଲିସ ଟ୍ରେନିଂରେ ଅନ୍ତତଃ ସେତିକି ଶିଖା ଯାଇଛି । ମାତ୍ର
ତୁମ୍ଭେମାନେ ଜାଣିଲ କିପରି ? ଅପରେସନ୍ ପାଇଁ ଆମର ଯାତ୍ରା
କାର୍ଯ୍ୟକ୍ରମ ତ ଅତ୍ୟନ୍ତ ଗୋପନୀୟ ଥିଲା ।"

"ଟ୍ରେନିଂରେ ତଥାପି ମଧ୍ୟ କିଛି ଭୁଲ୍ ରହିଯାଏ । ଅତି
ଦାମିକିଆ ଗାଡ଼ି ଏପଟେ ଝୁଲେ ନାହିଁ ବୋଲି ଶିକ୍ଷା ଦିଆଯାଇ
ନାହିଁ । ବାସ୍- ସେତିକି ଆମ ପାଇଁ ଯଥେଷ୍ଟ ।" ଅପରପକ୍ଷରୁ
ସ୍ମିତହାସ୍ୟ ।

X X X X

କବୀର ଜଣେ ପ୍ରକୃତିପ୍ରେମୀ ଉଚ୍ଚପଦସ୍ଥ ପୋଲିସ ଅଫିସର ।
ତାଙ୍କୁ ବଣ ପାହାଡ଼ ଭଲଲାଗେ । ରୁକିରିର ବ୍ୟସ୍ତତା ଭିତରୁ ବାହାରି

ଯାଇ ବଣ ଜଙ୍ଗଲର ବିଜନତା ଭିତରେ ହଜିଯିବାକୁ ବେଳେବେଳେ ମନ ଉଛାଟ ହୁଏ । ବିଶେଷକରି କୋରାପୁଟ ଜଙ୍ଗଲ ଯେମିତି ତାଙ୍କୁ ହାତଠାରି ଡାକେ । କିନ୍ତୁ ଏବେ ଆଉ ସେଇ ଜଙ୍ଗଲ ପ୍ରକୃତିପ୍ରେମୀଙ୍କ ପାଇଁ ନିରାପଦ ନୁହେଁ । ମାଓବାଦୀମାନଙ୍କର ଆଡ୍ଡାସ୍ଥଳୀ ପାଲଟିଛି ନିରୀହ ଜଙ୍ଗଲ । ଚାଲିଛି ପୋଲିସ ଓ ମାଓବାଦୀମାନଙ୍କର ବାଘବକରୀ ଖେଳ । ଜଣେ ଅନ୍ୟଜଣଙ୍କୁ ମାରିବାକୁ ବ୍ୟଗ୍ର । ଉଭୟ ପକ୍ଷ ଏହି ମାରଣ ଖେଳରେ ଦକ୍ଷ । ପାନରୁ ଚୂନ ଖସିଲେ ମୃତ୍ୟୁ ସୁନିଶ୍ଚିତ । କବୀରଙ୍କ ସହଧର୍ମିଣୀ ସୌମ୍ୟା ମଧ୍ୟ ସ୍ୱାମୀଙ୍କ ଭଳି ପ୍ରକୃତିପ୍ରେମରେ ପାଗଳିନୀ । ଅଭିଜାତ ଘରର ଅଳିଅଳୀ କନ୍ୟା, ପଦସ୍ଥ ଅଫିସରଙ୍କ ସ୍ତ୍ରୀ । କିନ୍ତୁ ପୁରୁଣା ଡାକବଙ୍ଗଲାରେ ରହିବାକୁ, ଜଙ୍ଗଲ ପାଖ ରାସ୍ତାକଡ଼ରୁ' ଦୋକାନର କାଠ ବେଞ୍ଚରେ ବସି ଚ୍ୟା ପିଇବାକୁ, ବରା ପକୁଡ଼ି ଖାଇବାକୁ ସେ କୁଣ୍ଠାବୋଧ କରନ୍ତି ନାହିଁ । କୁଲୁକୁଲୁ ଝରଣା ଜଳରେ ପାଦ ନଚାଇ ନୃତ୍ୟ ଛନ୍ଦରେ ଫଟୋ ଉଠେଇ ଭିଡ଼ିଓ କରିବା ତାଙ୍କର ନିଶା । ସାପ, ତେଲୁଣିପୋକ, ବିଛା, କୀଟପତଙ୍ଗକୁ ସୌମ୍ୟାଙ୍କର ପ୍ରାଣେ ଡର । ମାତ୍ର ବଣ ଜଙ୍ଗଲରେ ଭ୍ରମଣ କଲାବେଳେ କଳ୍ପନା କରନ୍ତି ଯେ, ତାଙ୍କ ଗସ୍ତ କାର୍ଯ୍ୟକ୍ରମ ଖବର ପାଇ ପୋକ, ଜୋକ, ସାପ ଉଭେଇ ଯାଇଥିବେ ।

ସୌମ୍ୟାର ଅନ୍ତରଙ୍ଗ ବନ୍ଧୁ ଶ୍ୱେତା । ପୂର୍ବଜନ୍ମରୁ ବନ୍ଧୁତ୍ୱ ଥିଲା କି କ'ଣ? ସପିଂ, ଚାଟିଂ, ପାର୍ଟି ସବୁବେଳେ ମିଶି କରନ୍ତି । ଶ୍ୱେତାଙ୍କ ସ୍ୱାମୀ ସନ୍ଦୀପ ଜଣେ ଯୁବ ବ୍ୟବସାୟୀ । ସନ୍ଦୀପ ପ୍ରବୀରଙ୍କଠାରୁ ବୟସରେ ସାନ । ବ୍ୟବସାୟ କାମରେ ସବୁବେଳେ ବାହାରେ ବୁଲୁଥା'ନ୍ତି । କେତେବେଳେ ଦିଲ୍ଲୀ ତ କେତେବେଳେ ସାନ୍‌ଫ୍ରାନ୍‌ସିସ୍କୋ । ତେଣୁ ଅଧିକାଂଶ ସମୟ ଶ୍ୱେତା ସୌମ୍ୟାଙ୍କ ପାଖରେ ରହନ୍ତି । ଯେମିତି ଗୋଟିଏ ଜଏଣ୍ଟ ଫ୍ୟାମିଲି । ସନ୍ଦୀପ ଭୁବନେଶ୍ୱରରେ ଥିବାବେଳେ ନିଶ୍ଚୟ ଏକ ଭ୍ରମଣ ଯୋଗ ଘଟେ । ସମସ୍ତେ ସେଠର କୋରାପୁଟ ଜଙ୍ଗଲରେ ଘନଘୋର ବର୍ଷାକୁ ଉପଭୋଗ କରିବାକୁ ସ୍ଥିର କଲେ । ଆଗରୁ ଫୋରକାଷ୍ଟ ହୋଇଥିଲା । କେହି ଖାତିର କଲେ ନାହିଁ । କାରଣ ବର୍ଷା ସମୟରେ କୋରାପୁଟର ଦୃଶ୍ୟ ନିଆରା । ପଞ୍ଚ‌କୁପଞ୍ଚ କୁଣ୍ଡ‌କୁଣ୍ଡିଆ ପାହାଡ଼ ସୌମ୍ୟାର ଥାକଥାକ ଷ୍ଟାଇଲ‌କରା କେଶସଜ୍ଜା ଭଳି । ତା' ପଞ୍ଚ‌କୁ ନୀଳ ସବୁଜ ଘଞ୍ଚ ଜଙ୍ଗଲ, ଷ୍ଟେଚାର ଘନ କୁଣ୍ଠିତ କେଶ ଭଳି । ସ୍ଥାନେ ସ୍ଥାନେ କାଚକେନ୍ଦୁ ଝରଣା ଜଳର ଫୁଆର ସହରଠାରୁ ଦୂରରେ ଅଜ୍ଞାନତା ଓ ସରଳତାରେ ଛଳଛଳ ଆଦିମ ଜନଜାତି । ଅଙ୍କାବଙ୍କା ରାସ୍ତାରେ କିଲ୍‌କିଲିଆ ଥଣ୍ଡା ପବନର କୁତୁକୁତୁ ଖେଳ । ଲାଗୁଥାଏ କୋରାପୁଟ ନୁହେଁ, ସୁଇଜରଲ୍ୟାଣ୍ଡ କିୟା କାନାଡ଼ାର କୁବେକ ସିଟି । ଥରେ ପହଞ୍ଚିଲେ ରହିଯିବାକୁ ଇଚ୍ଛା ହୁଏ । ସକାଳ

ଛୁଆ, ସମସ୍ତେ ସନ୍ଦୀପଙ୍କର କଳା ପାଜେରୋ ଗାଡ଼ିରେ ବସିଲେ। ସନ୍ଦୀପ ଗାଡ଼ି
ଚଲାଉଥାଏ। ସମସ୍ତଙ୍କ ଆଖିରେ ସକାଳର ଛାଇ ନିଦ। ଟିକେ ଟିକେ ଭୁଲେଇ
ପଡ଼ୁଥା'ନ୍ତି ସମସ୍ତେ। ଆଗରେ ସନ୍ଦୀପଙ୍କ ସହ କବୀର ବସିଥା'ନ୍ତି। ଦୁହେଁ ମୃଦୁ
ଆଳାପ କରୁଥା'ନ୍ତି। ମଝି ସିଟ୍‌ରେ ସୌମ୍ୟା ଓ ଶ୍ୱେତା ଅଧା ଖୋଲା ଆଖିରେ
ଝୁଲାଉଥା'ନ୍ତି। ଯେମିତି ନିଶାଗ୍ରସ୍ତ ଅବସ୍ଥା। ଅଥଚ ସେମାନେ ବୋତଲ ଛୁଇଁଥିଲେ
ନାହିଁ। ପଛ ସିଟ୍‌ରେ ସୌମ୍ୟାର ଦୁଇ ପୁଅ ଓ କବୀରଙ୍କ ସାନ ଝିଅ। ଜଙ୍ଗଲ ରାସ୍ତାର
ରୋମାଞ୍ଚ ସବୁଠୁ ବେଶୀ ଉପଭୋଗ କରୁଥା'ନ୍ତି ଛୁଆମାନେ। ମିଛିମିଛିକା ଖେଳୁଥା'ନ୍ତି
"ହେଇ, ବାଘଟାଏ ଦେଖିଲି, ହାତୀଟାଏ ଦେଖିଲି, ସାପଟାଏ ଦେଖିଲି"।
"ମାଓବାଦୀଟାଏ ଦେଖିଲି" ପୋଲିସ କନ୍ୟା ତାନ୍ୟା କହିଲା। ସନ୍ଦୀପର ପିଲାମାନେ
ପଚାରିଲେ– ମାଓବାଦୀର କ'ଣ ମାମ୍ପ ଭଳି ରୁମୁରୁମିଆ ଶୁଙ୍ଢ ଅଛି ?"

ତାନ୍ୟା କହିଲା "ମତେ ଜଣା ନାହିଁ କିନ୍ତୁ ଭାରି ଭୟଙ୍କର ଜୀବ। ପାପା ଓ
ତାଙ୍କ ସାଙ୍ଗମାନଙ୍କଠୁ ଶୁଣିଛି, ଦେଖିନି କେବେ। ଆଜି ଦେଖା ପଡ଼ିଗଲେ ଭଲ ହୁଅନ୍ତା।
ସ୍କୁଲରେ ସମସ୍ତଙ୍କ ଆଗରେ କୁହନ୍ତେ।"

କବୀର ସତର୍କ କରାଇଦେଲେ "ଶୁଣ ଆମେ ଏବେ ମାଓବାଦୀ ଅଞ୍ଚଳକୁ
ଯାଉଛେ ଏବଂ ବଡ଼ ଗୋପନୀୟ ଭାବେ ଯାଉଛେ। ତେଣୁ ଆମମାନଙ୍କୁ ସାବଧାନ
ହେବାକୁ ହେବ। ଯେହେତୁ ଆମର ଏଇଟା ଘରୋଇ ଟ୍ରିପ୍‌। ଆମ ସହ ପୋଲିସ
ପ୍ରୋଟେକ୍‌ସନ ନାହିଁ। ତେଣୁ ଅଧିକ ସତର୍କ ହେବାକୁ ପଡ଼ିବ। ସବୁଠୁ ବଡ଼ କଥା
ହେଲା ଏ ଗାଡ଼ିରେ ଗୋଟିଏ ପୋଲିସ ଫ୍ୟାମିଲି ଅଛି ଏକଥା ଯେମିତି କେହି ନ
ଜାଣନ୍ତି। ମାଓବାଦୀମାନେ ଖବର ପାଇଲେ ଆମକୁ କିଡ୍‌ନାପ କରିନେବେ ଏବଂ
ତା' ପରେ ନାନାଦି ନାଟକ ଢଳିବ। ସରକାର ବି ଅଡ଼ୁଆରେ ପଡ଼ିବେ ଆମକୁ
ମୁକୁଳେଇବା ପାଇଁ। ଦଶଟା ମାଓବାଦୀଙ୍କୁ ହୁଏତ ହାଜତରୁ ଛାଡ଼ିବାକୁ ପଡ଼ିବ ନଚେତ୍‌
ଆମର ମୁଣ୍ଡକାଟ ହେବ। ଏ ହେଉଛି ଆମର ଜୀବନ ମରଣର କଥା। ସମସ୍ତେ
ମୋ କଥା ଧ୍ୟାନ ସହକାରେ ଶୁଣ। ସନ୍ଦୀପ ହେଲେ ବିଜ୍‌ନେସ୍‌ ମ୍ୟାନ୍‌। ସମସ୍ତେ
ଜାଣିବେ ଯେ ସନ୍ଦୀପ ଜଣେ ଛୋଟକାଟର ବ୍ୟବସାୟୀ ଏବଂ ମୁଁ ହେଉଛି ଜଣେ
କମ୍ପ୍ୟୁଟର ଇଂଜିନିୟର। ଆମେରିକାର ବଷ୍ଟବ ସହରରେ ଢକିରି କରେ।
ଭୁବନେଶ୍ୱରରେ ଘର ଏବଂ ଆମେ କୋରାପୁଟ ବୁଲି ଆସିଛୁ। ଜାଣିଶୁଣି ମୁଁ ସଙ୍ଗରେ
ପୋଲିସ ପରିଚୟପତ୍ର ଆଣି ନାହିଁ ଏବଂ ମ୍ୟାଡମ୍‌ ଦୁଇଜଣ ହେଉଛନ୍ତି ହାଉସ
ୱାଇଫ୍‌। ମୋ ଝିଅ ବଷ୍ଟବ ସହରରେ ପଢ଼େ ଏବଂ ସନ୍ଦୀପଙ୍କ ଦୁଇ ପୁଅ
ଭୁବନେଶ୍ୱରରେ ପଢ଼ନ୍ତି। ସେମାନେ କିଛି ଡ୍ରାମା କରିବା ଦରକାର ନାହିଁ। କେବଳ

ତାନ୍ୟାକୁ ଆମେରିକାନ୍ ଇଂଲିଶ ଆକ୍ସେଣ୍ଟରେ କଥା କହିବାକୁ ହେବ। ସେଇଟା ତା' ପାଇଁ ସମସ୍ୟା ନୁହେଁ। ଯଦି ଦରକାର ପଡ଼େ ଆମେ ସମସ୍ତେ ଟିକେ ଟିକେ ଅଭିନୟ କରିବା। ସମସ୍ତେ ବୁଝିଲ ତ!"

କବୀର ପୁନି କହିଲେ "ଦ୍ୱିତୀୟ କଥା ହେଲା ସବୁଠୁ ଗୁରୁତ୍ୱପୂର୍ଣ୍ଣ। ଯଦି କିଏ କେତେବେଳେ ଜଙ୍ଗଲ ଭିତରେ ହଜିଯାଏ, ତେବେ ଡୋଣ୍ଟ ବି ପ୍ୟାନିକ, କେହି ଡରିବ ନାହିଁ। ପ୍ରଥମେ ନିଜକୁ ଲୁଚାଇ ରଖିବ। କୌଣସିପ୍ରକାରେ ନିକଟସ୍ଥ ପୋଲିସ ଫାଣ୍ଡିରେ ପହଞ୍ଚିଯିବ ଓ ସାହାଯ୍ୟ ମାଗିବ। ମୋବାଇଲ ସାଙ୍ଗରେ ରଖିବ, ସମସ୍ତଙ୍କ ଫୋନ୍ ପୂରା ବ୍ୟାଟେରୀ ଚାର୍ଜରେ ଅଛି। ତେଣୁ ଚିନ୍ତା ନାହିଁ। ପାଖରେ କିଛି ଟଙ୍କା ଓ ଚକୋଲେଟ୍ ଅଛି। ମୋବାଇଲ ଯୋଗାଯୋଗ ପାଇଁ, ଚକୋଲେଟ୍ ଭୋକରୁ ରକ୍ଷା ପାଇବା ପାଇଁ ଏବଂ ଟଙ୍କା ଦ୍ୱାରା ଅନ୍ୟର ସହାୟତା ପାଇବା ପାଇଁ ଲୋଡ଼ା। ସନ୍ଦୀପର ଗାଡ଼ିରେ ତ ସବୁବେଳେ ଟାଙ୍କି ଫୁଲ୍ ପେଟ୍ରୋଲ୍ ଥାଏ। ଏତିକି ଜିନିଷ ମାନିଲେ କୌଣସି ବିପଦରେ ଅଧିକ ସମୟ ପର୍ଯ୍ୟନ୍ତ ଲଢ଼େଇ କରିହେବ।"

ଏକ ସୁଖଦ ଭ୍ରମଣକୁ ପୋଲିସ ଅଫିସରଙ୍କ ସତର୍କ ଚିହ୍ନଣୀ ଦ୍ୱାରା ଭୟଭୀତ ନ କରିବା ପାଇଁ ସନ୍ଦୀପ ସହସା ଏଫ୍.ଏମ୍ ରେଡିଓର ଭଲ୍ୟୁମ୍ ବଢ଼ାଇଦେଲେ ଓ ଗୀତର ସୁର ସହ ବେସୁରା ଗୁଣୁଗୁଣୁ ହେଲେ। ଏ ଭିତରେ ଗାଡ଼ି ବ୍ରହ୍ମପୁରରେ ପହଞ୍ଚି ଯାଇଥିଲା। ବାଟସାରା ଠାକୁର ଭୋଗ ଖାଇବା ପରେ କେଉଁଠି ବରା, ଇଟିଲି, କେଉଁଠି ପଇଡ଼, କେଉଁଠି ଚଣା ଛୁଟ ଖାଇ ଖାଇ ସମସ୍ତେ ଆନନ୍ଦରେ ସନ୍ଦୀପର ସାବଲୀଳ ଡ୍ରାଇଭିଂର ଆନନ୍ଦ ଉପଭୋଗ କରୁଥିଲେ। ମନୋରମ ସାଲୁର ଘାଟିରେ ପହଞ୍ଚିବା ବେଳକୁ ଆକାଶରେ କିଛି କଳା ବାଦଲ ଘୋଟି ଆସୁଥିବାର ଦେଖିଲେ। ଅସରାଏ ଧମକାଣି ବର୍ଷା ବି ବର୍ଷିଗଲା। ସାଲୁର ଘାଟିର ଲାଞ୍ଜ ନ ସରୁଣୁ ସୁଙ୍କି ଘାଟିର ମୁଣ୍ଡ ଆରମ୍ଭ। ସୁଙ୍କି ଘାଟ ବହୁତ ମନୋରମ। ଖୁବ୍ ଦୀର୍ଘ ଏବଂ ଉଚ୍ଚା ଘାଟି। ଉପରକୁ ଯେତେ ଉଠୁଥା'ନ୍ତି ସେତେ ଥଣ୍ଡା ଲାଗୁଥାଏ ଗାଡ଼ିର କାଚ ଖୋଲି ଏସି ବନ୍ଦ କରିବା ସତ୍ତ୍ୱେ। ମନ ଶାନ୍ତ ଓ ଉତ୍‌ଫୁଲ୍ଲିତ ହେଉଥାଏ। ପାହାଡ଼ର ଅପରୂପ ସୌନ୍ଦର୍ଯ୍ୟରେ ସମସ୍ତେ ବିମୋହିତ। ଗୋଟିଏ ପାଖରେ ପାହାଡ଼ର ଅଧା ବାଦଲରେ ଲୁଚି ଯାଇଛି ଏବଂ ଅନ୍ୟ ପାଖରେ ଖୁବ୍ ତଳେ ସୁନ୍ଦର ସମତଲ ଉପତ୍ୟକା। ସମସ୍ତେ ଗାଡ଼ିରୁ ଓହ୍ଲାଇ ପ୍ରାକୃତିକ ସୌନ୍ଦର୍ଯ୍ୟ ଉପଭୋଗ କଲେ ଏବଂ ଫଟୋ ସେସନ୍ କଲେ। ଫେସବୁକ୍ ଓ ହ୍ୱାଟ୍ସଆପ୍‌ରେ ଏସବୁ ନ ଦେଲେ ଭ୍ରମଣର ମୂଲ୍ୟ କ'ଣ? କବୀର କହିଲେ "ସୁଙ୍କି ଘାଟିରେ ବେଶୀ ସମୟ ନ ରହି ପଳାଇବା। ଦୁଇମାସ ତଳେ ସୁଙ୍କି ଘାଟିରେ ମାଓବାଦୀଙ୍କ ବୋମା ବିସ୍ଫୋରଣରେ ସାତଜଣ

ପୋଲିସ ସହିଦ ହୋଇଯାଇଥିଲେ। ଜାଗାଟି ଯେତେ ସୁନ୍ଦର ହେଲେ କ'ଣ ହେବ, ମାଓବାଦୀଙ୍କ ଉପଦ୍ରବ ଯୋଗୁଁ ଏବେ ସେତିକି ଅଧିକ ବିପଦଜନକ ହୋଇପଡ଼ିଛି। ଜୀବନର ଏଇଟା ହିଁ ନିରାଟ ସତ୍ୟ। ସୌନ୍ଦର୍ଯ୍ୟ ସହ ସବୁବେଳେ ବିପଦ ଯୋଡ଼ି ହୋଇ ରହିଛି। ପୋଲିସ ଚାକିରିରେ ଭର୍ତ୍ତି ହେବା ପୂର୍ବରୁ କବୀର ସୁନାବେଡ଼ା ମିଗ୍‌ବିମାନ କାରଖାନାରେ କାମ କରୁଥିଲେ। ସେଇଠାରେ ରହି ପରୀକ୍ଷା ପାଇଁ ପ୍ରସ୍ତୁତ ହୋଇ ଭାରତୀୟ ପୋଲିସ ସେବା ଚାକିରିରେ ଯୋଗଦେଲେ। ସେତେବେଳେ ସୁକ୍‌ ଘାଟିରୁ ଚଲି ଚଲି ସେ ପଟାଙ୍ଗିରେ ପହଞ୍ଚ ଯାଉଥିଲେ ଏବଂ ବୋମା ଘାଟିରୁ ଟ୍ରେକିଂ କରି ରାୟଗଡ଼ା ଚଲିଯାଇଥିଲେ। ମାତ୍ର ମାଓବାଦୀ ଆସିବା ପରେ ସବୁ କଥା ବଦଳିଗଲା। ଏବେ ଆଉ ଏକା ଏକା ଟ୍ରେକିଂ କରିହେବ ନାହିଁ। ଘାଟିରେ ଯେତେ ଉପରକୁ ଉଠୁଥିଲେ କବୀରଙ୍କର ପଞ୍ଚ କଥା ସେତେ ମନେପଡୁଥିଲା। ଏ ଭିତରେ ରାସ୍ତା ଯେତେ ସୁନ୍ଦର ଓ ମସୃଣ ହୋଇଛି ସେତିକି ବିପଜନକ ବି ହୋଇଯାଇଛି ମାଓବାଦୀଙ୍କ ପାଇଁ। ପଟାଙ୍ଗି, ସେମିଲିଗୁଡ଼ା ଓ ସୁନାବେଡ଼ା ପରେ କୋଲାବ ଡ୍ୟାମର ପାଣି ଦେଖାଗଲା। ଖୁବ୍ ସ୍ୱଚ୍ଛ ପାଣି। ପାଣି ଭିତରେ ପାହାଚଗୁଡ଼ିକ ଦ୍ୱୀପ ଭଳି ଫୁଟି ଦିଶୁଥାଏ। ସ୍ଥିର ପାଣିରେ ବୋଟିଂ କରିବାକୁ ଖୁବ୍ ମଜା ଲାଗନ୍ତା। ଏମିତି ଭାବୁ ଭାବୁ ଭ୍ରମୁରିପୁଟ ହୋଇ ଗାଡ଼ି କୋରାପୁଟରେ ପହଞ୍ଚିଲା। କୋରାପୁଟ ସର୍କିଟ ହାଉସ୍ ଗୋଟିଏ ଛୋଟ ପାହାଡ଼ ଉପରେ ଅବସ୍ଥିତ। ଗାଡ଼ି ପହଞ୍ଚିଲାବେଳକୁ କିଛି ପୋଲିସ ଅଫିସର ପୋର୍ଟିକୋକୁ ଆସିଗଲେ। କବୀର ଓ ଅନ୍ୟମାନଙ୍କୁ ପାଛୋଟି ନେଇ ସେମାନଙ୍କ ରୁମ୍ ଦେଖାଇଦେଲେ। ମୁହଁ ହାତ ଧୋଇବା ପରେ ସମସ୍ତେ ମୁକ୍ତାକାଶ ତଳେ ଖାଇବାକୁ ଆସିଗଲେ। ଗରମ ଗରମ ଖାଦ୍ୟ ସେମାନଙ୍କର ଭୋକ ବଢ଼ାଇ ଦେଇଥିଲା। ତୃପ୍ତିରେ ଖାଇଲେ ସମସ୍ତେ। ସତରେ କୋରାପୁଟ ହେଉଛି ଗୋଟିଏ ଶୈଳନିବାସ। ଖାଇବା ଶେଷରେ ଗରମ ଗୋଲାପଜାମୁ ଭଳି କୋରାପୁଟ ଶୈଳନିବାସ ମଧୁର କିନ୍ତୁ ଶୀତଳ।

ରାତି ଏସ୍.ପି.ଙ୍କ ଘରେ ଡିନର। ସମସ୍ତେ କିଛି ସମୟ ବିଶ୍ରାମ ନେଲେ। ସଂଧ୍ୟାରେ ଉଠି ହାଲୁକା ଗରମ କପଡ଼ା ପିନ୍ଧି ଏସ୍.ପି.ଙ୍କ କ୍ୱାର୍ଟର୍ସକୁ ବାହାରିଲେ। ପାହାଡ଼ ଉପରେ ଇଂରେଜ ଅମଲର ଏସ୍.ପି. ବଙ୍ଗଳା। ପୋଲିସ ଆଦର କାଇଦାରେ ରାତ୍ରି ଭୋଜନର ବ୍ୟବସ୍ଥା ହୋଇଥାଏ। ଜିଲ୍ଲା କଲେକ୍ଟର, ଟ୍ରେନି ଆଇଏଏସ ଓ ଆଇପିଏସ ଅଫିସରମାନେ ମଧ୍ୟ ନିମନ୍ତ୍ରିତ ହୋଇଥା'ନ୍ତି। ସେମାନଙ୍କ ପାଇଁ ନୂଆ ଚାକିରିର ନୂଆ ସ୍ୱପ୍ନ। ସମସ୍ତେ କବୀରଙ୍କୁ ଘେରିଯାଇ ଅନେକ ପ୍ରଶ୍ନ ପଚାରିଥିଲେ। କବୀର ଜେନେରେସନ୍ ଗ୍ୟାପକୁ ଚାହିଁ ଉତ୍ତର ଦେଉଥା'ନ୍ତି। ପୋଲିସ ବ୍ରାଞ୍ଚର

ମୃଦୁମାଦକତା ସହ ସମସ୍ତେ ଖାଇଲେ ଓ ନାଚିଲେ ମଧ୍ୟ। କିନ୍ତୁ ପୋଲିସ ଚୁକିରିରେ ସବୁବେଳେ ସମୟ ଠିକ୍ ଯାଏ ନାହିଁ। ହସଖୁସିରେ କାମ କରି ଫୁଲିବାର ଅଛି। ସମୟ ଉପରେ କ'ଣ ଭରସା? ଦିନର ସାରି ସମସ୍ତେ ଗାଡ଼ିରେ ବସିଲେ। ସଂଧାଟି ସୁଖଦ ହୋଇଥିବାରୁ ଏସ୍.ପି.ଙ୍କୁ ଧନ୍ୟବାଦ ଦେଲେ। ଆସନ୍ତାକାଲି ଲଙ୍କାପୁର ଯାଇ ଗୋଟିଏ ଟ୍ରାଭେଲ୍ କଟେଜ୍‌ରେ ରହିଣୀ ବୋଲି ଏସ୍.ପିଙ୍କ କାନରେ କବୀର କହିଲେ। ଗୋପନୀୟ ତଥା ଘରୋଇ ଗସ୍ତ ଭଳି ପୋଲିସ ପ୍ରୋଟେକ୍‌ନ ଦରକାର ନାହିଁ ବୋଲି ଏସ୍.ପି.ଙ୍କୁ ଜଣାଇଦେଲେ। ଏସ୍.ପି. ଚିନ୍ତିତ ହୋଇ କହିଲେ, "ସାର! ମାଓପ୍ରବଣ ଅଞ୍ଚଳ, ସତର୍କ ରହିବେ।"

କୋରାପୁଟରେ ଦ୍ୱିତୀୟ ଦିନ। ମାଛକୁଣ୍ଡ ପାଖରେ ରାସ୍ତା କଡ଼ରେ ଗୋଟିଏ ଟ୍ରାଭେଲ୍ କଟେଜ୍‌ର ନାମ ହେଉଛି "ଦେଶିଆ"। ପୁରା ଆଦିବାସୀ ଢାଞ୍ଚାରେ ନିର୍ମିତ। ଆଦିବାସୀ କୁଡ଼ିଆରେ ରହିବା ଭଳି ଅନୁଭବ ହେବ। ସେଠାରେ ରାତ୍ରିଯାପନର ବ୍ୟବସ୍ଥା କରାଯାଇଥିଲା। ମାଓବାଦୀ ଚଲପ୍ରଚଲର ହଟ୍ ବେଡ଼୍‌ରେ ସ୍ଥାନଟି ଅଛି। ଏସ୍.ପି.ଙ୍କଠାରୁ ଶୁଣିଥିଲେ କବୀର। ତେଣୁ ତାଙ୍କର ଅନ୍ତର୍ମନ କହିଲା ସେ ସ୍ଥାନରେ ରାତ୍ରିଯାପନ କରିବା ଠିକ୍ ହେବ ନାହିଁ। ସମସ୍ତଙ୍କୁ ଠିକ୍‌ଠାକ୍ ଘରକୁ ଫେରିବାର ଅଛି। ଯାହା ବି ହେଉ ରାତ୍ରିଯାପନ କରିବାକୁ ହେଲା। ଏବଂ ସକାଳୁ ସକାଳୁ କେରାପୁଟରୁ ବାହାରିଗଲେ। ଜୟପୁରରୁ ମାଛକୁଣ୍ଡ ରାସ୍ତାରେ ଯାଉ ଯାଉ ରାସ୍ତା ଭୁଲ୍ ହୋଇଗଲା। ଗାଡ଼ି ଫେରାଇ ପୁଣି ମାଛକୁଣ୍ଡ ରାସ୍ତା ଧରିଲେ। ମାଓପ୍ରବଣ ଜାଗାରେ ରାସ୍ତା ବଦଳାଇବା ଖୁବ୍ ଭଲ କଥା। ଏହା ନିରାପଦ। ମଝିରେ ପାତ୍ରପୁଟ ପୋଲ ପାଖରେ ସମସ୍ତେ ମକା ପୋଡ଼ା ଖାଇଲେ ଓ ଶୀଘ୍ର ବାହାରିଗଲେ। ଦୁଇପଟେ ଘଞ୍ଚ ଜଙ୍ଗଲ, ଧୂ ଧୂ ଖରାକୁ ଖାତିର କରୁନଥାଏ। ଶୀତଳ ପବନ ମୁହଁରେ ବୋଲିହୋଇ ନିର୍ଭୟ ଆଶ୍ୱାସନା ଦେଉଥାଏ। ଗାଡ଼ିଯାଇ ଲମତାପୁଟ ହାତରେ ପହଞ୍ଚିଗଲା। ସେଠାରୁ ଡ଼ାହାଣକୁ ଭାଙ୍ଗିଲେ ମାଛକୁଣ୍ଡ ଜଳଭଣ୍ଡାର। ସନ୍ଦୀପ କହିଲେ "ଗାଡ଼ି ଟିକିଏ ଟେକ୍ କରିବାକୁ ପଡ଼ିବ।" ଦେଖିଲାବେଳକୁ ପଛ ଚକଟି ପଙ୍କଚଟ୍ ହୋଇଯାଇଛି। ସନ୍ଦୀପ ହାତ ମଝିରେ ଗାଡ଼ି ରଖିକରି ଚକ ବଦଲାଇଲେ। ସେଦିନ ବହୁତ ଭିଡ଼ ଥାଏ। ଏଠିକା ହାତର ଦୃଶ୍ୟ ସମ୍ପୂର୍ଣ୍ଣ ନିଆରା। ଆଦିବାସୀମାନେ ଖୁବ୍ ଦୂରଦୂରାନ୍ତରୁ ହାଟକୁ ଆସନ୍ତି। କିଛି ଆବଶ୍ୟକ ଜିନିଷ କିଣି ହସ ଖୁସିରେ ଫେରିଯା'ନ୍ତି। ହାଟ ହିଁ ଆଦିବାସୀମାନଙ୍କର ଜୀବନ। ହାଟ ବନ୍ଦ ହୋଇଗଲେ ଜୀବନଯାତ୍ରାର ଖୁବ୍ ସମସ୍ୟା ହୁଏ। ସେମାନେ ଜିନିଷ ବିକି ପାରିବେ ନାହିଁ କି କିଣି ପାରିବେ ନାହିଁ। ହାଟ ଯେମିତି ତାଙ୍କର ହୃତ୍‌ପିଣ୍ଡ। କବୀର ଗାଡ଼ି ବାହାରେ ଛିଡ଼ା ହୋଇଥା'ନ୍ତି। ହଠାତ୍ ଯାତ୍ରୀବାହୀ ଜିପ୍ ପାସ୍ କଲା। ସେଥିରେ

ବସିଥିବା ଜଣେ ବ୍ୟକ୍ତି କବୀରଙ୍କୁ ପୋଲିସ କାଇଦାରେ ସାବଧାନ ହେଲା। କବୀର ମଧ୍ୟ ଅଭ୍ୟାସବଶତଃ ପୋଲିସ ଢ଼ାଞ୍ଚାରେ ସାବଧାନ ହୋଇ ସମ୍ମାନ ଜଣାଇଲା। କିନ୍ତୁ ପରକ୍ଷଣରେ ସେ ଚମକି ପଡ଼ିଲେ। କୋରାପୁଟର ଲମତାପୁତ ହାତରେ ତାଙ୍କୁ କେମିତି ଜଣେ ପୋଲିସ ବୋଲି ଚିହ୍ନି ପାରିଲା? ବୋଧହୁଏ ସେହି ବ୍ୟକ୍ତିଜଣକ କେବେ ତାଙ୍କ ସହ କାମ କରୁଥିବ। କିନ୍ତୁ ମାଓବାଦୀ ଅଞ୍ଚଳରେ ପୋଲିସ ବୋଲି ଚିହ୍ନାପଡ଼ିବା ଆଦୌ ଶୁଭ ଲକ୍ଷଣ ନୁହେଁ। ସେ ନିଜେ ସେତେବେଳେ ଭୁଲିଗଲେ ଯେ ସେ ଜଣେ କମ୍ପ୍ୟୁଟର ଇଂଜିନିୟର ବୋଲି ପ୍ଲାନ କରିଥିବା କଥା। ମସ୍ତବଡ଼ ଭୁଲ ହୋଇଗଲା। ସନ୍ଦୀପ ଗାଡ଼ି ଠିକ୍ କରି ଡାକିଲେ। ସମସ୍ତେ ଗାଡ଼ିରେ ବସି ମାଛକୁଣ୍ଡ ରାସ୍ତାରେ ବାହାରିଲେ। ମାଛକୁଣ୍ଡ ପହଞ୍ଚିବାର ପାଞ୍ଚ କିଲୋମିଟର ଦୂରରୁ "ଦେଶିଆ" କଟେଜ୍ ତାଙ୍କ ରହଣୀ ସ୍ଥାନ। ସେଠି ବିଦ୍ୟୁତ୍ ପ୍ରବାହ ନାହିଁ। ପ୍ରାକୃତିକ ପାରିପାର୍ଶ୍ୱିକ ପରିବେଶ ସମସ୍ତଙ୍କୁ ମୁଗ୍ଧ କଲା। ସେମାନେ ଗାଡ଼ିରୁ ଓହ୍ଲାଇବାମାତ୍ରେ କେତେଜଣ ଆଦିବାସୀ ଝିଅ ସେମାନଙ୍କୁ ପାଛୋଟି ନେଲେ। ଟେବୁଲ ଓ ଚେୟାର ପଡ଼ିଥିଲା ଖାଇବା ପାଇଁ। ଭାତ, ଡାଲି, ବାଇଗଣ ଭଜା ଓ ମାଛ ତରକାରି ବେଶ୍ ସ୍ୱାଦୁକର ଥିଲା। ପଙ୍ଖା ନ ଥିବାରୁ ଟିକେ ଆଶ୍ୱସ୍ତି ବୋଧ କରୁଥିଲେ ସମସ୍ତେ। ଠିକ୍ ଅଛି, ଯେ ଦେଶ ଯାଇ ସେ ଫଳ ଖାଇ। ଖାଇସାରି ସମସ୍ତେ ଙ୍ଗଲଛପର ଘରକୁ ଗଲେ ବିଶ୍ରାମ ପାଇଁ। ଙ୍ଗଲଘରଗୁଡ଼ିକ ବେଶ୍ ଥଣ୍ଡା ଥିଲା। ଗାଧୁଆ ଘର ଡ଼ିଜାଇନ୍ ସ୍ୱତନ୍ତ୍ର ଥିଲା। ସେଥିରେ ୱାସ ମେସିନ୍‌ଗୁଡ଼ିକ ତମ୍ବରେ ତିଆରି ଓ ସାୱାର ତଳେ ଗେବଲସର ଚଟାଣ। ସତରେ ଝରଣାରେ ଗାଧୋଇବାର କଳ୍ପନା। ପାଶ୍ଚାତ୍ୟ ଓ ଜନଜାତୀୟ ଶୈଳୀର ଅପୂର୍ବ ମିଶ୍ରଣର ପ୍ରୟାସ ସମସ୍ତଙ୍କୁ ଚକିତ କଲା।

କୋରାପୁଟର ସଲପ ରସ ଉପକୂଳ ଅଞ୍ଚଳର ଖଜୁରି ତାଡ଼ି ଭଳି ଏକ ପାନୀୟ। ସମସ୍ତେ ସଲପ ଚାଖିବାକୁ ରୁହିଁଲେ ତେଣୁ ଗାଡ଼ି ନେଇ ପାଖ ଗାଁକୁ ଗଲେ। ସେଠାରେ ସଲପ ମିଳୁଛି କି ନାହିଁ ପରିବାରର ପିଲାମାନେ କହିଲେ "ସଲପ ସକାଳେ ମିଳେ ସନ୍ଧ୍ୟାରେ ମିଳେ ନାହିଁ। ଆସନ୍ତାକାଲି ସକାଳେ ଆସିବେ ସଲପ ନିଶ୍ଚିତ ମିଳିବ।" କବୀର ସେତିକି ଶୁଣି ମାଛକୁଣ୍ଡ ଆଡ଼କୁ ଗାଡ଼ି ଚଲାଇବାକୁ କହିଲେ। ଗୋଟିଏ ଗାଁରେ ଅଧିକ ସମୟ ରହିବା ଏଠାରେ ବୁଦ୍ଧିମାନର କାର୍ଯ୍ୟ ନୁହେଁ। ସବୁ ଗାଁରେ ମାଓବାଦୀମାନଙ୍କର ଚର ଅଛନ୍ତି। ମାଛକୁଣ୍ଡ ବଜାରରେ ଗାଡ଼ି ରଖିଲେ, ସେତେବେଳକୁ ସନ୍ଧ୍ୟା ହୋଇଯାଇଥାଏ। ବଜାର ଛକରେ ମାଛକୁଣ୍ଡ ଥାନା। ଥାନା ପାଖରେ ଗାଡ଼ି ରଖି ସମସ୍ତେ ଘୁଲି ଘୁଲି ମାଛକୁଣ୍ଡ ପାଖରେ ଥିବା ଛୋଟିଆ ବ୍ୟାରେଜ ଆଡ଼କୁ ଗଲେ। ବ୍ୟାରେଜ ପାରି ହୋଇ ଅନ୍ୟ ପଟକୁ ଗଲେ। ବ୍ୟାରେଜ ତଳେ ପାଣିର

ସ୍ରୋତ ପ୍ରଖର- ଭୟ ଉଦ୍‌ବେଗକାରୀ। ଗୋଡ଼ ଖସିଗଲେ କୁଆଡ଼େ ଭାସାଇ ନେବ ଠିକଣା ନାହିଁ। ନଦୀର ଆର ପାର୍ଶ୍ୱରେ ଆନ୍ଧ୍ରପ୍ରଦେଶ। ସମସ୍ତେ ପୋଲ ପାରି ହୋଇ ଆନ୍ଧ୍ରପ୍ରଦେଶର ମାଟି ଛୁଇଁ ପୁଣି ଫେରିଆସିଲେ। ସ୍ୱାଧୀନତା ସମୟର ଡୁଡୁମା ମାଛକୁଣ୍ଡ ପ୍ରୋଜେକ୍ଟ ଆନ୍ଧ୍ର ଓ ଓଡ଼ିଶାର ସମନ୍ୱୟ ପ୍ରକଳ୍ପ। ଦୁହେଁ ଏହି ଜଳପ୍ରପାତରୁ ବିଦ୍ୟୁତ୍‌ ଉତ୍ପାଦନ କରି ବାଣ୍ଟି ନିଅନ୍ତି। ମାଛକୁଣ୍ଡ ବଜାରରୁ କିଛି ଚିପ୍‌ସ ଓ ମିକ୍‌ଚର କିଣି ସମସ୍ତେ ଗାଡ଼ିକୁ ଫେରିଲେ। ବଜାର ବନ୍ଦ ହେବାକୁ ବସିଥାଏ। ପାହାଡ଼ ଓ ଜଙ୍ଗଲ ଅଞ୍ଚଳରେ ବଜାର ଖୁବ୍‌ ଶୀଘ୍ର ବନ୍ଦ ହୁଏ। ସନ୍ଧ୍ୟା ପରେ ହୋ ହୋ ବଜାର ଖାଁ ଖାଁ ଲାଗେ। ସହରୀ ଲୋକଙ୍କୁ ଜଙ୍ଗଲୀ ରାତି ବଡ଼ କଷ୍ଟକର ଲାଗୁଥାଏ। କିଟିକିଟି ଅନ୍ଧାର ଭିତରେ ଗାଡ଼ି ଷ୍ଟାର୍ଟ କରି ସମସ୍ତେ ଦେଶୀଆକୁ ଫେରିଲେ। ଦେଶୀଆରେ ଗାଡ଼ି ରଖୁ ଦେଖୁଲେ ଯେ କିଛି ଯୁବକ ମୋଟରସାଇକେଲରେ ସେଠାରୁ ପଳାଇ ଗଲେ। ସେମାନେ ଖୁବ୍‌ ବଳିଷ୍ଠ ଥିଲେ। ସେମାନଙ୍କର ଭାବଭଙ୍ଗୀ ବେଶ୍‌ ସନ୍ଦେହଜନକ ଥିଲା। ପିଲାମାନେ ଗାଡ଼ିରୁ ଓହ୍ଲାଇ ନିଜ ନିଜ ରୁମ୍‌କୁ ଗଲେ। କବୀର ଖୁବ୍‌ ଶୀଘ୍ର ଗାଧୋଇପଡ଼ି ବାହାରି ଆସିଲେ। କବୀର ଓ ସନ୍ଦୀପ ସନ୍ଧ୍ୟା ପାଇଁ କିଛି ଡ୍ରିଙ୍କ୍‌ସ କାଢ଼ିଲେ। ଦେଶୀଆରେ ନିଯୁକ୍ତ ପିଲାକୁ ଗ୍ଲାସ ଆଣିବାକୁ କହିଲେ। ପିଲାଟି ଗ୍ଲାସ ସହ ଏକ ସ୍ୱାଇଟ୍‌ ବୋତଲ ଥୋଇଲା।

"ଏଥିରେ କ'ଣ ଅଛି?" କବୀର ପିଲାଟିକୁ ପଚାରିଲେ। ପିଲାଟି କହିଲା ଯେ- ଥାନା ବାବୁ ସେଥିରେ ସଲପ ପଠାଇଛନ୍ତି। କବୀର ଆଶ୍ଚର୍ଯ୍ୟ ହେଲେ ଥାନା ବାବୁ କିପରି ଜାଣିଲେ ଯେ ସେମାନେ ଏଠାରେ ଅଛନ୍ତି ବୋଲି? ତାଙ୍କ ଆସିବା କଥା ତ ଥାନା ବାବୁଙ୍କୁ କୁହାଯାଇ ନାହିଁ। ସେମାନେ ସଲପ ଖୋଜୁଥିବା କଥା କାହାରିକୁ ଜଣା ନାହିଁ। ଥାନା ବାବୁ କିପରି ଜାଣିଲେ? କବୀରଙ୍କର ମନ ଭିତରେ ଭୟ ସୃଷ୍ଟି ହେଲା। ସେ ବିବ୍ରତ ବୋଧ କଲେ। ପିଲାଟିକୁ ପଚାରିଲେ "ଥାନା ବାବୁ ଏଠିକି କାହିଁକି ଆସିଥିଲେ?" ପିଲାଟି କହିଲା "ଆପଣମାନେ ଯିବା ପରେ ଥାନାରୁ ଲୋକ ଆସିଥିଲେ ଏବଂ ଆପଣମାନଙ୍କ କଥା ପଚରୁଥିଲେ। ଆପଣ ରାତିରେ ଏଠି ରହିବେ ବୋଲି ଆମେ ସେମାନଙ୍କୁ କହିଲୁ। ତେଣୁ ସେ ଆପଣମାନଙ୍କ ପାଇଁ ସଲପ ବୋତଲ କହି ଏହି ସ୍ୱାଇଟ୍‌ ବୋତଲ ଦେଇଗଲେ।" ସେମାନେ ଯିବା ପରେ ଆଉ କିଛି ଯୁବକ ଆସି ଦୁଇଟିଯାକ ରୁମ୍‌ରେ କିଛି ଫଳ ଓ ଗୋଟିଏ ଲେଖାଏଁ 'ଗିଫ୍‌ଟପ୍ୟାକେଟ୍‌' ମଧ୍ୟ ରଖି ଯାଇଛନ୍ତି।

କବୀର ସଙ୍ଗେ ସଙ୍ଗେ ଚିକ୍ଚାର କରି ସମସ୍ତଙ୍କୁ ବାରଣ୍ଡାକୁ ବାହାରି ଆସିବାକୁ କହିଲେ। କୌଣସି ଜିନିଷ ଓ ପ୍ୟାକେଟ୍‌ ନ ଛୁଇଁବା ପାଇଁ ନିର୍ଦ୍ଦେଶ ଦେଲେ। ସନ୍ଦୀପ ଆବାକାବା ହୋଇ ରହିଥା'ନ୍ତି। ଯେମିତି ପ୍ରାଣହୀନ ମୂର୍ଚ୍ଛି। କବୀର ସନ୍ଦୀପଙ୍କୁ ଇସାରା

କଲେ ଜଲ୍‌ଦି ଗାଡ଼ି ବାହାର କରିବା ପାଇଁ। ସମସ୍ତଙ୍କୁ ତତ୍‌କ୍ଷଣାତ୍‌ ଗାଡ଼ିରେ ବସିବାକୁ କହିଲେ। ତରବରରେ ସୁଟ୍‌କେଶ୍‌ ଆଣି ଗାଡ଼ିରେ ରଖିଲେ ଏବଂ ଟାଣି ଆଣି ଗାଡ଼ିରେ ବସାଇଲେ। ଗାଡ଼ି ଦ୍ରୁତ ଗତିରେ ବାହାରିଗଲା। "ଦେଶିଆ"ର ଝିଅମାନେ ଅନୁରୋଧ କରୁଥା'ନ୍ତି ରାତ୍ରି ଭୋଜନ କରିସାରି ଯିବା ପାଇଁ। ଖାଦ୍ୟ ପ୍ରସ୍ତୁତ ହୋଇସାରିଛି ବୋଲି କହିଲେ। ମାତ୍ର କବୀର କୌଣସି ଅସ୍ୱାଭାବିକ ବ୍ୟବହାର ପ୍ରଦର୍ଶନ ନ କରି ଶାନ୍ତ ଭାବରେ କହିଲେ "ଘରୁ କାହାର ଅସୁସ୍ଥତା ଖବର ପାଇ ସେମାନଙ୍କୁ ସଙ୍ଗେ ସଙ୍ଗେ ବାହାରିଯିବାକୁ ପଡ଼ିବ।" ଆଖି ପିଛୁଲାକେ ସମସ୍ତେ 'ଦେଶିଆ' ଛାଡ଼ିଲେ। ପିଲାମାନେ, ସୌମ୍ୟା ଓ ଶ୍ୱେତା କିଛି ବୁଝି ନପାରି ସ୍ତାଣୁ ହୋଇ ବସିଥା'ନ୍ତି। ମାଛକୁଣ୍ଡରୁ ଜୟପୁର ଋଳିଶ କିଲୋମିଟର ରାସ୍ତା। ଜୟପୁରରେ ପହଞ୍ଚିଗଲେ ସେମାନେ ବିପଦମୁକ୍ତ ହୋଇପାରିବେ। ଜହ୍ନ ଆଲୁଅରେ ଗାଡ଼ି ଚଲାଇ ହେବ ତେବେ ହେଡ୍‌ ଲାଇଟ୍‌ ବନ୍ଦ କରିଦେବା ଭଲ ହେବ ବୋଲି ଉପଦେଶ ଦେଲେ। ଲମ୍‌ତାପୁଟ୍‌ ପୂର୍ବରୁ କିଛି ଲୋକ ରାସ୍ତାକଡ଼ରୁ ଗଛ କାଟୁଥିବାର ଦେଖିଲେ। କବୀର ସନ୍ଦୀପଙ୍କ କାନରେ ଚୁପ୍‌ ଚୁପ୍‌ କହିଲେ "ଗଛ ପଡ଼ିବା ପୂର୍ବରୁ ଗାଡ଼ି ବାହାରି ଯିବାର ଅଛି।" ସେଥିରେ ବିପଦ ଥିଲେ ମଧ୍ୟ ଦକ୍ଷ ଗାଡ଼ିଚାଳକ ସନ୍ଦୀପ ଗାଡ଼ି ଲାଇଟ୍‌ ବନ୍ଦ କରି ଦ୍ରୁତଗତିରେ ସେ ରାସ୍ତାରୁ ବାହାରିଗଲେ। ଠିକ୍‌ ପରେ ପରେ ଗଛଟି ରାସ୍ତା ମଝିରେ ଗାଁ ଗାଁ ହୋଇ ପଡ଼ିଲା। କବୀର ଆଖି ବନ୍ଦ କରି ରହିଗଲେ। ରାସ୍ତାରେ କିଛି ଲୋକ ଗାଡ଼ି ଅଟକାଇବାକୁ ହାତ ଦେଖାଉଥିଲେ, ମାତ୍ର କବୀରଙ୍କ ନିର୍ଦେଶରେ ସନ୍ଦୀପ ଗାଡ଼ି ନ ଅଟକାଇ ଦ୍ରୁତ ଗତିରେ ପାରି ହୋଇଗଲେ। ଅଳ୍ପ ସମୟ ଭିତରେ ସେମାନେ ବିପଦର ସୀମାରେଖା ଭିତରୁ ବାହାରି ଯାଇ ଜୟପୁର ବଜାରରେ ପହଞ୍ଚିଗଲେ। କବୀର ଏସ୍‌.ପି.ଙ୍କୁ ଫୋନ୍‌ରେ ଜେରା କଲେ "ତୁମେ ମାଛକୁଣ୍ଡ ଥାନା ବାବୁଙ୍କୁ କାହିଁକି କହିଲ ଯେ ଆମେ 'ଦେଶିଆ'କୁ ରାତ୍ରିଯାପନ କରିବା ପାଇଁ ଯାଉଛୁ ବୋଲି?" ଏସ୍‌.ପି କହିଲେ "ନାଇଁ ସାର୍‌, ମୁଁ ତ ଥାନା ବାବୁଙ୍କୁ କିଛି କହି ନାହିଁ। ସବୁକିଛି ଗୋପନୀୟ ରଖାଯାଇଛି। କିନ୍ତୁ ଆପଣ ଏବେ କେଉଁଠାରେ ଅଛନ୍ତି? ସବୁ ଠିକ୍‌ଠାକ୍‌ ଅଛି ତ? କିଛି ପ୍ରୋଟେକ୍‌ସନ୍‌ ପଠାଇବି କି?"

କବୀର କହିଲେ "କାଲି ଦେଖାହେଲେ କହିବି। ମାତ୍ର ଏବେ ମାଛକୁଣ୍ଡ ଥାନାବାବୁଙ୍କୁ କୁହ ସେ ଯେ 'ଦେଶିଆ' କଟେଜକୁ ଯାଇ କହିବେ ଯେ ସ୍ୱାଇଟ୍‌ ବୋତଲ କିୟ ରୁମ୍‌ରେ ଥବା ଗିଫ୍‌ ପ୍ୟାକେଟ୍‌ କେହି ଖୋଲିବେ ନାହିଁ।"

କବୀର ଓ ସନ୍ଦୀପ ଜୟପୁରରୁ କୋରାପୁଟ ଆଡ଼କୁ ନିରାପଦରେ ଫେରିଗଲେ। ଜୟପୁର ଘାଟି ଚଢ଼ୁ ଚଢ଼ୁ କୋରାପୁଟ ଏସ୍‌.ପି.ଙ୍କ ଫୋନ୍‌ ଆସିଲା। ସେ କହିଲେ

"ମାଛକୁଣ୍ଡ ଥାନାବାବୁଙ୍କୁ ଖବର ଦେଲି ଯେ 'ଦେଶିଆ'ର ଝଲଝରଟା ନିଆଁ ଲାଗିଯାଇଛି। ସେ କୌଣସି ଲୋକ 'ଦେଶିଆ'କୁ ପଠାଇ ନଥିଲେ। ଆପଣ ନିଜର ଉପସ୍ଥିତ ବୁଦ୍ଧି ଯୋଗୁଁ ନିଶ୍ଚିତ ବିପଦରୁ ପରିବାର ସହ ବଞ୍ଚିଯାଇଛନ୍ତି। ଈଶ୍ୱର ବଡ଼ ଲୋକ।"

ସନ୍ଦୀପର ନିରାପଦ ଗାଡ଼ି ଝଲନା ଯୋଗୁଁ କବୀର ତାକୁ ଧନ୍ୟବାଦ ଦେଲେ। ମନକୁ ମନ ଭାବିଲେ ଜୀବନର ପ୍ରତି ପଦପାତରେ ବିପଦ ଥାଏ ଓ ବିପଦକୁ ଚିହ୍ନିପାରିବାର ଶକ୍ତି ଈଶ୍ୱର ଦେଇଥା'ନ୍ତି। ଇନ୍ଟ୍ୟୁସନ୍ ମାଧ୍ୟମରେ ତାହା ସେ ଜଣାଇଦେଇଥା'ନ୍ତି। ଇନ୍ଟ୍ୟୁସନ୍ ସର୍ବଦା ଠିକ୍ ନ ହୋଇପାରେ କିନ୍ତୁ ଇନ୍ଟ୍ୟୁସନକୁ ଅବହେଳା କଲେ ନିଶ୍ଚିତ ଭାବରେ ବିପଦ ଘେରରେ ପଡ଼ିଯିବାକୁ ହୁଏ। କାରଣ ଇନ୍ଟ୍ୟୁସନ୍ ଭିତରେ ବହୁ ସମୟରେ ଈଶ୍ୱର ହିଁ ନିର୍ଦ୍ଦେଶ ଦେଉଥା'ନ୍ତି। ତା' ସତ୍ତ୍ୱେ ତାଙ୍କର ପୋଲିସ ମନ ପରାଜୟର ଗ୍ଲାନିରେ ହତସନ୍ତ ହେଉଥାଏ। ସେ ଭାବୁଥା'ନ୍ତି ଏତେ ସତର୍କତା ଓ ଗୋପନୀୟତା ସତ୍ତ୍ୱେ ଭୁଲ୍ ରହିଗଲା କେଉଁଠି? ବୋଧହୁଏ ସେ ଜାଣିପାରିଲେ ନାହିଁ ଯେ ସମୟ କେବଳ ବିପନ୍ନ ନୁହେଁ ଅରଣ୍ୟ ମଧ୍ୟ ବିପନ୍ନ। ଅରଣ୍ୟ ବିପନ୍ନ ହେଲେ ଜୀବନର ନିରାପଦ କାହିଁ?

ମଙ୍ଗଳାଯୋଡ଼ିର ମାଛରଙ୍କା

ରହ ରହ କ୍ଷଣେ ବାଷ୍ପୀୟ ଶକଟ
ଦେଖିବି ଚିଲିକା ଋରୁ ଚିତ୍ରପଟ।

ଏକଥା ଗାଇଥିଲେ ଦିନେ କବି ଗୋପବନ୍ଧୁ ବାଷ୍ପୀୟ ଶକଟର
ବାତାୟନ ଦେଇ ଚିଲିକା ଦର୍ଶନ କରି ।

ଆମେ କିନ୍ତୁ ଯାଉଥିଲୁ କାର୍‌ରେ । ଚିଲିକାରେ କିଛି ସମୟ
ରହିବୁ ଆଉ କବିଙ୍କ ପଦକୁ ଦୋହରାଇବୁ–

ସୁନ୍ଦର ତୃପ୍ତିର ଅବସାଦ ନାହିଁ
ଯେତେ ଦେଖୁଥିଲେ ନୂଆ ଦିଶୁଥାଇ ।

ଚିଲିକା କହିଲେ ସମସ୍ତେ ବରକୁଲ, ବାଲୁଗାଁ କିମ୍ବା
ସାତପଡ଼ା କଥା ଭାବନ୍ତି । ମାତ୍ର ଭୁବନେଶ୍ୱରରୁ ହାତ ପାହାନ୍ତାରେ
ଚିଲିକା ଅଛି ବୋଲି ଖୁବ୍ କମ୍ ଲୋକ ଜାଣନ୍ତି । ସ୍ଥାନଟିର ନାମ
ହେଲା– ମଙ୍ଗଳାଯୋଡ଼ି । କାର୍‌ରେ ଗଲେ ଘଣ୍ଟାକର ରାସ୍ତା । ମାତ୍ର
ଷାଠିଏ କିଲୋମିଟର । ଶୀତ ରତୁରେ ବିଚିତ୍ର ରୂପରଙ୍ଗର
ଭ୍ରମଣବିଲାସୀ ବିଦେଶୀ ପକ୍ଷୀ ଦଳ ଉଡ଼ି ଆସନ୍ତି ମନ ପରିବର୍ତ୍ତନ
କରିବା ପାଇଁ । ପୁଣି ଶୀତ ରତୁକୁ ସଙ୍ଗରେ ନେଇ ସେମାନେ
ନିଜ ଘରକୁ ଫେରି ଯାଆନ୍ତି । ଖାଦ୍ୟ ଅନ୍ୱେଷଣରେ ସେମାନେ
ହଜାର ହଜାର କିଲୋମିଟର ଦୂରରୁ ସମ୍ଭବତଃ ଆସନ୍ତି । ପୂର୍ଣ୍ଣଗର୍ଭା

ଚିଲିକାରେ ଗାଧୋଇପାଧୋଇ ଖାଇପିଇ ଟିକେ ମୋଟା ହୋଇ ଖୁସି ମନରେ ଦେଶକୁ ଲେଉଟନ୍ତି । ଅଲିଭ୍ ରିଡ୍‌ଲେ କଇଁଛ ଯେମିତି ଅଣ୍ଡାଦେବା ପାଇଁ ପ୍ରଶାନ୍ତ ମହାସାଗରରୁ ହଜାର ହଜାର କିଲୋମିଟର ଦୂରରୁ ଆସନ୍ତି ଫେମିଙ୍ଗୋମାନେ ସାଇବେରିଆରୁ ଉଡ଼ିଆସନ୍ତି । ଆଶ୍ଚର୍ଯ୍ୟ ! କେମିତି ସେମାନେ ବାଟ ଭୁଲନ୍ତିନି ଈଶ୍ୱରକୁ ଜଣା । ମସ୍ତିଷ୍କଧାରୀ ମଣିଷ ତ ସହରରେ ବୁଲିବା ପାଇଁ ଜିପିଏସ୍‌କୁ ଅନୁସରଣ କରେ । ଅଥଚ ଏଇ କ୍ଷୁଦ୍ର ମସ୍ତିଷ୍କଧାରୀ ପକ୍ଷୀମାନେ କେମିତି ରାସ୍ତା ମନେରଖ୍ ନିର୍ଭୁଲ ପଥରେ ଘରବାହୁଡ଼ା ଗୀତ ଗାଇ ଗାଇ ଫେରିଯାଆନ୍ତି ଆଉଥରେ ଆସିବେ ବୋଲି ଚିଲିକାକୁ ପ୍ରତିଶ୍ରୁତି ଦେଇ ? ସେତେବେଳେ ଗାଁ ଲୋକମାନେ କହନ୍ତି "ଦୁଃଖ ଦେଇ ଗଲ ବିଦାୟୀ ବନ୍ଧୁ" । ଦିନ ଥିଲା ଯେତେବେଳେ ମଙ୍ଗଳାଯୋଡ଼ିର ଗ୍ରାମବାସୀମାନେ ପକ୍ଷୀ ଶିକାର କରି ଜୀବିକା ନିର୍ବାହ କରୁଥିଲେ । କିନ୍ତୁ ଏବେ ସେମାନେ ପକ୍ଷୀପ୍ରିୟ ଏବଂ ସେମାନଙ୍କର ସଂରକ୍ଷଣରେ ପ୍ରୟାସୀ । ଏଥିପାଇଁ ବହୁତ ଅନୁଷ୍ଠାନ ସେମାନଙ୍କୁ ପୁରସ୍କୃତ କରିଛନ୍ତି ।

କେଦାର ଜଣେ ସରକାରୀ ଅଫିସର । ନୂଆଦିଲ୍ଲୀରୁ ବଦଲି ହୋଇ ଭୁବନେଶ୍ୱରରେ ଦାୟିତ୍ୱ ଗ୍ରହଣ କରିଛନ୍ତି । ବନ୍ଧୁମାନେ କହନ୍ତି "କେଦାର ଗୋଟିଏ ପ୍ରକୃତିପ୍ରେମୀ ପାଗଳ" । ପ୍ରକୃତରେ କେଦାର ଭାରତବର୍ଷର ସମସ୍ତ ଜାତୀୟ ପାର୍କ, ଜାତୀୟ ଉଦ୍ୟାନ ବୁଲି ସାରିଛନ୍ତି ନିଜ ଦରମାର ଅଧା ବୁଲାବୁଲିରେ ଖର୍ଚ୍ଚ କରିଦିଅନ୍ତି । ଛୁଟିଦିନଟିଏ ହାତରେ ପାଇଲେ ଆଖପାଖରେ କେଉଁଠିକି ହେଲେ ବୁଲିଯିବାର କାର୍ଯ୍ୟକ୍ରମ ତାଙ୍କର ଥାଏ । ସହରଠାରୁ ଦୂରରେ ପ୍ରକୃତିକୁ ଉପଭୋଗ କରିବା ପାଇଁ କିଣା ରଖିଥାଏ ଟେଣ୍ଟ, ସ୍ଲିପିଂ ବ୍ୟାଗ୍, ଫାଇବର ବୋଟ, ମାଉଣ୍ଟେନ ବାଇକ୍ ଇତ୍ୟାଦି ସରଞ୍ଜାମ । ଏଥିରେ ତାଙ୍କୁ ସାଥୀ ଦିଅନ୍ତି ଅନ୍ତରଙ୍ଗ ବନ୍ଧୁ ବିକ୍ରମ । ସେମାନେ ଦୁହେଁ ସାଇକ୍ଲିଂ କ୍ଲବ୍ର ସଦସ୍ୟ । ପୁନି ନଦୀରେ ଡଙ୍ଗା ରଖିଲା, ଗାଡ଼ି ଚଲାଇ ଜଙ୍ଗଲ ଭିତରେ ପହଞ୍ଚିଯାଇ ରାତ୍ରିଯାପନ ଦୁହିଁଙ୍କର ବିଳାସ । ସେତେବେଳେ ସହର ଜୀବନ ପ୍ରତି ବିତୃଷ୍ଣା ଓ ବୈରାଗ୍ୟର ଜୀବନଦର୍ଶନ ଉଦ୍‌ବେଲି ଉଠେ । ନିଜକୁ ଗୌତମବୁଦ୍ଧଙ୍କର ଅବତାର ବୋଲି ଭାବନ୍ତି ଆଉ ହସନ୍ତି, ହସନ୍ତି ।

ନୂଆବର୍ଷ, ଜାନୁୟାରୀ ମାସର ଶୀତ ସକାଳ । ଭୁବନେଶ୍ୱରରେ ପ୍ରବଳ ଥଣ୍ଡା । ସାରା ପୃଥ‌ିବୀ ହିମ ପ୍ରବାହରେ କମ୍ପିତ । ଏମିତିଆ ହାଡ଼ଭଙ୍ଗା ଥଣ୍ଡାରୁ ରକ୍ଷା ପାଇବା ପାଇଁ ସାଇବେରିଆ ଓ ମଙ୍ଗୋଲିଆର ଏଥର ବହୁସଂଖ୍ୟକ ପକ୍ଷୀ ଚିଲିକା ହ୍ରଦକୁ ଆସିଛନ୍ତି ବୋଲି ଖବର ମିଳିଥାଏ । କେଦାର ସ୍ଥିର କଲେ ନୂଆବର୍ଷ ସହ ରବିବାର ପଡ଼ୁଥିବାରୁ ମଙ୍ଗଳାଯୋଡ଼ି ଯାଇ ପକ୍ଷୀ ଦର୍ଶନ କରିବେ । ବନ୍ଧୁ ବିକ୍ରମକୁ

ମନକଥା କହିଲେ । ବିକ୍ରମ ଉଲ୍ଲସିତ ହୋଇ ପ୍ରସ୍ତାବ ଦେଲେ ତାଙ୍କର ବାନ୍ଧବୀ ଶ୍ରାବଣୀ ମ୍ୟାଡ଼ମ୍‌କୁ ସଙ୍ଗରେ ନେଲେ ଭ୍ରମଣର ମାଦକତା ବଢ଼ିବ । ବିକ୍ରମର ଭାବବିହ୍ବଳତାରେ କେଦାର ମଧ୍ୟ ସଙ୍ଗୋପନରେ ବିହ୍ବଳ ହେଲେ । ବିକ୍ରମ ଶ୍ରାବଣୀ ମ୍ୟାଡ଼ମ୍‌ଙ୍କ ସହ କଥାବାର୍ତ୍ତା କରି ଭ୍ରମଣ କାର୍ଯ୍ୟକ୍ରମ ଚୂଡ଼ାନ୍ତ କରିଦେଲେ । ସାଙ୍ଗରେ କେଦାର ଯିବେ ବୋଲି ବିକ୍ରମ ଫୋନ୍‌ରେ ଶ୍ରାବଣୀକୁ କହିପାରିନଥିଲେ । କେଦାର ପ୍ରସ୍ତାବ ଦେଲେ ଯେ ସେ ମଧ୍ୟ ସ୍ତ୍ରୀଙ୍କୁ ସଙ୍ଗରେ ନେବେ । ତା’ହେଲେ ଶ୍ରାବଣୀଙ୍କୁ ସଙ୍ଗୀ ମିଳିଯିବ । ବିକ୍ରମ ହସି ହସି କହିଲେ “ତୋ ଭଳି ବେରସିକ ସଂସାରରେ ନାହାନ୍ତି, ସବୁକଥାରେ ସ୍ତ୍ରୀଙ୍କୁ ସଙ୍ଗୀ କଲେ ଜୀବନରେ ଟିକିଏ ରସଭଙ୍ଗ ହୁଏ । ତୋତେ ମୁଁ ଚିହ୍ନିଥିବାରୁ ଶ୍ରାବଣୀକୁ କହିଥିଲି ତୋ ସ୍ତ୍ରୀ ମଧ୍ୟ ଯିବେ । ସେ କଥା ଶ୍ରାବଣୀ ରୋକ୍‌ଟୋକ୍ ମନା କରିଦେଲେ । ଏବେ କ’ଣ କରିବା ? ସଙ୍ଗରେ ବାନ୍ଧବୀ ନ ଥିଲେ ପକ୍ଷୀଯୁଗଳଙ୍କୁ ଦେଖି ନିଜକୁ ପକ୍ଷୀଠାରୁ ହୀନ ବୋଲି ଭାବିବା ନାହିଁ କି ? ଅନ୍ତତଃ ମଙ୍ଗଳାଯୋଡ଼ି ଭ୍ରମଣଟା ଟିକିଏ ରୋମାଣ୍ଟିକ୍ ହେବା କଥା । ଏବେ କିନ୍ତୁ ଶ୍ରାବଣୀକୁ ଆଉ ବୁଝାଇ ହେବ ନାହିଁ । ସମ୍ଭବତଃ କେଦାର ଅନ୍ତର ଭିତରେ ସେକଥା ରୁଣ୍ଡୁଥିଲେ । ମୁମ୍ବାଇରୁ ଆସିଥିବା ତାଙ୍କ ବାନ୍ଧବୀ ସମ୍ଭାବୀକୁ ନ ନେଇ ଶ୍ରାବଣୀକୁ ନେବାରେ ଲାଭ କ’ଣ ? ସମ୍ଭାବୀ ଆଧୁନିକା । ତାଙ୍କ ସହ ଗତ ରାତିରେ କେଦାର ଡିସ୍କୋ ପଏଣ୍ଟକୁ ଯାଇଥିଲେ ଏବଂ ବହୁତ ନାଚିଥିଲେ । ମଙ୍ଗଳାଯୋଡ଼ି ଯିବା କଥା ସେ ତାଙ୍କୁ କହିଛନ୍ତି ଏବଂ ସମ୍ଭାବୀ ସମ୍ମତ ଅଛନ୍ତି । ଯଦି ଶ୍ରାବଣୀ ମ୍ୟାଡ଼ମ୍ ନ ଯିବେ ତେବେ ସମ୍ଭାବୀ ଗଲେ ଆଦୌ ରସଭଙ୍ଗ ହେବ ନାହିଁ । ବିକ୍ରମ ରାଜି ହୋଇଗଲେ । ବାନ୍ଧବୀ ଶ୍ରାବଣୀଙ୍କର ଉଦାରତାକୁ ପ୍ରକାଶ କରି ସେ କହିଲେ ଶ୍ରାବଣୀ କିନ୍ତୁ ଆମ ପାଇଁ ସବୁ ବ୍ୟବସ୍ଥା କରିଦେଇଛି । ଡଙ୍ଗା, ବାଇଟ୍, ବ୍ରେକ୍‌ଫାଷ୍ଟ, ଲଞ୍ଚ ସବୁ ତା’ ତରଫରୁ ଆମ ପାଇଁ ଉପହାର ।” ବିକ୍ରମ କେଜାଣି କେମିତି ବାନ୍ଧବୀମାନଙ୍କୁ ବଶ କରି ରଖିଥାଏ । କଲେଜ୍ ସମୟରେ ତା’ର ଏ ପ୍ରକାରର ଆକର୍ଷଣୀ ଶକ୍ତି ଅଛି । ଏବେ ପିଲାଛୁଆର ବାପା ହେଲା ପରେ ବି ସେହି କଲେଜ୍ ହିରୋ ହୋଇ ରହିଛି । ଆର୍ମିରେ କୁଆଡ଼େ ହିରୋ ହୋଇ ରହିବାକୁ ପଡ଼େ – ଯୁଦ୍ଧରେ ହେଉ ବା ପ୍ରେମରେ ହେଉ । ଭୋର ପାଞ୍ଚଟା ବାଜିନି ବିକ୍ରମ ଆସି କେଦାରଙ୍କ କବାଟରେ କରାଘାତ କଲେ । କେଦାରଙ୍କୁ ଅଳସ ଲାଗୁଥିଲା । କ’ଣ ନା ଆର୍ମି ପଙ୍କ୍‌ଚୁଆଲିଟି । ଗାଡ଼ିରେ ଖାଦ୍ୟପେୟ, ବାଇନାକୁଲାର୍ ଇତ୍ୟାଦି ରାସ୍ତା ପାଇଁ ରଖାଗଲା । ସମ୍ଭାବୀ ତାଙ୍କ ହୋଟେଲରେ ବହୁ ପୂର୍ବରୁ ପ୍ରସ୍ତୁତ ହୋଇ ରହିଥିଲେ । ସେ ବି କିଛି କମ୍ ପଙ୍କ୍‌ଚୁଆଲିଟି ନୁହନ୍ତି । ଗୋଟିଏ ନାଲିରଙ୍ଗର

ଭିଷ୍ଟର ଜ୍ୟାକେଟ ପିନ୍ଧି ହେଢ୍ ସ୍କାର୍ଫ ମୁଣ୍ଡରେ ଦେଇ ସେ ମହମର ମୂର୍ତ୍ତିଭଳି ଦିଶୁଥିଲେ । ସମ୍ଭାବୀକୁ ଦେଖି ବିକ୍ରମର ମୁହଁରେ ହସ ଖେଳିଲା । ଚିହ୍ନା ପରିଚୟ ପୂର୍ବରୁ ସେ "ଗୁଢ଼ମର୍ଷି଼ଂ ସମ୍ଭାବୀ" କହି ତାଙ୍କୁ ଗୋଟାପଣେ କୁଣ୍ଠାଇ ପକାଇଲା । କେଦାର ମନେମନେ ଅସନ୍ତୁଷ୍ଟ ହେଲା । ଅଜଣା ଅଚିହ୍ନା ଝିଅକୁ କୁଣ୍ଠାଇବା କି ପ୍ରକାର ସୌଜନ୍ୟ ? ହ୍ୟାଣ୍ଡସେକ୍ କରିଥିଲେ ଚଳିନଥା'ନ୍ତା କି ? କେଦାର ଚିଡ଼ି ଯାଇଥିଲେ । ସେ ଦୁହିଁଙ୍କୁ ଏକାଠି ଛାଡ଼ିଦେବା ପାଇଁ ପଛ ସିଟ୍‍ରେ ବସିବାକୁ କହିଲେ ଏବଂ ନିଜେ ଗାଡ଼ି ଚଲାଇଲେ ।

ଜାତୀୟ ରାଜପଥରେ ଗାଡ଼ି ଗୁଲିଲା । ପଛ ସିଟ୍‍ରେ ମଧୁର ଆଲାପ । ସାମ୍ନା ସିଟ୍‍ରେ ନିରବତା । ସିନ୍ଦୂରା ଫାଟି ଆସୁଥାଏ । ରାସ୍ତାରେ କାଁ ଭାଁ ଟ୍ରକ, ଖୁବ୍ ଶାନ୍ତ ପରିବେଶ । ସକାଳର କୋମଳ ଖରାର ସ୍ୱର୍ଣ ବେଶ୍ ଅନ୍ତରଙ୍ଗ ଲାଗୁଥାଏ । ନୂଆ ଗାଡ଼ି, ଇନୋଭା କ୍ରେଟା ନିଃଶବ୍ଦରେ ମସୃଣ ରାଜପଥରେ ଯେମିତି ଭାସିଯାଉଥାଏ । ବ୍ରାହ୍ମ ମୁହୂର୍ତ୍ତ, ଅନ୍ତରଙ୍ଗ ବନ୍ଧୁ ଏବଂ ସକାଳର ଶୀତଳ ପବନ-ଭଗବାନଙ୍କର ଅପାର କରୁଣା ବିନା ମିଳିବା ଅସମ୍ଭବ ।

ବିକ୍ରମ ସମ୍ଭାବୀଙ୍କ ସହ ଅନ୍ତରଙ୍ଗ ହେବା ପାଇଁ କିଛି ଜୋକ୍ କହୁଥାଏ । ମଧୁର ଆଲାପରେ ଦୁହେଁ ବ୍ୟସ୍ତ କିନ୍ତୁ କେଦାର ପାହାଡ଼ ଉହାଡ଼ରୁ ସକାଳର ସୂର୍ଯ୍ୟ ମୁହଁ କାଢ଼ିବାର ଦୃଶ୍ୟରେ ମଗ୍ନ । ସ୍କୁଲ ବେଳର କଥା ମନେପଡ଼ୁଥାଏ । ସ୍କୁଲକୁ ଯିବା ରାସ୍ତାରେ ଦୁଇଟା ପାହାଡ଼ ମଝିରେ ସୂର୍ଯ୍ୟୋଦୟ, ଆକାଶରେ ଉଡ଼ିଗଲା ଚଢ଼େଇ, ମିଞ୍ଜିମିଞ୍ଜି ଗୋଟିଏ ଫିକା ତାରା ଇତ୍ୟାଦି ଇତ୍ୟାଦି... ।

ଜାତୀୟ ରାଜପଥ ଛାଡ଼ି ଟାଙ୍ଗି ଥାନା ରାସ୍ତା ଧରି ବାଙ୍କି ବଜାର ପାର ହୋଇଗଲେ ସମସ୍ତେ । ସାମ୍ନାରେ ଗୋଟିଏ ରେଲ ଫାଟକ । ଟ୍ରେନ୍‍ଟି ଆସୁଥାଏ । ଫାଟକ ବନ୍ଦ ଥାଏ । ସମସ୍ତେ ଗାଡ଼ିରୁ ଓହ୍ଲାଇଲେ ଓ ଅଣ୍ଟା ସଳଖିଲେ । କିଛି ସାଇକେଲ ଓ ମଟରସାଇକେଲ ଚଢ଼ାଳି ଫାଟକ ତଳେ ଗଳି ରେଲ ଧାରଣା ପାରିହୋଇ ଯାଉଥା'ନ୍ତି । ଏମାନେ ଜୀବନଟାକୁ ସବୁକଥାରେ ଇମର୍ଜେନ୍‍ସି ଡ୍ୟୁଟି ବୋଲି ଭାବନ୍ତେ ଭଲା ! କେତେବେଳେ ଯେ ମରଣଯନ୍ତାରେ ପଡ଼ିଯିବେ... ଛାଡ଼ ଶୁଭ ସକାଳରେ ଅଶୁଭ ଚିନ୍ତା ମନକୁ ଆଣିବା ଉଚିତ ନୁହେଁ । ରେଲ ଧାରଣା ପାଖରେ ଗୋଟିଏ ଧଳା ବଗ ଧାନମୁଦ୍ରାରେ ଏକଗୋଡ଼ିଆ ଠିଆ ହୋଇଥାଏ । ପକ୍ଷୀମାନେ ବି ଯୋଗ, ପ୍ରାଣାୟାମ କରନ୍ତି ? କେଡ଼େ ଶାନ୍ତ ସେମାନେ ? ଅଥଚ ମଣିଷ କେଡ଼େ ଅଶାନ୍ତ ? ଈଶ୍ୱର ମନୁଷ୍ୟକୁ ଚିନ୍ତା କରିବାର ଶକ୍ତି ଦେଇ ସବୁ ଅନର୍ଥ ଭିଆଇଛନ୍ତି । ପକ୍ଷୀ ଭଳି ମଣିଷ ସବୁବେଳେ ଖୁସି ନୁହେଁ, ଅଧିକାଂଶ ସମୟ

ଦୁଃଖୀ । କେଦାରଙ୍କ ଭାବନାକୁ ଗୋଟିଏ ଫୁତ୍କାରରେ ଉଡ଼ାଇଦେଇ ପାସେଞ୍ଜର
ଟ୍ରେନ୍‌ଟିଏ ସିଟି ମାରି ଫାଟକ ଅତିକ୍ରମ କରିଗଲା । ଫାଟକ ଉଠିବା ମାତ୍ରେ ଦଳଚକଟା
ହୋଇ ଲୋକେ ରାସ୍ତା ପାରି ହୋଇଗଲେ । ବିକ୍ରମଙ୍କ ଗାଡ଼ି ମଧ୍ୟ ସେହି
ପ୍ରତିଯୋଗିତାରେ ଭାଗ ନେଇଥିଲା । ବିକ୍ରମ ଶ୍ରାବଣୀ ଦେଇଥିବା ଫୋନ୍‌ ନମ୍ବରରେ
ମଧୁ ଗାଇଡ଼୍‌କୁ ଫୋନ୍‌ କଲେ । ମଧୁ ସମସ୍ତ ବ୍ୟବସ୍ଥା କରିଛନ୍ତି ବୋଲି ଉତ୍ତର
ଦେଲେ । ସେ ବୋଟ୍‌ ସହିତ ଜେଟି ପାଖରେ ଅପେକ୍ଷା କରିଥିଲେ । ଆବଡ଼ା
ଖାବଡ଼ା ରାସ୍ତା ଦେଇ ଗାଁ ପାରି ହୋଇଯିବା ପରେ ବିସ୍ତୀର୍ଣ୍ଣ ଚିଲିକା ହ୍ରଦ ଦେଖାଗଲା ।
ସକାଳର ସୂର୍ଯ୍ୟକିରଣ ଚିଲିକା ପାଣିରେ ପଡ଼ି ଦର୍ପଣ ଭଳି ଚିକ୍‌ଚିକ୍‌ କରୁଥାଏ
ଏବଂ ଦଳ ଦଳ ପକ୍ଷୀ ଉଡ଼ିଉଡ଼ି ନିଜର ମୁଁହ ଦେଖୁଥା'ନ୍ତି । ଫୋନ୍‌ରେ ମଧୁକୁ
ଡାକି ହାତ ଉଠାଇବାକୁ କହିଲେ ଏବଂ ମଧୁକୁ ଚିହ୍ନିବାରେ ସଫଳ ହେଲେ । ମଧୁ
ଡଙ୍ଗା ପାଖକୁ ପାଞ୍ଚୋଟି ନେଲା ସମସ୍ତଙ୍କୁ । ସମସ୍ତେ ଡଙ୍ଗାରେ ବସିଲେ । ଅନ୍ୟ
ପର୍ଯ୍ୟଟକଙ୍କ ଡଙ୍ଗା ମଧ୍ୟ ପାଣିରେ ଭାସୁଥାଏ । ଗୋଟିଏ ଡଙ୍ଗାରେ ମିଲିଟାରୀ
ପୋଷାକ ପିନ୍ଧି ଜଣେ ଯୁବକ ଏକ ବିରାଟ ଫଟୋ କ୍ୟାମେରା ଲଗାଇଥା'ନ୍ତି ।
ବିକ୍ରମ ଦେଖିବାମାତ୍ରେ ସେ ପରିଚିତ ଭଳି କହିଲେ "ଆପଣମାନେ ନିଶ୍ଚିତ
ଭୁବନେଶ୍ୱରରୁ ଆସିଛନ୍ତି, ମୋର ନାଁ ସମିତ୍‌ । ଶ୍ରାବଣୀ ମ୍ୟାଡମ୍‌ ଆପଣଙ୍କ ଉପରେ
ସୟନ ଦୃଷ୍ଟି ରଖିବା ପାଇଁ କହିଛନ୍ତି । ବେଳେବେଳେ ଚିଲିକାରେ ଡଙ୍ଗା ବି ଓଲଟି
ପଡ଼େ । କିନ୍ତୁ ମଧୁର ଡଙ୍ଗା କେବେ ଓଲଟି ନାହିଁ । ଆପଣ ନିଶ୍ଚିନ୍ତରେ ଜଳବିହାର
କରନ୍ତୁ ।"

ଡଙ୍ଗା ଭିତରେ କାଠପଟାରେ ବସିଲେ ସମସ୍ତେ । ବାଇନାକୁଲାରକୁ ଠିକ୍‌
ଜାଗାରେ ରଖାଗଲା । ସମସ୍ତେ ଡଙ୍ଗାର ଭାରସାମ୍ୟ ରକ୍ଷାକରି ବସିବା ପାଇଁ ମଧୁ
ଉପଦେଶ ଦେଲା । ବିକ୍ରମ ଓ ସମ୍ଭାବୀ ସାମ୍ନା କାଠପଟାରେ ବସିଲେ । ତାଙ୍କ
ପଛକୁ କେଦାର ଓ ଶେଷ ପଟାରେ ମଧୁ । ନଳବଣ ଦେଇ ଚିଲିକା ଭିତରକୁ
ଡଙ୍ଗାଟି ବାହାରିଗଲା । ବେଳେବେଳେ ଡଙ୍ଗା କାଦୁଅରେ ଲାଗିଯାଉଥାଏ । କେଦାର
ଟିକେ ବ୍ୟସ୍ତ ହେଲେ । ମଧୁ କହିଲା– ଏତିକି ଅଂଶରେ ଚିଲିକାର ଗଭୀରତା
କମ । ଆଉ ଟିକେ ଆଗକୁ ଗଲେ ସବୁ ଠିକ୍‌ ହୋଇଯିବ । ସତର୍ପଣରେ ଚିଲିକା
ଭିତରକୁ ଡଙ୍ଗାଟି ପହଁରିଗଲା । ସେଥିପାଇଁ ନାଉରିଆକୁ କେହି ଧନ୍ୟବାଦ ଦେଲେ
ନାହିଁ । ସେ ମଧ୍ୟ କାହାରି ଧନ୍ୟବାଦକୁ ଅପେକ୍ଷା କରେ ନାହିଁ । ତା' ପାଇଁ ଡଙ୍ଗା
ବାହିବା ବାମ ହାତର ଖେଳ । ଏବେ ଡଙ୍ଗାରେ ସେମାନେ ଆନନ୍ଦ ଲୁଟିବେ ଏବଂ
ପ୍ରଶଂସା ପାଇବ ସମ୍ଭାବୀ । ସବୁଠି ଏକଥା ଘଟେ । ମଙ୍ଗଳାଯୋଡ଼ିରେ ଚିଲିକା

ବହୁତ ଅଗଭୀର । ଘାସ ଓ ପାଣିର ଅପରୂପ ସମନ୍ୱୟ । ମଧୁ ଗୋଟି ଗୋଟିକରି ପକ୍ଷୀମାନଙ୍କୁ ଚିହ୍ନାଉଥିଲା – ଗଡ଼ୱିଟ୍, ୱ୍ୱାଗଟେଲ୍, ଟର୍ନ, ମୁରହେନ, ସ୍ୱାଲୋ ଇତ୍ୟାଦି ଇତ୍ୟାଦି… । କେଉଁ ଚଢ଼େଇ କେଉଁ ଦେଶରୁ ଉଠିଆସିଛି, କିଏ ମାଛ ଖାଏ ଓ କିଏ ଖାଏ ଘାସ ଓ ଦଳ, କିଏ ଗେଣ୍ଡା ଖାଏ ତ କିଏ ଝିଙ୍ଗିକା– ପୋକଜୋକ, କିଏ ପାଣି ଉପରେ ଭାସୁଥିବା ଜିନିଷ ଖାଏ ତ କିଏ ପାଣି ଭିତରେ ବୁଡ଼ି ବୁଡ଼ି ଖାଦ୍ୟ ଖାଏ ସବୁ ମଧୁର ନଖଦର୍ପଣରେ । ମଧୁର କହିବା ଅନୁଯାୟୀ, ଏଠାରେ ପକ୍ଷୀମାନେ ନିଜ ନିଜର ଅଭ୍ୟାସ ଓ ସୁବିଧା ମୁତାବକ ଖାଦ୍ୟ ଖୋଜି ନିଅନ୍ତି । ଚିଲିକାରେ ପର୍ଯ୍ୟାପ୍ତ ଖାଦ୍ୟ, ତେଣୁ ସେମାନଙ୍କ ଭିତରେ ଝଗଡ଼ାଝାଣ୍ଟି ଲାଗେ ନାହିଁ । ଏତେ ଦେଶର ଚଢ଼େଇ ରୂପରଙ୍ଗରେ ବିଭେଦ ରହିଛି କିନ୍ତୁ ଭାବରେ ଭେଦ ନାହିଁ । ଚଢ଼େଇଟିଏ ଡେଣା ଖୋଲି ଚୁପ୍‍ଚାପ୍‍ ବସିଥାଏ । କାରଣ ପଚାରିବାରୁ ମଧୁ କହିଲା, "ସେଇଟି ପାଣିକୁଆ, ମାଛ ଖାଇସାରି ଖରାରେ ଡେଣା ଶୁଖାଉଛି ।" ପକ୍ଷୀମାନଙ୍କର ପେଟ ପୂରିଗଲେ ସେମାନେ ଡେଣାର ଯତ୍ନ ନିଅନ୍ତି । ମଣିଷଙ୍କ ଭଳି ଦେହ ଖରାପ କରି ଡାକ୍ତରଖାନା ଦଉଡ଼ନ୍ତି ନାହିଁ । ଧନ ଅର୍ଜନ ନାହିଁ କି ଖର୍ଚ୍ଚ ନାହିଁ ।

କେଦାର ଚଢ଼େଇମାନଙ୍କୁ ନିରୀକ୍ଷଣ କରୁଥା'ନ୍ତି କିନ୍ତୁ ସମ୍ରାଟ୍ ଓ ବିକ୍ରମ ଗଛରେ ମଜ୍ଜି ରହିଥା'ନ୍ତି । ଚଢ଼େଇ ଦେଖାଇବା ବାହାନାରେ ବେଳେବେଳେ ସମ୍ରାଟ୍ ଉପରକୁ ଢିଲ ପକଥା'ନ୍ତି ବିକ୍ରମ । କେଦାର ମନେ ମନେ ହସିଲେ । ଏବେ ସେ ମଧୁ ସମ୍ପର୍କରେ ଅଧିକ ଜାଣିବାକୁ ଚୁହିଁଲେ ।

ମଧୁ ଜଣେ ପକ୍ଷୀଶିକାରୀ ଥିଲା । ଚିଲିକା ଭିତରେ ପକ୍ଷୀ ଶିକାର କରିବା ତା'ର ନିଶା ଥିଲା । ତାହାହିଁ ଥିଲା ତା'ର ଜୀବିକା । ପକ୍ଷୀଟିଏ ମାରିଲେ ସେ ଆନନ୍ଦିତ ହେଉଥିଲା । ନଳବଣରେ ଥିବା ଫରେଷ୍ଟ ଅଫିସରଙ୍କ ହାତରେ ପକ୍ଷୀଶିକାର ବେଳେ ଥରେ ସେ ଧରାପଡ଼ିଲା । ତାକୁ ରାତିରେ ଅଟକ ରଖୁ ନିର୍ଘୁମ୍‍ ବାଡ଼େଇଲେ । ଫରେଷ୍ଟ ଅଫିସରମାନଙ୍କର ଏଭଳି ବ୍ୟବହାର ତାକୁ କଷ୍ଟ ଦେଲା । ମୁକୁଳିବା ପରେ ପ୍ରତିଶୋଧପରାୟଣ ହୋଇ ସେ ନଳବଣର ହଜାର ହଜାର ପକ୍ଷୀ ମାରିଦେଲା । କେଦାର ପଚାରିଲେ "ହଜାର ହଜାର ପକ୍ଷୀ ଜଣେ ଲୋକ କେମିତି ମାରିଲା ?" ମଧୁ କହିଲା "ଭାରି ସହଜ । ପକ୍ଷୀ ଖାଦ୍ୟରେ ବିଷ ମିଶାଇ ପାଣିରେ ପକାଇଦେଲେ ଏକାଥରେ ହଜାର ହଜାର ପକ୍ଷୀ ମରିଯିବେ । ଏପରିକି ସେ ଫରେଷ୍ଟ ଅଫିସରଙ୍କୁ ଚ୍ୟାଲେଞ୍ଜ କରି କୌଶଳରେ ଖସି ଆସେ ଏବଂ ସେମାନେ ତାକୁ ଧରିପାରନ୍ତି ନାହିଁ । ସେ କୁଆଡ଼େ ଚିଲିକା ହ୍ରଦ ବୀରାସ୍ଥାନ ବୋନୀ ନିଜକୁ କହେ । ସବୁ ଚାପୁ, ସବୁ ପାଣି ରାସ୍ତା ତାକୁ ଜଣାଥିଲା । ତାକୁ କାବୁ କରିବା ପାଇଁ

ଫରେଷ୍ଟ ବାବୁମାନଙ୍କ ପକ୍ଷେ କାଠିକର ପାଠ ହୋଇପଡ଼ିଲା । ମଧୁ ଭଲି ପକ୍ଷୀ ଶିକାରୀମାନଙ୍କ ଦାଉରେ ପର୍ଯ୍ୟଟକମାନେ ମଙ୍ଗଳାଯୋଡ଼ିକୁ ଆସୁନଥିଲେ । ମଙ୍ଗଳାଯୋଡ଼ି ଚିଲିକାର ଏକ କଳଙ୍କ ହୋଇ ରହିଥିଲା ।"

ଦିନେ ମଧୁ ଜୀବନରେ ଏକ ମଧୁର ଘଟଣା ଘଟିଲା । ପକ୍ଷୀ ଶିକାର କରି କ୍ଲାନ୍ତ ହୋଇ ସେ ଦ୍ୱିପ୍ରହର ଖରାରୁ ରକ୍ଷା ପାଇବା ପାଇଁ ଗଛ ଛାଇରେ ବସିଥିଲା । ସେତିକିବେଳେ ଗାଡ଼ିଟିଏ ଆସି ସେଠାରେ ଅଟକିଲା । ଗାଡ଼ିରୁ ଜଣେ ତରୁଣୀ ଓହ୍ଲାଇଲେ ଏବଂ ମଧୁକୁ ପଚାରିଲେ ଚିଲିକାକୁ ଯିବା ପାଇଁ ସେପଟରେ ରାସ୍ତା ଅଛି କି ନାହିଁ ? ମଧୁ କହିଲା "ଆପଣ ବରକୂଲ ବା ସାତପଡ଼ା ବାଟେ ନ ଯାଇ ଏପଟେ କାହିଁକି ଆସିଲେ ? ତରୁଣୀଜଣକ କହିଲେ "ଗୁଗୁଲ୍ ମ୍ୟାପରୁ ଦେଖିଲି ଯେ ଭୁବନେଶ୍ୱରଠାରୁ ଏହି ରାସ୍ତାଟି ଚିଲିକାକୁ ପାଖ । ଏଠାରେ ପାଣି ଅଛି, ଟାପୁ ଅଛି, ନଳବଣ ଅଛି, ତେଣୁ ପକ୍ଷୀମାନଙ୍କର ଗହଳଚହଳ ବେଶୀ । ବିଦେଶୀ ପକ୍ଷୀ ଏଠାକୁ ଅଧିକ ସଂଖ୍ୟାରେ ଆସନ୍ତି । ପକ୍ଷୀମାନଙ୍କର ଫଟୋ ଉଠାଇବାକୁ ମୁଁ ଭଲପାଏ । ତୁମେ ଦେଖ୍‌ପାର ।" ନିଜ ଆଲବମରୁ ପକ୍ଷୀମାନଙ୍କ ଫଟୋ ସେ ଦେଖିଲେ । ମଧୁ ତରୁଣୀଙ୍କର ପକ୍ଷୀଶାସ୍ତ୍ର ଉପରେ ଜ୍ଞାନ, ରୁଚି ଓ ପକ୍ଷୀମାନଙ୍କ ପ୍ରତି ସ୍ନେହ ଦେଖ୍‌ ଭାବବିହ୍ୱଳ ହୋଇଗଲା । ପକ୍ଷୀମାନଙ୍କୁ ଦେଖ୍‌ ସେ ଜାଣିନଥିଲା ଯେ ପକ୍ଷୀ ଏତେ ସୁନ୍ଦର ! ଫଟୋ ଦେଖ୍‌ ସେ ସେକଥା ଜାଣିଲା । ତା' ହୃଦୟରେ ଏକ ଅଭୂତ ବିଷାଦ ଭାବ ଆସିଲା । ତା' ଆଖିରେ ଲୁହ ଜକେଇ ଆସିଲା । ତରୁଣୀ କିଛି ବୁଝିପାରିଲେ ନାହିଁ । ମଧୁ କୋହ ସମ୍ବରଣ କରି କହିଲା ଯେ "ସେ ଜଣେ ପକ୍ଷୀଶିକାରୀ ଏବଂ ନିଜ ହାତରେ ହଜାର ହଜାର ପକ୍ଷୀ ମାରିଛି, ମାତ୍ର ପକ୍ଷୀମାନଙ୍କର ସୁନ୍ଦର ଫଟୋ ଦେଖ୍‌ ସେ ଅନୁତାପ କରୁଛି । ଏବେ ଭାବୁଛି କାହା ପାଖରେ ନିଜ ଦୋଷ ପାଇଁ କ୍ଷମା ପ୍ରାର୍ଥନା କରିବି ? କିଏ ମୋତେ କ୍ଷମା ଦେବ ?"

ତରୁଣୀ ମଧୁର ହାତ ଧରିଲେ, କହିଲେ "ତୁମେ ମୋ ହାତ ଧରି କୁହ ଆଜିଠାରୁ ଆଉ ପକ୍ଷୀ ଶିକାର କରିବ ନାହିଁ ବରଂ ପକ୍ଷୀମାନଙ୍କୁ ଭଲପାଇବ ଏବଂ ସେମାନଙ୍କୁ ରକ୍ଷା କରିବ । ସେତିକିରେ ତୁମ ପାପର ପ୍ରାୟଶ୍ଚିତ ହୋଇଯିବ ।" ମଧୁ ପ୍ରତିଜ୍ଞା କଲା । ସେହିଦିନଠାରୁ ସେ କେବଳ ନିଜେ ନୁହେଁ ଗାଁ ଓ ଆଖପାଖର ସମସ୍ତଙ୍କୁ ପକ୍ଷୀ ଶିକାର ପାଇଁ ବାରଣ କଲା । କେତୋଟି ପକ୍ଷୀର ସୁନ୍ଦର ଫଟୋ ତରୁଣୀ ତାଙ୍କୁ ଦେଇଥିଲେ । ଗ୍ରାମ ଲୋକେ ସେ ଫଟୋକୁ ଦେଖ୍‌ ମୁଗ୍‌ଧ ହୋଇଗଲେ ଏବଂ ପ୍ରତିଜ୍ଞା କଲେ ଯେ ସେମାନେ ଆଉ ପକ୍ଷୀ ଶିକାର କରିବେ ନାହିଁ । ତରୁଣୀ ଜଣକ ନିଜ ନାମ ଶ୍ରାବଣୀ ବୋଲି କହିଥିଲେ । ପକ୍ଷୀମାନଙ୍କ ସମ୍ପର୍କରେ ଅଧିକ

ଜାଣିବା ପାଇଁ ବହିଟିଏ ବି ଦେଇଥିଲେ । ତା'ପରଠାରୁ ଶ୍ରାବଣୀ ବହୁଥର ଆସିଛନ୍ତି, ମଧୁ ତାଙ୍କୁ ନେଇ ଚିଲିକା ଭିତରକୁ ଯାଇଛି । ମଧୁ ଡଙ୍ଗା ଚଲାଏ ଏବଂ ଶ୍ରାବଣୀ ପକ୍ଷୀମାନଙ୍କ ଉପରେ ଗବେଷଣା କରନ୍ତି । ଧୀରେ ଧୀରେ ଶ୍ରାବଣୀ ମ୍ୟାଡମ୍‍ଙ୍କ କଥାରେ ଆଖପାଖର ଗାଁଲୋକେ ପକ୍ଷୀ ଶିକାର କରିବା ଛାଡ଼ିଦେଲେ । କାରଣ ତାଙ୍କ କଥାରେ କୁହୁକ ଥିଲା । ସେମାନେ କେବଳ ପକ୍ଷୀଙ୍କ ଭଲପାଇଲେ ନାହିଁ, ଶ୍ରାବଣୀ ମ୍ୟାଡମ୍‍ଙ୍କୁ ମଧ୍ୟ ଭଲପାଇଲେ । ମଙ୍ଗଳାଯୋଡ଼ି ପକ୍ଷୀମାନଙ୍କର ଅଭୟାରଣ୍ୟ ପାଲଟିଗଲା । ତା'ପରେ ମଙ୍ଗଳାଯୋଡ଼ି ହେଲା ପର୍ଯ୍ୟଟକମାନଙ୍କର ଶ୍ରେଷ୍ଠ ସ୍ଥଳ । ସେମାନଙ୍କୁ ଡଙ୍ଗାରେ ବୁଲାଇବା ଫଳରେ ଗାଁଲୋକଙ୍କର ବି ଉପାର୍ଜନ ବଢ଼ିଗଲା । ଏବେ ମଙ୍ଗଳାଯୋଡ଼ିରେ ଅନେକ କଟେଜ୍ ନିର୍ମାଣ ହୋଇଛି । ଓଡ଼ିଶା ସରକାର ମଙ୍ଗଳାଯୋଡ଼ିକୁ ପ୍ରକୃତିପ୍ରେମୀ ଗ୍ରାମ ବୋଲି ପୁରସ୍କୃତ କରିଛନ୍ତି । ବନବିଭାଗ ମଧୁକୁ ପକ୍ଷୀମିତ୍ର ଉପାଧି ଦେଇ ପୁରସ୍କୃତ କରିଛନ୍ତି । ଯେଉଁ ଫରେଷ୍ଟ ଅଫିସର ମଧୁକୁ ଆରେଷ୍ଟ କରିଥିଲେ ସେ ମଧୁକୁ ପୁରସ୍କାର ଦେଇ ଗଳାରେ ଲଗାଇଥିଲେ । ମଧୁ ଲୁହ ଛଳଛଳ ଆଖିରେ କହିଲା, "ମତେ ନୁହେଁ ବରଂ ଶ୍ରାବଣୀ ମ୍ୟାଡମ୍‍ଙ୍କୁ ପୁରସ୍କାର ଦେଇ ଅଫିସରଜଣକ ତାଙ୍କ ଗଳାରେ ଲଗାଇଥିଲେ ଖୁସି ହୋଇଥା'ନ୍ତି ।" କେଦାର ଚିହିଁକି ଉଠି କହିଲେ, "ନା, ନା ଶ୍ରାବଣୀ ମ୍ୟାଡମ୍ ଖାଲି କଥାରେ କହିଛନ୍ତି, ତୁମେ ତ କାମ କରି ଦେଖାଇଛ । ତାଙ୍କୁ କାହିଁକି ସେ ଅଫିସରଟା ଗଳାରେ ଲଗାଇଥା'ନ୍ତେ ? ମଧୁ କହିଲା "ଆଜି ଆପଣ ଶ୍ରାବଣୀ ମ୍ୟାଡମ୍‍ଙ୍କ ଗେଷ୍ଟ ବୋଲି ସେ ବହୁତ ଆନନ୍ଦିତ । ତାଙ୍କୁ ମୋର ନମସ୍କାର ଜଣାଇବେ ।"

ଏତେବେଲେକେ ବିକ୍ରମ ଗଦ୍‍ଗଦ୍ ସ୍ୱରେ କହିଲେ "ଦେଖ ମୋର ବାନ୍ଧବୀ ଶ୍ରାବଣୀ କେତେବଡ଼ ବ୍ୟକ୍ତିତ୍ୱ । ତାଙ୍କ ପାଇଁ ଆଜି ମଙ୍ଗଳାଯୋଡ଼ି କେବଳ ଭାରତ ନୁହେଁ ଭାରତ ବାହାରେ ମଧ୍ୟ ସୁପରିଚିତ । ଖାଲି ସେତିକି ନୁହେଁ ସେ ଏତେ ସୁନ୍ଦରୀ ଏବଂ ଏତେ ସୁନ୍ଦର ଇଂରାଜୀ କୁହନ୍ତି ଯେ ସେଥିରେ ସମସ୍ତେ ମୁଗ୍‍ଧ ହୋଇଯା'ନ୍ତି । ସେ ଭୁଲ କଥା କହିଲେ ବି ଲୋକେ ତାଙ୍କ କଥାରେ ବଶୀଭୂତ ହୁଅନ୍ତେ । ମାତ୍ର ଶ୍ରାବଣୀ କେବେ ଭୁଲ କଥା କୁହନ୍ତି ନାହିଁ । ସେଡେବେଳକୁ ସନ୍ଧ୍ୟାବ୍ରତଙ୍କର ମୁଡ୍ ଖରାପ ହୋଇଗଲାଣି । ବିକ୍ରମ ନିଜର ଭୁଲ ବୁଝିପାରିଲା । ସନ୍ଧ୍ୟାବ୍ରତ ମ୍ୟାଡମ୍‍ଙ୍କୁ ଖୁସି କରିବା ପାଇଁ ଉଠାଇଥିବା ଫଟୋ ସବୁ ଦେଖାଇଲେ । ମାତ୍ର ସନ୍ଧ୍ୟାବ୍ରତ ମୁହଁ ଭାରୀ କରି ବସିଥା'ନ୍ତି । ତାଙ୍କ ସାଙ୍ଗରେ ଡାକିଆଣି ଶ୍ରାବଣୀକୁ ପ୍ରଶଂସା କରିବାର ଅର୍ଥ କ'ଣ ? କେଦାର ଓ ବିକ୍ରମ ଦୁହେଁ ଆଶ୍ୱସ୍ତବୋଧ କଲେ । ସନ୍ଧ୍ୟାବ୍ରତ ଆସିଥିଲେ କେଦାରଙ୍କ ଅନ୍ତରଙ୍ଗ ବନ୍ଧୁ ହିସାବରେ । କିନ୍ତୁ ଡଙ୍ଗାରେ ବସି

ବିକ୍ରମ ସମ୍ଭାବୀଙ୍କର ଅନ୍ତରଙ୍ଗ ବନ୍ଧୁ ଭଳି ଆଳାପ କଲେ । କେଦାରଙ୍କୁ ସମ୍ପୂର୍ଣ୍ଣ
ଆଢେଇଦେଲେ । କେଦାର ବାଧ୍ୟ ହୋଇ ମଧୁ ସହିତ ଆଳାପ କଲେ ଏବଂ ଶ୍ରାବଣୀ
ମ୍ୟାଡ଼ାମ୍‌ଙ୍କ ଗୁଣଗାନ ହେଲା । ତା' ସାଙ୍ଗକୁ ବିକ୍ରମ ମିଠାରେ ମହୁ ଢାଳିଲେ ।
ଜଣେ ନାରୀ ସମ୍ମୁଖରେ ଆଉ ଜଣେ ନାରୀର ପ୍ରଶଂସା କରାଯାଏନି ବୋଲି ନାରୀ
ବିଶାରଦମାନେ କହିଛନ୍ତି । ବିକ୍ରମର ବାହାପିଆ ଗୁଣ ଯୋଗୁଁ ଏବେ ସମ୍ଭାବୀ
କାର୍ଯ୍ୟକ୍ରମର ଆନନ୍ଦକୁ ପଣ୍ଡ କରିଦେଲେଣି । ବିକ୍ରମ ଏବେ ବେଶ୍‌ ପଷ୍ଟାଉଥିଲା ।
ତା' ମୁହଁ ଦେଖି କେଦାର ମନେ ମନେ ହସିଲେ । ଭଲ ହୋଇଛି ଉପରେ ପଡ଼ି
ତାଙ୍କ ବାନ୍ଧବୀ ଉପରେ ପ୍ରଭାବ ବିସ୍ତାର କରିବାର ଫଳ ପାଇଛି । ଏବେ କେଦାର
ଦେଖିଲେ ଯେ, ସମ୍ଭାବୀ ମଧୁ ଆଡ଼କୁ ଢଳିଲେଣି । ନାରୀ ମାୟା ନାରାୟଣଙ୍କୁ
ଅଗୋଚର ।

ଏତିକିବେଳେ ଏକ ଅଭାବିତ ଘଟଣା ଘଟିଲା । ଗୋଟିଏ ରିଭରଟର୍ଣ୍ଣ ପକ୍ଷୀ
ପାଣିରୁ ମାଛଟିଏ ଧରି ଉଡ଼ିଯାଉଥିବାବେଳେ ମାଛଟି ତା' ମୁହଁରୁ ଖସିପଡ଼ିଲା ଏବଂ
ମାଛଟି ପାଣିରେ ପଡୁ ପଡୁ ଗୋଟିଏ ମାଛରଙ୍କା ପକ୍ଷୀ ଲଙ୍ଫ ମାରି ସେହି ମାଛଟିକୁ
ପାଣିରୁ ଉଠାଇନେଲା । ସମସ୍ତେ ଆହା ଆହା କହିଲେ । ମାଛଟା ବିଚରା ବଞ୍ଚୁ
ବଞ୍ଚୁ ପୁଣି ଯମରାଜ ଧରିନେଇଗଲେ । ମାତ୍ର ଏ କ'ଣ ହେଲା ? ହଠାତ୍‌ ଏକ
ଛଞ୍ଚାଣ ମାଛରଙ୍କାକୁ ଧରିବ ବୋଲି ମାଡ଼ିଆସିଲା । ମାଛରଙ୍କା ଜୀବନ ବଞ୍ଚାଇବାକୁ
ଯାଇ ମାଛକୁ ଛାଡ଼ିଦେଇ ପୁଣି ପାଣି ଭିତରକୁ ଲଙ୍ଫ ମାରିଲା । ଛଞ୍ଚାଣଟି ମାଛ ବା
ମାଛରଙ୍କା କାହାକୁ ନ ପାଇ ଉପରକୁ ଉଡ଼ିଗଲା । ଯାହାହେଉ ସମସ୍ତଙ୍କର ଜୀବନ
ବଞ୍ଚିଗଲା । ଆଖି ପିଛୁଳାକେ ଏ ସବୁ ଘଟଣା ଘଟିଗଲା । ଏହିପରି ଏକ ନାଟକ
ସକାଳୁ ଏପର୍ଯ୍ୟନ୍ତ କେଦାର, ବିକ୍ରମ ଓ ସମ୍ଭାବୀ ମଧ୍ୟରେ ଚଳିଛି । କିନ୍ତୁ ମଧୁ ଏଠି
ସମସ୍ତଙ୍କ ଭିତରେ ସମ୍ପର୍କର ସୂତ୍ର ହୋଇ ସମସ୍ତଙ୍କୁ ବଞ୍ଚାଇଛି । ଏତିକିବେଳେ ସୁବ୍ରତ
ପହଞ୍ଚିଗଲେ ଏବଂ ସମସ୍ତଙ୍କୁ ଗଡ଼୍‌ ଉଇଟ୍‌ କଟେଜ୍‌କୁ ନେଇ ଗରମ କଫି ପିଆଇବା
ପାଇଁ କହିଲେ । କେଦାର ଓ ବିକ୍ରମ ମୁହଁ ରୁହାଁରୁହିଁ ହୋଇ ମନାକଲେ ।
ସେମାନଙ୍କର ମନ ଭଲ ନଥିଲା । ସମ୍ଭାବୀ ହସିଦେଇ କଟାକ୍ଷ କଲେ "ସେମାନେ
ତ ମାଛରଙ୍କା ପାଟିରୁ ତ ଏବେ ଖସିଛନ୍ତି, ପୁଣି ଛଞ୍ଚାଣ ହାବୁଡ଼ରେ କାହିଁକି ପଡ଼ିବେ ?
ବରଂ ଘରକୁ ଯାଇ ସ୍ତ୍ରୀଙ୍କ ହାତରନ୍ଧା ଖାଆନ୍ତୁ । ଛୁଟିଦିନଟା ଭଲରେ କଟିବ ।
ପରେ ଆସି ସେମାନେ କଟେଜରେ ରହିବେ ଏବଂ ସୁବ୍ରତଙ୍କର ଆତିଥ୍ୟ ଗ୍ରହଣ
କରିବେ ।" ସମସ୍ତେ ଏକସଙ୍ଗେ ହସିଲେ । କେଦାର ପକେଟ୍‌ରୁ ପାଞ୍ଚ ଶହ ଟଙ୍କା
କାଢ଼ି ଗ୍ରହ ଶାନ୍ତି ପାଇଁ ମଧୁ ହାତକୁ ବକ୍ସିସ୍‌ ବଢ଼ାଇଦେଲେ । ମଧୁ ସଙ୍ଗେ ସଙ୍ଗେ

କହିଲା, "ଶ୍ରାବଣୀ ମ୍ୟାଡ଼ମ୍ ମନା କରିଛନ୍ତି ପଇସା ନେବା ପାଇଁ । ସ୍ନେହ ଶ୍ରଦ୍ଧାର ଦାମ୍ ମାତ୍ର ପାଞ୍ଚଶହ ଟଙ୍କା ?" କେଦାର କହିଲେ ଏଇଟା କାହାରି ଦାମ୍ ନୁହେଁ । ଏଇଟା ଗ୍ରହ ଶାନ୍ତି ପାଇଁ ଖର୍ଚ୍ଚ କର । ଆଜି ମାଛ ଓ ମାଛରଙ୍କାର ଜୀବନ ରକ୍ଷା ହୋଇଯାଇଛି । ତୁମ ଶ୍ରାବଣୀ ମ୍ୟାଡ଼ମ୍‌ଙ୍କୁ ଆମର ଶତଶତ ପ୍ରଣାମ ଜଣାଇଦେବ । ବିକ୍ରମଙ୍କ ମୁହଁରୁ କଥା ବାହାରୁ ନଥାଏ । ସୁବ୍ରତ କିଛି ବୁଝିପାରୁ ନଥିଲେ । ସମ୍ଭାବୀ କହିଲେ ପକ୍ଷୀମାନେ ନିଜ ବାସସ୍ଥାନକୁ ଉଡ଼ିଯିବା ଭଳି ଆମେ ସମସ୍ତେ ଫେରିଯିବା ନିଜ ନିଜ ଘରକୁ । କିନ୍ତୁ ଫେରିଯିବା ଏକ ସୁଖଦ ଅନୁଭବ ନେଇ । ସେହି ମାଛରଙ୍କା ପାଟିରୁ ମାଛଟି ଖସିଯିବା ଭଳି ଜୀବନର ପ୍ରତିଟି ମୁହୂର୍ତ୍ତ ଭୁଲ୍ ବୁଝାମଣାରୁ ଖସିଯିବାର ଏକ କଳା ହୋଇପାରିଲେ ଜୀବନର ପ୍ରତ୍ୟେକଟି ମୁହୂର୍ତ୍ତ ହେବ ଅନନ୍ୟ ।

ଅଧରସ୍ପର୍ଶ

ପୃଥିବୀରେ ସବୁଟି ସବୁ ଅଛି, କିନ୍ତୁ ଟିକିଏ ଶାନ୍ତି ଆଉ ଆନନ୍ଦ ମିଳୁନାହିଁ। ଆଜିର ମଣିଷ ଏତେ ସୁଖଲୋଭୀ ହୋଇଯାଇଛି ଯେ ସୁଖ ଓ ଆନନ୍ଦ ଭିତରେ ଥିବା ସୂକ୍ଷ୍ମ ପାର୍ଥକ୍ୟକୁ ବୁଝିବା ପାଇଁ ସାମର୍ଥ୍ୟ ନାହିଁ କିମ୍ବା ସମୟ ନାହିଁ। ଦୁଷ୍ମନ୍ତ ଦୁଃଖକୁ ଅଙ୍ଗେ ନିଭେଇଛି, ସୁଖକୁ ଅର୍ଜନ କରିଛି, କିନ୍ତୁ ଆନନ୍ଦ ଖୋଜି ଚାଲିଛି ଜୀବନସାରା। ସେ ଜାଣେ ଆନନ୍ଦର ଇଣ୍ଡେକ୍ରେ ସର୍ବୋଚ୍ଚରେ ଅଛି ହାତ ବଢ଼ାଇଲେ ଛୁଇଁବା ପରି ଗୋଟିଏ ପଡ଼ୋଶୀ ଦେଶ ଭୁଟାନ। ସେଠି ବସ୍ତୁବାଦୀ ସଭ୍ୟତାର ସମୃଦ୍ଧି ନଥାଇପାରେ, ବିଜ୍ଞାନର ଚରମ ଉପଲବ୍ଧି ନଥାଇପାରେ; କିନ୍ତୁ ସେଠି କୁଆଡ଼େ ସମସ୍ତେ ଆନନ୍ଦର ଉପଲବ୍ଧିରେ ଜୀବନଟା ବିତାଇ ଦିଅନ୍ତି। ଦୁଷ୍ମନ୍ତ ଭୁଟାନର ସ୍ୱପ୍ନ ଦେଖେ। କିନ୍ତୁ ଯିବାର ସୁଯୋଗ ଏଯାଏ ମିଳିନାହିଁ। ଯାଇଛି ଭୁଟାନର ସୀମା ପର୍ଯ୍ୟନ୍ତ ମାତ୍ର ସୀମାପାରି କରିପାରିନି। ଦୁଷ୍ମନ୍ତ ଏହି ମଣିଷ ହାତଗଣା ସୀମାରେଖାକୁ ମାନିଲେ ମଧ ପସନ୍ଦ କରେନାହିଁ। ସୀମାରେଖା ଯଦି ନଥାନ୍ତା ଯୁବ ଅଫିସର ଦୁଷ୍ମନ୍ତ ପିଲାଦିନ ଭଳି ଏକା କୁଦାକରେ ଏ ଦେଶରୁ ସେଦେଶକୁ ଡେଇଁପଡ଼ିଥାନ୍ତା ଏବଂ ଆନନ୍ଦର ଉପଲବ୍ଧି ପାଇସାରନ୍ତାଣି। ସେ ସୁଯୋଗକୁ ଅପେକ୍ଷା କରିଛି। କିନ୍ତୁ ତା' ଭଳି ଚଳଚଞ୍ଚଳ ଯୁବକ ସବୁବେଳେ ସେହି

ଅମାନିଆ ବାଲକଟିଏ ହୋଇ ରହିଗଲା। ପିଲାଦିନେ ସେଥ୍ପାଇଁ ମା'ଙ୍କଠାରୁ ସରୁ ଚଟକଣି ଖାଇଛି। ବାପାଙ୍କଠାରୁ ନିୟମ, ଶୃଙ୍ଖଳା ଏବଂ ଅଧ୍ୱସାୟ ସମ୍ପର୍କରେ ଉପଦେଶ ଶୁଣି ଏକାନରେ ପୂରାଇ ସେକାନରେ ବାହାର କରିଦେଇଛି ବୋଲି ଭାବୁଥିଲେ ମଧ୍ୟ ବାପାଙ୍କ ଉପଦେଶ ତା' ଭିତରେ କୋଉଠି ହେଲେ ଛପି ରହିଯାଏ। ଏଣେ ମା'ଙ୍କର ତା' ପାଇଁ ସ୍ୱପ୍ନ କାଲେ ଚଟକଣିର ମଲମ ହୋଇ ତାକୁ କାନଧରି ବସ୍ ଉଠ୍ କରାଇବ ସେଥିପାଇଁ ମଧ୍ୟ ଭୟଥାଏ। ସବୁ ମିଶିମିଶି ଚଗଲା ଦୁଷ୍ୟନ୍ତ ଭଲ ଛାତ୍ର ଭାବରେ ନାଁ କଲା। ଉଚ୍ଚପଦବୀରେ ଅବସ୍ଥାପିତ ହେଲା। ମା'ବାପାଙ୍କୁ ପାଖରେ ରଖି ଏବେ ତାଙ୍କୁ ସ୍ନେହର ଶାସନ କରୁଛି। ଏ ବୟସରେ ବି ବାପାଙ୍କର ଗୁଣ୍ଠିପାନ ଅଭ୍ୟାସ ଛଡ଼ାଇଦେଇଛି ଏବଂ ମଧୁମେହର ଆଶଙ୍କା ଥିବା ମା'ଙ୍କର ଅତ୍ୟଧିକ ମିଠା ଉପରେ ଅଙ୍କୁଶ ଲଗାଇଛି।

କିନ୍ତୁ ସେ ତା'ର ପିଲାଦିନର କେତେଗୁଡ଼ିଏ ଅଭ୍ୟାସ ଛାଡ଼ିପାରି ନାହିଁ। ତା'ର ଭଲଗୁଣ ହେଲା ଯେ ତା' ପକେଟରେ ପଇସା ରହେନି ଏବଂ ସେଥିପାଇଁ ମଧ୍ୟ ତା'ର ପରବ୍ୟୟ ନଥାଏ। ମାସ ଆରମ୍ଭରେ ବ୍ୟାଙ୍କ ଆକାଉଣ୍ଟରେ ଦରମା ଚଢ଼ିଲା ମାତ୍ରେ ବାବୁଙ୍କର ଏଟିଏମ୍ରୁ ପଇସା କାଢ଼ିବାକୁ ତର ସହେନାହିଁ। ପଇସା ଖର୍ଚ୍ଚର ଆଗୁଆ ହିସାବ ତା' ପାଖରେ ନଥାଏ। ଟଙ୍କା ଅଭାବରେ କାହାର ଚିକିସା ହୋଇପାରୁନି ତ ସେ ହସି ହସି ତା' ହାତରେ ଶକ୍ତି ମୁତାବକ ଅର୍ଥ ଗୁଞ୍ଜିଦିଏ। କାହାର ମୁହଁ ଶୁଖିଲା ଦିଶୁଛି ଦେଖିଲେ ଅଚିହ୍ନା ହେଲେ ବି ତା' ପାଖରେ ଠିଆ ହୋଇଯାଏ ଆଉ କଥା ଆରମ୍ଭ କରୁ କରୁ ତା' ଦୁଃଖର ପସରାଟିକୁ ପଦାକୁ କାଢ଼ିଆଣି ତା' ମନକୁ ହାଲ୍କା କରିଦିଏ। ଦୁଷ୍ୟନ୍ତର ଏ ସବୁ ଭଲଗୁଣ ବୋଲି ଅନେକ କହିଲେ ମଧ୍ୟ ସଂସାର କରିବା ପାଇଁ ଦୁଷ୍ୟନ୍ତ ଏପର୍ଯ୍ୟନ୍ତ ଯୋଗ୍ୟ ହୋଇନାହିଁ ବୋଲି ମା' କହନ୍ତି। ଦୁଷ୍ୟନ୍ତ ମଧ୍ୟ ସଂସାର କରିବା ପାଇଁ ମନ କରିନାହିଁ। ଦିନେ ମା' ଶାନ୍ତି ନାମକ ଏକ ଝିଅର ପ୍ରସ୍ତାବ ଦେଇ ତା'ର ସୁନ୍ଦର ଫଟୋଟି ଦେଖାଇବାରୁ ଦୁଷ୍ୟନ୍ତ ସେଥ୍ପ୍ରତି ଦୃଷ୍ଟିପାତ ନକରି କହିଥିଲା – ମୁଁ ଶାନ୍ତି ଖୋଜୁଛି ମା', ଶାନ୍ତି ନାମକ ଅର୍ଡିନାରୀ ଝିଅ ନୁହେଁ – "Nature is my first wife"। ମା' ଇଂରାଜୀ ବୁଝିପାରୁଥିଲେ ମଧ୍ୟ ସେ ଆଉଥରେ କହିଲା – "Nature"ର ଅର୍ଥ ବୁଝିପାରୁଛ ତ "ପ୍ରକୃତି"। ପ୍ରକୃତି ବ୍ୟତୀତ ଆଉ କୌଣସି ଝିଅ ମୋର ଏତେ ପସନ୍ଦ ହେବନାହିଁ।"

ମା' ଖୁସୀ ହୋଇଯାଇ କହିଲେ – "ହଁ, ପ୍ରକୃତି ବୋଲି ଝିଅଟିଏର ପ୍ରସ୍ତାବ ବି ଆସିଛି।"

"ତମେ ବୁଝିପାରିବ ନାହିଁ ମା" ଏମିତି କହି ଆଜିପର୍ଯ୍ୟନ୍ତ ସେ ସଂସାର କରିନି। କିଏ ବା ତା' ସାଙ୍ଗରେ ସଂସାର କରିବ? ଯେତେ ରୋଜଗାର କଲେ ବି ପକେଟ ଖାଲି, ସାଇକେଲ ଧରି ଭାରତ ଭ୍ରମଣ, ଏଣେ କଲେଜ ଛାତ୍ର ଭଳି ହିମାଳୟ ଆଦି ପାହାଡ ପର୍ବତରେ ଟ୍ରେକିଂ, ଲେହ-ମୋନାଲି, ଗାଙ୍ଗଟକ୍-ନାଥୁଲା, ଗଙ୍ଗୋତ୍ରୀ, ଯମୁନୋତ୍ରୀ ଆଦି ସ୍ଥାନ ଟ୍ରେକିଂରେ ବୁଲିସାରିଲାଣି। ପ୍ରତିବର୍ଷ ପୂଜାଛୁଟିରେ ନିଶ୍ଚୟ ସେ ଏକ ଦୂର ସ୍ଥାନକୁ ଭ୍ରମଣରେ ଯାଏ। ପ୍ରତିବର୍ଷ ହିମାଳୟ ତାକୁ ଡାକେ। ସେ ବର୍ଷ ତାକୁ ଭୁଟାନ ଅଥୟ କଲା। ତା' ଭିତରେ ଅଥୟପଣ ହାବୁଡ ମାରିଲେ ଆଉ କେହି ତାକୁ ଅଟକାଇପାରନ୍ତି ନାହିଁ। ଭୁଟାନ ଭ୍ରମଣରେ ବାହାରିପଡିଲା ଦୁଷ୍ମନ୍ତ। ଭୁଟାନର ପାରୋଠାରେ ଥିବା ଏୟାରପୋର୍ଟ ସମ୍ପର୍କରେ ସେ ଶୁଣିଥିଲା। ପାରୋ 'ପରୀ' ଭଳି ଏକ ସୁନ୍ଦର ସହର, ଯେଉଁଠି ହିମାଳୟର କନ୍ଦରରେ ଥିବା ଉପତ୍ୟକାରେ ଏୟାରପୋର୍ଟ, ଯେଉଁଠି ଉଡ଼ାଜାହାଜର ଡେଣା ଟିକିଏ ହିସାବ ଗୋଲମାଲ କରିଦେଲେ ଦୁଇପାର୍ଶ୍ୱର ପର୍ବତଶୃଙ୍ଗରେ ବାଜି ଦୁର୍ଘଟଣା ଘଟିବାର ଆଶଙ୍କାରେ ଯାତ୍ରୀମାନଙ୍କର ହୃଦ୍ସ୍ପନ୍ଦନ ବଢ଼ିଯାଏ, ପର୍ବତ କନ୍ଦରରେ ଥିବା ମୋନାଷ୍ଟିଗୁଡ଼ିକ ତାକୁ ଅଥୟ କରିପକାଇବ। ପୂଜାଛୁଟି ଆରମ୍ଭ ହୁଅନ୍ତେ ସେ ଟ୍ରେନରେ ଉଠିଲା। ପହଞ୍ଚିଲା ନିଉଜଲପାଇଗୁଡ଼ିରେ। ସେଠାରୁ ଗାଡିଟିଏ ଭଡ଼ାକରି ପୁଞ୍ଚସିଲିଙ୍ଗରେ ପହଞ୍ଚିଗଲା। ଚଟାପଟ ଜଳଯୋଗ କରିଦେଇ ବାହାରିପଡିଲା ପାରୋ ରାସ୍ତାରେ। ବାଟରେ ଗେଡ଼ୁ, ରୁପଟ୍ୟ, ଚୋଙ୍ଗା ଇତ୍ୟାଦି ସ୍ଥାନର ନାମ ପଢ଼ି ଭାବିଲା – ଭୁଟାନକୁ କ'ଣ ବହୁପୂର୍ବରୁ ଓଡ଼ିଆ ଲୋକମାନେ ଆସିଥିଲେ କି? ନଚେତ ଗେଡ଼ା, ଚେପା, ଟିମା, ପାରା ଇତ୍ୟାଦି ନାମ ଏଠାରେ କେମିତି ଆସିଲା। ଏମିତି ଭାବି ଭାବି ସେ ଆସି ପହଞ୍ଚିଗଲା ତା'ର ମଧୁଶଯ୍ୟାର ଉପତ୍ୟକା ପାରୋଠାରେ। ସେ ପହଞ୍ଚିବା ବେଳକୁ ଭୁଟାନ ସୁନ୍ଦରୀମାନେ ପାରୋନଦୀରେ ନିଶ୍ଚୟ ସ୍ନାନ କରୁଥିବେ ବୋଲି ସେ କଳ୍ପନା କରିଥିଲା। ମାତ୍ର ପାରୋ ନଦୀ ଏତେ ସୁନ୍ଦରୀ ଯେ ଭୁଟାନ ସୁନ୍ଦରୀମାନେ ତା' ପାଖରେ କାଲେ ମ୍ଲାନ ପଡ଼ିଯିବେ ସେଥିପାଇଁ ସେ ସେଠାରେ ସ୍ନାନ କରନ୍ତି ନାହିଁ। ସେହି ନଦୀ କୂଳରେ ଛୋଟ ସହର ପାରୋରେ ପହଞ୍ଚିବା ମାତ୍ରେ ଆନନ୍ଦର ଉପଲଣ୍ଢ କ'ଣ ସେ ବୁଝିବାକୁ ଆରମ୍ଭ କଲା।

ଘରଗୁଡ଼ିକ ରାସ୍ତା କଡ଼ରେ ଧାଡ଼ି ଧାଡ଼ି ହୋଇ ଶାନ୍ତ ଶୃଙ୍ଖଳିତ ଭାବେ ଠିଆ ହୋଇଥିଲେ। ସତେ ଯେମିତି ଘରଗୁଡ଼ିକ ଦୁଷ୍ମନ୍ତକୁ ପାଛୋଟି ନେବାକୁ ଠିଆ ହୋଇଥିଲେ। ପାରୋ ନଦୀ କୂଳରେ ଝୁଲୁ ଝୁଲୁ ସେ ପ୍ରଥମେ ଯେଉଁ ହୋଟେଲ ପାଖରେ ପହଞ୍ଚିଲା ନାଁ ତା'ର ଉତ୍ତମୟାରା। ପାଦ ତା'ର ସେଇଠି ଅଟକିଲା।

'ଉଭମ୍ୟାରା'ର ଅର୍ଥ କଲା ଦୁଷ୍ମନ୍ତ – ଉଭମବନ୍ଧୁ। ଆଉ ଆଗକୁ ଯିବାର ଆବଶ୍ୟକତା ନଥିଲା। ସେ ହୋଟେଲ ଭିତରକୁ ପ୍ରବେଶ କରିବାମାତ୍ରେ ସ୍ୱାଗତକକ୍ଷ ଦ୍ୱାରା ମୁହଁରେ ଅପେକ୍ଷାରତ ଏକ ସୁନ୍ଦରୀ ଡାକୁ ପାଛୋଟି ନେଲା। ତା'ର ହସ ହସ ମୁହଁ ସାଙ୍ଗକୁ ସୁତ୍ଳ ରୁହାଣୀ ଦୁଷ୍ମନ୍ତକୁ ଯେମିତି ଏକ ଅଡୁଆରେ ପକାଇଲା। ତରୁଣୀଟି ସହିତ ପଦେ କଥା ହେବା ପାଇଁ ତା'ର ମନହେଲା। ହୋଟେଲର ଭଡ଼ା କେତେ ପଚାରିବାରୁ ସୁନ୍ଦରୀ ସହ ଆଳାପ ଆରମ୍ଭ ହେଲା। ଭଡ଼ା ଅଧିକ ନଥିଲା। ତରୁଣୀଟି ଦୁଷ୍ମନ୍ତକୁ ପାଛୋଟି ନେଇ ୩୮୪ ନମ୍ବର ରୁମ୍ ଖୋଲିଦେଲା। ଦୁଷ୍ମନ୍ତ ସହ ସେ ମଧ୍ୟ କୋଠରି ଭିତରକୁ ପ୍ରବେଶ କଲା। ରୁମ୍‌ରେ ଥିବା ସମସ୍ତ ସୁବିଧାକୁ ଗୋଟି ଗୋଟି କରି ଦୁଷ୍ମନ୍ତକୁ ବୁଝାଇଦେଲା। ଏପରିକି ବାଥ୍‌ରୁମ୍ ଖୋଲି ଗରମ ପାଣି, ଥଣ୍ଡା ପାଣି ଇତ୍ୟାଦି ସଂପର୍କରେ ତାକୁ ଅବଗତ କରାଇଲା। ଆବଶ୍ୟକ ପଡ଼ିଲେ ରିସେପ୍ସନକୁ ଫୋନ୍ କରିବାକୁ କହି ତରୁଣୀଟି ବାହାରିଯିବା ବେଳକୁ ଦୁଷ୍ମନ୍ତ ତା'ର ନାମ କ'ଣ ପଚାରିଲା। ତରୁଣୀଟି ସ୍ମିତହସି ଦୁଷ୍ମନ୍ତର ବେଡ୍‌ସାଇଡ୍ ଟେବୁଲ୍‌ରେ ଥିବା ମିନେରାଲ୍ ପାଣିବୋତଲକୁ ଇସାରା କଲା। ଦୁଷ୍ମନ୍ତ କିଛି ବୁଝିପାରିଲା ନାହିଁ। କହିଲା – "ମୋର ଏବେ ପାଣି ଆବଶ୍ୟକ ନାହିଁ, ତୁମର ନାମ ଜାଣିବା ଆବଶ୍ୟକ। ଏହି ଅଜଣା ଦେଶରେ କେହି ତ ଜଣେ ଚିହ୍ନା ମଣିଷ ଥାଉ।"

ତରୁଣୀଟି କହିଲା – "ପାଣିବୋତଲର ନାମଟି ପଢ଼ନ୍ତୁ ନା!"

ଦୁଷ୍ମନ୍ତ ଆଶ୍ଚର୍ଯ୍ୟ ହୋଇ ପାଣିବୋତଲକୁ ରୁହିଲା, ଲେଖା ହୋଇଥିଲା – "କିନ୍‌ଲି"। ଦୁଷ୍ମନ୍ତ କିଛି ବୁଝିପାରିଲା ନାହିଁ। ଝିଅଟି ସେକଥା ଜାଣିପାରି କହିଲା – "ମୋର ନାମ ହେଉଛି 'କିନ୍‌ଲି'। ବୋଧହୁଏ ମୋର ପିତାମାତା ପ୍ରଥମକରି କିନ୍‌ଲୀ ପାଣିବୋତଲ ଦେଖିବା ସମୟକୁ ମୋର ଜନ୍ମ ହୋଇଥିଲା। ପାଣି ତ ଜୀବନ। ତେଣୁ ଅତିଶ୍ରଦ୍ଧାରେ ମୋର ନାମଟି କିନ୍‌ଲି ଦେଲେ ଯେ ବେଳେବେଳେ ମୋର ସାଙ୍ଗମାନେ ମତେ ବେଶ୍ ଚିଡ଼ାନ୍ତି। କିନ୍ତୁ ହୋଟେଲରେ କାମ କରିବା ପରେ ଗୋଟିଏ ସୁବିଧା ହୋଇଛି ଯେ ମୋର ନାମ କେହି ଭୁଲିଯାଆନ୍ତି ନାହିଁ। ଆପଣ ମୋର ନାମଟି ଯଦି ଭୁଲିଯିବେ ତେବେ ପାଣିବୋତଲକୁ ରୁହିଁଲେ ମନେ ପଡ଼ିଯିବ। ଦରକାର ହେଲେ ରିସେପ୍ସନକୁ ଫୋନ୍ କରି କିନ୍‌ଲିକୁ ଖୋଜିଲେ ମୁଁ ଆପଣଙ୍କର ଯାହା ଦରକାର ଯୋଗାଇଦେବି।" କର୍ତ୍ତବ୍ୟରତ ତରୁଣୀଟି ରୁଲିଗଲା।

ଦୁଷ୍ମନ୍ତ ମଖମଲି ଗଦି ଉପରେ ଲେଉଟିପଡ଼ିଲା ଓ ବଡ଼ ବଡ଼ ଝରକାରେ ଫାଇବର୍ ଗ୍ଲାସ୍ ଦେଇ ପର୍ବତର ଶୋଭା ଦେଖୁ ଦେଖୁ ତା'ର ଆଖିପତା ଲାଗିଗଲା। ରୁମ୍‌ର ଟେଲିଫୋନ୍ ବାଜିବାରୁ ଦୁଷ୍ମନ୍ତ ଫୋନ୍ ଉଠାଇଲା। ଅପରପଟୁ କିନ୍‌ଲିର

କଣ୍ଠସ୍ୱରକୁ ବାରିପାରିବା ମାତ୍ରେ ଦୁଷ୍ମନ୍ତ ଉଠିବସିଲା। କିନ୍ଲି ମଧୁରସ୍ୱରରେ ଆପଣାର ଲୋକ ଭଲି ପଚରିଲା – "ଆଜି ରାତ୍ରିଭୋଜନରେ ଆପଣ ଖାଇବେ କି ନାହିଁ? କିଛି ତ ଅର୍ଡର କଲେନାହିଁ?"

ଦୁଷ୍ମନ୍ତ କହିଲା – "ଅର୍ଡର କରିବାର କ'ଣ ଅଛି, ତୁମେ ତ ଦାୟିତ୍ୱରେ ଅଛ। କ'ଣ ଖାଇବାକୁ ମିଳିବ ନାହିଁ? ଏଠି କ'ଣ ଖାଇବାକୁ ଦେଇପାରିବ?"

"ଯଦି ମନେରଖିଲା ଭଲି ଖାଦ୍ୟ ଖାଇପାରିବେ ତେବେ ପରଷିବି ଥୁରାକା ଓ ଏମାଦସୀ" କିନ୍ଲି କହିଲା।

"ଯଦି ମନେରଖିବାର ପ୍ରଶ୍ନ ଉଠିଲାଣି ତେବେ ତାହା ହିଁ ଖାଇବି, ତେବେ ଏଠାରେ ରାତ୍ରିଭୋଜନ କେତେବେଳେ ପ୍ରସ୍ତୁତ ହୋଇଯିବ?" ପଚରିଲା ଦୁଷ୍ମନ୍ତ।

କିନ୍ଲି କହିଲା – "ସାତଟାରୁ ନଅଟା ଭିତରେ ଯେକୌଣସି ସମୟରେ ଆସିପାରନ୍ତି। କିନ୍ତୁ ତା'ଠାରୁ ବିଳମ୍ବ ହେଲେ ରେଷ୍ଟୁରାଣ୍ଟ ବନ୍ଦ ହୋଇଯିବ।"

ଦୁଷ୍ମନ୍ତ ପଚରିଲା – "ତୁମେ କ'ଣ ସକାଳୁ ସନ୍ଧ୍ୟା ପର୍ଯ୍ୟନ୍ତ କାମ କର? ତୁମର ଡ୍ୟୁଟି କେତେବେଳଯାଏ?"

କିନ୍ଲି କହିଲା – "ମୋ ସାଙ୍ଗର ଦେହ ଖରାପ ଥିବାରୁ ତା'ସାଙ୍ଗରେ ରାତି ନଅଟା ପର୍ଯ୍ୟନ୍ତ ଡ୍ୟୁଟି କରି ଘରକୁ ଫେରେ। ତା'ରି ଅନୁରୋଧରେ ମୁଁ ଓଭରଟାଇମ୍ କରୁଛି। ତାକୁ ମୁଁ ପ୍ରାଣଦେଇ ଭଲପାଏ।"

ଦୁଷ୍ମନ୍ତର ପଚରିବାକୁ ଇଚ୍ଛା ହେଲା – "ପୁଅ ସାଙ୍ଗ ନା ଝିଅ ସାଙ୍ଗ?" କିନ୍ତୁ ପଚରିଲା ନାହିଁ। ଏକ ଅତିଥି ଦେଶରେ ସ୍ୱଳ୍ପ ପରିଚିତା ତରୁଣୀଟିକୁ ଏପରି ପ୍ରଶ୍ନ ପଚରିବା ଶାଳୀନ ନୁହେଁ। ତା'ଛଡ଼ା ସେ ଯଦି ପୁଅସାଙ୍ଗ ବୋଲି ଉତ୍ତର ଦିଏ ତେବେ ଦୁଷ୍ମନ୍ତ ଟିକିଏ ନିରାଶ ହୋଇଯିବନି କି? ଏହି ସ୍ୱଳ୍ପ ରହଣୀ କାଳରେ ଯେଉଁ ଝିଅଟି ତାକୁ ପ୍ରଥମରୁ ଭଲ ଲାଗିଛି ତା'ର ଯେ କେହି ପୁଅସାଙ୍ଗ ନାହାନ୍ତି ଏତିକି ଭାବିନେଲେ ଆନନ୍ଦର ଉପଲକ୍ଷ୍ୟ ଟିକିଏ ଗଭୀର ହେବନି କି?

ଫୋନ୍ ରଖିବା ଆଗରୁ କିନ୍ଲି କହିଲା – "ଆପଣଙ୍କୁ ରାତ୍ରିଭୋଜନ କରାଇସାରି ମୁଁ ଘରକୁ ଫେରିବି। ଆପଣ ଆମ ବନ୍ଧୁଦେଶରୁ ଆସିଛନ୍ତି। ମୋର ପ୍ରିୟ ଅତିଥି। ସନ୍ତୋଷ ହୋଇ ଫେରିଗଲେ ମୁଁ ଖୁସୀ ହେବି।"

ଦୁଷ୍ମନ୍ତ ଧନ୍ୟବାଦ କହି ଫୋନ୍ ରଖିଲା ଏବଂ ଭାବିଲା ଆଗରୁ ଯଦି ଜାଣିଥାନ୍ତା ଯେ କିନ୍ଲି ସହ ଦେଖାହେବ ତା'ହେଲେ ତା'ପାଇଁ ଓଡ଼ିଶାର ହସ୍ତଶିଳ୍ପର କିଛି ଗୋଟିଏ ଉପହାର ନେଇ ଆସିଥାନ୍ତା। ଏବେ କିନ୍ଲିକୁ ଦେବ କ'ଣ? ଦୁଷ୍ମନ୍ତ ଖାଇବା ପାଇଁ ଯିବାବେଳେ ବ୍ୟାଗରୁ ବାହାରକଲା ଘରୁ ଆଣିଥିବା ରାସିଲଡ୍ଡୁର

ପ୍ୟାକେଟ୍‍ଟି । କିନ୍‍ଲିକୁ ଦେଖିବା ମାତ୍ରେ ତା' ହାତକୁ ବଢ଼ାଇଦେଇ କହିଲା –
"ଜାଣିନଥିଲି କିନ୍‍ଲି ଭଲି ଝିଅଟିଏ ସହ ଦେଖାହେବ । ତେଣୁ କିଛି ଉପହାର
ଆଣିନାହିଁ । ଏ ହେଉଛି ମୋ ମା'ଙ୍କ ହାତତିଆରି ଏକ ପ୍ରକାର ଶସ୍ୟ ଏବଂ ଗୁଡ଼ରେ
ତିଆରି ଲଡ଼ୁ । ଏହାକୁ କହନ୍ତି ରାଶିଲଡ଼ୁ । ତୁମେ ଖାଇଲେ ମୁଁ ଖୁସି ହେବି ।"

କିନ୍‍ଲି ଲଡ଼ୁ ପ୍ୟାକେଟ୍‍ଟିକୁ ହାତରେ ଧରି ସୁନ୍ଦର ଉଚ୍ଚାରଣ କରି କହିଲା
– "ରାଶି ଲଡ଼ୁ! ଭାରି ସୁନ୍ଦର ନାମ । ମୁଁ ବିବାହ କଲା ପରେ ମୋର ଯଦି ଝିଅ
ହୁଏ ତା'ର ନାମ ଦେବି ରାଶି, ଯଦି ପୁଅ ହୁଏ ନାମଦେବି ଲଡ଼ୁ ।"

ସେ ବିବାହିତା କି ନା ଦୁଷ୍ମନ୍ତ ପଚାରିଲା ନାହିଁ । କେବଳ ଏତିକି କହିଲା
– "ଆମ ଦେଶରେ ବି ଏହିପରି ନାମ ଝିଅପୁଅଙ୍କର ଅଛି ।"

କିନ୍‍ଲି ଲଡ଼ୁ ଖାଇଲା, ଦୁଷ୍ମନ୍ତକୁ ଧନ୍ୟବାଦ ଜଣାଇବା ସହ କହିଲା –
"ତୁମ ଦେଶର ଏହି ଲଡ଼ୁ ଭାରି ଟେଷ୍ଟି ।"

ଦୁଷ୍ମନ୍ତ କିନ୍‍ଲି ପରଷି ଦେଇଥିବା ଥୁରାକା ଓ ଏମାଦାସୀ ଖାଉ ଖାଉ କହିଲା
– "ତୁମ ଦେଶର ଏ ଖାଦ୍ୟ ବି ଭାରି ଟେଷ୍ଟି ।"

ଖାଇସାରିବା ପରେ ଦୁଷ୍ମନ୍ତ କିନ୍‍ଲିକୁ ଅନୁମତି ମାଗିଲା ତା' ସହ ଗୋଟିଏ
ଫଟୋ ଉଠାଇବା ପାଇଁ । କିନ୍‍ଲି ସହସା ରାଜି ହୋଇଗଲା ଏବଂ ଦୁହେଁ ଏକାଠି
ଛିଡ଼ାହୋଇ ଜଣେ ହୋଟେଲ୍‍ ବୟକୁ ଡାକିଲେ । ଦୁଷ୍ମନ୍ତ କ୍ୟାମେରା ବଢ଼ାଇଦେଲା
ତା' ହାତକୁ । ହୋଟେଲ୍‍ ବୟ ଫଟୋ ଉଠାଇବା ଆଗରୁ ପାଖକୁ ଲାଗି ଛିଡ଼ା
ହେବାପାଇଁ ଇସାରା ଦେଲା । କ୍ୟାମେରା ଲାଇଟ୍‍ ଦୁଇଥର ଫ୍ଲାଶ୍‍ ହେଲା ଏବଂ
ସୁନ୍ଦର ଫଟୋଟିଏ ଉଠିଲା ।

କିନ୍‍ଲିକୁ ଗୁଡ୍‍ନାଇଟ୍‍ କହିବା ଆଗରୁ ଦୁଷ୍ମନ୍ତ କିନ୍‍ଲିକୁ ଟାଇଗର୍‍ନେଷ୍ଟ
ମୋନାଲିକୁ ଯିବାପାଇଁ ରାସ୍ତା ପଚାରିଲା । ଓ ଚଢ଼ିବା ପାଇଁ କେତେ ସମୟ ଲାଗିବ
ବୋଲି ପଚାରିଲା ।

କିନ୍‍ଲି କହିଲା ଯେ ହୋଟେଲଠାରୁ ଦେଢ଼ଘଣ୍ଟାରୁ ଅଧିକ ସମୟ ଲାଗିବ
ନାହିଁ । କିନ୍ତୁ ସୂର୍ଯ୍ୟାସ୍ତ ପୂର୍ବରୁ ପାହାଡ଼ ଉପରୁ ତଳକୁ ଓହ୍ଲାଇ ଆସିବା ଆବଶ୍ୟକ
ଏବଂ ଅନ୍ଧାର ହେବା ପୂର୍ବରୁ ହୋଟେଲରେ ପହଞ୍ଚିଯିବା ଭଲ । ରାତିରେ ବେଶ୍‍
ଥଣ୍ଡା ପଡ଼ିବ । ପରଦିନ ଦୁଷ୍ମନ୍ତ ପାରୋ ସହର ବୁଲିସାରି ଟାଇଗର୍‍ନେଷ୍ଟ ମୋନାଷ୍ଟିକୁ
ଯିବା ପାଇଁ ସ୍ଥିର କଲା । ପାରୋ ସହରର ଗଳିକନ୍ଦି ତାକୁ ଭାରି ଭଲ ଲାଗିଲା ।
ୟୁରୋପୀୟାନ୍‍ ଢାଞ୍ଚାରେ ନିର୍ମିତ କୋଠାଗୁଡ଼ିକ ସହରଟିକୁ ଖୁବ ଶାନ୍ତ ଓ ସୁନ୍ଦର
କରିଦେଇଛି । ଓ‍ୱିଲୋ ଏବଂ ପାଇନ୍‍ ଗଛର ସମ୍ଭାରରେ ସହରଟି ସବୁଜ ସବୁଜ

ଲାଗୁଥାଏ । ଏକ ସୁନ୍ଦର ସାନ କାଫେଟାରିଆରେ ସକାଳ ଜଳଖିଆ ଏବଂ ଗରମ କଫି ପିଇସାରିବା ପରେ ଉଷ୍ମ ଖରାରେ ଝୁଲି ଝୁଲି ପାରୋ ନଦୀକୂଳରେ ସେ ବସିଲା ଏବଂ ପିଲାଦିନର ଅଭ୍ୟାସବଶତଃ ଭାବିଲା – ନଦୀରେ ଗାଧୋଇପଡ଼ିବ କି ? ପାଣିରେ ଗୋଡ଼ ବୁଡ଼ାଇଲା ଏବଂ ଚଟ୍‌କରି ଉଠାଇ ଆଣିଲା – ବରଫ ଭଳି ଥଣ୍ଡା ପାଣି । କାହିଁକି ଏତେ ଥଣ୍ଡା ପାଣି ବୋଲି ଛୋଟ ପିଲାଙ୍କ ଭଳି ନଦୀକୁ ଛୋଟବଡ଼ ପଥର ଫିଙ୍ଗିଲା । ସାମ୍ନାରେ ଉଚ୍ଚା ଉଚ୍ଚା ପର୍ବତମାଳା ମଣିଷର ଶକ୍ତି ପରୀକ୍ଷା ପାଇଁ ଯେମିତି ଆହ୍ବାନ ଦେଉଥିଲେ । ଦୂରରେ ଏକ ପର୍ବତ ଉପରେ ବରଫ ପଡ଼ି ଚକ୍‌ ଚକ୍‌ କରୁଥାଏ, ଯେମିତି ମଣିଷର ସୀମା ପରଖିସାରିଛି ବୋଲି ପର୍ବତ ଦାନ୍ତ ଦେଖାଇ ହସୁଥିଲା । ଏହିପରି ପ୍ରକୃତିର ପ୍ରେମରେ ସେ ସମୟ ଭୁଲିଗଲା ।

ଦେଖୁ ଦେଖୁ ଦୁଇଟା ବାଜିଗଲା । ତା'ର ମନେପଡ଼ିଲା ଯେ ତାକୁ ଟାଇଗର୍‌ନେଷ୍ଟ ମୋନାଷ୍ଟ୍ରି ଯିବାର ଅଛି । ଖୁବ୍‌ଶୀଘ୍ର ସେ ମୋନାଷ୍ଟ୍ରିର ବେସ୍‌କ୍ୟାମ୍ପକୁ ବାହାରିଲା । ପାହାଡ଼ତଳେ ପହଞ୍ଚିବା ବେଳକୁ ସମୟ ତିନିଟା ବାଜିଯାଇଥିଲା । ସୂର୍ଯ୍ୟଙ୍କର ତାପ ଧୀରେ ଧୀରେ କମିଆସୁଥାଏ । ଦୁଷ୍ମନ୍ତ ଗୋଟିଏ ବାଡ଼ି କିଣିଲା । ପାହାଡ଼ ଉପରକୁ ଚଢ଼ିବାକୁ ସାହାଯ୍ୟ କରିବ । ତା' ପରେ ପାହାଡ଼ ଚଢ଼ିବାକୁ ଆରମ୍ଭ କଲା । ଏହି ସମୟରେ ଯାତ୍ରୀମାନେ ପାହାଡ଼ ଉପରୁ ତଳକୁ ଫେରୁଥାନ୍ତି । କେତେଜଣ ଦୁଷ୍ମନ୍ତକୁ ଆଶ୍ଚର୍ଯ୍ୟ ହୋଇ ରୁହିଁଲେ । କହିଲେ – "ଆପଣଙ୍କୁ ଅଢ଼େଇଘଣ୍ଟାରୁ ଅଧିକ ସମୟ ଲାଗିବ । ଆପଣ ପହଞ୍ଚିବା ବେଳକୁ ଅନ୍ଧାର ହୋଇଯାଇଥିବ, କ'ଣ ଦେଖିବେ ?"

ମାତ୍ର ଦୁଷ୍ମନ୍ତ ନମ୍ରତା ସହ ପାହାଡ଼ ଚଢ଼ିବାକୁ ଲାଗିଲା । ପକେଟରେ ହାତମାରିଲା, ଛୋଟ ଟର୍ଚ ଲାଇଟ୍‌ ପାଖରେ ଅଛି । ଯାହାହେଉ ଓହ୍ଲାଇଲା ବେଳକୁ କାମରେ ଆସିବ । ସନ୍ଧ୍ୟା ହୋଇଆସୁଥିଲା, ଦୁଷ୍ମନ୍ତ ଟିକିଏ ଜୋର୍‌ରେ ଚଢ଼ିବାକୁ ଆରମ୍ଭ କଲା । ତା'ର ଛାତି ଧଡ଼ଧଡ଼ ହେଲା ଓ ପାଦ ଅପେକ୍ଷା ନିଶ୍ୱାସ ଦ୍ରୁତତର ହେଉଥିଲା । ପର୍ବତ ଉପରେ ଟାଇଗର୍‌ନେଷ୍ଟ ମୋନାଷ୍ଟ୍ରି ଖୁବ୍‌ ଚମତ୍କାର ଦିଶୁଥାଏ । ଅସ୍ତଗାମୀ ସୂର୍ଯ୍ୟର ନାଲି କିରଣରେ ଧଳା ମୋନାଷ୍ଟ୍ରିଟି ନାଲି ଦିଶୁଥାଏ । ସମୟ ପାଞ୍ଚଟା ବାଜିବାକୁ ଯାଉଥାଏ । ପାଞ୍ଚଟା ବେଳେ ମୋନାଷ୍ଟ୍ରି ବନ୍ଦ ହୋଇଯାଏ ବୋଲି କିନ୍‌ଲି କହିଥିଲା । ଆଗକୁ ଆଉ ପାଞ୍ଚଶହ ପାହାଚ ବାକିଥିଲା । ଦୁଷ୍ମନ୍ତ ଥକ୍କା ମାରିଲା, ଦୁଇଢୋକ ପାଣି ପିଇଲା । ଝାଳରେ ଓଦା ହୋଇଯାଇଥିବା ସାର୍ଟ ପବନ ବାଜି ଥଣ୍ଡା ଲାଗୁଥିଲା, ତଥାପି ସେ ପାହାଚ ଚଢ଼ିବାକୁ ଲାଗିଲା । ଆଉ ଶହେ ପାହାଚ ବାକିଥିଲା ସେ ଦେଖିଲା – ଜଣେ ଲାମା(ମୋନାଷ୍ଟ୍ରିର ମହନ୍ତ) ରୁବି ପକାଇ ପାହାଚରେ ଓହ୍ଲାଉଛନ୍ତି । ଦୁଷ୍ମନ୍ତ

ମନରେ ଝଟ୍କା ଲାଗିଲା, ସେ ହାରିଗଲା । ମହନ୍ତଙ୍କୁ ଜୁହାର କରି ସେ ପାହାଚ ଚଢ଼ିଲା । ମୋନାଷ୍ଟ୍ରିର ବନ୍ଦ ଦୁଆରେ ଆଣ୍ଠେଇପଡ଼ି ଜୁହାର ହେଲା । ପୁଣି ଛିଡ଼ା ହୋଇ ରୁରିଆଡ଼ ସୁନ୍ଦର ଦୃଶ୍ୟକୁ ଦେଖିଲା । ଆଜିର ନିର୍ଦୟ ସୂର୍ଯ୍ୟ ପାହାଡ଼ରେ ଲୁଟିଯିବାକୁ ବସିଲେଣି । ଦୁଷ୍ମନ୍ତର ପାଣି ବୋତଲ ଅଧା ହୋଇଯାଇଥିଲା । ଖାଇବା ଜିନିଷ କିଛି ବି ନଥିଲା । ସେ ଦେଖିଲା ଜଣେ ବୁଢ଼ୀ ପାହାଚଗୁଡ଼ିକୁ ଓଲାଉଛନ୍ତି । ସେ ବୁଢ଼ୀକୁ ଜୁହାର କଲା । ବୁଢ଼ୀ ତାକୁ ଇଙ୍ଗିତରେ ପାଖକୁ ଡାକିଲା, ତିନୋଟି ଚକୋଲେଟ୍ ଓ ଗୋଟିଏ ପାଣିବୋତଲ ଦେଲା । ପୁଣି ଗୋଟିଏ ନାଲି ସାଲ ମଧ୍ୟ ଦେଲା । ଇଙ୍ଗିତରେ କହିଲା – ସେ ବିକୁନାହିଁ, ଉପହାର ଦେଲା । ଦୁଷ୍ମନ୍ତ କୃତଜ୍ଞତା ଜଣାଇ ଚକୋଲେଟ୍କୁ ପକେଟ୍ରେ ରଖିଲା ଓ ପାଣିବୋତଲକୁ ହାତରେ ଧରି ତରତର ହୋଇ ପାହାଚରେ ଓହ୍ଲାଇଲା । ତାକୁ ଅନ୍ଧାର ପୂର୍ବରୁ ଯେମିତି ହେଲେ ପାହାଡ଼ ତଳେ ପହଞ୍ଚିଯିବାକୁ ପଡ଼ିବ । ରାତିରେ ପାହାଚ ଓହ୍ଲାଇବାର ବିପଦ ଓ କଷ୍ଟ ସମ୍ପର୍କରେ ତା'ର ଅଭିଜ୍ଞତା ଥିଲା । ଧୀରେ ଧୀରେ ଅନ୍ଧାର ମାଡ଼ିଆସିଲା । ସେ ପକେଟ୍ରୁ ଟର୍ଚ ବାହାର କଲା । ଟର୍ଚ ଆଲୋକରେ ଅତି ସଂକୀର୍ଣ୍ଣ ରାସ୍ତାରେ ଓହ୍ଲାଇବାକୁ ଚେଷ୍ଟା କଲା । ସକାଳେ ପାହାଡ଼ ପର୍ବତ ଯେତେ ସ୍ପଷ୍ଟ ଓ ସୁନ୍ଦର ରାତିକୁ ସେତିକି ରହସ୍ୟମୟ ଓ ବିପଜ୍ଜନକ । ବାଟ ଆବୁଡ଼ାଖାବୁଡ଼ା । ଗୋଟିଏ ପାଖରେ ପାହାଡ଼ ଓ ଅନ୍ୟପାଖରେ ଖାଇ । ଗୋଡ଼ ଖସିଲେ ମୃତ୍ୟୁ ସୁନିର୍ଦିଷ୍ଟ । ଦୁଷ୍ମନ୍ତ ବଡ଼ ସତର୍ପଣରେ ପାହାଡ଼ ଖସୁଥାଏ । ଶୀଘ୍ର ହୋଟେଲରେ ପହଞ୍ଚିପାରିଲେ କିନ୍ଲି ସହ ଦେଖାହେବ । ପ୍ରବଳ ଭୋକ ମଧ୍ୟ ହେଲାଣି । ଦୁଷ୍ମନ୍ତ ସବୁବେଳେ ଉସ୍ସାହର ସହ ଟ୍ରେକିଂ କରିଥାଏ । ଆଜି ଯେମିତି କିନ୍ଲି ସେହି ଉସ୍ସାହରେ ଆଉଟିକେ ରଙ୍ଗ ବୋଲିଦେଇଛି । ତା'ର ଉସ୍ସାହ ବଢ଼ିଗଲା ଏବଂ ସେତିକିବେଳେ ପାହାଚ ଉପରୁ ପାଦ ଖସିଗଲା । ସେ ଭାରସାମ୍ୟ ହରାଇ ଓଲଟିପଡ଼ିଲା, ଭୟରେ ଚିକ୍ରାର କଲା । ପାହାଚ ଉପରେ ଗଡ଼ି ଗଡ଼ି ଯାଉଥିବା ବେଳେ ସାହାଯ୍ୟ ପାଇଁ ପାଟି କରୁଥିଲେ ମଧ୍ୟ ପାଖରେ କେହି ନଥିଲେ । କିଛି ଧରିବାକୁ ଚେଷ୍ଟାକରି ଅଟକିଯିବା ପାଇଁ ରୁହିଁଲେ ମଧ୍ୟ ହାତପାହାନ୍ତାରେ କିଛି ନଥିଲା । ସେ ତଳକୁ ତଳ ଖସି ଖସି ଯାଉଥିବା ବେଳେ ଖାଇ ଉପରୁ ବଢ଼ିଥିବା ଗୋଟିଏ ଝଙ୍କା ଗଛଡ଼ାଳରେ ତା'ର ଗୋଡ଼ ଛନ୍ଦି ହୋଇଗଲା ଓ ସେ ସେଠାରେ ଅଟକିଗଲା । ହାତରୁ ଟର୍ଚ, କ୍ୟାମେରା, ପାଣିବୋତଲ ଅନେକ ଆଗରୁ ଖସିଯାଇ ସାରିଥାଏ । ତା'ର ମୁଣ୍ଡ ଫାଟି ରକ୍ତ ବାହାରୁଥିଲା, ଡାହାଣଗୋଡ଼ଟି ଉଠୁନଥିଲା । ଜଙ୍ଘ ପାଖରୁ ଭାଙ୍ଗିଯାଇଥିଲା କି ନ'ଣ? କିଛି ସମୟ ସେ ଗଛରେ ଅଟକି ରହିଲା । ରୁରିପଟେ ଘୋର ଅନ୍ଧାର । ବଞ୍ଚିବାର ଆଶାକୁ କ୍ଷୀଣ କରିଦେଇଥିଲା । ତା'ର ଉପରକୁ କି ତଳକୁ ଯିବାର ଉପାୟ

ନଥିଲା । ଏ ଦେଶରେ ତା'ର କେହି ବି ନଥିଲେ । କେବଳ ଥିଲା ଜଣେ କିନ୍‌ଲି । ବିପଦକାଳରେ ତା' କଥା ଦୁଷ୍ମନ୍ତ ମନେପଡ଼ିଲା । ଏହି ଦୁଇଦିନ ମଧ୍ୟରେ ସେ ଯେମିତି ତାକୁ ଭଲପାଇ ବସିଥିଲା । ତା'ର ସାନ୍ନିଧ୍ୟରେ ଆନନ୍ଦ ଓ ଶାନ୍ତିର ସ୍ୱର୍ଗୀୟତା ଅନୁଭବ କରୁଥିଲା । ସେହି ଅନ୍ଧାରରେ ସେ ମୁଣ୍ଡରୁ ରକ୍ତ ନେଇ ହାତବଡ଼ାଇ ପଥର ପାହାଚରେ ଇଂରାଜୀରେ 'କିନ୍‌ଲି' ବୋଲି ଲେଖିଲା । ଯେଉଁ ଝିଅଟିକୁ ସେ ପ୍ରଥମଦେଖାରେ ଭଲ ପାଇଥିଲା ତାକୁ ସେକଥା କହିପାରିଲା ନାହିଁ ବୋଲି ମନରେ ଅବସୋସ ଆସିଲା । ତା'ର ଆଖିପତା ପଡ଼ି ପଡ଼ି ଆସିଲା ଓ ସେ ଶୋଇପଡ଼ିଲା ।

ସେ ସ୍ୱପ୍ନ ଦେଖିଲା ଯେ, ତା' ପାଖଦେଇ ଗୋଟିଏ ବାଘ ଯାଉଛି, ସେ ବାଘକୁ ଡାକିଲା ଓ କହିଲା – ମତେ ଟିକିଏ କିନ୍‌ଲି ପାଖକୁ ନେଇଯା । ବାଘ କହିଲା – ନା', ଏ ଯେଉଁ ଟାଇଗର୍‌ନେଷ୍ଟ ମୋନାଷ୍ଟ୍ରି ଦେଖୁଛ ସେହି ଗୁମ୍ଫାରେ ମୋର ଘର ଥିଲା । ମଣିଷମାନେ ଆସି ସେଠାରେ ମୋନାଷ୍ଟ୍ରି କଲେ, ମତେ ଓ ମୋ ପିଲାଛୁଆଙ୍କୁ ବେଘର କରିଦେଲେ । ମଣିଷ କେଡ଼େ ନିର୍ଦ୍ଦୟ ସେକଥା ମୁଁ ଜାଣିଛି । ତେଣୁ ତୁମକୁ ମୁଁ ସାହାଯ୍ୟ କରିପାରିବି ନାହିଁ । ଏହାକହି ବାଘ ଲାଙ୍ଗୁଡ଼ ହଲାଇ ସେଠାରୁ ଚାଲିଗଲା ।

ତା'ପରେ ଦୁଷ୍ମନ୍ତ ଦେଖିଲା ଗଛ ଉପରେ ଗୋଟିଏ ବୁଲ୍‌ବୁଲ୍ ବସିଛି । ଦୁଷ୍ମନ୍ତ ତାକୁ କହିଲା – ତୁ ଟିକିଏ ଉଡ଼ିଯାଇ କିନ୍‌ଲିକୁ କହିପାରିବୁ କି ମୁଁ ପାହାଡ଼ ଉପରେ ପଡ଼ିଛି ବୋଲି । ବୁଲ୍‌ବୁଲ୍ କହିଲା – ନା', ମୋର ସାଥୀକୁ ଗୋଟିଏ ମଣିଷ ଧରିନେଇଯାଇଛି । ତାକୁ ନେଇ ମୋନାଷ୍ଟ୍ରେ ପିଞ୍ଜରାରେ ରଖିଛି । ସେ କେତେ ବିକଳରେ ମୋତେ ଡାକୁଛି ଏବଂ ଉଡ଼ିଆସିବାକୁ ଚାହୁଁଛି । ସେହି ନିର୍ଦ୍ଦୟ ମଣିଷମାନେ ମନ୍ତ୍ରପାଠ କରୁଛନ୍ତି, କିନ୍ତୁ ମୋ ସାଥୀକୁ ଛାଡ଼ୁନାହାନ୍ତି । ମୁଁ ଜାଣିଛି ମଣିଷମାନେ କେଡ଼େ ନିର୍ଦ୍ଦୟ । ମୁଁ ତୁମକୁ ସାହାଯ୍ୟ କରିବିନାହିଁ । ଏତିକି କହି ସେ ଉଡ଼ିଗଲା ।

ଦୁଷ୍ମନ୍ତ ପୁଣି ଦେଖିଲା ପାଖରେ ସାପ ଶୋଇଛି । ତାକୁ ପଚାରିଲା – ତୁ ମତେ ଟିକିଏ ସାହାଯ୍ୟ କରିପାରିବୁ କି ? ମୁଁ ଏଠାରେ ପଡ଼ିଛି ବୋଲି ଟିକିଏ ତୁ ମୋର କିନ୍‌ଲିକୁ କହିପାରିବୁ କି ? ସାପ ତତ୍‌କ୍ଷଣାତ୍ ଉତ୍ତର ଦେଲା – ସାହାଯ୍ୟ କରିବାକୁ ମୁଁ ରାଜି । କିନ୍ତୁ ମଣିଷମାନେ ମତେ ଏତେ ଘୃଣା କରନ୍ତି ଯେ ମତେ ହୋଟେଲ୍‌ରେ ଦେଖିବା ମାତ୍ରେ ବିନା ଦୋଷରେ ମାରିଦେବେ । ମୁଁ ତୁମକୁ ସାହାଯ୍ୟ କରିବାର ଅର୍ଥ ମୋର ମୃତ୍ୟୁ । ଏହା କହି ସାପ ଚାଲିଗଲା । ଦୁଷ୍ମନ୍ତ ଭାବିଲା ମଣିଷ ତା'ର ଅପକର୍ମ ପାଇଁ ଆଜି ସମସ୍ତଙ୍କ ପାଖରେ ଘୃଣ୍ୟ ହୋଇଯାଇଛି ।

ଏତିକିବେଳେ ଦୁଷ୍ମନ୍ତର ସ୍ୱପ୍ନ ଟୁଟିଗଲା ଏବଂ ସେ ଦେଖିଲା – ରାତିରେ

ଜଣେ ଲାମା କିଛି ପରିବା ଧରି ଟାଇଗରନେଷ୍ଟ ମୋନାଷ୍ଟିକୁ ଯାଉଛନ୍ତି। ସ୍ବଚ୍ଛ ଚନ୍ଦ୍ରାଲୋକରେ ସେ ସ୍ବଚ୍ଛନ୍ଦରେ ପାହାଡ଼ ଚଢ଼ିଯାଉଛନ୍ତି। ଏହା ତାଙ୍କର ନିତିଦିନିଆ ରାସ୍ତା। ତେଣୁ ତାଙ୍କର ଆଲୋକର ଆବଶ୍ୟକତା ନାହିଁ। କିଛିବାଟ ଯିବା ପରେ ଲାମା ଦେଖିଲେ ଯେ ରାସ୍ତା ଉପରେ ମନ୍ଦାଏ ଆଲୋକ ଦେଖାଯାଉଛି। ପାଖକୁ ଯାଇ ଦେଖିଲେ ଯେ ଗୋଟିଏ ଜଳନ୍ତା ଟର୍ଚ୍ଚ। ତାଙ୍କୁ ଲାଗିଲା ଘଟଣାଟା ସ୍ବାଭାବିକ ନୁହେଁ। ସେ ରୁରିଆଡ଼କୁ ରୁହିଁଲେ, କିଛି ଦୂରରେ ପଡ଼ିଥିଲା ଗୋଟିଏ କ୍ୟାମେରା। କ୍ୟାମେରାଟିକୁ ଅନ୍କରି ଦେଖିଲେ ଯେ ସେଥିରେ ଗୋଟିଏ ଝିଅ ଓ ପୁଅର ଫଟୋ ଅଛି। ଝିଅଟି ନିଶ୍ଚୟ ଭୁତାନ ଓ ପୁଅଟି ଇଣ୍ଡିଆନ୍ ଭଳି ଲାଗିଲା। ଲାମା ଟର୍ଚ୍ଚିକୁ ଟିକିଏ ନଜର ପକାଇବାରୁ ତା'ଉପରେ ଲେଖାଥିଲା ପରି ଲାଗିଲା। କ୍ୟାମେରାର ଲାଇଟ୍ ଉପରେ ଦେଖିଲେ ଯେ ଟର୍ଚ୍ଚ ଉପରେ କିନ୍ଲୀ ଓ ଗୋଟିଏ ମୋବାଇଲ୍ ନମ୍ବର ଲେଖାଯାଇଛି। ଲାମାଜଣକ କିଛି ଆଶଙ୍କା କରି ନିଜ ମୋବାଇଲରୁ ସେହି ନମ୍ବରଟିକୁ ଫୋନ୍ ଲଗାଇଲେ। ସେତେବେଳକୁ ସାତଟା ବାଜିଥାଏ। ଜଣେ ଝିଅ ଫୋନ୍ ଉଠାଇଲା ଓ ତା'ର ନାମ କିନ୍ଲୀ ବୋଲି କହିଲା। ଲାମା କହିଲେ ଯେ ସେ ଗୋଟିଏ ଟର୍ଚ୍ଚ ଲାଇଟ୍ ପାଇଛନ୍ତି ସେଥିରେ କିନ୍ଲୀର ନାମ ଲେଖା ହୋଇଛି ଓ ଫୋନ୍ ନମ୍ବର ଲେଖାହୋଇଛି। କିନ୍ଲୀର ଟର୍ଚ୍ଚ ଲାଇଟ୍ ଏଠାକୁ କିପରି ଆସିଲା ?

ଲାମାଙ୍କଠାରୁ ସବୁ ଶୁଣି କିନ୍ଲୀ ବ୍ୟସ୍ତ ହୋଇପଡ଼ିଲା। କହିଲା - ଟର୍ଚ୍ଚଟି ମୋର ନୁହେଁ, ଦୁଷ୍ମନ୍ତକର। ସେ ଇଣ୍ଡିଆରୁ ଆସିଛନ୍ତି ଓ ଆମ ହୋଟେଲରେ ରହୁଛନ୍ତି। ସେ ଆଜି ଟାଇଗରନେଷ୍ଟ ଯାଇଥିଲେ। ବର୍ତ୍ତମାନ ସୁଦ୍ଧା ହୋଟେଲକୁ ଫେରିନାହାନ୍ତି। ମୁଁ ତାଙ୍କୁ ଅପେକ୍ଷା କରି ରହିଛି। ତାଙ୍କ ଫୋନ୍ ନମ୍ବର ମୋ ପାଖରେ ନଥିବାରୁ ଫୋନ୍ କରିପାରିନାହିଁ। ସେ ନିଶ୍ଚୟ କିଛି ଅସୁବିଧାରେ ପଡ଼ିଛନ୍ତି। ଏବେ ମୁଁ ସାଙ୍ଗେ ସାଙ୍ଗେ ହୋଟେଲରୁ ଗାଡ଼ିମେଲ ଯାଉଛି। ସେ ଆମର ପ୍ରିୟ ଅତିଥି। ତାଙ୍କୁ ଖୋଜି ନେଇଆସିବା ଆମର କର୍ତ୍ତବ୍ୟ। କିନ୍ଲୀ ସେଠାରେ ପହଞ୍ଚିବା ପର୍ଯ୍ୟନ୍ତ ଲାମାଜଣକ ଅପେକ୍ଷା କରି ରହିଥିଲେ। କିନ୍ଲୀ ପହଞ୍ଚିବା ପରେ ସବୁଲୋକ ମିଶି ପାହାଡ଼ ଉପରେ ଖୋଜାଖୋଜି କଲେ। ଟର୍ଚ୍ଚ ଆଲୋକରେ ଦେଖିଲେ ଖାଇପାଖର ଏକ ଗଛରେ ନାଲିକପଡ଼ା ଓହଲିଛି। ପାଖକୁ ଯାଇ ଦେଖିଲେ ସେହି ନାଲିକପଡ଼ା ଝୁଲାଇ ହୋଇ ଦୁଷ୍ମନ୍ତ ଝୁଲି ରହିଛନ୍ତି ଗଛରେ। ଦୁଷ୍ମନ୍ତର ହାତ ଗୋଟିଏ ପଥର ଚଟାଣକୁ ସ୍ପର୍ଶ କରିଛି ଓ ସେଥିରେ ଲେଖାଯାଇଛି କିନ୍ଲୀ। କିନ୍ଲୀ ହାତଲଗାଇବାରୁ ଜାଣିଲା ଯେ ଦୁଷ୍ମନ୍ତର ନିଃଶ୍ବାସ ଚଳୁଛି। ଖୁସୀ ହୋଇ ସମସ୍ତେ ମିଶି ନାଲିସାଲ୍ଟିକୁ ଗଛରୁ କଷ୍ଟେମଷ୍ଟେ ଖୋଲି ଦୁଷ୍ମନ୍ତକୁ ତଳକୁ ଆଣି ପଥରଚଟାଣରେ ଶୁଆଇଲେ।

ସେଠି ଗଢ଼ୁଥିବା ପାଣି ବୋତଲ, କିଛି ଚକୋଲେଟ୍ ଓ କ୍ୟାମେରାଟିକୁ କିନ୍ଲିକୁ ଦେଲେ। କିନ୍ଲି ଦେଖିଲା ଯେ ପାଣିବୋତଲ ଓ ଚକୋଲେଟ୍ ଉପରେ କିନ୍ଲି ବ୍ରାଣ୍ଡର ନାମ ଲେଖାଯାଇଛି। ସବୁଟକ କିନ୍ଲି ଦୁଷ୍ୟନ୍ତ ପାଖରେ ଦୁଇଟି ଦିନରେ କେମିତି ପହଞ୍ଚିଗଲା ? ଏଡିକି ଭାବି କିନ୍ଲିର ଆଖିକୁ ଲୁହ ଆସିଗଲା। ସେ ଭାବିଲା– ତେବେ କ'ଣ ଏହି ଭାରତୀୟ ଅତିଥିଙ୍କୁ ସେ ଭଲପାଇ ବସିଛି ? ଦୁଷ୍ୟନ୍ତକୁ ପାହାଡ଼ରୁ ଖସାଇ ଆସି ଗାଡ଼ିରେ ବସାଇ ହୋଟେଲରେ ପହଞ୍ଚିଲା କିନ୍ଲି।

କିନ୍ଲିର ଶୁଶ୍ରୁଷାରେ ଦୁଷ୍ୟନ୍ତ ଆଖି ଖୋଲିଲେ। ତାଙ୍କର ବିଶ୍ୱାସ ହେଲାନାହିଁ ଯେ ସେ ବଞ୍ଚିଛନ୍ତି ବୋଲି। ପାଖରେ କିନ୍ଲିକୁ ଦେଖି କହିଲେ – "ତୁମେ ସତରେ କିନ୍ଲି। କିନ୍ଲି ବିନା ପ୍ରାଣରକ୍ଷା ସମ୍ଭବ ନୁହେଁ। ଦୁଷ୍ୟନ୍ତ କିନ୍ଲିକୁ ସବୁଘଟଣା ବର୍ଣ୍ଣନାକରି କହିଲା ଓ ସେ କିପରି ନାଲିସାଲରେ ଗୁଡ଼ାଇ ହୋଇ ଗଛରେ ଲଟକି ରହିଲା ତାହା ହିଁ ଆଶ୍ଚର୍ଯ୍ୟର ବିଷୟ ଥିଲା। ସେହି ବୃଦ୍ଧାଟି କିଏ ଏବଂ କାହିଁକି ତାକୁ ନାଲିସାଲ, ଗୋଟିଏ ପାଣିବୋତଲ ଓ କିନ୍ଲି ଲେଖାଥିବା ଚକୋଲେଟ୍ ଦେଇଥିଲେ ତା'ର ରହସ୍ୟ ଜାଣିପାରି ଦୁଷ୍ୟନ୍ତ କିନ୍ଲିକୁ ପଚାରିଲା। କିନ୍ଲି କହିଲା – "ଏହାର ରହସ୍ୟ ମୁଁ ମଧ୍ୟ ଜାଣେନାହିଁ। ସଂସାରରେ କ'ଣ ଆଉ କେଉଁ ବ୍ରାଣ୍ଡର ପାଣି ବା ଚକୋଲେଟ୍ ନାହିଁ ? ତୁମ ପାଖରେ ସବୁଗୁଡ଼ିକ କିନ୍ଲି ବ୍ରାଣ୍ଡ କିଏ କାହିଁକି ଦେଲା ? ବୋଧହୁଏ ପ୍ରେମ, ଆନନ୍ଦ ଏବଂ ଈଶ୍ୱର ସମସ୍ତେ ଗୋଟିଏ ଗୋଟିଏ ରହସ୍ୟ। ଏ ସବୁ ଆଜିର ଘଟଣା ସାଧାରଣ ଘଟଣା ନୁହେଁ।"

"ଆମେ ତ ଆନନ୍ଦ ଏବଂ ପ୍ରେମକୁ ଖୋଜିପାଇଛେ। କିନ୍ତୁ ପାଇନାହିଁ ଈଶ୍ୱରଙ୍କୁ, ଯିଏ ସେହି ବୃଦ୍ଧା ରୂପରେ ମୋର ପ୍ରାଣ ବଞ୍ଚାଇବା ପାଇଁ ସେହି ନାଲି ସାଲ୍‌ଟିକୁ ଦେଇଥିଲେ ଓ ତା' ସହ ଦେଇଥିଲେ ତୁମକୁ। ସେହି ଈଶ୍ୱର ସବୁଦିନ ପାଇଁ ରହସ୍ୟ ହୋଇ ରହିବେ। ତାଙ୍କୁ ଖୋଜି ଲାଭ ନାହିଁ" ଦୁଷ୍ୟନ୍ତ ଦାର୍ଶନିକ ଭଳି କହିଲା।

କିନ୍ଲି କହିଲା – "ଈଶ୍ୱର ନୁହେଁ, ଈଶ୍ୱରୀ। ତୁମେ ସବୁ ପୁରୁଷମାନେ କାହିଁକି ଈଶ୍ୱରୀମାନଙ୍କୁ ଚିହ୍ନିପାରନ୍ତି ନାହିଁ କେଜାଣି ?"

ଦୁଷ୍ୟନ୍ତ ସ୍ମିତହସି କହିଲା – "ଈଶ୍ୱରୀଙ୍କୁ ମୁଁ ଏହି ଆନନ୍ଦମୟ ଦେଶରେ ଚିହ୍ନିପାରିଛି।"

କିନ୍ଲି ଦୁଷ୍ୟନ୍ତର ବ୍ୟାଣ୍ଡେଜ୍‌ମରା କପାଳରେ ପ୍ରୀତିର ଅଧରସ୍ପର୍ଶ ରଖିଲା, ଯାହା ଦୁଷ୍ୟନ୍ତକୁ ଆନନ୍ଦର ଚରମ ଉପଲବ୍ଧରେ ପାର୍ଥିବରୁ ଅପାର୍ଥିବକୁ ନେଇଗଲା।

ଯାହା ତୁମର ଇଚ୍ଛା

ଆଶୀର୍ବାଦ ଲିସାଙ୍କର କରୁଣ ଆଖିକୁ ରହିଁ କହିଲେ "ଯାହା ତୁମର ଇଚ୍ଛା।"

ଲିସା କହିଲେ "ଗତ ଦୁଇବର୍ଷ ହେଲା ସେ ଆଲ୍‌ଫ୍ରେଡ୍‌ଙ୍କୁ ଖୋଜୁଛନ୍ତି ଏବଂ ଏଥର ମଧ୍ୟ ଲେହ ଯାଇଥିଲେ। ମାତ୍ର ତାଙ୍କୁ ପାଇଲେ ନାହିଁ। ଏ ଭିତରେ ମନାଲିରେ ସେ ଗୋଟିଏ ରେଷ୍ଟୁରାଣ୍ଟ ମଧ୍ୟ କରିଛନ୍ତି। ତା'ର ନାମ 'ଲିସାସ୍ ଚିକେନ୍'। ଆଲ୍‌ଫ୍ରେଡ୍‌ଙ୍କ ଦୟାରୁ ହୋଟେଲ୍ ବେଶ୍ ଲୋକପ୍ରିୟ ହୋଇପାରିଛି ଓ ବେଶ୍ ଭଲ ଚଳିଛି। ଆପଣଙ୍କୁ ଆଉ ଏକ ଅନୁରୋଧ, ଆପଣ ଏହି ବ୍ୟବସାୟରେ ମୋ ସହ ମିଶିବେ କି ?"

ଆଶୀର୍ବାଦ ଲିସାଙ୍କ କରୁଣ ଦୃଷ୍ଟିକୁ ରହିଁଲେ, ତାଙ୍କୁ ମନା କରିପାରିଲେ ନାହିଁ। କହିଲେ "ଯାହା ତୁମ ଇଚ୍ଛା।" ଲିସା ହସିଦେଇ କହିଲେ "ମୁଁ ଆଉ ଏକ ପ୍ରଶ୍ନ ପଚାରିବି ?" ଆଶୀର୍ବାଦ କହିଲେ "ଯାହା ତୁମର ଇଚ୍ଛା।"

ଲିସା କହିଲେ "ତୁମେ ବାହା ହୋଇଛ କି ? ଯଦି ନୁହେଁ ତେବେ ତୁମର ଗାର୍ଲ‌ଫ୍ରେଣ୍ଡ ଅଛନ୍ତି କି ? ମତେ ତୁମେ ବିବାହ କରିପାରିବ କି ?" ଆଶୀର୍ବାଦ ପାଖ ଚେୟାରରେ କିଛି ସମୟ ବସିପଡ଼ିଲେ। ଆଶୀର୍ବାଦ ନିରବତା ରକ୍ଷା କରିବାରୁ ଲିସା କହିଲେ "ସରି, ମୁଁ ଭାବବିହ୍ଵଳ ହୋଇ କିଛି କହିପକାଇଲି।"

ଆଶୀର୍ବାଦ କହିଲେ "ଯାହା ତୁମର ଇଚ୍ଛା। ଆଚ୍ଛା ଏଥରକ ମୁଁ ତୁମକୁ ଗୋଟିଏ ପ୍ରଶ୍ନ ପଚାରିବି କି ?"

ଲିସା କହିଲେ "ପଚାର।" ଆଶୀର୍ବାଦ କହିଲେ "ବର୍ତ୍ତମାନ ତୁମେ ଅଶୀ ମିଲିୟନ୍ ଡଲାରର ମାଲିକାଣୀ। ତୁମେ ମତେ କାହିଁକି ପ୍ରପୋଜ୍ କଲ ?" ଲିସା କହିଲେ "ଚଲ କଫି ସପରେ ବସିବା। ତୁମକୁ ମୁଁ ଗୋଟିଏ ଗପ କହିବି।"

ଦୁହେଁ କଫି ସପରେ ବସିଲେ। ଲିସା କହିଲେ "ମୁଁ ବ୍ଲାକ୍ କଫି ନେବି, ତୁମେ କ'ଣ ନେବ ?" ଆଶୀର୍ବାଦ କହିଲେ "ଯାହା ତୁମର ଇଚ୍ଛା।"

ଲିସା ଠୋ ଠୋ ହସିଲେ। ଆଶୀର୍ବାଦ ପଚାରିଲେ "ଏପରି ହସିବାର କାରଣ ?" ଲିସା କହିଲେ "ଗପଟି ଶୁଣ ଆଗେ–

ଗୋଟିଏ ରାଜ୍ୟରେ ଜଣେ ରାଜା ଥିଲେ। ତାଙ୍କ ମନରେ ଗୋଟିଏ ପ୍ରଶ୍ନ ଥିଲା ଯେ ସେ ରାଣୀଙ୍କୁ ଖୁସୀ କରିପାରୁଛନ୍ତି କି ? ତେଣୁ ତାଙ୍କୁ ଖୁସୀ କରିବାର ଉପାୟ କ'ଣ ବୋଲି ସମସ୍ତଙ୍କୁ ପଚାରିଲେ। ବିଭିନ୍ନ ଲୋକ ବିଭିନ୍ନ ଉପାୟ ବତାଇଲେ। ମାତ୍ର ରାଜାଙ୍କ ମନକୁ କୌଣସି ଉପାୟ ଉପଯୁକ୍ତ ମନେହେଲା ନାହିଁ। ରାଜା ଶେଷରେ ତାଙ୍କର ବୁଦ୍ଧିମାନ ମନ୍ତ୍ରୀଙ୍କୁ ଡାକି ପଚାରିଲେ। ଗୋଟିଏ ମାସ ଲାଗିବ ବୋଲି ମନ୍ତ୍ରୀ କହିଲେ। ରାଜା କହିଲେ "ଠିକ୍ ଉତ୍ତର ନଦେଲେ ମୁଣ୍ଡ କାଟ୍ ହେବ।"

ମନ୍ତ୍ରୀ ଆସନ୍ନ ମୃତ୍ୟୁର ଭୟ ଆଶଙ୍କାରେ ଘରେ ପହଞ୍ଚିଲେ। କାରଣ ରାଜାଙ୍କ ମନକୁ କେଉଁ ଉପାୟଟି ଉପଯୁକ୍ତ ମନେହେବ ସେଇଟା ରାଜା ସିନା ଜାଣନ୍ତି, ମନ୍ତ୍ରୀ କେମିତି ଜାଣିବେ ? ମନ୍ତ୍ରୀଙ୍କ ବୁଢ଼ୀ ମା' ମନ୍ତ୍ରୀଙ୍କ ବିଷାଦର କାରଣ ପଚାରିଲେ। ମନ୍ତ୍ରୀ ସବୁକଥା କହିଲେ। ବୁଢ଼ୀମା' କହିଲେ "ମାସଟିଏ ଆରାମରେ ବୁଲ୍। ଠିକ୍ ସମୟରେ ମୁଁ ଉତ୍ତରଟା କହିଦେବି।"

ମାସେ ପୂରିବାର ଦିନକ ଆଗରୁ ମନ୍ତ୍ରୀ ବୁଢ଼ୀମା'କୁ ଉତ୍ତର ପଚାରିଲେ। ବୁଢ଼ୀମା' କାଗଜରେ କିଛି ଲେଖିଲେ ଓ ଗୁଡ଼ାଇକରି ସୂତା ବାନ୍ଧିଲେ। ଖୋଲିକରି ଦେଖିବାକୁ ମନା କଲେ। ମନ୍ତ୍ରୀ ରାତିସାରା ଶୋଇପାରିଲେ ନାହିଁ। କେଜାଣି ବୁଢ଼ୀମା' କ'ଣ ଲେଖିଥିବ ? ରାତି ପାହିଲେ ନିଶ୍ଚୟ ତାଙ୍କର ମୁଣ୍ଡକାଟ୍ ହେବ।

ପରଦିନ ସକାଳେ ବୁଢ଼ୀମା'ଙ୍କ ଉତ୍ତର କାଗଜଟି ଧରି ରାଜ ଦରବାରରେ ଉପସ୍ଥିତ ହେଲେ ମନ୍ତ୍ରୀ। କହିଲେ – "ଉତ୍ତର ଏଥିରେ ଲେଖା ଅଛି।"

ରାଜା ଉତ୍ତର ଲେଖାଥିବା କାଗଜଟି ମନ୍ତ୍ରୀଙ୍କ ହାତରୁ ନେଇ ନିଜେ ନ ପଢ଼ି ରାଣୀଙ୍କ ହାତକୁ ବଢ଼ାଇଦେଲେ। କହିଲେ "ଏଥିରେ ତୁମକୁ ଖୁସୀ କରିବାର ଉପାୟ ଲେଖା ଅଛି। ତେଣିକି ଯାହା ତୁମର ଇଚ୍ଛା। ମନ୍ତ୍ରୀ ବଞ୍ଚିବେ କି ମରିବେ ତୁମ ଇଚ୍ଛା ଉପରେ ନିର୍ଭର କରେ।"

ରାଣୀ କାଗଜଟି ଖୋଲିଲେ ଏବଂ ଲେଖାଟି ପଢ଼ିଲେ । ମନ୍ତ୍ରୀଙ୍କ ମୁଣ୍ଡରୁ ଗମ୍ ଗମ୍ ଝଲ ବୋହି ପୋଷାକ ଓଡ଼ା । ହଠାତ୍ ଟୋ ଟୋ ହସିଉଠିଲେ ରାଣୀ । କହିଲେ "ତୁମେ ଯେ ମୋର ମତାମତ ପଚାରିଲ ସେଥିପାଇଁ ତ ତୁମକୁ ବାହାହୋଇ ଖୁସିରେ ଅଛି । ଆଉ ପୁଣି କ'ଣ ?"

ରାଜା ପଚାରିଲେ "କିନ୍ତୁ ସେ କାଗଜରେ କ'ଣ ଲେଖା ଅଛି ?

ରାଣୀ କହିଲେ ଲେଖା ଅଛି - "ଯାହା ତୁମର ଇଚ୍ଛା ।"

"ଅର୍ଥାତ୍ ?" ରାଜା ଆଶ୍ଚର୍ଯ୍ୟ ହୋଇ ପଚାରିଲେ ।

ରାଣୀ କହିଲେ "ଅର୍ଥାତ୍, ସ୍ୱାମୀ ପ୍ରତି କଥାରେ ନିଷ୍ପତି ନେବା ପୂର୍ବରୁ ସ୍ତ୍ରୀକୁ ପଚାରିବ ଯାହା ତୁମର ଇଚ୍ଛା । ଏଥିରେ କେଉଁ ସ୍ତ୍ରୀ ଭଲା ଖୁସୀ ନ ହେବ ।"

ଏତିକି ଶୁଣି ରାଜା ହସିବାକୁ ଆରମ୍ଭ କଲେ ଏବଂ ମନ୍ତ୍ରୀଙ୍କ ସମେତ ରାଜସଭାରେ ସମସ୍ତେ ହସିବାକୁ ଆରମ୍ଭ କଲେ । ରାଣୀ ଗଳାରୁ ରନ୍ହାର କାଢ଼ି ମନ୍ତ୍ରୀଙ୍କୁ ଦେଲେ । ମନ୍ତ୍ରୀ ରନ୍ହାର ସହ ସନ୍ତୋଷ ଘରେ ପହଞ୍ଚିବାରୁ ଚିନ୍ତାଟେ ଥିବା ସ୍ତ୍ରୀ ଖୁସୀ ହେଲେ । ପଚାରିଲେ "ଉତ୍ତରଟା କ'ଣ ଥିଲା ?"

"ଯାହା ତୁମର ଇଚ୍ଛା ।" ସ୍ତ୍ରୀ ବିରକ୍ତ ହୋଇ କହିଲେ "ମୋର ଇଚ୍ଛା ଗୋଟିଏ ରନ୍ହାର" । ମନ୍ତ୍ରୀ ସଙ୍ଗେ ସଙ୍ଗେ ହୀରାର ହାର କାଢ଼ି ସ୍ତ୍ରୀଙ୍କ ଗଳାରେ ପିନ୍ଧାଇଦେଲେ । ସ୍ତ୍ରୀ ହାରଟି ପିନ୍ଧି ପଚାରିଲେ "ଏବେ କୁହ ଏହି ହାରଟି ପିନ୍ଧି ମୁଁ ଅଧିକ ସୁନ୍ଦର ଦେଖାଯାଉଛି ନା ରାଣୀ ଅଧିକ ସୁନ୍ଦର ଦିଶୁଥିଲେ ?" ମନ୍ତ୍ରୀ କହିଲେ "ଯାହା ତୁମର ଇଚ୍ଛା ।"

ସ୍ତ୍ରୀ ରାଗିଯାଇ କହିଲେ "ଆଖି ତୁମର, ଉତ୍ତରଦେବ ତୁମେ ।" ମନ୍ତ୍ରୀ ଦଉଡ଼ିଲେ ବୁଢ଼ୀମା' ପାଖକୁ । ବୁଢ଼ୀମା' କହିଲେ "ଉତ୍ତର ବତାଇଦେଲି ମୁଁ, ଆଉ ହାରଟି ନେଇ ଦେଲୁ ସ୍ତ୍ରୀକୁ । ତୋ ମୁଣ୍ଡରେ ଅଛି ଗୋବର । ସ୍ତ୍ରୀକୁ ମୁଣ୍ଡରେ ବସାଇଲେ ସର୍ବନାଶ ହୁଏ । ଏବେ ଯାହା ଭଗବାନଙ୍କ ଇଚ୍ଛା । ଯା' ଖଣ୍ଡେ କଡ଼ା ପାନ ମତେ ଦେ ।"

X   X   X   X   X

ଗଳ୍ପଟି କହିସାରି ଲିସା କହିଲେ "ମୋର ସବୁ ପ୍ରଶ୍ନର ଉତ୍ତର ମଧ ତୁମେ ସେଇଆ ଦେଇଛ । ତୁମେ ଅଶୀ ମିଲିୟନ୍ ଡଲାର୍ ନିଜେ ରଖିପାରିଥାନ୍ତ । ମାତ୍ର ମତେ ଦେଇଦେଲ । ତେଣୁ ମୁଁ ତୁମକୁ ବିବାହ କରିବାକୁ ଇଚ୍ଛା କରୁଛି ।"

ଆଶୀର୍ବାଦକ୍ଷର ବୁଢ଼ୀମା'ଙ୍କ କଥା ମନେପଡ଼ିଲା- ସ୍ତ୍ରୀକୁ ମୁଣ୍ଡରେ ବସାଇଲେ ସର୍ବନାଶ ।

ସେ ଉତ୍ତରଦେଲେ "ଯାହା ମୋ ସ୍ତ୍ରୀଙ୍କ ଇଚ୍ଛା - ତାଙ୍କ ନାମ ଶାନ୍ତି ।"

ଓଁ ଶାନ୍ତି ଶାନ୍ତି ଶାନ୍ତି ।

ହୃଦୟସ୍ୱର

ସହରତଳି ଜଙ୍ଗଲଟିଏ। ବୁଦବୁଦିଆ ଜଙ୍ଗଲ ସେପାରେ ଛୋଟ
ନଦୀଟିଏ। ନଦୀ ସେପାରିରେ ଘଞ୍ଚ ଜଙ୍ଗଲ ଓ ଡେଉଡେଉକା
ପାହାଡ଼। ନଦୀ ଭିତରେ ଭଲିକି ଭଲି ମାଛ, ଜଙ୍ଗଲରେ ବାଘ,
ଭାଲୁ ଓ ଅନ୍ୟ କେତେ ଜାତିର ଜୀବଜନ୍ତୁ ବସବାସ କରନ୍ତି।
ଏପାରି ଜଙ୍ଗଲରେ ଠେକୁଆମାନେ ଓ ନଈ ସେପାରିରେ
ହରିଣମାନେ ଆନନ୍ଦରେ ବିଚରଣ କରନ୍ତି। ଠେକୁଆମାନେ
ଯେତିକି ସୁନ୍ଦର ଓ ତରକା, ହରିଣମାନେ ମଧ ସେତିକି ସୁନ୍ଦର
ଓ ତରକା। ଦୁଇ ଜଣଙ୍କର ଆଖି ସୁନ୍ଦର ଓ ଦେହ ମଖମଲି
ନରମ। ଏଇ ଦୁହିଁଙ୍କ ଉପରେ ସହରରେ ଥିବା ଶିକାରୀମାନଙ୍କର
ଖୁବ୍ ନଜର।

ଦିନକର କଥା, ରବିବାର ଥାଏ। ଶିକାରୀଟିଏ
ଘୋଡ଼ାରେ ବସି ଶିକାର କରିବାକୁ ବାହାରିଲା। ଅଣ୍ଟାରେ
ପିସ୍ତଲ ଓ କାନ୍ଧରେ ବନ୍ଧୁକ ଝୁଲୁଥାଏ। ସାଙ୍ଗରେ ଥାଏ ଶିକାରୀ
କୁକୁରଟିଏ। ସେମାନେ ଆସି ଜଙ୍ଗଲ ପ୍ରାନ୍ତରେ ପହଞ୍ଚିଲେ।
ଶିକାରୀ ଘୋଡ଼ାରୁ ଓହ୍ଲାଇ ଧୀର ପାଦରେ ଜଙ୍ଗଲରେ ପ୍ରବେଶ
କଲା। ସେ ଜାଣିଛି, ତାକୁ ଖୁବ୍ ସତର୍ପଣରେ ଯିବାକୁ ପଡ଼ିବ।
ଜଙ୍ଗଲୀ ଜନ୍ତୁମାନେ ଖୁବ୍ ତରକା। ଟିକିଏ ଆଭାସ ପାଇଲେ

ଉଭାନ ହୋଇଯିବେ। ସତର୍କତା ଅବଲମ୍ବନ ନକଲେ ଖାଲି ହାତରେ ଘରକୁ ଫେରିବାକୁ ପଡ଼ିବ।

ହଠାତ୍ ଗୋଟିଏ ଠେକୁଆ ଆଗରେ ଦୌଡ଼ି ଚାଲିଗଲା। ଶିକାରୀଟି ଦୁଃଖୀ ହୋଇଗଲା। ନିଜ ଭାଗ୍ୟକୁ ଧ୍କ୍କାର କଲା। ଭାଗ୍ୟରେ ଥିଲେ ସିନା ଭଦଭଦଲିଆ ଚଢ଼େଇଟିଏ ଦେଖ୍ଥାଆନ୍ତା, ଯାତ୍ରା ଶୁଭ ହେଇଥାନ୍ତା। ଶିକାର ପୂର୍ବରୁ ଠେକୁଆ ଦେଖ୍ଲେ ଆଗକୁ ଆଉ ଜନ୍ତୁ ମିଳିବ ନାହିଁ। ତଥାପି, ଶିକାରୀ ନିଜ ଭାଗ୍ୟ ଉପରେ ବିଶ୍ୱାସ ରଖି ଆଗକୁ ବଢ଼ିଲା। କିଛି ସମୟ ସତର୍ପଣରେ ଚାଲିବା ପରେ ନଦୀଟିଏ ଦୃଶ୍ୟମାନ ହେଲା। ଶିକାରୀଟି ଗୋଟିଏ ବଡ଼ ପଥର ପଛରେ ଲୁଚିକରି ବସିଗଲା। ନଦୀର ଧାରଟି ପଥର ଉହାଡ଼ରୁ ଠିକ୍ ଭାବେ ଦିଶୁଥାଏ। ଘୋଡ଼ାଟି ପାଖରେ ଛିଡ଼ାହୋଇ ପାଟି ପାକୁଲାଇଲା। ଶିକାରୀ କୁକୁରର ଆଖି ଓ ଶିକାରୀର ଆଖି ଚାରିପଟକୁ ଘୂରି ବୁଲୁଥାଏ। ଯେକୌଣସି ସମୟରେ କିଛି ନା କିଛି ଜନ୍ତୁ ନଇର ପାଣି ପିଇବାକୁ ଆସିପାରନ୍ତି। ଜନ୍ତୁ ଦୃଶ୍ୟହେବା ମାତ୍ରେ ଶିକାରୀକୁ ଗୁଲି ଚଲାଇବାକୁ ପଡ଼ିବ ଏବଂ ନିର୍ଦ୍ଦେଶ ପାଇଲା ମାତ୍ରେ ଶିକାରୀ କୁକୁରକୁ ଶିକାର ପଛରେ ଦୌଡ଼ିବାକୁ ପଡ଼ିବ।

ଏହି ସମୟରେ ଗୋଟିଏ ହରିଣକୁ ବହୁତ ଶୋଷ କଲା, ନଦୀ ପାଖକୁ ଯାଇ ତା'ର ଶୋଷକୁ ମେଣ୍ଟାଇବାକୁ ପଡ଼ିବ। ଆଜି ସେ ଏକା, ସାଙ୍ଗସାଥୀମାନେ ଥିଲେ ପାଣି ପିଇବାକୁ ଯିବା ସହଜ। ଦୁଇଟା ଆଖି, ଦୁଇଟା କାନଠାରୁ ଦଶଟା ଆଖି ଓ ଦଶଟା କାନ ସବୁବେଳେ ଭଲ। ଜଙ୍ଗଲରେ ତ ପାଦେପାଦେ ବିପଦ, ଟିକିଏ ସତର୍କ ନହେଲେ ଜୀବନ ହାରିବାକୁ ପଡ଼ିବ। ବିଶେଷତଃ ପାଣି ପାଖରେ ବିପଦ ଆହୁରି ଅଧିକ। ପାଣି ନପିଇଲେ ହଂସା ଉଡ଼ିଯିବ। ପାଣିପାଖକୁ ଯିବାର ଅର୍ଥ ବିପଦ ମଧ୍ୟରେ ପାଦଦେବା କଥା। ମଣିଷ ଭଳିଆ ଓ୍ଵାଟର ବଟଲରେ ପାଣି ପିଇବା ସେମାନଙ୍କ ଭାଗ୍ୟରେ ନାହିଁ। ପାଣି ପିଇବା ଭଳି ଗୋଟିଏ ଛୋଟିଆ ଜିନିଷ ପାଇଁ ମୃତ୍ୟୁ ସହିତ ଲଢ଼ାଇ କରିବା ସେମାନଙ୍କ ଦୈନନ୍ଦିନ ଜୀବନ ସଂଗ୍ରାମ। ସହରର ଚିଡ଼ିଆଖାନାରେ ରହିଥିଲେ, ଏ ସମସ୍ତ ସମସ୍ୟା ନଥାନ୍ତା। ଖାଇବାକୁ ଠିକ୍ ସମୟରେ ମିଳିଥା'ନ୍ତା ଓ ପିଇବାକୁ ପାଣି ମୁହଁ ପାଖରେ ଥାଆନ୍ତା। ବାଘ କିମ୍ବା ଅନ୍ୟ ଜନ୍ତୁମାନଙ୍କ ଆକ୍ରମଣର ଭୟ ଆଦୌ ନଥାନ୍ତା। ଏତିକି ଅସୁବିଧା ଯେ କେବଳ ଗୋଟିଏ ଚାରିପଟ ଜାଲିଘେର ମଧ୍ୟରେ ରହିବାକୁ ହୋଇଥାଆନ୍ତା। ହରିଣ ପୁଣି ଭାବିଲା, ଜଙ୍ଗଲରେ ଯେଉଁ ସ୍ୱାଧୀନତା ଏବଂ ସବୁଜିମା ଘେରା ପାହାଡ଼ପର୍ବତ ଓ ନଦୀ, ଜଙ୍ଗଲରେ ବୁଲିଲେ ଯେଉଁ ମଜା, ଏସବୁ ଚିଡ଼ିଆଖାନା ମଧ୍ୟରେ କେଉଁଠି

ମିଳିଥାନ୍ତା ? ଏଠି ମନଲଭା ବୁଲିବାର ଓ କଅଁଳ ଘାସ ଖାଇବାର ଆନନ୍ଦ କ'ଣ ଚିଡ଼ିଆଖାନା ଭିତରେ ଥିବା ହରିଣକୁ ମିଳିପାରୁଛି ? ତା'ସାଙ୍ଗରେ ବାଲୁଙ୍ଗାପିଲାଙ୍କ ଟେକାମାଡ଼ ଓ ଟିଟିକାରି, ଏ ଜଙ୍ଗଲରେ ନାହିଁ । ଜୀବନରେ ସ୍ୱାଧୀନ ଭାବରେ ବଞ୍ଚିବାର ଆନନ୍ଦ ସବୁଠୁ ବଡ଼ କଥା । ଜଙ୍ଗଲରେ ଅବଶ୍ୟ ମୃତ୍ୟୁ ଶୀଘ୍ର ହୋଇପାରେ, ମାତ୍ର ସ୍ୱାଧୀନତାର ସ୍ୱାଦ ଖୁବ୍ ଆନନ୍ଦଦାୟକ । ଭାବନା ରାଇଜରେ ବୁଲୁବୁଲୁ ହରିଣ ଦେଖିଲା, ତା'ର ତୃଷ୍ଣା ଶୁଖିଆସିଲାଣି । ଶୋଷ ବଢ଼ିଚାଲିଛି । ଆଉ କୌଣସି ଉପାୟ ନଦେଖି ସେ ନଦୀଆଡ଼କୁ ପାଦ ବଢ଼ାଇଲା । ଗଛ ଉହାଡ଼ରୁ ବାହାରି ନଦୀ କୂଳକୁ ଓହ୍ଲାଇଲା ।

ହଠାତ୍ ଶିକାରୀର ନଜର ହରିଣ ଉପରେ ପଡ଼ିଲା । ତଡ଼ିତ୍ ବେଗରେ ଅଣ୍ଟାରୁ ପିସ୍ତଲ କାଢ଼ି ହରିଣକୁ ଲକ୍ଷ୍ୟକରି ଗୁଳି ଫୁଟାଇଦେଲା । ଶିକାରୀ ମୁହଁରେ ଚେନାଏ ହସ ଖେଳିଗଲା । ଠେକୁଆ ଦେଖିଥିଲା ସତ, ମାତ୍ର ଶିକାର ମିଳିଗଲା । ମାତ୍ର ଏ କ'ଣ ହେଲା ? ଠେକୁଆ କଥା ସତ ହେଲା । ହରିଣ ଦୌଡ଼ିବାକୁ ଆରମ୍ଭ କଲା । ଅର୍ଥାତ୍ ଶିକାରୀର ଲକ୍ଷ୍ୟଭ୍ରଷ୍ଟ ହେଲା । ଶିକାରୀ ବଡ଼ ବନ୍ଧୁକରୁ ଆଉ ଗୋଟିଏ ଗୁଳି ଚଲାଇଲା । ତାହା ମଧ୍ୟ ଯାଇ ପାଖ ପଥରରେ ବାଜିଲା । ପଥରରୁ ଧୂଆଁ ବାହାରିଲା । ହରିଣର ଭାଗ୍ୟ ଖୁବ୍ ତେଜ୍ । ଦୁଇ ଦୁଇଟା ଗୁଳିରୁ ବର୍ତ୍ତିଗଲା । ବନ୍ଧୁକର ଶବ୍ଦ ପାଖ ପାହାଡ଼ରୁ ପ୍ରତିଧ୍ୱନିତ ହୋଇ ଘଡ଼ଘଡ଼ିମାରିଲା ପରି ଫେରିଲା । ପକ୍ଷୀମାନେ ଫଡ଼ଫଡ଼ କରି ଦୂରକୁ ଚାଲିଗଲେ । ଶିକାରୀ କୁକୁରକୁ ଇଙ୍ଗିତ କଲା । କୁକୁର ହରିଣ ପଛରେ ଦୌଡ଼ିବାକୁ ଲାଗିଲା । ଶିକାରୀ ଆଶ୍ୱସ୍ତ ହେଲା । ତା'ର କୁକୁର ଖୁବ୍ ପାରିବାର । ଜଙ୍ଗଲ ଭିତରେ ଖୋଜି ଯେକୌଣସି ଶିକାରକୁ ଗୋଡ଼ାଇ ଧରିବାରେ ସେ ଖୁବ୍ ପାରଙ୍ଗମ । ଦୀର୍ଘ ଛଅ ବର୍ଷ ହେଲା ତା'ସାଙ୍ଗରେ ବୁଲୁଛି । ତା'ର ଦକ୍ଷତା ଉପରେ ଶିକାରୀର ପୂରା ଭରସା ଅଛି । ଘୋଡ଼ା ଉପରେ ବସି ହରିଣ ଦୌଡ଼ିବା ରାସ୍ତାରେ ଶିକାରୀ ଆଗକୁ ବଢ଼ିଲା ।

ସେପଟେ ହରିଣର ଛାତି ଖୁବ୍ ଜୋରରେ ଧଡ଼ଧଡ଼ କରୁଛି । ତା'ର ବାପାମାଆ ଧନୁତୀର କଥା କହୁଥିଲେ । ମାତ୍ର ଏତେ ଶବ୍ଦ କରୁଥିବା ଗୋଟିଏ ଯନ୍ତ୍ରକଥା ସେମାନେ ତାକୁ କେବେ କହିନାହାନ୍ତି ।

ମଣିଷଙ୍କ କଥା କାହାକୁ ବା ଗୋଚର । ସବୁବେଳେ କିଛି ନା କିଛି ନୂଆ ଜିନିଷ ବାହାର କରିବେ ଓ ସମସ୍ତଙ୍କୁ ଚକିତ କରିଦେବେ । ଆଜି ସିନା ଜୀବନ ବଞ୍ଚିଗଲା; ମାତ୍ର ସେ ଗୋଟିଏ ନୂଆକଥା ଜାଣିବାକୁ ପାଇଲା । ସେ ଯାଇ ତା'ର ସାଙ୍ଗସାଥୀମାନଙ୍କୁ ଏପରି ଏକ ଯନ୍ତ କଥା କହିବ । ନହେଲେ ସେମାନେ ଅଯଥାରେ

ଜୀବନ ହାରିବେ। ସେମାନଙ୍କୁ ସମୟ ସହିତ ତାଳଦେଇ ବାହାର ଦୁନିଆ କଥା ଜାଣି ବଞ୍ଚି ରହିବାକୁ ପଡ଼ିବ। ଜ୍ଞାନ ହିଁ ଶକ୍ତି – ଦୁନିଆର ଖବର ରଖିଲେ ଜ୍ଞାନ ବଢ଼େ। ଆଗରୁ ସିନା ଥିଲା, "ଜୋର ଯା'ର ମୁଲକ ତା'ର" ବର୍ତ୍ତମାନ କିନ୍ତୁ "ଜ୍ଞାନ ଯା'ର ମୁଲକ ତା'ର"। ହରିଣ ନିଜେ ଆବହମାନକାଳରୁ ଜଙ୍ଗଲର ଅନୁଭୂତି ନେଇଆସିଛି। ତା'ର ଶ୍ରବଣ ଶକ୍ତି ପ୍ରଖର, ଦୌଡ଼ିବା ବେଗ ମଧ୍ୟ ଦ୍ରୁତ, ହେଲେ ତାକୁ ବନ୍ଧୁକର ଗୁଳିରୁ ଅଡ୍ଥରକ୍ଷା କରିବାର କୌଶଳ ଜଣାନାହିଁ। ତା' ପାଖରେ ତ ବୁଲେଟ୍ ପ୍ରୁଫ୍ ପୋଷାକ ନାହିଁ, ସେ ବଞ୍ଚିବ କେମିତି? ଏସବୁ ଭାବୁ ଭାବୁ, ସେ ଦେଖିଲା ପଛରୁ ଶିକାରୀ କୁକୁର ମାଡ଼ି ଆସୁଛି। ହରିଣ ଆହୁରି ବେଗରେ ପଥର ସନ୍ଧିରେ ଦୌଡ଼ିବାକୁ ଲାଗିଲା। ହରିଣ ଭାବିଥିଲା ଯେ ବିପଦଟା ଟଳିଗଲା ବୋଲି। ମାତ୍ର ଏ କି କଥା, ଗୋଟିଏ ବିପଦ ଯାଇଛି କି ନାହିଁ, ଆଉ ଗୋଟିଏ ବିପଦ ଆସି ହାଜର। ବଞ୍ଚିବାଟା ଏତେ ସହଜ କଥା ନୁହେଁ। ତାକୁ ଆହୁରି ବେଗରେ ଦୌଡ଼ିବାକୁ ପଡ଼ିବ। ଯଏ ପଳାୟତି, ସଏ ଜୀବତି। ତା'ର ମା କଥା ମନେ ପଡ଼ିଗଲା। ଏ ଜଙ୍ଗଲରେ ତ ସେ ବଡ଼ ହୋଇଛି, ସବୁ ପଥର ସନ୍ଧିକଥା ତାକୁ ଜଣା। କୁକୁର ତ ସହରର, ଜଙ୍ଗଲରେ ହରିଣ ସହ ସମକକ୍ଷ ହୋଇପାରିବ ନାହିଁ। ତା'ର ଛାତିରେ ସାହସ ଆସିଲା। ସେ ନଦୀ ଭିତରେ ଥିବା ପଥର ଉପରକୁ ଡେଇଁ ନଦୀ ସେପାରିକୁ ଲମ୍ଫ ମାରିଲା। କୁକୁରଟି ଅଟକିଗଲା। ହରିଣର ଲମ୍ଫକୁ ଦେଖି ତାଟକା ହୋଇ ରହିଗଲା। ନଦୀକୂଲରେ ଛିଡ଼ା ହୋଇ କୁକୁର ଧକେଇଲା।

କିଛି ସମୟ ପରେ ଶିକାରୀ ଆସି କୁକୁର ପାଖରେ ପହଞ୍ଚିଲା। କୁକୁର ନଦୀ କୂଲରେ ବସି ଧକଉଥିବାର ଦେଖିଲା। ତା'କୁ ପ୍ରଚଣ୍ଡ ରାଗ ଆସିଲା। ଶିକାର ନଧରି ନଦୀ କୂଲରେ ବସି ଆରାମ କରୁଛି। କୁକୁର ଶିକାରୀର ମନକଥା ଜାଣିପାରିଲା। କୁକୁର ସାଙ୍ଗେ ସାଙ୍ଗେ କହିଲା ଯେ ହରିଣ ଖୁବ୍ ଜୋରରେ ଦୌଡ଼ି ଦୌଡ଼ି ନଈ ଆରପାରିକୁ ଲମ୍ଫ ମାରି ପଳାଇଲା। ଶିକାରୀ ପଚାରିଲା, ଦୀର୍ଘ ଛଅ ବର୍ଷ ଧରି ଟ୍ରେନିଂ ଦବାର ମାନେ କ'ଣ ରହିଲା? ସବୁଦିନ ଖାଇବା ପିଇବା ଦେଇ ଅଳସୁଆ କୁକୁରଟା ପାଇଁ ଏତେ ଖର୍ଚ୍ଚ କରିବାରେ ଲାଭ କ'ଣ। ଶିକାରଟିଏ ମିଳିଥିଲେ, ତା'ର ମାସକର ଖର୍ଚ୍ଚ ଉଠିଥାନ୍ତା। କୁକୁର ମନେ ମନେ ଭାବିଲା ଆଜି ଶିକାରୀ ନିଜେ ଦୁଇ ଦୁଇଟା ଗୁଳି ବରବାଦ କରିଛି। ତା'ର ନିଜର ବି ଲକ୍ଷ୍ୟଭେଦ କରିବାର ଦକ୍ଷତା ନାହିଁ। ନିଜର ଭୁଲକୁ ଦେଖିବାକୁ ଶିକାରୀର ଆଖି ନାହିଁ। କଥା କିଛି "ସ୍ୱର୍ଗକୁ ନିଶୁଣି ନାହିଁ କି ବଡ଼ବଡ଼ିଆଙ୍କୁ ଉତ୍ତର ନାହିଁ।" କୁକୁର ଭାବିଲା, ସବୁସେ ଭଲା ଚୁପ୍। ତେଣୁ ସେ ଚୁପ୍ ରହିଲା। ତା'ର ନୀରବତାକୁ ଶିକାରୀ ସହିପାରିଲା

ନାହିଁ । ତା'ର ମୁଣ୍ଡକୁ ରାଗ ଚଢ଼ିଲା । ଖୁବ୍ ବଡ଼ ପାଟିରେ ପଚାରିଲା "କାହିଁକି ତୁ ହରିଣକୁ ଧରିପାରିଲୁ ନାହିଁ ?" କୁକୁର ଭାବିଲା ଆଉ ଚୁପ୍ ରହିଲେ କିଛି ଭଲ ହେବନାହିଁ । ତେଣୁ ସେ କହିଲା "ହରିଣ ତା'ର ଜୀବନ ପାଇଁ ଦୌଡ଼ୁଥିଲା ଓ ମୁଁ ମୋ ମାଲ୍‌କର ପାଇଁ ଦୌଡ଼ୁଥିଲି, ସେତିକି ହିଁ ତଫାତ୍ ।" ଏ ଉତ୍ତର ଶୁଣି ଶିକାରୀ ମୁଣ୍ଡକୁ ପିଉ ଚଢ଼ିଗଲା । ସେ ଅଣ୍ଟାରୁ ପିସ୍ତଲ କାଢ଼ିଲା ଓ କହିଲା "ଅବତକ୍ ତୁମ୍ ମେରା ନମକ୍ ଖା ରହାଥା – ଅଭି ଗୋଲି ଖା" । ଏସବୁ ନାଟକ ଦେଖି କୁକୁର ପ୍ରାଣ ବିକଳରେ ହରିଣ ପରି ନଈର ପଥର ଉପରେ ଗୋଟିଏ ଡିଆଁମାରି ନଈର ଆରପାରିରେ ଯାଇ ପଡ଼ିଲା । ଗୁଳିଟି ତା'ର କାନପାଖ ଦେଇ ଚାଲିଗଲା । ଶିକାରୀର ଅପାରଗତାକୁ ସେ ପ୍ରଶଂସା କଲା । କିଛି ସମୟ ଆଗରୁ ଯେଉଁଟାକୁ ସେ ନିନ୍ଦା କରୁଥିଲା, ସେଟା ତା' ପାଇଁ ଆଶୀର୍ବାଦ ଭଳି କାମ କଲା । ତେଣୁ ଭଗବାନ ଯାହା କରନ୍ତି, ପ୍ରାଣୀର ମଙ୍ଗଳ ପାଇଁ । ଦୁନିଆର କୌଣସି ଜିନିଷ ପୁରାପୁରି ଠିକ୍ ନୁହେଁ କି ସମ୍ପୂର୍ଣ୍ଣ ଭୁଲ୍ ନୁହେଁ । ସମୟ ହିଁ ସବୁଠାରୁ ବଳବାନ୍ । କୁକୁର ପୁଣି ଦେଖିଲା ଯେ ଶିକାରୀ ଘୋଡ଼ା ଉପରେ ବସି ନଦୀ କୂଳରେ ଅନାଇଛି । କୁକୁର ଜୀବନ ବିକଳରେ ହରିଣ ଭଳି ନିଜ ଅଜାଣତରେ ନଈକୁ ଡେଇଁ ପଡ଼ିଛି, ଅଥଚ ଘୋଡ଼ା ତା'ଭଳି ନଈ ଡେଇଁବାକୁ ସାହସ କରିପାରିନି, କୁକୁର ଆଶ୍ୱସ୍ତ ହେଲା – ଘୋଡ଼ାର ବଳ ଓ ସାମର୍ଥ୍ୟ ଥିଲେ ମଧ୍ୟ ସେ ଲଞ୍ଫ ମାରି ପାରିବ ନାହିଁ । କାରଣ ସମସ୍ତଙ୍କର ଜୀବନର ଲକ୍ଷ୍ୟ ଭିନ୍ନ ଓ ଶକ୍ତି ଭିନ୍ନ । ଯେତେବେଳେ ନିଜର କର୍ମ, ଜୀବନର ଲକ୍ଷ୍ୟ ସହିତ ଏକ ହୋଇ ପାରିବ, ସେତେବେଳେ ହିଁ ଜଣେ ଅସମ୍ଭବକୁ ସମ୍ଭବ କରାଇପାରିବ ।

କୁକୁର ଆଗକୁ ଚାହିଁବାରୁ ଦେଖିଲା ହରିଣ ଠିଆହୋଇ ହସୁଛି । କୁକୁର ଆଖିରେ ଲୁହ ଆସିଲା । ହରିଣ ଗୋଡ଼ତଳେ ଲମ୍ବ ହୋଇ ପଡ଼ିଗଲା ଓ ତାକୁ କ୍ଷମା କରିବାକୁ କହିଲା । ଆଗରେ ହରିଣ କହିଲା, "ସେଥିରେ ତୁମର କୌଣସି ଦୋଷତ୍ରୁଟି ନାହିଁ । ତୁମେ ତୁମର କର୍ତ୍ତବ୍ୟ କରୁଥିଲ । ମାଲିକର ଉଦ୍ଦେଶ୍ୟ ଖରାପ ଥାଇପାରେ ମାତ୍ର ତୁମର ଉଦ୍ଦେଶ୍ୟ ଖରାପ ନଥିଲା ।" ଏବେ କୁକୁର ପ୍ରଭୁ-ଭୃତ୍ୟ ସଂପର୍କର ବୋଝରୁ ମୁକ୍ତ । ବର୍ତ୍ତମାନ କୁକୁର ପାଖରେ ପୂରା ସ୍ୱାଧୀନତା ଅଛି । ସେ ନିଜ ମନ ଖୁସିରେ ଯାହା ପାରେ ତା' କରିପାରେ । ପୁଣି ଏହି ଘଟଣାକ୍ରମରେ ସେ ମଧ୍ୟ ନିଜର ଶକ୍ତି ଓ ସାମର୍ଥ୍ୟକୁ ହୃଦୟଙ୍ଗମ କରିପାରିଛି । ବିପଦରେ ପଡ଼ି ହରିଣ ଓ କୁକୁର ଏବେ ସାଙ୍ଗ ହୋଇଗଲେ । ପାଖରେ ବାଘଟିଏ ଶୋଇ ଗୁଞ୍ଜୁଡ଼ି ମାରିଥିଲା । କୁକୁର ଡରିଗଲା, ମାତ୍ର ହରିଣ ହସିଲା – କହିଲା, ବାଘର ପେଟ ପୁରିଛି । ସେ ଆମକୁ ଏବେ ଖାଇବ

ନାହିଁ। ହରିଣ କହିଲା – "ଆମେ ବର୍ତ୍ତମାନ ଜଙ୍ଗଲ ମଧ୍ୟରେ ଅଛୁ। ନଈ ସେପାରିରେ ସହର ଓ ଜଙ୍ଗଲ ମଧ୍ୟରେ ଆକାଶ ପାତାଳ ତଫାତ୍। ଜଙ୍ଗଲର ଆଇନ ସହରର ଆଇନଠାରୁ ଭଲ। ସହରରେ ଲୋଭ ମଣିଷକୁ କାବୁ କରି ରଖିଛି, ତେଣୁ ସେ ପାପ କରେ। ଜଙ୍ଗଲରେ ଯେତିକି ଲୋଡ଼ା ସେତିକି ହିଁ ଜୀବନ। ତେଣୁ ପଶୁ ବଞ୍ଚିବା ପାଇଁ ଯାହା ଲୋଡ଼ା, ସେତିକି କରେ। ସେଥ୍‌ରେ ରାଗ ଓ ଈର୍ଷା ନାହିଁ। ଜଙ୍ଗଲରେ ପଶୁପକ୍ଷୀ ଶାନ୍ତିରେ ବଞ୍ଚୁଛନ୍ତି। ମଣିଷ ବିଚାରର ସବୁଥାଇ ମଧ ଶାନ୍ତି ବୋଲି ପଦାର୍ଥଟି ନାହିଁ। ବିଚରା କେତେ ଦୟାର ପାତ୍ର!"

ଦୁହେଁ ଆନନ୍ଦରେ କୋଲାକୋଲି ହେଲେ। କୁକୁର କହିଲା, "ଭାଇ ଏଥର ସହରକୁ ସାବଧାନ। ମୁଁ ଏଣିକି ଜଙ୍ଗଲରେ ରହିବି। ଜଙ୍ଗଲୀ କୁକୁର ସ୍ୱାଧୀନତାର ସ୍ୱାଦ ମୁଁ ଚାଖ୍ ସାରିଲିଣି। ହଉ ପୁଣି ଦେଖାହେବ।" ହରିଣ ଗୋଟିଏ ଦିଗକୁ ଗଲା ଓ କୁକୁର ଅନ୍ୟ ଦିଗକୁ ଗଲା। କୁକୁର ପୁଣି ଫେରିଆସି ହରିଣକୁ କହିଲା "ଭାଇ ତୁମ ମୋବାଇଲ ନମ୍ବରଟି ମୁଁ ରଖିପାରେକି?" ହରିଣ ଠୋ ଠୋ ହସି କହିଲା – ସହରୀ ବଦ‌ଭ୍ୟାସ ଛାଡ଼ିବା ପାଇଁ ତୁମକୁ ନିଶ୍ଚୟ ସମୟ ଲାଗିବ। ମନେରଖ ଜଙ୍ଗଲରେ ଯାନ୍ତ୍ରିକ ନେଟ୍‌ୱର୍କ ନାହିଁ। ଏଠି ସବୁ ନେଟ୍‌ୱର୍କ ପ୍ରାକୃତିକ। ତୁମେ ଭୋ ଭୋ ଡାକ ମାରିଲେ ମୁଁ ହାଜର ହୋଇଯିବି। ଏଠି ସହରର କୋଲାହଲ ନାହିଁ। ତୁମ ହୃଦୟର ସ୍ୱର ମତେ ଶୁଭିଯିବ ଯେ – କାଲି ସୂର୍ଯ୍ୟ ଉଠିଲେ ଏଠିହିଁ ଦେଖାହେବ। ନଦୀତୀର ହିଁ ଆମର ମିଳନସ୍ଥଳ।

ଶୂନ୍ୟପୃଷ୍ଠାର କବିତା

ଅଙ୍କିତ୍ ଜଣେ ଏଣ୍ଟରପ୍ରିନର୍। ଓଡ଼ିଶାରେ ଏକ ଆଇଟି କମ୍ପାନୀର ମାଲିକ। ଇଞ୍ଜିନିୟରିଂ ପାସ୍ କଲାପରେ ନିଜ ଅଧ୍ୟବସାୟ ବଳରେ ଏକ ଭଲ କମ୍ପାନୀ ଗଢ଼ିପାରିଛି। ବାପା ଓ ମା ତା'ର ବାହାଘର ପାଇଁ ଖୁବ୍ ବିବ୍ରତ ମାତ୍ର ଅଙ୍କିତ୍ ସେଥିରେ ଆଦୌ ମନ ଦିଏ ନାହିଁ। ଅଙ୍କିତ୍ ଆମେରିକା ଓ କାନାଡ଼ାର କିଛି କମ୍ପାନୀ ସହିତ ବ୍ୟବସାୟିକ ସମ୍ପର୍କରେ ଆସିଛି। ସେମାନଙ୍କର କିଛି କାମ କରି ତାଙ୍କର ପ୍ରିୟପାତ୍ର ହୋଇପାରିଛି।

ସେମାନଙ୍କଠାରୁ ଅଧିକା କାମ ଆଣି ନିଜର କମ୍ପାନୀକୁ ଅଧିକ ବଢ଼ାଇବାର ପ୍ରୟାସରେ ସେ ମନପ୍ରାଣ ଦେଇ ଲାଗିଥାଏ। ତେଣୁ ବାହାଘର ଆଡ଼କୁ ତା'ର ମନ ନଥାଏ। ବ୍ୟବସାୟ ସମ୍ପର୍କିତ କାମରେ ଅଙ୍କିତ୍‌କୁ ମଝିରେ ମଝିରେ ବିଦେଶକୁ ଯିବାକୁ ପଡ଼ିଥାଏ। କାମ ସହିତ ପୃଥିବୀର କିଛି ଦେଶ ବୁଲିଯିବାକୁ ସେ ମଧ୍ୟ ଭଲପାଏ। ଅନେକ ଛୋଟବଡ଼ ଦର୍ଶନୀୟ ସ୍ଥାନ ମଧ୍ୟ ସେ ଏଇ ବାହାନାରେ ବୁଲିଆସେ।

ଏଥର ସବ୍‌ସଲରର କାମ ପାଇଁ ସେ କାନାଡ଼ାର ଟରୋଣ୍ଟୋ ସହରକୁ ଯାଇଥାଏ। ଟରୋଣ୍ଟୋରେ କାମ ସରିବାପରେ, ଦୁଇଦିନ ପାଇଁ ସେ କ୍ୟୁବେକ ସିଟି ବୁଲିବାକୁ ଯାଇଥାଏ। ଟରୋଣ୍ଟୋରୁ

ଏକ କାର୍ ଭଡ଼ା ନେଇ ସେ କ୍ୱବେକ ସହରରେ ପହଁଚିଯାଏ। କ୍ୱବେକର ସାତୋ ପ୍ରୁଷ୍ଣେନାକ ଏକ ଦର୍ଶନୀୟ ସ୍ଥାନ। ଗାଡ଼ିଟିକୁ ପାର୍କ କରିବା ପାଇଁ ସେ ଏକ ପାର୍କିଂ ଜାଗା ଖୋଜି ବୁଲୁଥାଏ। ଚଳଚଞ୍ଚଳ ସହରରେ ଗୋଟିଏ ପାର୍କିଂ ଜାଗା ପାଇବା କାଠିକର ପାଠ। ହଠାତ୍ ସେ ଏକ ପାର୍କିଂ ସ୍ଥାନ ପାଇଗଲା। ମାତ୍ର ଏହି ସମୟରେ ସାମ୍ନାରୁ ଆଉ ଗୋଟିଏ ଗାଡ଼ି ପାର୍କ ପାଇଁ ଅଟକିଲା। ଗାଡ଼ିଟିକୁ ଚଲାଉଥିଲା ଜଣେ ଝିଅ। ଭଦ୍ରତା ଦୃଷ୍ଟିରୁ ଅଙ୍କିତ୍ ଗାଡ଼ିଟିକୁ ସେଠାରେ ପାର୍କ କରିବା ପାଇଁ ସୁଯୋଗ ଦେଲା। ଏବେ ଅଙ୍କିତକୁ ଆଉ ଗୋଟିଏ ପାର୍କିଂ ଜାଗା ଖୋଜିବାକୁ ପଡ଼ିବ। ଭାଗ୍ୟକୁ ସାମ୍ନାରେ ଆଉ ଗୋଟିଏ ଗାଡ଼ି ବାହାରୁଥିଲା। ଅଙ୍କିତ୍ ନିଜ ଗାଡ଼ିଟିକୁ ସେହିଠାରେ ପାର୍କ ଗାଡ଼ି ରଖ୍ ଟିକେଟ୍ପାଇଁ ସେ ପାକିଂ ମେସିନ୍ ପାଖକୁ ଗଲା। ମେସିନ୍ରେ କାର୍ଡ କିମ୍ବା କ୍ୟାସ୍ ପ୍ରବେଶ କରାଇ ରସିଦ୍ ନେବାକୁ ପଡ଼ିବ ଏବଂ ଗାଡ଼ିର ଝରକାରେ ରଖିବାକୁ ପଡ଼ିବ, ନଚେତ୍ ଭୁଲ୍ ପାର୍କ ପାଇଁ ଫାଇନ୍ ଲାଗିଯିବ। ଅଙ୍କିତ୍ ପାର୍କିଂ ରସିଦ୍ ଆଣି ଗାଡ଼ିର ଝରକାତଳେ ବାହାରକୁ ଦେଖାଯିବା ଭଳି ରଖିଲା। ଗାଡ଼ିଟିକୁ ଲକ୍ କରି ପାଦଚଲା ରାସ୍ତାରେ ଚାଲିଲା। ସାମ୍ନାରେ ଦେଖିଲା ଗୋଟିଏ ଝିଅ ପାର୍କ ମେସିନ୍ ପାଖରେ ବିଚଳିତ ହୋଇ ଛିଡ଼ା ହୋଇଛି। ସ୍ୱୟଂଚାଳିତ ମେସିନ୍ ଅଟକିଯିବା ପରି ଅଙ୍କିତର ପାଦ ଝିଅଟି ପାଖରେ ଅଟକିଗଲା। ସେ ଝିଅଟିକୁ ପଚାରିଲା – ମୁଁ ଆପଣଙ୍କୁ ସାହାଯ୍ୟ କରିପାରେକି ? ଝିଅଟି କହିଲା – ହଁ, ମୁଁ ଏଇ ସହରକୁ ନୂଆ ଆସିଛି। ପାର୍କିଂ ପଇସା କେମିତି ଦିଆଯାଏ ମୁଁ ଜାଣିପାରୁନି ?' ଅଙ୍କିତ୍ ପ୍ରଥମେ ପାର୍କିଂ ଜାଗାର ନମ୍ବର ପାର୍କ ପୋଷ୍ଟରୁ ଦେଖିକରି ଆସିଲା। ଆରେ ଏଇ ଝିଅଟିକୁ ତ ସିଏ ପାର୍କିଂ ପାଇଁ ଜାଗା ଛାଡ଼ିଥିଲା। ଫେରି ଆସି ମେସିନ୍ରେ ପାର୍କିଂ ଜାଗାର ନମ୍ବର ଦେଲା । ଝିଅଟିକୁ କହିଲା, ''ଦୁଇ ଡଲାରର କ୍ୟାସ୍ କିମ୍ବା କ୍ରେଡ଼ିଟ୍ କାର୍ଡ ଦରକାର ହବ। ଝିଅଟି ତା'ର କାର୍ଡ ଦେଲା । ସେଥିରେ ଝିଅଟିର ନାଁ ଲେଖା ହୋଇଥିଲା 'ଅଲିଭିଆ'। ମେସିନ୍ରେ କାର୍ଡ ପ୍ରବେଶ କଲା, ମାତ୍ର ମେସିନ୍ଟି ସେହି କାର୍ଡକୁ ଗ୍ରହଣ କଲାନାହିଁ । ଏମିତି ବହୁତ ଜାଗାରେ ଅନେକ ମେସିନ୍ କିଛି କିଛି କାର୍ଡ ଗ୍ରହଣ କରନ୍ତି ନାହିଁ। ଅଙ୍କିତ୍ ନିଜ କାର୍ଡରୁ ପଇସା ଦେଇ ପାର୍କ ରସିଦ୍ କାଢ଼ି ଝିଅଟିକୁ ଦେଲା । ଝିଅଟି ଗଦଗଦ ହୋଇଗଲା ଏବଂ ମର୍ସି ବୁକୁ କହିଲା। ଅଙ୍କିତ୍ କହିଲା ''ସେ ମୋ ପ୍ଲେଜର ଅଲିଭିଆ''। ଝିଅଟି କହିଲା ''ତୁମେ ମା ନାଁ କେମିତି ଜାଣିଲ ?' ଅଙ୍କିତ୍ କହିଲା – ''ମୁଁ କହିବି ନାହିଁ।''

ଅଙ୍କିତ୍ ନିଜ ରାସ୍ତାରେ ଚାଲିବାକୁ ଲାଗିଲା। ସହରର ସମସ୍ତ ଜାଗା ବୁଲିବା

ପାଇଁ ସେ ରେଡ୍ ବସ୍ ଟ୍ରାଭେଲ୍‌ରେ ଟିକେଟ୍ କରିଥାଏ। ରେଡ୍ ବସଟି ଆଉ ତିରିଶ ମିନିଟ୍ ପରେ ଆସିବ। ତେଣୁ ସେ ଏଣେତେଣେ ବୁଲାବୁଲି କରି ଅପରାହ୍ନ ଚାରିଟା ତିରିଶ ମିନିଟ୍‌ରେ ସାତୋ ଫୁଣ୍ଟେନ୍‌କ୍‌ରେ ପହଁଚିଲା। ବସ୍‌ଟି ଆସି ଯାଇଥାଏ। ସେ ବସ୍‌ରେ ଚଢ଼ି ଗୋଟିଏ ସିଟ୍‌ରେ ବସିଲା। କିଛି ସମୟ ପରେ ଜଣେ ଝିଅ ଆସି ତା'ପାଖ ସିଟରେ ବସିବା ପାଇଁ ଅନୁମତି ମାଗିଲା। ମୁଣ୍ଡ ଉଠାଇ ଦେଖିଲା ଝିଅଟି ଅଲିଭିଆ। ଫେରକା ଆଡ଼କୁ ଟିକିଏ ଆଉଜିଯାଇ ସେ ଅଲିଭିଆକୁ ବସିବାକୁ କହିଲା। ଅଲିଭିଆ ଗୋଟିଏ ଷ୍ଟ୍ରଙ୍ଗ୍ ପରଫ୍ୟୁମ୍ ବ୍ୟବହାର କରିଥିଲା। କିନ୍ତୁ ଅଙ୍କିତ୍‌କୁ ଭଲ ଲାଗିଲା। ବାହାର ଦେଶରେ ସମସ୍ତେ ପ୍ରାୟତଃ ପରଫ୍ୟୁମ୍ ବ୍ୟବହାର କରନ୍ତି। ପରଫ୍ୟୁମ୍ ଏଠି ନିତ୍ୟବ୍ୟବହାର୍ଯ୍ୟ ଜିନିଷ । ସେଥିପାଇଁ କିଛି କିଛି ପରଫ୍ୟୁମ୍‌ର ଦାମ ଆକାଶଛୁଆଁ। ସେ ଯାହାହେଉ, ବସ୍ ଗାଇଡ୍ ଫରାସୀ ଭାଷାରେ ବୁଝାଉଥାଏ। ଅଙ୍କିତ୍‌କୁ କିଛି ବୁଝା ପଡ଼ୁନଥାଏ। ଅଲିଭିଆ ତାହା ଜାଣିପାରିଲା ଓ ଅଙ୍କିତ୍‌କୁ ସବୁ ଇଂରାଜୀରେ ବୁଝାଇବାକୁ ଲାଗିଲା। ଅଙ୍କିତ୍ ଗୋଟେ ଛୋଟପିଲା ଭଳି ଅନେକ ପ୍ରଶ୍ନ ପଚାରି ଚାଲିଥିଲା ଏବଂ ଅଲିଭିଆ ଧୈର୍ଯ୍ୟର ସହ କହି ଚାଲିଥାଏ। ଅଲିଭିଆ ବେଶ୍ ସୁନ୍ଦରୀ, ଆକର୍ଷଣୀୟା ନିଶ୍ଚୟ। ସେ ପତଳା ଡ୍ରେସ୍‌ଟିଏ ପିନ୍ଧିଥିଲା। ଏତେ ପାଖରେ ବସି ଥିବାରୁ ଅଙ୍କିତର ଭାରତୀୟ ମନ ସଂକୁଚିତ ହୋଇପଡ଼ୁଥିଲା। ମାତ୍ର ଅଲିଭିଆର ସେଥିପ୍ରତି ନଜର ନଥିଲା। ଏ ଦେଶରେ ଛୋଟ ଛୋଟ ଡ୍ରେସ୍ ପିନ୍ଧିବା ସାଧାରଣ କଥା। ଅଲିଭିଆ ବୁଝାଉ ବୁଝାଉ ଅଙ୍କିତ୍ ଉପରେ ଢଳି ପଡ଼ୁଥିଲା। ରକ୍ଷଣଶୀଳ ଓଡ଼ିଆ ପୁଅ ଅଙ୍କିତ୍ ଅସ୍ୱସ୍ତି ଅନୁଭବ କରୁଥାଏ ମାତ୍ର ସେ ବେଶ୍ ରୋମାଞ୍ଚ ଅନୁଭବ କରୁଥାଏ। ଅଙ୍କିତକୁ ସହରର ଘରଗୁଡ଼ିକର ଫ୍ରେଞ୍ଚ ଓ ବ୍ରିଟିଶ ସ୍ଥାପତ୍ୟକଳାର ଯୁଗଳବନ୍ଦୀ ବେଶ୍ ଚମକ୍ରା ଲାଗୁଥାଏ। ତା'ର ମୁଗ୍ଧ ଦୃଷ୍ଟି ଘରଗୁଡ଼ିକୁ ନିଜ ସହିତ ଉଡ଼ାଇ ନେବାକୁ କହୁଥାଏ। ଅଙ୍କିତ୍ ଅନ୍ୟ ଏକ କଳ୍ପିତ ପୃଥିବୀରେ ହଜି ଯାଇଥାଏ। ବସ୍ କ୍ୟୁବେକ୍‌ର ବନ୍ଦର, ପାର୍ଲିଆମେଣ୍ଟ ହାଉସ୍, ବ୍ୟାଟଲ୍ ଫିଲ୍ଡ ଦେଖାଇସାରି ଶେଷରେ ସାତୋ ଫୁଣ୍ଟେନାକ୍ ପାଖରେ ଆସି ଅଟକିଲା। ସେତିକିବେଳେ ହଠାତ୍ ବର୍ଷା ହେବାକୁ ଲାଗିଲା। କ୍ୟୁବେକ୍‌ର ପାଗ ଖୁବ୍ ଅନିଶ୍ଚିତ, କେତେବେଳେ ଖରା ତ କେତେବେଳେ ଶୀତ, କେତେବେଳେ କନକନିଆ ଶୀତଳ ପବନ ତ କେତେବେଳେ ଅଚାନକ ବର୍ଷା। ଅଙ୍କିତ୍ ପାଖରେ ଖୁବ୍ ବଡ଼ ଛତାଟିଏ ଥାଏ। ଛତା ଖୋଲି ଅଲିଭିଆକୁ ଛତା ତଳକୁ ଆସିବାକୁ କହିଲା ଓ ଦୁହେଁ ଗାଡ଼ି ପାର୍କିଂ ସ୍ଥାନକୁ ଚାଲିବାକୁ ଲାଗିଲେ। ଅଙ୍କିତକୁ ଲାଗୁଥାଏ ଯେମିତି ସେମାନେ ଦୁହେଁ କେତେକାଳର ଅତି ପ୍ରିୟ ସାଥୀ। ଅଲିଭିଆ କହିଲା ଯେ ତା'ର ହୋଟେଲ

କାଫାଟେଲରେ ରୁମ୍ ରିଜର୍ଭ ଅଛି ଏବଂ ତାକୁ ସାତଟା ପୂର୍ବରୁ ପହଞ୍ଚିବାର ଅଛି । ଅଙ୍କିତ୍ ପଚାରିଲା– ''ରାସ୍ତା ଜଣା ଅଛି ତ ?'' ଅଲିଭିଆ କହିଲା ''ନା''। ଅଙ୍କିତ୍ କହିଲା, ''ତେବେ ମୋ ଗାଡ଼ି ପଛରେ ଆସ ।'' ଅଙ୍କିତ୍କୁ ମଧ ହୋଟେଲ କାଫାଟେଲ୍ ଯିବାର ଥିଲା । ସେଠାରେ ତା'ର ମଧ ରୁମ୍ ବୁକ୍ ହେଇଥିଲା । ତା' ପାଖରେ ହୋଟେଲ କାଫାଟେଲର ପୋଷ୍ଟାଲ ଆଡ୍ରେସ ଥିଲା ଏବଂ ଜିପିଏସ୍ ନ୍ୟାଭିଗେଶନ ମାଧ୍ୟମରେ ସେ ଯାଇ ହୋଟେଲରେ ପହଁଚିଯିବ । ଅଲିଭିଆ ପାଖରେ ଜିପିଏସ୍ ନ୍ୟାଭିଗେଶନ୍ ନଥିଲା । ଅଙ୍କିତ୍ ଅଲିଭିଆର ମୋବାଇଲରେ ଗୁଗୁଲ୍ ନ୍ୟାଭିଗେଶନକୁ ଯାଇ କାଫାଟେଲ ହୋଟେଲର ଠିକଣା ସେଟ୍ କରିଦେଲା । ଅଲିଭିଆକୁ କହିଲା ଯଦି ପିଛା କରୁକରୁ ଟ୍ରାଫିକ୍ ନିୟନ୍ତ୍ରଣ ଯୋଗୁଁ ଦୂରେଇଯାଏ ତେବେ ଗୁଗୁଲ ନ୍ୟାଭିଗେଶନ୍ ସାହାଯ୍ୟରେ ସେ ଡାଇରେକ୍ସନ୍ ଶୁଣି ହୋଟେଲରେ ପହଁଚିବାରେ ଅସୁବିଧା ହେବନାହିଁ। ଅଲିଭିଆ କିଛିବାଟ ଅଙ୍କିତର ପଛରେ ଆସିଲା ମାତ୍ର ମଝିରେ ଟ୍ରାଫିକ୍ ଯୋଗୁଁ କିଛି ଗାଡ଼ି ତାଙ୍କ ମଝିକୁ ଚାଲିଆସିଲା ଓ ଦୁହେଁ ଅଲଗା ହୋଇଗଲେ । ଅଙ୍କିତର ବିଶ୍ୱାସ ଥିଲା ଯେ ଅଲିଭିଆ ନିର୍ଦ୍ଦିଷ୍ଟ ଭାବରେ ଗୁଗୁଲ ନ୍ୟାଭିଗେଶନ ମାଧ୍ୟମରେ ହୋଟେଲରେ ପହଁଚିଯିବ । ତାହାହିଁ ହେଲା । ହୋଟେଲରେ ପହଁଚିବାପରେ ଅଙ୍କିତ୍ ଚେକ୍ ଇନ୍ କରୁ କରୁ ଅଲିଭିଆ ମଧ ପହଞ୍ଚିଗଲା ଏବଂ ଠିକ୍ ପହଞ୍ଚିଗଲା ବୋଲି ଅଙ୍କିତର ଚିବୁକରେ ଏକ ହାଲ୍କା ଚୁମ୍ବନ ଦେଲା । ଅଙ୍କିତ୍କୁ ରୁମ୍ ନମ୍ବର ୪୦୩ ଓ ଅଲିଭିଆକୁ ରୁମ୍ ନମ୍ବର ୪୦୨ ମିଲିଲା । ଅଙ୍କିତ୍ ରୁମରେ ପଶି ସାରାଦିନର ବୁଲାବୁଲି ପରେ ସୁନ୍ଦର କୋମଲ ଶଯ୍ୟାରେ କ୍ଲାନ୍ତ ଶରୀରକୁ ଲୋଟାଇ ଦେଲା । ୫ରକାର କାଚ ଦେଇ ହାଇଓ୍ୱେରେ ଖୁବ୍ ଚମ୍କାର ଦୃଶ୍ୟ ନଜରକୁ ଆସୁଥିଲା । ଗାଡ଼ିଗୁଡ଼ିକ ରାସ୍ତାରେ ଖୁବ୍ କ୍ଷିପ୍ର ଗତିରେ ଯିବାଆସିବା କରୁଥିଲେ । ଅଙ୍କିତ୍ ବେଡ଼ ଲ୍ୟାମ୍ପ ଓ ଟେବୁଲ୍ ଲ୍ୟାମ୍ପକୁ ଜଳାଇବାକୁ ଚାହିଁଲା, ମାତ୍ର ପାରିଲା ନାହିଁ । ବଡ଼ ବଡ଼ ହୋଟେଲ ଟେବୁଲ ଲ୍ୟାମ୍ପ ଓ ବେଡ଼ ଲ୍ୟାମ୍ପ ଜଳାଇବାପାଇଁ ଅନଭ୍ୟସ୍ତ ଅତିଥିକୁ କିଛି ସମୟପାଇଁ ମଗଜ ଖଟାଇବାକୁ ହୁଏ । ପ୍ରତ୍ୟେକ ହୋଟେଲ ଭିନ୍ନ ଭିନ୍ନ ଯାନ୍ତ୍ରିକ ପ୍ରଣାଳୀ ଅବଲମ୍ବନ କରିବାକୁ ପଡ଼େ । ରୀତିମତ ଟ୍ରାଏଲ ଏଣ୍ଡ ଏରର ପଦ୍ଧତି । କେଉଁଠି ସ୍ପର୍ଶ କଲେ ଜଳେ ତ କେଉଁଠି ଚିପିଲେ ଜଳେ ତ ଆଉ କେଉଁଠି ମାଡ଼ିଲେ ଲାଇଟ୍ ଜଳେ । ଅଙ୍କିତ୍ ଚେଷ୍ଟାକରି ଥକିପଡ଼ିଲା ଓ ବିରକ୍ତ ବି ହୋଇଗଲା । ଯାନ୍ତ୍ରିକ ଉତ୍କର୍ଷର ଏ ଏକ ଅହଂକାର ଭଳି ମନେହେଲା । ଲାଇଟ୍ ଦୁଇଟି ଜଳିଲା ନାହିଁ । ରୁମ୍ ଭିତରେ ଅନ୍ଧାର, ବାହାରେ ଢେର୍ ଆଲୁଅ । ଏଠି ଆଦୌ ବାହାର ଓ ଭିତର ମଧ୍ୟରେ

ସାମଞ୍ଜସ୍ୟ ନାହିଁ। ଅଙ୍କିତ୍ ବାଥରୁମ୍ ଭିତରକୁ ଯାଇ ସାୱାରଟିକୁ ଚଲାଇବାକୁ ଚେଷ୍ଟା କଲା। ସେଠାରେ ମଧ୍ୟ ଚେଷ୍ଟା ପ୍ରଚେଷ୍ଟାର କୁସ୍ତି କସରତ ଚାଲିଲା। ଗରମ-ଥଣ୍ଡା ପାଣି ମିଶାଇବା କଳ ମଧ୍ୟ ଅଚଳ ହୋଇଯାଇଥିଲା। କ୍ରୋଧ ଜାତ ହେବା ସ୍ୱାଭାବିକ କଥା। ଅଙ୍କିତ୍ ନିଜକୁ ଖୁବ୍ ବୁଦ୍ଧିମାନ ବୋଲି ମନେକରେ। ଯେକୌଣସି ଇଲେକ୍ଟ୍ରୋନିକ୍ସ ଯନ୍ତ୍ରକୁ ଅନାୟାସରେ ଚଲାଇଦିଏ, ସେଥିପାଇଁ ସେ ଗର୍ବ ଅନୁଭବ କରେ। ମାତ୍ର ସାଧାରଣ ଗୋଟିଏ ଟେବୁଲ ଲ୍ୟାମ୍ପ ଓ ବାଥରୁମ୍ ସାୱାରକୁ ନ ଚଲାଇପାରିବାରୁ ନିଜକୁ ଟିକିଏ ଧିକ୍ ମନେକଲା। ହୋଟେଲର ରିସେପସନରକୁ ଫୋନ୍ କରି, ସେସବୁକୁ କିପରି ଚଲାଇହେବ ତାହା ବୁଝିବାପାଇଁ ଭାବିଲା। ମାତ୍ର ତା'ର ଇଗୋ ତାକୁ ଟିକିଏ ବାଧା ଦେଉଥାଏ। ହଠାତ୍ କବାଟରେ କେହି ମୃଦୁ ଖଟ୍‌ଖଟ୍ କଲା। ଅଙ୍କିତ୍ କବାଟ ଖୋଲି ଦେଖିଲା ଯେ ଅଲିଭିଆ ଛିଡ଼ା ହୋଇଛି। ଅଲିଭିଆ କହିଲା ଯେ ସେ ତା'ର ମୋବାଇଲରେ ହୋଟେଲ ୱାଇଫାଇକୁ ଲଗାଇପାରୁନାହିଁ ଏବଂ ଅଙ୍କିତ୍‌ର ସାହାଯ୍ୟ ଚାହିଁଲା। ଅଙ୍କିତ୍ ଅଲିଭିଆର ଫୋନ୍‌ଟିକୁ ମାଗିଲା। ଫୋନ୍‌ଟିକୁ ଅଲିଭିଆ ହାତରୁ ନେଇ ଆଖି ପିଛୁଲାକେ ୱାଇଫାଇ ଲଗାଇଦେଇ ଅଲିଭିଆକୁ ଫେରାଇଦେଲା। ଅଲିଭିଆ ଫୋନଟିକୁ ପରୀକ୍ଷା କଲା ଏବଂ ହତବାକ୍ ହୋଇଗଲା। ଅଲିଭିଆ ପଚାରିଲା– ଏତେ ଶୀଘ୍ର କିପରି ତୁମେ ସେ ଫୋନ୍‌ଟିକୁ ସେଟ୍ କରିଦେଲ? ପୁଣି ହସିକରି କହିଲା ''ତୁମେ ବହୁତ ବୁଦ୍ଧିମାନ''। ଏହା କହି ଅଙ୍କିତ୍ ଗାଲରେ ଏକ ସୁଷ୍ମ କିସ୍ ଦେଲା। ଅଙ୍କିତ୍ କହିଲା– "ତୁମେ ମୋତେ ଗୋଟିଏ ସାହାଯ୍ୟ କରିପାରିବ? ମୋର ବେଡ ଲ୍ୟାମ୍ପ ଓ ଟେବୁଲ ଲ୍ୟାମ୍ପକୁ ଜଳାଇ ଦେଇପାରିବ କି?" ଅଲିଭିଆ ରୁମ୍ ଭିତରକୁ ଆସିଲା ଓ ଲାଇଟ୍ ଦୁଇଟିକୁ ଜଳାଇଦେଲା। ଅଙ୍କିତ ପଚାରିଲା କେମିତି କଲା? ଅଲିଭିଆ ହସିକରି ଲ୍ୟାମ୍ପ ପଛରେ ଥିବା ଛୋଟ ସ୍ୱିଚଟିକୁ ଦେଖାଇଦେଲା। ଅଙ୍କିତ୍ ଅଲିଭିଆକୁ କହିଲା – "ତୁମେ ବି ଅତି ବୁଦ୍ଧିମତୀ, ମୋତେ ଆଉ ଗୋଟେ ସାହାଯ୍ୟ କରିପାରିବ କି? ଗାଧୋଇବା ସାୱାରଟିକୁ ଟିକେ ଚଲାଇଦେବ କି?" ଅଲିଭିଆ ସାୱାର ହ୍ୟାଣ୍ଡଲକୁ ମୋଡ଼ାମୋଡ଼ି କଲା। ହଠାତ୍ ସାୱାରରୁ ପାଣି ଚାଲି ଆସି ଅଲିଭିଆ ମୁଣ୍ଡରେ ପଡ଼ିଲା। ସାୱାରଟିକୁ ବନ୍ଦ କରୁ କରୁ ଅଲିଭିଆ ଅଧା ଓଦା ହୋଇସାରିଥିଲା। ଏହା ଦେଖି ଅଙ୍କିତକୁ ଖରାପ ଲାଗିଲା। ସେ ଗୋଟିଏ ତଉଲିଆ ଆଣି ଅଲିଭିଆର ମୁଣ୍ଡ ପୋଛିଦେଲା। ଅଲିଭିଆକୁ ଟିକେ ଟିକେ ଅଠୁଆ ଲାଗିଲା। ତା'ର ଗୋଲାପି ଗଣ୍ଡର ରଙ୍ଗ ଗାଢ଼ା ଦିଶିଲା। ଅଙ୍କିତ୍ କହିଲା, "ହୋଟେଲବାଲା ଏ ସବୁ ଜିନଷକୁ ସହଜ କାହିଁକି କରନ୍ତିନି – ସମସ୍ତଙ୍କୁ ଏତେ କଷ୍ଟ କରିବାକୁ ପଡ଼ୁଛି।" ଅଲିଭିଆ

କହିଲା– "ଏଇଥିପାଇଁ ଯେ ଏହାଦ୍ୱାରା ଜଣେ ଅନ୍ୟ ଜଣଙ୍କର ସାହାଯ୍ୟ ମାଗିବ ଏବଂ ଜଣାପଡ଼ିବ କିଏ କେତେ ବୁଢ଼ିଆ କିମ୍ୱା ନିର୍ବୁଦ୍ଧିଆ।" ଏହା କହି ଦୁହେଁ ଖୁବ୍ ହସିଲେ। ଏହାପରେ ଦୁହେଁ ଖୁବ୍ ନିକଟତର ହୋଇଗଲେ। ଏକାଟି ବୁଲାବୁଲି ସହ କ୍ୟୁବେକ୍‌ର ସୌନ୍ଦର୍ଯ୍ୟକୁ ପ୍ରାଣଭରି ଉପଭୋଗ କଲେ। ଅଲିଭିଆ ଗୋଟେ ଆଉଟ୍‌ଡୋର ଝିଅ ଥିଲା। ଛୋଟବେଲୁ ଟ୍ରେକିଂ, ହାଇକିଂ, ସ୍କିଇଂ, କ୍ୟାମ୍ପିଙ୍ଗରେ ସମୟ ବିତାଇଛି। ଅଙ୍କିତ୍ ଭାବିଲା, ଭାରତରେ ଆମେ କେବଳ ପଇସା ସଂଚୟ କରି ରଖୁ। ଏ ସବୁ ଜିନିଷରେ ଆଦୌ ପଇସା ଖର୍ଚ୍ଚ କରୁନାହୁଁ। ଅଲିଭିଆ ସବୁବେଳେ କହେ ଅନୁଭୂତି, ଅଭିଜ୍ଞତା ଓ ଉପଭୋଗ ପାଇଁ ପଇସା ଖର୍ଚ୍ଚ କରିବା ଉଚିତ। କେବଳ ଗୁଡ଼ାଏ ଏଣୁତେଣୁ ସଞ୍ଚି କରି ପଇସା ଖର୍ଚ୍ଚ କରିବା ଅନୁଚିତ। କେବେ କାମରେ ଲାଗୁନଥିବା ଜିନିଷ ଜୀବନରେ ଗୋଟେ ଗୋଟେ ବୋଝ। ମାତ୍ର ଅଭିଜ୍ଞତା ଜୀବନରେ ମଣିମୁକ୍ତା ଭଳି। ଅଭିଜ୍ଞତା ଆନନ୍ଦ ଦିଏ ମାତ୍ର ଜିନିଷଗୁଡ଼ିକ ଦୁଃଖ ଦିଏ। କହିବା ଛଳରେ ଅଲିଭିଆ ଅଙ୍କିତକୁ କହେ– ତୁମର ଟେକ୍‌ନୋଲୋଜିରେ ବେଶ୍ ଉନ୍ନତ ହୋଇଛି। ମୋବାଇଲ ଫୋନ, ଜିପିଏସ ନାଭିଗେଶନ, ଇଣ୍ଟରନେଟ ସର୍ଫ ଇତ୍ୟାଦିରେ ଏତେ ବୁଡ଼ିକରି ରହିଛ ଯେ, ରାସ୍ତାଘାଟ ବା ଟେଲିଫୋନ ନମ୍ବର ମନେ ରଖୁନାହୁଁ। ସବୁକଥାରେ ଇଣ୍ଟରନେଟ୍, ୱାଇଫାଇ ଦରକାର, ନହେଲେ ମୁଣ୍ଡ ଖରାପ ହୋଇଯାଏ। ଏତେ କଥା ଶୁଣି ଅଙ୍କିତ୍ ଟିକେ ଚିଡ଼ିଯାଇ କହିଲା – "ତୁମ ହାତରେ ଯେଉଁ ରାଟେଲ ସ୍ନେକ୍‌ର ଟାଟୁ ଅଛି ତା' ମୋତେ ଭଲ ଲାଗେ ନାହିଁ, ଟାଟୁ କରିବା ମଧ୍ୟ ଭଲକଥା ନୁହେଁ।" ଅଲିଭିଆ କହିଲା ଯେ ତା'ର ଜଣେ ବୟସ୍‌ଫ୍ରେଣ୍ଡ ଥିଲା – ପିଟର, ଦୁହେଁ ମିଶି ହାତରେ ଏହି ରାଟେଲ ସ୍ନେକ୍‌ର ଟାଟୁ କରିଥିଲେ। ପିଟରକୁ ସ୍କିଂ ବହୁତ ଭଲ ଲାଗୁଥିଲା। ଥରେ ସେମାନେ ଏହି କ୍ୟୁବେକ୍‌କୁ ଆସିଥିଲେ। ନର୍ଦର୍ଷ ମାଉଣ୍ଟେନରେ ସ୍କିଂ କଲାବେଳେ ଆଭାଲାଂଚ ଆସି ପିଟର ପୋତି ହୋଇଗଲା। ତା'ର ମୃତଦେହ ମଧ୍ୟ ମିଳିଲା ନାହିଁ। ତାକୁ ମନେ ପକାଇ ଏଥର ସେ କୁବେକ୍ ଆସିଛି। ବରଫର ପର୍ବତରେ ପିଟରର ମୁହଁ ଦେଖିବାକୁ ଚେଷ୍ଟା କରୁଛି। ଏକଥା ଶୁଣି ଅଙ୍କିତର ଆଖିରେ ଲୁହ ଆସିଗଲା ଏବଂ ଟାଟୁ କଥା କହିଥିବାରୁ ଅଲିଭିଆ ପାଖରେ କ୍ଷମା ମାଗିଲା।

ଆଜି କ୍ୟୁବେକ୍‌ରେ ଶେଷ ଦିନ। ଦୁହିଁଙ୍କୁ ଫେରିବାର ଥିଲା। ଦେଖୁ ଦେଖୁ ସମୟ କେମିତି ଚାଲିଗଲା। ଅଙ୍କିତର ମନ ଟିକିଏ ଦୁଃଖ ଥାଏ। ସେ ବ୍ରେକଫାଷ୍ଟ ପରେ ହୋଟେଲରୁ ଟିକିଏ ବାହାରିଗଲା। ସକାଳର ପାଗ ଖୁବ୍ ଅନୁକୂଳ ଥିଲା। ପ୍ରଶ୍ଣା ପବନ ବୋହୁଥାଏ। ଅନ୍ୟମନସ୍କ ଭାବରେ ଅଙ୍କିତ ଚାଲୁଥାଏ। ଅଲିଭିଆ

ସହିତ ଘନିଷ୍ଠତା ପୁଣି ତା'ର ବୟସ୍‌ଫ୍ରେଣ୍ଡ ପିଟର କଥା ଭାବି ଭାବି ଅନ୍ୟମନସ୍କ ଭାବେ ବୁଲୁଥାଏ। ହଠାତ୍‌ ଏକ ଗାଡ଼ି ହର୍ଷରେ ସେ ପ୍ରକୃତିସ୍ଥ ହେଲା। ରାସ୍ତା ମଝିରେ ସେ ଅନ୍ୟମନସ୍କ ଭାବରେ ବୁଲୁଥିଲା। ଗାଡ଼ିଟି ସତରେ ମାଡ଼ି ଯାଇଥାଆନ୍ତା। ଅଙ୍କିତ୍‌ ଗାଡ଼ି ଡ୍ରାଇଭରକୁ କ୍ଷମା ମାଗିଲା। ଘଡ଼ିକୁ ଦେଖିଲା। ସମୟ ୧୨ଟା ହୋଇଯାଇଛି। ଏହା ମଧ୍ୟରେ ସେ ଦୁଇଘଣ୍ଟା ଚାଲିଛି। ସେ ପକେଟରେ ମୋବାଇଲ୍‌ଟିକୁ ଖୋଜିଲା ନିଜର ଲୋକେସନ୍‌ ଜାଣିବାପାଇଁ। ଆରେ ଏ କ'ଣ ହେଲା, ମୋବାଇଲ୍‌ଟିକୁ ହୋଟେଲର ବ୍ରେକ୍‌ଫାଷ୍ଟ ଟେବୁଲ ଉପରେ ଛାଡ଼ି ଆସିଛି। ଏବେ ହୋଟେଲ୍‌କୁ କିପରି ଫେରିବ, ଅଙ୍କିତ୍‌କୁ କିଛି ବୁଝିବାଟ ଦେଖାଗଲା ନାହିଁ। ଜିପିଏସ୍‌ ଉପରେ ଭରସା କରି ତାକୁ କିଛି ବାଟ ଜଣାନଥିଲା। ଅଲିଭିଆର ଚେକ ଆଉଟ ସମୟ ମଧ୍ୟ ୧୨ଟା ଥିଲା। ତା'ପରେ ସେ ଏୟାରପୋର୍ଟକୁ ଯିବ। ଅଙ୍କିତ୍‌କୁ ବିବ୍ରତ ଲାଗିଲା ଓ ସେ କାନ୍ଦ କାନ୍ଦ ହୋଇଗଲା। ଏପଟ ସେପଟ ହୋଇ ଇଆଡେ ସିଆଡେ ଦୌଡିବାକୁ ଲାଗିଲା। ଅଲିଭିଆକୁ କେତେ କଥା କହିବାର ଥିଲା। ଦୌଡ଼ୁଥିବା ସମୟରେ ହଠାତ୍‌ ଜଣେ ବୃଦ୍ଧା ଆସି ପହଞ୍ଚିଲେ। ସେ ତା'ର ବ୍ୟସ୍ତତାର କାରଣ ପଚାରିଲେ। ଅଙ୍କିତ ତାଙ୍କୁ ହୋଟେଲ କାଫାଟେଲରେ କିପରି ପହଞ୍ଚିବ ବୋଲି ପଚାରିଲା। ବୃଦ୍ଧା ଜଣକ ନିଜର ମୋବାଇଲ କାଢ଼ି ହୋଟେଲ କାଫାଟେଲ୍‌ ସର୍ଚ୍ଚ କଲେ ଓ ମୋବାଇଲରେ ଡାଇରେକସନ ଅଙ୍କିତ୍‌କୁ ଦେଖାଇଲେ। ଅଙ୍କିତ୍‌ ଦେଖିଲା ବୃଦ୍ଧାଙ୍କର ହାତରେ ମଧ୍ୟ ରାଟେଲ ସ୍ନେକର ଟାଟୁ ଥିଲା। ବୃଦ୍ଧା କହିଲେ ତୁମ ହୋଟେଲ ଦୁଇ କିଲୋମିଟର ଦୂରରେ ଅଛି। ଅଙ୍କିତ ଖୁସି ହୋଇ ବୃଦ୍ଧାଙ୍କୁ କହିଲା "ମୋ ବାନ୍ଧବୀ ଅଲିଭିଆ ହାତରେ ମଧ୍ୟ ରାଟେଲ ସ୍ନେକର ଟାଟୁ ଅଛି, ମାତ୍ର ସେ ମୋବାଇଲରେ ଜାଗାର ଡାଇରେକ୍ସନ ଦେଖିପାରେ ନାହିଁ। ବୃଦ୍ଧାଙ୍କୁ ଧନ୍ୟବାଦ ଦେଇ ହୋଟେଲ ଆଡ଼କୁ ଦୌଡ଼ିଲା। ହୋଟେଲ ବ୍ରେକ୍‌ଫାଷ୍ଟ ଟେବୁଲରେ ତା'ର ମୋବାଇଲଟି ପଡ଼ିଥିଲା। ମୋବାଇଲରେ ଅଲିଭିଆର ଦଶଟି ମିସ୍‌କଲ ଥିଲା। ଅଙ୍କିତ୍‌ ରିସେପସନରେ ଅଲିଭିଆ କଥା ପଚାରିଲା। ରିସେପସନିଷ୍ଟ କହିଲେ, ଅଲିଭିଆ ୧୨ଟାରେ ଚେକ୍‌ ଆଉଟ୍‌ କରି ଦେଇଛନ୍ତି ଏବଂ ଏକ ଲଫାପା ଆପଣଙ୍କ ପାଇଁ ଦେଇଯାଇଛନ୍ତି। ଅଙ୍କିତ କମ୍ପିତ ହାତରେ ଲଫାପାଟିକୁ ଖୋଲି କାଗଜଟିକୁ ବାହାର କଲା। ସେଥିରେ ଲେଖାଥିଲା - "ଦୟାକରି ମୋତେ ଆଉ ଖୋଜିବ ନାହିଁ - କିନ୍ତୁ କ୍ୟୁବେକ୍‌କୁ ଆଉ ଥରେ ନିଶ୍ଚୟ ଆସିବ"। ଅଙ୍କିତ ମୋବାଇଲରେ ଅଲିଭିଆକୁ ଫୋନ୍‌ କଲା। ମାତ୍ର ସେପଟୁ ଫୋନ୍‌ଟି ଅନ୍‌ରିଚେବଲ୍‌ ଦେଖାଇଲା। ବୋଧହୁଏ ଅଲିଭିଆର ପ୍ଲେନ ମାଟିରୁ ଆକାଶକୁ ଉଠିଗଲା। ଅଙ୍କିତ ଦୁଃଖରେ

ମ୍ରିୟମାଣ ହୋଇଗଲା । ଆଖିରୁ ଲୁହ ଝରିଆସିଲା । ସବୁଯାକ ଅଘଟଣ ଏକା ସାଙ୍ଗରେ ଘଟିଲା କାହିଁକି । ଅଙ୍କିତ୍ ସଙ୍ଗେ ସଙ୍ଗେ ଚେକ୍ ଆଉଟ୍ କରି ଏୟାରପୋର୍ଟକୁ ବାହାରିଗଲା । ଗାଡ଼ିଟି ରେଷ୍ଟାଲରେ ଫେରାଇ ଟେରେଷ୍କୁ ବିମାନ ଧରିଲା । କାନ୍ଦ କାନ୍ଦ ଆଖିରେ ଝରକା ବାହାରକୁ ଦେଖୁଥିଲା । ଏୟାର ହୋଷ୍ଟେସଙ୍କ ମଧୁର ସମ୍ବୋଧନରେ ତା'ର ଚେତା ପଶିଲା । ଏୟାର ହୋଷ୍ଟେସ ତାକୁ ପାଣି ବଢ଼ାଇଲେ । ଏୟାର ହୋଷ୍ଟେସର ନାଁ ପଢ଼ି ଚମକି ପଡ଼ିଲା ଅଙ୍କିତ୍ । ନାଁଟି ଥିଲା 'ଅଲିଭିଆ' । ତା' ହାତରେ ମଧ ରାଟେଲ୍ ସ୍ନେକ୍ର ଚାଟୁ ଥିଲା । ଅଙ୍କିତ୍ ତାକୁ କହିଲା – "ମୁଁ ଜଣେ ଅଲିଭିଆକୁ କ୍ୟୁବେକରେ ଭେଟିଥିଲି, ତା' ହାତରେ ମଧ ତୁମ ଭଳି ଚାଟୁ ଥିଲା ।" ଏୟାର ହୋଷ୍ଟେସ ଅବାକ ହୋଇ କହିଲା – ତା'ର ନାମ ଉଲିଭିଆ ମାତ୍ର ତା'ର ଛୋଟ ଭଉଣୀ ନାଁ ଅଲିଭିଆ । ଅଙ୍କିତ୍ ବିହ୍ବଳ ହୋଇଗଲା, ଯେମିତି ସେ ଅଲିଭିଆକୁ ପାଇଗଲା । ଅଙ୍କିତ୍ ଉଲିଭିଆକୁ ଅଲିଭିଆର ଠିକଣା ମାଗିଲା । ଉଲିଭିଆ ଛଳଛଳ ଆଖିନେଇ ସେଠାରୁ ପଳାଇଗଲା । ଅଙ୍କିତ୍ ଉଲିଭିଆ ପଛେ ପଛେ ଉଡ଼ାଜାହାଜର ପଞ୍ଚପଟକୁ ଗଲା । ଉଲିଭିଆ କାନ୍ଦି କାନ୍ଦି କହିଲା – ଦୁଇ ବର୍ଷ ତଳେ ଅଲିଭିଆ ତା'ର ବୟଫ୍ରେଣ୍ଡ ପିଟର ସହ କ୍ୟୁବେକ୍ରେ ସ୍କିଂ ପାଇଁ ଯାଇଥିଲା । ବରଫ ସ୍ଖଳନରେ ଦୁହିଁଙ୍କ ମୃତ୍ୟୁ ହୋଇଗଲା, ମାତ୍ର ସେମାନଙ୍କ ମୃତଦେହ ବରଫ ତଳୁ ଉଦ୍ଧାରକରି ହେଲା ନାହିଁ । ତା' ଭଉଣୀକୁ ମନେ ପକାଇବା ପାଇଁ ସେ ରାଟେଲ ସ୍ନେକ୍ର ଚାଟୁ କରିଛି । ଉଲିଭିଆ ଭ୍ୟାନିଟି ବ୍ୟାଗରୁ ଗୋଟିଏ ଫଟୋ କାଢ଼ି ଅଙ୍କିତକୁ ଦେଲା । ଅଙ୍କିତ୍ ଫଟୋଟିକୁ ଦେଖିଲା ଓ ନିଜ ସିଟ୍କୁ ଫେରିଆସିଲା । ପକେଟ୍ରେ ଥିବା ଲଫାପାଟିକୁ ବାହାରକଲା । ସେଥିରୁ କାଗଜଟିକୁ କାଢ଼ିଲା । କାଗଜରେ କିଛି ଲେଖା ନଥିଲା । କିନ୍ତୁ ଅଙ୍କିତକୁ ଝାପସା ହୋଇ କେତୋଟି ଶବ୍ଦ ଦୃଶ୍ୟ ହେଲା – କିମ୍ବା ତା' ମନର ଭାବନା ! ସେ ପଢ଼ିଲା – ମୋ ପାଇଁ ଦୁଃଖ କାହିଁକି ? ଜୀବନଟା ତ ବଞ୍ଚିଥିବାବାୟ ଲେଖା ସରିଥିବା କବିତା ଆଉ ମରଣ ପରେ ଗୋଟିଏ ଶୂନ୍ୟପୃଷ୍ଠା ! ଦିନ କେଇଟାରେ ସମୟ ଉଡ଼ାଇନିଏ ସେଇ ଲିଭିୟାଇଥିବା କବିତାର ଶୂନ୍ୟ ପୃଷ୍ଠାକୁ – ପୁଣି ଲେଖାଯାୟ ନୂଆ କବିତା । ବସନ୍ତରେ ବରଫ ତରଳିଗଲେ ଘାସ ଭିତରେ ଫୁଟି ଉଠିଥିବା ନୂଆଫୁଲ ପରି କ୍ଷଣିକ ହେଲେ ବି କେତେ ସୁନ୍ଦର ଏ ଜୀବନ !

କିମ୍ବଦନ୍ତୀର ନାୟିକା ସ୍ୱର୍ଗପରୀ

ମୃତ୍ୟୁଞ୍ଜୟ ବାବୁ ସମ୍ବାଦଟି ଶୁଣି ବିଷଣ୍ଣ ହୋଇଗଲେ। ମାର୍ଚ୍ଚ ମାସ ୨୩ ତାରିଖ ସନ ୨୦୨୦ ସନ୍ଧ୍ୟା ୭.୩୦ ମିନିଟ୍। ସେତେବେଳକୁ ଓଡ଼ିଶା ସରକାର ରାଜ୍ୟକୁ କରୋନା ଭୂତାଣୁ ସଂକ୍ରମଣରୁ ମୁକ୍ତ ରଖିବା ପାଇଁ ଲକଡାଉନ୍ ଘୋଷଣା କରିସାରିଲେଣି। ଲୋକମାନେ ଘର ଭିତରେ ରହିବା ପାଇଁ ପୋଲିସ ନିୟୁକ୍ତ ହେଲେଣି। କେତେକ ସ୍ଥାନରେ ଅମାନିଆ ଲୋକଙ୍କ ମୂର୍ଖତା ଯୋଗୁଁ ଟିକେ ଶକ୍ତି ମଧ୍ୟ ପ୍ରୟୋଗ କରିବାକୁ ପଡୁଥାଏ। ସକାଳୁ ଅହରହ ଡ୍ୟୁଟି ଚାଲିଛି। ପୋଷାକ ବଦଳାଇବା ପାଇଁ ମୃତ୍ୟୁଞ୍ଜୟ ଘରକୁ ଯାଇଥାନ୍ତି। ଘର ଗେଟ୍ ପାଖରେ ଗାଡ଼ି ରଖିଲାବେଳକୁ ଡ୍ରାଇଭର ଉଦୟ ଜୋରରେ ବ୍ରେକ୍ କଷିଲା। ମୃତ୍ୟୁଞ୍ଜୟ ବାବୁ ଗାଡ଼ିରୁ ଓହ୍ଲାଇ ଦେଖିଲେ ଯେ ସୁନ୍ଦର ଚଢ଼େଇଟିଏ ରାସ୍ତା ଉପରେ ବସିଛି। ଆଉଟିକେ ଆଗେଇଥିଲେ ଚଢ଼େଇଟା ଚକା ତଳେ ପଡ଼ି ଯାଇଥାନ୍ତା। ବୋଧେ ଉଡ଼ିପାରୁନଥିଲା। ଗୋଡ଼ରେ ଟିକିଏ ମାଡ଼ ଲାଗିଛି। ଉଠାଇଲାବେଳକୁ ମୁନିଆ ଥଣ୍ଡରେ ଖୁମ୍ପି ମଧ୍ୟ ଦେଲା। ଚଢ଼େଇଟା ଯତ୍ନରେ ଗୋଟିଏ କାର୍ଟନରେ ରଖାଗଲା। ପାଣି ଦେବାରୁ ସେ ଟିକିଏ ପିଇଲା। ରାତିରେ କାର୍ଟୁନରେ ରଖିଲେ ବିଲେଇ ଖାଇଦେଇପାରେ। ସେତେବେଳକୁ କରୋନା ଭୟରେ

ଡାଲି, ଚାଉଳ ଦୋକାନ ଛାଡ଼ିଲେ ଅନ୍ୟସବୁ ଦୋକାନ ବନ୍ଦ। ପିଣ୍ଢରାତିଏ ମିଳିବା କଷ୍ଟ। ଯାହାହେଉ ଗୋଟିଏ ବାଉଁଶ ଝୁଡ଼ି ମିଳିଲା। ତାକୁ ଘୋଡ଼ାଇବା ପାଇଁ ଗୋଟେ ଢାଙ୍କୁଣୀ ମଧ୍ୟ ମିଳିଲା। ଆମର ତ ସବୁକିଛି ଯୁଗାଡ଼ରେ ଚାଲେ। ବିରି ନଥିଲେ ବରାରେ ସୁଜି ମିଶାଅ। ଡାଲି ନଥିଲେ ପେୟ ମିଶାଅ।

ଚଢ଼େଇକୁ ଧରିବାକୁ ଡର ଲାଗୁଥାଏ। ପୁଣି ଖୁମ୍ପ ଦେବ। ଅକାଳେ ନିୟମ ନାହିଁ। ତାକୁ ଧରି ଝୁଡ଼ି ଭିତରେ ଛାଡ଼ି ଦିଆଗଲା ଓ ଢାଙ୍କୁଣୀ ମଡ଼େଇ ଦିଆଗଲା। ଏଥର କିନ୍ତୁ ସେ ଖୁମ୍ପିଲାନି। ବୋଧେ ଭରସା ପାଇଗଲା। ଝୁଡ଼ିଟିକୁ ଚାରିଟା ରଶିରେ ବାନ୍ଧି ଶୀକା ଭଳିଆ ଝୁଲାଇ ଦିଆଗଲା। ଆଉ ବିଲେଇ କି କଟାଶ କିଛି କରିପାରିବନି। ଟିକିଏ ଚାଉଳ ଗୋଟିଏ ଗିନାରେ ରଖିଦିଆଗଲା।

ତା'ପରଦିନ ସକାଳ ହେଲା। ସକାଳୁ ଦେଖିଲା ବେଳକୁ ଚଢ଼େଇଟି ଘର ଭିତରେ ମୁହଁ ଫୁଲେଇକି ଶୋଇଛି। ମୃତ୍ୟୁଞ୍ଜୟ ତାକୁ ଟିକିଏ ଡାକିଲେ। ବାହାରୁ ଫୁଙ୍କିଲା ପରେ ଚଢ଼େଇଟି ଡାଙ୍କୁ ଅନେଇଲା। ଖୁବ୍ ସୁନ୍ଦର ଚଢ଼େଇଟା। କପର ସଲଫେଟ୍ ରଙ୍ଗର ପର, ମୁଣ୍ଡରେ ମୁକୁଟ ଭଳି ତୁଲ – ଶୁଆ ଥଣ୍ଡିଆ ଚଢ଼େଇଟା। ବୋଧହୁଏ ଶୁଆ ଜାତୀୟ ହୋଇଥିବ। ତା'ର ଫଟୋ ଉଠାଇ ମୃତ୍ୟୁଞ୍ଜୟ ଜଣେ ସାଙ୍ଗଙ୍କ ପାଖକୁ ପଠାଇଲେ, ସେ ଜଣେ ବାର୍ଡ ୱାଚର ହୋଇଥିବାରୁ କହିଲେ, ଚଢ଼େଇର ନାଁ ହେଲା କାକଟେଲ। ଆରେ ସିଏ ଖାଇବ କ'ଣ, ବାର୍ଡ ୱାଚରକୁ ଫୋନରେ ପଚରାଗଲା। ତାଙ୍କୁ ଜଣାନାହିଁ, ବଡ଼ ଅଡ଼ୁଆ ହେଲା। ଚାଉଳ ଗିନାରେ ସେ ମୁହଁ ମାରିନି, ଭାବିଲା ବେଳକୁ ମନେ ପଡ଼ିଲା – ସଂଗୀତା ଅପାଙ୍କ ବଡ଼ ଭାଉଜ ବହୁତ ଚଢ଼େଇ ତାଙ୍କ କଟକ ଘରେ ରଖିଛନ୍ତି। ତାଙ୍କୁ ପଚରାଯାଉ। ସଂଗୀତା ଅପାଙ୍କୁ ଫୋନରେ ପଚରାଗଲା। ସେ କହିଲେ – ଚଢ଼େଇର ଫଟୋ ପଠାଅ – ଭାଉଜଙ୍କୁ ପଚାରି ବୁଝିବା।

ୱାଟସ୍ଆପରେ ଫଟୋ ପଠାଗଲା। ପାଞ୍ଚ ମିନିଟ୍ ପରେ ଉତ୍ତର ଆସିଲା ସେ ଚଢ଼େଇ ଚୁଡ଼ା ବତୁରା ଖାଇବ, ନଚେତ ଝୁଡ଼ଙ୍ଗ କାଟି ଦେଲେ ଖାଇବ କିମ୍ବା ଶାଗ ପତର ଖାଇବ। ଅଥବା ଚଡ଼େଇ ଦାନା ଆରାମରେ ଖାଇବ। ମାତ୍ର ଏବେତ ଦୋକାନ ବଜାର ବନ୍ଦ। ଦେଣୁ ଶାଗ, ଝୁଡ଼ଙ୍ଗ ଚେଷ୍ଟା କରାଯାଉ। ସତରେ ସେ ଝୁଡ଼ଙ୍ଗ ଖୁସିରେ ଖାଇଲା ଓ ପାଣି ପିଇଲା। ମୃତ୍ୟୁଞ୍ଜୟଙ୍କ ମନରୁ ଶଙ୍କା ଟିକିଏ ଗଲା। ସେ ଡିଉଟିରେ ବାହାରିଯିବା ବେଳକୁ ତାକୁ ଟିକିଏ ଅନେଇଦେଲେ। ଯାହେଉ ଘରେ ବନ୍ଦ ଥିବା ସମୟରେ ନିଃସ୍ୱାର୍ଥ ସାଥୀଟିଏ ମିଳିଛି। ଆଗରୁ କେବେ ଚଢ଼େଇ ରଖିନଥିଲେ। ତେଣୁ ତାଙ୍କୁ ମଜା ଲାଗୁଥିଲା।

ଛୋଟବେଲେ ଗୋଟିଏ କୁକୁର ଛୁଆ ରଖିବାକୁ ଇଚ୍ଛା ଥିଲା। ମାତ୍ର ମା'
ମନାକଲେ। କେଉଁଠାରେ ଏସ.ପି. ଥିବାବେଲେ ଗୋଟିଏ ମୟୂର ଛୁଆ
ରଖିଥିଲେ। ମାତ୍ର ଡି.ଏଫ.ଓ. କହିଲେ, ମୟୂର ରଖିହେବ ନାହିଁ। ୱାଇଲ୍ଡଲାଇଫ୍
ଆକ୍ଟରେ ପଡ଼ିବ। ଆଜି କାକଟେଲ ନିଜ ମନକୁ ଆସିଛି। ଦେହ ଭଲ ହେଲେ
ଇଚ୍ଛା ହେଲେ ରହିବ ନହେଲେ ଉଡ଼ିଯିବ। ମାତ୍ର ମୃତ୍ୟୁଞ୍ଜୟଙ୍କର ଚଢ଼େଇ ପ୍ରତି
ଟିକେ ମୋହ ଓ ସ୍ନେହ ଆରମ୍ଭ ହେଲାଣି। ଗାଧୋଇବା ବେଲେ କି ଖାଇବା
ବେଲେ ମନଟା ସେଇ ଚଢ଼େଇ ପାଖରେ, ସତେ ବା ପ୍ରଥମ ପ୍ରେମ।

ଝିଅ ଈଶାର ମଧ୍ୟ ଚଢ଼େଇ ଉପରେ ମାୟା ଲାଗିଯାଇଥାଏ। ସେ ତା'
ମାଆକୁ କହୁଥାଏ, "ଚଢ଼େଇର ଗୋଟେ ନାଁ ଦିଅ।" ମୃତ୍ୟୁଞ୍ଜୟ କହିଲେ, ମିତୁ
ନାଁ ଦେବାକି? କନ୍ଭେଣ୍ଟ ପଢ଼ୁଆ ଈଶାର ମା କହିଲେ ରୁହମ, ମୁଁ ଗୋଟେ ନାଁ
ବାଛେ। ଡିଉଟିରୁ ଆସି ମୃତ୍ୟୁଞ୍ଜୟ ପଚାରିଲେ, ନାଁ କ'ଣ ବାଛିଲ। ଈଶାର ମା
କହିଲେ "ପିଓନି", ପିଓନି ମାନେ କ'ଣ? ହୁଇସ୍କି ପିଓନି, ବିଅର ପିଓନି; ନା
ତା ପିଓନି, ମୃତ୍ୟୁଞ୍ଜୟ ଅଳ୍ପ ପରିହାସ କରି ପଚାରିଲେ। ଈଶାର ମା ସିଓନି କହିଲେ
ମୋ ନାଁ ସାଙ୍ଗରେ ମ୍ୟାଚ କରିକି ତା'ର ନାଁ ପିଓନି ଦେଲି। ସେ ମୋର ସାନ
ଝିଅ। ଲକଡାଉନ ସରିଲେ ଗୋଟିଏ ବଡ଼ ପଞ୍ଜୁରି ଆଣିବ। ଏବେ ଯାଉଣୁ ଆସୁଣୁ
ସମସ୍ତେ ତାକୁ ପିଓନି ପିଓନି ଡାକିବାକୁ ଲାଗିଲେ। ଖୁବ୍‌ଶୀଘ୍ର ସିଏ ଘରର ଗୋଟିଏ
ସଦସ୍ୟ ଭଲି ହୋଇଗଲା। ବେଲେବେଲେ ରାବିବା ମଧ୍ୟ ଆରମ୍ଭ କଲା। ପିଓନିର
ସ୍ୱର ସ୍ତ୍ରୀ ସିଓନିଙ୍କ ସ୍ୱର ଭଲି ମଧୁର ଥିଲା।

ସେଦିନ ରବିବାର ଥିଲା। ରାସ୍ତାରେ ଲକଡାଉନ ଚେକିଂ ଚାଲିଥାଏ।
ଦିଲ୍ଲୀରୁ ଖବର ଆସିଥାଏ କିଛି ଲୋକ ଧର୍ମ ସଭାରେ ପ୍ରାର୍ଥନା ସାରି ଦେଶର
ବିଭିନ୍ନ ପ୍ରାନ୍ତକୁ ଚାଲିଯାଇଛନ୍ତି ଏବଂ ସେମାନେ ସମ୍ଭବତଃ କରୋନା ଭାଇରସରେ
ଆକ୍ରାନ୍ତ। ବିଚଲିତ ଲାଗିଲା। ଏହି ସମୟରେ ଘରୁ ଫୋନ ଆସିଲା ଯେ
ଖାଇବାକୁ ଦେବାବେଲେ ପିଓନି ଉଡ଼ି ପଲାଇଲା। ଈଶା ଘରେ କାନ୍ଦୁଛି। ମା'
ସମସ୍ତଙ୍କ ଉପରେ ରାଗୁଛନ୍ତି। ମୃତ୍ୟୁଞ୍ଜୟଙ୍କ ମନ ବହୁତ ଖରାପ ହେଲା। ଗୋଟିଏ
ପଞ୍ଜୁରି ମିଲିଥିଲେ ଏମିତି ହୋଇନଥାନ୍ତା। ମନ ଦୁଃଖରେ ଖଣ୍ଡଗିରି ଛକରେ ଗାଡ଼ି
ଚେକିଂ କରୁଥାନ୍ତି। ଟ୍ରକ୍ ଓ ଟ୍ୟାକ୍‌ରମାନେ ପୁଲିସ ବ୍ୟାରିକେଡ୍ ପଛରେ ଛିଡ଼ା
ହୋଇଥାନ୍ତି। ହଠାତ୍ ସେ ଦେଖିଲେ ଗୋଟିଏ ଟ୍ୟାଙ୍କର ଉପରେ ପିଓନି ଭଲିଆ
ଚଢ଼େଇଟିଏ ବସିଛି। ମୃତ୍ୟୁଞ୍ଜୟ ଭାବିଲେ ସେ ସ୍ୱପ୍ନ ତ ଦେଖୁ ନାହାନ୍ତି। ସେ
ତାକୁ ଦେଖିବା ପାଇଁ ଗାଡ଼ି ଆଡ଼କୁ ଦୌଡ଼ିଲେ। ପୁଲିସ ଆସିବା ଦେଖି ଟ୍ରକ୍‌ର

ଡ୍ରାଇଭର ଗାଡ଼ିରୁ ଡେଇଁ ଦୌଡ଼ିବାକୁ ଆରମ୍ଭ କଲା। ସେ ଦ୍ୱନ୍ଦ୍ୱରେ ପଡ଼ିଲେ, ଡ୍ରାଇଭରକୁ ଗୋଡ଼ାଇବେ ନା ପିଓନିକୁ ଧରିବେ। ପୁଲିସ ଟ୍ରେନିଙ୍ଗ ପ୍ରଭାବ ନିଷ୍କାମ ସେବା, ଦୌଡ଼ିଯାଇ ଡ୍ରାଇଭରକୁ ଧରିଲେ। ଗାଡ଼ି ପାଖକୁ ଫେରିଲା ବେଳକୁ ଦେଖିଲେ ଯେ ପିଓନି ଗାଡ଼ିର ଟାଙ୍କି ଉପରେ ବସି ଢାକୁଣିକୁ ଖୁଲୁଛି। ସେ ବୋଧେ କିଛି କହିବାକୁ ଚାହୁଁଥାଏ। ଟ୍ୟାଙ୍କର ଢାକୁଣି ଖୋଲି ଦେଖିବାରେ ସେଥିରେ କିଛି ନଥିଲା। ମାତ୍ର ଟର୍ଚ ମାରିବାରୁ ଦେଖାଗଲା ଯେ ଟ୍ୟାଙ୍କର ଭିତରେ କିଛି ଲୋକ ଅଛନ୍ତି। ଡ୍ରାଇଭରକୁ ଦୁଇ ବାଡ଼ି ପକାଇବା ପରେ ସେ ସତ କଥା କହିଲା। ଦିଲ୍ଲୀରୁ କୋଡ଼ିଏ ଜଣ ଲୋକଙ୍କୁ ନେଇ ସେ ପାରାଦୀପ ଯାଉଥିଲା। ଦିଲ୍ଲୀରେ ତାଙ୍କର ଧର୍ମ ସଭା ହେଉଥିଲା। ତାହା ସରିଲା ବେଳକୁ ଦେଶରେ ଲକଡାଉନ ହୋଇଗଲା। ତେଣୁ ସେମାନେ ଲୁଚି କରି ପାରାଦୀପ ଯାଉଛନ୍ତି। ଏକଥା ଶୁଣିବା ମାତ୍ରେ ମୃତ୍ୟୁଞ୍ଜୟଙ୍କର କାନ ଛିଡ଼ା ହୋଇଗଲା। ଧର୍ମସଭାରେ ଅଢ଼େଇ ହଜାର ଲୋକ ଥିଲେ। ସେଥିରେ ବାହାର ଦେଶର ଲୋକ ମଧ୍ୟ ଥିଲେ। ଇତି ମଧ୍ୟରେ ସେମାନଙ୍କ ମଧ୍ୟରୁ ଶିହେରୁ ଊର୍ଦ୍ଧ୍ୱ ଲୋକ କରୋନାରେ ଆକ୍ରାନ୍ତ ହୋଇଛନ୍ତି ଏବଂ ହଜାରେରୁ ଅଧିକ ଲୋକ ବିଭିନ୍ନ ଜାଗାକୁ ବାହାରି ଯାଇଛନ୍ତି। ସେମାନଙ୍କର ଟେର ପୁଲିସ ପାଇପାରୁନି। ଡ୍ରାଇଭରକୁ ଇଣ୍ଟେରୋଗେସନ୍ କରିବାରୁ ଜଣାପଡ଼ିଲା ଯେ ସମସ୍ତେ ତେଲ ଟ୍ୟାଙ୍କର ଭିତରେ ପଶିକରି ଦୂର ଦୂରାନ୍ତକୁ ଚାଲିଯାଇଛନ୍ତି। ମୃତ୍ୟୁଞ୍ଜୟ ଗାଡ଼ିଟିକୁ କ୍ୱାରେଣ୍ଟାଇନ ସେଣ୍ଟରକୁ ପଠାଇଦେଲେ ଓ ସମସ୍ତଙ୍କର ଡାକ୍ତରୀ ମାଇନା କରିବାକୁ ନିର୍ଦ୍ଦେଶ ଦେଲେ। ସେ ସଙ୍ଗେ ସଙ୍ଗେ ସମସ୍ତ ଜିଲ୍ଲା ଓ ଅନ୍ୟାନ୍ୟ ପ୍ରଦେଶର ପୁଲିସ କଣ୍ଟ୍ରୋଲ ରୁମକୁ ଖବର ପଠାଇଦେଲେ। ସମସ୍ତ ତେଲ ଓ ପାଣି ଟ୍ୟାଙ୍କରକୁ ଚେକ୍ କଲେ, ଦିଲ୍ଲୀ ଧର୍ମସଭାକୁ ଯାଇଥିବା ସମସ୍ତ ବ୍ୟକ୍ତିଙ୍କୁ ଧରାଯାଇ ପାରିବ ଏବଂ ଏକ ବଡ଼ ମହାମାରୀକୁ ରୋକାଯାଇପାରିବ।

ଦେଖୁ ଦେଖୁ ଗୋଟିଏ ଦିନ ମଧ୍ୟରେ ଅଧିକାଂଶ ଲୋକଙ୍କୁ ବିଭିନ୍ନ ପ୍ରଦେଶର ପୁଲିସ ଧରିପାରିଲା। ଏହି ସଫଳତା ପାଇଁ ମୃତ୍ୟୁଞ୍ଜୟଙ୍କୁ ପୁଲିସ ପଦକରେ ସମ୍ମାନିତ କରିବା ପାଇଁ ଭାରତ ସରକାର ଘୋଷଣା କଲେ। ଆସନ୍ତା ସ୍ୱାଧୀନତା ଦିବସରେ ଏହି ପଦକ ପ୍ରଦାନ କରାଯିବ। ମୃତ୍ୟୁଞ୍ଜୟ ମନ ଭିତରେ ପିଓନିକୁ ବହୁତ ଖୋଜୁଥାନ୍ତି। ସବୁ ସଫଳତାର ଶ୍ରେୟ ପିଓନିର। ଯାଉଣ୍ଟୁ ଆସୁଣ୍ଟୁ ତାଙ୍କର ଆଖି ଗଛ ଡାଲରେ ଖୋଜି ହେଉଥାଏ ପିଓନିକୁ। ମାତ୍ର ପିଓନିର ଦେଖା ନଥାଏ। ବୋଧହୁଏ ତା'ର ଜୀବନ ରକ୍ଷା କରାଯାଇଥିବାରୁ ସେ ହଜାର ହଜାର ଲୋକଙ୍କର ଜୀବନ

ରକ୍ଷା କରିଦେଲା। ଭଲ କାମ କରି ଭୁଲିଯିବା କଥା। ବୋଧେ ପିଓନି ତାହା ପାଳନ କରୁଛି।

ସ୍ୱାଧୀନତା ଦିବସର ପଦକ ପ୍ରଦାନ ଉତ୍ସବର ଭବ୍ୟ ସମାରୋହରେ ମାନ୍ୟବର ମୁଖ୍ୟମନ୍ତ୍ରୀ, ରାଷ୍ଟ୍ରପତିଙ୍କ ତରଫରୁ ମୃତ୍ୟୁଞ୍ଜୟଙ୍କୁ ପୁଲିସ ପଦକରେ ମଣ୍ଡିତ କଲେ। ମୃତ୍ୟୁଞ୍ଜୟଙ୍କର ପ୍ରଶସ୍ତି ପତ୍ର ମଧ ପାଠ କରାଗଲା। କିପରି ସେ ସଫଳତାର ସହିତ ନିଜର ବିଚକ୍ଷଣ ବୁଦ୍ଧି ବଳରେ ଦେଶକୁ ଏକ ଆସନ୍ନ ମହାମାରୀରୁ ରକ୍ଷା କଲେ, ଇତ୍ୟାଦି ଇତ୍ୟାଦି।

ମୃତ୍ୟୁଞ୍ଜୟ ପଦକ ପିନ୍ଧି ଗାଡ଼ି ପାଖକୁ ଆସୁଥାଆନ୍ତି, ଟିକିଏ ଅନ୍ୟମନସ୍କ ଥାଆନ୍ତି। ହଠାତ୍ ଗଣମାଧ୍ୟମର ପ୍ରତିନିଧି ଦଳ ତାଙ୍କୁ ଘେରିଗଲେ ଏବଂ ନିଜର ପ୍ରତିକ୍ରିୟା ପ୍ରକାଶ କରିବା ପାଇଁ ପ୍ରଶ୍ନ କଲେ "ଏହି ପଦକର ଶ୍ରେୟ କାହାକୁ ଦେବେ"? ଜଣେ ଟିଭି କ୍ୟାମେରାମ୍ୟାନ କହିଲା, ସାର୍ ଆପଣଙ୍କୁ ଅଭିନନ୍ଦନ ଜଣାଇବାକୁ ଗୋଟିଏ ସୁନ୍ଦର ଚଡ଼େଇ ଆପଣଙ୍କ ଡାହାଣ କାନ୍ଧରେ ବସିଛି। ମୃତ୍ୟୁଞ୍ଜୟ ଉଲ୍ଲସିତ ହୋଇ ଦେଖିଲେ "ଆରେ ତାଙ୍କ କାନ୍ଧରେ ତ ପିଓନି ବସିଛି।" ତାଙ୍କ ଆଖିରୁ ଆନନ୍ଦାଶ୍ରୁ ବହିଗଲା। ଗଣମାଧ୍ୟମ ପାଇଁ ଉତ୍ତର ମିଳିଗଲା "ସବୁ ଶ୍ରେୟ ଦେଉଛି ଏହି ମୁକ୍ତ ପକ୍ଷୀଟିର। ଏହା ସାଧାରଣ ପକ୍ଷୀ ନୁହେଁ, ମଣିଷ ପାଇଁ ସ୍ୱର୍ଗପରୀ ହିଁ ଥିଲା।" ସେତିକି ବେଳେ ପିଓନି ମୁକ୍ତିର ଗୀତ ଗାଇ ଦୂର ଆକାଶକୁ ଉଡ଼ି ଯାଇଥିଲା। ପିଓନିର କାହାଣୀ ସେ ଅଞ୍ଚଳେ କହିଦେଲେ। ପିଓନିର କାହାଣୀ କିମ୍ବଦନ୍ତୀରେ ପରିଣତ ହୋଇଗଲା।

ସମୟ ସଂକେତ

ସହରର ସବୁଠୁ ବଡ଼ ମଲ୍‍-ଗ୍ରାଣ୍ଡ ସିନାତ୍ରା। ସେଠାରେ ନାମିଦାମୀ ବ୍ରାଣ୍ଡର ଦୋକାନ ସବୁ ଅଛି। ସବୁଆଡ଼େ ଚକ୍‍ମକ୍। ପଶିଗଲେ ଭାରତରେ ଅଛ କି ବିଦେଶରେ ଅଛ ଜାଣି ହେବନି। ମଲ୍ ଭିତରେ ପ୍ରାୟତଃ ଯୁବକ ଯୁବତୀମାନଙ୍କର ଭିଡ଼। ସମସ୍ତେ ଯୋଡ଼ି ଯୋଡ଼ି ହୋଇ ହାତକୁ ହାତ ଧରି ବୁଲନ୍ତି। କିନ୍ତୁ ସ୍ୱାମୀ-ସ୍ତ୍ରୀ ଛଡ଼ାଛଡ଼ି ହୋଇ ଏକା ଏକା ବୁଲନ୍ତି। ସ୍ତ୍ରୀ ଆଗରେ ତ ସ୍ୱାମୀ ପଛରେ। ହାତ ଧରାଧରି ହୋଇ ବୁଲିବା ଦୂରର କଥା। ବାହାଘରର ପ୍ରଥମ ଛଅ ମାସ ପର୍ଯ୍ୟନ୍ତ ହାତ ଧରାଧରି ତା'ପରେ ହାତ ଛଡ଼ାଛଡ଼ି। ଯେଉଁ ବାଟରେ ଯିଏ, କେବଳ ସେଲଫି ଉଠାଇଲାବେଳେ କୋଲାକୋଲି। ଏ ହେଲା ସବୁ ପରିବାରର କଥା। ଏଥିରେ କିଛି ଲୁଚାଇବାର ନାହିଁ।

    ସୁବୋଧବାବୁ ମଲ୍ ସିନାତ୍ରାର ମାଲିକ। ସେଦିନ ସେ ମଲରେ ନିଜ ରୁମରେ ବସିଥିଲେ। ମନ ବେଶ୍ ଖୁସି ଥିଲା। ଷ୍ଟାରବକ୍‍ର ବ୍ଲାକ୍ କଫି କପଟିଏ ପିଉଥିଲେ। ହଠାତ୍ ମଲର ମ୍ୟାନେଜର ଶ୍ରୀକାନ୍ତ ରୁମକୁ ପଶିଆସିଲେ। ମୁଣ୍ଡରୁ ତାଙ୍କର ଝାଳ ବୋହିପଡ଼ୁଥାଏ। ଖୁବ୍ ବିଚଳିତ ଜଣାପଡ଼ୁଥା'ନ୍ତି। 'କ'ଣ ହେଲା ଶ୍ରୀକାନ୍ତ?' ସୁବୋଧ ପଚାରିଲେ। ଶ୍ରୀକାନ୍ତ ଥା,ଆ,ମା,ମା ହୋଇ କହିଲେ- ବିଲ୍ କାଉଣ୍ଟରର ସୋନିଆ ପାଞ୍ଚ ଲକ୍ଷର ହାରକୁ ବିନା ପେମେଣ୍ଟରେ ଜଣେ ଗ୍ରାହକକୁ

ଦେଇଦେଇଛି । ସେନ୍‌ସର ଟ୍ୟାର୍‌ କାଢ଼ିଦେଇଥିବାରୁ ଗେଟ୍‌ର ସିକ୍ୟୁରିଟି ମଧ ଜାଣିପାରିଲା ନାହିଁ ।

ସୁବୋଧବାବୁ ତତ୍‌କ୍ଷଣାତ୍‌ କହିଲେ– "ସୋନିଆକୁ ସଙ୍ଗେ ସଙ୍ଗେ ରୁକିରିରୁ ବିଦା କରିଦିଅ ଏବଂ କ୍ୟାପିଟାଲ ଥାନାରେ ଗୋଟିଏ ଏଫ‌ଆଇଆର‌ଲା ଦେଇଦିଅ ।" କିଛି ସମୟ ପରେ ସୋନିଆ ଆସି ସୁବୋଧଙ୍କୁ ଦେଖାକରିବାକୁ ରୁହିଲା । ମାତ୍ର ସୁବୋଧବାବୁ ସୋନିଆର କୌଣସି କଥା ଶୁଣିବାକୁ ପ୍ରସ୍ତୁତ ନଥିଲେ । ଏହି ସମୟରେ ଥାନାବାବୁ ଆସି ପହଞ୍ଚିଲେ ଓ ସୋନିଆକୁ ପଚରାଉଚରା କରିବା ପାଇଁ ନେଇଗଲେ । ଗଲାବେଳେ ସୋନିଆ କହୁଥିଲା– "ସାର୍‌, ମୋ କଥା ଟିକିଏ ଶୁଣିଥିଲେ ଭଲ ହୋଇଥାନ୍ତା, ମାତ୍ର ଆପଣ ଶୁଣିଲେନି ।"

ତା' ପରଦିନ ସନ୍ଧ୍ୟାବେଳେ ସୁବୋଧ ନିଜ ଚାମ୍ବରରେ ବସିଥାଆନ୍ତି । ହଠାତ୍‌ ଶ୍ରୀକାନ୍ତ ରୁମ୍‌ ଭିତରକୁ ପଶିଆସିଲା । ତା' ମୁହଁରେ ପ୍ରସନ୍ନତାର । "କ'ଣ ହେଲା ଶ୍ରୀକାନ୍ତ ଖୁବ୍‌ ଖୁସି ଦେଖାଯାଉଛ" ସୁବୋଧ ପଚାରିଲେ । ଶ୍ରୀକାନ୍ତ କହିଲେ– "ସାର୍‌, ହାରତି ମିଳିଗଲା ।"

"ଆରେ ବାଃ, କେମିତି ମିଳିଲା" ସୁବୋଧ ଆଶ୍ଚର୍ଯ୍ୟ ହୋଇ ପଚାରିଲେ ।

ଶ୍ରୀକାନ୍ତ କହିଲେ "ଯେଉଁ ଗ୍ରାହକ ଜଣକ ହାରତି ନେଇଥିଲେ ସେ ଆସି ଫେରାଇ ଦେଇଛନ୍ତି । ଯେହେତୁ ତାଙ୍କ କ୍ରେଡ଼ିଟ୍‌କାର୍ଡ଼ରୁ ପଇସା କଟିଲାନି, ସେ ସନ୍ଦେହ କରି ହାରତିକୁ ଫେରାଇବାକୁ ଆସିଛନ୍ତି ।" "ବାଃ ଖୁବ୍‌ ଭଲ କଥା । ମୁଁ ସେହି ଗ୍ରାହକଙ୍କୁ ଭେଟିବାକୁ ରୁହେଁ" ସୁବୋଧ କହିଲେ ।

ଶ୍ରୀକାନ୍ତ କହିଲେ "ହଁ ସାର୍‌, ମୁଁ ତାଙ୍କୁ ଡାକି ଆଣୁଛି ।"

ଜଣେ ଗୋରା ତକ୍‌ ତକ୍‌ ସ୍ମାର୍ଟ ଯୁବକଙ୍କୁ ନେଇ ଶ୍ରୀକାନ୍ତ ଆସିଲେ । ସେ ନିଜର ନାଁ 'କବୀର' କହି ସୁବୋଧଙ୍କ ସହ ହାତ ମିଳାଇଲେ । ସୁବୋଧ କହିଲେ– "ହାରତି ଆସି ଫେରାଇ ଦେଇଥିବାରୁ ଆପଣଙ୍କୁ ବହୁତ ଧନ୍ୟବାଦ । ଆପଣଙ୍କ ଭଳି ସନୋଟ ମଣିଷ ଆଜିକାଲି ମିଳିବା କଠିନ ।"

କବୀର ସ୍ମିତହାସ୍ୟ କରି କହିଲେ "ଅନ୍ୟର ଧନ ଓ ଅନ୍ୟର ସ୍ତ୍ରୀ ଉପରେ ସେ ନଜର ପକାଇ ନାହିଁ ।" ଏହା ଶୁଣି ସୁବୋଧ ଟିକିଏ ସଂକୁଚିତ ମନେକଲେ କାରଣ ତାଙ୍କର ଗୋଟିଏ ଦୁଇଟା ଆଫାୟାର ରହିଛି । ତେଣୁ ସେ କଥା ନ ବଢ଼ାଇ କହିଲେ "ମୁଁ ଆପଣଙ୍କୁ କିଛି ସାହାଯ୍ୟ କରିପାରେ କି ?"

କବୀର କହିଲେ "ଏତିକି ଅନୁରୋଧ କରିବି ଯେ, ଯଦି ପୋଲିସକୁ କହି ସୋନିଆକୁ ଛାଡ଼ିଦିଅନ୍ତେ ତେବେ ଭଲ ହୁଅନ୍ତା । ମୋର ଅନ୍ୟମନସ୍କତା ପାଇଁ ଗୋଟେ ନିରୀହ ଝିଅ କାହିଁକି ଶାସ୍ତି ପାଇବ ।"

ସୁବୋଧ କହିଲେ "ନିଶ୍ଚୟ । ସେତିକି କାହିଁକି ତାକୁ ପୁଣି ରୁକ୍‍ସିରେ ରଖିଦେବି ।
ଆପଣ ନିଶ୍ଚିତ ରୁହନ୍ତୁ, ମୁଁ ପରଟି ପାରେକି ଆପଣ କ'ଣ କରନ୍ତି ?"

କବିର କହିଲେ "ମୁଁ ଆମାଜନ୍ ଇଣ୍ଡିଆର ସପ୍ଲାଇ ଚେନ୍‍ରେ ଜଣେ ମ୍ୟାନେଜର
ଅଛି ।"

ସୁବୋଧବାବୁ ହସିକରି କହିଲେ "ଯଦି ଆପଣ କିଛି ନ ଭାବିବେ ତେବେ
ଆମ ମଲ୍‍ରେ ପ୍ରକ୍ୟାରେମେଣ୍ଟ ମ୍ୟାନେଜର ଭାବେ ଜଏନ୍ କରିପାରନ୍ତି । ଆମାଜନ୍‍ଠାରୁ
ଅଧିକ ପ୍ୟାକେଜ୍ ଦେବୁ । କାରଣ ଆପଣଙ୍କ ଭଳି ଜଣେ ସଚୋଟ ମଣିଷ ଆମକୁ
ଦରକାର । କୋଟି କୋଟି ଟଙ୍କାର କିଣାବିକା ଏଠାରେ ହେଉଛି । ତେଣୁ ମୋ କଥା
ଆପଣ ରଖିବେ ବୋଲି ମୁଁ ଆଶା କରୁଛି ।"

କବୀର ସ୍ମିତ ହସି କହିଲେ "ମୋତେ ଦୁଇଦିନ ସମୟ ଦିଅନ୍ତୁ । ମୁଁ ଟିକେ
ଭାବିକରି କହିବି ।"

ଏହା ଭିତରେ କବୀର ସିନାତ୍ରା ମଲ୍‍ରେ ଗୋଟିଏ ବଡ଼ ପୋଷ୍ଟରେ ଜଏନ୍
କରିଥିଲେ । ସୋନିଆ ମଧ୍ୟ ବିଲ୍ କାଉଣ୍ଟରରୁ ପ୍ରମୋସନ ପାଇ କ୍ୟାସ ସେକ୍ସନର
ମ୍ୟାନେଜର ହୋଇଗଲାଣି । କବୀର ଓ ସୋନିଆ ଏ ଭିତରେ ଲିଭିଇନ୍ ରିଲେସନ୍‍ରେ
ରହୁଛନ୍ତି । କବୀର ଏବେ ସୁବୋଧବାବୁଙ୍କର ସବୁଠୁ ପ୍ରିୟ ମ୍ୟାନେଜର ହୋଇସାରିଛନ୍ତି ।
ବିଚରା ଶ୍ରୀକାନ୍ତ ଯେଉଁ ପୋଷ୍‍ରେ ଥିଲେ ସେଥିରେ ଅଛନ୍ତି । ଭାଗ୍ୟ କାହାକୁ ସହାୟ
ହୁଏ ତାହା ଛାର ମାନବକୁ ଅଗୋଚର । ଏବେ ସମସ୍ତେ ଜାଣନ୍ତି ସିନାତ୍ରା ମଲ୍ ହେଉଛି
କବୀରବାବୁଙ୍କର । ସବୁ କଣ୍ଡ୍ରାକ୍, ସବୁ ବିଲ୍ ବାବୁଙ୍କ ଦ୍ୱାରା ହିଁ ହୁଏ । ସୁବୋଧବାବୁ
ମଧ୍ୟ ସବୁ ଦାୟିତ୍ୱ କବୀରଙ୍କ ଉପରେ ନ୍ୟସ୍ତ କରି କଲିକତାରେ ପ୍ରାୟତଃ ରହୁଛନ୍ତି ।
ମାସକୁ ଥରେ ଅଧେ ଆସି ବୁଲିଯାଉଛନ୍ତି ।

ସିନାତ୍ରା ମଲ୍ ପାଖରେ ଗୋଟିଏ ଖୋଲାଜାଗାରେ ଆଉ ଗୋଟେ ସେଣ୍ଟ୍ରାଲ
ମଲ୍ ଖୋଲିଲା । ଦେଖୁ ଦେଖୁ ଦୁଇ ମଲ୍ ଭିତରେ ପ୍ରତିଯୋଗିତା ବଢ଼ିଲା । ଧୀରେ
ଧୀରେ ଗ୍ରାହକମାନେ ସେଣ୍ଟ୍ରାଲ ମଲ୍ ଆଡ଼କୁ ମୁହାଁଇଲେଣି । ସେଣ୍ଟ୍ରାଲ ମଲର ନୂଆ
ନୂଆ ଅଫର, ସୁନ୍ଦର ସୁନ୍ଦର ସେଲ୍ସ ଗାର୍ଲ ଗ୍ରାହକମାନଙ୍କୁ ଆକୃଷ୍ଟ କରୁଛନ୍ତି । ସିନାତ୍ରା
ମଲ୍‍ର ପ୍ରଫିଟ୍ କମିବାକୁ ଲାଗିଲା । ସୁବୋଧବାବୁଙ୍କ ଚିନ୍ତା ଘାରିଲାଣି । ଯେତିକି ବ୍ୟାଙ୍କ୍
ଲୋନ୍ ନିଆ ହୋଇଥିଲା ତା'ର ପରିଶୋଧ ହୋଇ ନାହିଁ । ସୁଧଭାର ବଢ଼ି ବଢ଼ି
ଚାଲିଛି । ତେଣୁ କେମିତି ପ୍ରଫିଟ୍ ବଢ଼ିବ, ସେ ବିଷୟରେ ସେ କବୀରଙ୍କ ସହ ସର୍ବଦା
ବିଚାରବିମର୍ଶ କରୁଥା'ନ୍ତି । ଏହା ମଧ୍ୟରେ ଶ୍ରୀକାନ୍ତ ମଧ୍ୟ ସୁବୋଧଙ୍କୁ କିଛି ବୁଝାଇବାକୁ
ଚେଷ୍ଟା କରୁଥା'ନ୍ତି ମାତ୍ର ସୁବୋଧବାବୁ ଶ୍ରୀକାନ୍ତର ଉପଦେଶକୁ ଆଦୌ ଗ୍ରହଣ

କରୁନଥା'ନ୍ତି । ପ୍ରଫିଟ୍ କମିବା ସହ ତାଙ୍କର ବ୍ଲଡ୍‌ପ୍ରେସର ବଢ଼ୁଥାଏ । ହଠାତ୍ ଡାଏବେଟିସ୍ ବାହାରିପଡ଼ିଲାଣି ।

ଥରେ ଶ୍ରୀକାନ୍ତ ଆସି କହିଲେ "ସାର୍ ! ସୁନିଆ ଯାଇ ସେଣ୍ଟ୍ରାଲ ମଲରେ ମ୍ୟାନେଜର ପ୍ରକ୍ୟୋରମେଣ୍ଟ ଭାବେ ଜଏନ୍ କଲାଣି । ତେଣୁ କବୀରଙ୍କୁ ଆଉ ବିଶ୍ୱାସ କରନ୍ତୁ ନାହିଁ ।"

ସୁବୋଧବାବୁ ସଙ୍ଗେ ସଙ୍ଗେ କବୀରଙ୍କୁ ଡାକି ସଂଗେ ସଂଗେ କହିଲେ "ସୋନିଆ ସେଣ୍ଟ୍ରାଲ ମଲରେ ଜଏନ୍ କରିବାଟା କିଛି ଠିକ୍ ହେଲାନି । ସେମାନେ ଆମର କମ୍ପିଟେଟର । ଆମର ଷ୍ଟ୍ରେଟେଜି ସେମାନେ ଜାଣିଯିବେ । ତେଣୁ ଆମର ମାର୍କେଟ ସେୟାର ଆହୁରି କମିଯିବ ।"

କବୀର କହିଲେ "ସାର୍ ! ସୋନିଆ ସହ ମୋର ଆଉ ଭଲ ପଡ଼ୁନାହିଁ । ଆମେ ଖୁବ୍ ଶୀଘ୍ର ଅଲଗା ହୋଇଯିବୁ ବୋଲି ସ୍ଥିର କରିଛୁ । ଆପଣ ଚିନ୍ତା କରନ୍ତୁ ନାହିଁ । ମୁଁ ସବୁପ୍ରକାର ଉଦ୍ୟମ କରୁଛି ଯେପରି ସନାତ୍ରା ମଲ ପୁଣି ପୂର୍ବ ଅବସ୍ଥାକୁ ଫେରି ଆସିବ । ଆପଣ କଲିକତା ଯାଇ ଆରାମ କରନ୍ତୁ । ସ୍ୱାସ୍ଥ୍ୟର ଯତ୍ନ ନେବା ଅଧିକ ଜରୁରୀ ।"

ଯାହାହେଲେ ବି ସୁବୋଧବାବୁ ଜଣେ ପୋଖତ ବ୍ୟବସାୟୀ । ତେଣୁ ସୁବୋଧ ତାଙ୍କୁ କଲିକତା ଯାଇ ଆରାମ କରିବାକୁ କାହିଁକି କହିଲା ଭାବି ତାଙ୍କ ମନରେ ସନ୍ଦେହ ହେଲା । ତେଣୁ ସେ କଲିକତା ଯାଇ ସେଠାକାର ଏକ ନାମୀ ରୁଟାର୍ଡ ଆକାଉଣ୍ଟାଣ୍ଟଙ୍କୁ ଆଣି ସିନାତ୍ରା ମଲର ଅଡ଼ିଟ୍ କରାଇଲେ । ଗୋଟିଏ ମାସ ମଧ୍ୟରେ ଅଡ଼ିଟ୍ ସରିଲା । ଅଡ଼ିଟ୍ ରିପୋର୍ଟ ଦେଖି ସୁବୋଧବାବୁଙ୍କ କପାଳ ଝାଳରେ ଓଦା ହୋଇଗଲା । ୩୪ ମାଙ୍ଗ ଗଡ଼୍ ! କବୀର ଆସିବା ପରଠାରୁ ହିଁ ସିନାତ୍ରା ମଲର କ୍ଷତି ଆରମ୍ଭ ହୋଇଛି । ପ୍ରକ୍ୟୋରମେଣ୍ଟରେ ଅନେକ ଜିନିଷ ଇନ୍‌ଭେଣ୍ଟରିରେ ଚଢ଼ି ନାହିଁ । ବିଭିନ୍ନ କମ୍ପାନୀର ଯ୍ରି ଅଫର୍‌ଗୁଡ଼ିକରେ ଜାଲିଆତି ହୋଇଛି । ଜିନିଷଗୁଡ଼ିକ ମଲକୁ ନ ଆସି ଅନ୍ୟଆଡ଼େ ଡାଇଭର୍ଟ କରାହୋଇଛି । ସପ୍ଲାୟର୍‌ମାନଙ୍କୁ ପେମେଣ୍ଟ ମଧ କରାହୋଇ ନାହିଁ । ଏହି କଥା ଅନେକ ଥର ଶ୍ରୀକାନ୍ତ କବୀରବାବୁଙ୍କୁ କହିଥିଲା । ମାତ୍ର ସେ କବୀରଙ୍କୁ ବିଶ୍ୱାସ କରି ସବୁ ଆଖିବୁଜି ଦେଇଥିଲେ । କମ୍ପାନୀର ବାଲାନ୍ସ ସିଟ୍ ମଧ ମାନିପୁଲେଟ୍ କରାଯାଇଛି । ପାଞ୍ଚ ବର୍ଷ ମଧ୍ୟରେ ସମୁଦାୟ କ୍ଷତି ପଚାଁତିରିଶ କୋଟି ହୋଇସାରିଛି । ସେଟିକିରେ ତାଙ୍କର ବ୍ୟାଙ୍କ ଲୋନ୍, ପେମେଣ୍ଟ ହୋଇ କମ୍ପାନୀ ପ୍ରଫିଟ୍‌ରେ ରହିଥିଲାଆଡ଼ା । ମସ୍ତବଡ଼ ଭୁଲଟାଏ ସେ କରିଦେଇଛନ୍ତି ।

ସୁବୋଧ ସଙ୍ଗେ ସଙ୍ଗେ କବୀରଙ୍କୁ ଡକାଇଲେ । ମାତ୍ର କବୀର ରୁମ୍‌ରେ ନଥିଲେ ।

ଫୋନ୍ ଲଗାଇଲେ, ଫୋନ୍ ସ୍ୱିଚ୍ ଅଫ୍ ଥିଲା। କବୀର କ'ଣ ଫେରାର୍ ହୋଇଗଲା
କି! ସୁବୋଧବାବୁ ଅଡ଼ିଟ୍ ରିପୋର୍ଟ ଧରି କ୍ୟାପିଟାଲ୍ ଥାନାରେ ଏତଲା ଦେଲେ।
ସେତେବେଳକାର ଥାନା ଇନ୍‌ସପେକ୍ଟର ରାଜୀବଲୋଚନ ଏବେ ଏସ୍.ପି.
ହୋଇଗଲେଣି। ସେ ଥାନାରେ ଉପସ୍ଥିତ ଥିଲେ। ଅଡ଼ିଟ୍ ରିପୋର୍ଟ ଦେଖି କହିଲେ
"ସୁବୋଧବାବୁ ମନେପକାନ୍ତୁ ସେଦିନ କଥା। ଆପଣ ନିଜେ ସୋନିଆକୁ ଛାଡ଼ିଦେବାକୁ
କହିଥିଲେ। ମୁଁ କହିଥିଲି ଯେ କେସ୍‌ଟିକୁ ଆଗକୁ ନେବା ଉଚିତ, କାରଣ ସୋନିଆ
ପାଞ୍ଚ ହଜାର ଟଙ୍କା ଦରମା ପାଏ କିନ୍ତୁ ତା'ର ଆକାଉଣ୍ଟରେ ପାଞ୍ଚ ଲକ୍ଷ ଟଙ୍କାର
ଟ୍ରାନ୍‌ଜାକ୍‌ସନ ଅଛି। ଆପଣ ମୋ କଥା କିଛି ଶୁଣିଲେନି। କବୀର କଥାରେ ପଡ଼ି
ତାକୁ ପୁଣି ରଖିରି ଦେଲେ। କବୀରକୁ ମଧ ନିଜ ମଲ୍‌ରେ ବଡ଼ ପଦବୀରେ ରଖିଲେ।
ଘରେ ନାଗନାଗୁଣୀଙ୍କୁ ପାଳିଲେ। ବେଳହୁଁ ସାବଧାନ ହୋଇଥିଲେ ଆପଣଙ୍କର ଏ
ଅବସ୍ଥା ହୋଇନଥାନ୍ତା।"

ସୁବୋଧବାବୁ ଶ୍ରୀକାନ୍ତଙ୍କ କାନ୍ଧରେ ଢଳିପଡ଼ିଲେ। ତାଙ୍କର ବ୍ଲଡ଼ପ୍ରେସର ହଠାତ୍
ବଢ଼ିଯାଇଥିଲା। ଶ୍ରୀକାନ୍ତ ସୁବୋଧବାବୁଙ୍କୁ ତୁରନ୍ତ ହସ୍ପିଟାଲକୁ ନେଇଗଲା।
ରାଜୀବଲୋଚନ ସଙ୍ଗେ ସଙ୍ଗେ କବିର ଓ ସୋନିଆଙ୍କ ବିରୋଧରେ ଲୁକ୍‌ଆଉଟ୍
ନୋଟିସ ଜାରି କରି ଭୁବନେଶ୍ୱର ଏୟାରପୋର୍ଟ ଦିଗରେ ଜିପ୍ ନେଇ ବାହାରିଗଲେ।

ରାସ୍ତାରେ ଭାବୁଥିଲେ ପ୍ରତାରଣାର ସମୟରେ ସୁବୋଧବାବୁ ସମୟର ସ୍ୱର
ଶୁଣିପାରିଲେ ନାହିଁ ଅଥଚ କବୀର ଭଳି ହିତ ଶତ୍ରୁର ମଧୁର ଛଳନାକୁ ବିଶ୍ୱାସ କଲେ।
ତେଣୁ ଏବେ ସ୍ୱାସ୍ଥ୍ୟ ହରାଇଲେ ଏବଂ ସମ୍ପତ୍ତି ହରାଇଲେ। ତାଙ୍କଭଳି ଲୋକ ବ୍ୟବସାୟ
କରିବାର ନଥିଲା। ଏ ଯୁଗରେ କବୀର ଓ ସୋନିଆମାନଙ୍କୁ ଧରିବା ସହଜସାଧ୍ୟ
ନୁହେଁ।

ବିଷଣ୍ଣ ବିଜୟୀ

ସେମାନେ ଖୁବ୍ ଅନ୍ତରଙ୍ଗ ସାଙ୍ଗ– ବରୁଣ, ସୁନୀଲ, ଅଙ୍କିତ ଏବଂ ଏକଲବ୍ୟ ।

ବରୁଣ ଆଣ୍ଡି ଏଣ୍ଡରଗ୍ରେନର୍, ସୁନୀଲ ଆର୍କିଟେକ୍, ଅଙ୍କିତ ଏୟାରଫୋର୍ସରେ କମାଣ୍ଡିଂ ଅଫିସର ଏବଂ ଏକଲବ୍ୟ କାର୍ଡିଓଲୋଜିଷ୍ଟ । ଚାରିବର୍ଷ ଆଗରୁ କେହି କାହାକୁ ଚିହ୍ନି ନଥିଲେ । ଭୁବନେଶ୍ୱର ଗଲ୍ଫ କୋର୍ସରେ ଚିହ୍ନା ପରିଚୟ । ବହୁତ ଦିନରୁ ସେମାନେ ଗଲ୍ଫ କ୍ଲବ୍ର ମେମ୍ବର । ମାତ୍ର ଗଲ୍ଫ ଖେଳିବା କଥା କେବେ ଭାବିନଥିଲେ । ଜାନୁଆରୀ ମାସର ଏକ ଶୀତୁଆ ସକାଳରେ ସେମାନଙ୍କର ଗଲ୍ଫ ଖେଳ ଶିଖିବା ଆରମ୍ଭ ହୁଏ । ପ୍ରତ୍ୟେକ ଗଲ୍ଫ କ୍ଲବରେ ମେନ୍ ଗଲ୍ଫ କୋର୍ସ ଏବଂ ପ୍ରାକ୍ଟିସ୍ ରେଞ୍ଜ ସ୍ୱତନ୍ତ୍ର ଭାବରେ ଥାଏ । ସେମାନେ ପ୍ରଥମେ ପ୍ରାକ୍ଟିସ୍ ରେଞ୍ଜକୁ ଯାଇ ଗଲ୍ଫ ସ୍ୱିଙ୍ଗ ଶିଖିଲେ । ପ୍ରଥମେ ପ୍ରଥମେ ବଲ ମାରିବାବେଳେ ଛୋଟିଆ ଗଲ୍ଫ ବଲ୍ ମୋଟେ ଲାଗିଲା ନାହିଁ । ଯଦି ବା ଲାଗିଲା ତେବେ କଜଳପାତି ଉଡ଼ିଲା ଭଳିଆ ବାଆଁ ଡାହାଣ କିମ୍ବା ଉପରତଳ ହୋଇ ଲାଗିଲା । ଦୁଇଜଣ ପୋଖତ ଇନ୍ସ୍ଟ୍ରକ୍ଟର ଇସଲାମ୍ ଏବଂ ବିଚିତ୍ରାନନ୍ଦ ସେମାନଙ୍କୁ ଗଲ୍ଫ ସ୍ୱିଙ୍ଗର ସମସ୍ତ ପଦ୍ଧତି ମନଯୋଗ ସହକାରେ ଶିଖାଉଥାଆନ୍ତି । ପରିଣତ ବୟସରେ କୌଣସି ଖେଳ ଶିଖିବାକୁ

ହେଲେ ସମୟ ତ ଲାଗିବ। କିଛିଦିନ ପ୍ରାକ୍ଟିସ୍ ଚାଲିଲା। ପ୍ରାକ୍ଟିସ୍ କଲାବେଳେ ଅଙ୍କିତ୍ ଏବଂ ବରୁଣଙ୍କ ଭିତରେ ପରିଚୟ ହେବା ପରେ ଘନିଷ୍ଟତା ବଢ଼ିଲା। କେମିତି ଜଲ୍‌ଦି ଶିଖିସାରି ମେନ୍ ଗଲ୍‌ଫ କୋର୍ସରେ ଖେଳିବେ ସେଥିପାଇଁ ଦୁଇବନ୍ଧୁ ଅଧିକ ଉତ୍ସୁକ ଥିଲେ। ନୂଆ ଖେଳାଳିମାନେ ପ୍ରାୟତଃ ରୁଧିମାସ ପ୍ରାକ୍ଟିସ୍ କଲାପରେ ଯାଇ ମେନ୍ ଗଲ୍‌ଫ କୋର୍ସରେ ଖେଳିପାରନ୍ତି। କାରଣ ନୂଆ ଖେଳାଳିଙ୍କର ବଲ ବାଁ ଡାହାଣ ଯାଇ ଅନ୍ୟ ଖେଳାଳିଙ୍କୁ କ୍ଷତ ବିକ୍ଷତ କରିବାର ସମ୍ଭାବନା ଥାଏ। ହିସାବ ଅନୁସାରେ ଗଲ୍‌ଫ କୋର୍ସରେ ଗଲ୍‌ଫ ବଲ ବାଜି ଯେତେ ଖେଳାଳି ମରନ୍ତି– ସେତିକି ଲୋକ ଉଡ଼ାଜାହାଜ ଦୁର୍ଘଟଣାରେ ମରନ୍ତି ନାହିଁ। ପଥର ଭଲି ଗଲ୍‌ଫ ବଲ୍‌ଟି ପଚାଶ କିଲୋମିଟର ବେଗରେ ଆସି ମୁଣ୍ଡ କିମ୍ବା ଛାତିରେ ବାଜିଲେ ପ୍ରାଣ ରୁଲିଯିବାକୁ କେତେ ସମୟ ବା ଲାଗିବ ? ସବୁ ଖେଳ ଭଲି ଗଲ୍‌ଫ ଖେଳରେ ମଧ ରିସ୍କ ଅଛି। ସାଧାରଣତଃ ଗଲ୍‌ଫ ଖେଳାଳିମାନେ ପଞ୍ଚାଅଶୀ ବର୍ଷ ପର୍ଯ୍ୟନ୍ତ ବଞ୍ଚନ୍ତି। ତା'ର କାରଣ ହେଲା– ଗଲ୍‌ଫ ଖେଳରେ ସାଙ୍ଗସାଥୀ ଗୁଲିଖଟି ସାଙ୍ଗରେ ଦୁଇଘଣ୍ଟାରେ ପାଞ୍ଚ କିଲୋମିଟର ରୁଲିବାକୁ ହୋଇଥାଏ। ତା' ସହିତ ସବୁଜ ଘାସ, ଗଛପତ୍ର, ଫ୍ରେସ୍ ଏୟାରରେ ସମୟ କାଟିବାର କିଛି ସୁଫଳ ତ ମିଳିବ ହିଁ।

ବରୁଣ ଏବଂ ଅଙ୍କିତ୍ ପ୍ରାକ୍ଟିସ୍ କରିବା ସମୟରେ ଆଉଜଣେ ଯୁବକ ଆସି ସେମାନଙ୍କ ସହ ଯୋଗ ଦିଅନ୍ତି। ଧୀର ସ୍ଥିର ସ୍ୱଭାବର ସ୍ୱଳ୍ପଭାଷୀ ଯୁବକ ଏକଲବ୍ୟ, ଆପୋଲୋ ହସ୍ପିଟାଲରେ ହାର୍ଟ ଡକ୍ଟର। ଖୁବ୍‌ଶୀଘ୍ର ଗଲ୍‌ଫ ସ୍ୱିଙ୍ଗ ଶିଖିଗଲେ। ଇସ୍‌ଲାମ୍ ମାଷ୍ଟର ତାଙ୍କୁ ବହୁତ୍ ପ୍ରଶଂସା କଲେ। ଅଙ୍କିତ୍ ଏବଂ ବରୁଣ ଟିକିଏ ଈର୍ଷାନ୍ୱିତ ହେଲେ। ମାତ୍ର ଏକଲବ୍ୟର ପ୍ରଭାବଶାଳୀ ବ୍ୟକ୍ତିତ୍ୱ ଯୋଗୁଁ ଏ ଦୁହେଁ ଖୁବ୍‌ଶୀଘ୍ର ତାଙ୍କର ବନ୍ଧୁ ହୋଇଗଲେ। ଦୁଇମାସ ମଧରେ ସମସ୍ତେ ଭଲ ଖେଳାଳି ସ୍ତରକୁ ଆସିଗଲେ। ସେମାନଙ୍କୁ ମେନ୍ ଗଲ୍‌ଫ କୋର୍ସତେ ଖେଳିବା ପାଇଁ ଅନୁମତି ମିଳିଗଲା।

ପ୍ରଥମ ଦିନ ସେମାନେ ଯାଇ ମେନ୍‌କୋର୍ସରେ ଖେଳ ଆରମ୍ଭ କଲେ। ସେଠାରେ ସେମାନଙ୍କର ଦେଖାହୁଏ ସୁନୀଲଙ୍କ ସହିତ। ସୁନୀଲଙ୍କର ଗଲ୍‌ଫ ଖେଳରେ ବାର ବର୍ଷର ଅଭିଜ୍ଞତା। ସେ ଆମେରିକାରେ ଥିବାବେଳେ ଗଲ୍‌ଫ ଶିଖିଥିଲେ। ତେଣୁ ସେ ନୂଆ ତିନିଜଣଙ୍କୁ ଗଲ୍‌ଫ କୋର୍ସରେ ମ୍ୟାନର୍ସ, ଏଟିକେଟ୍‌ସ ଏବଂ ରୁଲ୍‌ସ ସମ୍ପର୍କରେ ବୁଝାଇଲେ। ସେ କହିଲେ ଯେ, ଗଲ୍‌ଫ ହେଉଛି ଗୋଟିଏ ଜେଣ୍ଟିଲ୍‌ମ୍ୟାନ୍‌ର ଖେଳ। ଦେଖ୍‌ରଖିହିଁ ସବୁ ନିୟମମାନି ଖେଳିବାକୁ ପଡ଼ିବ। ମ୍ୟାନର୍ସରେ ସାମାନ୍ୟ ଭୁଲ୍ ହେଲେ ପୁରୁଣା ଖେଳାଳିମାନେ ନାକଟେକି ଦେବେ। ତେଣୁ ଗଲ୍‌ଫ କୋର୍ସର ମୋଟୋ ହେଲା 'ଆଲୋ ସଖ୍ୟ ଆପଣା ମହତ ଆପେରଖ୍।' ଗଲ୍‌ଫ ଏକା ମଧ ଖେଳି ହେବ

କିମ୍ବା ଏକା ସାଙ୍ଗରେ ଚାରିଜଣ ମିଶି ଖେଳିପାରିବେ। ତେଣୁ ଏହି ଚାରିଜଣ ବନ୍ଧୁ ମିଶି ଗୋଟିଏ ଛୋଟ ଗ୍ରୁପ୍ କରିଦେଲେ। ଗ୍ରୁପ୍‌ର ନାଁ ମଧ୍ୟ କରିଦେଲେ ଭାଇଙ୍କ ଗ୍ରୁପ୍। ଭାଇଙ୍କ ଗ୍ରୁପ୍‌ର ଗୋଟିଏ ଲୋଗୋ ଡିଜାଇନ୍ କରି ଗେଞ୍ଜିରେ ପ୍ରିଣ୍ଟ କରିଦେଲେ ଏବଂ ସେହି ଗେଞ୍ଜି ପିନ୍ଧି ଗଲ୍‌ଫ ଖେଳିଲେ। ଅନ୍ୟମାନେ ଏମାନଙ୍କର ହାବଭାବ ଦେଖି ଖୁବ୍ ଖୁସି। ଭାଇଙ୍କ ଗ୍ରୁପ୍‌ର ଖେଳାଳିମାନେ ସବୁବେଳେ ଭଲ ଖେଳୁଥାନ୍ତି। ତେଣୁ ଅନ୍ୟମାନେ ଭାଇଙ୍କ ଗ୍ରୁପ୍‌କୁ ପ୍ରଶଂସା କରୁଥାନ୍ତି। ଗଲ୍‌ଫ ଗୋଟିଏ ଗମ୍ଭୀର ଏବଂ ଦୁଃଖୀ ଖେଳ ମଧ୍ୟ। ଦୁଃଖର କାରଣ ହେଲା କାମନା। ଗଲ୍‌ଫ ଖେଳରେ ଖେଳାଳି ଅଧିକ ଆଶାବାଦୀ ହୋଇଯାଏ। ଖେଳାଳି ଚାହେଁ କେମିତି ଅଳ୍ପ ଷ୍ଟ୍ରୋକ୍‌ରେ ଖେଳ ଶେଷ କରିଦେବ। ଗଲ୍‌ଫ ଖେଳରେ ସମସ୍ତେ ନିଜ ବଲ୍‌କୁ ମାରି ଖେଳନ୍ତି। ଖେଳ ଆରମ୍ଭ ହୁଏ ଟି ଅଫ୍ ଜାଗାରୁ। ୩୦୦ କିମ୍ବା ୪୦୦ ମିଟର ଦୂରରେ ଗୋଟିଏ ଛୋଟ ଗାତ ଥାଏ। ଯେମିତି ସମୁଦ୍ର କୂଳରେ କଙ୍କଡ଼ା ବୁଲୁଥାଏ ଏବଂ ଶତ୍ରୁ ଆସିଲେ ଦୌଡ଼ିଯାଇ ଗୋଟିଏ ଛୋଟିଆ ଗାତରେ ପଶିଯାଏ, ସେହିପରି ଗଲ୍‌ଫ ଖେଳରେ ବଲ୍ ମାରି ଗୋଟିଏ ନିର୍ଦ୍ଦିଷ୍ଟ ଛୋଟିଆ ଗାତରେ ପକାଇବାକୁ ପଡ଼େ। ବିଶେଷତଃ ପାଞ୍ଚଟି କିମ୍ବା ଛଅଟି ଷ୍ଟ୍ରୋକ୍‌ରେ ବଲ୍‌ଟିକୁ ଗାତ ଭିତରେ ପହଞ୍ଚାଇବାକୁ ପଡ଼ିଥାଏ। ଯଦି ବଲ୍‌ରେ ଠିକ୍ ଭାବରେ ମାଡ଼ ନ ଲାଗେ ତେବେ ବଲ୍ ଯାଇ ବଣ, ଜଙ୍ଗଲ, ପାଣି କିମ୍ବା ବାଲି ବଙ୍କର ମଧ୍ୟରେ ପଡ଼ିପାରେ। ଜାଣିଶୁଣି ଗଲ୍‌ଫ କୋର୍ସରେ ବଣବୁଦା, ପାଣିଟାଙ୍କି ବାଲି ବଙ୍କର ଇତ୍ୟାଦି କରାଯାଇଥାଏ। ଭିଡିଓଗେମ୍‌ରେ ଯେମିତି ଜଣେ ସୈନିକ ସବୁକିଛି ବାଧାବିଘ୍ନ ପାରି ହୋଇଯାଇ ସାମ୍ଭାବ୍ୟ ଯାଗାରେ ପହଞ୍ଚିଥାଏ, ସେମିତି ଗଲ୍‌ଫ କୋର୍ସରେ ଖେଳାଳି ମାପିଚୁପି ବଲ୍‌କୁ ଠିକ୍ ଠାକ୍ ମାରି ଗ୍ରୀନ୍‌ରେ ପହଞ୍ଚାଇଦିଏ। ଗ୍ରୀନ୍‌ର ମଝି ଯାଗାରେ ଛୋଟିଆ ଗାତଟିଏ ଥାଏ, ଗାତ ଉପରେ ପତାକାଟିଏ ଲାଗିଥାଏ। ସେହି ପତାକାକୁ ଲକ୍ଷ୍ୟକରି ବଲ୍ ଖେଳାଯାଏ।

ଗଲ୍‌ଫ ଖେଳରେ ମୂଳକଥା ହେଲା ଲକ୍ଷ୍ୟଧାର୍ଯ୍ୟ। କେତେ ଜୋର୍‌ରେ ମାରିବାକୁ ହେବ ଅନ୍ଦାଜ କରି ଠିକ୍ କରିବାକୁ ପଡ଼େ। ଦୂରତାକୁ ଦେଖି ୫, ୬ କିମ୍ବା ୮, ୯ ଆଇରନ୍ କ୍ଲବ୍‌ରେ ମାରିବାକୁ ହେବ ସେ କଥା ହିସାବ କରିବାକୁ ହୁଏ। ଜଣେ ପିଲା ଯାହାକୁ କ୍ୟାଡ଼ କୁହାଯାଏ ସେ ସାଙ୍ଗରେ ବେଠିଆ ଭଲିଆ ବ୍ୟାଗ୍‌କୁ ଟାଣିଟାଣି ନେଉଥାଏ। ଅନେକ ସମୟରେ କ୍ୟାଡ଼ିମାନେ ପୋଖତ ଖେଳାଳି ଥାଆନ୍ତି ଏବଂ ଗଲ୍‌ଫ କୋର୍ସରେ ସେମାନେ ହିଁ ଖେଳାଳିକୁ ଖେଳ ଶିଖାନ୍ତି। ଖରାପ ଖେଳିଲେ କ୍ୟାଡ଼ି ହିଁ କ'ଣ ଭୁଲ ହେଲା କହେ ଏବଂ କମେଣ୍ଟ ମଧ୍ୟ ଦିଏ – "ସାର୍ ଆଉ ଟିକିଏ ପ୍ରାକ୍ଟିସ୍ କରନ୍ତୁ, ବଲ୍ ଉପରେ ନଜର ରଖନ୍ତୁ, ସ୍ୱିଙ୍ଗ୍ ଛୋଟ କରନ୍ତୁ, ଅଣ୍ଟାଟା ଠିକ୍

ବୁଲାନ୍ତୁ – ଇତ୍ୟାଦି ଇତ୍ୟାଦି ।" ଖରାପ ସ୍ୱିଙ୍ଗ ହେଲେ ନିଜକୁ ତ ଖରାପ ଲାଗେ । ତା'
ଉପରେ କ୍ୟାଚ୍‌ର କମେଣ୍ଟ କଟା ଘା'ରେ ଚୁନ ଦେଲା ଭଲି ଲାଗେ । କ୍ୟାଚ ଉପରେ
ଖୁବ୍ ରାଗ ଲାଗେ । ମାତ୍ର ଗଲ୍‌ଫ ଖେଳରେ କାହାକୁ ଦୋଷ ଦେଇହେବ ନାହିଁ ।
କ୍ରିକେଟ୍ ଖେଳ ହୋଇଥିଲେ ବୋଲର୍‌ ସ୍ପିନ୍ କଲା କିୟ ପିଚ୍ ଖରାପ ଥିଲା କହିହେବ ।
ମାତ୍ର ଗଲ୍‌ଫରେ ସେ ସବୁ କିଛି ନାହିଁ । ବଲ୍‌ଟି ଚୁପ୍‌ଚାପ୍ ମାଟିରେ ପଡ଼ିଥିବ – ନିଜେ
ଧୀର ସ୍ଥିର ଚିତ୍ତରେ ଠିକ୍ ଭାବେ ମାରିବାକୁ ହେବ । ଗଲ୍‌ଫ ଖେଳରେ ଦଶଟା ସ୍ଟ୍ରୋକ୍‌ରେ
ଆଠଟା ଖରାପ ଭାବରେ ବାଜିବ । ମାତ୍ର ଦୁଇଟା ବଲ୍‌ରେ ଭଲ କନେକ୍ ହେବ ।
ତେଣୁ ଖୁସିଠାରୁ ଦୁଃଖ ଅଧିକ । ମାତ୍ର ଦିନେ ଦିନେ ୧୦ଟାରୁ ୧୦ଟା ଭଲ କନେକ୍
ହେବ ଓ ଗର୍ବରେ ଛାତି କୁଣ୍ଠେମୋଟ ହୋଇଯିବ । ନିଜକୁ ଲାଗିବ ଯେମିତି ପୃଥ୍‌ବୀର
ଶ୍ରେଷ୍ଠ ଗଲ୍‌ଫ ଖେଳାଲି । ମାତ୍ର ଠିକ୍ ପରଦିନ ୧୦ଟାରୁ ୮ଟା ଖରାପ ବାଜିବ । ତେଣୁ
ଗଲ୍‌ଫ ଖେଳକୁ ଜୀବନ ସହିତ ତୁଳନା କରାଯାଇପାରେ । ଦୁଃଖ ପରେ ସୁଖ ଏବଂ
ସୁଖ ପରେ ଦୁଃଖ ଏମିତି ହିଁ ଚକ ବୁଲିଚାଲିଥିବ । ତେଣୁ ଭଲ ଖେଳିଲେ ଅନ୍ୟକୁ
ହତାଦର କରିବା କଥା ନୁହେଁ କିୟ ଖରାପ ଖେଳିଲେ ମୁହଁ ଶୁଖାଇବା କଥା ନୁହେଁ
ବୋଲି ସେମାନେ ବୁଝିଗଲେଣି ।

ଏ ଭିତରେ ଏକଲବ୍ୟ ଖୁବ୍ ଭଲ ଖେଳିଲେଣି । ତାଙ୍କର ହାଣ୍ଡିକ୍ୟାପ ୨୪ରୁ ଖସି
୧୪ ହୋଇସାରିଲାଣି । ସେ ବଡ଼ ଥଣ୍ଡା ମିଜାଜର ପିଲା । ତାଙ୍କର କ୍ୟାଚି ମଧ ଆହୁରି
ବଢ଼ିଆ । ତେଣୁ ଏକଲବ୍ୟ ଭାଇଙ୍କ ଗ୍ରୁପରେ ଏକ ନମ୍ବର ଆଡ଼କୁ ଅଗ୍ରସର ହେଉଥାନ୍ତି ।
ସୁନୀଲ୍ ମଧ ପନ୍ଦର ବର୍ଷ ଖେଳି ହାଣ୍ଡିକ୍ୟାପ ୧୦, ମାତ୍ର ଏକଲବ୍ୟ ଗୋଟିଏ ବର୍ଷ
ଭିତରେ ୧୪ରେ ପହଞ୍ଚିଥିବାରୁ ସୁନୀଲଙ୍କ ମନ ଭିତରେ ଟିକିଏ ଈର୍ଷା ହେଉଥାଏ ।
ଏକଲବ୍ୟଙ୍କୁ ଦେଖି ବରୁଣ ମଧ ନିଜ ଚେଷ୍ଟାରେ ଲାଗିଥାନ୍ତି । ମାତ୍ର ହାଣ୍ଡିକ୍ୟାପରୁ
୨୦ତଳକୁ ଖସୁନି । ଚତୁର୍ଥ ଖେଳାଲି ହେଲେ ଅଙ୍କିତ । ଚାରି ଦଉଡ଼ି କଟା ମଣିଷ ।
ଧୈର୍ଯ୍ୟ କହିଲେ ମୋଟେ ନାହିଁ । ଭଲ ପତଳା ଫିଗର, ଚାହିଁଲେ ଭଲ ଖେଳିପାରିବେ ।
ମାତ୍ର ସବୁବେଳେ ଖାମ୍‌ଖିଆଲି ଗୁଣ । ହାଣ୍ଡିକ୍ୟାପ ୨୪ରୁ କମୁନି ମାତ୍ର ସେଥିପାଇଁ
ଲଜ୍ଜା କରିବାର ବି ନାହିଁ । କ୍ୟାଚି କିଛି କହିଲେ ଫୋ କରି ହସି କଥାଟାକୁ ଉଡ଼ାଇ
ଦିଅନ୍ତି । ଚେଷ୍ଟାକରୁଛି କାଲି ଭଲ ଖେଳିବି ବୋଲି କୁହନ୍ତି । ଆଜି ଘରେ ଘରଣୀ ଗାଳି
ଦେଇଛନ୍ତି । ତେଣୁ ଖେଳ ଖରାପ ହେଉଛି ବୋଲି ବକ୍ତବ୍ୟ ରଖନ୍ତି । ମାତ୍ର ଦିନେ
ଦିନେ ସେ ଖୁବ୍ ଭଲ ଖେଳନ୍ତି । ସମସ୍ତଙ୍କୁ ତଟସ୍ଥ କରିଦିଅନ୍ତି । ଏପରିକି ସୁନୀଲ୍ ଏବଂ
ଏକଲବ୍ୟ ମଧ ଚମକି ପଡ଼ନ୍ତି । ସମସ୍ତେ କୁହନ୍ତି "ଅଙ୍କିତ ତମର ଭଲ ଖେଳିବାର

ପୋଟେନ୍‌ସିଆଲିଟି ଅଛି। ଟିକେ ଧୀରସ୍ଥିର ମନରେ ଖେଳିଲେ ସିନା ହେବ।" ମାତ୍ର ଅଙ୍କିତ ଖେଳିବା ବେଳେ ଖୁବ୍ ହସନ୍ତି ଏବଂ ଅନ୍ୟମାନଙ୍କୁ ମଧ୍ୟ ହସାନ୍ତି।

ଭାଇଙ୍କ ଗ୍ରୁପ୍‌ରେ ଟିକିଏ ମୋଡ଼ ପରିବର୍ତ୍ତନ ହେଲା। ଗଲ୍‌ଫ କୋର୍ସରେ ଜଣେ ସୁନ୍ଦରୀ ଝିଅ ଆଞ୍ଜନା ଆସି ଖେଳିବାକୁ ଆରମ୍ଭ କଲେ। ଆଞ୍ଜନା ବରୁଣଙ୍କୁ ଆଗରୁ ଜାଣନ୍ତି। ବରୁଣଙ୍କ ମାଧ୍ୟମରେ ଅନ୍ୟମାନେ ମଧ୍ୟ ଆଞ୍ଜନାଙ୍କ ସହ ପରିଚିତ ହେଲେ। କିଛିଦିନ ପରେ ଆଞ୍ଜନା ମଧ୍ୟ ଭାଇଙ୍କ ଗ୍ରୁପ୍‌ରେ ମିଶି ଖେଳିବାକୁ ଇଚ୍ଛା ପ୍ରକାଶ କଲେ। ଗ୍ରୁପ୍‌ରେ ଝିଅମାନେ ଖେଳିଲେ ଖେଳ ଖରାପ ହୋଇଯିବ ବୋଲି ବରୁଣ କହିଲେ। ମାତ୍ର ଅଙ୍କିତ ଏବଂ ସୁନୀଲ୍ କହିଲେ "ଜଣେ ଝିଅ ଖେଳିଲେ ଗ୍ରୁପ୍‌ର ସ୍ଟାଟସ୍ ବଦଳିବ।" ଏ ସବୁ ଶୁଣି ବରୁଣ କହିଲେ ହଉ ଯାହା ତୁମମାନଙ୍କର ଇଚ୍ଛା। ମାତ୍ର ସେ ଅଙ୍କିତ ଏବଂ ସୁନୀଲଙ୍କୁ ଗୋଟିଏ ଭବିଷ୍ୟବାଣୀ ଦେଲେ "ଦେଖ ସବୁଠୁ ଭଲ ଏକଲବ୍ୟ ଖେଳୁଛି। ସେ ଚୁପ୍‌ଚାପ୍ ଏବଂ ଶାନ୍ତଶିଷ୍ଟ ପିଲା। ମନୋଜ କୁମାର ଭଲି ଲମ୍ବା ନାକ। ଆଞ୍ଜନା ତାଙ୍କୁ ଶେଷରେ ଭଲ ପାଇବ ଏବଂ ତୁମେ ଦୁଇଜଣ କଟକ ନଲାରେ ଯାଇ ପଡ଼ିଥିବ।" ଶେଷରେ ଆଞ୍ଜନା ଭାଇଙ୍କ ଗ୍ରୁପ୍‌ରେ ଖେଳିଲେ। ସମସ୍ତେ ଭାଇଙ୍କ ଗ୍ରୁପ୍‌କୁ ଈର୍ଷା କଲେ। ଝିଅକୁ ପ୍ରଭାବିତ କରିବା ପାଇଁ ସମସ୍ତେ ଭଲ ଖେଳିବାକୁ ଚେଷ୍ଟା କଲେ– ଖେଳିଲେ ମଧ୍ୟ। ଏକଲବ୍ୟ ୧୦/୧୨ ହାଣ୍ଡିକ୍ୟାପ୍‌ରେ ଖେଳିବାକୁ ଲାଗିଲେ। ବରୁଣ ଯେମିତି କହୁଥିଲେ ସେମିତି ହେଲା। ଆଞ୍ଜନା ଟିକିଏ ଏକଲବ୍ୟ ଆଡ଼କୁ ଢଳିଲେଣି। ସୁନୀଲ ଯେତେ ଭଲ ଖେଳିଲେ ମଧ୍ୟ ଆଞ୍ଜନାଙ୍କ ମନକୁ ଛୁଇଁ ପାରୁ ନଥିଲେ। ଅଙ୍କିତ ମଧ୍ୟ ଚେଷ୍ଟାରେ ଥିଲେ। କିନ୍ତୁ ଏକଲବ୍ୟ ତୁଳନାରେ ଖୁବ୍ ପଛରେ ଥିଲେ। ଆଞ୍ଜନାଙ୍କ ଅନୁପସ୍ଥିତିରେ ସମସ୍ତେ କୁହନ୍ତି "ଚାଲ – ଏକଲବ୍ୟର ଆଙ୍ଗୁଠି ମାଗିନେବା। ତା'ର ଖେଳ ଖରାପ ହେଲେ ଅଙ୍କିତଙ୍କୁ ଟିକିଏ ଚାନ୍ସ ମିଳିବ। ଅବଶ୍ୟ କେତେବେଳେ କେମିତି ଆଞ୍ଜନା ଅଙ୍କିତଙ୍କୁ ପ୍ରଶଂସା କରନ୍ତି, ଆଉ ସେଥିରେ ଅଙ୍କିତ ସମସ୍ତଙ୍କ ପାଇଁ ବିୟର ମଗାଇ ଦିଅନ୍ତି।"

ବର୍ଷ ଶେଷର ଡିସେମ୍ବର ମାସ। ଏତିକିବେଳେ ଗଲ୍‌ଫ ଟୁର୍ଣ୍ଣାମେଣ୍ଟର ସମୟ। କର୍ପୋରେଟ୍ ଟୁର୍ଣ୍ଣାମେଣ୍ଟ, ଅଡ଼ି ଟୁର୍ଣ୍ଣାମେଣ୍ଟ, ହୋଇନ୍ ଓ୍ୱାନ୍ ଟୁର୍ଣ୍ଣାମେଣ୍ଟ ଇତ୍ୟାଦି ଇତ୍ୟାଦି। କର୍ପୋରେଟ୍ ଟୁର୍ଣ୍ଣାମେଣ୍ଟରେ ଭାଇକିଙ୍ଗ ମଧ୍ୟ ନାମ ଲେଖାଇଥାଏ। ଗ୍ରୁପ୍ ସିଲେକ୍ସନ୍‌ରେ ଏକଲବ୍ୟ, ଅଙ୍କିତ, ଆଲବର୍ଟ ଟିର୍କୀ ଏବଂ ବରୁଣ ଗୋଟିଏ ଗ୍ରୁପ୍‌ରେ ଥାଆନ୍ତି। ୨୫ ଡିସେମ୍ବରର ଶୀତ ସକାଳ ଟୁର୍ଣ୍ଣାମେଣ୍ଟରେ ୨୬ଜଣ ପୋଖତ ଖେଳାଳି ଭାଗ ନେଇଥାନ୍ତି। ସମସ୍ତେ ଭଲ ଡ୍ରେସ୍‌ରେ ଆସିଥାନ୍ତି। ସକାଳ ୭ଟାରେ ଖେଳ ଆରମ୍ଭ ହେଲା। ଆଞ୍ଜନା ମଧ୍ୟ ଆସିଥାନ୍ତି ଭାଇଙ୍କ ଗ୍ରୁପ୍‌କୁ ଚିଅର୍‌ଅପ୍ କରିବା ପାଇଁ।

ଆଲବର୍ଟ ଟିକ୍ନୀ ଜଣେ ପ୍ରଫେସନାଲ ଖେଳାଳି। ଅନେକ ଚାମ୍ପିଅନ୍‌ସିପ୍ ଟ୍ରଫି ନେଇଛନ୍ତି। ଏଥର ମଧ ନେବାର ସମ୍ଭାବନା ଅଛି। ତେଣୁ ବରୁଣ, ଅଙ୍କିତ ଏବଂ ଏକଲବ୍ୟ ଟିକିଏ ସିରିୟସ୍ ଥାଆନ୍ତି। ଖେଳ ଆରମ୍ଭରେ ଆଲବର୍ଟ ଏବଂ ଏକଲବ୍ୟ ଖୁବ୍ ଭଲ ଖେଳୁଥିଲେ। ସମସ୍ତେ ପାଖାପାଖି ସ୍କୋର୍‌ରେ ଥିଲେ। ଦେଖାଗଲା ଯେ ଅଙ୍କିତ ମଧ ଭଲ ଖେଳିବାକୁ ଆରମ୍ଭ କରିଛନ୍ତି। କାଳିଦାସଙ୍କ କଣ୍ଠରେ ସରସ୍ୱତୀ ବିଦ୍ୟେକଲା ଭଲି ଅଙ୍କିତଙ୍କ ହାତରେ ବାବା ପର୍ଶୁରାମ ଉଭାହେବା ଭଲି ମନେହେଲା। ବରୁଣଙ୍କ ସାଙ୍ଗରେ ଆଜ୍ନା ଚାଲୁଥାନ୍ତି। ବରୁଣଙ୍କ ଖେଳ ଭଲ ହେଉ ନଥାଏ। ସେ ଟିକିଏ ଡିପ୍ରେସନ୍‌କୁ ଚାଲିଗଲେ। ତେଣୁ ଆଜ୍ନା ଏକଲବ୍ୟଙ୍କ ସହିତ ଚାଲିବାକୁ ଲାଗିଲେ। ୯ ହୋଲ ଖେଳିସାରିବା ପରେ ସମସ୍ତେ ବ୍ରେକ୍‌ଫାଷ୍ଟ କଲେ। ତା'ପରେ ଆଉ ୯ଟି ହୋଲ ଖେଳିବାର ଅଛି। ଏତିକିବେଳକୁ ଜଣାପଡିଲା ଯେ ଖେଳର ବଲ କଷାକଷି ଚାଲିଛି ଅଙ୍କିତ, ଏକଲବ୍ୟ ଏବଂ ଆଲବର୍ଟଙ୍କ ମଧ୍ୟରେ। ଟ୍ରଫି ପାଇବେ ତ ଏହି ତିନିଜଣଙ୍କ ମଧ୍ୟରୁ ଜଣେ ପାଇବେ। ୧୦ନମ୍ବର ହୋଲୁରୁ ୧୫ନମ୍ବର ହୋଲ ପର୍ଯ୍ୟନ୍ତ ଆଲବର୍ଟ ଖୁବ୍ ଭଲ ଖେଳିଲେ। ସେ ଜଣେ ଚାମ୍ପିଅନ ଭଲି ଖେଳୁଥାନ୍ତି। ଏକଲବ୍ୟ ମଧ ଭଲ ଖେଳୁଥାନ୍ତି। ଅଙ୍କିତ ଚେଷ୍ଟାକରି ପାଖାପାଖି ରହୁଥାନ୍ତି। ଆଜ୍ନା ଏକଲବ୍ୟଙ୍କୁ ଅଧିକ ସପୋର୍ଟ କଲେ ମଧ ମଝିରେ ମଝିରେ ଅଙ୍କିତଙ୍କୁ ସାନ୍ତ୍ୱନା ଦେଉଥାନ୍ତି। ୧୫ ନମ୍ବର ଏବଂ ୧୭ନମ୍ବର ହୋଲରେ ଅଙ୍କିତ ଅଚାନକ ଚମକ୍ରାରିତା ଦେଖାଇଲେ। ଅସମ୍ଭବ ଭାବରେ ଭଲ ଖେଳିଲେ ଏବଂ ନମ୍ବର‌ଡ଼ାନ୍‌କୁ ଆସିଗଲେ। ଏଥର ୧୮ନମ୍ବର ହୋଲରେ ଖେଳ ଆରମ୍ଭ ହେଲା। ଏହା ହେଉଛି ଶେଷ ନମ୍ବର ହୋଲ। ଏଥିରେ କିଏ ଚାମ୍ପିଅନ୍ ହେବ ଜଣାପଡ଼ିବ। ୧୮ନମ୍ବର ହୋଲ ପାଇଁ ଟି ଅଫ୍ ହେଲା। ଅଙ୍କିତଙ୍କର ସୁନ୍ଦର ଟି ଅଫ୍ ହେଲା, ଏକଲବ୍ୟଙ୍କର ମଧ ଭଲ ହେଲା। ମାତ୍ର ଆଲବର୍ଟଙ୍କର ବଲ ଯାଇ ପାଣିରେ ପଡ଼ିଲା। ତେଣୁ ବର୍ତ୍ତମାନ ଏକଲବ୍ୟ ଏବଂ ଅଙ୍କିତଙ୍କ ମଧ୍ୟରେ କମ୍ପିଟିସନ। ଆଜ୍ନା ବର୍ତ୍ତମାନ ଦୋ ଦୋ ପାଞ୍ଚ ଅବସ୍ଥାରେ। ସେ ବିଶେଷତଃ ଏକଲବ୍ୟଙ୍କ ପାଖରେ ରହୁଥାନ୍ତି। ଅଙ୍କିତଙ୍କ ମନରେ ଟିକିଏ ବ୍ୟଥା ହେଉଥାଏ। ଏତେ ଭଲ ଖେଳି ମଧ କିଛି ଲାଭ ନାହିଁ। ଏହା ଭିତରେ ଆଲବର୍ଟ ଗୋଟିଏ ଭଲ ସ୍କୋକ୍ ମାରି ଆସି ଗ୍ରୀନ୍‌ରେ ପହଞ୍ଚିଗଲେ। ବର୍ତ୍ତମାନ ୪ଟି ସ୍କୋକ୍‌ରେ ଆଲବର୍ଟ, ଅଙ୍କିତ ୩ଟି ସ୍କୋକ୍‌ରେ ଏବଂ ଏକଲବ୍ୟ ମଧ ୩ଟି ସ୍କୋକ୍‌ରେ ଅଛନ୍ତି। ଯିଏ ଦୁଇଟି କିୟା ତା'ଠାରୁ କମ୍ ସ୍କୋକ୍‌ରେ ଗାତରେ ପକାଇବ ସେ ଚାମ୍ପିଅନ୍ ହେବ। ୧୦ଲକ୍ଷ ଟଙ୍କାର ପ୍ରାଇଜ୍। ଏକଲବ୍ୟ ୭ଟି ସ୍କୋକ୍‌ରେ ଗେମ୍ ସାରିଲେ, ଆଲବର୍ଟ ୬ଟି ସ୍କୋକ୍‌ରେ ସାରିଲେ। ଏବେ ଅଙ୍କିତ ଦୁଇଟି ସ୍କୋକ୍‌ରେ ସାରିଲେ ଚାମ୍ପିଅନ୍ ହେବେ। ଅଙ୍କିତ ଖୁବ୍ ସୁନ୍ଦର

ସଟ୍ ମାରି ଚତୁର୍ଥ ଷ୍ଟ୍ରୋକ୍‌ରେ ଗାତ ପାଖରେ ଆସି ପହଞ୍ଚିଗଲେ। ସମସ୍ତେ ତାଲିମାରି ତାଙ୍କୁ ଉତ୍ସାହିତ କରୁଥାନ୍ତି। ପଞ୍ଚମ ଷ୍ଟ୍ରୋକ୍‌ରେ ନିଜେ ଜିତିବେ ଏବଂ ୧୦ଲକ୍ଷ ଟଙ୍କା ନେବେ। ଅଙ୍କିତଙ୍କ ମୁହଁରେ ଅଚାନକ ଗମ୍ଭୀରତା ଆସିଗଲା। ପଞ୍ଚମରେ ସେ ମାରିବାକୁ ଯାଇ ହୋଲ୍‌ଠାରୁ ଦୂରେଇଗଲେ। ଆରେ ଏମିତି କ'ଣ କଲେ ବୋଲି ଆଜ୍ଞାନା ପାଟି କରୁଥାନ୍ତି। ଷଷ୍ଠରେ ପଟ୍ କର – ତା'ହେଲେ ଜଏଣ୍ଟ ଚାମ୍ପିଅନ୍ ହେବ। ମାତ୍ର ଏଥର ମଧ ସେ ହୋଲ୍ ମିସ୍ କଲେ ଏବଂ ଅଷ୍ଟମରେ ପଟ୍ କଲେ। ଆଲବର୍ଟ ଚାମ୍ପିଅନ୍ ହେଲେ, ଏକଲବ୍ୟ ରନର୍ସଟ୍ରଫି। ଏକଲବ୍ୟ ଆସି ଅଙ୍କିତଙ୍କୁ ପଚାରିଲେ କାହିଁକି ଜାଣିଶୁଣି ହାରିଲ? ଭାଇକିଂର ନାଁ ଉଜ୍ଜ୍ୱଳ ହୋଇଥାନ୍ତା। ଅଙ୍କିତଙ୍କ ଆଖିରେ ଟିକିଏ ଲୁହ ଜକେଇ ଆସୁଥାଏ ଏବଂ କହିଲେ "ଯଦି ଜିତିବାରେ ସବୁକିଛି ମିଳୁଥାନ୍ତା – ତେବେ ମହୁମାଛି ମହୁ ନିଜେ ପିଉଥାନ୍ତା। ଆଲବର୍ଟ ତ ଚାମ୍ପିଅନ୍ – ତାଙ୍କର ହାଣ୍ଡିକ୍ୟାପ୍ ୧ ଏବଂ ମୋର ୨୪।"

ଖେଳ ସରିଲା, କକ୍‌ଟେଲ୍ ପାର୍ଟି ଆରମ୍ଭ ହେଲା। ଟ୍ରଫି ଆନାଉନ୍ ସେଷରେ – ଆଲବର୍ଟଙ୍କ ନାମ ଘୋଷଣା କରାଗଲା। ଆଲବର୍ଟ ଟ୍ରଫି ନେଇ ବୁଲୁଥିଲେ। ଲାଗୁଥିଲା ଯେମିତି କାହାକୁ ଖୋଜୁଛନ୍ତି। ହଠାତ୍ ଆଜ୍ଞାନାକୁ ଦେଖିଲେ – ସେ ମଧ କାହାକୁ ଖୋଜୁଥିଲେ।

BLACK EAGLE BOOKS

www.blackeaglebooks.org
info@blackeaglebooks.org

Black Eagle Books, an independent publisher, was founded as
a nonprofit organization in April, 2019. It is our mission to
connect and engage the Indian diaspora and the world at large
with the best of works of world literature published on a
collaborative platform, with special emphasis on
foregrounding Contemporary Classics and New Writing.

Writing Selves
in Diaspora

Series Editor
Sonia Ryang, University of Iowa

New Asian Anthropology offers a forum for theoretical debate and empirical contributions toward a new anthropology of Asia. Books in the series provide critiques of existing studies and frameworks, and draw on radically new ethnographic data. Proposed subject matter ranges from fieldwork methodology to epistemology to fresh interpretations of the classics. The geographical area is broadly defined as Asia, including the Middle East, Central Asia, South Asia, Southeast Asia, East Asia, and diasporic Asia. The series provides a forum for dialogue among indigenous Asian and non-Asian anthropologists and other social scientists who address anthropological issues.

Titles in Series:

Writing Selves in Diaspora

Ethnography of Autobiographics of Korean Women in Japan and the United States

Sonia Ryang

LEXINGTON BOOKS

A division of
ROWMAN & LITTLEFIELD PUBLISHERS, INC.
Lanham • Boulder • New York • Toronto • Plymouth, UK

LEXINGTON BOOKS

A division of Rowman & Littlefield Publishers, Inc.
A wholly owned subsidiary of The Rowman & Littlefield Publishing Group, Inc.
4501 Forbes Boulevard, Suite 200
Lanham, MD 20706

Estover Road
Plymouth PL6 7PY
United Kingdom

British Library Cataloguing in Publication Information Available

Library of Congress Cataloging-in-Publication Data

Ryang, Sonia.
  Writing selves in diaspora : ethnography of autobiographics of Korean women in Japan
and the United States / Sonia Ryang.
    p. cm.
  Includes bibliographical references and index.
  ISBN-13: 978-0-7391-2901-2 (cloth : alk. paper)
  ISBN-10: 0-7391-2901-5 (cloth : alk. paper)
  ISBN-13: 978-0-7391-2902-9 (pbk. : alk. paper)
  ISBN-10: 0-7391-2902-3 (pbk. : alk. paper)
  eISBN-13: 978-0-7391-3028-5
  eISBN-10: 0-7391-3028-5
  1. Koreans—Japan. 2. Koreans—United States. I. Title. DS832.7.K6R938 2008
  305.48'8957052—dc22   2008020197

Printed in the United States of America

In memory of Miriam Silverberg (1951–2008)

Contents

Preface and Acknowledgments

More than a decade has passed since the publication of my first book on Koreans in Japan, *North Koreans in Japan: Language, Ideology, and Identity* (Westview 1997). During the interim period, the world has changed—and so have I. A reconfiguration has taken place in the way I relate to my field, both in relation to the immediate site of ethnographic fieldwork and the broader context of the academic discipline of social anthropology. Above all, however, it is my people (if I may describe them thus)—the people that I have closely worked with as an anthropologist for nearly two decades—who are different today. They are survivors, having risen to the enormous challenge of retaining and/or regaining their dignity in a world where only those with clear national affiliations are deemed truly human. Many of my people, Koreans in diaspora, have precarious or ambivalent national affiliations with a number of nation-states, including, for example, the two Koreas, Japan, and the U.S. As such, they continue to face the question of where to locate the self in a world in which the boundaries of nation-states are incessantly reinforced in the name of globalization. This process continues to be played out in a variety of contexts. In the case of the so-called global war against terror, attempts are made to outlaw certain national states and curtail domestic political freedoms in the name of security. In other cases, such boundaries may assert themselves in economic contexts, for example in debates surrounding the relationship between immigrant labor and trade deficits, reinforcing structures that intensify levels of exploitation of undocumented workers through human trafficking. The result is what we have in the world today: hatred and suspicion toward non-nationals.

Today, the privilege of national citizenship is the norm, and those unable to identify exclusive allegiance towards one nation-state continue to be faced with an ontological crisis. This is the reality for Koreans in diaspora. My earlier work, *North Koreans in Japan,* focused on Koreans in Japan who claimed an ideological association with North Korea despite the fact that no North Korean has ever lived in Japan. In this book, I expand the parameters to encompass Japan, the U.S., and beyond, primarily in response to my discovery of similarities and differences between Koreans, and particularly Korean women, in Japan and the U.S. in their ongoing diasporic lives.

I dedicate this book to the many Korean women in Japan and the US that have inspired and helped me, directly and indirectly, to write this book, through times of joy and suffering. I myself have faced a few personal and professional crises while preparing this book. My friends, Korean and otherwise, were there for me at such times, many becoming the "informants" for this book. As such, this book has been a truly inter-subjective and interactive endeavor; while all the credit it may attract should be directed to the women that helped me produce it, I must accept complete responsibility for any of its faults or shortcomings.

During the final stages in the preparation of this book, my friend and colleague Miriam Silverberg passed on after a long struggle with illness. As the reader will soon see, this book is about human worth and dignity, concepts that Miriam's departure led me to deeply reflect upon. My loving memory for Miriam is carried within this book.

Many individuals helped me in the production of this book. First and foremost, I'd like to acknowledge the eight women whose autobiographic writings appear in this book for their generosity and willingness to be part of this study. Bearing the pseudonyms Anmi, Mina, Risa, Songrae, CR, Yuki, Ryjung, and Jacey, these women and their voices form the core of this book. As the author of this book, I hope to have done justice to their admirable lives. Without their dedication and loyalty, without their inspiring words, and without their immense kindness, this book would not have come into being.

I thank my colleagues in the University of Iowa Department of Anthropology who were participants in the faculty reading group, notably Nanette Barkey, Laura Graham, Adi Hastings, Erica Prussing, and Scott Schnell, and the organizer of the group, Rudi Colloredo-Mansfeld. Their careful reading of parts of my text and constructive comments helped to add force and originality to my work. I also wish to thank The Center for Asian and Pacific Studies, University of Iowa, for allowing me to present the contents of this book at its seminar series, and the colleagues and students in my audience whose input further enhanced the book in many ways.

A portion of the content of chapter 2 "Love and Diaspora: A Romantic Autobiography of a Korean Woman in Japan" was presented in a panel organized by Janet Shibamoto Smith and Cindi Strutz as part of annual meetings of

Association for Asian Studies in April 2006. I thank panel organizers and audience for that session and I am particularly thankful for helpful comments by a discussant for the panel, Nobue Suzuki. I have also presented parts of this book in formal and informal settings at the Universities of Toronto and Sycney. I thank the audiences on those occasions for their attentiveness and interest, and for their suggestions and comments.

I wish to express my gratitude to Patrick Dillon of Lexington Books, whose enthusiasm made the publication of this book possible, and to copy editor Jonathan Caws-Elwitt. I would also like to thank Dr. Donald Cameron, who further refined the text with his excellent copyediting. My endowments from the C. Maxwell and Elizabeth M. Stanley Family and the Korea Foundation also played a crucial role in facilitating the publication of this book. I acknowledge the generosity of the above organizations with deep appreciation.

Last, but most certainly not least, my family deserves special mention: Bradley, Samantha, and Thomas for their endurance, patience, and company. My children, Samantha and Thomas, continue to teach me lessons about the beauty and strength of life itself. This book is written for them, and all those who will grow to make the world a better place.

Introduction

The Sacred Text in the Making

The Korean Diaspora and Autobiographic Writings

> The world is not humane just because it is made by human beings, and it does not become humane just because the human voice sounds in it, but only when it has become the object of discourse.... We humanize what is going on in the world *and in ourselves* only by speaking of it, and in the course of speaking of it we learn to be human.[1]

In the words of Hannah Arendt presented above, we might find the key to understanding why people write about themselves: people experiencing feelings of supreme joy or glory, having perhaps gone through a self-transforming event, but above all, people facing the tremendous challenges and difficulties presented by life. This is especially the case for those who have been displaced and dehumanized, going through the most trying of times which test the limits of humanity: survivors of concentration camps, the victims of slavery, colonialism, and racism, and those exiled and banished from their homes—people in diaspora. Dispersed and displaced, uprooted and homeless people in diaspora have lost their links with their homelands, the homelands where their ancestors were born, where their parents grew up, and where they and their offspring would have raised their families. The lost homeland symbolizes the loss of, say, meaningful life or, indeed, humanity. As such, speaking about it and, in some ways more significantly, writing about it are acts which preserve life by keeping open the window through which the authors can glimpse their lost homes and homelands, and the life contained in them—that is, their precarious humanity. They are, in other words, at once acts of remembrance and mourning. If, as Arendt states, discursivizing is an effort to humanize the horrors and tragedies of life (and here I would include not only the act of speaking the unspeakable but also the act of writing the unwritable), then the autobiography of diaspora is a record of humanity which has been stripped of national affiliation—only the memory of culture, the history of families, and an insecure future in a foreign land remain. Hence the importance of reclaiming the self through writing.

It was George Steiner who evidently recognized the text as the crucial foundation upon which the diasporic Jews could build the imaginary edifice of home. For Jewish people, the existence of the sacred books—"Dead Sea scrolls and priceless biblical papyri"—is a legitimation of their sacred home, and the search for it in its turn is imminently justified precisely because of the textuality of the identity that the books guarantee.[2] But for others in diaspora, especially in modern diasporas (in plural form, as proposed by James Clifford[3]), the situation can be radically different. To begin with, not every people is in possession of a text, which speaks to their common origin, mythically and heroically, and is filled with uplifting sagas of miracles and exodus. For many, myths are still new, memories still raw, diasporic origins still painfully contested; in other words, their sacred texts are not yet written and, if anything, are still in the making. The process of creating diasporic archives begins with writing about one's diasporic world, by humanizing it, as suggested by Arendt.

This book is part of such an endeavor. My attempt to do so relies on a glimpse into the autobiographic reflections of Korean women in diaspora. Through interactions with autobiographic writings of Korean women in Japan and the U.S., I unfold the way their selves are choreographed through both spoken and written discourses combining auto-analysis and auto-interpretation. My method has its origins in anthropology.[4] By this I mean to say that in writing this book, I combine ongoing interlocutions and exchanges with my "informants" and their autobiographic writings, while what anthropologists conventionally call "field data" are located not in the foreground, as is usual practice in ethnography, but in the background of autobiographic texts.[5]

In this book, I place women's writings from diverse diasporic locations at the center of my discussion, and consider the ways in which autobiographic writings and the ontology of diaspora intersect, permeating each other in meaningful ways. As such, this is not so much a study of autobiographies per se as of the act of writing autobiographically. This does not mean that I have come up with a ready-to-use manual for constructing or deconstructing the unified autobiographical subject, such as, for example, the feminine, the displaced, or the Korean. Rather, each chapter contains a transgression of genre, one way or the other, and, therefore, disrupts the view of the autobiography as a coherent, authoritarian, and truthful account of one's life, instead proposing that we see it as a genre full of promiscuous interpenetrations of mixed texualities and realities. Each chapter, therefore, touches upon the notion of the multiple aspects of the autobiographic subject and explores the concept of self as constructed, performed, and lived in diaspora. (See below.)

Before I communicate to the reader what each chapter is about, I must present a brief account of the historical and contemporary background of the Korean diaspora in Japan and the U.S., in order to assist the reader with identifying the location of autobiographic scripts and voices in this book. This will be followed by a discussion of diasporic Korean women's literature, closely informed by autobiographic elements. I elect to focus on two key works: *Yuhi*, the autobiographic work of fiction by the late Lee Yangji, an award-winning Korean female writer in Japan; and the late Theresa Hak Kyung Cha's *Dictee*, now an iconic text of Korean American feminist literature. Looking at them in comparative ways will highlight questions of truthfulness of diasporic locution and authenticity of diasporic identity. This will form the backdrop for the chapters to follow, each of which is based on or informed by selected autobiographic writings by diasporic Korean women in the U.S. and Japan.

THE KOREAN DIASPORA

The existing models of diaspora, in their extreme versions, are divided into what I might call the politico-classical model and the personal-modern model. The first, found for example in the cases of the Jewish and Armenian diasporas, is premised upon ethnic persecution as the cause of eternal dispersal and the loss of homeland. It is characterized by strong connections to the lost home (or homeland), which have been suffered collectively by the dispersed population. This may manifest in forms such as collective memory, myths, nostalgia, a desire to return, organized action toward or commitment to homecoming, efforts to preserve the original culture and mythical heritage, and insistence on difference from the host population. Ongoing ethnic persecution becomes an ontological precondition for diasporic communities.[6] As such, diaspora in this context often takes the form of an organized, political, and group-oriented movement.

The second model is concerned with ontological insecurity and an ongoing crisis of identity, generally associated with modernity and the consequent rise of the reflexive self, but in this case more specifically related to the loss of the original homeland or home (real or imaginary). This loss may be perceived either as a historical event or as an ongoing contemporary experience. In this model, therefore, the person's diasporic self-consciousness and his or her self-designation as a homeless, displaced, and dislocated subject become critical in identifying a diasporic form of life. As such, this model relates to ontological conditions, and presupposes an irreducible diasporic emotion or state of mind carried by individuals as a decisive criterion.

These models are not to be too starkly contrasted: in reality, most diasporas combine elements of both. This combination, however, is not easily discerned.

How do we, for example, justify deeming experiences and existences that are primarily personal as diasporic, when (as according to the first model) the concept supposedly relates to a collective orientation? Can one be diasporic when one has long forgotten about one's ancestral home and does not personally feel persecuted, in spite of one's family having historically experienced the loss of its ancestral homeland and the violent uprooting from one place to another— that is to say, when the person's subjectivity does not register the diasporic consciousness, while historical conditions of diaspora exist on the collective level of the group that the person primarily belongs to?

If the first model relates to the phylogeny of diaspora, the second describes the ontogeny of diaspora. But the two models are not as far apart as they first appear to be, as they are contiguous or consubstantial as far as their relation to home and home*land* is concerned. There are people in diaspora for whom the original exodus is no longer significant. There are people who have been destroyed by their recent exile. Some diasporas are unable to trace their origins in one country, since they originate from various parts of an entire continent that was later divided into several nations. Other diasporas are the result of colonial rule or recent civil wars among postcolonial nations. Yet others may be able to trace the routes of ancestral journeys of dispersion in various parts of the world, due to the multiple experiences of persecution and displacement they have been subjected to over many centuries. Refugees in camps may eventually form diasporic populations. Wars of invasion and conquest may turn original inhabitants into slaves and homeless people in their own lands. The common thread here is that in all these cases, ties to the homeland have been cut off—a process accompanied by varying levels of violence, a process characterized by disaster or catastrophe. If terms such as *immigration* or *transnational migration* include a connotation (even if perhaps only hinted at) of voluntariness, terms such as *exile, refugeedom, banishment*, and *diaspora* do not.

Where is the Korean diaspora located in the above topography? It was toward the end of Korea's last kingdom, under the heavy influence and intervention of foreign powers in the late nineteenth century culminating in colonial rule by the Japanese, that Koreans first moved to faraway lands in large numbers. These included Japan, Manchuria, Russia, North and South America, and the Pacific islands and Southeast Asia during the war. Leaving their homeland in search of survival was a difficult and complex endeavor. During the colonial period, tens of thousands moved to Japan, others to Northeast China and Siberia, yet others to the island of Sakhalin. Their dispersion bore distinctly modern characteristics, accompanied as it was by institutions, elements, possibilities, and forms of life that had not hitherto been part of their lives: wage labor, private ownership of plots of land, and opportunities for receiving formal education on the one hand; and financial debt, the estrangement and dispersal of families, and scattering of cultural assets on the other.

When the Japanese began governing Korea in 1910, Koreans quickly discovered that they did not own the land that they had cultivated for generations. Korean peasants did not traditionally have a notion of individual land-ownership, as all the land under the sky was believed to belong to the royal sovereign. Through the land survey completed by the Japanese Government-General of Korea, most arable land was securely placed in the hands of Japanese colonial authorities, Japanese corporations, and Japanophile Korean landlords. As with all indigenous colonized peoples whose livelihoods have been robbed by colonialists or conquerors, Koreans became landless and penniless in their own land, the land where their ancestors were born and their lineages were established, and in which they had entertained no doubts regarding the permanence of their existence as a people. Their departures were not of a one-time nature, for people who have to leave their homeland cannot usually do so with a firm resolve to either return in future or to permanently remain abroad. They leave, hoping to come back someday, possibly soon; when they do, they are soon forced out again after facing the reality of a deprived and unstable existence upon their return.

Once the Pacific War began in 1941, a great many Koreans were literally forced out of their homes and their homeland. Furthermore, they were hunted down and shipped out as a labor force to various destinations in Japan proper and beyond and as sex slaves for the Japanese military. After the war's end in 1945, their homeland was artificially partitioned into two halves, thereby complicating the conditions of homecoming for Koreans overseas. Subsequently, there was the civil war (1950–1953, the Korean War): millions of refugees moved from North Korea into South Korea, while it remains unclear how many went to North Korea from South Korea as displaced (or even kidnapped) persons.[7]

In all of these places of exile, including the colonial metropolis, the continent far and near, and the partitioned halves of the peninsula itself, new generations were born, made up of individuals who were born as strangers or aliens to the lands which ended up becoming their cultural and practical homes, but not their home*land*. There is a noticeable difference in diasporic ethos between native- and foreign-born generations, although it is ultimately true that neither has been able to achieve the goal of recovering the homeland. In other words, if the first generation set the mold for the phylogeny of the Korean diaspora, it is the foreign-born generations who are confronted with the ontogeny of diaspora. In both cases, the whereabouts of homeland remains an important, unanswered aspect of life.

Koreans only lost their homeland for the thirty-six years of Japanese colonial rule (1910–1945). The postcolonial Korean diaspora was a product of national partition, the civil war that followed, and the eventual tensions of the Cold War. For many, it was too complicated and painful to return to a homeland that was now split in two, and in which each side confronted the other with all-consuming hatred. Today, after sixty years of partition, hostility, and confrontation, Korea is a different place. South Korea is rapidly transforming: after decades of brutal military dictatorship, effectively an extended period of martial law, characterized by the direct, blatant, and violent oppression of dissent, the last decade or so has witnessed a dramatic transformation of its society on various levels. A burgeoning middle class and expanding market economy have developed since the reinstatement of civilian government, and the population has begun to enjoy the possibilities of new forms of social interaction, becoming, so to say, ever so modern—if not Western.[8]

North Korea, behind its strangely anachronistic and surreal behavior, its nepotism, its stagnant economy, its concentration camps, and its famine, nevertheless embodies a version of national identity that can also be characterized as modern. As Arendt notes, "Even the emergence of totalitarian governments is a phenomenon within, not outside, our civilization."[9] North Korea is a society where individuals are directly connected to the sovereign, formerly the Great Leader and today the Dear Leader. As such, the so-called traditional institutions such as kinship, ancestor worship, or community have disappeared, along with religions, meaning that in a peculiar and paradoxical way, it is a society of individualization and individualism, with individuals solely responsible for the inner purity of their loyalty to the leader.[10]

Neither of the two Koreas—as I hope the reader is able to see—is close to the original primordial home of millions of Koreans dispersed around the world today. For Koreans, modernity and diaspora are thus antithetical yet inseparable, as diasporic Koreans have been touched by modernity away from their homeland.

In sum, therefore, the Korean diaspora does not align neatly with either of the two models that I earlier alluded to, but falls somewhere in between. The Korean diaspora traverses colonialism and different types of war—World War II, civil war, and the Cold War—each event resulting in displacement of a different scale and nature. According to one source, there were as of 1995 some 4,938,345 Koreans permanently residing overseas, including 1,661,034 in the U.S. and 659,323 in Japan. The 2000 U.S. Census recorded 1,077,000 Koreans and the 2004 survey, 1.25 million, while 2004 Japanese Ministry of Justice statistics documented 607,419 Koreans registered as aliens in Japan.[11] Most Koreans in Japan do not have Japanese nationality. Considering, as Arendt emphasizes, that status as a national citizen has become a prerequisite for obtaining human rights in the post–World War II world—no longer can bare, naked humans, i.e. humans with no national affiliation and civic status, claim human rights—peculiarities prevailing among Koreans in Japan should merit attention.[12] It will be helpful here to compare the case of Koreans in Japan with that of Koreans in the U.S.

In a most striking coincidence, the years 1952 and 1965 marked profoundly meaningful turning points for Koreans in both Japan and the U.S., although the effects of measures taken in these years were very different for the respective communities. In 1952, with the McCarran-Walter Immigration and Nationality Act, migrant workers, including the majority of Koreans staying in the U.S., were granted U.S. citizenship; in 1952, Koreans in Japan became completely stateless, formally losing the hitherto-ambiguous affiliation with their former colonial master, Japan, which did not recognize either of the two states in Korea (i.e. South Korea and North Korea) as a sovereign nation. In 1965, with the liberalization of U.S. immigration policies, the Korean community in the U.S. expanded enormously in size; in 1965, with the normalization of diplomatic relations between Japan and South Korea, South Korean nationality became available, and this became the prerequisite for obtaining permanent residence in Japan. But unlike U.S. permanent residence, the Japanese counterpart had no potential to be upgraded to full citizenship. The history—especially the post–World War II history—of Koreans in Japan and the U.S. touches upon, in very different yet mutually engaging ways, the notion of what it means to be a human—a bare human being—in a world tightly compartmentalized into nation-states.

There is a fundamental difference, however, that divides Koreans in Japan from those in the U.S.: if the latter are discriminated against and marginalized as less-entitled and less-culturally-assimilated citizens inside the U.S. federal-national polity, the former, with their high degree of acculturation and assimilation to Japanese culture, are not discriminated against inside Japanese national polity; if the latter are treated as second-class citizens, the former are not treated as any kind of citizens whatsoever—or humans, for that matter, as I shall argue subsequently.

It needs to be emphasized that Koreans in the U.S. are an expanding population—for example, the number of Korean-born immigrants from Korea to the U.S. grew by more than 50 percent between 1990 and 2000 (from 568,397 to 864,125), bringing the total number of Koreans in the U.S. up to a little over two million.[13] By way of contrast, rushed repatriation immediately following the war led to a drastic and rapid reduction in the number of Koreans in Japan. From a population of 2.4 million at the end of World War II, numbers have languished between 600,000 and 650,000 ever since around 1946.[14] There are various reasons for this situation, with naturalization ranking highly: currently about ten thousand Koreans every year are naturalized as Japanese.[15] This itself, as the reader may have noticed, illustrates an interesting yet fundamental disparity between Koreans in Japan and Koreans in the U.S. In the U.S., ethnic heritage is at least acknowledged, and one is supposed to be able to identify oneself as a "such-and-such American" while being a U.S. citizen at the same time. By contrast, in Japan, the divide between Japanese and non-Japanese is final and definitive—there is no such category as Korean-Japanese (or any other hyphenated identity involving Japanese) in the customary understanding of ethnic identities. Here, the normative pretension has it that one is either Japanese or non-Japanese in an all-inclusive or all-exclusive way in terms of citizenship, cultural heritage, personal identity, and sometimes blood. The majority of Koreans in Japan today were born in Japan. But due to the *jus sanguinis* principle of the Japanese nationality law, as opposed to the *jus solis* U.S. principle, their birth on Japanese soil does not grant them Japanese citizenship.

In my view, a comparison between these two communities of diasporic Koreans in Japan and the U.S. leads to an important discussion on where the parameters of human rights, the rights that being human is supposed to secure, begin and end. As such, it is a crucial key to understanding what diaspora can ontologically mean in today's world, and for Koreans in particular. Let us refer again to Arendt:

> The declaration of the Rights of Man at the end of the eighteenth century was a turning point in history. It meant nothing more nor less than that from then on Man, and not God's command or the customs of history, should be the source of Law. Independent of the privileges which history had bestowed upon certain strata of society or certain nations, the declaration indicated man's emancipation from all tutelage and announced that he had now come of age.[16]

This famed opening statement of Arendt's "The Perplexities of the Rights of Man" is the point from which I'm going to open my discussion. In Arendt's text, this initial celebratory mood is soon to be replaced with the chilling observation that in fact, and especially during the mid-twentieth century, what were supposed to be the inalienable rights of man were not only alienable but also not even bestowable—unless one was the member of a national polity. Arendt further notes:

> Not only did loss of national rights in all instances entail the loss of human rights; the restoration of human rights, as the recent example of the State of Israel proves, has been achieved so far only through the restoration or the establishment of national rights. The conception of human rights, based upon the as-

sumed existence of a human being as such, broke down at the very moment when those who professed to believe in it were for the first time confronted with people who had indeed lost all other qualities and specific relationships—except that they were still human. The world found nothing sacred in the abstract nakedness of being human.[17]

The year 1952, the year the U.S. occupation of Japan ended with the signing of the San Francisco Treaty between Japan and the U.S., became a turning point in relation to the status of Koreans in Japan as human beings. It was through this treaty that the Japanese people, not the Emperor, regained their sovereign right to self-government. This treaty, characteristically, did not include Korea or Taiwan among its signatory powers, because the national sovereignty of either entity had not been restored in the eyes of the Japanese government. It unilaterally freed Korea and Taiwan from Japan's colonial government, while simultaneously freeing Japan from any responsibility for postcolonial settlement for the peoples of the former colonies that stayed on in Japan. What this meant was that, with sovereignty returning to the Japanese— and Japanese only—former colonial subjects remaining in Japan, whose homeland had not been restored or elevated to the position of nation-state in the eyes of the Japanese government, were rendered completely stateless.[18] Thus, with the end of the U.S. occupation, Japan became a nation predominantly of Japanese by birth.

At the same time, it is interesting to observe that, due to the continuing pronatalist population policy originally launched in 1940 under the national eugenics law, and despite the devastation of wartime defeat, Japan's population carried on growing until the late 1960s. This meant the country was able to avoid the kind of labor shortage that in other nations would typically have been met by immigrant workers during the period of accelerating modernization. As the defeated party in World War II and the former colonial master of Asia, Japan did not face an influx of refugees from other parts of Asia either. This meant that former colonial subjects, the majority of whom were Korean, were clearly marked out as the only stateless persons in Japan until very recently, the ramification being that they were destined to fill up the ranks of the lowest paid workers.[19]

While Koreans had been confined in Japan in the postwar decades as stateless people, North Korea offered a welcome to those Koreans wishing to be relocated from Japan to North Korea. In 1959, the repatriation of Koreans from Japan to North Korea was agreed upon between the North Korean Red Cross and the Japanese Red Cross. This was dubbed a "humanitarian" arrangement, strictly based on "voluntary" will. The Japanese government cordially responded to the North Korean gesture, as it potentially allowed it to rid itself of non-Japanese former colonial subjects, while also suiting its philosophy of postwar nation-building—notably, the building of a new Japan consisting only of the Japanese. It was a one-way journey, due to the lack of diplomatic relations between the two countries—and it remains so to this day. Between 1959 and 1976, a total of 92,749 persons (including 6,600 Japanese nationals, mostly wives) were repatriated from Japan to North Korea. From then on, until very recently, though on a dramatically diminished scale, repatriation has continued. (See chapter 3.)[20]

In the U.S., with the passage of the McCarran-Walter Act of 1952, the status endured by Koreans and other Asians, that is, "aliens ineligible for citizenship," was now revised. Post-1952 immigrants were admitted with the potential to become U.S. citizens, although the initial arrival of Koreans was not numerically overwhelming: from 1952 to 1964, only about 14,000 Koreans immigrated to the U.S., consisting mostly of "war brides" from the Korean War.[21] This seemingly welcoming act on the part of the U.S. government was clearly a product of the Cold War. Critics argue that the Act racialized Asians, subjecting them to stereotypes and deep cultural prejudices on the one hand, while on the other imposing strict ideological controls by clarifying that any alien that did not conform with the ideological values and behaviors of the majority of Americans in the polarized Cold War context would be deported or detained.[22] It was not until 1965 that the number of Korean immigrants began to multiply, as the Immigration and Nationality Act (influenced by the civil rights movement) abolished national origin quotas for immigrants, thereby making Asians into a major immigrant category in the U.S.

It was also after 1965 that Koreans in Japan gained access to a nationality; but unlike in the case of Koreans in the U.S., who were now eligible to become citizens of their host society, Koreans in Japan were now eligible to become "Korean," that is, to have the nationality of their own homeland. With the agreement between the Republic of Korea and Japan normalizing diplomatic relations, South Korean nationality became an option for Koreans in Japan. What is extremely interesting is that permanent residence in Japan was granted along with South Korean nationality. As stated by Arendt above, clearly, only when a person acquires a nationality through an arrangement between nation-states do human rights begin to be given to that person—in this case, residential security in Japan (part of basic human rights) was only accorded when South Korean nationality was acquired.

Morally speaking, this measure was grossly unjustifiable: why should the Japanese government have only compensated those Koreans in Japan who applied for South Korean nationality, when colonial rule had encompassed all of the Korean peninsula? This is an enigma until one considers the Cold War political environment. The U.S.-dominated international power network in

Asia allowed this measure (and many other similar and comparable injustices) to pass. This meant that the 1965 treaty left the stateless status of those Koreans in Japan who did not opt to identify themselves with South Korea intact. Here again, we see another instance of what Arendt describes: "Man, it turns out, can lose all so-called Rights of Man without losing his essential quality as man, his human dignity. Only the loss of a polity itself expels him from humanity."[23] With today's globe sliced into sovereign national states, nonnationals or the denationalized are stateless, homeless, and right-less; that is to say, they are bare human beings. In other words, they are right-less not because they are legally discriminated against, but because they are outside of the law. In a way, a jailed criminal who is a national citizen has more normal human rights than the denationalized.

It needs to be also added that a great difference between Koreans in Japan and those in the U.S. has been that ever since the early years of the postwar decades, Koreans in Japan have been polarized into two groups: supporters of North and South Korea respectively. Despite the fact that the majority of Koreans in Japan came from the southern provinces, the popularity of the postliberation Northern regime meant that a strong majority of them was politically sympathetic toward the latter. Both the aforementioned repatriation to the North, starting from 1959, and the 1965 option for South Korean nationality need to be understood in this light. The intensifying Cold War tension in Asia and mutual antagonism between the two halves of the Korean peninsula ensured that the two groups of Koreans in Japan continued to view each other with unrelenting animosity.

Meanwhile, in the U.S., the 1965 Immigration and Nationality Act opened the door to a large wave of Korean immigrants. In the decades to follow, Koreans became the third largest immigrant group, after Mexicans and Filipinos. From 1981 to 1990, 338,800 Koreans immigrated to the U.S., making Korea the fifth most common country of birth for foreign-born immigrants after Mexico, the Philippines, Vietnam, and China; while in 2004, Koreans had the lowest nativity rate among Asian Americans (about 24 percent of all Koreans), naturalized Korean-born individuals amounted to 41.5 percent of all Koreans, and unnaturalized Korean-born occupied 34.3 percent.[24] Of course, this does not in any way mean that their settlement was painless or easy, as assimilation and acculturation are time-consuming processes: indeed, the 2004 survey shows that the number of non-English-speaking Korean households reached a level of about half the number of all Korean households.[25] But such a datum itself attests to the fundamental difference between Korean diaspora in Japan and that in the U.S. Whereas Koreans continue to arrive in the U.S., regardless of their linguistic ability and cultural proficiency, mainly in order to secure better prospects for their children, in Japan, until the late 1980s,

hardly any Koreans arrived as new immigrants, while despite full acculturation Koreans continue to be outsiders to Japanese society. It will suffice to
note the difference between a *jus solis* ethos that promises migrants that their
children will be able to claim citizenship by being born in the host country,
and the displacement experienced by people confined to the soil of their former colonial ruler with no nationality or citizenship under *jus sanguinis* and
forced to hand down the fate of statelessness to their children and grandchildren.

A peculiar twist of the *jus sanguinis* principle of the Japanese nationality
law is aptly depicted in Zygmunt Bauman's words:

> If birth and nation are one, then all the others who enter or wish to enter the na-
> tional family must mimic, or are compelled to emulate, the nakedness of the
> newborn.
> The state—the guardian and prison guard, the spokesman and the censor-in-
> chief of the nation—would see to it that this condition was met.[26]

It is more than interesting to remember that those persons who are naturalized
are called *shin-Nihonjin*, or new Japanese, as if to indicate rebirth or the start
of a new life. This is all too deceptive, yet predictable: a person who is only
a naked human, bare life, is not a human in terms of rights and entitlements,
while a person who becomes a national is now treated as human for the first
time. Bare life, therefore, is not life; only national life is true life in today's
global order of nation-states. And whereas in the U.S., in which for better or
worse the foundation myth of the nation has it that the U.S. is a land of immigrants (of course, it is not), in Japan, the presupposed legal philosophy is
that Japan is fundamentally the land of the Japanese and the Japanese only.

In 1981, due to Japan's ratification of the International Covenants for Human Rights, Koreans in Japan who did not have South Korean nationality
were given permanent residence in Japan, which was called *tokurei enjūken*,
or special exceptional permanent residence. Accordingly, the Japanese immigration bureau issued a reentry permit to the holders of this status. Many Koreans whose family members had been repatriated to North Korea after 1959
were now able to travel to North Korea to be reunited temporarily with their
families. (This was made possible not because Japan and North Korea had entered diplomatic relation but because of "humanitarian" reasons—the same
rhetoric that was used in 1959—as will be discussed in chapter 3.) But due to
Cold War tensions between the two halves of the Korean peninsula, it still remained impossible to visit both North and South—it had to be an either/or decision. The reentry permit does not exactly work like a passport. It does not
grant entry to countries that have visa-waiver agreements with Japan. Therefore, whenever a Korean in Japan travels outside of Japan with this document,

he or she needs to have a prestamped entry visa prior to travel, the application process for which takes several months, with the added concern of a possibility of rejection due to the uncertain and unknown nature of this document
in the eyes of the embassies and consulates of other nations.

It was toward the end of the 1980s that some changes took place in relation
to Koreans in Japanese society. First, there was an influx of Koreans from
South Korea after the 1988 liberalization of overseas travel by the South Korean government. Second, inside the Korean expatriate movement, there was
a considerable easing in the hitherto confrontational positions upheld by the
South Korea supporters and the North Korea supporters, in light of global
moves toward ending the Cold War. Third, and connected with the above, the
Korean community in Japan increasingly came to realize and accept that the
homecoming wish of the first generation was not going to be achieved, as
Japanese-born generations came to realize that they and their children would
live (and die) in Japan.

In 1992, all Korean permanent residents, both those who had acquired this
status through the 1965 treaty and those who acquired it from 1981 on, were
grouped into a category of special permanent residents, or *tokubetsu eijūsha*.
This change was accompanied by various improvements in the residential status of Koreans in Japan, including a softening in deportation regulations in
cases where a felony had been committed. But, it should be emphasized that
unlike in the case of U.S. permanent residence, which is widely seen as a
bridging measure between foreign status and that of citizenship, special permanent residence in Japan has no such flexibility. It is a form of permanent
status, and under no circumstances will Japanese citizenship be granted on
this basis. It is only through naturalization that Japanese citizenship can be
obtained for foreign-born individuals; whether or not a person holds permanent residence, or for how long he or she has done so, is not taken into consideration.

In the meantime, Koreans in Japan continue to be plagued by an ambiguous
sense of national affiliation. It remains uncertain whether those with South Korean nationality, while holding South Korean passports, have national membership in relation to South Korea, or what type of membership this entails.
For example, a holder of South Korean nationality in Japan does not have a
South Korean resident registration number, a thirteen-digit ID, initiated about
four decades ago, which combines date of birth, gender, a code for the region
where the individual was first registered, and so on.[27] This ID number is com-
puterized, and is required for completion of basic routines in South Korea,
such as Internet registration. Unless one has a number that can be identified in
the Korean Information and Security Agency database, one is practically not a
national. Koreans in Japan who have South Korean nationality do not bear

such a number and do not appear in the database. For this reason, if the South Korean passport carried by a Korean traveler from Japan expires while he or she is abroad, the South Korean embassy in the given country cannot renew or reissue it.[28] The current conditions under which Koreans in Japan retain South Korean nationality also have it that they are exempt from military service and domestic taxation; in exchange, they are not eligible to vote or stand for election. Thus, their political entitlements in South Korea are of a precarious nature, and this makes one wonder if their South Korean nationality is of dubious sort.

On the other hand, those Koreans in Japan who do not have South Korean nationality, who today constitute a minority, remain stateless. But rather than being recognized as stateless persons in the media and other lay usage in Japan, they are regarded as "North Koreans." North Korean nationality does not exist at any level of Japan's legal and juridical establishment, since North Korea is not recognized by Japan as a proper state. Yet the Cold War ideology of non–South Korean equaling North Korean lingers on, triggering abuse and violence by Japanese perpetrators against those who do not have South Korean nationality and/or who are affiliated with the North Korea supporting expatriate organization (Chongryun, in the Korean abbreviation) whenever any hostility arises between the Japanese and North Korean governments. After the September 17, 2002, revelation that North Korean agents had secretively kidnapped a total of thirteen innocent Japanese from the shores of Japan during the 1970s and 1980s, Koreans in this category became the most vulnerable.[29] It would be this group of stateless Koreans, nakedly human and lacking the official stamp of any nation-state, that would be first loaded onto trucks, possibly given one hour to pack their bags, with the allowance of one bag per person, and sent away to the camps.

In the U.S. also, if not to the extent affecting Koreans in Japan, the Cold War and national partition interfered with the Koreans' lives. According to Erin Chung, South Korea's first postwar president Syngman Rhee systematically monitored the political allegiance of overseas Koreans. Later, while Korea was under the military dictatorship of Park Jung Hee and his successors, Koreans in the U.S. had to exercise caution, as they could be seen as points of contact with an "undesirable element" such as a North Korean agent, for example.[30] In the recent history of Koreans in the U.S., there have been significant turning points. The mass murder of citizens in the southwestern city of Kwangju in May 1980 had a profound effect on the lives of Korean Americans. Most notably, the Los Angeles riots of 1992 (or the "4.29 incident") carved even a deeper mark, revealing the generation gap inside the Korean American community and highlighting the way that the younger generation asserted its identity as American, demanding equal civil rights from the state and society.[31] Today, Koreans in the U.S. are divided along the lines of class, level of acculturation, and size of cultural capital, reflecting multiple factors such as circumstances of arrival, family migration history, economic status back in the homeland, and, to some extent, whether or not the family originated in the northern provinces—hundreds of families that had left North Korea during the Korean War as refugees were unable to settle in South Korea, eventually leaving Korea for the U.S. and other destinations.

After all, then, behind the differences in citizenship and possession of rights as humans/nationals, Koreans in the U.S. and Koreans in Japan find themselves on similar ground: the former, often patronizingly referred to as a model minority, are made to feel as if they were second-class citizens, despite their full citizenship under national-standard cultural domination of the U.S.; the latter, with adept acculturation and a highly skilled understanding of Japanese society and culture, continue to face the struggle for citizenship and civil rights. Historically also, as Jiyeon Yuh argues with regard to Korean migration, the ripple effect of the devastation of the Korean War and the lingering, temporary nature of the ceasefire (not the closure of war) created conditions which either led Koreans, in both the U.S. and Japan, to leave Korea or make it impossible for them to return to Korea.[32] These similarities, however, cannot be taken as fundamental: one struggles within the civil milieu where equality guaranteed by law is failing; the other struggles to enter such a milieu in the first place. If one is about resistance against discrimination and oppression, the other is about the fight to obtain the rights to be oppressed—that is, to be oppressed as citizens, not naked, mere humans.

LOCATION AND LOCUTION OF TRUTH

It is feminist and postcolonial writers of autobiographies who have challenged the hitherto-dominant figure of autobiographic writers, such as theologians and literary masters, as predominantly male. Post-1970s feminist intervention in the genre of autobiography with attention given to African American women and women of color—and when I refer to *feminists*, these include African American feminists and feminists of color themselves—has revealed both the subversive potential as well as the limitations of autobiography as a literary and political genre. In this debate, two closely intertwined points of consideration seem to be at stake: autobiography's (ambivalent) position vis-à-vis collective politics and its (equally twisted) relationship with truth-telling.

When a person who belongs to an oppressed collectivity, such as an African American woman or an indigenous person in Latin America, writes about his or her life, it often happens that the reader is unable to avoid the expectation that such a text should and naturally would speak to the misery, injustice, and pain that the collectivity suffers. Within the parameters of these expectations, African American women's autobiographies, for example, must necessarily denounce, if not directly in radical or politicized prose, at least by way of simply showing how they lived, racial oppression carried out by whites and sexist oppression carried out by both white and black men. Often, however, such expectations are betrayed or at least not fulfilled.

Linda Anderson draws our attention to the case of Zora Neale Hurston's *Dust Tracks on the Road*.[33] Hurston, a prominent African American anthropologist and writer, instead of speaking from the position of one truthful representation of African American women's selves, "draws attention to the autobiographical self as a fiction."[34] Hurston resists giving in to the multiple posited presumptions expected of an educated and outspoken African American woman. She omits certain factual events (such as her second marriage) in her autobiography, while she dramatizes her life. Here, we see the two points of concern that I suggested earlier intersecting with and permeating each other in muddy and messy ways. If an oppressed collectivity is one's community of origin, and if one is sensitive enough to see and understand it, it would not be truthful not to write from the political position of antioppression. At the same time, it is entirely up to the autobiographer herself whether to see her life being connected with larger collective politics or not, and how this connection is formed or not formed.

The controversy over truthfulness of autobiographic testimonial by Rigoberta Menchú is a case in point. As is well known, the Nobel laureate's life history was presented as the story of all poor Guatemalans. Her story—filled with details of the brutalities committed by the government and military, the exploitation and dehumanization of indigenous peoples, and the violence and torture that activists and guerrilla fighters were subjected to when captured by the authorities—had an earth-shaking impact on the entire world of conscience. The tragic and extreme poverty, unimaginable violence, and unbearable denigration that Menchú and her people suffered in their own land, the land where their ancestors were born and had built their homes, truly horrified the concerned minds of the world, effectively creating strong momentum and political pressure to end injustice and maltreatment in Guatemala.[35]

As we also know well, more than a decade after the publication of Menchú's life history, David Stoll refuted it, denying the details it contains one by one, on the basis of his own independent research and interactions with Guatemalans, many of whom were Menchú's neighbors and fellow villagers. According to Stoll, it was not that Menchú intentionally forged her identity, but that her political will might have resituated her recollections of the past. Stoll collected counterevidence which appeared to confirm, for example, that, contrary to Rigoberta's claims, her family had not been dirt-poor and had, instead, owned some land; her father had not been a prominent leader of the resistance, but a mere follower; and Menchú had not been deprived of opportunities for learning and had, instead, been educated by nuns in a Catholic establishment.[36]

Does this mean both Menchú and Hurston told lies? What does "to tell truthfully" mean, and what does it mean "to lie"? What, in other words, is the nature of autobiographic truth? Inevitably, an autobiographer relies on her memory, and we know that memory differs from objective documentation. Rather, the act of remembering, revisiting the past, and reunderstanding it involves interpretation, reenactment, reevaluation, and reregistration of certain facts and events, while forgetting or omitting others, rendering one's recollection largely subjective and, empirically speaking, unreliable. Yet this should not mean such a recollection is fake, since when one relives the past, the reliving itself is a meaningful performance through which one can be related to events that have already taken place in time and space; as such, the act of remembering, including reflections, reinterpretations, recompartmentalization, and recomprehension, is made real, if not wholly truthful. Which could be more truthful to the autobiographer: to include one's second marriage in the text, or to elaborate on how one felt about some fragments of one's past from today's vantage point? Which could be more truthful, when telling one's life history: to try to be objective in recounting past events, or to reveal one's ideological position and political inclinations? For anyone's life, the second exercise is more lifelike and, hence, true to one's self-understanding, as opposed to the option of recounting whether one has included all of the factual events that could have possibly happened in one's life. Furthermore, it is not possible for any human being to recall one's past completely, without missing any one snapshot and without making any memory errors. Thus, autobiographic truth requires a new way of registering events, selecting meaningful moments, and understanding the truth as something the existence of which cannot be empirically and objectively proved or substantiated by way of fact-checking.

With this in mind, I'd like to discuss texts by two Korean women in diaspora—one a writer, and the other an artist. The first is *Yuhi*, an award-winning autobiographical work of fiction by a Korean writer in Japan, Lee Yangji, and the second, *Dictee,* by Theresa Hak Kyung Cha, a Korean American artist. Both died young and prematurely: Lee died of an aneurysm at the age of thirty-seven in 1992, while Cha was murdered in 1982, at the age of thirty-one. With *Yuhio*, Lee won what is arguably the most prestigious literary award in Japan, the Akutagawa Prize. It was the first time that the prize had gone to a Korean woman in Japan. If Lee's *Yuhi* is an autobiographic work of fiction, Cha's *Dictee* is a collage of fragments, some autobiographic, some not. If *Yuhi* is a work written away from home, away from kinship and family, away from the bounds of collectivity, and adamantly from the position of the personal, *Dictee* is a text that was born from within the collectivity (including kinship and family), created by one person by touching upon many (hundreds of) others' lives through literally diverse and mixed media. As I shall argue, if *Yuhi* is a story about aphasic failure in acquiring a language, one's true tongue or mother tongue, *Dictee* is a text that performs aphasia itself, short of grammar, syntactically defunct, yet semantically ripe. If *Yuhi* is a lucid, unified fiction of true personal events, *Dictee* is an unstable, dislocated, subversive, and private form of conveying public truth.[37]

Their texts are, in ways that inform this whole volume, products of the collaboration between the collective and the personal. Against the background of increasing attention to Asian American women's identity and literary and artistic production/self-expression, Western academe has sustained the interest in Cha's text. At the same time, her text remains to be deciphered and is largely unheeded, as she was quintessentially unique in form and sensitivity. Lee also was a pioneer—a lone pioneer—in that, despite much attention having been given to *zainichi bungaku*, or Korean literature in Japan, Lee was the first woman to write about the complex love-hate relationship between gender and national displacement, gently but completely ignoring the hitherto dominant theme of patriotism and patriarchy. Furthermore, she was the first *zainichi* Korean author (Korean author in Japan) who won wide recognition in Japan and held Japanese nationality.

a.

Lee Yangji was born in 1955 to a Korean family that lived in Yamanashi prefecture in central Japan. Her parents were naturalized when she was nine, despite the opposition of her older brother (who was sixteen at that time). Her parents did not get along, and their hostile and difficult divorce, accompanied by a bitter and prolonged court battle, profoundly affected Lee during her childhood. In the end, having repeatedly run away from home, Lee gave up attending high school, an unusual path to take in Japan, where the predominant majority of middleschool graduates go on to receive high-school education. She became an apprentice maid in an inn in Kyoto, the owner of which arranged for her to be able to attend high-school classes held at the local night school. There, she met a history teacher, who encouraged her to pursue her interest in Korean history. Having earned the high-school diploma, she entered Waseda University, one of the top private colleges in Tokyo. Her thirst for learning about Korea led her to contact the Korean students' association on campus, but the association refused to grant her membership due to the fact that she was a Japanese national. Eventually, she went to South Korea to study, entering Seoul National University in 1983 at the age of twenty-seven, and it was around this time that she began writing novels. In 1988, her novel *Yuhi* won the Akutagawa Prize. After graduating from SNU, she entered Ehwa Woman's College graduate program, studying dance performance.[38]

Yuhi focuses on a South Korean family in Seoul that had accepted a girl called Yuhi, a Korean from Japan, as a home-stay student. As depicted in the beginning of the novel, Yuhi has already returned to Japan—the story takes the form of a series of recollections by Yuhi's home-stay aunt (hereafter referred to as Aunt) and niece (whom Yuhi called *eonni,* older sister; hereafter referred to as Eonni). Yuhi comes to Aunt and Eonni in her junior year of study at "S University," presumably SNU. Aunt's late husband was a graduate of SU, and Aunt feels something special for this girl. Yuhi also appears to be very happy and relieved to have found this house. The first thing she mentions about her room is how warm it is. But Aunt has just turned on the *on-dol,* the traditional central floor-heating system, and therefore the room is actually still heating up. Aunt and Eonni gather that Yuhi must have been treated poorly in the numerous boarding houses in which she has previously stayed. Indeed, Yuhi has seen many different parts of Seoul and its suburbs, and many different Korean families, due to her inability to stay in one place. Always, she has faced bad situations. In one family, while the parents were out, two teenage sons began a fistfight for some unknown reason, which escalated into a scene of broken glasses and a bloodied nose and mouth. Yuhi, badly shaken, called for an ambulance. The violence was too hideous for Yuhi to bear.

But, Yuhi's misery is first and foremost related to the language, or, more precisely, its enunciation. She endlessly struggles with her Japanese accent, and agonizes over the lack of authenticity in her pronunciation of Korean words. More importantly, Yuhi is unable to find beauty in the Korean language as spoken in South Korea today. Her failure in becoming Korean in Korea, the obstinate existence of Japaneseness within her, and her frustration and anger with herself indeed coincided with the agonies that Lee herself had faced. Korea was, for Lee, no longer the home that she thought she had lost or safe haven where she could recover her true identity: it was as foreign as it was possible to be, and Yuhi's (and Lee's) desire to belong and be accepted was not reciprocated.[39]

Here, aphasia, or loss of language, is a clue to understanding Lee's displaced identity. Her desire to love Korea was not only unattainable, but also wrong—wrong in the sense that she realized that love for the homeland was not a given or something that one was born with, but rather something that one had to acquire or earn. The homeland, in other words, did not automatically love her in return just because she had traced her ancestral origins to Korea. On the contrary, her one-sided love was rejected at every turn she made in Korea, and her predicament was usually related to language.

Let us, for example, consider the scene where Yuhi and Eonni, who shares Aunt's second floor with Yuhi, go out to buy a writing desk for Yuhi. They have to use a bus route that they never have taken before. Eonni, about ten years Yuhi's senior, does not know much about certain areas of Seoul, due to her protected upbringing. They are both uneasy, but Yuhi more profoundly so. When the bus becomes crowded and clamorous, the radio playing at high volume (a common subject of complaint by bus passengers in Seoul), and a peddler who has just jumped onto the bus begins to hawk small knives, explaining repetitively and in detail the superior aspects of his merchandise (also apparently a common scene on Seoul buses), Yuhi collapses on the floor, crying and covering her ears with both hands. Eonni, who has been suggesting that they should get off the bus, leaving the purchase of the desk for another day, declares that both of them must get off the bus at the next stop. Yuhi utters fragmented words in reply: "Eonni, Go, Desk, Want to buy." Just like an aphasic, Yuhi loses her syntax, and her words are mutilated, like limbs fallen off a body, hanging in fragile and dangling isolation. She is unable to cope with hearing the sound of Korean any more.[40]

Normally, study abroad means studying in a foreign country. But Yuhi's — and Lee's — destination was her homeland. Her personal pain is the pain of not being able to find her self — the self that she expected to be true, her true Korean self in her homeland.

One night, Eonni is woken by a voice counting, or chanting to be precise, from one to four, again and again. She opens Yuhi's door and discovers Yuhi, at 3:00 A.M., in a drunken stupor, listening to *taegeumsanjo*, the traditional Korean musical genre of her favorite wind instrument, the *taegeum,* and chanting numbers to it, tapping the desktop at the same time. She has almost emptied a bottle of grain wine, which normally contains a high volume of alcohol. Worried and angered, Eonni reproaches Yuhi, calling her unwomanly. Yuhi turns to her and writes the following words in Korean on a sheet of paper:

Eonni,

I am a hypocrite.
I am a liar.
Our country
I am unable to love.
Taegeum *beautiful.*
Taegeum *sound is our language.*

She writes these words in tears, wetting the paper and trembling in pain. She begins hurting herself by banging her head against the wall. Eonni holds Yuhi close in order to protect her, while Yuhi continues to alternately sob and cry. Eonni is at a loss, having no means to either comfort Yuhi or understand her behavior.[41]

After Yuhi's departure, Aunt reminisces that Yuhi used to say that the *taegeum* was the most honest of instruments because it is played as if it is speaking, directly transforming human breath into musical sound as if to vocalize human mind truthfully. Aunt remembers that Yuhi thought that the sound of the *taegeum* was that which inspired the original utterance of "our language," Korean; the sound of Korean was the sound of the *taegeum*, the most beautiful of sounds.[42]

While staying with the two women, Yuhi often comments what a good and proper form of Korean Aunt and Eonni speak to each other, how gentle it sounds. Yuhi tells them she's never met a Korean family that speaks so beautifully to each other inside the home. Yuhi's written Korean, Eonni soon discovers, is much more sophisticated than her spoken Korean. Eonni also finds out, to her dismay and bewilderment, that Yuhi does not read Korean books unless it is necessary in order to prepare for exams and papers. Yuhi spends the rest of her time reading Japanese books, which she owns in far greater volumes than Korean books. She does not watch South Korean TV, either. She appears, at times, critical of the way Korean is spoken and written today in South Korea. She points out to Eonni Korean's lack of passive voice and, by implication, its lack of subtlety, as if it is a valid reason for dissatisfaction Further, she complains about the oddity of writing Korean horizontally, as is the norm today in South Korea, as opposed to the vertical format found in the original *hunminjeongeum* (correct sounds to be taught to people), invented under the initiative of King Sejong in the fifteenth century.

Her frustration peaks in relation to the practice of having to write papers about Korea and things Korean by referring to Korea as *uri nara,* our country. *Uri nara,* or, more precisely, the Korean possessive pronoun *uri* (our), comes with a distinctly emotional baggage of attachment, ownership, oneness, and collectivity, when uttered in Korean. Under Japanese colonial rule, Koreans could not call Korea *uri nara.* After the partition of the nation, neither half's utterance of *uri nara* was complete, and this was proof of the historical severing of the nation by the Korean War and the Cold War. And for someone like Yuhi, a Korean girl born and raised in Japan, speaking Japanese, writing Japanese, reading in Japanese, to call South Korea *uri nara* required a change of heart, a mutation of a grave sort, a commitment of a serious kind, the weight of which would be difficult to imagine for Korean natives who had been born and grown up in Korea, calling Korea, unquestionably, *uri nara.*

Yuhi's struggle ends miserably by her quitting the prestigious university six months before graduation. The novel emphasizes the massive effort demanded of Korean families wishing to send their children to SU. In order for their children to successfully pass the entrance exams, families devote enormous amounts of money, time, and personal and emotional resources. Yuhi, on the other hand, has entered the institution by way of a special admission quota open only to overseas-born Korean applicants. Was this special-quota-based form of entry perhaps a curse, leading to her eventual self-negation and self-condemnation as a liar and hypocrite? Or, more deeply, perhaps her birth in Japan, not simply a foreign land but the land of the nation's mortal enemy, the former colonial master, may have tainted her blood, no matter how Korean her parents may have been. Was Yuhi's (and Lee's) agony the expiation of sins committed by previous generations of her family in diaspora, a punishment for their having left the homeland? As if unable to shake off this curse, Yuhi finds refuge in the Japanese language amidst the chaos and clamor of the Korean language, the language she is unable to call her own, the language that stubbornly remains foreign to her.

b.

> Mother, you are eighteen years old. You were born in Yong Jung, Manchuria and this is where you now live. You are not Chinese. You are Korean. But your family moved here to escape the Japanese occupation.[43]

Unlike Yuhi, Cha's mother, who is eighteen in the epic, is considered more unproblematically Korean, despite the fact that her motherland Korea is now a colony of Japan. Her native tongue, Korean, is her refuge from Japanese and Chinese. The latter is the language of the locals; she is a schoolteacher in Manchuria, a land to which tens of thousands of Koreans migrated before and during the colonial period. Toward this young and frail teacher, the reader is made to feel imminently protective.

At the time of Cha's mother's exile to China—presumably the 1930s—Japan was steadily extending its aggressive ambitions beyond the Korean-Chinese border on multiple fronts, including military occupation and cultural domination. The latter was most effectively undertaken through the dissemination of Japanese language education in schools. As Lisa Lowe has noted, education plays a prominent role in *Dictee*, the title itself reflecting the author's own education in a French Catholic institution during her formative years; similarly, according to Anne Anlin Cheng: "Cha's text suggests that [diverse] levels of interpellation—from infantile development to national to colonial to religious indoctrination—in fact mime each other."[44] But education here is both accepted and challenged; it is portrayed as something that makes one and that which one, in turn, constructs. One senses that it was through education that Cha's obedience and docility, as well as her determinedly questioning stance, were cultivated.

Theresa Hak Kyung Cha was born in Pusan, a city in the southeastern tip of Korea, in 1951, in the middle of the Korean War. The family migrated to the U.S. in 1961. Cha was educated at Berkeley and in Paris, increasingly attracting attention as a rising star in the fields of performing and mixed-media art; but her career was cut short by her murder in 1982 in New York City. It was mainly posthumously that *Dictee* and her other works attained the status of icons.

Unlike in the case of Lee, Cha's art and writing often feature her parents, especially her mother. Mother figures prominently in *Dictee*. Ordinarily, *Dictee* is referred to as (at least partially) an autobiographic work, but in what way it is so is not as self-evident as the critics might hope it to be. The volume contains writings of heterogeneous genres, including poems, symbols, what resemble secret codes, composition pieces, excerpts from historiography, and fragmentary recollections, among others, and these are written in more than one language. What seems to repeatedly emerge in this collage is the figure of Mother or Woman. While it is understandable that an autobiographer may start by reflecting on a person whom one deems to have played an important role in one's personal development, a person who has exerted a major influence on determining one's life course, there is no obvious clue as to how and why, in the case of Cha, her mother is chosen.

More intriguing is the fact that the book opens by referring to Yu Guan Soon (Gwan-Sun), a female anti-Japanese martyr who was arrested, tortured, and eventually executed at the age of seventeen by the Japanese in 1920, in the wake of the nationwide anti-Japanese rebellion in Korea in 1919. References to colonialism abound in *Yuhi* as well, but in a different way. Yuhi, to begin with, is a living legacy of colonial rule, just like Lee herself. Torn between the two cultures and identities, the colonial exiles and their descendants find themselves in a dead-end—in their host culture, which is their native culture, they are foreigners; in their home culture, which is their natal culture, they are foreigners.

Often, an idealized version of home and homeland is brutally shattered by the reality of the homeland itself—as in the case of Yuhi's observation that the Korean language spoken in Korea has lost what to her is its authenticity and primordial connection with the sounds of the *taegeum*. Equally often, the hope of recovering her true self, which has been lost through her foreign upbringing and the foreign language, is taken away—as in the case of Yuhi continuing to identify herself as a liar in her homeland. The double failure of not finding home and not being able to find one's true self marks the story of Yuhi, and the colonial past lies in the background of every failure Yuhi faces in her Korean homeland. Or, more precisely, Yuhi's disappointment is not about not finding home, but not being able to love it. Her yearning for an authentic Korea is betrayed by today's South Korean society, culture, and language, but this yearning is, perhaps, misconceived in the first place.

Whereas Lee works against the nationalized colonial past by strenuously insisting on the personal level in her endeavor to recover her Korea, Cha's reference (or embrace) of the martyr Yu seems oddly conformist to the nationalist reclamation of the past as a collective endeavor. Yu is often referred to as a Korean Joan of Arc, symbolizing Korean resistance to the Japanese, treasured in orthodox history textbooks in both North and South Korea. As such, it would not be too off the mark to detect in the way Yu is cherished the mechanism by which Yu's feminine agency has been appropriated by the corpus of male-dominant, male-centered nationalist historiography, making Yu into an orthodox, standard nationalist figure. How can this conventional national figure appear in the overture of a text as unconventional, unlocatable, subversive, and unmistakably feminist as *Dictee?* Or is our supposition that *Dictee* is radically feminist misconceived—just like our irresistible expectation that Rigoberta Menchú's or Zora Huston's words be collectively representative?

What is interesting in Cha's writing, in relation to both Yu and Cha's mother, is that she writes about them from the point of view of a woman who is older than they are. Yu at seventeen and Mother (in Epic Poetry) at eighteen are captured by Cha at ages older than these (although Mother emerges repeatedly on later pages at varying ages). In this way, one can argue, Cha is trying to see her younger days in juxtaposition to the past lives of these two women, lives lived during the colonial period—one was executed as an anticolonial rebel, while the other was banished beyond the national borders as an exile. Death and exile—these were the two options that Korean women faced under colonialism. But can this be only about colonialism? How about her reference to *"her"* in her writings about the anti-military government movements at the times of the 4.19 Incident in 1960 and the Kwangju Massacre in 1980? There, her mother appears briefly, in the letter Cha addresses to this very Mother, as someone trying to stop her older brother from joining the anti-establishment demonstrators out in the street; her older brother pushes past her mother and heads out to the demonstration.[45]

April 19—the sound of it evokes the notion of the sacred among certain generations of Koreans (perhaps those above forty years of age). It is the date of the youth rebellion in 1960 which overturned the government of Syngman Rhee, the man who had been in power since Korea's independence in 1945 with the tension-ridden, yet unmistakable support of the U.S. government and its military presence in South Korea. It was one year after this rebellion that Cha's family left Korea for the U.S. Cha pays a return visit to Korea for the first time, after nearly twenty years have elapsed since the family's emigration, in 1980, which happens to be the year of the popular uprising and subsequent massacre of thousands of citizens in Kwangju, and writes, again, taking the form of a letter addressed to her mother. But first, she acknowledges the distance between her and her motherland:

> I am here for the first time in eighteen years, Mother. We left here in this memory still fresh, still new. I speak another tongue, a second tongue. This is how distant I am. From then. From that time.[46]

Cha juxtaposes the 1960 student movement and the 1980 massacre of mostly young people and students in the city of Kwangju in such a way as to deliberately suppress or compress the twenty-year period in between. At the same time, she stresses how distant she herself has become from Korea during this period, now speaking English at ease. And she repeatedly invokes the mysterious figure, "*her*," among fellow Koreans.

> Her name. First the whole name. Then syllable by syllable counting each inside the mouth. Make them rise they rise repeatedly without ever making visible lips never open to utter them.
>
> ....
>
> Violation of *her* by giving name to the betrayal, all possible names, interchangeable names, to remedy, to justify the violation. Of *her.* Own. Unbegotten. Name. Name only. Name without substance. The everlasting, Forever. Without end.[47]

Does "she" overlap with her own mother or any Mother, Korean Mother, and her motherland, Korea? Or, is "her" name freedom, *jayu*, or reunification, *tongil*, both keywords in the 4.19 Incident and in Kwangju, longed for by the students in their demonstrations?: "*Urie soweoneun jayu, kkumedo soweoneun jayu . . . Jayuyeo eoseo ora jayuyeo ora* (Our wish is freedom; even in our dreams, our wish is freedom. . . . Come freedom, come quickly)," as went the 1980 Kwangju street song.

Strangely, Cha's fragmented phrases are rather a precise depiction of the confusion and chaos created through the revolts by Kwangju citizens and the brutal and bloody suppression that ensued. Under martial law, free broadcasts of the Kwangju massacre in May 1980 were not allowed. It was broadcast, in fragments yet more extensively, in Japan (I witnessed this as a college student in Japan at the time) — scenes which included a female student being clubbed to death, a row of male students being bundled up by wire and rushed off to some unknown destination by heavily armed soldiers, two little boys being taken away by soldiers at gunpoint, and the blackened corners of a street piled up with bodies and blood. These fragments corresponded neatly with Cha's disjointed utterances. Kwangju in 1980 was exactly that—one confusing space where life was no longer life, words were no longer words, and death was everywhere. Many weeks later, pictures of wailing mothers, clad in white traditional funeral attire, throwing themselves over the coffins of their children, were shown on TV—that, too, corresponded with Cha's cry for Mother, her writings to Her.

From a distance, Cha invites her mother into the scene, saying:

> I feel the tightening of the crowd body to body now the voices rising thicker I hear the break the single motion tearing the break left of me right of me the silence of the other direction advance before. . . . They are breaking now, their sounds, now new, you [Mother] have heard them, so familiar to you now could you ever forget them not in your dreams, the consequences of the sound the breaking.[48]

Reading *Dictee* last decade, Lowe commented: "The subject of *Dictee* continually thwarts the reader's desire to abstract a notion of ethnic or national identity."[49] Reading it in this century, not many readers would hesitate to accept the reality that many of us live more than one identity, elusively situated and constantly shifting. But more than that: *Dictee* closely knits Cha's personal identifications with those of others, including Mother, Woman, and the Nation, using a technique commonly found in autobiographies of diasporic subjects. Was not Menchú in exile when she recounted her story to Elisabeth Burgos-Debray in Paris, claiming her story was that of all poor Guatemalans? Why is her diasporic existence often overlooked when critics deal with her testimonials? In other words, should we not allow the consideration that a diasporic subject's autobiography might be different in terms of the conception of this very notion of "the subject" as opposed to the nondiasporic (and even oppressed) subject/autobiographer? Seen this way, the profound significance of *Dictee*, it seems, lies rather in its unprecedented form—as art—performing diaspora through constant locational and locutional shift.[50]

We seem to be approaching the paradox: *Yuhi*, obviously an autobiographic novel, is nowhere near as autobiographic as *Dictee*, which does not first appear as apparently autobiographic. The difference, it seems, at least partially resides in the presence of kinship references or the lack thereof. Yuhi quintessentially appears alone, despite her use of the sisterly term Eonni. Her family of origin (supposedly in Japan) is never mentioned, and her host family in her "homeland" exists only temporarily in time and space. Cha's kinship, on the other hand, exists ubiquitously—in connection to her mother, Yu, the demonstrators, the Nation. The connection among them is intensified due to Cha's diasporic positionality. References to kinship (metaphoric, as in the case of the Nation, or metonymic, as in the case of Mother) deployed by Cha make her textual self interconnected, woven into the thick national network of kinship; yet in this way, Cha's self emerges more securely than Yuhi's to the surface level of engagement. After all, autobiographies are written that way: to depict oneself in connection with others, yet always separated from others by a thin veil of self-consciousness.

c.

Both *Dictee* and *Yuhi* are multilingual, multivocal texts. What emerges from these is a subject, a diasporic subject, who is displaced between/among plural languages and is constantly struggling to avoid being drowned under the waves of "the foreign," while resisting "the national." References to the organs of speech abound in both. Take the example of the tongue as referred to in *Dictee*. an organ that is required to make correct enunciations, the tongue suffers in *Dictee,* being bitten between the teeth and becoming swollen, cracked, and broken. The torture of the tongue is a subtext for the torture that the Korean language suffered under the Japanese—bitten, swollen, cracked, and broken, as in references such as the following: "Tongue inside the mouth inside the throat inside"; "There. Later, uncertain, if it was the rain, the speech, memory"; "To bite the tongue. Swallow. Deep. Deeper. Swallow. Again even more"; and "Sentences. Paragraphs. Silent . . . Pages and pages in movement."[51] Fragmented and tormented, the tongue becomes speech, writing, and language.

The ethos of the lost tongue, the pathos of the lost or hidden self, and the sadness that is completely private and hard to verbalize overlap with those of Yuhi in inversion, whose true, secure language remains Japanese, yet who wants to recover her mother tongue, the language of everyday life in South Korea, which comes to her as only an incomplete means of self-expression. Furthermore, Yuhi's inability to love the Korean language as spoken in today's South Korea precipitates her to look toward the past (the time of King Sejong, i.e., the fifteenth century), the authenticity of which exists only in the imaginary, merely exacerbating her predicament. If Lee writes about the torture of the tongue (read "language") through Yuhi's aphasic pain, Cha is performing an aphasic act in *Dictee*. If *Yuhi* is about the insufficiency of the mother tongue, *Dictee* is about the partial efficacy of all languages that the user (Cha) can claim. The reality of diaspora gave Cha many different languages, each insufficient and each incomplete, including her mother tongue; it gave Lee one language, Japanese, in its utmost beauty and completion.

There is also Yuhi's obsession with the *taegeum*, an instrument that forces the player to assume a kissing posture in motion. Yet, as if to mimic two lovers in tension, a hair-splitting space is maintained between the player's mouth and the instrument, a space that is empty and filled with force at the same time. Just as the *taegeum* requires the player to breathe with all his or her heart, from deep down in the gut, the tongue one loves fills one's heart, sometimes making one utter words with care—like gentle kisses—and at other times taking control of the speaker in passion or anger. Yet, again, the player's lips never touch the flute. It is the breath that produces the sound, not the babbling. The Korean language for Lee was precisely that—the unproducible sound, the sound produced neither by lips nor the tongue, but by the soul. Yuhi's (Lee's) obsession with the authenticity of enunciation is touched upon in the last scene of the novel, which depicts Yuhi's struggle to say the Korean word *pawui* (rock). The pronunciation of this word would be an insurmountable challenge for a native speaker of Japanese and, as such, the challenge to do so crystallizes the unattainable desire to be born with the mother nation's soul.

Being home is speaking and also, I would suggest, following our discussion of Lee and her work, writing. Being home, in other words, is using the language, living in and inside the language that one feels at home with. A woman born on foreign soil as a stateless person—as of 1955, the year of Lee's birth, Japan acknowledged neither Korea—Lee was homeless, nationless. Her parents had adopted a foreign national identity, which became her legal nationality, yet she was unable to accept it, traveling to the original homeland only to find herself spurned, and unable to find herself the home she yearned for. When one engages in further reading of Lee's works, however, it becomes obvious that what is being evoked here is not simply the ethno-national dyadic opposition between Korea and Japan and the diasporic agony attached to it. The way her pain seeps through her words is also related to her upbringing, her less-than-happy childhood in a dysfunctional, eventually broken home, in which frequent violent clashes between her parents ended in an ugly divorce battle—in a word, a torment of kinship.

An aversion to writing about her parents or any parents manifests in Lee's work; when referred to at all, parents appear as immature, irresponsible, and irrational individuals who only know how to express themselves through anger and violence. In the closing scene of one short story, *Aoiro no kaze* (Blue breeze), the parents of Takako, a little girl and the protagonist, begin engaging in a fistfight while seated in the front of the family car. Father hits Mother with his left arm while holding on to the steering wheel with his right hand (Japanese cars drive on the left). Mother is retaliating, although she is being badly beaten and is unable to compete with Father's strength. Mother's painful screams and the sound of Father's forceful punches terrify Takako, who is frozen with fear, just like in the many other fight scenes that take place in the story. Then, gradually, she begins to see a cow and an old lady, the images she has seen before in dreams and dazed visions among many thoughts about killing herself. In a daze, she throws herself between the two front seats of the car. Consequently, she is severely beaten on the right side of the head and the left side of the neck by her parents, who are deeply absorbed in an explosion of hostility, having forgotten that they have a little girl in their lives. The story ends with Takako dreaming and being curious, in her fading consciousness traveling to another world, wondering why everyone is looking so serious . . .[52]

It would be safe to say that this chilling story reflects Lee's perception of her own parents. From this, one can imagine that not only did Lee lack a homeland, but she also never had a home in which she felt secure and protected. Family heritage, it would appear, is perceived differently in Cha. The caring and protective manner in which she writes for and about her mother (at the age of eighteen) changes, as Mother in *Dictee* grows older and Cha (as in the piece on the 4.19 Incident and the 1980 massacre) becomes the daughter again. But transposing roles, paying or repaying the loving gaze that surely (the reader is made to think) Cha would have received from her as a child, is an eloquent testimonial to her relationship to Mother. This is utterly missing in Lee's work. Both diasporic, both lost and in search of self, having or not having Mother makes a difference. Whereas Lee writes from the position where no family exists—in fact, she almost writes against family in other stories depicting extramarital affairs or infidelity—Cha writes as an individual connected with family, Mother, and Nation. Lee's national connection is rigidly framed—so rigidly that it breaks easily—as she tries to recover it alone and by herself, away from the parents who deserted it by opting for naturalization; Cha's national consciousness is mother-given, nurtured inside the family first. Does the difference between the two remind us of the fact that diaspora is primarily a family phenomenon embedded in kinship, rather than an individual experience? And is this how diasporic individuals are connected to national or ethnic identity—that is, through kinship among other forms of connections?

The collective uprootedness and multiple displacements suffered by a community of people permeates individuals to the core, and this permeation is itself multi- and transgenerational. Diaspora necessarily traverses generations, in other words. Even if, as in Lee's case, one is disappointed in one's parents and tries to abandon one's own family, the tracks followed by preceding generations in diaspora haunt the protagonist—as we will see in the following pages. Similarly, the multiple displacements that Cha's family suffered, first as war refugees and then as immigrants, were family experiences, though the degree and mode of impact on each of its members varied—as we will also see in the following pages. Diasporic autobiographies are thus ridden with internal tensions between collective (including family) memories and personal contentions, as children in diaspora grow up being fed family romances relating to a "return" or a "lost land," while oscillating between the embrace of such a dream and a denial of such an ideal as one belonging not to them, but to their parents—as we shall see in chapter 5. *Dictee* and *Yuhi,* each in very differing ways, speak to such an ethos of diaspora. This gives us a key to opening the door to the world of women depicted in this volume.

WOMEN IN THIS BOOK

I began collecting autobiographies of Koreans in Japan, while conducting interviews related to their life histories, from around 1992. Since my appointment to the faculty of a U.S. university in 1997, the scope of my autobiographic research has expanded to include Korean Americans. I have read about eighty autobiographies by women and about fifty by men. A great many of them were class assignments. The others were written by the volunteers for my ethnic identity project *Voice/Life: Making Asian American Archives* (2003–2005), as well as by volunteers from among Koreans in Japan. For *Voice/Life,* I interviewed about forty Asian and Asian American students, including Korean and Korean American students, on campus. After the initial round of interviews was over, I selected individuals and asked each of them to write an autobiography for me. In the case of Korean young adults in Japan, I conducted the data collection in a more random manner: in some cases, I asked individuals to write their autobiographies first, and followed up with an interview, while in other cases, the order was reversed. For most of the college students, I discovered, writing an autobiography became a meaningful act of self-reflection and self-understanding.

My slightly older informants were mostly born between the years 1955 and 1965, and all come from Japan. Initially, they were often rather reluctant to write an autobiography, since they found it to be embarrassing or to be something requiring a lot of time and effort. But, once they began writing, many discovered it to be cathartic, and their autobiographies often ended up being much longer and more detailed than those of the college students. Numerically speaking, I have read many fewer autobiographies written by this group, which consisted entirely of women. The women, I was told, found that writing autobiographically allowed each of them to recover one way or another a part of their past that they had nearly forgotten, helping them to realize the roles they had played in contributing to a larger collective and communal cause—be it the family or children's education, expatriate politics, or a personal career. Understandably, their autobiographies were more introspective, retrospective, and reflexive than the forward-looking and speculative writings of the college students. But, simultaneously, the occasion of writing about the past also permitted them to entertain new possibilities for the future.

Arendt once wrote: "Each time we talk about things that can be experienced only in privacy or intimacy, we bring them out into a sphere where they will assume a kind of reality which, their intensity notwithstanding, they never could have had before."[53] Similarly, according to Jerome Bruner: "The Self as narrator not only recounts but justifies."[54] If so, Cha's and Lee's respective narrative selves are utterly justifiable as autobiographical subjects, for they pay no homage to objectivity or the singularity of truth and/or experience. But surely, the autobiographic self is different from the fictional or poetic self. Nevertheless, the act of telling and retelling (or writing and rewriting) reveals the self. In Lee's fiction, the author is ruthlessly exposed despite her adoption of other names such as Yuhi. In Cha's subversive challenge, her vulnerability is revealed; that is, the vulnerability of her love for Mother and the fragility of the indoctrinated belief system, be it Catholicism, patriotism, or filial piety. Each time, as stated by Arendt, one is new, different, yet authentic: each protagonist in Lee's autobiographic novel is another incarnation of herself, and each disjointed page of Cha is made of herself. The same also goes for my "writers" (rather than "informants"): each time they wrote—as some wrote many short pieces for me—and each time they read—as I asked a few of them to read and reread a portion of their writings—each of the slightly different truths about their selves was generated, reconfigured, and sometimes re-created.

Thus, in the following chapters, I explore selves as they reveal their multiple authenticities, just as we read in the works of Lee and Cha. I try to locate how memory is formed, reflecting the multiple displacements and global relocations many of my writers and their families have gone through. At the same time, I map out how the ontology of diaspora formulates and constructs particular selves. I am, however, not trying to suggest that there could be such a thing as a "Korean self" simply as an outcome of Korea's collective history, its colonial past, or the present-day diaspora. On the contrary, as the reader will soon see, I am skeptical of the idea of "such and such a self of such and such a culture," as in the cases of the "Japanese self" or "Western self." These labels are in themselves reifying in terms of the way in which they relate to who individuals are and what their lives are about. In this book, instead of labeling the (let us say) culturalist (or culture-determinant) self, I adopt the strategy of letting individuals think, speak, and write about themselves with the language and expressions that they prefer and choose. Looking at Lee's and Cha's respective texts, we get the clue that diasporic self-formation and identification (rather than the stark concepts of "self" and "identity") are closely intertwined with family (with or without love), nation (imaginary or real), and language (lost or gained)—all of which concepts evoke home and homeland in many different yet meaningful ways. The complex interplay between these concepts forms the subtext for each chapter.

Three young women aged between nineteen and twenty-two are the storytellers in chapter 1, "Many Ways to Be Korean—and Something Else: An Inquiry into the Self." All of them have early yet acute memories, and therefore understandings, of the experience of moving from one culture to another—the first of them having moved from Korea to the U.S., the second having moved from unawareness (of her ethnic identity) to hyperawareness by reclaiming her lost Korean identity in the U.S., and the third having moved between the Korean ethnic enclave in Japan and the Japanese mainstream. Each story contains border-crossing, real or symbolic, at an early age. We learn from their stories the role played by language or, more precisely, multiple languages, in the formation of ethnically positioned, gendered, and maturing identities, not through the even utilization of different languages, but through the losing and gaining, hyperutilization and suppression of languages at each border crossing, with each experience being heterogeneous in nature and functioning as a test of (and something that forms) self and identity.

How does diaspora affect personal life, not simply in terms of daily matters, but in relation to life events with long-term implications, such as love and marriage? Chapter 2, "Ethnic Love Story: A romantic Autobiography of a Korean Woman in Japan," takes up this issue. I address the question of the possibility or availability of a socially and politically meaningful life in the confines of a diasporic community in connection to love. I also explore the way in which love is made irrelevant, due to male-dominant and ancestor-land-oriented notions of human congregation (mainly between men), or relevant, as long as it works to reproduce the social values of the diasporic community. A close focus on the language of love and the ethnicization of the romantic self is the theme of this chapter. My discussion will rest in particular on the institutionalized production of a certain set of values inside the ethnic community, by what I call *romantic discipline*, that takes place inside Korea University of Tokyo, operated by Chongryun, the North Korea supporting expatriate organization of Koreans in Japan.

Chapter 3, "A Letter from Afar: Totalitarianism, Neoliberalism, and Self-Reference," is inspired by and built around a letter that a Korean woman in Japan wrote to a former high-school classmate who had chosen to be repatriated to North Korea in the late 1970s in order to pursue her dreams. In this chapter, I explore totalitarianism and the mechanism of self-reference; I also consider the biopolitical formation of self in North Korea, and compare all of the above to the recent discussion of neoliberalism. We will discover uncanny similarities emerging between the two systems of neoliberalism and totalitarianism. I also consider the notion of the camp as proposed by Giorgio Agamben, wherein the structure of power assumes radically arbitrary arrangements.[55] Between the totalitarian homeland and its derivative diasporic community, we will see, there is hardly any meaningful exchange or viable communication, while both derive their potency from the notion of exile — exile from home, exile from the world, and exile from humanity — as ontological foundations of community. It is this separation, paradoxically speaking, that reinforces romantic longing for the oppressive homeland, as we will see in the woman's letter.

Chapter 4, "Diaspora and the Ethic of Care: A Note on Disability, Aging, and the Vulnerability of the Denationalized," takes up the theme of care and caregiving in connection to diaspora, disability, and aging, as well as what I might call the ethnic reasoning of justice or morality. Using the autobiography of a Korean woman in Japan as a guide, I search for the aspect of morality in the diasporic community, which is underexplored or unexplored in the existing studies of diaspora. Ties to family and close kin, or other such (personal) relationships, may well demonstrate moral prerogatives that take precedence over abstract principles of justice. This is most clearly seen in the area of caregiving for the vulnerable, such as the disabled and the elderly, when the members of an ethnic community of stateless people have long since given up on relying on the notion of the common social good in the host society. Drawing on feminist debates on moral development and the ethics of care, with special attention to the works of Carol Gilligan, Joan Tronto, and Eva Kittay, I synthesize the interjection (or lack thereof) of the personal and the political inside the diasporic community.

The final chapter, "*Terra Incognita*: Family Maps of Diaspora," weaves the stories of two young Korean American women's families. The diasporic dispersion of people creates an alternative cartography, mapmaking of an entirely unrecorded sort. It is quintessentially unpredictable, yet concretely traceable, not simply in rather unreliable phenomena such as memory, but more succinctly in the recording of loss, damage, and destruction. That I am avoiding medical or medicalized terms such as "trauma" or "pain" is intentional: I am joining Ian Hacking in his study of a nineteenth-century transient mental illness called the fugue (or "mad travels") in France and Germany in my effort to resist the medicalization of diaspora discourse.[56] This does not mean that I would do away with the metaphors of health, medicine, or pain, or that I would come up with a replacement approach substituting the medical terms. Rather, my modest goal in this short, final segment of the book is to posit questions about the overuse of medicalized discourse when viewing collective suffering such as that found in diaspora. Family mapmaking that reveals consistent footprints of diasporic Koreans will tell us what could be involved in the incessant repetition of departures and arrivals.

Each chapter is a testimonial to this outcome: that the location of self in diaspora is never settled, and is sometimes migratory and isolated, at other times strongly connected with the family, ethno-political community, and the lost motherland, as well as with the newly found home. While this much has already been said by many, this book does more: each chapter will force us to think about the interrelationship between diaspora and autobiographic writing, and about the way in which self is claimed against this interrelationship.

What differentiates my text from autobiographical works of literature such as those by Cha and Lee is its methodology—more precisely, its ethnographic aspect. Unlike fictional works, which come with a story constructed more often than not (although, of course, not always) in advance, ethnography works in close relation with the tension between anticipation and tangentials, as noted by Marilyn Strathern: "Rather than devising research protocols that will purify the data in advance of analysis, the anthropologist embarks on a participatory exercise which yields materials for which analytical protocols are often devised after the fact."[57] The study that I present here is of precisely this nature. Some of the contingencies and turns of event which emerged or, indeed, sometimes erupted unexpectedly throughout the course of the research for this book, intimate conversations and interviews with the women, and solicitation of their autobiographic knowledge in writing often challenged my expectations, not infrequently forcing me to reshape or abandon my preconceived ideas and, therefore, rendering my data impure. Yet in retrospect, this outcome was more than logical—after all, no one's life is as predictable as any sophisticated research protocol can ever predict.

This unpredictability is nevertheless a productive digression. Strathern again: "Out of this comes a social sensibility, familiar at least to the anthropological fieldworker. Where research involves 'human subjects,' researcher and subject are likely to *share* problems."[58] Indeed, the individuals who have helped me produce this book have known me for a long time in one capacity or another. This does not compromise the "purity" or "objectivity" of my data, as such things are not my primary interest here. This book is not about the science, the statistics, the clinical observation, or even the generality of autobiographic selves in diaspora. On the contrary, it is my purpose to do precisely the opposite—to reveal life's contingencies, complexities, and coincidences, as they are affected by the intersection of gender and identity in diaspora. For this exercise, as I hope the reader will see, relying and expanding on autobiographic writings and reflections has proved to be fruitful. The reader will have noticed that I avoid the term "autobiography," while preferring to use "autobiographic writing." This is because, to me, the former denotes the bounded, canonical text, while the latter indicates the incomplete nature of a text, that is, the text in the making. Also, generically, not all of my texts can be considered as autobiography; indeed, the text I use in chapter 3 is a letter.[59]

Each chapter relies on the personal writings of Korean women. These are heterogeneous texts: some are lengthy and complete, some fragmentary, and others written piece by piece. Using women's own writing—albeit fragmented and sometimes only too partial—provided an illuminating entry point into their lives. Although I followed up with interviews and e-mail communications with most of the writers, inevitably there is a gap between what they wrote for me and what I discovered and interpreted about their lives. As I began writing this book, I realized that the fact that they opted to write certain things about their lives and opted out of writing others needed to be respected. Rather than probing into the parts of their lives that they had decided not to write about, and rather than trying to (artificially) fill the gaps that had been noticed in their writing, I chose to leave them as they were. The reader will find that I do not always support or verify the informants' words with additional data, and that I do not always confirm the truthfulness or falsity of the information given in their writings. These are, in other words, not my concerns in this book.

Their writings were, moreover, given to me as tokens of goodwill—gifts—not as research samples or some kind of data, although they *became* data. However, the imparting of one's own words, especially written words, is an extremely personal act, delicate and fragile in itself. The protocol (if there is any) in this case might involve handling and presenting their words in protective, not revelatory, ways. In other words, at times demanding more information in relation to certain elements of their writing would have been too intrusive and out of turn. Instead, these texts became guides allowing me to look at their worlds, both through and beyond their personal lives.

As such, my role as a researcher may have been unorthodox (seen from the medico-scientific notion of research, which has done much damage to sociocultural anthropology today), but I have retained my intention of trying to maintain the morality of a human relationship with my informants, rather than trying to dig out information which they may have intentionally or subconsciously refrained from including in their writing. I do not believe that merely supplying exhaustive information makes a good ethnography, as opposed to supplementing the given (limited) information with enriching interpretation. Furthermore, a few of my autobiographers wrote in Japanese, meaning that the inclusion of their writings in this volume necessitated their translation into English. I tried not to Anglicize the information they had provided by inserting convenient cultural equivalents. The reader might feel that I am intentionally less than kind at times, but I hope it will be understood that my moral obligation is not only toward the reader but also to my writer-informants. This does not mean that I do not critique or analyze the autobiographic writings offered to me. As the reader will see, I weave through the meander of multiple roles I am assigned on the pages to follow — including researcher, interpreter, analyst, listener, and friend.

This leads me to the point I need to communicate to the reader before we proceed further. In writing about the lives of Korean women in Japan and the U.S., I am often unable to divorce myself from their lives and life histories. I myself am a Korean from Japan, now settled in the U.S. — whether this settlement is temporary or not, I do not yet know. I have no nationality, since in Japan, one has to be born to Japanese(-blooded) parents to be Japanese. As stated earlier, the end of the postwar U.S. occupation of Japan in 1952 saw Koreans in Japan lose all entitlements to membership of the Japanese national polity, while Japanese nationality law does not grant nationality according to place of birth. I do not have South Korean nationality either, since my parents did not opt to apply for it when it became available in 1965 for Koreans in Japan: this was during the heightened tension of the Cold War, and they did not want to support the then-current military dictatorship in South Korea.

My first exit out of Japan to the West was in 1985. It was a lonesome endeavor, a singular act of resistance against Japanese society, where, as a Korean educated in Korean schools in Japan, I did not have many chances to pursue my desire for graduate study in Japan. Upon arriving at London Heathrow, my heart began pounding and my cheeks becoming warm at the sight of the uniformed immigration officers. (I would have this same bodily reaction whenever I crossed the national borders thereafter.) I carried only a makeshift travel document issued by the Japanese government, a document which had become available only a few years earlier and with which only a few Koreans from Japan had traveled to Europe before me. Prior to my departure from Tokyo's Narita International Airport, an airline official had warned me that the airline could not guarantee my entry to the UK due to the peculiar nature of the document which I carried, and informed me that in the event of my entry being denied, I would have to take the first available flight back to Japan, paying all costs. Contrary to my expectations, my entry to the UK was noneventful. The immigration officer let me in easily, most likely because I had a legitimate UK student visa, which had been issued after a three-month wait, and the bank statement to prove my family's financial capacity. After finding myself thrown into the labyrinth of London streets, I got on a train headed north to York, where I eventually obtained my first graduate degree in the UK.

More than twenty years have passed since that day. My efforts to return to Japan have been consistently unsuccessful. In the meantime, willingly or not, I have been forced to build my career in the West—in Britain, in Australia, once more in Britain and in Australia, and then in the U.S. This is not a track record of a jet-setting international intellectual, but rather the trajectory of one struggling woman pushed from one continent to the other, in her endeavor to find a place to study and work. My diasporic ontology did not stop at my being a stateless Korean born and raised in Japan; by making my exit to the UK, Australia, and the U.S., the complexity of my diasporic ontology was infinitely augmented. My current position as tenured faculty with endowment at a reputable U.S. higher education and research institution is only a transitional point from which to register the statelessness (and, by extension, homelessness) of my existence.

Nevertheless, it is only in very recent times that I have realized and registered the fact that I am multiply displaced. When my previous employer, in what to me (and to many) was an unjustifiable act of authoritarianism, denied me tenure, the livelihood, health, and well-being of my children, as well as my career prospects, became jeopardized. The termination of my employment would have meant the loss of my daughter's health insurance, thereby seriously endangering her life. Having severe physical disability and medical complications, including a history of pediatric cancer, she would have lost access to critical health care and therapeutic treatment. My diasporic instinct perceived the crisis with an acute sense of despondency. I, a woman with no nationality, no national government to rely on, was the easiest to dispose of. My vulnerability as a mother, as an academic, and as a human being was augmented by the added insecurity of my diasporic existence, not simply because I was subjected to what to me was a grotesque injustice, but because—as Arendt precisely stated—my nationless status immediately made me not simply unemployed, but unequivocally devoid of a place to go, to live, and to raise children. Diaspora works this way, does it not, by making one realize that one has no recourse, no home to return to, in a world divided along the borders of nation-states.

In diaspora, betrayal, disillusionment, indignation, outrage, and loss are feelings that come with sharpened edges. The women whose stories and life histories are introduced in this volume have all experienced these emotions, to different degrees and in different directions, but nevertheless always underpinned by diasporic vulnerability. The reader will find a close overlap between their stories and mine. My stories are theirs, and theirs, mine. I will not conceal the extent to which their stories overlap with my own, and how closely I relate to them in terms of sensitivities, perceptions, and actions. Our intersubjectivity is, in this sense, a constitutive element of this book.

This intersubjectivity, however, is not unmediated. It is formulated interactively through the use, choice, or refusal of certain language(s). It is not simply in the sense of certain wording or expressions, but also in the sense of language choice, that we can find clues to their diasporic existence. The fact that I am writing this book in English is a reflection of one such choice in exchange for the renunciation of other possibilities, and this choice is not unrelated to the reality of my past twenty years of multiple displacements in the English-speaking world—just like Lee wrote in Japanese only. The fact that I choose certain words as opposed to others also reflects exclusive decisions that do not allow substitution. The fact that women, when talking with me and writing for me about themselves, use one language as opposed to another is based on selections (whether forced on them or not) that they make within the confines of diasporic vulnerability and the conditions under which languages compete for a hegemonic position in constituting their diasporic subjecthood. Not surprisingly, multilinguality often mirrors the political map of diasporic identity formation—as in the case of Cha. If the reader notices—as I hope she does—that I pay incessant attention to language use throughout this book, it is for this reason.

Finally, I must refer to the incompleteness of this volume. Only certain portions, aspects, and glimpses of the women's lives are contained in this volume, and no one is depicted in an exhaustive or exclusive way, unlike in many life-history books or biographies. I adopted this method in order to let the plural women's lives emerge as relayed, partially overlapping, multivocally represented, and mutually interjecting. Above all, I wanted their stories to live and stay alive, rather than be killed off in the text. Partiality is a good reminder of that. Moreover, I do not mean, in a mechanical and naïve manner, to insist on typicality. Rather, my strategy is to evoke the shared uncertainties of life, each vulnerable and fragile, yet each supple, resilient, and beautiful, each struggling for meaning and purposefulness—that is to say, the ontology of enormous complexity. Now, let us turn the page to meet these women.[60]

NOTES

1. Hannah Arendt, *Men in Dark Times* (New York: Harcourt Brace, 1993), 24, emphasis added.

2. George Steiner, "Our Homeland, the Text," *Salmagundi* 66 (1985): 4–25.

3. James Clifford, "Diasporas," in *Routes: Travel and Translation in the Late Twentieth Century* (Cambridge, MA: Harvard University Press, 1997).

4. During the 1990s, anthropology had moments for autoethnography and other forms of self-inquiry. These were focused mainly on anthropologists themselves in professional settings, and were distinguished from native anthropology, by which an ethnographer studies his/her own culture, by way of writing about one's ontological ambiguity as anthropologist. The most representative example would be Behar (1996), but see also Reed-Danahay (1997), Okely (1996), and Okely and Callaway (1992) for a more specific inquiry into intersection of ethnography and autobiography. I maintain my previous stance critical of these writings. See Ryang (2000a, 2005).

5. By no means am I the first one to do this. Mintz ([1960] 1974), in *A Worker in the Cane*, uses Don Taso's autobiography.

6. A good example of this school of thought can be found in Safran (2004). For a summary of recent studies of diaspora, see Kokot, Tölölyan, and Alfonso (2004) and also Ong (1999), who offers an astute outline.

7. There is a slew of literature and research emerging in the area of historical routes that Korean diasporas took. For Koreans in Manchuria during the colonial period, for example, see Hyun Ok Park's study (2003). As for the early Korean (both naturalized and migrant) involvement in Russian/Soviet politics in Siberia, see the now classic Scalapino and Lee (1972). For the history of Koreans in Japan, the forced labor mobilization they were subjected to, and the expatriate politics among them, see the corpus of Pak Kyeong-Sik (1992, for example). For the much-debated issue of the so-called Korean "comfort women," or sex slaves to the Japanese military, see Yoshimi (2000) or Choi (1997), to cite only two. Contemporary discussions on Korean diasporas in the U.S. and Japan offer comprehensive yet concise overviews of history as well. See my *Koreans in Japan* (Ryang 2000) and *North Koreans in Japan* (Ryang 1997), and Abelmann and Lie (1995) and Hur (1988) for the Koreans in the U.S. For the Korean War, see the monumental study by Cumings (1980).

8. For a comprehensive study of sociohistorical dynamics of South Korea, see John Lie, *Han Unbound: The Political Economy of South Korea* (Stanford, CA: Stanford University Press, 1998).

9. Hannah Arendt, *The Portable Hannah Arendt* (New York: Penguin, 2000), 44.

10. Family's collective responsibility in case of political failure is still at work, as for example families are often sent to concentration camps as one unit, while "revolutionary pedigree" remains intact, as can be seen in the leadership nepotism. See Ryang (1992, 2002) and see more on North Korea in chapter 3.

11. See Tai-Hwan Kwon, "International Migration of Koreans and the Korean Community in China," *Korean Journal of Population and Development* 26, no. 1 (1997), www.ncbi.nlm.nih.gov/entrez/query.fcgi?cmd=Retrieve&db=PubMed&list_uids=12293072&dopt=Abstract (accessed March 3, 2006); U.S. Census Bureau, "Population: Table 24: Resident Population by Region, Race, and Hispanic Origin 2000," in *Statistical Abstract of the United States 2005*, 2007, www.census.gov/prod/2006pubs/07statab/pop.pdf (accessed March 1, 2007); U.S. Census Bureau, *The American Community—Asians: 2004*, American Community Survey Reports (Washington, DC: U.S. Department of Commerce, February 2007), 4; and Ministry of Justice, Japan, "Registration of Foreign Residents," *Immigration Bureau*, 2004, www.moj.gov.jp/ENGLISH/IB/ib-01.html (accessed March 1, 2007).

12. Arendt's stance is most clearly encapsulated in her *Origins of Totalitarianism* (1958a). Here, I use excerpts contained in Arendt (2000).

13. See Jennifer Yau, "The Foreign Born from Korea in the United States," *Migration Information Source*, 2004, www.migrationinformation.org/feature/display.cfm?ID=273 (accessed February 2006). As of 1990, 72.7 percent of Koreans in the U.S. were foreign born, of which 41 percent were born between 1980 and 1990 (U.S. Department of Commerce, Bureau of Census 1993: 3).

14. Statistics from Edward Wagner, *The Korean Minority in Japan: 1904–1951* (New York: Institute of Pacific Relations, 1951), 96.

15. Chikako Kashiwazaki, "The Politics of Legal Status: The Equation of Nationality with Ethnonational Identity," in *Koreans in Japan: Critical Voices from the Margin*, ed. S. Ryang (London: Routledge, 2000), 29.

16. Arendt (2000: 31).

17. Arendt (2000: 41).

18. The Japanese government's immigration bureau is on record stating that neither *kankoku* (South Korea) nor *chōsen* (North Korea), each of which appeared in the alien registration cards of Koreans in Japan, meant a nationality or the name of a state, since Japan did not recognize either (Ryang 1997: 122).

19. From the cultural point of view, postwar reconstruction of Japan's national-cultural identity was avidly put together by using clusters of discourses focusing on Japan's racial homogeneity and cultural uniqueness. For a critique on this, see Ryang (2004: chap. 5).

20. Sonia Ryang, "The North Korean Homeland of Koreans in Japan," in *Koreans in Japan*, 38. Morris-Suzuki's recent work reveals that the Japanese government was considerably more enthusiastic about the Korean repatriation to the North than has previously been understood, while the International Committee of the Red Cross endorsed it (Morris-Suzuki, 2007 forthcoming). For more on repatriation and North Korea, see chapter 3.

21. Sucheng Chan, *Asian Americans: An Interpretive History* (Boston: Twayne, 1991), 140; Eui-Young Yu, "Koreans in America: An Emerging Ethnic Minority," *Amerasia Journal* 4, no. 1 (1977): 120. A rather different comparison between Koreans in Japan and Koreans in the U.S. can be found in Chung (forthcoming).

22. This was recently resurrected in the Patriot Act (Cole 2002: 953). See Campi (2004) for a brief, but useful, study.

23. Arendt (2000: 38).

24. Yau (2004); U.S. Census Bureau, "Population: Table 8: Immigrants by Country of Birth 1981 to 2005," in *Statistical Abstract of the United States 2005*; U.S. Census Bureau (2007c: 13).

25. U.S. Census Bureau (2007c: 14). Kim and Yu (1996) offer an extensive collection of memorable life histories of Koreans in the U.S.

26. Zygmunt Bauman, *Liquid Love* (Cambridge, England: Polity, 2005), 130.

27. Tae-gyu Kim, "New Individual Identification System Sought," *Korea Times*, February 24, 2005, //search.hankooki.com/times/times_view.php?term=new+individual+identification+system+sought++&path=hankooki3/times/lpage/tech/200502/kt2 005022420180211800.htm&media=kt (accessed February 14, 2006).

28. I owe this information to Youngmi Lim.

29. See Ryang (1997) for more details on Chongryun. See also chapters 3 and 5. For the Japan-North Korea animosity, see McCormack (2002, 2006), for example.

30. See Erin Chung, "The Politics of Contingent Citizenship: A Comparative Study of Korean Political Engagement in Japan and the United States," in *Diaspora without Homeland: Being Korean in Japan*, ed. S. Ryang and J. Lie (Berkeley: University of California Press, forthcoming).

31. See Abelmann and Lie (1995) and Chang and Leong (1994) for the LA riots. As for the discussion on the Kwangju massacre, see Shin and Hwang (2003).

32. For further discussion, see Ji-yeon Yuh, "Moved by War: Migration, Diaspora and the Korean War," *Journal of Asian American Studies*, October 2005: 277–291.

33. Zora Neale Hurston, *Dust Tracks on the Road* (Urbana: University of Illinois Press, 1984). See Walker's (1984) comment.

34. Linda Anderson, *Autobiography* (London: Routledge, 2001), 107.

35. Elisabeth Burgos-Debray's intense, one-week interview with Menchú in Paris resulted in the Spanish original of *Me llamo Rigoberta Menchú y así me nació la conciencia*, which was translated into English as *I, Rigoberta Menchú, an Indian Woman in Guatemala* (Burgos-Debray 1984). The book has been translated into at least eight languages and has sold tens of thousands of copies worldwide.

36. The Menchú controversy knows no end. See Arias (2001) and particularly the important essay by Pratt (2001), which connects Stoll's position (Stoll 1999) with the political economy of contemporary college education.

37. Lee Yangji, "Yuhi," in *Yuhi* (Tokyo: Kōdansha, 1989a); Theresa Hak-Kyung Cha, *Dictee* (Berkeley: University of California Press, 2001).

38. See Hayes (2000) for a brief biographical note in English on Lee.

39. One of the most powerful impacts that *Yuhi* delivered to the Korean literary tradition in Japan was its new light on gender. The existing *zainichi* literature had been male-centered, male-produced, and predominantly male-narrated. Surely, the figure of enduring mother existed as a pairing protagonist to the figure of violent father. But that was a subject with no original voice, assigned only to occupy a position that was derivative of the violent husband, whose existence bore witness to the scar of the colonial past, the hardship of ethnic discrimination, and the misery of marginalization, and, hence, whose anger exploded on the bloodied body of his wife. This stereotype of (mostly first generation) Korean women was turned upside down by a sensitive, hesitant, ambivalent, and speechless figure of Yuhi. (In Lee's other works female protagonists are also sensually portrayed, with their sexuality and eroticism explored.) Yuhi's inability to communicate with her compatriots, of course, corresponded to Lee's own inability, which she eventually overcame by adopting (quite ingenuously) an alternative medium—dance. In her other short novel, *Koku* (time), Lee also depicts a *zainichi* woman in South Korea, whose main means of self-expression is to play the *kayageum*, a Korean traditional musical instrument that resembles a harp in structure, but which is set across the lap of the player instead of standing against her. For *Koku*, see Wender (2000b). For a pioneering commentary on Korean women's literature in Japan, see the now classic article by Field (1993).

40. Lee (1989a: 60–69).

41. Lee (1989a: 79–85).

42. Lee (1989a: 106).

43. Cha (2001: 45).

44. See Lisa Lowe, "Unfaithful to the Original: The Subject of *Dictee*," in *Immigrant Acts: On Asian American Cultural Politics* (Durham, NC: Duke University Press, 1996); and Cheng (2001: 159).

45. Cha (2001: 83).

46. Cha (2001: 85).

47. Cha (2001: 87–88), emphasis in the original.

48. Cha (2001: 81–82).

49. Lowe (1996: 129).

50. To my mind, enough is said about *Dictee*'s generic resistance and transgression with reference to conventional textual forms (Lowe 1996; Min 1998; and Cheng 2001, for example); whereas not much is explored about the constructivist effect of *Dictee* with regard to national identity, with references to iconic events or persons such as Yu and the April 19 uprising, and the role such identifications play in diaspora remains to be discussed.

51. Cha (2001: 67–75).

52. Lee (1989b).

53. Hannah Arendt, *The Human Condition* (Chicago: University of Chicago Press, 1958b), 50.

54. Jerome Bruner, *Acts of Meaning* (Cambridge, MA: Harvard University Press, 1990), 121.

55. Giorgio Agamben, *Homo Sacer: Sovereign Power and Bare Life* (Stanford, CA: Stanford University Press, 1995). See chapter 3.

56. Ian Hacking, *Mad Travellers: Reflections on the Reality of Transient Mental Illnesses* (London: Free Association Books, 1998).

57. Marilyn Strathern, *Commons and Borderlands: Working Papers on Interdisciplinarity, Accountability and on the Flow of Knowledge* (Oxford: Sean Kingston, 2004), 5–6.

58. Strathern (2004: 11), emphasis in the original.

59. My approach is similar to, but different from, that of Abelmann's *Melodrama of Mobility,* an excellent work focusing on the personal realm of Korean women and Abelmann's own close interaction with them, in that, though I am much inspired by Abelmann, my focus rests more on the act and product of writing. See Abelmann (2003).

60. All personal names of the women I introduce in this volume are fictive, for the purpose of protecting their privacy.

Chapter One

Many Ways to Be Korean—and Something Else

An Inquiry into the Self

How do we grow up to become ourselves? This question remained central in American anthropology for the good part of the twentieth century, particularly in its major branch, the culture and personality school. Franz Boas is widely seen as the founding father of this school, but in effect it was his students, and especially two women—Margaret Mead and Ruth Benedict—who actually established its intellectual footing and carried on and expanded its entrepreneurial repertoire and parameters. Their major conviction was that a culture produces a corresponding personality, and that it would be possible, therefore, to portray a typical personality as long as we understood the culture that this personality belonged to.[1] With the name of the school itself logically tautologous, culture and personality scholars were thus strongly inspired by psychology and a belief in the strong correlation between culture and psyche, and were deeply interested in studying childhood as the foundation upon which the culturally specific adult personality is formed. In today's anthropological studies of culture, no longer do we directly and unproblematically establish connections between culture and personality, childhood and adulthood, and the individual and society. However, one connection that is largely derived from the culture and personality school, and now housed in the subfield of psychological anthropology, is alive and well: the connection between self and culture.[2]

Among the most prolific subbranches is that relating to the study of Japan, in which it is possible to find an almost inexhaustible supply of constructs dealing with the self. At a glance, this subfield appears to exhibit coexisting polarizing tendencies: "deconstructionist," showing how the Japanese self is diverse, contested, multiangled, and multifunctional, and always involves negotiation; and "constructionist," showing how the Japanese self is unified, essential, culturally consistent, and reducible to a set of finite traits.

1

The former trend is represented by Dorinne Kondo, whose work focuses on the multiple dimensions found in discourses of the Japanese self.[3] Informed by postmodernist moments of fragmentary consciousness and reflexivity, Kondo traces the subtle and diverse strategies of self-making, and the deployment and appropriation of discursive tools available to individuals in a small confectionery factory in Tokyo.

The latter trend often presents the Japanese self to be synonymous with national character, as if the boundaries of the nation-state themselves, and the birth and development of the individual within them, constituted the key elements in the formation of the self. This enterprise is taken up avidly by social psychologists and is found, for example, in the works of Hazel Markus and Shinobu Kitayama and their collaborators, but it can trace its intellectual origin in the concept of *amae* (dependence or interdependence) proposed by psychiatrist Takeo Doi in postwar Japan.[4] According to these scholars, the Japanese self is primarily interdependent, sociocentric, self-evasive, and homogeneous, as compared to its most obvious opposite, a Western self that is independent, egocentric, self-assertive, and heterogeneous.

Upon closer examination, the divide between these two trends is not fundamental in nature. This is because as long as one sets the boundaries of the "Japanese" self, and as long as the conceptual premise calls for the imagination of a set of cultural boundaries called "Japan," we are forced to see the self as always, already, and only culturally (and nationally) conditioned as Japanese. The difficulty is as follows: Where does the "Japan" of the Japanese self start and end? Does "the Japanese" mean Japanese-speaking individuals or Japan's citizens, excluding Japan-born foreigners and diasporic Japanese? None of the researchers offer any clarification. Furthermore, set in this way, the question of "who is Japanese?" emerges as a dubious endeavor, impregnated with suspicious nuances relating to racial uniqueness and genetic makeup. It has long since become common practice in anthropology not to assume an essentialized identity or self, especially after the intervention of postmodernism. Nevertheless, even the "deconstructionist" trend as represented by Kondo rests on the premise of discursive cultural constructs such as *uchi no kaisha* (our company) and other idioms firmly rooted in the discourse of Japanese cultural uniqueness. Kondo shows the multifaceted use of these idioms, but such deployment is itself premised upon the parameters of the boundaries of a Japanese self or selves in Japan, as if to assume a conceptual unity of Japan as a national territory and Japanese psyche as a cultural location, returning us to the above question: "who is Japanese?"

The peril of lumping together people who presumably fall under one convenient ethnic, cultural, or national category, such as Japanese, Korean, or American, and then referring to a Japanese, Korean, or American "self" is not so much that it simplifies intragroup diversity—such an exercise is often necessary as the starting point of an investigation—as that it uses head as tail, giving the starting point of investigation the status of conclusion. In this way, that massive bundle of fine tapestry, into which individuals are woven in many different ways, sometimes overlapping with each other, sometimes disconnected from each other, yet interacting in an unpredictable and unstructured way—the entity that we might call the ambiguity of everyday life—vanishes from the research.

As long as we cling to the showcasing of "such-and-such" a self, we not only miss which self we are trying to know, but also end up collecting the categories that we, the researchers, have given them, the informants; that is, the study becomes about the research itself, not the self of others. This is particularly evident in social psychology projects, where the primary investigative mode takes the form of multiple-choice questionnaires: these, in fact, reveal more about the researchers, who have come up with the categories and questions in the first place, than the consciousness of informants.[5]

In this chapter, I'd like to critique the national or cultural configuration of self, not by setting it aside or eliminating it as an investigative category *in toto*, but by focusing on diasporic and transnational movement of the self that crosses national and cultural borders and embraces multiple locations. As such, the cultural and national references (such as Korean, American, or Japanese) are kept in what is to follow, but only insofar as the border-crossing person perceives them to be meaningful.

Three young women aged between nineteen and twenty-two are the writers/storytellers of this chapter. All of them have acute memories and experiences of having to understand what it is like to move from one culture to another—the first of them moving from Korea to the U.S.; the second woman moving from a lack of awareness (or refusal to be aware) of her ethnic identity to awareness by reclaiming her lost Korean identity in the U.S.; and the third woman moving between the Korean ethnic enclave in Japan and the Japanese mainstream. Each story includes a border crossing at an early age: two actual and one figurative or, more precisely, two national and one cultural. We learn from their stories the crucial role played by language, or multiple languages, in the formation of ethnically positioned, gendered, and maturing identities. Not through the even utilization of different languages, but in losing and gaining, hyperutilizing and suppressing languages upon every border crossing does each experience present them with tests and challenges, in their constant and conscious struggle to maintain their dignity and deepen their self-understanding.

In what follows, I synthesize the (written) autobiographical accounts and (spoken) self-reflections of three young women. As I write here, they are either attending college or have just graduated, and their primary ethnic self-identification is Korean. The first woman, whom we shall call Anmi, was born in Korea and initially came to the U.S. alone, as an overseas student at a girls' boarding school. The second, Mina, was born and raised in the U.S. by her Korean parents, never visited Korea, and does not speak Korean, although she comprehends it. The third, Risa, was born and raised in Japan, educated in Korean ethnic schools up to the ninth grade, and went on to attend Japanese senior high and college. All three share interesting understandings of multiple, yet at times equally singular, identities as Korean. Of course, as I have emphasized, what it means to be "Korean" for each woman is different, never fixed, and in a state of constant readjustment. This is because, for them, "being Korean" is merely a point of departure for being something else while at the same time not completely relinquishing what each takes as being Korean, since there are times when they rely on a (how else shall I say this?) essentialized notion of Koreanness, in order to be self-sufficient.

I shall first present what these three women externalized about themselves through their interactions with me and also in their autobiographic essays. I then conduct a comparative analysis of their lives, letting their selves emerge in such a way as to illustrate elements of commonality and difference. In so doing, I rely on a few medical and psychosomatic conditions as analogous references. I use these analogies only as tools to further illuminate our understanding of the women's selves, and not in order to diagnose or medically categorize them, which would privilege medical knowledge over the sociocultural interpretation of human connections (see chapter 5). Following this, I shall lean toward the approach taken by Paul Eakin: that every self has its own stories to tell; that is, every self is autobiographically formulated— auto (self), bio (life), and graph (writing).[6] In the same vein, it will be important to see how different languages impact differently on the formation of self, as they work to configure and reconfigure memories of the past, understanding of the present, and projections of the future. Furthermore, by focusing on the recollections and experiences of relatively young women, I hope to shed light on lives that are still very much in the making, rather than focusing on what they say about themselves in retrospect, a more common approach in autobiographic texts. In the final segment of the chapter, I shall briefly return to the issue of the self in relation to cultural categories, as in the cases of the "Japanese self" or "Korean self" and, by reflecting on these women's cases, test the viability of such an approach. With these thoughts in mind, let us first meet Anmi, followed by Mina and Risa.

A GIRL WHO LOVED NUMBERS

Soon after I came to America, the economic crisis in Korea caused the exchange rate to double.... it became impossible for my parents to pay my private school tuition. My parents, who would do anything for my education, decided to move to America. Our family moved to the countryside, and since we were not citizens or residents, I was not allowed in the public school system. So I attended a small, private school, where I won many first places in the state math league and became the "math wiz," as my teacher noted in my report card.

Anmi's decision to go to a U.S. high school was a surprising one in the eyes of her peers. She had been accepted into South Korea's most prestigious high school that excels in science education. Graduates from this school occupy the highest proportion of science majors at the prestigious Seoul National University in Korea. But the summer school in which Anmi participated right after her acceptance to the science high school changed the course of her life. It was held in the northwestern U.S.; her fascination with the culturally unfamiliar environment, communicating using the lingua franca, English, though with a lot of struggle, excited her and ignited in her a great sense of being challenged and a determination to take that challenge. Perhaps, Anmi tells me, it was somewhat similar to discovering the brand-new "me"—the self that is expressed through an unprecedented medium, a foreign language—and the use of this new language, in which Anmi was not yet fluent, forced her to search hard for the right word to deploy in order to express what she wanted to say, a process that troubled Anmi, but also fulfilled her. Surely it was a challenge; but Anmi was, in her words, "ready to take it on" and move on to the brave new world of an English-speaking high school education.

But contrary to Anmi's high hopes—yet perhaps quite predictably in retrospect—her experience at this upper-class boarding school in New England was one of enormous bewilderment from day one. There were no other students from Korea apart from Anmi. Her peers, who were well provided for and recruited from privileged families around the world, spoke much better English than she did. She not only felt materialistically and culturally inferior, but she also found it hard to get over her loneliness. There was no one with whom she could talk in the language she felt most at home in—Korean. Apart from the expensive international calls to her parents in Korea, she was reduced to muteness. In addition, the sense of loss—the sense that she had made a mistake in not having gone on to attend that prestigious high school in Seoul, instead coming all the way to the U.S. only to feel miserable—was tremendous.

She felt as if she were gasping for air. Amid all this, it was the math class, where she easily exceeded the abilities of her peers, that kept her going. It was as if the numbers functioned as a third language for her—Anmi's command of math was accorded full merit and recognition at school, unlike her Korean heritage, which did not earn her much of a perk in comparison to her peers from western Europe, for example. Outside math classes, she felt as if she had lost her power of speech—similarly to being aphasic—because of her lack of English proficiency. This statement needs a qualification: it is not to say that she did not speak good enough English; but she was unable to express her deep and intricate feelings using English. This frustrated her and isolated her from her peers. She felt defeated: her family had paid so much money and sacrificed so much in order to send her to the U.S. to study; she had even given up entry to one of the most prestigious and competitive high schools in Seoul; and yet, was this all she could do? Often she would just keep quiet and let others express themselves. It felt as if she had come to assume a different personality and identity—the identity of an aphasic, a person who has lost language, the process that is recounted (paradoxically) in an eloquent fashion in the autobiography of Jasvinder Khosa, an aphasia patient (see below).[7] And when she spoke, she would first mentally put words into the right order, check where to place the definite or indefinite articles, and rehearse the sentence in her mind prior to uttering it, as if she had difficulty in constructing sentences, just like aphasics might.[8]

Anmi's experience closely resembles my own. When I first arrived in England from Japan as a graduate student, my English was so poor that I had no choice but to get by through smiling rather than talking. I found it hard to stay awake during seminars when I understood only about 30 percent of the content, for example. Often, I would break into tears after a tutorial, because of immense feelings of humiliation and stress due to my lack of confidence. I would have to write Christmas cards many times, since my spelling of "Merry Christmas" was wrong. And that first Christmas was the loneliest time in my entire life, when there were only three overseas students left in the empty dormitory. The sense of loss of self, loss of direction, engulfed in the thick and foggy English weather, would have been utterly unbearable had it not been for my determination to make it. Even more significant was my awareness that my study abroad had cost my family an enormous amount of money due to the then-still-disadvantageous exchange rate between Japanese yen and sterling pound, as well as my knowledge that I could not possibly go home empty-handed in light of the family sacrifice. All these factors resonate with Anmi's situation.

Anmi compares her years at the boarding school to childhood. She felt as if she had to start all over again, reliving her childhood—feeling like a toddler who is constantly frustrated since no one clearly understands her. Anyone who has raised a child will know that for a few years during the infancy of their child, parents have to constantly play guessing games in order to figure out what their child is saying. Anmi did not have words to describe that wordlessness, the state of being utterly at a loss, having no language to express herself. She emphasizes that all that was there was her gaze, as if her eyes (by seeing) had to undertake the part of communication that normally the speaking of words would fulfill.

During my initial period in England, I was made into the little child of the dormitory, as a few well-meaning dorm mates were eager to teach me how to cook English dishes and how to pronounce certain words with a proper English accent. I quickly became an interesting project for my friends who cared to educate me in the English way of life. It was only after a couple of years that I realized that the "education" I had received from my upper-class friends was heavily class-bound and had nothing to do with the "English" way, as there was no such a thing as the supraclass English way in general. The lack of critical intention and the eagerness to absorb—just like a child who is learning quickly, absorbing an enormous amount of information each day— characterized my early months in Britain. And just as a toddler observes, mimics, echoes, copies, and learns, I did the same: I listened carefully and imitated my friends' accent, I adopted their dress code, I even walked like they did; and I learned to become one of them. But the most painful process involved the acquisition of a proper English accent. I would manipulate my tongue, lips, jaw, and mouth in ways I had never had to before. It was indeed a rehabilitation of the musculature of my face and larynx. In the end, I was rehabilitated—to a great degree—but the process of domestication of my language was a clear reminder of my wildness. Whenever I was told, "your English is very good," I understood how barbaric and untamed I was in their eyes.

Furthermore, the reality was that acquiring or imitating "proper" English would not grant me membership in British society. Even after many years of living in England, both as a graduate student and as faculty (and, therefore, as a taxpayer), I encountered numerous occasions where I was deemed an outsider. My worth lay, in other words, in being a docile foreigner.

About a year into her stay at the school, as stated by Anmi at the beginning of this chapter, the economic situation in South Korea changed, and Anmi's parents joined her in the U.S. Anmi and the family moved to the rural mid-Atlantic region, but her struggle continued in the area of academic achievement. It was not that she lagged behind; on the contrary, she continued to excel, particularly at math and science, and the new environment in which she found herself—less urban and less competitive—suited her better than the upper-class boarding school in New England. Of course, the fact that she now lived with her family was a decisive plus for her security. At the same time, in retrospect, with her parents living with her, she felt more pressure to do well at school, which augmented her existing feelings of having to achieve more.

It was not until five years later that the family visited Korea. Anmi had by then been admitted to a high-ranking college on the East Coast. She regards this visit as having been the most important occasion for her to make up her mind about her future. She recalls:

> One day, I was watching a documentary program on television with my family. It was about an Indonesian worker in Korea who had been staying illegally. He had left his wife and one-month-old baby in Indonesia to come to Korea to work. For nine years, he never went back to his country, because he could not come back to Korea once he left, due to his illegal status. He worked at a factory, where he had a hard and risky job that other Koreans avoid and worked more than twelve hours a day. However, he got paid very little wages, most of which were sent to his family in Indonesia. Thus, for three years, though he was in pain from an inflammation of the liver, he never went to the hospital for proper medical treatment because he had no money and insurance. When he was finally brought to the hospital by a coworker, it was too late. He was dying. The day before he was [to be] taken to his family by the people from the [humanitarian] program, he died. After watching, I got so mad and cried. I still do not know at whom I was mad. I think I was just able to relate to him more than anyone else, as I know how hard it is to be far away from family in a foreign country, especially when you are sick.

After this encounter, she was determined to pursue a career in medicine. After this visit to Korea, Anmi also felt that she understood better who she was and where she belonged. That long-term sense of being an outsider in the U.S. was finally going away, while that desperate feeling of trying to remember what Korea was like had also lost its intensity. Anmi was, perhaps, coming to terms with her existence in the two worlds. While visiting Korea, upon being reunited with former peers from her middle school in Seoul, Anmi was constantly told that she had become a different person: she was now, in the eyes of her former peers, a quiet person, while she had been a very active, lively, and leading character in class prior to her departure for the U.S. She connects this to her experience of not having the language of self-expression in her New England boarding school. She does not resent this, but is amazed at how much one can change oneself when one is forced to adopt a role that one knows full well is not in line with one's own character.

She graduated from her college in three years with a high GPA and, at the time of my writing here, is working as a researcher at a research institute while preparing to be admitted to the medical school of her choice. She continues to love math, but feels she is no longer dependent on numbers when thinking about herself as a person.

A GIRL WHO FOUND HIDDEN TEARS

"I grew up quite unaware that my sisters and I are Korean," Mina reminisces in her writing.

My family lived in a severely Caucasian neighborhood; we were one of two families of color that I can remember. The other family was also Korean and, incidentally, lived right next to us. I guess we subconsciously stuck together. My childhood as I lived it was normal; my younger sister, by a year, and I played with these blond twins that were my sister's age and lived across the street. We were practically inseparable until I was five. Then, gradually, they would make up excuses to not go out and play. I vaguely remember curbside conversations about why our eyes were different, or why our hair was black. Or perhaps I am only dreaming of a context to explain what would happen to us in the years to come.

Mina's parents didn't socialize with any of the parents in the neighborhood:

How could they? They could not speak English that well at the time, and most of their days were consumed by twelve-hour workdays, while the other parents trickled in around five o'clock in order to prepare dinner and play catch in the yard. My parents didn't have the time and energy to worry about our neighbors anyway; we were supposed to be in a safe, quaint neighborhood. And it was; there were trees, and a creek, and lots of room to ride bikes. It was an idyllic scene to raise children, only apparently it was for every child but their own. As the ties of friendships ceased to exist, the ugly head of cruelty began to emerge. One day my older sister opened our mailbox only to find it stuffed full with grass, dirt, and a letter stating the fact that we did not belong here and that we should leave, only in the more colorful language of ignorant teens. We recognized some of the handwriting; she used to be our friend, an older girl with a huge dog. My older sister wrote her own letter and taped it to our mailbox for all to see. I wish I could remember exactly what she wrote, but even at an early age, she was quite proficient with four-letter words. My parents were unsure of what to do, but hoped for emotions to dwindle.

Mina's parents ran a store in the inner city, a very tough neighborhood, in order to raise their children in a relatively safe suburb which was, however, not nearly happy enough for the family.

Mina told me about what happened one afternoon, when her younger sister came running home from the bus stop, tears streaming down her face. "We never really got the full story from my younger sister about what happened, but it was enough for her to swear to never to return to school again." As I listened and took note, I could not miss an uncharacteristic silence—a very brief silence—followed by a long sigh. I raised my eyes and saw her face. Tears were running down her cheeks. Mina apologized, and I asked her not to. She kept saying she did not know why, but all of a sudden, the emotion had taken such a firm grip of her body. She was not able to speak for a little while, her body appearing rigid, almost shaking in pain. Then, she continued:

We . . . we did know who one of the main attackers was, a boy three years older than her, who made up half of an evil dynamic duo, the other half being a hard-faced girl, who incidentally is the sister of our former twin playmates. My sisters and I went to confront the boy and explain his deed to his mother. Would you be surprised to know that she did not seem too concerned about the fact her son took pleasure in tormenting little children?

Mina's pain came back, not through refined language or graceful prose, by detailed scientific description or sharp analysis—but instead in the way her body felt or, more precisely, the way her body remembered how it had felt, how the rage had made it rigid and frozen and shaken at the same time, and how mortified she had been at the sight of her baby sister in tears. The scene reminded me of Maggie Scarf's account of bodily memory (see below). But, according to Mina, her reaction to these harassments was, sadly (as she recalls): "try to be white." And her "internal drive to be part of homogenized society" continued into college.

But of course, this option was hard to sustain. She and her sisters were often needed to help out with the operation of their parents' small liquor store in the inner city. Before dark, Mina would go help her parents in the store, where her family was exposed to verbal insults by almost every customer, most of these being racial slurs. Mina feels that her lack of love for her own self developed gradually and steadily throughout her adolescence as a product of her hatred of people at large, starting with her parents' customers. Mina writes:

> If only I knew early in my life the simple fact of my value as a human. I was weak, something I do not want to admit, but it is obvious. My only comfort is that I became stronger, first in words, and then gradually in mind, and I was always quick to defend anything that meant the slightest bit to me, which can be a virtue that severely handicaps at times. My efforts mostly consisted of my version of reverse racism, going to an ignorant extreme by making fun of anyone not Asian. Not the most laudable action, but I progressed. I stopped using jibes and verbal punches as a means to an end and realized that inward action was required. This epiphany was the result of a fateful meeting with a professor in my senior year who interviewed Asians about their experiences in America. I usually never talk to anyone, save my sisters, about the details of my childhood laid forth, but as we shared stories of humorous and equally egregious events, I became increasingly animated, and, really, why the hell not talk about it?[9]

Interestingly, her journey to recover or, perhaps, discover, her own self also gave her the chance to think about others as well—including those underprivileged people she had had to deal with in the inner city. She realizes that such a frame of mind also strengthens her justification and motivation to pursue a career in medicine. Now that her premed requirements were fulfilled and her MCAT results satisfactory, she found herself able to devote her time to something that would be helpful for herself as well as others like her. Since there were very limited options for taking Korea-related courses on campus (at the institution where I was previously employed), despite the fact that Asian Americans accounted for almost 25 percent of the entire student body at that time, she led the Korean Students Association to campaign for an increase in the number of such courses. They drafted a petition letter, collected signatures, and met with the deans. The campaign was not wholly successful: although college administrators promised that they would do something to enhance the Korea-related curriculum, nothing concrete followed. But for Mina, personally at least, it was a fruitful political experience. At least she now feels she has done something to redeem her lost past, where she had tried to live without an identity. Furthermore, she had done something not simply for herself, but something that would help others like her. The campaign provided Mina and her fellow KSA members with a multifaceted lesson and valuable experience. By recognizing her own self-worth, Mina came to recognize the worth of others and the value of collective action.

A GIRL WHO WROTE TO LIVE

Risa is a sophomore who was intending to major in business and management at the time of our meeting. She is the only student that her high school—a Japanese high school—recommended to this particular college to be accepted through *suisennyūgaku*. This is a system whereby admission is granted on the basis of meritorious performance at high school, and the student is therefore not required to endure the trials associated with the standard (and often painful) entrance examination. Risa was by no means the first student that her high school, a middle- to high-ranking public school in metropolitan Tokyo, had sent to college by way of *suisennyūgaku*. But she *was* the first *Korean* student that the school accorded the privilege of *suisennyūgaku*. Risa wrote upon acceptance to the college:

> Thinking about my three years in high school, I can tell I became a different person than who I had been up until middle school. I feel I've become closer to my own self (*Jibunjishin ni chikazuita toiu kanjiga shimasu*). I've come to feel more comfortable with myself. This is strange, considering that I'm Korean and yet, I did not feel like myself in the past in Korean [elementary and middle] schools.

Risa was educated up to middle-school level at a Korean school operated by the Chongryun (see the introduction and chapter 2). Her paternal grandparents were colonial immigrants to Japan. They worked hard in order to earn a living for themselves and their children, without regard for the danger and degrading nature of the jobs. By the time Risa's mother married their youngest son, the family owned a very successful retail business in Tokyo. Her grandparents were important benefactors to the Korean school Risa attended, and therefore her decision to apply to a Japanese high school came as a surprise and a disappointment to her teachers. Some teachers bitterly viewed her decision as a betrayal, and harassed her by way of encouraging her classmates to criticize her choice. But Risa (and her mother) persevered, and she eventually left the Korean ethnic education system by successfully passing the entrance examinations to a Japanese high school of her choice.

The reason that she left the Korean school for a Japanese school is not easy to explain. She was not unhappy in the Korean ethnic school environment. But there was one problem. Risa is an avid writer: she enjoys writing short stories and literary essays. But what she enjoys most is her diary. She has kept a journal since she was thirteen years old. It was around that time that she began taking a great interest in writing. At first, she tried to write in Korean, but it did not work: "It felt as if I was writing about someone else," Risa tells me. This is because Korean is for her the school language and, therefore, associated with classes, learning, and tests and, by extension, with discipline and public presentation. By default, this makes the Korean language a disciplinary language of an official and performative nature. She cannot relax in Korean or be truthful to herself—she thinks. Her language at home, her private language that can express her feelings and the intricacies of her everyday life, is Japanese. It is in this language—not in Korean, her official mother tongue—that she reads novels and poems, expresses in writing her emotional ups and downs, and talks to the individuals close to her. Unlike Anmi's case of struggling to communicate in English, which was manifested in syntax, Risa's problem was predominantly with Korean semantics, given that Korean and Japanese are syntactically identical.[10]

While the problem of a linguistic split and uneven distribution of competence in Korean and Japanese is widely found among Korean students at Chongryun schools in Japan, the characteristics of Risa's case, with her drive to write personally, seem to have been closely related to recent changes in her life. It was when she was thirteen that her parents' strained marriage ended in divorce. At school, nobody except Sanghi, her best friend, showed genuine sympathy for her situation: Sanghi's parents had each previously divorced before remarrying and having Sanghi. Although in Japan the divorce rate is generally on the rise, among Koreans in Japan, divorce is still rare and seen as taboo.[11] Risa was deeply hurt by this, as she wrote: "I was not able to talk to anyone, I felt ashamed about my parents' divorce, and was very lonely all day, all night." From then on, her mother had to work extra hard to support her education, and it was around this time that the idea of going to a Japanese high school was born, not just as a result of her desire for linguistic freedom, but also for financial reasons. Korean schools are independently financed and therefore, compared to Japanese public schools, charge substantially higher fees. Journal writing, which began around the time of her parents' divorce, may well have been Risa's coping mechanism: she had no other outlet for her feelings, since she did not want to ask her mother about the details of the divorce, although she never blamed her. For Risa, therefore, the change of environment from a Korean school to a Japanese one may have also symbolized, at least on one level, a fresh start.

This does not mean that Risa prefers Japanese to Korean. She does not necessarily think that Japanese is superior to, or more beautiful than, Korean. For one thing, she is not interested in Japanese literature as her career or lifelong profession. She just needs, according to her, a language that can express her feelings, capture the details and complexities of life, and, above all, fulfill her desire to keep diary entries in a natural way. Of course, one can suspect her lack of proficiency in Korean. It is true that teachers at Korean schools are not native speakers of Korean, and their enunciation and knowledge of Korean tend to be heavily influenced by Japanese, their first language. Nevertheless, it would be fair to say that Risa was not in any sense a student who struggled to perform adequately at the Korean school. On the contrary, she maintained her place in the upper ranks throughout her nine years of study there. For her (and many others attending Korean schools), school-related activities were conducted in Korean due to the strict disciplinary implementation of Korean as the language of instruction and the language to be used within the school premises. On the other hand, once students are outside the school, they switch to Japanese, and it is this latter sphere that Risa mainly writes about in her diary, that is, her personal record.[12]

Since turning thirteen, every day she would come home, do her homework, eat her TV dinner all alone, and look forward to sitting down and writing about her thoughts, her day, her encounters, her losses, her gains, her disappointments, her sources of joy, and so on. Because of her mother's long hours, she would spend much time on her own at home, bored and lonely. Writing gave her a moment of self-reclamation, a moment which she could have all to herself, yet not feel alone. Risa's case might recall the symptom described by Alice W. Flaherty, a neurologist, as *hypergraphia*: just like a person who has been diagnosed as (nonepileptic) hypergraphic, which often occurs at times of personal and emotional crisis, Risa had to write in order to regain her near-lost self and identity (see below). Could this also be related to the experience of Lee Yangji's, though in inversion, in that Lee was multiply rejected by Korean students in Japan on the grounds of her official nationality, by her parents' divorce, and by the homeland where she struggled to blend in; whereas Risa embarked on an endeavor to leave what had been officially conferred on her as her own ethnic properties?

After she started her high-school study in a Japanese-language setting, however, something interesting happened to Risa. Whereas she continued to write her journal mostly in Japanese, she had an urge to do some writing in Korean, using genres other than her journal. Just as Yuhi continues to read in Japanese in South Korea except for her college coursework and exams, for which she reads the Korean-language materials, Risa wrote poems and personal essays in Korean and inserted them in her diaries, which she predominantly continued to write in Japanese. Oddly, therefore, her diary became bilingual. Overall, her desire to achieve a consistency and unity of private language and public language was realized after her switch to the Japanese high school. But then, her Korean ability came to provide her with a special, inner space, which she could occupy all to herself, often offering her a helping hand in enriching the dynamic narratives of her personal development.

Risa gave a speech at her high-school graduation ceremony, as the representative of all the graduating seniors. Her Japanese teachers spoke highly of her in the ceremony, which made Risa's mother very proud. Risa is excited about the prospect of learning more in her years at college, and she wants to work for a financial corporation while continuing to write privately in various genres, either in Japanese or Korean.

ANALOGOUS FRAMEWORKS

As the reader will have noted, the processes used by these women to reclaim their pasts and move forward led me to use frameworks analogous to psychosomatic conditions: aphasia, bodily memory, and hypergraphia. Each of these conditions involves a deep contemplation of, or at least an effort to contemplate with, the self. *Aphasia* literally means a complete absence of speech, and is commonly recognized among stroke victims. Therefore, in the case of Anmi's initial experiences with speaking English, the term *aphasia*, strictly speaking, is not applicable; the more accurate term would be *dysphasia*, that is, "lack of coordination in speech" and "difficulties with speech."[13]

But the conditions associated with aphasia occurred to me as analogous to Anmi's experiences (and my own) when I encountered the autobiography of Jasvinder Khosa, whose life has been filled with tension between attempts at acculturation and diasporic displacement in every possible sense. Khosa, an Indian from the Punjab, grew up in Northern Ireland, moving between Protestant and Catholic neighborhoods. The family tried to return to India at least twice, but failed to do so for various reasons, primarily economic and cultural. Khosa's mother stayed behind in India, trying to facilitate the family's permanent return, while their father raised Khosa and his siblings single-handedly. When Khosa was in middle school, his father's mental health deteriorated: many years of hard work, trying to make enough money for the family to eventually go back to India, which in any case never happened, had taken its toll on his health. Khosa was sent to live with his older sister, who was married to a middle-class English husband. For Khosa, moving from a working-class Irish-Panjabi background (speaking English with an Irish accent) to a middle-class family in Nottingham was not easy—it was almost like moving to a foreign land. Once he had grown up, he settled in the north of England as a professional, but then suffered a brain hemorrhage and became aphasic. Since he received rehabilitation therapy only in English, his Panjabi has almost completely disappeared. Yet amid this tumultuous life, Khosa has discovered the oasis of a new identity:

> The use of language both gives rise to and kills meaning. Words label. Words can name and create meaning, bringing experience and understanding. However, they capture precisely what "is," and not as an adage as experienced by that individual at that particular time. They are abstract maps and not sensory reality— moving instantly to objectify without allowing the subjective (in other words, the emotional truth experienced by that individual) to settle. Whereas aphasia allows me time to just "be."[14]

From within this amazing tale of losing and gaining language and identity multiple times, Khosa emerges as the one with an identity, and not just an identity, but an identity that is absolutely unique and original, that is, his own. There is a connection here with Anmi's journey—losing Korean, learning English, and regaining Korean, finding help and refuge along the way in mathematical symbols. Although, technically, Anmi never lost any language even once, in reality, her acquisition of the new language (English) changed her use of the old one (Korean) and consequently made her into a new person. Just like Khosa's realization that the use of language can kill meaning, Anmi realizes that her lack of English did not necessarily makes her any less of a person; the opposite is quite possible. Paradoxically, therefore, loss is gain. Of course, ultimately, it is the personal strength displayed by Anmi and Khosa that made this happen in each case. But these are not extraordinarily unusual tales in the context of diaspora. Hundreds and thousands of immigrants go through such experiences. One strongly wonders if Khosa's positive turnaround after having lost language(s) came precisely from his personal experience of having grown up as an immigrant, a member of a diasporic family, an experience that preceded his hemorrhage and aphasia.

The immigrant experience is, borrowing from Khosa, "sensory reality," and this is clearly seen in the example of Mina and her life story. The sisters were racially harassed, while their parents worked twelve-hour days in the inner

city. When they were older, they helped their parents, being exposed to verbal
abuse all the time by customers. As a child, Mina could not verbally express
her anger very well and had to fight all throughout her childhood and adolescence, if not always face to face with the racists, then with her own defeatist
self. In the meantime, she also experienced what Leanne Hinton has identified
as "involuntary language loss" among Asian American immigrants. Just like in
Hinton's sample, a group of linguistic autobiographies written by Asian American college students, Mina's Korean has never reached a proficient level: she
understands her parents' words, but cannot converse freely in Korean.[15] This
may have contributed to Mina's sense of inadequacy and feelings of personal
inauthenticity while growing up. It took her close to sixteen years in school,
until she had almost completed her college education, to finally turn back and
face her self as a diasporic Korean American.

Mina's case also strongly reminded me of the story of science journalist
Maggie Scarf, due to the element of self-denial that was embodied, rather
than discursivized or articulated. Scarf grew up in an abusive household with
a neglectful and indifferent mother and a father who was prone to frequent,
illogical, and violent outbursts. However, she spent her whole life in denial of
the fact that her family was dysfunctional, trying to live up to the ideal of the
happy American home. Scarf was finally forced to face the reality when her
mother completely ignored Scarf's efforts to impress her. However, this realization, too, came rather late. For a long time, Scarf could not figure out why
her jaw so often froze up, to the extent that she could not open her mouth in
the morning to brush her teeth, or when this had begun to happen. Through
therapy, she came to terms with her reclaimed memory of one fatal day when
her mother dismissed her first *New York Times* article, saying that she had better things to read. Once she had connected her jaw pain with this experience,
the pain gradually went away, and she no longer woke up in the morning with
a frozen jaw.[16]

Mina's tears while telling me about her sister's ordeal had a similar effect
of connecting the dots. She had found her hidden tears: she had had to pretend to be tough and, in a way, had truly become tough when facing down
bullies and racists, later adopting a strategy of trying to become white. This
strategy, however, had been an emotionally costly one, and telling me the stories of her childhood—I simply asked how she grew up—made her realize
that there had been many events which she would recall with regret, anger,
and tears. Her crying was a cathartic release, just like Scarf's coming to terms
with the reality of her childhood home, since Mina was finally able to face a
past where she had tried hard to become someone other than herself. Her recovery or discovery of her self was cotemporal to her leadership role in ad-
vocating the need for Korea-related courses on campus, her energetic partic-

ipation in the activities of the Korean Students Association, and her being able to live with herself as a Korean. Of course, this is an ongoing process of authenticating her identity; but it seems that Mina has turned an important corner.

Being Korean in Japan never caused a personal problem for Risa in that, despite severe ethnic discrimination against Koreans, Risa was raised protectively inside the Korean ethnic enclave; but being primarily a Japanese speaker while trying to write in Korean and be Korean did cause a degree of emotional stumbling inside her. When faced with the personal crisis of her parents' divorce, her mother's long working hours, and the long, lonely evenings, alone and bored, Risa began writing almost compulsively. Now she enjoys writing, but back then, she had a strong urge to write in order to feel safe and secure. This I compared with Alice W. Flaherty's account of hypergraphia. Hypergraphia, what neurologist Flaherty terms "the incurable disease of writing," is, clinically speaking, an interictal symptom of epilepsy, that is, one of the symptoms found between seizures. But there are many who suffer from a nonclinical yet powerful form of hypergraphia—just like Risa.[7] Flaherty, herself hypergraphic and once briefly institutionalized, began recognizing her symptoms after losing the prematurely born twins she had given birth to while overworking as a resident at a hospital. Her drive to write provided her with relief from the pain of loss, bereavement, and extinguishment of hope.

In a way, writing is a survival for Flaherty and other hypergraphics. According to her:

> What do I need? It is not to have those tiny babies back. They were too small for me to remember; they have vanished like soap bubbles. . . .
>
> In fact, during my postpartum break I discovered a mystery: I loved my sorrow. It was as if I had been preparing all my life for that event, that I had entered into my birthright. . . .
>
> I no longer know whether it is my children that I long for or my sorrow. I have an irrational belief, left over from my sensible past, that if I tell enough people about this knot that is always pulled tight, someone somewhere will be able to loosen it. But my new self needs it always to be pulled tight. I don't write to forget what happened; I write to remember.[18]

For Risa also, we may analogically reason, writing is a salvaging of the lost happy home life when she was growing up—that three-level home, unusually large even for Tokyo's choicest residential district; her parents decorating it with tiles that they had bought on their trip to Europe; and the extended family on her father's side, whom she used to visit all the time. Writing gave her a chance to hold on to all that was trying to escape from her memory. Just like

Flaherty's, Risa's self needed to be "pulled tight," which she expressed through writing.

Interestingly, the cases that I have referred to of aphasia, bodily memory, and hypergraphia all stem from the protagonist's autobiographical recollection and experiences. As in the cases of Khosa, Scarf, and Flaherty, their efforts to autobiographically capture their selves gave these three women, Anmi, Mina, and Risa, an opportunity to contemplate a lost past, the reclamation of which provided them with the strength to build a more solid sense of self. If this is not all about growing up, it certainly is in part about it. This process, it seems, is inherently dialectical—denial of denial, that is, overcoming the self-denial and self-doubt that one did not have the courage or maturity to admit in the past. This process is far too complex and rich to be captured in fragments or in isolated or incomplete terms—surely not in simplified labels referring to a "Japanese," "Korean," or "American" self, for example. Furthermore, the diasporic existence of the individuals in question intensifies this process of self-authentication.

THE EMERGENCE OF THE STORIED SELF

Drawing on Jean-Paul Sartre, Paul Eakin writes that "we are always writing our lives in the act of living them" and that "narrative disorders and identity disorders go hand in hand."[19] At the same time, he warns us of what to me appears as a Western logocentrism, that is, the assumption that the ability to narrate is good and that there is something wrong with a person when he or she cannot narrate; in other words, good narrative denotes health and normality. The works of Oliver Sacks, for example, offer abundant examples in which the nonnarrative self is a self that is different, yet not necessarily abnormal or impaired.[20] Similarly, as can be seen in the case of Khosa above, aphasia can give one a new and different, yet meaningful and reflexive, identity.

As I have shown, the cases of the three women demonstrate that losing is gaining—not having one certain language or culture can give one multiple languages and cultures. In Risa's case as well as in Mina's, what society conventionally imposes as the mother tongue may not function as one's personal language: it may be that it is one's foreign language (categorically speaking) that provides one with a sense of authenticity and truthfulness. In Anmi's case, the process by which she became fluent in her second language, English, was akin to growing up all over again. For those whose lives encompass more than one culture/language set—and there are many of those in the diasporic world—"narrative disorders" are part of everyday life. In other words, one might not be competent or confident in any particular language, while being, say, half-competent in diverse aspects of multiple languages, to uneveː degrees, with uncoordinated distribution of vocabulary and skill, for example Moreover, language can be dysfunctional altogether: Mina's experience of re- claiming the past was in part achieved by way of a bodily (nonnarrative) re- action, where language had failed.

In all three cases, being Korean, or the received sense of ethnic identifica- tion as Korean, plays a key role in determining who they are. However, as caː be seen in the above discussion, such a sense is never fixated on one point anċ is always moving around. Sometimes, as in the case of Mina's rejection, be- ing Korean is a burden loathsome enough to get rid of; on the other hanċ, even when one wants to consciously retain it, as in the case of Anmi after sh_ moved to the U.S., the energy expenditure required to acculturate for survivaː in the foreign environment transforms it in unexpected directions, leading her old classmates to comment that her personality has changed. In the case of Risa, being Korean has been a double-faced issue, due to her lack of abilit̠ to reflect personally in the Korean language, while being fully aware of anċ accepting of the belief that she is ethnically Korean, a point of reference thaː made her distinguish herself from the rest of Japanese society. In all threɛ cases, being Korean is not an absolute and all-consuming part of their iden- tity, but nevertheless is an important, meaningful, and indispensable compo- nent. The notion I deploy here, the notion of being Korean, is first and fore- most a discursive and nominal strategic moving target, for or against whicː individuals construct, critically and reflexively, their senses of self. As such, this is in contrast to the social-psychological endeavor to preconstruct a con- cluding point of the self as "Japanese" or "Western," which works only to fiː those frameworks with teleologically collected attributes such as interde- pendency or independence. Instead, I am using an ethnicized attribute as onɛ of many tools with which the self is being constructed, perceived, and en- acted. Moreover, it is being Korean *in diaspora* that defines the association c̠ Anmi, Mina, and Risa with Korean identity. Here, national borders have be- come irrelevant or relevant only in the sense of negativity and ambivalence, their "Koreanness" being an attribute deriving from the transnational, trans- border form of life of diasporic peoples.

Eakin, relying on the work of developmental psychologists, stresses thɛ link between the extended self, that is, the self in time, and autobiographicaː memories.[21] In this understanding, children and adults are equally competeɾː in their authorship of autobiographies; the continuity between the childhooċ stories that we write (mentally or actually) for ourselves comes to form thɛ basis for our mature selves, and from within this whole process emerges thɛ extended self.[22] Seen this way, the three women's autobiographies are onl̠ part of the corpus of stories that they have written and will write in the coursɛ

of their lives. And, of course, we are not talking about something new to anthropology: anthropologists have always paid attention to autobiographic accounts and writings when engaged with life histories.[23] It is simply a matter
of emphasizing that we need to make a conscious connection between life
histories, autobiographies, and inquiries into the self.

In addition to the sense of extendedness, continuity, and constant transformation as stated above, in the contemporary context of transnationalism, immigration, migration, and diaspora, stories that construct the self are likely to
be ingrained in more than one culture, language, and society, as well as in the
nation-state, stretching across many borders and different terrains. It will not
have escaped the reader that the three women display, to a significant degree,
evidence of overlapping identity formation with regard to their transnational,
transcultural, and translinguistic experiences. All three have traveled from
one cultural realm to the other, either physically and linguistically or in terms
of positional orientation, and the personal, the cultural, and the national are
intertwined in many unpredictable ways. Put in the life span of the individuals, and such intertwining creates an infinite number of reconfigurations of
priorities and orders of experiences in the formation of the self. At the same
time, the direct impact of kinship and family on these reconfigurations is
enormous, as can be seen in the cases of all three women.

DIASPORA AND CULTURED SELF

The shortcomings of the notion of a cultured self, such as the Japanese self or
Western self, should be clear by now. This is because none of these can possibly capture the multiple, complex stories that construct the self, especially the
self in diaspora: they seize upon fragmentary words and labels related to only
one part of the lives of individuals as if they were only living one story. The
anthropologist of Japan might still insist that my cases relate to members of
(ethnic) minority groups, and that mainstream, majority Japanese do not fall
into this category of the multiply storied self. But even the most homogeneous-
looking Japanese live through more than one story simply by growing up and
facing different selves at every turn on their journeys through life. All of the
three women that I have introduced in this chapter primarily identify themselves as Korean, but this "Koreanness" is, as stated above, laden with thick
ambiguity and multiply disconnected and simultaneously overlapping points
of reference to ethnicity, politics, and culture, all traversing transnational, transcultural spheres. In other words, their stories demonstrate that there are many
ways to be Korean and something else at the same time.

How does the above discussion implicate itself in our inquiry into diaspora?
Needless to say, people in diaspora are not the only people who write about

their lives. But the stories they tell about themselves, the languages they learn and forget, and the selves they construct broadly espouse multiple national boundaries and disrupt cultural borders which might otherwise be secure and firmly drawn, especially in the eyes of the mainstream, nondiasporic population. As can be seen in the cases of the three women I introduced in this chapter, even when people in diaspora try not to register their diasporic positionality, being willing to assimilate and associate themselves with the mainstream population (as in the case of Mina), their earlier life histories are never completely disposed of or smoothly absorbed by the ongoing present: at times, the past sticks out as an unresolved issue. At the same time, as in the case of Anmi, even when they have established their national-cultural identity, the mode of self-identification is radically altered and rearranged as they begin to live their everyday lives in a foreign language and their selves in diaspora begin to form. These very selves are rendered heavily unstable in terms of a single form of identification. On the other hand, as in the case of Risa, the diasporic dispersion of the previous generations under colonialism is responsible for limiting, yet simultaneously expanding, the horizons of their self-formation.

The truism of modernity—that the self is located, formed, and activated in multidirectional, complex, and reflexive ways—remains so insofar as one does not take into consideration that the history and reality of diaspora are lived through by generations and families, as well as selves, as will be demonstrated further in this book. For the journeys into the unknown taken by the families of Anmi, Mina, and Risa were historically and geopolitically prestructured by the international power relations manifested either in the colonial relations between Korea and Japan or in the postwar economic, political, and military relations between South Korea and the U.S. Thus, at least in the cases of the three women, multiplicity of self has not only been conditioned by personal(ized), individual(istic) development, but has also been heavily molded by kinship relations, the family's displacement from the homeland, generational interrelations, and other (say) non- or anti-individualistic instances of diasporic life. Let us move on, then, to see how the consequences of diaspora and the traversing of multiple languages pan out in a more personal and introspective story—the romantic autobiography of a Korean woman in Japan.

NOTES

1. For example, Mead (1953a); and Ruth Benedict, *Patterns of Culture* (Boston: Houghton Mifflin, 1934). The culture and personality school became instrumental in providing the enemy profiling during World War II, which paved the way for its rapprochement with national character studies during the Cold War. See for example, Bateson and Mead (1942), Benedict (1946), Mead (1953b), Mead and Metreaux (1953),

Gorer (1942, 1948, 1967), and Haring (1956). As for critique, see Mandelbaum (1953), Martindale (1968), Neiburg and Goldman (1998), and Ryang (2004: chap. 1). For Boas and his career, see Kuper (1988).

2. I'm not saying this transformation was simple or clear-cut; rather, I'm suggesting that the legitimate heir of the culture and personality school is most likely the subbranch of psychological anthropology. See, for example, Hsu (1961, 1972), Barnouw (1963), and Shweder (1979a, 1979b). Of course, the focus on self emerged as an important key in the intervention of feminist anthropology and Melanesian anthropology, as shown by Strathern (1988, for example) and Weiner (1976).

3. See Kondo's *Crafting Selves* (1990) and an article critically reflecting on Lebra's work (1985). There are others whose works fall somewhere between the two trends I mention, although some in the list are much closer to the "constructionist" in approach. See Mathews (1996), Plath (1980), Lebra (1976), Rosenberger (1992), and Dissanayake (1996), for example. See, for a comprehensive critique, Ryang (2004: chap. 6). Again, the Japan field is not the only subfield in which the inquiry into the self is active and lively. Melanesia is another; see note 2 above and also Battaglia (1995), for example.

4. See Sonia Ryang, *Japan and National Anthropology: A Critique* (London: Routledge, 2004), 170–71, for historical background of the birth of this concept. The representative book of Doi's that was published in English is Doi (1973). See Doi (1962, 1988) and Markus and Kitayama (1994). As for the works of sociocultural anthropologists and other scholars that fall into the category of "constructionist," see Caudill (1961), Caudill and Doi (1963), Caudill and Weinstein (1969), and Lebra (1973, 1983). While clearly inheriting the culture and personality school's approach, works that come after Doi's influential theory of *amae*, or dependence, form their own stream in their disproportionate emphasis on Japanese uniqueness. See Ryang (2004: chap. 6), Gjerde and Onishi (2000), Kusserow (1999), and Spiro (1993) for a critique. For a study that stands on the view of Japanese self based on the primordial (pre-)national formation, see Ohnuki-Tierney (1993), and see also Hudson's (1999) critique.

5. See survey questions, for example, in Kitayama, Markus, and Lieberman (1995); Kitayama, Markus, Matsumoto, and Morasakkunkit (1997); and Kitayama, Markus, and Kurokawa (2000). For a lucid critique, see Lindholm (1997), and for a more succinct critique of dichotomy between American self and Japanese self, see Lindholm (2007: 210–17).

6. For a full discussion, see Paul J. Eakin, *How Our Lives Become Stories: Making Selves* (Ithaca, NY: Cornell University Press, 1999).

7. The study of bilingual aphasia can be found in Michel Paradis, ed., *Aspects of Bilingual Aphasia* (New York: Pergamon, 1995). See especially the chapter by Sasanuma and Park. For Khosa, see below in the text.

8. I have already used this disorder as an analogy in the introduction, in relation to *Yuhi* and *Dictee*, referring to Lee Yangji and Theresa Hak Kyung Cha, respectively. Aphasia can broadly be divided into two types: Broca's and Wernicke's. Broca's aphasia manifests itself in difficulty with syntax, while in the case of Wernicke's, the manifestation pertains to semantics. Considering that English and Korean are very

different syntactically, we might usefully consider Anmi's (and Yuhi's) difficulties in parallel reference to the symptoms of Broca's aphasia. See Jakobson (1968, 1971) and Jakobson with Santilli (1980) for Broca's and Wernicke's aphasia.

9. Mina is referring to my project *Voice/Life: Making Asian American Archives*, which I had been conducting for about a year or so by the time I met Mina. See my introduction. I should also add that through the interaction with my Asian American students on campus (in my previous institution), I was made to realize how many female students of diverse class backgrounds assumed or imagined their hair was blond and their eyes, blue during their childhoods. This gives us an interesting glimpse into our society, where a standard type of beauty, as propagated among and hence imposed on children, represents a western European female prototype.

10. It will, however, be inappropriate to approximate Risa's trouble with the Korean language with Wernicke's aphasia, given that her command of Korean is as good as that of her Japanese. Rather, it will be more illuminating to remind ourselves of Jakobson's distinction between the aphasia of the failing metaphor and that of the failing metonym, which Jakobson associates, respectively, with Wernicke's and Broca's. In this chart, Risa's failing Korean applies to both metaphor and metonym. See Jakobson (1968, 1971) and Jakobson with Santilli (1980).

11. The number of divorces in Japan was 69,410 in 1960 and 95,937 in 1970, steadily increasing to 284,906 in 2003—still a very low rate for an advanced industrial nation (Nihon fujin dantai rengōkai 2004: 192).

12. My past research details this. See Ryang (1997), for example.

13. Lesley Jordan and Wendy Kaiser, *Aphasia: A Social Approach* (London: Chapman & Hall, 1996), 7. I'm not trying to pathologize the experiences of Anmi and others that I introduce in this chapter. The use of psychosomatic references does not go beyond the confines of analogy, I reiterate.

14. Jasvinder Khosa, "Still Life of a Chameleon: Aphasia and Its Impact on Identity," in *Aphasia Inside Out: Reflections on Communication Disability*, ed. S. Parr, J. Duchan, and C. Pound (Maidenhead, England: Open University Press, 2003), 19.

15. Hinton (1999) asked the Asian American students at the University of California, Berkeley, to write the linguistic autobiography. These show that the loss of heritage language (parents' language) in the process of growing up later frustrated and inconvenienced the speakers. It will be interesting to investigate how the loss of heritage language affects the sense of self.

16. Maggie Scarf, *Secrets, Lies, Betrayals: The Body/Mind Connection* (New York: Random House, 2004).

17. Alice W. Flaherty, *The Midnight Disease: The Drive to Write, Writer's Block, and the Creative Brain* (Boston: Houghton Mifflin, 2004), 23.

18. Flaherty (2004: 204–5).

19. Eakin (1999: 123, 124).

20. For example, Oliver Sacks, *An Anthropologist on Mars: Seven Paradoxical Tales* (New York: Vintage, 1995).

21. Fivush and Reese (1992), Nelson (1989), and Fivush (1988), for example. See Eakin (1999: 113).

22. Eakin (1999: 113); Catherine Snow, "Building Memories: The Ontogeny of Autobiography," in *The Self in Transition: Infancy to Childhood*, ed. D. Cichetti and M. Beeghly (Chicago: University of Chicago Press, 1990); Dennie Wolf, "Being of Several Minds: Voices and Versions of the Self in Early Childhood," in *The Self in Transition*.

23. Sidney Mintz, *Worker in the Cane: A Puerto Rican Life History* (1960; repr. New York: Norton, 1974); Vincent Crapanzano, *Tuhami: A Portrait of a Moroccan* (Chicago: University of Chicago Press, 1980); Marjorie Shostak, *Nisa: The Life and Words of a !Kung Woman* (New York: Vintage, 1981), to cite only a few. Mintz has been particularly inspiring for the present study, as it includes the autobiography written by the informant himself, supplemented by Mintz's own interpretation and accounts, which expand on the informant's life history. For a recent study outside of anthropology that pays attention to the self's development and autobiographic stories with some reference to diaspora, see Cavell (1994).

Chapter Two

Love and Diaspora

A Romantic Autobiography of a Korean Woman in Japan

Do people fall in love in diaspora, and if so, do they do so differently? What does diaspora have to do with love? By relying on what I call the romantic autobiography, I address in this chapter the question of romantic love in relation to diaspora. Intuitively, we are inclined to think about romantic love as a personal experience. But if, as Joan Scott has asserted, experience is a process by which subjecthood is constructed, and if, as Sidonie Smith and Julia Watson have stated, autobiographical subjects "do not predate experience," then how are we to understand love as an experience that constitutes the loving subject?[1] Furthermore, how should we recognize the specificity of romantic agency in diaspora, if there is any, that is?

In this chapter, I'd like to identify the process by which the autobiographic subject emerges through romantic experiences in close connection to the language of love available to her under the ontological condition of diaspora. I introduce what I call the romantic autobiography of a Korean woman born and raised in Japan who is bilingual in Japanese and Korean yet also fluent in English, having received a Korean ethnic education in Japan before going to study in Britain—let us call her Songrae. My purpose in focusing on love in this chapter is also to explicate the way in which what we tend to think of in the West as personal and therefore endogenous is intricately and intrinsically compounded with that which is thought of as exogenous—examples being community, diaspora, and the nation, for example.

In understanding Songrae's linguistic (and extralinguistic) handling of love, it is important to point out at the outset that the Korean language education she received in her Korean ethnic schools was heavily influenced by the official state language of North Korea, which is filled with "revolutionary" clichés (see below). From this, we may predict that this form of Korean is rather limited in its variety of expression and flexibility of vocabulary. This is due to North Korea's totalitarian mechanism, which by default restricts individual citizens' personal lives by subjecting them fully to state-initiated indoctrination. (See more on this in chapter 3.) Conversely, although Japanese is taught in Korean schools as a foreign language, Koreans living in Japan use the language extensively outside the classroom. Unlike those Koreans who migrated from South Korea after that nation's liberalization of overseas travel in 1988, the numerical minority among Koreans in Japan today, often referred to as "newcomers," the majority of Koreans in Japan are colonial (i.e., pre-1945) migrants and their descendants. They were born in Japan and speak Japanese as their first language, use the language both at home and, of course, outside the home in the Japanese social milieu. This means that their private feelings and affairs are expressed and mediated predominantly in Japanese (as in the case of Risa in chapter 1), although differences in levels of education and income, socialization patterns, cultural capital, and so on would result in different mode of employment of both Korean and Japanese languages. On this basis, I specifically ask whether Songrae's binguality plays any role in her love choices. And, if it does, exactly what role?

To begin with my conclusion, I must state here that my findings are not consistent, in that Songrae, who is fluent in Korean and Japanese, seems generally unable or, perhaps, unwilling, to capture the fine details of her emotions, desires, and loves when speaking and writing in either Japanese or Korean. Of course, being "unable" and being "unwilling" are different, the former referring to a capacity and the latter to an intention not to use a capacity, even though one might have this capacity. But are they so far apart as we might first think? If one were to avoid the use of certain words, such as, for example, profanities or pornographic words, would this kind of avoidance be due to unwillingness or a lack of capacity? Would it not be conceivable that the repeated avoidance of certain utterances could lead to the attrition of the capacity to make such utterances itself? Can we say that a lack of intention leads to a lack of capacity, or in fact is it the other way around—when one does not have a word (and the encapsulated concept), is one still able to enact or visualize the reality that the concept brings out? In Songrae's case, is a certain structure inherent to her binguality constraining her capacity to express herself? And how about when a third language is added to her capacity—as indeed is the case for Songrae with her English? How is multilinguality connected to love in diaspora, if at all? Furthermore, what can we grasp about selves in diaspora by looking at her recollections of past loves?

It would not take too much to assert to the reader that Japanese popular culture is replete with romanticism. We know in the West that Japanese popular culture is appreciated abroad not simply for Pokemon or Nintendo, but also for romantic movies, novels, and *manga*, or comic books, which range from girly fantasy to aggressive lovemaking. In a manner that intellectual labeling would assume to be orientalist, Japanese culture goods such as the movie *Shall We Dance?* are imported and adapted to the Western cultural market, stirring up desires and arousing romantic passions.[2] If Songrae is being exposed to the mainstream products of Japanese popular culture, surely she can be expected to deploy tools that are available in this milieu when romantically expressing herself. But she does not, and she seems to constantly struggle to look into her own self introspectively within the framework of romantic love. And it is here that I wish to emphasize the possibility of problems deriving from the extralinguistic realm, and wish to connect the ontological reality of diaspora of Koreans in Japan to what is arguably the most personal realm of their lives, that involving love and romance. I hope to show how the personal and the political are not easily separated. However, I also hope to show how, unlike in the case of earlier feminist slogans endorsing the political nature of personal issues affecting women, Songrae's case comes with the drawback of creating an arid and materialistic personal life, where love enjoys only limited communication, and sociality within the *oikos* is deprived (in the Aristotelian sense) of discourse.

On one hand, this consequence may be closely connected not simply to diaspora in general but intricately to the Korean diaspora in Japan in particular—its historical entanglement through the tensions of the Cold War, which prestructured the decolonization of the Korean homeland, as well as the Korean diasporic community in Japan, in a distinctly male-dominant fashion. If so, how have the ensuing diasporic gender relations shaped the love and romantic agency of women? On the other hand, a substitution of material exchange with discursive one inside the love relationship, as we will find in Songrae's case, may be the result of distinctly capitalist economic structure in Japan and the formation of relationships it dictates, and inevitably, the denationalized diasporic population (Koreans) inside this structure is affected. If so, how does the level of material comfort in diaspora assign the place of women inside the home? Put directly, does money give a diasporic woman a secure home?

In order to explore these issues, I shall first briefly capture how language is treated in currently-available studies of love, in the section "The Language of Love"; this is followed by a reading of Songrae's autobiographic reflection, entitled "Ethnic Love Story." In "The Politics of Love," I will present a historical overview of the Korean language education in Japan that Songrae and others like her were subjected to, with an eye on the expatriate political movement supporting North Korea carried out by Chongryun. I explore the mechanism by which the language and norms of love are produced and reproduced inside the Korean diasporic community, with the focus on Korea University of Tokyo operated by Chongryun, where Songrae and hundreds of others like her have been educated. In order to provide the reader with a better background, I preface this section with a short account of the history of postwar Korean ethnic education in Japan, "Chongryun and Korean Language Education." In the following two sections, "Songrae's Case" and "Love and Language," I'll discuss the interrelationship between love and the language of love, as embedded in ethnic identity and the politics of diaspora. A short reflection on love and home (or the loss thereof) in diaspora, arrived at by returning closely to a consideration of Songrae's case, is also included in this section. In the final segment of the chapter, "Love, Political Life, Home," I address the point of how ethnicity, diaspora, and other factors that bear upon the formation of the self play key roles in shaping romantic ideals in articulation with the home as a place where, paradoxically, political life takes place.

I shall contend that inside a diasporic community, love is not a matter of personal choice or feelings, as we are often (mis)led to believe in our (Western) society, since for people in diaspora (and, especially, in a politicized one) personal choices can involve grave consequences in terms of sociality, as they classify and declassify individuals with regard to their topos inside (or outside) the diasporic community. With this in mind, I inquire into the complex choreography of the diasporic self's formation through self-reference, with a focus on romancing endeavors or lack thereof. I shall touch upon the question of whether, then, women like Songrae, who married inside the diasporic community, have found "home"—as in a place where socially and politically meaningful life (*bios*) is attainable—or, whether "home" for these Korean women is *oikos* as opposed to *polis*, where life is merely *zoē*—simple, basic life that all living beings have even when they have no social or political role, just because of the necessity of living. I shall argue that the peculiar statelessness of the Korean diaspora in Japan reconfigures the separation between *polis* and *oikos*, or the public and the private, in such a way as to undermine both spheres for women.

THE LANGUAGE OF LOVE

It appears that, with or without an emphasis on literacy, love, as is the case with many other concepts, institutions, and experiences humans possess, is closely connected with language (spoken or written). But exactly how are they connected? If language plays a contributing, constructive, and positive role in enhancing and deepening loving feelings, or, conversely, if its role is to rationalize and at times offer comfort in relation to unachieved romantic

desire, then can those who speak more than one language have a richer experience with regard to love? Further still, how does the proclivity or internal
structure of a certain language that individuals possess precondition their romantic experiences, both through encouraging them to take certain actions
and also through dissuading them from taking others?

Since antiquity, humanity has engaged with the question of love. In the
cases of most major literate cultures, a large proportion of available historic
documents and writings concern love, revealing a fascination and a sense of
enthrallment with diverse forms of love, from romantic passion to familial affection, true friendship, or care of neighbors. Where cultures did not possess
their own writing systems, the tradition of telling and retelling love epics
played the role of the archive.

Scholars have, in various guises and with greater or lesser levels of commitment, argued that for love, especially romantic love, to be born, literacy
plays an important, or decisive, role. They have held the dissemination of
writing and literacy to be responsible for the birth of romantic love among
people who used to be located outside the realm of passionate romance — non-
literate and lower-class peoples. Lawrence Stone, for example, notes that
"public admiration for marriage-for-love" rose out of the romantic movement
of late eighteenth-century Europe, "only winning general acceptance in the
twentieth [century]." Stone regards the birth of a popular new literary genre,
the novel, or more precisely the romantic novel, as an important factor leading to the idea of falling in love becoming accepted as a positive event in life.[3]

Jack Goody emphasizes literacy as the major culprit in the formation of romantic love. In thinking about the culture and tradition of love, Goody asserts
that Eurasia, with its long history of literacy, forms one group, while Africa,
where literacy was traditionally not found, forms another: whereas traditions
of writing about romantic love are found in Eurasian cultures, no such equivalent is found in African oral traditions. Furthermore, when love is literally
expressed in the latter context, it is transformed into something other than
orally expressed sentiments — something more solid and permanent.[4]

Anthropologists — unlike literary critics, psychoanalysts, historians, and so-
ciologists — have, by and large, lagged behind in the race to study love, or in
framing the study of love and romantic relations in the analytical paradigms of
their own discipline.[5] Anthropologists have always discussed sex, copulation,
mating, matchmaking, and, above all, marriage under the rubric of kinship and
ritual, yet they have curiously tended to ignore love.[6] Why? This appears to be
related to the dominant intellectual tradition, according to which love was seen
as an emotion that accompanied only a certain level of civilization. Hence, just
as medieval, illiterate peasants were supposed not to have fallen in love, but
simply to have copulated and procreated, the "primitives" that anthropologists

studied were not seen as being capable of, or interested in, falling in love. This type of perception saw love as a distinctly high-cultural phenomenon—pertaining to the realm of noble emotions—or a sophisticated sentiment. Also, this perception was underpinned by the assumption of love's clear-cut separation from sex, according to which love functions logocentrically and sex, carnally. When no word for love (or none corresponding to the meaning of the term in the Western language) could be found in the native vocabulary, it became more or less common practice to deem that that particular culture was devoid of love. Goody's aforementioned example attests to this.

In recent years, however, romantic relations have captured the eyes of anthropologists, and they are rapidly proving to be a theme worthy of fieldwork. This is not only because there is no longer really a "culture" that has not been touched by Western cultural domination and modernization (or the aspiration to modernize) and, perhaps more directly, infiltrated by Hollywood-type versions of various native romantic mass products such as novels and movies; it is also (if not more so) because anthropologists have begun to recognize that native discourses of love may present themselves quite differently—both semantically and syntactically—from those of the West. For example, by taking a more culturally relativistic approach, William Jankowiak and Edward Fischer document that 146 out of 166 sampled cultures have words corresponding to the Western notion of love.[7]

Focusing on the poetic expression of Bedouin women, Lila Abu-Lughod has explored how deep feelings that Bedouin women could not normally display in public were conveyed using the vehicle of poetry. More recently, Laura Ahearn has analyzed the use of letter writing—or, more precisely speaking, love-letter writing—in relation to changing courtship practices within a Nepalese village, especially since the introduction of compulsory education, with the resulting improvements in literacy among villagers, particularly young females. Nicole Constable's study of international couples who met through online dating showes that whether online or not, (Western) men and (non-Western) women can meet and enter fulfilling relationships and marriage.[8]

In all of these studies, literacy and the appropriation of certain literary genres have been shown to play a key role in courtship. The Nepalese lovers Ahearn studied achieved their romantic ambitions through the writing of love letters, contriving to express their personal feelings within the prestructured limitations of kinship euphemisms and terminology—I must not say "limitations," since the kinship terminology used by lovers to address each other was at once convention and creation, in that each utterance was laden with personally appropriated meanings attached to generalized terms; as such, the conventional letter-writing format became an effective vehicle for expressing each unique form of agency and each unique action and emotion. In other words, a knowledge of the kinship system, its relationships, and, above all, its terms plays a decisive role in Nepalese love-letter writing. For Constable's international couples, English literacy on the part of the women in the Philippines and Hong Kong was a prerequisite for entering into online communication. Here, literacy was required in two areas: English and computers. Considering that Internet use itself presupposes the possession of knowledge relating to e-mail communication — standard practices, codes, abbreviations, signs, etc. — and is not simply a matter of replicating conversational (verbal) English, for global romance to be consummated, complex literacy becomes imperative. In the case of the poetic form of self-expression captured by Abu-Lughod, this particular genre, the recitation of poems, becomes a prerequisite for love. Or, should we say, it is only within the framework of this formula that Bedouin women are allowed to convey their loving sentiments and longing desires. Conversely, within this genre, women can express sentiments that it is otherwise taboo to publicize.

The use of language, or words, both spoken and written, enunciated with passion behind customary forms of kinship address, codified in highly private and clandestine poetry, and hidden in the paradoxically public and widely accessible context of the World Wide Web and e-mail, offers crucial insights which researchers may use when preparing the groundwork for their fieldwork and, later, conducting their analyses. This method, though of course logical, stands on a certain intellectual (or perhaps cultural) premise — the premise that love is to be confessed and expressed through words; saying is loving. Hidden in poetic disguise, handwritten under candlelight, or sent by the click of a mouse, the most crucial assumption in this body of research (and, indeed, most of the existing anthropological studies of love and romance) is that love is (needs to be, rather) spoken, written about, that is to say, discursivized. Note here that the paradigm has not shifted — whereas, in the past, the lack of a language of love was deemed equivalent to the absence of love, the discovery of a native love language is deemed equivalent to the discovery of native love. For, unless expressed, how is love meant to live? Unless enunciated, how are men and women supposed to be romantically awoken so that they may begin a relationship? But is this all it takes to know, understand, and study love, that is, love's language?

What is curious in these studies is that the question of how we can actually capture the intricacies contained in the interrelationship between love and the discourses of love is, to a large degree, left unaddressed, it being simply assumed that what people tell (admit in words) about love is the truth about love. On the one hand, the role of language in love and romantic relationships is underexplored; on the other hand, language has been routinely relied upon

in the studies of love as a priori data. This renders the whole approach circu-
lar.[9] The underlying methodological assumption is that language is a medium
through which men and women express love. Here, the love inside one's heart
precedes the language of love that flows from one's mouth, pencil, or keyboard. That which waits to be exposed is the following: what happens when
love's performative orientation is premised upon radically limited linguistic
resources in the first place? Can love grow or be conveyed using a language
in such a situation?

AN ETHNIC LOVE STORY

"An Ethnic Love Story": entitling this section in this manner, I do not in any
way suggest that there is an ethnically specific way to fall in love, or that
there is a form of love that one ethnic culture can claim as its own. It is, however, my intention to suggest that ethnicity, or the types of ethnic relations,
sense of difference, and identity within which one lives one's life, is no small
factor, guiding one to fall in love with certain persons and not fall in love with
certain others. Seen from different angles, ethnic identicality can posit both
positive and negative factors in romantic relations. In many cultures, it is pre-
scribed that ethnicity forms the limits of endogamy. Strict rules of clan exogamy are often accompanied by the rules of ethnic endogamy. This is to say,
rather than assuming some essential endowment unique to an ethnic community, that men and women who are eligible for romance within an ethnic community are overtly and covertly disciplined into embracing some individuals
and eliminating others as possible suitors.

But the rules of ethnic endogamy, of course, do not interfere with, or re-
duce, the level of passion. Similarly, this rule does not successfully discour-
age transgression: in Japan, currently over 80 percent of all marriages involving Korean persons are marriages between a Korean and a Japanese, with
Korean-to-Korean marriages constituting an extreme minority of cases.[10]
Arranged marriages between Koreans and Japanese are unheard of; in other
words, we can be certain that marriages between Koreans and Japanese are
so-called "love marriages." It is quite impressive, in light of the ethnic discrimination against Koreans and the general proclivity in Japanese society toward the exclusion of non-Japanese Asians as desirable marriage partners,
that these transethnic lovers persevere and beat the odds.

Whether this passion is spontaneous or not, or genuine or not, is quite a
separate matter. Or, perhaps, this statement itself is falsely postulated. Just as
in Pierre Bourdieu's concept of habitus, the way an individual falls in love
with a certain person appears to be simultaneously spontaneous and struc-

turally predetermined, due to the internalized norms and value systems that are imposed upon and absorbed by individuals, and improvised and acted upon by them.[11] The following autobiography will show that who is chosen, from what ethnic, cultural, class, occupational, or other socially categorizable group, depends heavily on cultural values, personal knowledge, social conventions, or, in a word, one's upbringing within a family; disciplines given in school; and antitransgression admonitions insidiously embedded inside the community, and internalized by individuals themselves. This, again, is never available as a free, personal choice; and yet, at the same time, choices are often made which conflict with the regularity and predictability that ready-made statistics may suggest.

This, of course, is expressing a truism, but suffice it to add here that the reality of modern diasporas appears to intensify the extent to which love is predetermined or prelimited, incurring the need for self-justification on the part of the lovers who are, like it or not, fully equipped with the romantic potential available in modernity. In other words, contrary to what might seemingly be projected, internationalization or contact with and exposure to other cultures and educational institutions (including through study abroad) and other border-crossing experiences during the period when one is, generally speaking, romantically active may not result in the expansion of one's field of love choices—in fact, it might narrow it in the case of individuals in diaspora, or a particular form of Korean diaspora in Japan, as will be shown below. I'd also like to further demonstrate that the language of love (or indeed the absence thereof) takes individuals down and along interesting paths, behaving not as a mere carrier or mediator of meanings, but at times as an active interventionist, guide, and creator of meanings, no matter how impoverished these meanings may be. And it is on this point that I shall reinvoke the title of this section, "An Ethnic Love Story," in the context of an analysis of what I call romantic autobiography of a Korean woman in Japan.

Songrae was born to an intellectual family of Koreans in Japan. She belongs to a rather unusual subgroup of Koreans in Japan, who went to study abroad in the late 1980s—this was still very rare in those days. She received all of her education in Korean schools from the elementary to the college level, prior to her study abroad in Europe. At the time of her writing the following autobiographic account, her two daughters were studying at a Korean elementary school. She wrote a brief autobiography for me, referring to her romantic history, and provided me with further information via e-mail. This was combined with the repeated, informal person-to-person interviews and conversations I had with her (often over the phone) over close to a decade. The following is a synthesis of all of the correspondence I've had with her, although the core content comes from her original autobiography.

When it comes to my romantic history, it does not go back very far. I was a tomboy and was not interested in dating for the longest time. I would think that I was popular with boys mainly because I was the only girl in my class at the engineering department of Korea University that year. But nothing romantic happened with anybody. It would have to have been after graduation that I became romantically involved with someone. It was a Japanese person from a prominent politician's family. He and I happened to be in the same section of the firm. I was working as a software engineer. He, Mr. O, was a very cordial, polite, well-educated gentleman. We had a couple of dinner dates, went to watch movies together, and realized that we were talking about our personal future in very close proximity to each other.

But, perhaps, it was clear to me from the very beginning that there was no future together for us. He was from a publicly recognized family [in Japan] and he was destined to stand in the metropolitan district elections, running for office, just like his father, uncles, and grandfather. He was sincere with his feelings toward me and I, with mine, toward him, but it was not possible. On the one hand, I could not accept the idea that I might be permanently removing this man from his destined career, or family business, if you like. As we know, in Japan, if one were to marry a Korean, one could forget about one's public and political career. But on the other hand, ultimately, I did not think I could be married to a Japanese. That would have been such an extreme deviation from my Korean upbringing. Regardless of how rich or powerful this man might have been, my family would have seen it as a calamity, and my friends, indeed, the Korean community that I grew up in, would have ostracized me. I did not think I would be able to bear such a consequence. I suggested to him that we should go our separate ways. When I think about it now, I doubt it was love. I was fascinated with Mr. O's unique family background, but how much I was attracted to him as a person I'm not sure anymore. I was fresh out of college and too young to know what love (*koi*) was.

It was a year or so later that I got an opportunity to study abroad in England. I was admitted to the master's degree course in computer science at a rather prestigious university in the north of England. I struggled initially, as I spoke very poor English. It was then that I met E, who later became my boyfriend. E came from the south of England. His family was a bit like mine—not very wealthy, but well educated. He was very patient with me and helped me get used to English university life. He would correct my grammatical errors very gently and patiently, so that I would not be offended or made to feel inferior. After one and a half years of dating, thanks to E, I became quite a good English speaker.

When I was done with my study, it was very clear in my mind that I'd not spend the rest of my life with E. In retrospect, I could argue that the cultural distance between us was a large factor, in addition to the difficult prospect of having to live in England away from my family in Japan. But frankly, I don't think, even to myself, that I loved him in any convincing way. I found it almost awkward whenever he said, "I love you." For me, it was a mystery why he had to say that like some kind of mantra, as if saying this was more important than showing affection through behavior. Either way, there was not a strong enough bond between us, I think. In fact, when I say "love" (*ai*) when talking about that relationship, I can feel immediately that this is the wrong word.

After I came back to Japan, I dated a couple of Korean men, introduced through former classmates. In the end I got married to my husband, whose family background is very similar to mine, although his family is a lot wealthier than mine. My husband and I were both educated in Korean ethnic schools up to college level. We both enjoy downhill skiing and road trips. Still, we are very different in terms of values. Of course, again, I'm speaking in retrospect. I'm not saying, turning my comment on E upside down, that it is purely because of ethnic education and cultural proximity that I married him [i.e. her husband]. I guess I fell in love (*koi shiteita*) — but saying this feels very remote from me now. I wanted to be comfortable after marriage, so I would not have to pretend to be anyone other than myself. And in this sense, it just seemed most appropriate that I marry a Korean from a similar background to my own. It was based on my choice — nobody forced this marriage on me. Love (*ai*) sounds foreign to me now, though. We stick with each other due to mutual trust, a sense of duty towards our children and, most importantly, familiarity. *Suki toka kirai toka iunodewa nakute, isshoni kurasiteikeru aite toiu tokoro deshōka* . . . (Rather than liking or not liking, should I say my husband is a companion with whom I can continue to live day-to-day.)

Songrae and her husband had just celebrated the tenth year of their marriage. Her husband had bought her a French designer handbag, which was added to Songrae's already extensive collection. She told me it was a good means to get even, since he had spent a lot of money on his cosmetic surgery without prior consultation with her. An expensive handbag thus resolved the tension that had risen up after that surgery. The best adjective to describe Songrae's life — as part of an economically stable family with healthy children, living with all the urban amenities that the average Japanese would deem to be ideal — would perhaps be *satisfactory*. As Songrae herself said, whether or not it is love that governs her relationship with her husband, however, remains to be verified. Unlike her older sister, who had an arranged marriage, Songrae never experienced a formal introductory meeting. She thinks it was because her parents were not sure what to do with her, as she was highly independent and had already taken an unusual path in contrast to her peers — for example by going to England to receive a graduate education. She believes that they have no idea about her premarital involvement with Japanese or English men and that they are content with her marriage, although they are not as close to her in-laws as they are to those of her sister. Back to Songrae, again:

I did not realize how difficult it would be for me to write about love. When I was a student at Korean schools, I really do not remember even fancying anyone

(*Darekani akogareta kotomo nakattato omoimasu*). Growing up, I had a lot of friends, both male and female. Although now I keep in touch mainly with the girls, I've always loved my friends, all of them. In a way, I feel I'm the kind of person who values friendship (*yūjō*) more than romantic love (*renai*) and that could be why I struggle to write about love. Also, I've never had to write something like this before and my Japanese is not used to capturing this. Shall I say, it's very awkward and I'm unable to find the right words (*Nandaka totemo gikochinai to iuka, kotobaga umaku detekonai toiu kanjidesu*). But, this does not mean my Japanese is ill-equipped: I would feel much worse if I were to write about love in English or Korean. I must say I'm simply not used to it. I'd do anything for my children and I'd have no problem writing about my devotion for them. But when it comes to romantic love, I'm at a loss and I really don't know what to write about (*Nanio kaite iinoyara yoku wakaranaishi tomadotte shimaimasu*). All I know is that I have always known that I had to marry a Korean in Japan (*Zainichi chōsenjin to kekkonsuru to iu kotowa zutto wakatteitanodato omoimasu*).

Songrae never used Korean in her autobiography. In our phone conversations, too, she spoke predominantly in Japanese, except for the rare occasions when she talked about the Korean ethnic education she had received, when reproducing the North Korean clichés that she had acquired through that education.

CHONGRYUN AND KOREAN LANGUAGE EDUCATION

Songrae's marriage, though belonging in an extreme minority in the large picture of Korean marriages in Japan, is not so unusual among the Koreans in Japan who grew up inside the Chongryun, an expatriate ethnic organization that supports North Korea (see the introduction). Needless to say, it would not be surprising to find an ethnic, expatriate, and diasporic organization promoting ethnic intermarriage. What is surprising in this case is that this ethnic movement in Japan supports North Korea, despite the fact that the predominant majority of Koreans in Japan came originally from provinces that belong to today's South Korea. Chongryun, or, formally in Korean, *chaeilbon choseonin chongryeonhaphoe* (the General Association of Korean Residents in Japan) fashions its organizational apparatuses after North Korea's state institutions for totalitarian indoctrination. In the ideological operation of Chongryun, love, or more precisely romantic love, plays no small part. It may be surprising to some readers to imagine that love has anything to do with an ideological operation fashioned after North Korean style totalitarianism.[12] In order to explain this, I must make a detour by looking into the Chongryun ideological apparatus in question, notably in the context of its ethnic education, and by conducting a particularly close examination of its system of higher education.

Chongryun was founded in 1955. The Korean expatriate movement in Japan had faced a difficult and tumultuous decade following the end of World War II. Right after Japan's defeat at the end of the war, it has been said that there were about 2.4 million Koreans remaining in Japan.[13] The majority of these instantly lost their livelihoods at the end of the war: they had either been forced to come to Japan to work in war-related industries or had come to Japan semivoluntarily looking for the work that was available at a time of war. The repatriation package that was offered by the U.S. occupation authorities and the Japanese government was inadequate, inconsistent, disorganized, and ill-planned (or not planned at all, in many cases). Most Korean repatriations at this time were the result of efforts on the part of the Koreans themselves, and these often turned out to be chaotic. Even if they succeeded in making their exit from the devastation in Japan, they often found the situation in Korea equally unstable, if not worse. Mass repatriation, nevertheless occurred, and by 1947, the Korean population in Japan had shrunk to 529,907; in 1948, it was around 590,000.[14]

Upon Japan's defeat, the Allies partitioned Korea—a historical consequence of World War II, the rationale behind which no one seems able to explain to this day. If any nation needed to be partitioned in East Asia, it was Japan, because of its past aggression. Yet due to rising Cold War tensions in East Asia, Japan's national integrity was not only saved but also nurtured by the U.S., while its former colonies and the territories it had invaded and occupied ended up being devastated and divided: Korea, China, and Vietnam, for example. Partition divided the Korean peninsula into the Soviet-occupied North and the South under the American military government. Three years after the war, in 1948, upon the withdrawal of the Soviets and the American military government (although a heavy U.S. military presence remained in South Korea), northern and southern Korea held separate elections and established mutually antagonistic regimes.

As stated, the vast majority—98 percent—of first-generation Koreans in Japan came from the southern provinces.[15] But the postwar left turn of Japanese society (at least in the initial year or so under the U.S. occupation) attracted the majority of Koreans remaining in Japan to the Communist movement and the Sovietized North. As soon as the war was over, in October 1945, Koreans formed their own leftist organization and entered into sisterly relations with the newly reconstructed Japanese Communist Party. This organization, *chaeil-bon choseonin ryeonmaeng* or the League of Koreans in Japan, defined itself as an interim organization that would help all Koreans repatriate to the peninsula and, in the meanwhile, teach Korean adults and children Korea's own language, culture, and heritage. The reason the League of Koreans conspicuously defined itself as an interim organization was that Koreans (and perhaps many other peoples in the world) believed that the partition of their motherland was only temporary and that, once the Americans and Soviets were out, it would be unified. In other words, at this point, the left and right split within Korean expatriate nationalism in Japan did not reflect exclusive allegiances of loyalty to either regime—the partition line was vague and only temporarily drawn in the mental map of Koreans in Japan, who in large part assumed that all Koreans would eventually be repatriated and that they would not continue living in Japan, their colonial metropolis, indefinitely.

The League of Koreans constructed many makeshift Korean language schools all around Japan. Most of them did not have permanent building structures, and they were often unofficial gatherings of children and grown-ups under anybody who could teach the Korean language. Such schools were numerous, however: according to Pak Kyeong-Sik, as of October 1949, the League sponsored a total of 578 primary, middle, and high schools spread across almost all of the prefectures in Japan, with about 50,000 students in total. It also issued a total of 912 textbooks on various subjects and in various grades, written in Korean, to be used in these schools.[16] Due to the accelerating polarization of the Korean peninsula in the context of the Cold War, however, the schools under the League were increasingly seen as subversive by the authorities, both the U.S. occupation forces and the Japanese.

On January 24, 1948, the Ministry of Education of Japan issued an order stipulating that all Korean children in Japan must attend accredited schools approved by the prefectural governments, meaning that Korean schools needed to follow the Japanese standard curriculum as stipulated by the ministry or else risk closure. Accreditation for an academic institution in the eyes of the ministry meant that all teachers must be certified and licensed by the Japanese government; all schools must use textbooks approved by the government; and the schools must be subjected to regular inspections by the government. If Korean schools wished to be accredited as academic institutions, their language of instruction had to be Japanese, and their teaching of Korean had to be placed outside the formal curriculum. It virtually amounted to a declaration of closure for all of the Korean schools that existed. The League and the Korean schools resisted, insisting that they had the right to teach Korean students the Korean language. As the deadline for accreditation drew near, violence erupted on the premises of Korean schools in many locations in Japan. The fiercest battle took place in April 1948 in Kobe, where Koreans and Japanese (mostly Communist) supporters occupied the mayor's office, demanding permission to continue Korean ethnic education, upon which martial law was declared and the U.S. military and Japanese police raided Korean schools and neighborhoods. At least one Korean male student was shot to death on the spot; a Korean schoolgirl sustained head injuries and later died;

and one Korean teacher was killed in his prison cell after arrest. Hundreds were wounded, and mass arrests followed.[17]

Following this, in September 1949, the League of Koreans in Japan was subjected to the Prevention of Destruction Law, the incident being the first time that this law had been applied in postwar Japan. The League's premises and properties, along with cash savings and other assets, were confiscated by the authorities, and its leaders were banned from political activity. Its schools, following the Kobe incident, had become defunct. Many of them were closed down, while a handful retained their continuity through incorporation as providers of noncredit extracurricular classes subordinate to the Japanese public school system. This was a major blow for Korean expatriate nationalism in postwar Japan.

Chongryun, upon its foundation in 1955, adopted the pragmatic strategy of avoiding the direct confrontation with authorities that the League had suffered from. It declared itself to be an organization of overseas nationals of North Korea, openly pledging loyalty to that country. At the same time, it publicly defined itself as a law-abiding organization in Japan; and, as an organization representing North Korea overseas, it endorsed its renunciation of all activities interfering with Japan's domestic politics and affairs. From this position, Chongryun-affiliated Koreans withdrew their membership from political organizations in Japan, including the Communist Party, trade unions, and radical student groups. Within its self-accorded extraterritoriality, Chongryun tried to reconstruct the League's Korean schools and secure legal status for them. But in order to obtain such status under the terms stipulated by the Japanese Ministry of Education, Chongryun would have had to abandon all instruction in Korean language, history, and culture at the compulsory education level. The alternative to accreditation as fully academic schools was to seek accreditation for Chongryun schools as nonacademic, yet fully legal, schools. Thus, Chongryun schools submitted applications to be accredited as nonacademic "miscellaneous" schools (such as would be the case for beautician's schools or culinary schools, for example).

One by one, the Chongryun schools were granted such accreditation, making them legitimate institutions in the eyes of the Japanese law. In exchange for legitimacy, Chongryun schools now completely lost all powers of authorization in relation to the issuing of academic degrees and certificates. To this day, therefore, no Chongryun school graduate is seen as having received a formal education in Japan. Furthermore, Chongryun schools receive no subsidies or rebates, and indeed no form of funding from the Ministry of Education. Yet Chongryun has simultaneously secured for itself an advantageous niche away from the Ministry of Education: due to the nonacademic standing of its schools, they are now located outside the reach of ministry tenets. The

Ministry of Education cannot inspect or investigate what Chongryun schools teach, what kind of textbooks they use, and what qualifications their teachers have. Thus, the Chongryun's education system became an autonomous realm inside the Japanese nation-state, within which pedagogical endeavors in support of North Korea flourished. At its peak, Chongryun boasted a total of more than 150 Korean ethnic schools under its control, encompassing all grades from K to 12, in addition to college and graduate programs.

THE POLITICS OF LOVE

What is most relevant to our discussion in this chapter is the college run by Chongryun, Korea University. It is here that young men and women are intensively educated and trained to become future Chongryun leaders. It would not be an exaggeration to say that Korea University is—as Chongryun's official discourse refers to it—a nurturing cradle of the future Chongryun cadre. At the same time, it is here also that the young men and women of Chongryun fall in love and find their future spouses. So how is romance born in the intensified political setting of the Korea University campus? Korea University upholds a position that discourages dating among its students. Yet, as I shall argue below, such repression comes hand in hand with an open embrace of romantic admiration of certain male and female character types. These are designed, projected, and heavily marketed by the Korea University authorities, represented by the Youth League Committee (YLC), which is staffed by professional Chongryun activists and oversees student life in general.

When Korea University was founded in Tokyo in 1956, it had no lecture rooms or buildings of its own and was loaned a portion of the Tokyo Korean High School (also under Chongryun) athletic field, on which it built a shabby wooden hut. At first, it only offered two-year teacher training courses, in order to secure the provision of teachers for Korean schools in Japan. During the initial years, Korean students recruited from around Japan took room and board with Korean families nearby, since Korea University did not yet have a dormitory. Starting from 1957, North Korea began sending educational funds to Chongryun. The first remittance was spent on building the Korea University campus in the suburbs of Tokyo. By the late 1950s, Korea University was equipped with lecture rooms, dormitories, a library, a refectory, an auditorium, and other basic facilities, and had extended its curriculum to that equivalent to a four-year liberal arts college. From that time, all students came to be accommodated on campus. Korean parents from all corners of Japan sent their sons and daughters to Korea University, excited about the prospect of sending their children to college and eventually making them leaders of Chongryun's *aegugundong*, or patriotic movement.

Although the Ministry of Education has never acknowledged KU to this day, the university obtained special accreditation from the newly elected mayor of Tokyo, Minobe Ryōkichi, in 1967. Minobe, a Communist/Socialist coalition candidate, allowed the continued existence of Korea University and its production of Korean school teachers and Chongryun's cadre. (Many of his policies were later reversed by the current mayor of Tokyo, Ishihara Shin-tarō, although even anti-Korean rightist Ishihara cannot seem to alter the protections granted to Korea University by his predecessor.) Thus, from the 1960s, KU came to stand on a relatively secure footing. Its funding comes in part from tuition fees paid by students' parents, but mostly from donations by Koreans in Japan. This is due to the fact that its very existence has been something that Chongryun-supporting Koreans have taken great pride in, despite North Korean funding having ceased sometime during the 1960s. Indeed, Korea University grew in size during the 1970s and 1980s, and this period also saw an intensification of its ideological education, its commitment to the North Korean leadership, and its disciplinary organization of student life. I shall place the focus of my discussion on these decades, as they were the times during which Songrae studied at Korea University.

The 1970s and 1980s were a time when more Korean families began sending their daughters to Korea University. In the past, if a family had to choose a child to send for higher education, it had to be a son, due to the Korean custom of putting sons first. Now, however, as general living standards among Koreans were improving, daughters began obtaining entry to Korea University in larger numbers, making the male-female ratio on campus almost equal by the late 1970s. It was at around this time that the dating code came to be imposed on students. Dating was not encouraged, and was sometimes even criticized and banned, as it was seen as a private affair and, hence, antirevolutionary or counterrevolutionary. Men and women were supposed to devote their passions to the North Korean Great Leader, and deviation of time and energy toward an individual of the opposite sex was not seen as emblematic of a sound lifestyle from Chongryun's point of view.

The organization that directly concerned itself with the dormitory and campus life of Korea University students was the YLC. The YLC consisted of professional activists who staffed supervisory positions and student officers who were given disproportionate executive-decision-making power in relation to the consciousness-raising of fellow students, resulting in hostile and stressful peer-pressure routines that turned out to be very effective in terms of student self-governance on campus. Each academic department had its YLC subcommittee, which oversaw sub-subcommittees in each class. So, for example, the class of 1982 of the Department of Foreign Languages had one class committee, which was supervised by the departmental committee, which was then placed under the direct command of the YLC.

Korea University students in those days led a rule-bound life, confined to their campus and inside their dorm rooms. There were numerous curfews, which had the effect of minimizing opportunities for student life outside the campus. During the 1980s, Wednesday afternoons from 3:00 to 5:00 P.M. and Sundays from 9:00 A.M. to 8:00 P.M. were the only times during which students could leave campus without permission. A student wishing to leave campus at any other time had to obtain the signatures of his or her dorm-room leader, class committee officer, and departmental committee officer; the YLC officer; a junior faculty member; and the head of the department. Daily wake-up time was set at 6:20 A.M., announced every morning by the North Korean music broadcast from the loudspeaker with which every dorm room was equipped. By 6:40, everyone was lined up in the quad performing North Korean "people's gymnastics." A canteen breakfast followed, and the first class of the day began at 8:30. Extracurricular activities began at around 3.00 P.M., after classes were done. Between 8:00 P.M. and 9:00 P.M., a mandatory hour was spent studying the revolutionary works of the Great Leader. Students sat down collectively in formal clothes in their dorm rooms and read out from the *Kim Il Sung Selected Works.* Bathing was available three days a week from 3:00 P.M. to 10:00 P.M. in a large public bathhouse (one for women and another for men). A review of the day took place at 10:30 P.M. First, the dorm-room leader would summarize elements of a checkpoint chart detailing the behavior of room members during the day. These included a study quota based on the self-reported number of hours during which students had studied the subjects in which they were majoring; and performance in relation to the 100-percent Korean-speaking goal—whether or not one had uttered any Japanese words and, if so, how many words, needed to be reported at this time—and in relation to the general code of good moral behavior. Every night, all lights had to be turned off by 11:20.

A more select ideological corps operated behind the scenes in all of the open committees, and also played a key role in the regulation of dorm life. Men and women from the families of Chongryun's cadre and high-profile financial donors were selected for membership in this unit, called the *hakseup-pan,* or study group. This was supposed to be a secret organization, although its existence was widely known among nonmember students by the early 1980s. Those men and women selected as members of the study group were given special martial arts training. They met every week in order to check on each other's level of ideological purity through self-criticism/group-criticism (*pipangwa jagipipan*) sessions; spent extra hours late at night clandestinely studying the teachings of the Great Leader, which were said to have been made available specially for this unit and not to the general student body; and held (supposedly) underground meetings to discuss special issues (usually taken up with mostly benign and boring lectures given by obscure figures from Chongryun's Central Committee). Every such meeting closed with a solemn pledge of loyalty, and oaths committing attendees to sacrifice their own lives, if necessary, in order to defend North Korea's leaders.

I know this firsthand, since I was a member of this unit. I was not an exemplary member, though, and my tendency to read foreign books—my major was French—was usually an object of severe peer criticism. I was often called a "bourgeois" and accused of imbibing corrupt Western ways, which was proof that I did not love my nation and was not prepared to sacrifice myself for the Great Leader. At some point, it became impossible for me to bear this treatment, and I requested to the authorities that I be expelled from the unit. I boycotted martial arts training sessions and did not show up for study/discussion and criticism meetings. My foot-dragging only led in turn to an augmentation of the criticism. I do not mean to suggest, however, that my years at Korea University were therefore horrible and miserable. On the contrary, I enjoyed learning and was able to strengthen my ability to focus. In fact, there were to be many times later in my life that I was made to feel grateful for this experience of trial and struggle, since it prepared me for much worse treatment to come, as related in the introduction of this book.

Unlike the general code of dating restriction on campus, which was guarded by the YLC officers, yet often violated by the students, inside the *hakseuppan,* dating between male and female members was absolutely prohibited. When any member was found to be dating anyone, either inside or outside the *hakseuppan,* the punishment took the form of nightly peer criticism, administered on an individual basis. So, for example, my cohort, a *hakseuppan* member who was dating another *hakseuppan* member (who is now her husband), was forced to get out of bed every night after the 11:20 lights-off and was taken to the girls' bathroom to be subjected to individual criticism by her *hakseuppan* comrades. According to this woman, she was incessantly told to end the relationship, while her boyfriend was not criticized by any of his comrades. This was because, as she told me, the *hakseuppan* had a policy of putting pressure on female partners, under the belief that such forms of corruption as dating were mainly the fault of the female and that once the female partner got over her infatuation, the relationship would naturally dissolve.

This does not mean that Korea University and the Chongryun authorities were indifferent to, or against, love and marriage. On the contrary, Chongryun saw ethnic intermarriage among members of the younger generation as an important fortress in securing its sociopolitical future. During the 1980s, it placed prominent emphasis on *aegukjeok kajeong,* or the patriotic family, partly because of the fact that generational change was replacing first-generation cadres with middle-aged male officers born and raised in Japan. In this light, it was part of the mission of KU to prepare its students for future "patriotic marriage" based on *hyeongmyeongjeok tongjiae*, or love between revolutionary comrades.

Thus, YLC officers were constantly involved in a public marketing campaign targeted at carefully selected types of men and women on campus. Both male and female types were subdivided into categories such as (let us say) prince, princess, working-class hero, and female warrior. A prince was a physically attractive, academically successful, high-ranking YLC member with "manly" looks; a princess was not necessarily a committee member, but was aesthetically exquisite and visually pleasing and most likely an outstanding practitioner of traditional Korean performing arts, such as dance and singing. The working-class hero was a less physically attractive man who nevertheless had a good athletic record and/or was known for comedic talent, endearing him to all; the female warrior was typically chubby or big and not beautiful in a conventional way, yet was capable of delivering stunning speeches at public gatherings.

These four types of individual were given the chance to speak in front of hundreds of students whenever spontaneous or prearranged meetings took place—denunciation meetings (which rallied against U.S. imperialism or the South Korean "puppet clique") or morals-enhancing meetings (which were held in order to achieve the set goals of an "exemplary revolutionary movement"). A working-class hero type would go on first, setting up an energetic, bright, and enthralling mood, followed by a princess type, who would deliver a feminine, quiet, adorable, yet intelligent speech. A female warrior type would then respond, showing off her impressively talented, warm, and powerful speech, and a suitably majestic prince type would conclude with a well-composed, lucid, and utterly artful speech. The pattern was evidently aimed at marketing these types as the most desirable and most ideal potential future spouses; that is to say, although dating was prohibited, marriage was definitely on the horizon. These men and women were not permitted to date while they were still studying at Korea University, but pairing and mating within the framework of marital legitimacy were seen as key elements for locking individuals into family units in the Chongryun network.[18]

During the 1970s and 1980s, Korean daughters in Japan were sent to Korea University so that they would be able to attach a good record from the university to the introductory note and portrait to be submitted to the matchmaker in preparation for arranged marriage. They worked at the Chongryun offices for a couple of years after graduation in order to acquire a good reputation as an office worker (typically assigned to making tea and coffee for everyone, in addition to other routine, menial work such as answering phones), again in order to improve their chances of good matchmaking later. It was said, during these decades, that the best outcome for a wealthy *aeguk-*

jeok sanggongin (patriotic industrialist and entrepreneur) was taking a Chongryun cadre's daughter as daughter-in-law: she would be able to speak Korean and would be polite and obedient. Above all, she would not do outrageous things, as she would be aware of the need to maintain her father's reputation and good standing in the community.

In many Chongryun offices in those days, a common form of harassment suffered by unmarried women when they reached the age of twenty-five or so and had no immediate prospects of marriage was to be constantly told to get married by colleagues, superiors, and sometimes even younger female coworkers. The good moral standing of such women, their job skills, their contributions to the patriotic cause, and their willingness to serve the organization became irrelevant at that age. It was their marriageability that counted—just like in any Jane Austen novel. Therefore, when a woman employee successfully moved on from her service to Chongryun by marrying up (i.e., to a wealthy and powerful suitor), her wedding ceremony, the size of the diamond in the engagement ring, the honeymoon location, and other details were talked about with great delight in Chongryun offices.

The vast majority of female students in Korea University were enrolled in the two-year teacher-certification programs. They were sent out to the large number of Chongryun elementary schools that were dotted throughout all the prefectures of Japan. The women who graduated from four-year undergraduate programs with majors and specializations in particular fields became upper-level schoolteachers, journalists, office workers (as mentioned above), and full-time Chongryun activists. These career paths were not voluntarily chosen. One day before the graduation ceremony, the graduating seniors had "assignment allocation meetings," that is, meetings where individuals' allocated duties were read out in front of the other members of the class. Typically, few personal wishes were taken into consideration. Many a student broke down in tears from despair upon hearing that she would be working in a city far away from her home or, worse, far away from her dating partner. But proper convention dictated that one receive one's assigned duty with honor, standing upright in a calm and collected manner and responding by saying, "It is my greatest honor to receive this assignment. I will work hard to contribute to the patriotic cause of Chongryun and will remain loyal to our Great Leader."

Of necessity, there were exceptions. In my year, for example, there were about thirty of us in the class. Those cadre members of *hakseuppan*, who were quite numerous, got the toughest assignments and were sent away from their hometowns, because on our graduation trip to North Korea, they had had the honor of being met by Kim Il Sung and Kim Jong Il in Pyongyang. I was sent to Chongryun's English-language newspaper office—since I had not had the honor of meeting the two Kims, I was able to stay in Tokyo, my hometown. A daughter of the then Chongryun chairman was assigned to graduate study, although she, too, had met with the two Kims and her academic scores were not outstanding. Another girl, whose mother had come to campus prior to her graduation and had met with YLC officers (most likely presenting them with a sumptuous payment), was "assigned" to go home and live with her family. In retrospect, the Korea University YLC campaign for patriotic marriage was insidiously successful, since despite these assignment policies, Korea University graduates overall ended up marrying Chongryun Koreans. Some met prospective suitors in remote cities, while others kept their relationships long distance. (Out of close to twenty women in my class, I am the only one who did not marry Korean, had more than one marriage, and had children outside wedlock: the rest of the women married Korean, and none is divorced to this day.)

Both students and parents alike responded well to the orchestrated efforts to encourage marriage between Chongryun's young men and women. Indeed, a key element motivating many parents to send their children to Korea University was the hope that it would help them find a good Korean future son-in-law or daughter-in-law. Love in the Chongryun political community was—I use the past tense intentionally, since it is by and large no longer the case today—a distinct type of construction, perhaps the most significant and effective one that the organization has managed to produce. It was a productive and reproductive institution that enabled Chongryun to formulate and consolidate its family-based foundation, according to which loyalty toward the family would overlap with loyalty toward the organization, North Korea, and the Great Leader. Just like *nous autre victoriens,* as depicted by Foucault in his *History of Sexuality,* Korea University students in the 1970s and 1980s were, in practice, not at all repressed—just as the Victorian repression went hand in hand with scientific encoding of sex as knowledge in that period, repressive rules prohibiting dates inside Korea University may have taught students to say they were repressed; but in reality, every day they were exposed to an intensive, massive, highly public, and insidious form of romantic indoctrination, and disciplined to fantasize about an ideal-typical revolutionary hero in the hope of achieving eventual sexual and marital union.[19] In an almost Quixotic thrust, Korea University students in those days became infatuated with idealized revolutionary types, resulting in utterly successful marriages with fellow Chongryun Koreans; these couples called each other "comrade." Songrae, indeed, was, and is, one of them—but with qualifications.

SONGRAE'S CASE

Songrae's case differs slightly from the experience of the majority of female students at Korea University at the time. As she wrote, she was the only female student in the class. Furthermore, her department, the engineering department, was exempt from assignment allocation by the YLC. This reflects the unique origin of the department itself. The engineering department was established in the late 1970s in response to the strong wishes of Korean parents in Japan, who wanted their children (mainly their sons) to be able to work for midsize Japanese firms. Such parental wishes reflected a surge in the job supply in the prebubble Japanese economy, especially in software-related industries. Overall, the so-called organizational routine in this department was lenient. For example, in contrast with her peers in other departments, Songrae does not have bitter memories of participation in criticism sessions. After graduation, Songrae and all of her classmates sought employment in either Japanese or Korean firms, and none became a full-time Chongryun employee. In this sense, it would be safe to say that Songrae was subjected to a less intense degree of romantic indoctrination within Korea University. Yet she still married in accordance with Chongryun's preset framework of ethnic marriage. Why?

In comparison with the possibilities that one of her earlier partners could have offered her, Songrae's husband, a Korea University graduate, can only offer a relatively narrow and mundane existence. Songrae rationalizes this, saying: "I wanted to be comfortable after marriage, so I would not have to pretend to be anyone else other than myself. And in this sense, it just seemed most appropriate that I marry a Korean from a similar background to my own." She then emphasizes, as has been shown, that it was her own choice, although love (*ai*) seems remote from her marriage now.

Upon closer examination, however, Songrae and her husband do not share particularly similar backgrounds: Songrae's parents are highly educated, though not wealthy, while none of her in-laws are college educated. They are wealthier than Songrae's parents, and seem to enjoy a more consumption-oriented lifestyle, including sightseeing trips to Hawaii, Canadian skiing tours, koala-bear hugging in Australia, bungee jumping in New Zealand, and so forth. In terms of family values and lifestyles, the two families are far apart. For example, Songrae's parents would watch TV sparingly, mainly to learn the news and discuss international events in their living room. Her in-laws would leave the TV on all day on sports and entertainment channels.

Songrae is in a state of constant disagreement with her husband regarding how to raise and educate their daughters. She, for example, thinks it would be possible for her children to go abroad to study, possibly to the U.S. Her husband thinks—and I quote from him—"everyone in the U.S. has a gun and does drugs. I'm not going to send my kids to a place like that." Songrae worries that if her daughters did not achieve good academic standing and failed to be transferred later to good Japanese upper schools (they are currently studying at a Korean school), their future would be doomed, as they would have no option but to marry well. Her husband thinks that such a future would be perfectly acceptable. In a way, Songrae wants her children to have social recognition—despite the obvious difficulties arising from their status as Koreans living in Japan. Her husband could not care less—for him, the small circle of his extended family is all that matters. Nevertheless, Songrae justifies her marriage. We all do that—it is difficult for a rational individual to fundamentally alter the lifestyle that he or she is embedded or entrenched in. But is this all there is to this picture?

Songrae, who was never herself a big fan of North Korea oriented indoctrination, nevertheless regarded it as imperative to marry a Korean. Marrying and having children with someone else—such as a Japanese—would bring calamity not only upon herself, but also upon her family and the community at large. This type of self-prohibition was typically implemented side by side with what I may call romantic discipline, whereby individuals were trained to be self-monitoring lovers in the North Korea oriented expatriate community. Thus, despite several encounters and romantic involvements with non-Korean men, Songrae "always knew [she] had to marry a Korean man." Do we see here the workings not only of indoctrination of a narrow political kind, but also of a larger, more insidious mechanism, by which a diasporic community operates in controlling its ethnic reproduction?

The irony—and I hope the reader was able to detect it in the preceding section—is that inside Korea University, romantic discipline took on a distinctly logosuppressive form; that is to say, life at Korea University for Songrae's cohorts was devoid of romantic language. As stated above, students were subjected to a strict rule allowing them to speak in Korean only. For Korea University students, Korean, in its turn, was not a private language within which they could identify and convey their personal sentiments and emotions. Inside Korea University due to the total intrusion of organizational norms, there was hardly any distinction between the private and the public. For four years, students ate together, bathed together, and learned and lived together, literally showing their naked bodies to each other. Furthermore, the mandatory self-revelation of thoughts, which was institutionalized in the form of self-criticism/group-criticism sessions, rendered the art of the suppression of the private almost complete. The institutionalized and mandatory exposure of their living space, in which only Korean, their public and political language, was allowed, radically reduced love-related choices for Korea University students, who were at the same time heavily subjected to the projection of a finite set of ideal male and female types by the YLC. Herein seems to lie the secret of the successful intra-ethnic marriage rate among Chongryun Koreans of Songrae's generation.

After marriage, however, life for women like Songrae seems to remain devoid of political elements. Songrae and her cohorts from Korea University, with their Chongryun affiliations, now generally live financially stable, if not very secure or opulent, lives. Like Songrae, many of the Korean women in Japan that I know and who originally came from a Chongryun background have distanced themselves from Chongryun and North Korea. Even though their children may currently be attending Chongryun-operated elementary or middle schools, most Korean parents (including Songrae) have long-term plans to transfer their children to Japanese schools, either when they reach high school level or earlier. It is very likely that Korea University, just like other Korean schools, will eventually face a shortage in enrollments.

Chongryun schools are indeed facing a serious crisis, now that second- and third-generation Korean parents are moving away from Chongryun schools. It must also be added that, unlike in the 1990s or earlier, during which time the Japanese government was relatively happy to leave Chongryun alone, now, in the aftermath of the 2002 revelation that North Korean agents had kidnapped Japanese citizens during the 1970s and 1980s in order to use them in espionage training, Korean schools and Chongryun offices face the acute danger of persecution. Already, the Japanese authorities have prosecuted many Chongryun individuals and offices for embezzlement and tax evasion involving illegal transactions with North Korea.[20] This is all very ironic, considering that since the mid-1990s, Chongryun has undertaken extensive and fundamental curricular reforms, eliminating all mention of Kim Il Sung and Kim Jong Il, and references to other North Korean hegemony; and abolishing hitherto paramount and sacrosanct academic subjects, such as the Revolutionary History of the Great Leader Marshal Kim Il Sung and the Childhood of Our Father Marshal Kim Il Sung.[21]

Songrae's two girls currently attend an evening cramming program in order to prepare them for Japanese upper-level school entrance examinations. Beyond a vague sense of anticipation in relation to her children's future, and despite her experience of having studied abroad and having earned a higher degree, Songrae does not have a much larger vision of her life — at least as far as she tells me. How is this form of life related to the way women like Songrae talk (or don't talk) about love?

LOVE AND LANGUAGE

Scholars of love emphatically argue that romantic love is the domain of women. As the major consumers of romantic novels, Anthony Giddens notes, women have advanced much further than men in their linguistic mastery of the culture of romance.[22] It is not hard to see this if one considers how much Jane Austen's novels were — and continue to be — loved and read by women in many societies, including our own. Indeed, in the spirit of Austen, whatever society deems to be good marriage tends to be a goal to be attained along the path of romantic love. Talk of love, in this vein, is everywhere: in popular songs, in soap operas, in poetry and literature, and between close friends and confidantes. Love, it seems, is one of the words most frequently on the tips of the tongues of modern, young, educated, men and women. But what we see in Songrae's case is different: she is wary of talking about love and romance. When she mentions love, *ai* or *koi* in Japanese, it is usually in denial of this concept.

When I embarked on the project of collecting romantic autobiographies of Korean women in Japan, it turned out to be very difficult—not because they would not write them for me, but because they would not write about love in the manner I had expected, that is in a romantic manner. Of the women who wrote autobiographies for me (some in very fragmented form), none, except for Songrae, wrote about their romances that did not lead to marriage. All women are now in their forties, all are married to Koreans, and all were exposed to Chongryun's Korean education. Songrae is the only one who wrote about encounters with men other than her current husband and/or men who were not Korean. This does not mean that she is the only one who had romantic involvements with men other than her husband prior to marriage. Yet the other women decided not to write about these or decided that these were not worth noting—it was a matter of unwillingness, rather than inability, in my reckoning. This became clear to me when I talked with the women away from their writing: they told me about their premarital dating endeavors, but did not want to note them in writing. Also, characteristically, none of them (including Songrae) touched upon sexual aspects of their romantic pasts. I did not make any explicit requests in this regard and, therefore, it is understandable that no one would write about such things. But it is not difficult to imagine that had I made such a request, the respondents would have reacted altogether differently—most likely, negatively—to my request, to the extent that I could not have obtained any of the romantic autobiographies.

Most interestingly, the women who responded to my request of telling me about their love stories completely avoided telling me details of their first love, either in writing or during our conversations. At a glance, none appears to have had one. As we have seen, Songrae claims that she was a "tomboy" who did not fall in love with anyone until after she left college; even then is skeptical, refusing to accord the status of first love to any of a series of relationships. First loves are often characterized by strong infatuation and overwhelming mental and physical reactions—your heart throbs, your pulse accelerates, and you seem to lose your power of speech. Your head is filled with intrusive thoughts about the other, and you feel unbearable pain at the thought that the other may not be interested in you.[23] The women do not note any experience of anxiety, worry, or pain, on the one hand, or elation and over-joyousness, on the other, in the context of first or even later loves, for that matter. I do not, however, believe that it is because they did not have such experiences. Rather, I regard this as a clue that leads us to understand what they see as love or, more precisely speaking, what they are willing to talk or write about as love.

For Songrae (and others), love that is worth the mention is love that has been delivered as the result of long-lasting forms of mutual bonding such as marriage. Memories of dates and perhaps brief encounters with a special person are quietly brushed aside as peripheral data, as a non-love, or as a not-quite-love, while the sense of trust and mutual dependence felt toward the husband, if not described as love, is considered most important, as part of a relationship worth mentioning. Songrae retrospectively rationalizes that she was, after all, not in love (or not in love enough) with her Japanese and English boyfriends. And just like in *Pride and Prejudice,* good marriage (meaning upwardly mobile hypergamy to a rich man) is taken as the final scene in the real-life drama of romance and affection.

Furthermore, in Songrae's account, there is, so to say, a fatalism about having to marry a Korean, no matter what. Songrae, who had sufficient opportunities to go outside of the Korean enclave, nevertheless preconceived (perhaps retrospectively) her ultimate love/marriage to be with a Korean. Love in diaspora, as it were, is thus ethnicized. Her love's identity, in other words, is in sync with the identity of the Korean diaspora in Japan.

It is clear that Songrae deems that once one is married, love becomes irrelevant. Such an image does not deviate from what may be called the standard image of Japanese marriage: for Japanese women of Songrae's generation and older, once married, love is not to matter or be talked about; but the commitment and routine flow of life, year after year, is seen as a sufficient bond to hold matrimony together.[24] However, whereas among Japanese women, by default, personal choices—albeit within the constraints and pre-structured field of cultural indoctrination as to what is seen as good marriage—are more widely available, among Korean women like Songrae choices are limited—extremely limited; and perhaps this limit is to some extent self-imposed. For Korean women in Japan of her generation, who grew up amid the confrontations of the Cold War, an ideal husband would have to have been someone with a Chongryun educational and political background and orientation. Ideally, he would also have been someone who could trace his regional origins to the same province as the would-be bride, but who absolutely must not come from the same clan as hers, as this would have been completely taboo according to Korean kinship rules. Furthermore, he would have been someone who could provide well for her, and preferably better than the bride's maiden family itself.

It would be helpful to remember that Songrae and other women whom I have mentioned in this chapter belong to an extreme minority—as stated earlier, the predominant majority of Koreans in Japan marry Japanese. It should also be noted that, as a consequence, arranged marriages between Koreans of this group (i.e., those aspiring to marry fellow Koreans) often involve awkward situations, as many of the young men and women introduced to each other through matchmakers come from the same school as each other or may have also been introduced to each other's former classmates, for example. In the case of these women, educated in Korean schools and ending up with the aspiration or predetermined idea of marrying a Korean person, the pool from which to choose a spouse would be particularly severely restricted. Yet what seems to win out in the end is the consciousness of the inevitability of marrying a Korean. This evidently reflects the effects of Chongryun's romantic discipline, which promoted the idea of intra-ethnic marriage by projecting and marketing certain types of male and female as ideal and charismatic.

From another angle, how to raise a family in Japan inside a diasporic community of Chongryun-affiliated Koreans ultimately becomes a more important question than whom to love, for Songrae and others like her. Interestingly, for them, children are not seen as the fruit of the love they share with their husbands—as is so easily and unproblematically believed in the West— but rather as an inevitable yet logical consequence of marriage. A childless marriage, in other words, is a tragic unthinkable in the Korean diasporic community in Japan. They marry in order to have children, and it has to be in that order and in that sequence. Therefore, marriage without children and children without marriage are viewed both as heterodoxy and sacrilege. This in itself is not unusual, globally speaking. It is Western (and especially U.S.) culture that is in the minority among the romantic cultures of the world, with its strenuous insistence on a linear, causal connection between romantic love and marriage. But in the cases of Songrae and the other women I encountered, all of them from a Chongryun-educated background, growing up in the 1960s and 1970s and getting married in the 1980s, it was imperative that no matter what happened, marriage should be with a Korean and should reproduce Korean diasporic children in Japan. In this process, love either became irrelevant at some point or was not the most important element to begin with.

Songrae wrote her autobiography in Japanese. It appears that Songrae does not possess the kind of romantic language through which she can explore her marital relationship—either in Korean or in Japanese. Songrae has distanced herself considerably from the North Korea oriented linguistic zone, and now conducts her life more or less exclusively in Japanese. Yet she would not apply the romantic clichés available in the realm of Japanese popular culture, to which she is exposed every day through TV, music, novels, billboard ads, and so forth. She is wary of using even the most basic among these, such as *koi* or *ai,* either heavily qualifying such use or denying its existence. While "love" is not within the repertoire of Japanese speech for Songrae, she does not possess a private language of love in Korean either, since the Korean language education she received located Korean as the school language, the language that she learned and was trained in so as to be able to lead a school (or institutionalized) life. And we have already seen that inside Korea University, romantic discipline was given in a distinctly logosuppressive manner.

Would it be too outlandish to imagine that Songrae is resisting revealing her most vulnerable personal feelings to the Japanese language, while not being able to find an alternative in Korean, either? More precisely, is she afraid of sounding like a Japanese, rather than a Korean woman in Japan, by utilizing a standard set of Japanese romantic clichés? What kind of forces and conditions drive her to do so, and what is preventing her from succumbing to the mainstream Japanese romantic culture that is available to her?

This enigma appears to point to the path that love and romance in Korean diaspora are destined to follow. Entangled between homeland-oriented politics and ethnic and political discrimination in the host society, the personal life choices of diasporic Koreans in Japan of Songrae's background become extremely limited, as stated. They know that casual encounters with Japanese in public spaces would not lead to romance, or that repeated dating with Japanese would not lead to marriage. Men and women in the Korean diaspora in Japan, or, more precisely, those placed directly under the Chongryun tenets, are made to feel morally obligated to their elders, and are expected to reproduce offspring of their own kind, that is, their own diasporic kind. Songrae adopts a strategy of nondeployment of love language in her self-characterizations, which tend to be linguistically poor. This is different from strategic silence. For she is not silent in any sense; but her reduced semantic scope reminds me of the dysphasiac condition of speech impairment. An aphasiac child loses a sound and does not recover it in the process of growing up. This precipitates the loss of words containing that sound, incurring the loss of the meaning of those words from the child's comprehension of the world. Similarly, in the world inhabited by Songrae and other Chongryun-educated women, the notion/word "love" (as we might imagine it) has been deactivated to the extent that it has become dormant. In this milieu, love is talked about only when referring to fatherly love of the Great Leader or revolutionary camaraderie. Hence, in response to my request to personally recount their experiences of love, their romantic histories turned out to be arid and poorly expressed. As Roman Jakobson has written in relation to aphasia, "the active use of the word as interpreter of the concept is impaired."[25]

The ability of my women informants to (say) syntactically express their relationships as romantic, while remaining unable to semantically flesh them out with meaningful words, appears to indicate an ontological analogy to their diasporic existence. This is to say that the skeleton of each woman's life exists in Japan, yet its meaning is not validated in Japanese society in any participatory context, whether it be politics, economics, or culture—including romantic culture.

As I stated earlier, more Koreans in Japan marry Japanese than Koreans, and it is easy to imagine that those who marry Japanese would use passionate Japanese language of romance to express their love. In this sense, Koreans are *not* excluded from the Japanese love scene just because they are Korean. Here, however, it is interesting to note that most Koreans who marry Japanese tend to eventually be naturalized as Japanese citizens, and also that the majority of children born to interethnic marriages tend to receive their entire education in mainstream Japanese schools. In this way, they become members of the Japanese nation, albeit in a qualified way, but at least in a far more legitimate way than those who remain excluded from Japanese national membership, confined in the Korean-dominated environment, with intra-ethnic marriage choices, education at Chongryun schools, and lack of nationality and national status (as in Songrae's case). It is as if to say that the lack of national membership deprives one of romantic ability. And how could it not be the case? If, as Arendt insists, the loss of nationality brings about the loss of human rights, the right to love—one of the basic human rights in modernity—is also taken away from the denationalized.

LOVE, POLITICAL LIFE, HOME

What I am trying to suggest is that love embodies a compounded predicament in the case of Chongryun-affiliated Korean women in Japan. As gentrification progressed among Chongryun Koreans, their living standards rose (albeit belatedly) and hypergamy inside the diasporic community became possible due to increasing economic and social stratification within this group of Koreans in Japan, attrition of women in the patriotic movement, or *aegugundong,* became notable. Women of Songrae's cohort typically dropped out of full-time service for the expatriate organization, despite their Korea University education, upon marriage or childbirth. Once out of the expatriate movement, they have been unable to find avenues in which to participate in the alternative political movements available inside Japanese society, be it the environmental movement or grassroots civil-rights activism, due to their hitherto-confined existence within the ethnic enclave of Chongryun. Thus, despite their successfully marrying Korean husbands, an act that embodies an important element of political life within the Korean diaspora in Japan, women ironically end up distancing themselves from participation in politics. I hasten to mention that their inability to join existing political and social movements and groups within Japan does not derive one-sidedly from the limitations placed upon them through their Chongryun education and indoctrination. Japanese feminism, for example, is to this day confined within its own national ethnic class boundaries, and has consistently failed to incorporate, enter into dialogue with, or express solidarity with non-Japanese women in Japan and Japanese women who are less educated, are of lower class, and/or are disabled.[26]

The youthful passion and romantic energy of Chongryun women was in effect manipulated and channeled by the realities of the politicized diaspora under Chongryun's influence, persuading them that they were necessarily fated to marry Koreans and produce Korean families. Their romantic potential was robbed by diasporic political constraints. Even when they try to remember their romantic pasts, by way of writing autobiographically, they adopt passive, almost self-canceling postures toward love, while their language tends to be prosaically banal and impoverished. This makes their approach to romance almost (if not entirely) anti-love. I am not suggesting that these Korean women living under Chongryun's umbrella are unique: humans, both men and women, often rationalize their limited choices, convincing themselves that any particular choice is the only one available. And people fall in love in extremely limited and demographically endangered environments. Still, in the case of the Chongryun-affiliated Korean women in Japan, the partition of Korea, the division of expatriate communities, Cold War tensions, the weight of a diasporic future, and the Chongryun-initiated indoctrination of "correct" love as seen in Korea University life are all factors bearing down upon them when they fall in love.

Thus, if their "love" seems weak or evasive, negative or antithetical, this is closely related to the limited life choices that the Korean diaspora in Japan creates. Needless to say, it is not my intention to judge their love. For so-called romantic love in our (Western) society is more often than not preconditioned by financial calculations, concern over social status, racial politics, ethnic proximity or distance, religious identicality, Hollywood-projected images of beauty, and many other considerations that we don't usually associate with romantic love or its essence. Nevertheless, the autobiography of love, I stress, becomes grossly impoverished in the case of the Korean diaspora in Japan, where individuals are taught to steer their passions in certain ways because of the marginalization suffered in the host society and also because of the political pressures and assumptions that they have acquired while growing up within a highly politicized diasporic community. Songrae is a stateless person, a national of neither Japan nor Korea (either Korea, that is). In an uncanny, yet rather brutally obvious manner, her lack of a language of love reveals her lack of national belonging.

It is in this connection that I'd like to address the issue of home and the lack thereof, and this issue, in my view, is related to the poverty of language—both private and public. I specifically invoke the necessity of political life for the modern reflexive self inspired by Giorgio Agamben's emphasis on the distinction between two Greek words denoting life, *bios* and *zoē*. *Bios* meant politically and socially meaningful life—most likely granted and enjoyed by (male) citizens (patricians) of the *polis; zoē* was used to denote basic, simple life with no social or political existence—even insects have it.[27] Meaningless life does not require a society or political participation. Political life, in other words, is a privilege enjoyed by those who securely belong to, and have membership in, the public sphere.

Does this mean that *bios* exist only in *polis* and *zoē,* in *oikos?* Perhaps the matter is not so simple, especially in the modern world, where reflexive and critical agency has become available for all and sundry—even for women and other hitherto marginalized populations. Having said this, one still needs a footing, a home base, in which one is raised and nurtured and from which one is able to make an entry into politicosocial participation. Indeed, no one acquires a social existence without belonging somewhere. Then again, what does life become when modern subjecthood is combined with an ancient, primordial form of human displacement, that of losing the land called home? Will life ever be the same again? Is life going to continue? For life without a homeland is, as it was for the originally dispersed Jewish population, unspeakably lost—lost in such a definitive and final way that, perhaps, life without a homeland may not even be considered life: it reduces one's life to *zoē*. For political life, according to Arendt, cannot be attained without a terrain that one can call home, and hence, for her, loss of political life is loss of home.[28]

But, what *is* home? Songrae lives comfortably, financially speaking. Her husband owns a midsize IT company, in addition to a couple of commercial real-estate properties that procure regular income. Her in-laws' business is going very well, and, despite Japan's long-lasting recession, it is not showing any sign of weakening. But is her home *home?* For if she is unable to enact her self in a fulfilling manner (seen in her case, for example, in the way that she tries not to think about her relationship with her husband), can such a realm still be home? If her ideals in life revolve solely around child-rearing or obtaining more designer purses, how does she reconcile the fact that her self is placed, as it were, on a kind of extended hold, while she endures a nonromantic, or even nonaffectionate and nonattached, relationship with her husband? Furthermore, if she has no arena in which she can be a politicosocial actor in such a way as to enact her *bios,* inside or outside the home, how can she claim herself to have an existence of her own, her own self?

One can easily see that the blueprint of traditional Korean male-dominated values preserved in the diasporic community is reproduced in her views toward life. Since Greek antiquity, those who did not have a political life—barbarians, slaves, minors, and women, above all—did not have a home to which they fully belonged. They were only half-members, half-human, often the property of others. In this context, it is interesting to note that among Koreans in Japan, the colonial diaspora had a fundamentally different meaning for men and women: for men, the lament of leaving their ancestral home is a major cause for grief; for women, the loss of the ancestral home is not genuinely theirs, since they never had such a home that they belonged to in the first place. But then, I wonder, how uniquely diasporic can the problem of unfulfilled self-realization inside the home be? Is this a problem unique to diasporic marriage, or is it an aspect of modern marriage in general? Is this specifically a Korean problem (in Japan), or is it not?

On the other hand, in the case of Songrae (and many others like her), the attrition in use of the Chongryun-engineered, North Korean style Korean language seems to be of significance when thinking about self and love in diaspora. Despite the years of Chongryun education in Korean that she received, Songrae now has hardly any opportunity to speak, read, or write in Korean. Songrae even uses Japanese with teachers at the Korean school that her children go to—young Chongryun schoolteachers are also unable to communicate adequately and at ease in Korean. And unlike the elderly women informants that I worked with in the past, who were more than willing to reproduce and echo Chongryun's political prose when referring to their sense of self,[29] my middle-aged, Korea University-educated informants are unable or unwilling to reproduce such discourses—meaning that their organizational language, the language they learned and in which they expressed their loyalty to North Korea, has ceased to exist. It was through this language that they had recognized and registered their belonging to the ethno-political community—that is to say, it was in this language that they had lived political life, albeit within a precarious, twisted, and male-dominant sphere of diasporic nationalism. With the attrition of this language, they lost the material as well as psychosomatic basis of sociopolitical belonging. And this process was unequivocally accompanied by the loss of political life. Their life, in other words, is imminently being reduced to *zoē*.

As Arendt has suggested, if true friendship, love among equals, is possible only in *polis* and, in contrast, domination and power of the household head make social relationships (including love) in *oikos* fundamentally unequal and, hence, unfree, then women who do not have access to public life (such as Korean diasporic women in Japan) are eternally deprived of free love. Or, conversely, is love in diaspora possible only among "unequals"? Is it only when power and authority are unevenly distributed that romance can be born? In the scheme of the mainstream West, romance is seen as a relationship that free individuals enter into by their own choice, and the two partners in such relationships are at least ideally considered equal. In such a scheme, love's language infinitely mimics the equal exchanges between free citizens of the *polis*—praising each other's capacities, physicality, possessions, achievements, beauty, and so on. Paradoxically, however, in the modern West, love routinely resides in the private, the *oikos*. Romantic love, in other words, is an affair that is quintessentially private. In antiquity, as Arendt has stated, the private was viewed with contempt due to its association with the basic livelihood needs required for humans to survive, while the public was a sphere in which men could truly claim their individually unique existence. But, as she has also stated, "love, in distinction from friendship, is killed, or rather extinguished, the moment it is displayed in public."[30]

What if loving people do not have a distinction between public and private—not in the way that, as Arendt claims, modernity collapses these into the social realm, but in the sense of disenfranchisement from the public realm of the society they live in, as in the case of Koreans in Japan? I suspect that under such circumstances, love's inequality—as in the case of an *oikos* dominated by the disproportionate and absolute despotism of the household head—prevails. I further speculate that such examples of love are inherently loveless, in that, as in the private realm in antiquity, necessity comes first in life, rather than ideals, dreams, and a desire for wholesome fulfillment. In light of Arendt's words above, "love" in this instance is constantly displayed in public—as in the Chongryun Koreans' discussion of the size of diamonds on engagement rings—and, therefore, simultaneously killed—as in the arid, materialistic marital life seen in Songrae's case. Love in such cases is less dignified and not free—indeed, free choice is never possible. In other words, love in disapora is not the same as love in a society of people who have an equal franchise and participatory capacity in political life. Love within the Korean diaspora in Japan, therefore, is unique, in that it constitutes the desperate endeavor of a disappearing and endangered community intent on salvaging and securing its future. But the reality is that this endeavor is failing, and in fact has been failing for some time: even many of the Chongryun Korean school parents that I have interacted with no longer believe that it is important for their children to marry fellow Koreans. Many of them have confirmed to me that they would accept any type of romantic relationship or marriage in the lives of their children, as long as it brought their children happiness. Songrae is one of them: she says she'd be happy if her daughters were to pursue love and romance regardless of ethnic and political constraints. Whether such romance would stand on the equality between the lovers, however, is another question. Still, when that happens, it will be time to talk to Songrae about love again.

NOTES

1. Joan Scott, "Experience," in *Feminists Theorize the Political*, ed. J. Butler and J. Scott (New York: Routledge, 1992), 27; Sidonie Smith and Julia Watson, *Reading Autobiography: A Guide for Interpreting Life Narratives* (Minneapolis: University of Minnesota Press, 2001), 25.

2. There are numerous works on Japanese popular culture in English. See, for example, Kelly (2004) and Allison (2006). Also, for a more gendered perspective, see Miller and Bardsley (2005). For orientalism, see the now-classic Said (1978). *Shall We Dance?* a Japanese movie featuring a married, overworked middle-aged man's romanticizing of his young, female dance teacher, has been adapted and remade for an all-star-cast Hollywood production (*Shall We Dance?* 1996, 2004).

3. Lawrence Stone, "Passionate Attachments in the West in Historical Perspective," in *Passionate Attachments: Thinking about Love*, ed. W. Gaylin and E. Person (New York: Free Press, 1988), 18, 19. This view is pretty much endorsed by Gidders (1992), though with the emphasis on gender differences.

4. Jack Goody, "Love, Lust and Literacy," in *Food and Love: A Cultural History of East and West* (London: Verso, 1998), 112.

5. Outside cultural anthropology, and for more recent examples of studies of love, see, for example, Tennov (1979), Person (1988), Sternberg (1998), Gaylin and Person (1988), and Verhaeghe (1998) in psychology and psychoanalysis; in sociobiology, Fisher (1992) and Liebowitz (1983); and in sociology, Walsh (1991), Illouz (1997), and Swidler (2001), to cite only a few. More classical, important examples include Fromm (1956) for psychology; Mercuse (1966) for social analysis; Weil (1951), Nygren (1953), and Lewis (1960) for theologically informed studies of love, if not romantic love per se; and Macfarlane (1986) for ethnologically informed history. See also, for a brief but illuminating analysis, Lindholm (1998a). Of course, Freud (e.g., 1963) can be cited here as the archetypal study of love and sexuality. See Nicholi (2002) for Freud on love.

6. It is indicative to see that Malinowski's (1926) classical study is entitled *The Sexual Life of Savages* and not "love life of," although the book is full of data about what today we would call love.

7. William Jankowiak and Edward Fischer, "A Cross-Cultural Perspective on Romantic Love," *Ethnology* 31, no. 2 (1992): 149–55. See also Jankowiak (1995), for fuller exploration.

8. Lila Abu-Lughod, *Veiled Sentiments: Honor and Poetry in a Bedouin Society* (Berkeley: University of California Press, 1986); Laura Ahearn, *Invitations to Love: Literacy, Love Letters, and Social Change in Nepal* (Ann Arbor: University of Michigan Press, 2001); Nicole Constable, *Romance on a Global Stage: Pen Pals, Virtual Ethnography, and "Mail-Order" Marriages* (Berkeley: University of California Press, 2003).

For relevant studies, see Kendall (1996), Rebhun (1999), and Yan (2003). Sahlins (1985) offers insights into the ethnographic taking of love as an institution, as presented in ancient Hawai'ian verses of loyalty, worship, and adoration for the royals, and Crapanzano (1980) discusses love in a broader humanistic perspective, with the focus on a Moroccan tile-maker and his spirituality.

9. Swidler (2001) is a good example of tautologous study of love, using "talks," that is, the data that she and her research assistants collected by way of prestructured interviews, for the starting point as well as end result of the research.

10. Kim Yeong-dal, "Hoshō: kaisetsu to tōkei no hosoku" [Supplement: Explanation and supplementation of statistics], in *Sūji ga kataru zainichi kankoku chōsenjin no rekishi* [History of Koreans in Japan seen from statistics], ed. Y. Morita (Tokyo: Akashishoten, 1996), 179.

11. See Bourdieu (1991, 1990), for example, on habitus.

12. In fact love, sexuality, and totalitarianism in North Korea are symbiotically connected—just like in *1984* (Orwell 1983).

13. Edward Wagner, *The Korean Minority in Japan: 1904–1951* (New York: Institute of Pacific Relations, 1951), 95.

14. Morita Yoshio, *Sūjiga kataru zainichi kankoku chōsenjin no rekishi*, 103; Wagner (1951: 95). The chaotic and often life-threatening situation of Korean repatriation immediately after the war is well reconstructed in Caprio and Yu (forthcoming). The rise of the Korean population by about 60,000 between 1947 and 1948 (as can be seen in the text) may be attributed to return migration from Korea and also to the people previously unaccounted for.

15. According to statistical data, as of 1959, only 1.7 percent of the entire population of Korea-born Koreans in Japan came from the North, while 1.1 percent came from Kangweon Province, which was divided into North and South in 1945 (Morita 1996: 40).

16. Pak Kyeong-Sik, *Kaihōgo zainichi chōsenjin undōshi* [History of Korean movement in Japan: After the liberation] (Tokyo: Sanichishobō, 1989), 31; Kim Yeong-Dal, *GHQ Bunsho kenkyū gaido: zainichi chōsenjin kyōiku mondai* [A research guide for documents on Korean ethnic education in Japan issued by the General Headquarters for Allied Occupation] (Kobe, Japan: Mukugeshobō, 1989), 37; Fujii Kōnosuke, "Kaihōgo nihon ni okeru chōsenjin gakkō no kokugo kyōkasho" [Korean textbooks in Korean schools in Japan after the liberation], *Zainichi Chōsenjinshi Kenkyū*, June 1980, 90–91. See Ryang (1997: 84–86) for a summary.

17. See Hiromitsu Inokuchi, "Korean Ethnic Schools in Occupied Japan, 1945–52," in *Koreans in Japan: Critical Voices from the Margin*, ed. S. Ryang (London: Routledge, 2000); and Yukiko Koshiro, *Trans-Pacific Racisms and the U.S. Occupation of Japan* (New York: Columbia University Press, 1999) for this.

18. Love and romance, which lead to marriage, constitute an effective ideological state apparatus. I have discussed this in the context of the Japanese nation-state (Ryang 2006a).

19. Michel Foucault, *The History of Sexuality,* vol. 1 (Harmondsworth, England: Penguin, 1977).

20. The news about North Korea's past kidnappings of innocent Japanese citizens was thrown in the face of the then Japanese prime minister Koizumi by Kim Jong Il, the North Korean leader, during their first ever meeting in September 2002. Since then, the pressure, both overt and covert, from Japanese authorities on Chongryun has been increasing dramatically, which is rendering it gradually impossible for Chongryun offices and schools to operate at normal pace. See McCormack (2005) and International Crisis Group (2005) for Japan-North Korea animosity and its aftermath Recently, reports abound in Japanese media about Chongryun's illegal activities, as well as its defeat in courtrooms. See, for example, "Court Axes Tax Cuts for Chongryun Hall" (2006); "Police Search Chongryun Affiliate over '80 Abduction"(2006); "Pro-Pyongyang Group Searched" (2006); and "Sin Guan-Su's North Korean Spy Ring under Investigation" (2006). The real extent of what Chongryun did or did not do with regard to North Korea's past abductions or its illegal transactions is hard to determine at this point, not least because of the media's sensationalistic take on this issue.

21. See, for details, Sonia Ryang, *North Koreans in Japan: Language, Ideology, and Identity* (Boulder, CO: Westview Press, 1997), chaps. 1, 2.

22. Anthony Giddens, *Transformation of Intimacy: Sexuality, Love and Eroticism in Modern Societies* (Cambridge, England: Polity Press, 1992), 41–48. Giddens here is referring to the early stage of modernity. While referring to much more recent times, Giddens sees love as being separated from lust in a rational manner, and as soon to be superseded by sexual plasticity, which would be a more dominant form of interpersonal relations of our time. Lindholm offers critical comment on this view (Lindholm 1998).

23. Dorothy Tennov, *Love and Limmerence: The Experience of Being in Love* (New York: Stein and Day, 1979) and Helen Fisher, *The Anatomy of Love: A Natural History of Mating, Marriage, and Why We Stray* (New York: Fawcett Columbine, 1992) detail the state of infatuation.

24. I detail this as a historical effect of postwar purity education (*junketsukyōiku*), implemented under the U.S. occupation in Japan. See Ryang (2006a: chaps. 3, 4).

25. Roman Jakobson, *Child Language: Aphasia and Phonological Universals* (The Hague: Mouton, 1968), 36.

26. A prophetic example can be found in a series entitled *Nihon no feminizumu* [Feminism in Japan], edited by Inoue Teruko, Ueno Chizuko, and Ehara Yumiko (1994), all leading figures of Japanese feminist scholarship and critique. In its first volume, *Ribu to feminizumu* [Lib and feminism], the book collates diverse voices of feminists from the margin, including a Korean feminist in Japan and a Japanese feminist with a disability. The irony is that the diversity is simply (and irresponsibly) presented, while little effort is made internal to the text to bridge the gaps between these voices from the periphery and mainstream feminism.

27. Giorgio Agamben, *State of Exception* (Chicago: University of Chicago Press, 1995).

28. Hannah Arendt, *The Origins of Totalitarianism* (New York: Harcourt Brace, 1958a). See also Xenos (1993).

29. Sonia Ryang, "Nationalist Inclusion or Emancipatory Identity? North Korean Women in Japan," *Women's Studies International Forum* 21 (6): 581–97; Ryang (1997: chaps. 3, 4).

30. Hannah Arendt, *The Human Condition* (Chicago: University of Chicago Press, 1958b), 51–52.

Chapter Three

A Letter from Afar

Totalitarianism, Neoliberalism, and Self-Reference

Unlike the Jewish diaspora, the history of the Korean diaspora is short. There is no sacred text and no biblical myth of exodus, and, strictly speaking, Koreans only lost their homeland for a very short period—thirty-six years, to be precise—while under Japanese colonial rule from 1910 to 1945. But like the Jewish case, despite significant efforts, recovery of the Korean homeland in the post–World War II period has proved to be extremely difficult and complicated. If Israel, as symbolically meaningful as it may be as the modern Jewish homeland, seems forever plagued by feuds with its Arab neighbors, Korea, divided into northern and southern halves, appears to be eternally incapable of restoring itself into one nation. In their own land, a peninsula surrounded by sea on three sides, in the land where their ancestors were born and their forefathers were brothers, Koreans have become bitter enemies of each other. The three-year civil war (1950–1953), and the fratricidal atrocities that accompanied it, set the scene for a half century of division. Long after the Americans relinquished power in the South and the Soviets withdrew from the North, the divided Koreans have continued to confront each other, right up to the present day. While no sacred text exists, a sacred ideal has been created by national partition: Korean reunification. This became the supreme goal, the ultimate utopia, and signified the recovery of the true homeland for all Koreans. The geography of reunification, an imaginary landscape with no line drawn in the middle of the peninsula, has become the sacred map of the long-lost homeland.

As with any myth of a lost homeland, this one involves post-scripting. The current territorial boundaries of the Korean peninsula, which the two halves have claimed wholly as theirs from primordial times, were formed relatively recently, beginning to emerge in the seventh century A.D., and consolidated in the tenth century with the foundation of the Koryeo kingdom. Although neither North Korea nor South Korea would readily acknowledge as much in their official national histories, significant invasions by neighboring countries took place, leading to a mixing of peoples, a blurring of boundaries, and a steady flow of material goods. All of the above were accompanied with pillaging and destruction, which would paradoxically lead to the further encoding of national identity as autochthonous and primordial.

There was the century-long usurpation and control of the Korean royal court by the Mongolians during the thirteenth and fourteenth centuries, which eventually culminated in the demise of Koryeo, to be replaced by Yi Korea or Choseon (1392–1910). At the end of the sixteenth century, a massive Japanese army invaded the peninsula in order to use it as a stepping-stone in its attempt at taking Ming China, the grand scheme designed by Toyotomi Hideyoshi. Premodern Korea was divided into mutually insular provinces and regions, and diet, dialects, rituals, and customs, to cite only a few aspects, varied vastly among them. Thus, there was no such a thing as a culturally homogeneous, historically unified, and quintessentially primordial homeland for all Koreans. Indeed, it is very doubtful that such a place ever existed— hence my claiming the myth of a primordial, unitary Korea to be a post-script.

In this sense, the imaginary homeland of the Korean diaspora paradoxically came about hand in hand with the reality of national partition: when two Koreas were formed through partition, one homeland emerged by way of desire. This perception was strongly manifested among Koreans in Japan. Postwar, postcolonial, postliberation, and postpartition Koreans in Japan came to realize that homecoming was no longer simply a matter of making a journey—instead, it became a matter of making numerous decisions and choices, such as that of which political entity—North or South—one would identify oneself with, regardless of (yet also constrained by) one's regional origin prior to colonial dispersion. Koreans in Japan, remaining in Korea's former colonial metropolis and, hence, more laden with antagonism and contradictions of a very complex kind, themselves came to embody their nation's torn circumstances inside their torn communities, at the very core of their personal existence.

As stated in the introduction, Koreans in Japan came predominantly from the southern provinces, but it was North Korea that strongly attracted their support during the initial decade following the war. The secret of Northern popularity was related to the historical coincidence between a radical surge of anti-Japanese (and retrospectively anticolonial) sentiments among Koreans and the eruption of mass support for leftist forces in postwar Japan. Prior to 1945, Koreans were prominent in the Japanese trade-union movement; although Korean activists were treated as second-class participants and had a hard time obtaining trust and gaining leadership positions inside the labor movement, their participation was sizable and influential.[1] Furthermore, prior to the total suppression of the Japanese Communist Party in the 1930s, Korean members had played a significant role inside the party. Koreans joined the Japanese Communist Party according to the Comintern policy then in practice of promoting one party per nation; since Korea was a colony of Japan, a separate party for Koreans was deemed unnecessary. Under the (one-time) liberal policies during the early years of the postwar U.S. occupation, Korean prewar communists, such as Kim Cheon-Hae, were released from jail by amnesty and quickly became iconic figures in the expatriate nationalist movement in Japan. Koreans remaining in Japan thus associated leftist forces with the stance of demanding national reunification and complete independence for Korea and, therefore, joined Japan's leftist movement with enthusiasm.

Among Koreans in Japan, thirty-three-year-old Kim Il Sung in the North was far more popular than the U.S. returnee Syngman Rhee in the South, because of the former's sustained record of having fought in Manchuria without once having been apprehended by the Japanese authorities. As I have mentioned in chapter 2, from 1945 to 1955 the Korean nationalist movement in Japan went through, first, the turmoil of being divided into supporters of North and South; then the suppression of the leftist League of Koreans by the authorities in 1949; and then a further intensification of the internal split due to the outbreak of the Korean War. In 1955, as has also been stated earlier, a new form of leftist Korean expatriate nationalist organization, Chongryun, emerged: a characteristic of Chongryun was that it declared itself to be solely an organization for overseas nationals of North Korea. By renouncing any unlawful activities in Japan, this declaration effectively accorded Chongryun self-granted extraterritoriality in the eyes of the Japanese authorities: as long as North Korea supporters simply supported the North and did not cause any unlawful trouble to the Japanese authorities, then peaceful coexistence with these forces would become possible. It also coincided with the rise of what historians of Japan call the *1955 system*, in which Japanese left- and right-wing political forces came to coexist without overtly confronting each other through subversive activities.

Following its foundation, Chongryun became a formidable mass organization, ensuring support for North Korea. According to one piece of Japanese intelligence data, at the time of Chongryun's emergence, almost 90 percent of Koreans in Japan supported North Korea.[2] We have seen in the preceding chapter that it effectively and energetically reconstructed the Korean schools of its predecessor, the League of Koreans, and turned them into an effective ideological apparatus to enhance commitment to North Korea. One significant event boosting the popularity of Chongryun and North Korea among Koreans in Japan (who were originally southerners) was North Korea's acceptance of

Koreans in Japan as fellow countrymen and women, and the related opening up of a route for repatriation in 1959, as stated in the introduction above. This was at a time when the South Korean government was flatly refusing to accept any Korean deportees from Japan; these were detained in a camp in southwestern Japan, worsening an already severe situation that Koreans in Japan faced (see below). Chongryun aggressively recruited volunteers to be repatriated to the North, its policy in perfect (albeit ironic) alignment with the Japanese government's goal of ridding Japan of poor Koreans (see below). In time, however, it also came to be known that Koreans from Japan were systematically discriminated against in their own fatherland's *el norte* (also see below). Approximately 3,000 Koreans were relocated from Japan to North Korea in December 1959 on the first repatriation boat, which was provided by the USSR as a token of friendship. Subsequently, about 49,000 made the journey in 1960, and a further 22,000 in 1961. By 1967, a total of 88,611 had left Japan for North Korea.[3] No return entry of repatriates is allowed, since Japan and North Korea have no functioning diplomatic relations (but see below).

Was this repatriation repatriation? Was it not, rather, a phenomenon that comes closer to "exile"? According to Nico Israel, *exile* means banishment by "an institutional act of force," but it also, contradictorily, contains an implication of "a matter of will," as connoted in its Latin etymology, *ex salire*, or leaping out.[4] As we shall see, the background, in which Koreans in Japan were not only pushed out by institutional force on the part of the Japanese government and Chongryun but also willing to leave Japan to be repatriated, seems to qualify their exodus as exile.

The term *repatriation*, on the other hand—meaning rejoining, or returning to, the fatherland, *la patrie*—implies the conclusion of a journey, the return to where one originally departed from. Does this, however, also imply a matter of will, as in the case of *ex salire*; or can it be forced, making it look more like institutional banishment? What was it that made Koreans in Japan believe that their exile in Japan was to end felicitously by taking the repatriation boat to North Korea? What persuaded them to cross the ocean in search of a utopic paradise, deemed to be their authentic homeland? Why, for example, did they not go back to South Korea, which was their home? And what happened to those who did not return and remained behind in Japan? As we follow this chapter's story, we will see these terms, *exile* and *repatriation*, begin to resemble each other, rather than being the opposites they first appeared to be.

REPATRIATION AND EXILE

In the traditional Korean penal system modeled after the Chinese penal code, banishment or exile was a routine form of punishment handed down to bureaucrats or literati who had committed crimes not as serious as treason. The latter would have meant execution—not only for the criminal himself, but for his entire family and often his extended family, including children, in order to conclusively terminate the lineage. The decapitated heads and headless bodies of the executed were typically put on public display, representing the worst form of punishment, that is, dismemberment and defiling of the corpse, which was believed to prevent the revival of the dead souls in any form. As opposed to the above type of capital punishment, premodern penal exile at least permitted the hope of an eventual, possible return. At the end of a painful period of absence from society and public service following the deprivation of one's title and political office, having been shamed and ostracized by the community, one hoped to recover one's political role and social functions, and hoped that one's good name (along with those of one's ancestors and offspring) would be restored. Considered from this comparative historical perspective, paradoxically, exile begins to look hopeful.

Repatriation, on the other hand, depends very much on which *patrie* one is returning to. If one's fatherland were a land of insularity and solipsism, one would experience a similarly closed-off existence following repatriation, a life that would begin to resemble exile from the rest of the world. This possibility was further aggravated in the case of Koreans in Japan, considering that the vast majority of the first generation originally came from the southern provinces that today form part of South Korea. Without the hope of, or belief in, the utopia of reunification, the eventual union of the two halves of Korea, therefore, the repatriation of Koreans from Japan to North Korea could not have happened, and could not have been understood as "repatriation," even by the repatriates themselves.

Moreover, it would be appropriate to describe the situation in which Koreans in Japan were placed following the end of the war as "dual exile." This is because of the way in which Koreans, former colonial subjects remaining in their former colonial metropolis, Japan, were made stateless between 1945 and 1952, a condition which for many lasted at least until 1965, and for others until 1981 (see the introduction). Koreans were officially excluded from Japanese national status in 1952; and it was not until 1965, when Japan and the Republic of Korea (South Korea) concluded formalization of diplomatic relations, that Koreans in Japan gained the eligibility to apply for South Korean nationality, as stated earlier in this book. Meanwhile, many Koreans in Japan have remained virtual detainees or prisoners in Japan, with no legal access to the outside world, due to their total lack of travel documents and civic status. Reentry permits to Japan began being issued in 1981, enabling bearers to travel abroad, albeit with restrictions. In principle, however, as I argued in the introduction, their status in relation to a particular national polity remains far from clear.

The choice of either North or South at the height of the Cold War was final, definitive, nonnegotiable, and mutually exclusive, and was made primarily for politico-ideological reasons. The division—both within the peninsula and inside the expatriate community—was no longer reversible in the aftermath of the fratricidal Korean War. Thus, acquiring South Korean nationality after 1965 meant politically siding with the South *tout court,* rather than simply identifying one's regional origins. This predicament eloquently speaks to the situation in which Koreans in Japan were first exiled as a result of colonialism and the subsequent postcolonial settlement, and then exiled due to national partition in the postwar period through the decisions of the superpowers. Both cases involved institutional force, that is, they involved the affected people's involuntary subjection to the consequences of imposed decisions made external to their own will; but at the same time, both cases also involved *ex salire,* elements of a will to leap.

What I mean is that, just as Nico Israel's definition of exile has a double meaning, in the case of Koreans, too, exile was in some ways voluntarily imposed. They rejected Japanese nationality after 1945, and many among them who were associated with North Korea rejected South Korean nationality after 1965. In the postwar, postliberation minds of Koreans in Japan, retaining any legal or political ties to Japan was to cling to the humiliation of the colonial era. Hence, it was deemed just and necessary to cut off all connections with Japan as soon as the war was over.[5] For many who supported the North, rejection of South Korean nationality was also a form of resistance. They viewed the action of the Japanese and South Korean governments, pairing South Korean nationality and Japanese permanent residence (as discussed above), as a cunning trick used by their Cold War enemies, since these enemies knew that the majority of Koreans in Japan came from the south and continued to worry and wonder about their families there, with whom they had not been able to make contact for at least two decades.

Chongryun waged a strong campaign based around resisting this temptation, not only condemning the authorities' measure as a callous trick, but also insinuating that applying for South Korean nationality would be a cardinal betrayal—thus further polarizing Koreans in Japan along the Cold War divide. This polarization lasted somewhat longer than historians might assume: as late as 1979, only 370,000 Koreans in Japan had South Korean nationality, out of a Korean population of around 600,000 in Japan.[6] This figure had fallen to around 320,000 by 1990, presumably because many in this group had become naturalized as Japanese citizens. Today many estimate that the majority of Koreans in Japan hold South Korean nationality, while naturalization continues to increase.[7] Unofficially, a Chongryun official informed me that as of October 2006, internal research by Chongryun deemed that fewer than 50,000 Koreans in Japan still did not hold South Korean nationality. As stated in the introduction, adopting South Korean nationality today does not itself wholly solve the predicament of exile. But half a century earlier, in 1959, the solution was sought in a totally different manner.

EXILE AFTER EXILE

The 1959 opening of repatriation to North Korea was in part the result of North Korea's efforts to outdo South Korea, when the latter was experiencing difficulties with Japan in negotiations aimed at achieving diplomatic normalization. Chongryun and the Koreans affiliated with it lobbied for the repatriation of Koreans from Japan to the North, a move that coincided with the Japanese government's goal of ridding Japan of Koreans. Especially targeted were poor Koreans who were recipients of destitution welfare issued by local municipalities, the number of which was estimated by the government to be around 60,000.[8] In her recent, seminal work, Tessa Morris-Suzuki underscores the significance of this figure, which was used by the Japanese government as a target to be achieved when recruiting Koreans to be sent away to North Korea. Morris-Suzuki, researching recently declassified International Committee of the Red Cross papers, highlights the complicity of the organization in assisting the Japanese government in the latter's concerted effort to rid its territory of poor Koreans.[9]

The Japanese government was not wrong to assume that poor Koreans would be happy to be repatriated to the North. According to 1963 data, about 4,200 out of 6,000 Korean repatriates to the North who had jobs were day laborers, while 7,800 repatriates were unemployed.[10] Just as a barometer, considering that there were a total of about 89,000 repatriates for the years 1959 to 1967, and subtracting the 3,000 in 1959 (since there was only one trip in December), the yearly average was around 12,000.[11] Adding 7,800 unemployed Koreans and 4,200 day laborers would amount to exactly 12,000, meaning that the predominant majority of Korean repatriates were destitute, had unstable or precarious jobs, or were unemployed.

For the many Koreans supporting North Korea, it was, however, repatriation in the political sense that mattered in the end. Many firmly believed that national partition would soon be over, eventually rendering their repatriation to the North identical to repatriation to one, whole Korea. And, in this sense, it is more than understandable that many families that were not poor chose to be repatriated or sent their children to North Korea, hoping that the rest of the family would join them shortly. North Korea's initial enthusiastic welcome of repatriates from Japan, advertised using all possible channels of the media directed toward the external world—and fanned by Chongryun, which called it "exodus from capitalism to socialism"—played no small part in the decision-making of Koreans in Japan.[12] In other words, many opted to be repatriated with an entirely different motivation from simply trying to make a living. Many wanted to let their children pursue professional careers not available to them in Japan, in fields such as medicine, art, public service, and academia. Many others deemed it noble to live and work in their own homeland, no matter how comfortably they had lived in Japan. For those who opted to be repatriated, living in Japan was considered a form of exile, and the only way to end it and live as complete human beings was to allow themselves to be embraced in the bosom of their homeland.

Notable was a family strategy of sending the children first while they were minors. Repatriating neighbors or relatives were made their ersatz guardians. Japanese family law basically did not interfere with these arrangements, since upon the registration of an application for repatriation, the Japanese government and municipalities considered the treatment of applicants as outside of their responsibilities. No social worker was assigned (to ensure that no abuse or exploitation was taking place), and no medical examination was administered (to assess the health of repatriates). This was basically due to the fact that Japanese authorities wanted to hastily remove Koreans from their soil.

Morris-Suzuki records one incident in which a thirteen-year-old girl was entrusted to a repatriating neighborhood family, since the girl had no parents in Japan and her older sister and brother-in-law were broke, because of her sister's tuberculosis among other things. It was only during the final check at Niigata, the port from which the first repatriation boat was to depart, that the legitimacy of this informal adoption was questioned.[13] Surely, the local municipality's alien registration office was involved in enabling this girl to depart with her neighbors, yet the lawfulness of this arrangement was never raised until they got to Niigata. This episode reveals the hasty manner in which repatriating Koreans were treated. Behind the facade of celebrating their repatriation as a humanitarian deed, the Japanese authorities' approach was guided by the ultimate goal of ridding Japan of Koreans, no matter what.

Families, when opting to send their children first, tended to send sons rather than daughters, this being quite understandable in light of the preference for sons, or male-centrism, found in Korean kinship. Parents were hopeful that if their sons were repatriated to the fatherland sooner, they would benefit more from (what was described to them as) the egalitarian, high-standard, and free eleven-year compulsory-education system in North Korea. This would enable their sons to make best use of their talents and gifts, allowing them to become medical doctors, research scientists, philosophers, concert pianists, educators, politicians, and so on and on. The homeland, or so it was thought, was the only place where one could become a man and live like a man by gaining political membership, a cultural franchise, and equal access to an active social and public milieu. Unfortunately, many were mistaken.

The family of world-renowned soprano Chon Wolson belonged to this group. Chon's four brothers, aged ten to seventeen, were repatriated in 1960, accompanying repatriating relatives. In 1969, all four were sent to a labor camp on suspicion of spying for Japan. In the camp, the second oldest was tortured, and died. The other three brothers were released in 1978. The family learned of this only in 1980, when Chon's mother visited North Korea. In 1985, Chon was invited to perform in front of Kim Il Sung, and, on that visit, she was able to be reunited with her surviving three brothers. The reunion was awkward, due to the brothers' worry about being watched and listened to. Saddened by this reunion, Chon has never again visited North Korea. Her oldest brother died in 1990, and the second youngest in 2001; the cause of their deaths is not known to her, and, in the meantime, Chon has stopped hearing from the youngest and still does not know what has happened to him.[14] We now know that Chon's family is not atypical. Repatriation to the North turned out to be an exile after exile, a more authentic and, hence, utterly hopeless exile, the truest form of banishment from humanity at large. It is still not clear how many repatriates from Japan were banished to concentration camps, becoming stateless in the land they believed to be the motherly bosom, as the propaganda had it, in which they would become true human beings.

The camp is where the state of exception prevails. For the *exception* here derives from *ex capere*, meaning "outside," and the state of exception is a state in which the law makes itself known by suspending itself. This is an effective way to control a population that exists outside ordinary law. Camp labor in North Korea, from what one can discern from the accounts of defectors, is not utilitarian, but is organized purely for the purpose of dehumanizing inmates.[15] To be precise, they are not enslaved—they do not have the status of slaves. In the camps, they are forced to engage in meaningless forms of labor, designed solely to dehumanize detainees. Unlike the ethnic discrimination Koreans suffer in Japan, which they can at least criticize, denounce, and be indignant about, camp labor is not even talked about—it is not something anyone should feel emotional about, since doing so might just endanger a material existence which has already been made so precarious. Inside the camps, many simply expire.

Institutions such as concentration camps were most likely able to come into existence in North Korea because of the extended martial-law-like conditions in place there since the Korean War ceasefire. Under the rubric of a national emergency—the unfinished war—that has prevailed since 1950, whoever is deemed a traitor or enemy of the state can face arbitrary forms of retribution.

Expiation is possible only by submission to punishment, not by counterevidence or self-justification.

It is only in recent years that information about the existence of concentration camps in North Korea and the reality of life inside the camps has begun to leak out beyond its national borders. For a long time, it was believed that North Korea was, all in all, a good place to be repatriated to, and that it was a state deserving of respect—after all, it remained the fatherland, *choguk,* for the Koreans in Japan who supported it. It was after 1981 that this imagery began to be readjusted: a change in opinion started slowly, accompanied by resistance and denial, but snowballed rapidly and incrementally, eventually causing an avalanche. The reason why I rather precisely mark 1981 as the year in which change began to be noticed is (ironically, in retrospect) related to unprecedented changes that took place in Japan around that period: the Japanese government ratified the International Covenants for Human Rights in 1979. These developments directly implicated the lives of Koreans in Japan who supported North Korea. Starting from 1981, they could obtain permanent residence in Japan without having to simultaneously obtain South Korean nationality, as well as reentry permits to travel abroad and come back to Japan (as discussed in the introduction).[16]

It was simply natural that families whose members had been repatriated to North Korea would travel there to be temporarily reunited with their loved ones. The pro–North Korea Chongryun fully capitalized upon this situation, monopolizing travel arrangements and acting as a liaison office between Koreans in Japan and the North Korean authorities. For many, the initial visit to North Korea proved overwhelming: finally, it was believed, they were to set foot on the soil of their fatherland and witness a miracle of human history, the glorious socialist paradise on earth, *sahoejueui chisangragweon*—just as the North Korean propaganda had repeatedly claimed.

Exactly how many visited North Korea from Japan is hard to determine—neither the Japanese Immigration Bureau nor Chongryun publicizes such figures, and it is not even certain whether they documented such figures in the first place. According to my calculations from yearly statistics issued by the Immigration Bureau, there was an increase in travel abroad during the 1980s by Koreans with reentry permits residing in Japan: from 4,273 in 1980 to 9,070 in 1986. In 1989 and during the early 1990s, the annual figure remained in the 15,000 range. Not all of these individuals were visiting North Korea, obviously. Considering that North Korean passenger ships entered the Japanese port of Niigata on the Sea of Japan, we can get a rough sense of the number of Korean visitors to North Korea by studying the figures for this port. Up through 1985, about 3,300 to 3,500 Koreans residing in Japan left Japan via Niigata. In 1986, the figure was 3,851, increasing to 4,532 in 1987. The figures for subsequent years were 3,953 (1988), 5,246 (1989), 4,392 (1990), and 4,686 (1991). The figure for 1992—the year of Kim Il Sung's eightieth birthday—was 5,067, falling to 3,344 in 1993 and rising again to 4,249 in 1994—the year of Kim Il Sung's death.[17] All in all, it appears that an average of about four to five thousand Koreans in Japan visited North Korea every year during the 1980s and early 1990s. The number of repatriates was already in severe decline by the beginning of the 1980s.

Not all of the trips to North Korea were reunion trips by the relatives of repatriated family members. Chongryun organized various kinds of trips, broadly divided into three categories: reward trips, reeducation trips, and family reunion trips. The first category consisted of trips given as rewards for hard work, as recognition of devotion or achievements, or in relation to promotions received by activists, employees, schoolteachers, and students. The second category included study trips by Korea University seniors; tutorial trips for Chongryun's performing artists (during which they received close tutelage by North Korean experts); short- or long-term reeducation programs for Chongryun cadres, as well as rank-and-file members; and retraining trips for schoolteachers, especially Korean-language teachers. The third category consisted of fortnightly reunion-visit package tours, which included basic sightseeing and four to seven days of visits to the repatriated families. All visits were placed under the mandatory supervision of North Korean officials, who accompanied all visitors to the repatriated families.

In the beginning, North Koreans welcomed the visitors from Japan with sincerity and enthusiasm. Boats entered via the port of Weonsan, which had been designated to receive visitors from Japan and, hence, was consciously prepared so as to give visitors a good first impression of the long-lost and now-recovered fatherland. Upon my first visit there in 1981, Weonsan looked like a new city, renovated and refurbished, distinctly characterized by its Soviet-style buildings, parks, and public plazas. The pier was filled with a welcoming crowd that had been mobilized by the party. It is most likely that new clothing had been supplied to them for the purpose of greeting visitors from Japan, as seen from the identical design and fabric of their outfits. Men, women, and children of all ages lined up and made an orderly human wall on the pier, to orchestrate the first sight of the fatherland for the visitors from Japan. Live music was played, and the Young Pioneers welcomed the ship's captain home with a salute and a bouquet. People were in tears, and whenever possible they would come closer to the visitors and offer kind words, such as: "I am so happy to have you here—you must be suffering so much under Japanese capitalism," or "Welcome to the warm bosom of our fatherland—congratulations upon your first experience of witnessing our great achievement under the wise guidance of our Great Leader." They would hold the visitors' hands and shake them with passion, conveying a genuine welcome and the joy of greeting them. Their faces were tanned, dry, and deeply wrinkled, yet shining with tears of joy, full of pride at their being members of "the glorious socialist fatherland." Often, teary faces were seen on both sides. Such a heartfelt welcome by the fatherland brought tears to the eyes of the Chongryun visitors, moving and overwhelming them. It was a sad scene, viewed in retrospect. After all, North Koreans themselves exist in a kind of stern exile in their own land, left in benighted ignorance about the outside world as well as their own—in a way, banished from the rest of the world.

Nico Israel captures diaspora as the curse of the postexodus Moses with an admonition that disobedience of the Lord's teachings would be met with the fate of eternal dispersion of the Jews among the Gentiles. He adds the claim that diasporic removal is associated with "a perpetual otherness amid others" and "a spreading that weakens."[18] If, however, as we touched upon earlier, exile can be somewhat temporary and may leave a ray of hope for return, diaspora as a scattering that weakens may imply permanence. On the other hand, does a spreading always weaken a people, I wonder? North Koreans are certainly not in diaspora, and they live in their homeland, but they, as a people, are extremely weakened.

By the time I visited North Korea for the third time, in 1985, as a reporter for Chongryun's newspaper, members of the welcome party were no longer as passionate as they had been in 1981. One teenager approached me, calling me *eonni,* older sister, and instead of congratulating me upon my visit to the fatherland, told me that her mother was sick and that she needed 2,000 Japanese yen to enable her to buy her mother medicine. I was shocked, and tried hard to think whether I knew the girl or not. In the end, I gave her the money, but my feelings were mixed in the face of such a naked testimony regarding how hard things in fact were in North Korea, which at that time I had heard only as hearsay. When I recounted this story to my colleagues in Chongryun's newspaper office back in Tokyo, I was surprised to discover that most of them had had similar encounters in North Korea.

THE LOGIC OF THE CAMP

The recent CNN production on North Korea, *Undercover in the Secret State* (first aired on November 13, 2005), showed public executions, a glimpse into the concentration camps, street crime, and a poster declaring that Kim Il Sung was assassinated by his son Kim Jong Il due to the former's inclination toward an open-door policy for the country, among other scenes. These were not wholly surprising and may even have been predictable. It is in a way expected that a totalitarian society such as North Korea would have public executions of traitors and domestic enemies—George Orwell has already shown that, albeit in a fictional way. The most chilling imagery was not of these extraordinary events but, rather, of mundane reality.

One piece of footage caught a brief encounter between a young female transportation officer and two middle-aged women passengers on a train. When the officer checked their papers—no North Korean citizen is allowed to travel from one town to another without a written permit from the authorities—the women's permit turned out to be not in order. The officer hysterically ordered them out. Realizing that despite repeated orders issued in a shrill voice the women were dragging their feet, the officer began pulling at their bags, which perhaps were filled with food they had purchased from other towns for their families to eat, or for them to trade for goods that their families needed in order to survive. The women, perhaps the officer's mother's age, who were exhausted and whose faces were tanned and emaciated, held on to their bags, each one covering her face with one hand and quietly sobbing and murmuring, submissively asking the officer why she was treating them in this way. The officer began hitting the women on their heads and slapping their faces, while the women submitted without protest.[19]

This footage showed that the personal safety of North Korean individuals depends not on the rule of law but on the temperament of the officers, administrators, and other uniformed representatives of the authorities. Their well-being is left at the mercy of the officers they encounter, dependent on the latters' mood on that particular day and at that particular moment. This precarious lawlessness in the name of the law is precisely what Agamben has called the *logic of the camp*, where power is invested arbitrarily in the person of uniformed officialdom, just as it is under martial law or in a state of emergency.[20]

The form of social institution that is most closely associated with the camp is, needless to say, totalitarianism. In contrast to today's object of global intellectual fascination, neoliberalism, totalitarianism appears imminently obsolete and otherworldly. But are they so clearly unrelated to each other? David Harvey, in his recent work on neoliberalism, states that: "the neoliberal state should favour strong individual private property rights, the rule of law, and the institutions of freely functioning markets and free trade."[21] Harvey is quick to point out that, unlike in the above type of theoretical postulate, the real-life neoliberal state is faced with the eternal burden of intervention, at times strong and sometimes repressive, in order to monitor and guard against moves by the masses toward a collective utopic society; it therefore tries to keep the masses as individualistically oriented as possible.[22]

The paradox of neoliberalism reveals itself most nakedly in times of war, as can be witnessed in the U.S. since the opening of the "war on terror"—the sectors of the U.S. neoliberal economy represented by oil companies continue to benefit enormously from the war in Iraq, while the vast American middle class is sandwiched between higher taxes and lower wages. In this type of situation, the government must check the population's frustrations and its ensuing desire to question the government's accountability, while guarding against organized antiwar, antigovernment activities. These goals are usually addressed by way of public persuasion and economic incentive within the parameters of civil rights, but sometimes they are addressed by going beyond those boundaries—that is, by using methods akin to those typical of totalitarian regimes, including random phone-tapping of citizens, unlawful imprisonment, and even summary execution.

The post-9/11 U.S. homeland security policy, represented by the Patriot Act, is a good example of a permanent state of emergency. Time and again, we are told that there is no end to the war against terror. Under this act, there has been an exponential increase in the decision-making powers accorded to the U.S. President. This gets translated into the unlimited detention of suspects and "enemies." Meanwhile, despite the trendy fad of embedding journalists within military units, we are left with very little information regarding who is killing whom, how they are killing them, and on what grounds. Disregard of the Geneva Convention, for which the Japanese had been denounced in relation to Japan's treatment of Western POWs during World War II, features prominently in Bush-Cheney courses of action. Thus, an unprecedented expansion in the executive powers of the president is justified in the name of war.

We must not overlook, either, that recent energetic moves toward the amendment of Article Nine of the Japanese Constitution signal the potential for a similar outcome in that country: that is, for unlimited power to be placed in the hands of the sovereign in the name of emergency. In the post–World War II world, the supreme emergency takes the form of the national emergency. It is in the current atmosphere, charged with a revived ultranationalism, that Japan's former Prime Minister Abe rejected in 2007 accusations that Japan coerced Asian (mostly Korean) and other women into military sexual slavery during World War II. Indeed, his denial has been described as "the clearest so far" when compared to those of his predecessors.[23]

According to Agamben, war is also the key to understanding modern totalitarianism. In his words:

> modern totalitarianism can be defined as the establishment, by means of the state of exception, of a legal civil war that allows for the physical elimination not only of political adversaries but of entire categories of citizens who for some

reason cannot be integrated into the political system. Since then, the voluntary creation of a permanent state of emergency (though perhaps not declared in the technical sense) has become one of the essential practices of contemporary states, including so-called democratic ones.[24]

In the above-quoted description, with the concentration of disproportionate power in the hands of a supreme leader, a propaganda-like denial of the past, and a rewriting of history, so-called neoliberal states begin to look more like totalitarian states.

In an uncanny coincidence, persecution of Koreans in Japan in Japan's modern history often took place at a time of martial law, during a state of emergency. In 1923, following a strong earthquake that devastated Tokyo and its vicinity, Koreans were lynch-mobbed, tortured, and mass-murdered in a public frenzy by Japanese citizens—under martial law—resulting in the death of 6,000 Koreans.[25] Twenty-five years later, in 1948, in the wake of mass protests by Koreans against the decision to forcibly close independent ethnic Korean schools, martial law was declared in the western Japanese city of Kobe by the U.S. military (then occupying Japan) and Japanese authorities, resulting in at least three deaths and innumerable injuries and police arrests, in addition to the destruction of school buildings.[26]

Is there any connection between the persecution of Koreans and the power to suspend ordinary law (as through the imposition of martial law)? How did these two instances of martial law in the twentieth century influence the formation of the Korean diaspora in Japan? By asking these questions, I'm not simply problematizing the forms of cultural or ethnic discrimination or prejudice that any Korean person might be subjected to in Japan; rather, I am questioning the nature of *topos* in relation to a Korean in Japan's social order. At the same time, I am referring to the notion of the undeclared legal civil war mentioned by Agamben earlier. Whenever Koreans became a problem in the eyes of the authorities in Japan, martial law was declared—what does this tell us, I reiterate? Does this not tell us about the *topos* of Koreans in the Japanese nation-state, as a population that needs to be first and foremost placed under "protective custody" in a space created in separation from the ordinary, regular order; that is, a space where the rule of law is suspended, where law governs by suspending itself, that is to say, a camp? Furthermore, is not this population topographically and topologically placed in a peculiar position—as bodies that can be killed without murder charges being incurred against the murderer, as lives that may or may not belong within the ordinary order, and as people whose documentation is incomplete or missing? Modern human history has repeatedly shown the destination for this kind of population to be the concentration or extermination camp.

If the declaration of martial law is a neoliberal means of suspending the law, in totalitarianism such a declaration itself becomes redundant. What is unique about totalitarian society and its concentration camps is that, in a fashion that goes against utilitarian principles, "superfluous" human beings or "undesirable" elements are not put to work or made to produce materials for the society, but are incarcerated with no obvious apparent purpose other than to be dominated and subjugated by the authorities.

Is this alien to neoliberalism, though? I would answer otherwise. Globally speaking, not one of the so-called neoliberal states is free of refugees, illegal immigrants, and undocumented aliens. Upon their apprehension, they, too, are housed in institutionalized incarceration in refugee camps, detention centers, and prisons—that is, camps under the custodial control of the nation-state and its uniformed officers. Their fate is sometimes decided swiftly, through deportation or amnesty, for example; but in most other cases, they are left to stagnate, incarcerated ad infinitum at the mercy and discretion of state authorities, possibly because of a lack of personnel, or perhaps simply because of a lack of interest in their fate. It is no secret that the ongoing U.S. "war against terror" has produced a large population in this category, including the POWs in Guantanamo Bay. The ongoing debate regarding illegal aliens and the pros and cons of their detention in camp-like facilities in the U.S. is another such example. Routinely, they are denied, or restricted in their access to, legal representation, on the basis that they are enemy nationals or simply because they are not national citizens.

Japan used to have a designated camp for the detention of illegal border crossers and offenders of the Alien Registration Law while they awaited deportation. Non-Japanese offenders used to be detained at Ōmura shūyōjo, or the Ōmura camp, for years with no trial, no clear plan for their relocation, no access to legal representation, and no schooling, for school-age detainees. The bulk of the detainee population was Korean.[27] When two International Committee of the Red Cross officers, William Michel and Eugène de Weck, visited the camp in 1956, as part of a fact-finding mission related to the repatriation of Koreans in Japan to North Korea, it was enclosed by a high wall, with watchtowers on all four corners. At that time, it held a total of 1,467 Korean detainees, belonging to two major categories: those who had completed sentences for past criminal offences (the minority) and people who had been arrested for illegal entry (the majority). Among the detainees, there were 140 children under the age of fifteen, thirty-one of whom had no accompanying parents. They were detained in limbo with no access to legal representation, as neither the Japanese nor South Korean governments claimed responsibility for them.[28]

The fact that the Ōmura camp has since been relieved of its special duty of detaining Koreans, and instead houses illegal immigrants from diverse national groups today, does not mean that Koreans no longer face the possibility of this form of detention. In the case of a national emergency, such as in the war that Japan's current political climate is rather eager to have the option of, nonnationals or enemy nationals would be the first to face detention in the name of national security.

In 2002, during the historic, first-ever meeting between North Korean and Japanese heads of state, North Korean leader Kim Jong Il revealed to the then Japanese Prime Minister Koizumi that, during the 1970s and 1980s, North Korea's secret agents had kidnapped a total of thirteen innocent Japanese citizens in order to utilize them for the training of North Korean spies. Ever since this revelation became public, Japanese authorities, including taxation and immigration officials, local municipal authorities, and intelligence and police officials — as well as mass-media outlets — have been conspicuously making concerted efforts to dehumanize Koreans in Japan in retaliation. Numerous arrests, searches, and random inspections have taken place and continue to take place today, on the basis of even remote suspicions of past involvement with North Korea through donations to the pro–North Korean Chongryun. On April 25, 2007, the police searched the Tokyo home of a woman alleged to be a former North Korean agent, in relation to her involvement in the 1973 abduction of two children in Hokkaido, the northernmost of Japan's four main islands. On the same day, in a manner that reminds the observer of the postwar raiding and suppression of the League of Koreans in 1949, police stormed Chongryun premises housing a Chongryun-affiliated research office. Such a high-handed, forceful treatment of Chongryun would have been unthinkable even ten years ago, due to concerns over possible protests by Japanese leftist or pacifist groups. But today, the Japanese government appears to be comfortable carrying out this kind of direct action against Chongryun, since there is hardly any recognizable opposition force in Japan's political and civic arenas. Chongryun protesters resisted on-site, resulting in numerous arrests on the basis of the obstruction of justice.[29]

Given the heated hostility toward North Korea that we have been witnessing on an ongoing basis ever since 2002, be it in relation to North Korea's past kidnapping of Japanese citizens, its missile launching, or its more recent nuclear weapons program and the crisis surrounding its nuclear detonation, it would not be an overreaction to sense the possibility of reactivating the mission of the Ōmura camp, targeted at Koreans in Japan, especially those associated with North Korea.[30] Or should we recognize that the Japanese state has already declared legal civil war against Koreans in Japan, reminding us of the instances of martial law of 1923 and 1948, and augmenting the possibility of the application of protective custody to Koreans in the name of national emergency? Fundamentally speaking, then, there is not much difference between the camp population (both actual and potential) under neoliberalism and that under totalitarianism.

TOTALITARIANISM AND SELF-REFERENCE

Harvey also notes that under neoliberalism, while "personal and individual freedom in the market place is guaranteed, each individual is held responsible and accountable for his or her own actions and well-being."[31] Anthropologists have noticed this for some time, particularly in relation to what some call the *audit culture*. Marilyn Strathern emphasizes that in the audit culture, new demands for accountability are made in relation to academics in Western higher-education institutions, continually increasing the need for self-reference and self-study.[32] Indeed, individuals in late capitalism are made increasingly accountable for their own conduct, multiplying the number of occasions that oblige us to engage in self-analysis and self-examination, including, but not limited to the following: tenure and promotion dossiers or grant applications in academe; medical history questionnaires or therapeutic counseling for patients; resume-writing for job applicants; and, of course, tax returns for all. It was Michel Foucault who established the historical significance of the self-reflexive confession as an institution making individuals accountable for their conduct, causing them to reflect upon it and judge it by themselves. Anthony Giddens, on the other hand, strenuously emphasizes the importance of reflexivity and critical self-consciousness as the key to understanding modernity and the modern self. Self-accountability has come to flourish as a modern way of life, penetrating the lives of all and sundry as global modernity intensifies under neoliberalism.[33]

In this sense, it is wholly logical that self-focused "life-writing," including the writing of autobiographies, has become a genre embraced by modern, reflexive individuals.[34] Self-writing, as I might call it in contradistinction to life-writing, has also played an important role in relation to resistance in oppressive and devastating situations. Anne Frank's diary, for example, continues to give hope and inspiration to humanity, through the courage and strength of mind and spirit vis-à-vis dehumanizing conditions that it embodies.[35] As is widely known, it was written while Frank was in hiding, as the Nazis gradually but steadily forced Jewish families in Amsterdam like her own into precarious living conditions, ultimately bringing about their deaths in unspeakably inhumane ways and leaving only an untraceable debris of corpses.

But there are also plenty of examples of self-focused writing that serves the purpose of narcissistic self-aggrandizement and self-advertisement. Writing that involves self-reference thus comes as a double-edged sword: some examples of self-writing are narrowly self-obsessed, while others are capable of reaching beyond the personal confines of the writer to make an impact on the lives of millions. From this, we might recognize that the neoliberal ethos of personal accountability and responsibility, equipped in particular with the armory of a self-diagnostic, self-psychologizing, and self-analyzing nomenclature (*codependency, depression, anxiety disorder, hypochondriac, repressed memory, genetic makeup, childhood trauma, dissociative disorder*—indeed, you name it), comes with an antitotalitarian effect of rendering a focus on self rather distinctly liberating.

Furthermore, autobiographic practice, in our understanding, especially when deployed by the weak and the oppressed as a vehicle to carry their voices, is an effective weapon in asserting the manifesto of the powerless. The genre that comes closest to this type of self-writing of resistance would be the testimonio. As I touched upon in the introduction, one of the most powerful examples of this subgenre in recent decades is Rigoberta Menchú's life history, which is usually seen as a paragon of the testimonio, a genre of Latin American oral history told by an oppressed and silenced individual, speaking on behalf of a larger community of oppressed and disenfranchised individuals. As I also mentioned in the introduction, truthfulness constitutes the major element in making the testimonio legitimate, even though what to regard as truthful may radically differ depending on who is writing and who is reading. In other words, the credibility and accountability of the testifier is crucial in authenticating his or her testimonies—it is an inherently tautologous process of self-validation.

While this self-referential culture may be the constituent component of neoliberalism, it is also one of the strongest elements of a culture of totalitarianism. The reader might find it intriguing at a glance that I am approximating our familiar and much loved practice of self-writing with totalitarianism, which we are used to thinking of as foreign and "not-us." Yet self-accountability with regard to truthfulness is an institution heavily utilized in totalitarian states such as North Korea. There, the population is subjected to an incessant process of mental purification, according to which individuals must hold themselves accountable not only for their conduct, but also for their inner beliefs and state of mind in the ubiquitous eyes of the Great Leader. Every New Year's Day, men and women, the old and the young, write New Year's pledge letters addressed to the Great Leader. At the end of every day, week, month, and year, the population goes through a ritual of self-review for each work unit, organizational unit, or school classroom. What is judged in these sessions is whether one is able to recount, interpret, and judge one's own conduct, verbally and/or in writing; present it in front of one's comrades; and then gratefully receive the

critical verdict of the group. In this context, how to make a retrospective, public self-presentation becomes a more important criterion for the judgment of
good moral-political character than what one actually did in reality.

Just like in neoliberal economies—where one's skill in managing one's retirement funds, for example, and not the state's management of its centralized
pension fund, determines whether or not one experiences a financially comfortable retirement—in totalitarianism, one's capacity to deliver proof, rhetor-
ically in this case, of one's faithfulness to the regime becomes a decisive factor in determining one's level of well-being or ill-being, sometimes even
becoming a matter of life and death. Here, one is alone and is solely responsible for his or her own conduct. Back to back with the family-oriented and
pseudokinship terminology utilized by the North Korean state, especially in
its references to Kim Jong Il as the nation's father and Kim Il Sung as its
grandfather, individuals are not even in a position to trust members of their
own families, precisely because when one commits a crime in the eyes of the
authorities, the entire family is sent into exile—just as in the premodern Korean penal code. Thus, in the North Korean totalitarian society, the self and
the rest exist in a random mixture of insecure connection and disconnection.
The only certainty exists in the direct connection the self has with the Great
Leader through the channel of loyalty toward him.[36] Arendt's words capture
this well:

> The disturbing factor in the success of totalitarianism is rather the true selfless-
> ness of its adherents: it may be understandable that a Nazi or Bolshevik will not
> be shaken in his conviction by crimes against people who do not belong to the
> movement or are even hostile to it; but the amazing fact is that neither is he
> likely to waver when the monster begins to devour its own children and not even
> if he becomes a victim of persecution himself, if he is framed and condemned,
> if he is purged from the party and sent to a forced-labor or a concentration camp.
> On the contrary, to the wonder of the whole civilized world, he may even be
> willing to help in his own prosecution and frame his own death sentence if only
> his status as a member of the movement is not touched.[37]

In the North Korean context, when writing a self-review report, referred to
as *chonghwamun*, one first needs to be able to assess the strength of one's loyalty, commitment, and dedication to the leadership; love for the country; level
of participation in teamwork; and self-sacrificing performance in relation to
task fulfillment, hard work, level of dedication, and so on. One then proceeds
to critically recount in which aspects one has been lacking in effort; in which
ways one has not sufficiently prepared or not sufficiently improved oneself
since the previous criticism session; in what directions one is distracted and
why; what kinds of bad influences one is unconsciously receiving; in what

work department one needs to strive harder; and so on. The key here is to maintain consistently and strenuously that one's loyalty to the leadership and love for the country, the party, and the masses is intact, while admitting that one happened to pay insufficient attention to one's speech or conduct, or somehow failed to be vigilant in relation to one's own weakness. It is imperative that one present an immaculate example of self-criticism. Indeed, this becomes a genre in itself, since, as noted above, it is more important to be able to criticize oneself in public in a proper and coherent manner, and according to the established format, than to actually do the job well. In fact, if one deviates from the formulaic language of the review by way of being too original, this itself is seen as a liability, becoming the object of a new round of group criticism.

There is one canonical criterion for a good *chonghwamun:* the correct and extensive citation of the words of Kim Il Sung or Kim Jong Il. North Koreans memorize both leaders' writings, word by word, sentence by sentence, from *The Works of Kim Il Sung* and *The Works of Kim Jong Il.* The ability to learn either Kim's words by heart and recite them correctly is the best demonstration of the pledge of one's commitment and sincerity toward the revolutionary and patriotic cause of North Korea. Conversely, if one were to misquote either of the Kims' sacred words, the consequences could be catastrophic (even life-threatening), since this would be seen as a sign of lack of loyalty or, worse still, a false claim of loyalty toward the leaders.

The climax of many an allegorical story, film, or TV drama in North Korea features an example of self-criticism by a hitherto nonexemplary, semireactionary, and problematical comrade, as every North Korean can recognize and relate to this type of situation. By the same token, it is believed that if one fails to make a proper and sincere public display of self-criticism, one's sins are not cleansed and one sets oneself up for punishment and humiliation. In this way, in North Korea's leader-focused totalitarianism, self-reference becomes a life-and-death concern for citizens. This mechanism in its turn maintains the moral-ideological accountability of the population toward the leader, as well as the individual's accountability to his or her own conscience. Although it is imagined in the West that under totalitarianism there is no concept of the individual or the self, and that the population merely submits to whatever the state (or the authorities) demand of it, a totalitarian society such as North Korea's works on the basis of the self's atomization and its autonomous isolation from the rest of society, each individual being responsible for monitoring his or her own conduct and loyalty toward the leader. In North Korea, the self and its actions (including self-enactment, self-criticism, reflexion, self-analysis, and self-assessment) are thus crucial parts of the ideo-

logical and socioeconomic mechanism/process by which the society reproduces itself.[38]

Thus, though operating in very different directions and with different effects, self-accountability is the key to understanding the workings of both the
North Korean brand of totalitarianism and the kind of neoliberal audit culture
found in advanced Western capitalism: both presuppose a disciplinary regime
of incessant antiheretic self-inquisition. Only what is seen as heresy differs in
these societies. It is with this in mind that I introduce a letter written by a Korean woman in Japan, addressed—but never posted—to a high school classmate who was (voluntarily) repatriated to North Korea in the late 1970s. I
shall consider the process by which self-writing as a form of self-reference
works as an uncanny reminder of the way that the diasporic reality and the
system of nation-states effectively make denationalized individuals hold
themselves responsible for life's misfortunes and the unexpected and undesirable twists and turns of history. I withhold the writer's background until a
later section, in order to focus the reader's attention on the letter itself and to
allow its autobiographic mode of self-inquiry to inform us of the dilemmas
and agonies faced by people caught in a historical abyss created in the shadows of Cold War politics.

A LETTER FROM AFAR

Dear SH—

Close to thirty years have passed since you were repatriated to North Korea. You
have lived in North Korea longer than you have in Japan by now. None of us
knew, did we? That we would end up never seeing each other again, or even
hearing about each other, in this strange, incomprehensible way. Words have no
power, however, and I just have to simply resign myself to imagining what has
become of you, me, all of us. Do you still remember our class? Thirty-six girls—
all full of character and personality, full of life. We had among us some really
gifted ones, smart ones, truly kind ones, exceedingly beautiful ones, and really
funny ones. Our class was unusually endowed with unique people. And our
teacher, Ms C. Remember? On our graduation day, before any of us had broken
into tears, she was already crying.

But by far, you were the most impressive of us all—all of us would agree to
that. Your singing, acting, reciting, reading—all of those incredible perform-
ances you could present so spontaneously and so immaculately. It came, therefore, as no surprise when you declared that upon graduation you would be repatriated in order to pursue your dream of becoming a People's Actress
(*inminpaeu*) in North Korea—or maybe, maybe I was not just surprised, perhaps
I was jealous. I was jealous of your noble decision. It was, yes, "cool" that you

made such an incredibly heroic, courageous decision. I was also, I'm sure you did not fail to notice, disappointed in myself. I was made to realize how unimaginative and passive I'd been in thinking about my own future—simply going to Korea University, just like about one-third of us did, as it was the safest, most secure way to the future. I did, of course, dream about my future—I have been a dreamer, as you know, since I was little. I wanted to become a diplomat, then a concert violinist, and then, an interpreter. But I did not know how to be any of these, and before I knew it, I was graduating from high school. I simply opted, as I said, for the one safe path that was open.

But your decision! The decision to be repatriated in order to pursue your dream towered like a giant in front of me. Of course, it meant—all of us knew— you would never see your parents, your friends, your street, your home again. All those seemed irrelevant, though, did they not? All those little sentimental inconveniences embarrassed us, did they not, because of their triviality?

We were only eighteen, but what an eighteen-year-old you were! You embodied the hopes and dreams of us all. Sometimes, I feel I was more mature, wiser, and braver when I was eighteen than I am now, but compared to you, I feel belittled. It took about three years after we had sent you off from Ueno station platform, chanting "Long Live our Great Leader Kim Il Sung!" and "Long Live our fatherland," for me to see you on the big screen. I saw your cameo appearance in a scene where a group of women were singing in the movie Korea's Star [a North Korean feature movie]. At first, I could not believe it—but of course it was meant to happen. Why not? I did not doubt your success, never. Yes, you've done it, SH—I cheered you on. I was so very proud of you.

The next time, also to this day the last, that I saw you was in the Pyongyang No. 1 Department Store. It was during our college senior tour to North Korea. I remember, as I was window-shopping, that someone called my name from behind. I turned around and you were standing there. You were wearing a beige duster coat and a pair of black leather pumps, which were obviously Japanese-made—your parents must have been sending you goods from Japan regularly, I gathered. I was relieved to see that you looked healthy and that your material life did not seem too limited. We just chatted a little bit, after greeting each other. But we knew it, didn't we, that we were no longer classmates, that we no longer shared life's dreams, that we even spoke different Korean languages. What a cold meeting that was . . . There was no warm embrace, no screaming, no fooling around . . . you had mastered the rules of North Korean behavior and almost instantaneously warned me with your eyes and voice not to show my excitement. I complied, or at least tried to, speaking minimally and quietly. It was awkward and painful.

Only many years later, I felt sadness about this encounter. It took me a long time to figure out exactly what had happened then. You remembered how naïve I had been and immediately took my tendency to express my emotion directly as a potential harm, a factor that could endanger your safety. At that time, Kim Il Sung was still alive and his reign was stable—or at least it looked that way. How strange it is now to have thought about North Korea as an even remotely livable place? Beyond that: we thought it would be our sanctuary. Your parents, dedicated to your success, believed that repatriation would open up a bright new future for you—a future that those of us, Koreans in Japan, could not even dream about while living in Japan.

I remember you told me that your parents sent with you a lot of gifts and cash for the North Korean acting school, in order to ensure your well-being. You said, jokingly, since you did not come from a cadre family like mine, that your parents were showing their loyalty [to North Korea] by opening their purse. What a strange turn of events we are witnessing, then. A rich, beautiful, free-spirited, and gifted girl like you now lives in the world's poorest and last-remaining Stalinist country, where goods are scarce and policies unpredictable. And I, the one who always pledged eternal loyalty [to North Korea] more eagerly than anyone else, live a life of material abundance under capitalism.

SH—

I heard that you were married to a North Korean-born actor and that you left acting more than ten years ago. After that brief appearance, I never again saw you in any of the North Korean movies. Yes, it was twenty-five years ago that I saw you in Pyongyang one last time. Will we meet again? Why did you quit acting? Were you forced? Were you discriminated against, because of your Japanese upbringing? Were you treated well, or at least fairly? Are you healthy? Are you happy? Are you alive? Have you ever been sent away to a re-education camp? Why are we not hearing from you?

Even today, some old people in Chongryun are still defending North Korea and its leadership. I do not blame them—it was the only life they had had: when they got rid of colonialism, they found in their participation in Chongryun's expatriate movement in support of North Korea the momentum to regain their life, new life. The Cold War fixed their position much too long and much too rigidly and what had been a heroic life became (as seen by us) a fool's endeavor. I'm sorry for them, too. But they are dying off and, in a way, they've had a good life—a meaningful life. It is our generation that I'm worried about, and of course, our children's. Do you have children, SH? I don't even know that.

SH—

After close to thirty years, I'm writing to you—remembering our youthful days, songs we sang together again and again, coffee shops we frequented, over-criticizing and badmouthing grown-ups, insisting on stupid little details of our school uniforms or hairstyles. We were happy kids then. But why does this pain me this much, to think about it? SH, I do hope your womanhood was not robbed—indeed, I do hope your humanity is not harmed. Of course, who am I to say this? Why should I assume that my world should preserve my humanity? It is not like that. It is a constant struggle to refresh one's sense of integrity and principles. I see cowards, I see deception, I see pathetic humans, I see individuals with greater power refuse to assume greater responsibility, I see the highly prestigious establishment completely losing its decency and crushing the pow-erless, I see all these everyday and yet, more often than not, am unable to make any difference. I fail miserably, compromising and patronized, or indulging in petty personal revenge. It infuriates me when that happens, but at least I have the freedom to get indignant about my unpreparedness, lack of abilities, weak sense of politics, or what have you. My frustration with myself derives from my own set of moral criteria and the discrepancy from it in my actual deeds. Or, at least, I'm able to believe so.

I hope North Koreans, all my repatriated friends, and you above all, are not so fragile. I do hope that, behind the vulnerability, there is resilience. We don't break so easily, do we?

Recently, I'm hearing more about isolated cases in which former repatriates have come back to Japan using back-alley routes. I wonder if you are consider-ing such an escape, granted that it is indeed possible, and sometimes wonder if you're already back in your parents' home without letting any of us know . . . but the question I'm haunted with is: "were we so wrong when we were eight-een?" Were we? No one can answer that.

So long, SH. I wish you all the very best. Wherever you are, some day, may we find each other again.

CR

GIFT OF LOYALTY

As the letter tells us, the writer, CR, comes from a Chongryun cadre's family. She and SH were classmates in a Korean high school operated by Chongryun. The two women grew up in the 1960s and 1970s and, toward the end of high school, they were eternally separated, as CR went to study at Chongryun's Korea University and SH was repatriated to North Korea in order to pursue her dream of becoming an actress. SH was the last classmate CR sent off to North Korea. The late 1970s may sound rather recent for such a decision to live in North Korea (and never come back to Japan) to be made. But based on the experience of many (myself included), it was not unusual. As stated ear-lier, the repatriated population was diverse, and SH represented many others whose parents were eager to help their children achieve their dreams. Like SH's parents, many also sent their children off with an impressive range of gifts, as if it were a kind of dowry toward their future in an unknown land. I must add that unlike during the 1960s, when the majority of repatriates who went to North Korea were families seeking a better life, by the time SH was repatriated—that is, by the late 1970s—the repatriating population was min-imal, consisting of select individuals like SH who wanted to pursue specific goals in North Korea, reflecting the general improvement in living standards among Koreans in Japan. SH's repatriation at the end of the 1970s was one of the last of this kind, since merely a few years later, the Japanese government decided to issue reentry permits to Koreans in Japan, allowing them to visit North Korea. SH could have taken this route, instead of being (eternally) repatriated, but of course, no one could have predicted such a turn of events.

Indeed, many were mistaken. SH was perhaps relatively lucky, since, at least, according to CR, she appeared once in a film and then retired from professional life. Others were not so fortunate. I know of one family that had been promised residence in Pyongyang prior to departure, but was sent to a remote mountain village upon arrival. I have known other cases where repatriated family members disappeared one by one, losing contact with each other; after a long period of silence, news of their deaths was delivered to the family in Japan. We have already noted the fate of Chon Wolson's brothers.

If this type of occurrence is somehow predictable and rather well-known in the cynical sense, more problematical was the way that Chongryun used the repatriation route as a supply channel for the North Korean leaders. For Kim Il Sung's sixtieth birthday in 1972—an important landmark for commemorating long life in Oriental calendar cycles—Chongryun loaded repatriation boats with multiple batches of goods, which were shipped to North Korea. These included hundreds of imported vehicles, including Mercedes-Benz cars, in addition to (then still costly) color TV sets, various kinds of industrial machinery, home electrical appliances, trucks, bulldozers, excavators, agricultural machinery, an assortment of Japanese luxury goods, rarefied treasures from all over the world, cash, jewelry, silk, delicacies, and even abalones and the famed Niigata rice (of Japan), to cite only a few examples. Kim Chan Jung, a former Chongryun journalist and long-time Chongryun-watcher, believes that Chongryun collected a total of five billion yen from Korean residents in Japan for Kim Il Sung's sixtieth birthday.[39]

But the most expensive, or rather priceless, gift offered by Chongryun for Kim's sixtieth birthday in 1972 was a group of about one hundred young men and women, selected on the basis of academic record, pedigree, behavior, moral character, and degree of "revolutionary" commitment. Inclusion in this delegation was seen as the utmost honor and privilege, and those included were treated as celebrities in the Chongryun community. While in Japan, they were organized into motorcycle brigades and given special training on how to ride motorbikes in perfectly choreographed formation. Upon their arrival in North Korea, the members began their journey toward Pyongyang on their motorcycles. Every North Korean city they passed through extended them a heartfelt welcome. Upon finally reaching Pyongyang, they had the honor of parading their motorcycles into a stadium, in perfect formation, to receive a passionate and enthusiastic welcome by citizens who had the honor of attending Kim Il Sung's sixtieth birthday celebrations, with Kim himself present. The Chongryun motorcycle brigade had the ultimate honor of being received by Kim Il Sung in person. Photos of these ceremonials were disseminated via the Korean Central News Agency in Pyongyang and relayed by Chongryun's news agency in Tokyo. (Satellite and Internet were not available then.) For many years, the honor received by the brigade was talked about in Chongryun offices and schools. At lower-grade schools, teachers would recognize any student whose older sibling had been a member of the motorcycle brigade and congratulate him or her in front of the class as belonging to a most "revolutionary and patriotic" family.

The point I need to emphasize is that this event took place in 1972, at a time when no one could enter North Korea and then reenter Japan. As stated above, the reentry permit for Japan, which would enable Chongryun Koreans (who did not have South Korean nationality and, therefore, did not have permanent residence in Japan either) to visit North Korea and come back to Japan, became generally available only after 1981. These outstanding young men and women were, thus, sent as a human gift of loyalty (or as sacrificial victims) dedicated to Kim Il Sung. To this day, no one from this legendary group is known to have attained an executive or leadership position in the North Korean government or the ruling Korean Workers' Party.

In a word, the repatriation route functioned not simply as a channel for repatriation, but also as a conduit for mass flows of gifts of loyalty, including human beings and material goods. In return, Chongryun Koreans received misrepresentation, misrecognition, illusory deception, and moral discipline to revere and be grateful for North Korea and Kim Il Sung. The flow of gifts, in a word, was an effect of a complex structure of ideological reproduction. Yet CR's letter is full of personal remorse, and alludes to the perception of her friend's repatriation as a consequence of her (i.e., CR's) individual conscience—in other words, CR is holding herself (at least partly) responsible and accountable for the repatriation of SH and others. Why?

I first approached CR with a request for her to write her autobiography for me almost ten years ago. She did provide me with one rather incomplete piece, which went into my file and sat with the others in my drawer. Recently, during a conversation between the two of us, CR asked if she could write another piece for me. Elated, yet curious, I asked her why. She told me that there was one event that she felt she must write about. CR's letter, then, is not so much a letter as a form of written self-reflection. She obviously did not intend to send it to SH in the first place. Nor did she write this only for/to SH. Certainly, she wrote it for me, understanding that I would try to publish it in English some day; hence, additional background information is given at times. But above all, she wrote it for herself—she wrote it in order to connect the unconnected ends and disentangle the entangled connections; in order to think about what became of her friend; and in order to (if she could) settle this memory inside herself, as she continues to feel she had a part to play—albeit an indirect and innocent part—in SH's life.

I can personally relate to this. Beginning in first grade at the Chongryun Korean school I attended in Japan, every year one or more of my classmates would be repatriated to North Korea, usually with their families. When I was a sixth-grader, in the early 1970s, my good friend KT was repatriated with his mother and younger brother so that they could all join his father, who had been repatriated some years earlier. KT's father was a scientist, and he had been invited to participate in a conference in Eastern Europe as a member of the North Korean scientific team. He had left Japan with a one-way air ticket, since the Japanese government refused to grant him reentry to Japan. The family was aware of the consequences of doing this and had planned to join him by later being repatriated.

It was customary at school for us to hold a class send-off gathering. We collected money and bought a small gift. We sang school songs together and wrote one paragraph each in a notebook that was given to KT as a souvenir. And we went to see the family off at the nearest railway station, just like CR would later do for SH. A few times, a letter from KT reached our class from North Korea; but as the years passed, we lost contact—as happened with many others who were repatriated. Later, I heard a rumor that his father had been purged and the family had been moved to an unknown location, deep in the mountains. To this day, I have never again heard from them or heard about their situation.

KT is only one among many of my former classmates who were repatriated. Whenever it happened, those of us who were left behind in Japan had an ambivalent feeling. It was a mixture of envy and fear—envy, because they were leaving for what was supposed to be a paradise on earth, our own country; and fear, because even as kids we knew it was a one-way journey and that no change of mind was allowed. Because of this finality of departure, the class was made to feel complicit in the fate of their repatriating friends. Because of the way their repatriation was celebrated and accepted as a source of "honor and happiness for us all," it was not simply seen as "their" business. This goes some way toward explaining why CR holds herself to have been involved with, and accountable for, SH's repatriation. This is despite the fact that, unlike KT, SH was repatriated on her own, as a result of a voluntary, individual, and independent decision. Nevertheless, CR continues to be vexed by her classmate's repatriation. There is no doubt that the repatriation changed SH's life forever, but it permanently altered CR's life as well.

In another light, the way CR and others feel a collective, yet acutely personalized, form of responsibility toward those who were repatriated may also be connected to the North Korean style institution of criticism and self-criticism as a routine mental exercise within Chongryun. When young (i.e., in fourth grade and above at elementary school, or in middle school), all students join the Young Pioneers; in high school and above, they are mandatorily made members of the Youth League. At the age of twenty-eight, women join the Women's Union. Men, at around their mid-thirties, move on to join the main body of Chongryun. Throughout all these units, from the fourth grade on, every individual within the Chongryun structure is subjected to regular self-criticism sessions. I have already described how these are carried out inside Korea University (see chapter 2). If one stays on as a full-time employee of Chongryun, one participates in mutual criticism sessions within one's professional unit.

Regularly, once every two years or so, employees are sent to a *kangseup*, literally, a lecture and learning session, which takes place at a secluded facility called a *hagweon*, or study center. Chongryun used to own several *hagweon*—including one that was centrally located in Tokyo and accommodated high-ranking cadres, and several others in important locations such as Osaka and Kyushu. (Today, Chongryun owns no such facilities, due to a need for financial restructuring which led to the recent sale of many of its assets.) Cadres and cadre reserves typically take longer, more intense courses, such as six-month courses. During this period, participants are confined in what Irving Goffman called a "total institution."[40] However, in Chongryun's reeducation courses, unlike in North Korea, the penal system is verbal in nature, enforced through mutual criticism sessions. Just like in North Korea, how and how well one is able to assess and criticize oneself holds the key to either success or failure. But unlike in North Korea, Chongryun's criticism sessions do not actually endanger one's life; in North Korea, life is vulnerable, naked, with no defenses in the face of total domination.

Nevertheless, good self-inquisition skills become equally important attributes for participants in Chongryun and North Korean criticism sessions. Supervisors are trained to detect superficial criticism, which itself leads to harsher criticism. Therefore, however awkward, participants are forced to reveal to other participants their upbringing, mental weaknesses, professional shortcomings, and lack of revolutionary will. While in American self-analysis, blame can be attributed to external or unavoidable elements or factors, such as one's somatic makeup (proclivity towards alcohol abuse, for example); a hereditary chemical imbalance (such as depression that runs in the family); or even the immaturity of one's parents, in North Korean style self-criticism, all blame is to be borne solely by oneself—one's lack of will power, of determination, of patience, of courage, of strength, and so forth. Organizers and supervisors would deem such an outcome to be evidence of a successful session—an orderly, exhaustive, eloquent, formulaic, yet individually unique process of self-inquiry and self-reference, resulting in the admission of personal guilt.

In her letter, CR is blaming her moral failures, compromises, and lack of integrity, as if to suggest that her personal qualities and attitudes toward life are, to an extent, connected to what has happened to SH. This incessant routine of self-reference is a product of Chongryun training—in CR's case, years of education and reinforcement of self-criticism at Chongryun schools. But this practice was nowhere nearly as successful, thorough, or complete as in North Korea itself, where the goal appears to be total domination of the population. The state of emergency based on an unfinished war makes such a thing possible in North Korea. It was in this context of a heightened sense of national emergency, which has been sustained for decades, that Kim Il Sung was elevated to a position of absolute power, able to eliminate all of his opponents and designate his son as heir while alive. And, after his death, he has been permanently installed as the eternal Great Leader who lives with North Koreans for ever and ever. It was also under such conditions that it became possible to encamp the entire population under the control of an arbitrary yet formidable type of domination.

THE ENCAMPED BODY

The British filmmakers Daniel Gordon and Nicholas Bonner have documented close to one year in the lives of two young state-trained gymnasts in Pyongyang, North Korea. Pak Hyon Sun, thirteen at the time of filming, and Kim Song Yun, eleven, were selected by the government following a request by the filmmakers. Hyon Sun and Song Yun, along with thousands of others living in Pyongyang who range in age from five or six to their early thirties, practice mass games day in and day out, all year around. They are highly accomplished gymnasts who are already richly rewarded at their young age. The families of both girls are given the privilege of living in a well-appointed apartment in Pyongyang with modern amenities, such as a TV set, as a reward for their participation in the mass games. As the film goes on to show the actual mass games in which the two perform, the viewer is mesmerized by the flawless unity of hundreds and thousands of individuals, whose bodies look and move like one body. Bent, stretched, and spinning, the bodies of these men, women, and children make the unthinkable into a visual reality. A perfectly synchronized, choreographic masterpiece challenging the angular lim-

itations of human bodies makes one forget that these are in fact an aggrega-
tion of thousands of different individual bodies.[41]

Anthropologists have long explored the sociality and symbolic properties
and meanings of the body away from or against the biomedical gaze.[42] In a
society like North Korea, the body is always socially appropriated and never
individually owned, while individuals are held responsible for its mainte-
nance, improvement, and transformation. Thus, even bodies in concentration
camps are not desocialized (although they may be dehumanized)—they are
social in that their redundancy and excess of life as a form of existence on the
extreme margins of life's boundaries constitute a strong nexus for the state in
its managerial concern to work on more extensive (if not effective) forms of
domination.

Discursively, body-oriented rhetoric abounds in North Korea. From around
the 1970s, Kim Il Sung's doctrine, entitled *Juche,* came to dominate North
Korean ideological discourse. Combining the Chinese characters *ju* (meaning
"main" or "master") and *che* (meaning "body"), *Juche,* ironically (or perhaps
logically), means subject—that is to say, people are the subjects of their own
society as well as subjected to the society. In itself, it is rather an innocuous
doctrine, mainly because of its lack of intellectual sophistication and system-
atic and coherent internal structure. Nevertheless, seen hand in hand with the
way the North Korean population is placed vis-à-vis its sovereign, the Great
Leader, it begins to emerge as one of the most dreadfully lethal doctrines of
totalitarianism. Under this catch-all phrase, the population identifies itself
closely with the Leader, but not merely that: they do so by identifying themselves as the originary point of self-subjection to the sovereign. One of the favorite banners of North Koreans reads: "Let us all become revolutionaries
whose body has only the *Juche* type blood." The corpus of the population is
at once individualized and collectivized—individuals are held responsible for
making themselves into better and purer North Korean subjects by way of
self-referential criticism and ideological cleansing. Most importantly—and I
shall risk a contradictory statement—they are made to do this voluntarily. As
a consequence, they are to form one organic body in their march to attain the
goals set out by the Great Leader.

National sovereignty, in this totalitarian structure, completely overlaps with
the sovereign Leader, and the *corpus populi* with the body of the sovereign. In
this type of society, life is extremely politicized, and, paradoxically, supreme
political life is achieved only through death. One North Korean war tale tells
the story of Hero Li Su-Bok, a teenager who sacrificed himself in suicide-
bomber fashion during the Korean War, in order to destroy a U.S. tank. His
story appears in elementary school textbooks, children's stories, and songs.
The main point of such references is encapsulated in the term *jeongchijeok*

saengmyeong, or political life. Despite his death, or rather precisely because of his death, Hero Li acquired eternal political life—that is to say, he is with us forever. The inversion of life and death, or the acquisition of life by way of death, is characteristic of North Korean totalitarian discourse.

This practice is epitomized in the way in which the late Kim Il Sung is referred to as being eternally alive. But if the death of Kim Il Sung (in 1994) was exceptional in being that of the sovereign, the way in which his son Kim Jong Il succeeded him as supreme leader was less than banal. In my view, however, nepotistic anomalies are less relevant in thinking about North Korean totalitarianism than other aspects of its society, such as the way the population is disciplined into a form of self-repeating, self-referential existence. Nevertheless, Kim's son's ascendance to the leadership position posits an enigmatic question about sovereignty, or, more precisely, the exception of the sovereign. If, as Carl Schmitt has stated, "Sovereign is he who decides on exception," Kim Jong Il is the exemplary case: he *is* the law and is therefore excepted from subjection to the rule of law.[43] But the way the population relates to him has been made extremely personal and peculiarly self-oriented. All news broadcasts are dedicated to him—one recognizes this easily in the way newsreaders enunciate words, with utmost care and upward-looking eyes, as if to confirm the offering of a piece of news to the sacred being. The aforementioned two young gymnasts, Hyun Sun and Song Yun, were very distressed when they learned that Kim Jong Il, yet again, failed to view their mass game performance. Kindergarteners learn about how thrifty or caring toward friends Kim Jong Il was as a child, absorbing his virtues as theirs. At the same time, the North Korean population is continually told that the people are the masters of their own society. The rhetoric of self-mastery is repeated ad infinitum: when they play no part in decision-making—such as by participating in mandatory voting for the single candidate preselected by the state—they are told all the decisions are theirs.

The discourse of masterhood penetrates the population so effectively that the population becomes self-repeating. I emphasize self-repeating as opposed to self-reproducing. For, in the setting of North Korean political life, the meaning of life is no longer allowed to expand: the population must manage by recycling words from the thesaurus containing the limited vocabulary that the authorities have deemed to be valid. Moreover, the whereabouts of authority remains endlessly unclear. Does authority lie with Kim Jong Il? Does authority lie with the ruling Workers' Party of Korea? What kinds of authority do they have, then? In a society where the population is made into self-replicating bodies whose life is politicized to the extent that there is little distinction between *polis* and *oikos* (meaning that even members of your own family, ultimately, can betray you), no longer is authority required in reality.

Sustained martial law is sufficient for society to remain in existence; that is to say, life in North Korea can be described as simultaneously the most politicized and most naked.

In North Korea, we are witnessing one of the most effective and efficient examples of biopolitics in modern history. As Agamben has written:

> If there is a line in every modern state marking the point at which the decision on life becomes a decision on death [. . .] this line no longer appears today as a stable border dividing two clearly distinct zones . . . [C]ertain events that are fundamental for the political history of modernity (such as the declaration of rights), as well as others that seem instead to represent an incomprehensible intrusion of biologico-scientific principles into the political order (such as [. . .] the contemporary debate on the normative determination of death criteria), acquire their true sense only if they are brought back to the common biopolitical (or thanatopolitical) context to which they belong. From this perspective, the camp—as the pure, absolute, and impassable biopolitical space (insofar as it is founded solely on the state of exception)—will appear as the hidden paradigm of the political space of modernity, whose metamorphoses and disguises we will have to learn to recognize.[44]

As archaic as it may appear to some, North Korea (and totalitarianism, for that matter) is a modern phenomenon—just like parliamentary democracy or neoliberalism. As far as the effects of biopolitics are concerned, that is to say, in the way in which state decision-making is deeply implicated in the life and death of the population, and in the way in which bare life and politicized life have become almost indistinguishable, therefore, North Korea is not bizarre or different—it stands in logical continuity with societies such as the U.S., a state that grants its president the "right" to infringe other nations' sovereignty at his or her will, and Japan, a state whose leaders continue to publicly deny its historic brutal violation of other nations' sovereignty. In this sense, also, it is not surprising that scholars have closely approximated and genealogically associated biopolitics and neoliberalism. For, after all, as I have indicated, totalitarianism and neoliberalism as political systems stand not in opposition but in continuity. If, indeed, as Aihwa Ong asserts, neoliberal technology should be traced to a biopolitical mode of governing "that centers on the capacity and potential of individuals and the population as living resources that may be harnessed and managed by governing regimes," totalitarian technology should also be traced to a biopolitical form of government, with an emphasis that in this latter case, the difference is that the life and death of the population are more directly subjugated to the domination of the governing regime.[45]

This can also be seen in the human trafficking and other transactions across the shores of Japan and North Korea that have been hitherto kept clandestine.

These instances reveal the neoliberal-totalitarian symbiosis in uncomfortable yet unmistakable ways. CR wonders, toward the end of her letter, whether SH might have quietly returned home, that is, to Japan, in order to be reunited with her family. She may not be wrong, as it is true that cases of return entry to Japan by former repatriates have been reported recently. What she omits, however, is the fact that such a return would have necessitated the use of family assets and involved the transfer of a substantial amount of cash, just like when SH's family included a substantial donation at the time of her repatriation.

As we have already seen, many types of visits have been made from Japan to North Korea since the 1980s, through arrangements made by Chongryun. One category of visit was the family reunion package, as has also been stated. While there was a standard formula for such visits, payment of an additional amount would enable visitors to modify the package to some extent to their own liking. An overnight stay with relatives would cost an additional amount per night, for example. Payments were typically made in cash, in Japanese yen, and were arranged through the ad hoc mediation of a Chongryun officer in charge, who would transfer them to the North Korean office. Cash-based transactions, in other words, were always part of the family reunion business venture jointly operated by Chongryun and the North Korean government.

Recently, it was reported that some families in Japan whose members had been repatriated were able to invite their repatriated kin from North Korea to Japan for visits. Such visits required Pyongyang's authorization, in addition to the payment of substantial amounts on the part of the families in Japan. Such a human flow was made possible due to the fact that, prior to the 2006 ban on port visits by North Korean passenger ferries to Niigata, Japan, North Korean crew were allowed to enter Japan while their ship was being prepared for departure. Most likely, those repatriated relatives were able to enter Japan by this route.

A Korean woman in Japan recalls that her family "donated" 100 million yen (approximately one million U.S. dollars) to Chongryun in exchange for a one-week visit by one of her relatives. The same woman invited a total of ten relatives in 2005. At that time, Chongryun lowered the price, and she paid several million yen per person.[46] What we see in these transactions is the neoliberal ethos of the free market, where prices are set in correlation with supply and demand, and where any individual can enter as a free agent into negotiations for a transactional contract, as long as he or she has money. In the North Korean version of totalitarianism, we would assume that it would be one's political pedigree and political standing that would accord one more power and prestige. This may be true, but free-market economic logic operates hand in hand with such thinking and penetrates the political milieu. Consequently, what would normally be defined as a matter requiring a purely political decision, such as whether or not a repatriated individual should be allowed to return to Japan in order to visit his or her family, is placed on the market, and the deal priced at market value. The purchase and sale of visitation rights are made possible thanks to the coexistence of totalitarianism and neoliberalism across the Sea of Japan.

"Do you have children, SH?" asked CR. Do children grow in North Korea? one wonders. Are they born to live or die? one wonders. For life in a camp society such as North Korea is, in the final analysis, unbearably indistinguishable from death. Given especially the international isolation of North Korea, any human rights, civil rights, or political rights that North Koreans may have within their national boundaries have already been nullified in the eyes of other nations. Thus, if and when North Koreans become refugees, they do not become bare human beings, as they already are nothing other than bare life in their own land. In this vision, the fate of Koreans who were repatriated (exiled) to North Korea—orphans of diaspora—is rendered hopelessly precarious. At the same time, as I have interpreted in this chapter, global neoliberal economics and political logic are undoubtedly keeping North Korean totalitarianism alive and well, in spite of discourses promoting human rights and freedom for all, or perhaps, precisely because of these discourses. As long as this symbiosis continues, the exile of Koreans in Japan will know no end.

NOTES

1. See for example, Iwamura Toshio, *Zainichi chōsenjin to nihon rōdōsha kaikyū* [Koreans in Japan and the Japanese working class] (Tokyo: Azekurashobō, 1972).

2. Hiroyama Shibaaki, "Minsen no kaisan to chōsensōren no keisei ni tsuite" [On the dissolution of Minjeon and the emergence of Chongryun], *Kōanjōhō* 22 (1955): 5–11.

3. Sonia Ryang, "The North Korean Homeland of Koreans in Japan," in *Koreans in Japan: Critical Voices from the Margin*, ed. S. Ryang (London: Routledge, 2000b), 38.

4. Nico Israel, *Outlandish: Writing between Exile and Diaspora* (Stanford, CA: Stanford University Press, 2000), 1.

5. See Chikako Kashiwazaki, "The Politics of Legal Status: The Equation of Nationality with Ethnonational Identity," in *Koreans in Japan*.

6. Ōnuma Yasuaki, "Zainichi chōsenjin no hōteki chii ni kansuru ichi kōsatsu" [An examination of the legal status of Koreans in Japan], part 4, *Hōgaku kyōkai zasshi* 97, no. 2 (1980): 217–21.

7. Sonia Ryang, *North Koreans in Japan: Language, Ideology, and Identity* (Boulder, CO: Westview Press, 1997), 122–23.

8. No public welfare was available for Koreans out of the Japanese governmental resources. However, local municipalities often did not discriminate against Koreans in providing the minimum welfare designed to support the lowest-income and no-income families in the locality. This is called *seikatsuhogo*, or livelihood protection.

9. See Tessa Morris-Suzuki, "Freedom and Homecoming: Narratives of Migration in the Repatriation of *Zainichi* Koreans to North Korea," in *Diaspora without Homeland: Being Korean in Japan*, ed. S. Ryang and J. Lie (Berkeley: University of California Press, forthcoming).

10. Hōmushō [Ministry of Justice, Japan], *Shutsunyūkoku kanri—sono genkyō to kadai* [Immigration control: Current situation and future tasks] (Tokyo: Hōmushō, 1976), 53–55.

11. Calculated from Hōmushō [Ministry of Justice, Japan], *Hōmunenkan* [Justice Ministry yearbook] (Tokyo: Hōmushō, 1967), 196.

12. A similar campaign was waged by the women's organizations closely associated with or affiliated to the Japanese Communist Party to encourage Japanese women who were married to Korean men to accompany their husbands and children in being "repatriated" to North Korea. The issues of the so-called "Japanese wives" were long neglected, although some made their return back to Japan recently, after what turned out to be ineffective and transient rapprochement between Japanese and North Korean governments in the early 2000s. For a historical background to this issue, see Aoki (2005).

13. Morris-Suzuki (2007: 4–10).

14. Hiroshi Matsubara, "Cover Story: Money Game," *Asahi.com*, January 3, 2007b, www.asahi.com (accessed February 22, 2007); also, Chon's own memoir (2006).

15. For example, Chol-hwan Kang, *The Aquariums of Pyongyang: Ten Years in the North Korean Gulag* (New York: Basic Books, 2002).

16. Prior to 1981, permits were rare and were issued on a case-by-case basis, rather than as an entitlement. It needs to be stressed that even though reentry permits to Japan were to become available, entry to another country would require a pregranted visa. It goes without saying that, while not impossible, it is extremely difficult and time-consuming to obtain a visa with this document, as no consulate gives it a recognition equivalent to a passport. Also, initially, issuance of the permits entailed cumbersome procedures, which took months to complete, involving frequent visits to the immigration offices, which were found only in a limited number of locations. Often encounters with immigration officers were humiliating. Scenes of an immigration officer verbally abusing applicants were commonly witnessed in those days.

17. Ryang (2000b: 40).

18. Israel (2000: 2).

19. "Video Shows Execution, Life inside North Korea," *CNN.com*, November 14, 2005, www.cnn.com/2005/WORLD/asiapcf/11/13/nkorea.hiddenvideo/index.html (accessed November 22, 2006).

20. Giorgio Agamben, *Homo Sacer: Sovereign Power and Bare Life* (Stanford, CA: Stanford University Press, 1995), chap. 7; Giorgio Agamben, *Means without End: Notes on Politics* (Minneapolis: University of Minnesota Press, 2000), 37–45.

21. David Harvey, *A Brief History of Neoliberalism* (Oxford: Oxford University Press, 2005), 64.

22. Harvey (2005: 69).

23. Norimitsu Onishi, "Abe Rejects Japan's Files on War Sex," *New York Times*, March 2, 2007, www.nytimes.com/2007/03/02/world/asia/02japan.html?ex=1330491 600&en=46b8ee3c003bb079&ei=5088&partner=rssnyt&emc=rss (accessed May 5, 2007).

24. Agamben (2005: 2).

25. I have detailed this elsewhere. See Ryang (2003).

26. Yukiko Koshiro, *Trans-Pacific Racisms and the US Occupation of Japan* (New York: Columbia University Press, 1999); Hiromitsu Inokuchi, "Korean Ethnic Schools in Occupied Japan, 1945–52," in *Koreans in Japan*. See chapter 2 of this book.

27. For example, Pak (1969), Yoshitome (1977), and Park (1983), on the Ōmura camp.

28. Morris-Suzuki (2007: 125–26). See Morris-Suzuki (2007: chaps. 11, 12) for more background information.

29. "Police Raid N. Korea-Related Facilities," *Asahi.com*, April 26, 2007. www.asahi.com/ (accessed May 8, 2007).

30. For North Korea's nuclear detonation, see "North Korea Claims Nuclear Test," *BBC News*, October 9, 2006, news.bbc.co.uk/2/hi/asia-pacific/6032525.stm (accessed November 22, 2006). See also the recent series of articles that the *Asahi* carried, covering the difficult situation that Chongryun Koreans are placed in (Matsubara 2007a, 2007c).

31. Harvey (2005: 65).

32. Marilyn Strathern, "Introduction: New Accountabilities," in *Audit Cultures. Anthropological Studies in Accountability, Ethics, and the Academy*, ed. M. Strathern (London: Routledge, 2000).

33. Michel Foucault, *The History of Sexuality*, vol. 1 (Harmondsworth, England: Penguin, 1977); Anthony Giddens, *Modernity and Self-Identity: Self and Society in the Late Modern Age* (Stanford, CA: Stanford University Press, 1991).

34. Sidonie Smith and Julia Watson, *Reading Autobiography: A Guide for Interpreting Life Narratives* (Minneapolis: University of Minnesota Press, 2001), 1-4.

35. Anne Frank, *The Diary of A Young Girl: The Definitive Edition* (New York: Doubleday, 1995). See also Ryang (2000b).

36. Upon its foundation in 1948, the North Korean state abolished the Korean traditional ancestral worship in all forms, including the clan exogamy rules, ancestral memorial services and accompanying feasts, and the practice of compiling each clan's multigenerational family trees. While it is difficult to clearly identify the North Korean population registration system under the current regime, which claims that it even abolished all forms of taxation, it would be appropriate to assume that for ordinary people, the trace of lineage does not go back beyond the point of Kim Il Sung's anti-Japanese resistance, starting from the 1930s. The North Korean authorities recognize and most heavily favor the descendants of Kim's close associates from the prewar era. Immediately below them are the bereaved families of high-ranked officers and agents who were killed during the Korean War and the subsequent, post–Korean War anti–South Korean espionage and other subversive operations. Children from this group are educated in *hyeongmyeonghagweon*, or the revolutionary school. The

abolition of clan ancestral worship articulates with North Korea's practice of deeming Kim Il Sung to be the originary point of the nation, a concept that fundamentally clashes with Korean traditional kinship ideology, including the aversion to incest.

37. Hannah Arendt, *The Origins of Totalitarianism* (New York: Harcourt Brace, 1958a), 307.

38. Sonia Ryang, "Critical Synthesis on North Korea as Embodied Ideology," *Social Epistemology* 6, no. 1 (1992): 3–12 ; Sonia Ryang, "Technologies of the Self: Reading North Korean Novels from the 1980s," *Acta Koreana* 5, no. 1 (2002): 21–32.

39. Hiroshi Matsubara, "Korean Residents in Anguish: Broken Dreams," *Asahi.com*, January 4, 2007c, www.asahi.com/ (accessed January 4, 2007).

40. Erving Goffman, *Asylums: Essays on the Social Situation of Mental Patients and Other Inmates* (Chicago: Aldine, 1962).

41. *A State of Mind,* directed by Daniel Gordon (2004).

42. One of the earliest and most influential of such works is Margaret Lock and Nancy Scheper-Hughes, "The Mindful Body," *Medical Anthropology Quarterly* 1 (1987): 6–41.

43. Carl Schmitt, *Political Theology: Four Chapters on the Concept of Sovereignty* (Chicago: University of Chicago Press, 1922), 5. How this happens, its process and logical foundation, needs to be explored. I intend to do this in a book on North Korea's totalitarianism with the focus on the 1990s, before and after Kim Il Sung's death in 1994. The replacement of the North Korean sovereign is, in my view, not a matter simply of political rearrangement, but an instance that requires logical, philosophical, and ethnological inquiry. (Ryang, in preparation).

44. Agamben (1995: 122–23).

45. Aihwa Ong, *Neoliberalism as Exception: Mutations in Citizenship and Sovereignty* (Durham, NC: Duke University Press, 2006), 6.

46. Matsubara (2007b).

Chapter Four

Diaspora and the Ethic of Care

A Note on Disability, Aging, and the Vulnerability of the Denationalized

Why do we care for each other, when, according to the morality of individualism, we should simply be concerned with our own well-being? As in the case of CR, the writer of the letter we read in the previous chapter, we care about friends, worry about their misfortune, and hope to be able to help them. We blame our own shortcomings and moral failings when we realize that our efforts to extend our goodwill to others have been inadequate or not sufficiently generous. If all of us could take care of ourselves, there would be no need to think about others in society. But the reality is very different: no one, not even the richest or the most powerful, can be completely self-sufficient throughout his or her entire life, requiring no help from others. As long as we live in a society, we require the morality of mutual assistance, care for the community, and concern for the greater social good—conversely, our good moral character is necessarily born through our engagement with others, the public.

Concern for the public good—how is this virtue formed in diaspora, especially in a diasporic community of stateless people such as the Koreans in Japan? When people do not have access to political participation in the greater (host) society, how can we envision their moral development? Are they by default more individualistically oriented, concerned only with their personal well-being, distanced from engagement with the greater social good? How about more immediate groups, such as family, friends, and neighbors? And, how and why should these people—stateless, diasporic people—care for each other when in need?

These seemingly prosaic questions inform the discussion in this chapter, for they force us to look into unexpectedly profound areas of inquiry, particularly when viewed up close through the eyes of Yuki, a Korean woman in

Japan in her late forties whose autobiography I shall introduce shortly. She is a permanent resident of Japan and does not possess South Korean nationality. The story of her life makes us wonder about the ethical foundations not only of Japanese society but also of other societies, including our own, in relation to care for the needy, including the young, the aged, and the disabled, especially when these latter do not belong in our own national polity. I shall introduce Yuki's story primarily in order to share it with the reader, but also in order to rely on it as a window for opening up a deeper exploration and discussion on morality, justice, and the ethic of care, themes that have been the subject of lively debate in many circles and particularly among feminist scholars.

It was Carol Gilligan's seminal work in the early 1980s that drew our attention to the differences between men and women in terms of moral growth and development. Critically deconstructing Lawrence Kohlberg's work on developmental psychology, Gilligan reinterpreted the hitherto-held assumption that women were less capable of developing justice-oriented reasoning than men. She instead highlighted the fact that women place more emphasis on personal relationships than on impersonal, abstract principles. Developmentally, in other words, girls form their mature selves in close connection and continuation with their mothers and caregivers, according to Gilligan, while boys' mature selves are formed through a series of separations from the people around them.[1]

This does not mean that girls and women are incapable of justice-oriented reasoning. As Grace Clement argues, the need for discussion, rather, arises in the area of what we see justice to be and how we view it.[2] A moral obligation to the people close to one, either structurally or emotionally, is an important issue for women, while to men it often appears that the consideration of personal relations is an obstacle in the path of fair and objective justice for all. Thus, whereas women's maturity may mean the capability to take care of others in a compassionate manner, men's maturity may correspond to the ability to sever themselves from the web of personal relationships.

How much of this, however, is unique to the Western, Judeo-Christian cultural tradition? For an interesting parallel can regularly be drawn between the (Western) female self—the interdependent self concerned with immediate personal relations, situated within a concentric web of moral obligations—and the Japanese self (as opposed to the Western male self), in academic discourses on the formation of the self. As I touched upon in chapter 1, ever since the concept of *amae* (dependence or interdependence) was proposed as a pivotal aspect in the formation of the Japanese self, cultural, linguistic, and psychological anthropologists, social psychologists, and psychiatrists, among others, have avidly participated in the enterprise of exploring and establishing the culturally situated self in Japan.

Does the kind of "Japanese self" much discussed by researchers include the self of Koreans in Japan also? And, if so, how far does their interdependency go? Does it, for example, extend to include Japanese social circles and the public milieu as well? And how is this observation implicated in the theme of this chapter, that is, the ethic and morality of care and their workings under the conditions of diaspora? These are the questions I'd like to think about in this chapter.

It is known, for example, that in Japan, caring for others is mainly the domain of women. Japan is not an exception in this regard: in many cultures, including our own, whether it be a stereotype or not, women are expected to care more for those in need than men. Less well-known are the effects of an aging population and changing kinship relations and residential arrangements in Japan, and their implications for the caregiving situation. For example, in 2002, in 21.1 percent of households consisting only of a husband and wife, both were aged sixty-five or above. Life expectancy at birth in Japan in 2004 was 78.64 years for males and 85.59 for females.[3] Japanese society thus faces a serious need to consider social security, health insurance, and caregiving for its population in the new millennium.

It can be assumed that the Korean population in Japan largely follows the Japanese demographic pattern, due to its long-term residency and acculturation in Japan. While it is hard to concretize this assumption, due to the Japanese government's policy of not including non-Japanese residents in its census and other domestic statistical surveys, it is not difficult to infer that aging is also a serious concern for Koreans in Japan.[4]

In order for me to think about the morality of care in a diasporic community, I would like to make a detour into two sub-areas. First, I would like to explore the formation of the ethnic self and the development of the morality of justice among Koreans in Japan, which is closely connected to the lack of public life for Koreans in Japanese society. These issues will be discussed in the third section below. Second, I would like to examine the ethic of care and the related feminist debate, which will be considered in the context of the situation faced by Korean women in Japan. These themes will be covered in the fourth section below. In the final section, I will come back to Yuki's story, in order to address the question of the ethic of care in diaspora. Let us, however, first read Yuki's autobiography, which precedes all the other sections.

YUKI: A MOTHER AND A DAUGHTER

I am a mother and a daughter. This fact was brought home to me lately very vividly through my mother's illness, and it gave me an unexpected opportunity to reflect on my life. I am not certain if I can deliver this story well, but I shall simply write as my pen carries me.

I was born the only child of a Korean family living in Japan at the end of the 1950s. In those days, it was unusual for a Korean family to have an only child. Koreans value sons over daughters, and so, I can only imagine how much my parents were disappointed. My mother, I understand, was implicitly blamed for the lack of a male heir (well, heirs in Korean families are always male) by her parents-in-law and other members of the in-law family. I am certain many people assumed my mother was "defective" because she did not give birth to multiple children. It was fortunate that my father was not the oldest male in the family.

When growing up, I was spoilt by the standards of Korean families of the day. The family was neither rich nor poor, but I had some exquisite items as my childhood treasures. It was always my mother who bought me those—she worked at part-time menial jobs and she must have saved her earnings to buy me those. My father did not approve of lavishing me with expensive goods or giving me excuses not to study. He must have been worried about spoiling me as an only daughter, since if I were to acquire a reputation of being spoilt, my marriage prospects would not have looked good. My father worked for a business owned by a Korean family. In his spare time, he also helped the local Korean ethnic organization [Chongryun] as a branch officer [with no stipend].

I graduated from a Korean high school [operated by Chongryun] and entered a Japanese private vocational school [*senmongakkō*] in order to gain a basic accounting qualification. I had the option of going to Korea University [operated by Chongryun], but my parents did not want to put me into the strictly organized dormitory life of Korea University. I, personally, was attracted to the two-year degree [teacher's certificate course] at Korea University, but I also hesitated at the prospect of having to live away from my parents, especially my mother, and so we settled on the vocational school option.

At the age of twenty, I got married to my (former) husband through an arrangement [i.e., an arranged marriage]. This was an early age, even by Korean standards of the day. The match was arranged by my father's employer. The family [of her husband-to-be] had a very good reputation overall. I know my mother felt sad that I was leaving her at such a young age, but the advantage of the match was undeniable for her and my father. My husband was a middle child in a total of nine children. All his brothers and sisters were brilliant, known either for their intellectual achievements or financial success, but my husband was heavily overshadowed by his capable older and younger brothers and sisters, and growing up, I think, he was made to think of himself as inferior to the rest of his siblings. After graduating from a Korean high school, he worked in the family business under his father and older brother. Come to think of it, it was this aspect of his personality, notably his lack of self-confidence, that eventually became a problem for our marriage.

I did not become pregnant for the first four years of marriage. My in-laws, particularly my mother-in-law, minded this greatly. My mother-in-law would take me to the shaman who would visit her from South Korea to offer her services: sometimes, it was a cleansing ritual after a death in the family; other times, it was a ritual to wish for the family's prosperity. Right in front of the family, in one of these rituals, the shaman declared that I brought bad luck to the family. The family business was slowly declining at that time and, in addition, the youngest brother of my husband was having marital problems. I felt awful, but I was also certain that it was an excuse that the shaman had made up and knew I was being made a scapegoat because of my childlessness. Family suspicions of me lingered on from that time.

Then, soon after that, I became pregnant. (The shaman of course took the credit for this.) After the excruciatingly painful hours of labor, I gave birth to a baby girl. She was a big, healthy baby with a beautiful face. I thanked the world for her birth, and all my pain vanished at that moment. My husband and I were ecstatic and my parents, understandably, relieved. My husband and I were proud and felt so much love toward each other. Raising our daughter, my husband was really a good father—generous and kind. For the first time since my marriage, I felt I had a family of my own. Nothing else mattered—the continuing harassment from my mother-in-law and sisters-in-law, the constant nagging about the fact that we only had one child and that it was a girl—did not matter. We were happy.

In a few years, however, my father-in-law passed on. Unlike my other in-laws, my father-in-law had loved me and trusted me. He had protected me whenever a strange, unfounded blame was placed on me. I could tell, in a way, he was grateful I had married his awkward son who lacked self-confidence, and that he loved our daughter, always giving her extra-special treatment among close to twenty grandchildren in all.

After his death, my in-laws' family started to fall apart. The family business encountered serious difficulty. It could have survived and could have been restructured, I think, had it not been for my sisters-in-laws' bickering at each other. But, unfortunately, after many years of internal fighting among themselves, they decided to put all of the blame on my husband. My brother-in-law, the oldest of the children, had already left the family business after the death of his father, because he had been fed up with his sisters' intervention. My husband was forced to resign from the position of manager and was told that if he wanted to continue working for the family firm, he would have to start from the lowest rung of the salary ladder. He quit and was unemployed for a while.

I decided to work at that point. I borrowed money from friends and from a bank and made a down-payment for the lease of a small retail space in a cooperative market. That is how I started this current business of mine—selling decorative goods and souvenirs. I was not used to selling things, let alone being in charge of my own business. My husband was against the idea and did not help me. But many people helped me. Especially, a female friend of mine, a Korean, who was in a very similar position to myself, went out of her way to act as guarantor for my bank loan. Without her help, I would not have been able to start this business.

A little while after I opened my business, my husband began working as a bar tender. He does not drink and I don't know to this day how he thought of that vocation, but he is still working as a bar tender and, by now, is very experienced—I find it amusing and somehow good. I do think it was good that he found his vocation, since it was taking him a long time to recover from the treatment he suffered at the hands of his sisters. But, inevitably, the schism between us became deeper and deeper.

What disappointed me was that I did not receive much, if any, support from my parents, and especially my mother [in order to open my own business]. She seemed only worried about the risk that I was taking, and kept telling me to be cautious. Come to think about it now, I understand my mother was being protective towards me. But I had spent ten years of my marriage being cautious and nothing good had resulted from it. My parents, especially my father, were also a little angry that I had decided to go out on my own, running my own store, rather than doing something together with my husband or trying to reconcile with my in-laws. My birth family is small and we never had complicated domestic problems. Therefore, my parents did not understand how things could be so complicated and nasty inside a large, wealthy family that was facing a decline in its fortunes. Furthermore, they had no idea how unreliable my husband was. Had I simply depended on him, I would not have been able to provide for my daughter. When I opened the store, my sisters-in-law took offence and came to the store, screaming at me, creating quite a scene. My neighboring storeowners came over and told them strongly that if they did not leave right then, they would call the police. After this incident, they have pretty much left me alone. I have no contact with them whatsoever.

But our marriage was unable to be saved — after two or three years of leading separate lives, my husband and I were divorced. My daughter lived with me, regularly visiting or getting together with my husband. When I faced the possibility of divorce, I talked to the friend who had helped me open the store. She had also been divorced. Upon her suggestion, I did not initially disclose my divorce to my parents. When she got a divorce, her parents almost disowned her and she regretted that she had not taken enough time in preparing her parents for this outcome. I knew my parents would see my divorce as a failure on my part and, worse still, a betrayal. I was particularly aware of my mother's possible reaction. She would have said, "you could have lived just fine if you had silently endured [the situation]."

But I was not able to prepare my parents to face my divorce. After all, how does one "prepare" one's parents for such news? Predictably, they were very upset when they found out about it from someone else. They called me many times at my apartment and store, but every time I was either with customers or too busy to get engaged in deep conversation. So, it took me close to one year to visit them to sit down and talk it out. My mother was bitterly disappointed. She kept asking me why I had left such a strong, well-regarded, and prosperous family. She had no idea how cruel and bad things were inside this so-called well-regarded family. My father, on the other hand, was surprisingly understanding and concerned more about how I was able to raise my daughter virtually single-handedly. My daughter had just entered middle school, and I was keenly aware that she needed to be attended to [carefully] at her sensitive age. Divorce among Koreans in Japan was still a taboo in those days, and it was fully understandable that my father was so concerned. I, too, was not certain as to whether I was going to be able to financially sustain [my efforts to provide for] my daughter's life. But all I had left to do was try. I did not expect any financial aid from my parents, but the first thing my mother said was that she did not have any money she could loan me, while my father simply asked how I was going to financially manage. I was deeply hurt by my mother's preemptive refusal to help in the face of my crisis. I am her only daughter. How could she do this to me? I did not talk to her for quite a long time after that.

But, either way, I was not able to keep in touch with my parents regularly for close to a decade to come. I did not intend this, but I was overwhelmed by my struggle to manage my small business and raise my daughter. Occasionally, I was terribly sad whenever I remembered how close my mother and I had been in the past, and the realization of how fragile our closeness had been nearly destroyed me. But, really, I did not have much time to lament—I had so much to do regarding my responsibility toward my daughter. My daughter must have found it hard, but she coped admirably well with the change of life, including the financial adjustment. It was fortunate that she was only a little child when the family was wealthy as, while growing up, she did not really enjoy many luxuries and was not spoilt as the granddaughter of a big merchant family. My daughter has been the source of my strength.

Of course, I do wish I had never had to work this hard, standing on the floor of my store from 9:30 A.M. to 9:30 P.M., except for a monthly one-day break, and wish I had more time to share with my daughter. Although she has many friends, having time with one's own mother is always special. I know this painfully well, because I myself grew up as an only child and can say so from my own memories of growing up close to my mother. Since my mother worked only part-time, she was always available so that we could do many things together. My daughter grew up knowing no such thing and [enjoying] no substantial time together with her mother. I feel terrible about that. I was envious of some of my Korean friends who had strong families that were mutually supportive and tightly knit. What was doubly hurtful was that I could not talk to these friends about my situation too much. They were of course sympathetic, but their disgust at the way I was treated made me more miserable. I guess it is quite unusual for a Korean woman in Japan like me to be totally left alone to look after her child and herself because, one way or another, there is normally someone in the Korean extended family that would volunteer to help. In the long run, however, this experience has made me into a much stronger person than I used to be.

I did not fully reconcile with my mother for a long time. While my father came to visit us many times and I regularly sent gifts and greetings to my parents via a department store's home delivery service, my mother's visits to our apartment were extremely rare. In fact, I think she visited us only once. According to my father, my mother felt guilty about this entire turn in my fortunes. She was the one who had first asked the matchmaker that ended up marrying me to my former husband (Yuki is referring to her arranged marriage mentioned earlier). She was the one who had always told me to put up with my in-laws. Amazingly, she had even asked me whether I could have another child—she herself had an only girl. I resented this. Years went by without any meaningful conversations between us.

In the meantime, I noticed whenever father came to visit us that he had begun to look very tired and almost sick. He was retired by then, and he and my mother lived humbly on his pension and savings, while he still occasionally helped the Korean ethnic community whenever he could. I also noticed that his hair had rapidly turned gray and that he was walking with labored steps. He would hurry to go back to my mother and would not like to talk too much about her, obscuring the ends of his sentences when asked about her. Then, he stopped coming to see us altogether. I finally decided to call. My father's voice on the other end of the line was barely audible—I asked point blank what was wrong with my mother. She had been, it turned out, suffering from acute back pain for about six months. Although the doctors thought it was a kind of osteoporosis, there were many uncertain symptoms. "Your mother," I still clearly remember my father's voice, "has become disabled. She has been unable to walk or sit up on her own for some time." My first reaction was anger—strange, but I did not quite know why—perhaps because of my own neglect of my aging mother. Come to think of it, my mother was close to seventy. I closed my store, packed an overnight bag, and took a night train to my parents' home.

It was a sad day—my mother, who had always been active and supple, had become unable to walk. She lay in front of me as I sat in their living room. My father had bought a single bed to be placed in the living room so that my mother did not have to use the stairs. When I saw a small urn under the bed, allowing my father to assist with her bathroom needs, I could not contain my tears any more. My father, too, looked very tired. No doubt—he had to bathe my mother, wash her hair, cook for her, take care of her bathroom needs, do the laundry, wash the dishes: in a word, all those things that he had never had to do before. He was exhausted, and both of them were terribly worried about their remaining future. I asked them why they had not even told me right away. Their answer was that they had hoped mother would recover soon. I felt awful—it was obvious that they did not want to burden my life with this additional factor, and I also realized how they had felt when, years ago, I did not tell them about my divorce right away.

I wanted to help them immediately with anything, everything, I could offer. But it was not that simple. In fact it turned out that I, their only daughter, was not in a position to help my disabled mother in any effective way. My store was basically managed, staffed, and run all by myself. I do everything from planning wholesale orders to sweeping the shop floor. Occasionally, I employ temporary part-timers, but in times like this, when businesses all around are facing tight budgets, I cannot afford that. I could not leave my store unattended even one day. Furthermore, at that time, my daughter was preparing to face her college entrance examinations. Since I never received a college education, it was my strong wish that she go to study at college. I was torn between my filial obligation towards my mother and my parental obligation towards my daughter.

My parents' health insurance could pay for most of the medical care my mother required, but since my mother's condition quickly became chronic, it was of more concern that her daily life be managed through therapeutic intervention. Through internet research, with a lot of help from my daughter, I was able to find out about what kind of services were offered by the local municipality they live in, whether mother was eligible for those services as a disabled person and, if so, what level of care and services, and combined with her age factor, how many services, including massage therapy, day nursing, and doctor's home visits, could be obtained at what cost, and so on. I discovered that my mother was entitled to receive many of those services due to her age [and also her permanent residence] on a subsidized basis.

My parents were not comfortable having strangers coming into their home. Despite my repeated requests, they would not arrange home-visits from therapists and nurses. For example, they would not borrow a handicap-adapted toilet seat, insisting that these had been used by other people and that they found it better and easier to stick with their under-the-bed urn. In particular, they made it clear to me that they did not want any Japanese person coming into their home. They said that even having to engage in small talk with a Japanese massage therapist was awkward, as if they were speaking to a foreigner. I joked, telling them that indeed they were foreign to each other. I found it interesting that ethnicity was such an important factor for them in a situation where they really required care from any qualified person. But, at the same time, I fully understood their feelings. What was most frustrating for me, however, was that they would only accept *my* visits and my occasional services, such as housecleaning and laundry, simply augmenting my burden.

About six months into this situation, my father was invited to visit North Korea as a member of a delegation. I was furious—how could [Chongryun] bring such a matter to him at a time like this, when my sick mother absolutely required his care? I was even more furious at my father—he was wanting to go. I was amazed. Hadn't he so devotedly taken care of my mother and, therefore, didn't he know better than anyone else that if he were to leave my mother now, there would be nobody to take care of her? My father and I had a few angry exchanges of strong words over the phone. I was shocked when he insisted that it would be the one last public service in his life [for the Korean community]. "Look at mother," I entreated. "How can you leave her? She cannot even go to bathroom on her own." Father said, determinedly, that I should be the one to take care of her and should move in with her for the two weeks that he was going to be gone.

I was frantic. I was angry. But first, I had to find some way of placing my mother into a temporary care facility. The only place I could think of was N Clinic. I knew the owner of the clinic personally, and thought I should ask him for a personal favor. I did, and he was willing to help me by hospitalizing my mother for the period that my father was to be away. I felt immensely relieved and, at the same time, indebted to him and only vaguely worried about the financial consequences of this arrangement. Right after this arrangement was agreed upon, my father's trip was cancelled for a reason not known to me. He was deeply disappointed, but what could he do, when he had someone who was in need of constant care at home? Before long, he was back to the caregiving routine. My mother was very hurt by all this—the idea that my father was going to abandon her, even temporarily. But she kept saying that she wanted my father to go. At the same time, she kept also saying that she could not have made the trip to N Clinic. In retrospect, I can understand that my father was tired, just so tired of having to take care of my mother, day in and day out, all day and all night. He is an old man, too. Many nights, he could not sleep because my mother could not sleep due to the pain. The North Korean trip was a convenient opportunity that landed on his lap [permitting him] to take a short break from an ongoing caregiving situation. I had to pay quite a sum of money for my mother's hospitalization arrangement and I could not have it reimbursed, but I accepted this loss as a necessary consequence.

Within about a year or so, my mother's condition slowly improved. My mother was able to move between her bed and the bathroom, alleviating father from the burden of having to empty the urn. I was cautiously happy. Above all, I was immensely impressed by the resilience of my mother, as well as the devotion of my father. He became a first-rate caregiver to my mother. She made discoveries about herself—her dependency, fragility, and human bonds, her connection with my father. As for myself, I rediscovered what a beautiful relationship my parents had, but also, I think that it is not that they always had it, but that they learned about each other through my mother's illness and made their relationship into one that became beautiful. I wished that, even once, I had had such a close connection with my former husband.

I wonder how I am going to be cared for and by whom. Would it be my daughter or would it be professional caregivers? I definitely have not done enough for my mother and father, and in the years to come, I may have opportunities to care for them one way or the other. When and if I am financially better off, I may be able to invite them to live with me. And, in the meantime, my daughter will grow. She will see me getting old and will face the situation where she has to care for me. And, just like it was for me, for her also, when she wants to care for me, she may not be able to, because of her other obligations. Just like I did, she will also have days when she is made to realize that she, too, is a mother and a daughter.

THE MORALITY OF JUSTICE IN DIASPORA

What can we learn from the above autobiography by Yuki? A Korean, a woman, a divorcee, a single mother, a stateless person in Japan, with not many people to turn to for help, unable to care for her parents as much as she would like to, working twelve hours a day with one day off each month . . . Between the multiple dilemmas that weave through the human connections in which she is placed, we can try to read an undercurrent of principles and judgments that reflect her sense of justice, concern, and care. How are they related to her diasporic existence? Her gender? Her sense of self? As stated in the beginning of this chapter, in this section and the next I will make two detours in order to excavate clues to help answer these questions, notably in the areas of morality and justice on one hand, and the ethic of care on the other.

The feminist critique of moral justice has relied first on male-female differences (as suggested by Gilligan) in terms of judgment, care, and relationships. Initially, as in the case of theorists such as Nel Noddings, this was done in such a way as to rely on essentialized notions of female gender and motherhood. It did not take long, however, for this approach to be revised by more critical theorists, such as Joan Tronto, who succinctly argued that the feminine ethic of care and the feminist ethic of care constitute two different ethical positions.[5] However, importantly, the feminist critique of the dominant ethic of justice and its attempt to highlight the ethic of care was launched firmly from within the position of the national citizen, i.e., the member of a national polity, and it still faces the challenge of how to substantiate the ethic of care in regarding the denationalized population.[6]

Membership in a national polity grants entry to political life. No matter how constrained and discriminated against they are and no matter how frustratingly unsuccessful they may be, women can raise their concerns and voice their criticisms through structured channels of civic participation and the exercise of citizens' political rights, such as their right to vote, so long as they are the members of a nation-state. Without such prior eligibility, their voices do not reach the political realm as legitimate voices—no matter how justified they may be in their opinions and criticisms. Nonnational, noncitizen women (and men) do not have a direct access to political life equal to that of national citizens in the current world, subdivided as it is into sovereign nation-states. Furthermore, this division is oddly being strengthened in the name of globalization, in the sense that the global is strenuously taken as a coalition of the national, rather than as a mechanism that strives to transcend national borders.

Stateless residents in a national polity have little means to elevate their private concerns to the level of public debate. Neither do they have much access to the ethos of envisioning their ethical concerns in close connection to the common social good, due mainly to their stateless status as outsiders in relation to mainstream society. This structurally forces them to have to take care of each other away from the public resources and welfare programs offered by the (host) national state. How should we, then, understand the sense of justice and the ethic of care embodied by women, mothers, and daughters who are also stateless persons existing outside of the national state order (such as Yuki)? To state my conclusion first: I do not think that the same configuration of justice and care that has been eloquently argued and suggested by existing theorists and ethicists concerned with the feminist ethic of care can be applied to nonnationals, or denationalized women, as long as we are lacking an ethicotheoretical position that can critically transcend the current world constituencies of nation-states and human rights bestowed on the premise of national membership.

When the prospect of a disability or chronic illness affecting a denationalized family member arises, the understanding that this would need to be managed using the family's private resources is prelinguistic. The first question in this case may be from which uncle the family can borrow money, rather than which benefit program offered by the government the family can apply for. In reality, there is a wide array of options between a search for the help of relatives and one for public subsidies, and many of us settle somewhere in between, by resorting to such resources as employer-provided or private health insurance, combined with family income and savings.

However, aside from the U.S. habit of typically obtaining health insurance through employment, we must remember that there is a vast number of nations, including most of those in northwestern Europe and Australia, in which health insurance is nationalized, that is to say, it comes as part of the prerogative of national citizenship. Foreign residents are often required to purchase different sets of policies from their own pockets in these societies. Furthermore, beyond health insurance, there will be an array of care needs that arise one by one, including child care, while the caregiver is caring for the sick inside his or her family. Again, in many societies, child care is nationalized and public, i.e., available primarily and in principle for national citizens to raise national children. Evidently, the burden of the caregiver is multiplied in the denationalized family, as opposed to that of a national citizen's family in the same situation, although this is not to play down the complex pressures and constraints that families of national citizens face in similar circumstances.

Would the moral formation of the denationalized be inevitably constrained in situations where they were allowed no access to public life in the host society? Here, the diverse ways in which the denationalized are formed need to be borne in mind. Some stateless persons are refugees of war or political crisis and may or may not have a strong collective will to return to their homeland, as they have risked their lives in order to escape. Rather, their priority in life may be shifted towards the achievement of eventual integration into the prospective host society, about which they have become familiar by way of contact with NGOs or international relief programs, for example.

On the other hand, the case of denationalized, diasporic groups of long-term residents, such as the Koreans in Japan, presents a different situation. The majority of Koreans in Japan, it is true, have a nationality—that of the

Republic of Korea (South Korea). As stated in the introduction, the form of South Korean nationality granted to Korean applicants in Japan exempted them from military service in South Korea and made them ineligible to vote or stand for election at all levels of public office—local, municipal, or national politics—in South Korea. They are not entitled to participate in the national pension or social security, either. In other words, although a legitimate overseas travel document in the form of a passport has become available to them, the form of South Korean nationality acquired by Koreans in Japan does not bestow upon them the citizens' prerogatives of political and national participation and other entitlements within the public milieu of South Korean society.

Needless to say, the form of permanent residence that Koreans in Japan acquired in 1965 does not allow them to participate in civic and public life in Japan either, as long as Japan upholds one of the world's strictest principles of *jus sanguinis* (bloodline) in relation to national political membership. Thus, although the majority of Koreans in Japan today do have South Korean nationality along with Japanese permanent residence, curiously, their participation in political life continues to be blocked in both Japan and South Korea. Under these conditions, children grow up knowing that they will not be eligible for public service appointments or public office, understanding that they will not be diplomats internationally representing any nation, and assuming that they will eventually either have to inherit their parents' Korean restaurant business or find work in an ethnic enclave, in the employment of a well-to-do Korean entrepreneur. For girls, as touched upon in chapter 2, ethnic hypergamy becomes a top priority when envisioning a secure future.

In the postwar Japanese education system, moral education is closely connected with the development of an understanding of the apparatuses of the nation-state, teaching children how to be good and proper members of postwar democratic Japanese society. Education in personal moral responsibility progresses hand in hand with teaching of civic responsibility in Japan. Social studies classes, in which the pedagogy of justice and morality is put into practice in the Japanese public elementary education system, teach children to gradually become conscious of their positions as members of their neighborhoods, of their local municipalities, of their wards or cities, of their prefectures, and finally, of their national state. This situation gives rise to an issue which has been addressed by Eriko Aoki, writing about Korean students in Japanese schools—namely, how is a Korean child who is not a full member of any of these units expected to develop a moral capacity and sense of responsibility toward these Japanese public entities?[7] It appears that the moral development of Korean children is consequently curtailed or suspended, leaving them in an undeveloped or underdeveloped state vis-à-vis awareness of their moral duty, sense of public justice, and will and capacity to participate in political life. In an ethnic community where all individuals know that they need to somehow finance their old age out of their own pockets, that they have no public safety net in the case of bankruptcy, and that they cannot get public funding at an advantageous interest rate when trying to set up small businesses—while being obligated to pay municipal, residential, and business taxes—it is hard to develop a sense of moral obligation in relation to the common good in the form of national strength and prosperity.

As stated in earlier chapters, a slow but steady shift has occurred in Japan since around the 1980s. For example, in the early 1980s, those Koreans in Japan who had not applied for South Korean nationality after 1965 (thereby retaining their stateless status in a purer form since the 1952 forfeiture of their membership of the Japanese nation—see the introduction) were granted "special exceptional permanent residence." As mentioned in the preceding chapter, this measure enabled Koreans in Japan in this category to obtain a travel document (in the form of a reentry permit to Japan) allowing them to go overseas and return to Japan. In 1985, Japanese nationality law was reformed, altering the hitherto exclusively patrilineal succession of nationality and enabling a Japanese mother's nationality to be inherited by a child born to an international marriage. This resulted in a sizeable number of Koreans in Japan who had been born to a Korean father and Japanese mother retrospectively obtaining Japanese nationality. This development is reflected in statistics showing that the total number of Koreans in Japan registered as aliens dropped from 683,313 in 1985 to 677,959 in 1986, and then to 673,787 in 1987.[8]

In the early 1990s, through a series of immigration law reforms, all holders of permanent residence in Japan under the category of former colonial subjects (mainly first-generation Koreans and Taiwanese and their descendants living in Japan) were made "special permanent residents," regardless of the previously diverse statuses of their permanent residence. With this reform, greater leniency was granted to the holders of permanent residence. For example, if a special permanent resident committed a felony resulting in a sentence of less than seven years, he or she would not now be deported; previously, the cutoff point for deportation had been three years. Permanent residents of Japan (including Koreans) were now eligible to apply for the national pension program (though with significant restrictions—see below). Their reentry permits were made more flexible: previously, they had needed to be renewed every year in person at the nearest immigration bureau; now, the permit functioned as a multiple reentry permit and was valid for four years (although under the former Prime Minister Abe, in 2006, the system reverted to one in which permits were issued on a year-by-year basis).

With these changes, Koreans in Japan came to experience a notable shift in internal dynamics, especially in the area of collective consciousness of citizenship rights. Small-scale, locally oriented groups of Koreans began engaging in activities that, in principle if not in action, resembled more the U.S. civil rights movement of the 1960s than the ethnic-identity activism traditionally waged by Korean organizations in Japan. The reader is reminded that Chongryun, upon its emergence in 1955, renounced all acts of domestic interference in Japanese national politics, effectively self-alienating Koreans in Japan from the Japanese public milieu, looking only to North Korea in its identification of public life for Koreans in Japan (see chapters 2 and 3).

In the 1990s, however, the stance of demanding rights for resident aliens (if not for citizens) as contributors to the well-being and strengthening of local communities in Japan captured the imagination of sporadic grassroots ethnic movements. These groups emerged demanding voting rights for Koreans in local elections. Progressive Japanese municipalities and solidarity organizations expressed support. Today, numerous local municipalities in Japan grant some kind of limited pseudo–civil rights, duties, and benefits to their Korean (non-national) residents who are holders of special permanent residence. In light of the increasing presence of new immigrants in Japan, Korean (and other former colonial) residents thus receive somewhat differentiated treatment on both legal and social levels. Their acculturation is more or less complete, and with their residence in Japan extending to almost five generations, culturally they are more at home in Japan than in either North or South Korea. It should be clear, however, in the final analysis, that this does not mean that Koreans in Japan have achieved legal, civil, and political integration into Japanese society.[9]

How is the foregoing exposition reflected in the formation of the Korean ethnic self in Japan in relation to the self's moral development? It would be helpful here to consider the feminist revision of the developmental psychology of classical theorists such as Jean Piaget.[10] According to classical developmental psychology, girls will often abandon a game if a dispute arises over the rules, whereas boys will insist on continuing the game, often quarreling and arguing over the rules in order to justify their own positions to each other, and eventually resolving disagreements. Past psychological studies have concluded from this that the sense of self for boys and girls develops differently. Notably, they have argued that girls typically exhibit weak autonomy, viewing themselves as being intermeshed with others and strongly influenced by their relationships, while boys are characterized by strong autonomy, viewing themselves as independent agents, pursuing causes while being less influenced by others or by their relationships. As stated earlier, the feminist intervention since the 1980s under the intellectual initiative of Gilligan has sufficiently revised such labeling and rearranged the theory of the development of the self into one that focuses on different orientations.

Feminists have argued (successfully) that the self that rests on an abstract sense of justice, typically found in male reasoning, is not necessarily superior or more justified than the self that rests on a concrete sense of relationship and attachment. Furthermore, the abstract and the concrete are not so far apart when looked at carefully in connection to justice.[11] The key notion that feminists focus on when rearranging the existing ethic of justice is *care*. Care here is not supposed as an alternative to justice, but either as a viable, effective, and practical companion or as a partner, each strengthening the other. In fact, as Virginia Held has succinctly stated: "Few would hold that considerations of justice have no place at all in care."[12] The issue is, rather, where to place the priority, in addition to when, and how. In the ethic of care, personal and concrete relationships take precedence over the abstract and formal logic of justice; but, again, these are not mutually exclusive. From a care perspective or care orientation, the self will develop by way of attachment to, and personal interaction with, others—reminding us of the discussion on the contrast between the Japanese self and Western self that I briefly mentioned at the beginning of this chapter.

For Korean boys and girls who grow up in an ethnic enclave and for those who grow up in isolation within Japanese society, there are typically two different senses of self in relation to ethnicity that will developmentally emerge. For example, for children in Korean schools, who learn the Korean language as their national language, Korean history as their national heritage, and Korean culture and art as their own tradition, the sense of self that emerges vis-à-vis Japanese society is characterized by feelings of separation. This does not mean that boys and girls in Korean schools know nothing about contemporary Japan, or its language and culture: they are well versed in these. However, they are capable of possessing a social realm that is separate from Japanese contemporary events, not only by way of identifying themselves and their families as Koreans, but also by imagining the wider collectivity of the diasporan community, as well as the imaginary homeland. Such imaginings do not have to rely on reality—immersion in the nationalistically oriented Chongryun school education system, for example, would provide a sufficient foundation for the establishment of such an ethos. In other words, even if a child were fully acculturated in Japanese culture and society and aware that she and her family would not be repatriated to Korea, her sense of self-integration into Japanese society would not be assured. She would identify her family, her Korean friends and neighbors, and the greater Korean community as the primary objects of her loyalty. Thus, her sense of justice would primarily be concerned with her ethnic community. Such a prerogative is able to coexist unproblematically with the ethos of law-abidingness vis-à-vis Japanese state apparatuses that Chongryun has consistently sustained and implemented within its organizations, including its schools. As a consequence, students at Chongryun's Korean schools develop a sense of passive indifference toward

Japanese civic life, that is to say, an understanding that Japan's civil society is not deemed to be part of their own public space.

We need to remember that Koreans in Japan, especially those affiliated with Chongryun, have little prospect of obtaining a voice in the public arena of Japanese society. Instead, their sphere of public justice is formed inside the ethnic community. Interestingly, here, personal relationships (just as in the case of the girls in the Western psychological studies) become very important, in that, practically speaking, it is family members, Korean friends and neighbors, and the ethnic organization and community that will ultimately help them in times of need. The aspect of personal orientation is highlighted inside this community, as people tend to know each other, directly or secondhandedly, through a web of kinship, acquaintances, school contacts, business partnerships, and so on. Indeed, one of Chongryun's traditional roles was to provide staff for the funerals of Korean persons in the community. Similarly, it was common to see a local Chongryun chairperson delivering a speech at a wedding ceremony for a Korean bride and groom. When a baby was born, Chongryun officials would make sure that a bouquet was sent to the mother's hospital bedside. Evidently, Chongryun is a political organization, but ethnic politics and its public sphere require close attention to personal relationships, support, emotional ties, and solidarity, especially given Koreans' exclusion from the rights and benefits of Japanese citizenship.

In such a community, therefore, regardless of gender, personal and kinship relations carry more weight than a bundle of abstract principles of justice. In this sense, the development of the Korean ethnic self would come closer to the development of the girl (as opposed to that of the boy) as conventionally understood in Western developmental psychology. This, of course, is not to say that Koreans in Japan live in a realm where everyone helps each other and no deception or exploitation exists. To the contrary, stories of ethnic exploitation and mutual animosity resulting from unfortunate business transactions, for example, abound within the community. But the sanction here—rather than the penitence in accordance with a state legal system—takes the form of ostracization and the ruining of one's reputation, that is to say, a personally oriented and relationship-based form. This, of course, can have serious economic consequences, given that a great many Korean businesses operate inside the ethnic enclave, revolving around personal reputations and trust. Yuki's in-laws' internecine dispute and the resulting punishment of her husband attest to this.

On the other hand, Korean boys and girls who grow up among Japanese, attending Japanese schools, would undergo an entirely different process in relation to their cultivation of a sense of self. Young Koreans belonging to this category can, roughly speaking, be further divided into two subtypes. The first subtype includes those boys and girls, typically living in ethnic neighborhoods, who are fully aware that they are Korean, and who do not hesitate (when necessary) to reveal to their Japanese peers that they are Korean. The second subtype includes boys and girls who may or may not be aware that they are Korean—the first alien registration in person takes place at the age of fourteen—and who, in cases where they know they are Korean, will hide this knowledge from their Japanese peers. Because of phenotypical (skintype) identicality, as well as their high level of acculturation, it would be completely possible for these boys and girls to pass as Japanese, as long as they used Japanese-style passing names.

Individuals who can be described as the first subtype, moreover, may or may not use ethnic names. The use of ethnic names has been an acute political issue among Koreans in Japan, due in part to Korea's colonial history, one episode of which saw the forced adoption of a Japanese-style system of family registration and clan nomenclature in 1939. Many Korean families in postwar Japan, when sending their children to Japanese schools, carried on using this name, which would make them appear Japanese to unsuspecting peers. During the 1970s and 1980s, left-leaning Japanese teachers saw in the use (or recovery) of ethnic names the hope of cultivating positive self-esteem among Korean students, and they campaigned for the use of *honmyō*, or true (i.e., ethnic) names, aggressively encouraging students to declare their Korean names in front of the class. This tendency to equate the use of ethnic names with the gaining of (positive) ethnic self-consciousness was echoed in a later decade by Korean activists in Japan who had been naturalized as Japanese citizens and had lost their original Korean names upon naturalization. These individuals were typically the children of parents who had opted for naturalization; that is to say, they did not opt for naturalization themselves—the reader is reminded of Lee Yangji's case, discussed in this volume's introduction. One period saw a nationwide expansion in networking among former Koreans who equated the recovery of their ethnic names with the recovery of ethnic pride and a positive sense of self. These so-called "born-again Koreans" had typically suffered acute developmental pains associated with their self-negation as Korean, and I class them in the second subtype.[13] Between the first and second subtypes, there is a vast array of Koreans living in Japan whose ethnicity-conscious selves are formed in a variety of ways, developmentally speaking. Some are lone wolves who compensate for their ethnicity by being good bullies among their Japanese peers; some try to excel academically; others pour their energies into the cultivation of specialized talents, such as classical piano or athletic ability; yet others become lost and victimized in a sinister environment.[14]

What is commonly said, both about Korean children who grow up deeming Korea to be their homeland and about Korean children who grow up hiding their ethnic identity, is that they all end up being made conscious of their status as outsiders in relation to Japanese society. For these children, a sense of justice and feelings of engagement by the self with the greater social good must develop outside of the Japanese state apparatuses. This is due to their stateless status and the heavily compromised nature of their existence in Japanese society. This type of developmental process posits a significant challenge. For, in the measure of compartmentalization, their "public" really is "private," seen from the Japanese state's point of view. As has been stated by Arendt, "private" means it is deprived of something—in this case, political life, a kind of life that is more highly valued and deemed more significant for humans to fully develop.[15]

Ethnic justice may emerge, in different configurations, in distinction from the Japanese nation-state's idealized and codified morality, while the moral ethic for Koreans in Japan may take on a different set of values from that of the Japanese. Similarly, gender differences recognized in American samples may convey a different signification in a different culture, while the reality and constraints of diaspora often create a rather different kind of moral dilemma from that found in mainstream society. As Tronto has emphasized in her critique of Gilligan, any theory of moral development (or of the self, for that matter) that does not take into consideration the political, social, and economic conditions that existed prior to the location of the subject as a morally developing self—in other words, any theory of moral development that looks only at those who were already privileged (even if they were viewed differently, from the perspective of gender, for example)—will inevitably reproduce the moral values held by the already privileged class of people, and exclude the working class, the minimally educated, racial and ethnic minorities, and immigrants: in Gilligan's study, intragender stratification along race and class lines is grossly omitted.[16] I would add one more category of minority to Tronto's list: that of the stateless, the diasporic, and the other outsiders located on the margins of political life in the modern nation-state—such as the Koreans in Japan. For they present a form of life that other marginalized people (including immigrants) do not present—whereas an immigrant typically has the nationality of the home country, the denationalized diasporic do not.

I shall close this section by commenting on the Japanese self and the ethnic Korean self in Japan in comparison. At the beginning of this chapter, I suggested that characterizations of the Japanese self—and the ethnic Korean self in Japan—as interdependent correspond to aspects of Western models of girls' development, owing to their placing emphasis on person-to-person relations, including family, kinship, and friends. Does this also remind the informed reader of the *ie*, or household society, that Japan used to be known for—where, particularly during the 1970s and 1980s, big business management took on the distinct private idiom of family or *oikos*?[17] Furthermore, does this mean that the ethnic Korean self in Japan, therefore, now seems imminently close to the Japanese self, with both prioritizing personal relationships over abstract notions of justice, for example? A superficial observer would happily notice numerous striking parallels between stereotypical characterizations of the Japanese self and Japanese society and characterizations of the Korean ethnic self and community, as depicted in this chapter—including the interdependence of the self, a household- or family-oriented approach to solving larger problems, and so on. One must not, however, forget that the fundamental topoi for these two entities are located far apart, in different terrains. One group—the Japanese—are members of a nation-state and a national-political-public society; the other—the ethnic Koreans in Japan—are outsiders in relation to the order of nation-states, and only hold membership in a community that is disenfranchised and that sustains itself largely in an ideological manner, reflecting the prolonged partition of the homeland. Sense of self, morality, and justice take inevitably different paths of development for these two groups.

Suffice it here to state that the way in which the Japanese self is currently studied, that is, by excluding long-term resident aliens, despite their near-complete acculturation, eloquently attests to the legal and topological excommunication of Koreans in Japan by the Japanese state, which is felicitously replicated by uncritical researchers. As has also been emphasized earlier in the chapter, the fact that concrete relationships are prioritized over abstract principles does not imply inferior morality or a lower quality of moral capacity. Conversely, however, if, in an ideal world, host societies of denationalized and diasporic people were to uphold higher moral standards, not discriminating against people of difference or lack (such as the lack of nationality), the ethnic logic of morality and sense of self of these people, as well as their sense of a greater social good, would develop along a different path—more in convergence with the moral aspirations of the host society, assuming that the moral values upheld by the host society were not of the narrow-minded nationalist kind. Let us think more about this in the next section, where we focus on the ethic of care.

THE ETHIC OF CARE IN DIASPORA

What is care, and how is this relevant to our understanding of Korean diasporic women in Japan? Simply put, care may start inside the home, between a mother and her newborn. The mother's labor in taking care of the newborn is often neither compensated for nor reciprocated by the baby itself for many months or years, at least not in the form of a direct mutual acknowledgement of caregiving and care-receiving. In the earlier, narrower version of the ethic of care, theorists such as Noddings strongly identified care with the dyadic relationship between mother and child. This was in opposition to Kantian moral philosophy, according to which one was supposed to strive for perfection oneself and where, therefore, helping others to achieve perfection was a contradiction. Noddings writes: "We must be exquisitely sensitive to that ideal of perfection and, in the absence of a repugnance overwhelming to one-caring, we must as ones-caring act to promote that ideal [i.e. the ideal of helping and caring for others]."[18]

Noddings, while anchoring her ethical foundations of care in the mother's care for the newborn, assumes that as long as each one of us cares for our loved ones, a society should (automatically or naturally) eventually become a caring one. In other words, it is our individual and personal initiative, responsibility, practice, and inclination that matter in promoting care. Hence her conditional clause: "in the absence of a repugnance overwhelming to one-caring." What would, one wonders, create a repugnance overwhelming to one-caring? Is it created in the eyes of the beholder? Does this effectively mean that cultural and ideological predilections and prejudices are acceptable for Noddings, as long as they come as personal choices? No personal choices, however, are purely personal — they are simultaneously constrained by the sociocultural, historical, economic, and, above all, political conditions one has been exposed to and formed by. If we begin to acknowledge personal choices as relative, no matter how politically harmful such choices might be considered by the public at large, it becomes acceptable for a racist nurse to ignore a sick patient of the race other than hers in a pediatric ward, because of the personal repugnance that overwhelms her. The priority placed on the personal thus ultimately privileges the already-privileged, preserving and replicating the uneven power relations existing in society. The lack of sensitivity toward the structurally disprivileged and marginalized population constituted a prominent weakness of early feminist assertions relating to the ethic of care, where care was largely imagined to be a value and an activity of well-educated, economically better-off, and personally motivated white women in mainstream America.

Although the emphasis on the ethic of care was born from within the critique of the assumption behind liberal individualism, early exploration of the ethic of care contained weaknesses similar to those found in the doctrines it was fighting against. For it preserved the assumption that society consists of autonomous individuals, all equally capable of entering into social contracts as independent selves based on free will, an assumption that is male-oriented and inherently discriminatory toward women, the lower class, and diverse minorities, whose participation in political life is limited from the outset.

Among many influential works of feminism that attempted to revise these earlier weaknesses, interventions made by Tronto and by Eva Kittay stand out as the most effective, contemporaneously as well as historically; and it is these thinkers' works that I'd like to rely on when considering the question of care in connection to the denationalized, including Koreans in Japan such as Yuki. Both Tronto and Kittay address the weaknesses of the early feminist take on the ethic of care and, through their works, they contribute toward critically reconfiguring the ethic of care. On the one hand, they build it into a more sophisticated argument against liberal individualism, while, on the other hand, they liberate it from the confines of the private by trying to deconstruct the boundaries between public and private.

Tronto defines *care* as, first, a reaching out to something other than the self and, second, the prospect of leading to some type of action. She elaborates on these points, along four definitive positions:

1. Care is not restricted to human interaction with others.
2. Care is not restricted to dyadic, individualistic relations.
3. Care is culturally conditioned.
4. Care is ongoing.[19]

On the basis of this, Tronto proposes four elements of care:

1. Attentiveness: The absence of attentiveness is a moral failure, as noticing other's needs is the first task.
2. Responsibility: An alternative to a more rigid notion of obligation, a flexible notion of responsibility reinforces the political dimension of care.
3. Competence: The inclusion of this element would hold accountable the bureaucratic systems by which many of us are controlled.
4. Responsiveness: This element requires that we remain alert and sensitive to the possibilities for abuse of the vulnerable.[20]

By suggesting that these elements be positively included in our new thinking about care, Tronto extends the notion of care into the political sphere, enmeshing it with the private realm and the personal sphere.

In my view, Tronto's redefinition of care offers an effective tool for elevating the ethic of care beyond the family and the private. Of particular importance is her emphasis on overcoming dyadic reciprocity—supposedly naturally given—when understanding care, as it redefines the scope of the previous, limited notion of care by the mother of the newborn suggested by Noddings. In Noddings's formulation, only when care is acknowledged by the person being cared for is the care relationship complete. This brings Noddings's position close to liberal individualism, with its foundation on the social contractarian principles of the autonomous self and egalitarian, equivalent exchange between equal citizens. However—as Tronto points out—in many caregiving situations, a direct exchange of acknowledgement or complete reciprocity is not possible.[21] What about those who do not have the capacity to respond in the way our convention would have us expect—such as autistic children or people with Alzheimer's disease? Are we unable to care for these persons, or do we abandon their care?

Insofar as we narrowly focus on the dyadic, individual care relationship, the moral grounds for caring for those who cannot respond become precarious. Tronto's four elements of care enable us to go beyond such confines of the personal and the private. Furthermore, we also have plenty of documentary evidence within our reach that in deprived and oppressive societies, regardless of what mothers want or do not want, their relationships with the young take on drastically different forms compared to the U.S. conventions so unproblematically embraced by Noddings.[22] In other words, there is nothing universal or innately human about a mother taking care of her newborn or infants.

According to Tronto: "To be a morally good person requires, among other things, that a person strives to meet the demands of caring that present themselves in his or her life. For a society to be judged as a morally admirable society, it must among other things, adequately provide for care of its members and its territory."[23] Of course, the question that arises in relation to our inquiry in this chapter would be whether or not nonnationals or the denationalized still count as "members" of society. Furthermore, when "the public" of the denationalized diasporic community is ultimately "the private," when seen from the host nation's point of view (as I argued earlier), how does one politicize care that takes place inside the homes and the communities of these marginalized nonnationals? How do we hold the bureaucracy responsible, when, from the point of view of the nation-state, it has no obligation to provide care for the nonnationals? Evidently, negotiations with the system of service provision would take on different dimensions in this case—we shall see this in the final section, when we closely reexamine Yuki's case from this perspective. Meanwhile, let us move on to consider Kittay's views.

Kittay's work is significant in that it incorporates the feminist ethic of care into a concern for those who are most vulnerable in many societies—the disabled. Drawing on the irrefutable fact that everyone is some mother's child, Kittay urges us to look at the needs of the new mother, a woman who has just given birth to a new life. From the first moment of postpartum, she takes care of the newborn, regardless of her own physical discomfort. Then, asks Kittay, who takes care of her? Kittay reminds us of the Greek practice of assigning a *doula,* a slave or servant who exclusively attended to the needs of the postpartum mother, while the latter devoted her energies to ensuring a beneficial start to the life of the baby. She extends this ethic into the public sphere and the common good—improvising from the term *doula,* Kittay proposes the ethic and practice of *doulia,* by which the needs of those who meet the needs of others by taking care of them are met.[24] Kittay transfers a practice that took place inside *oikos* into *polis*; or, more precisely speaking, she deconstructs the divide between *oikos* and *polis* and proposes that a good society must be able to take care of the person who attends to the needs of the other (or others), who, without receiving her care, might not thrive or even survive.

Groups within the population that come to the fore in this list of the vulnerable include children, the sick (especially those who are chronically ill), the elderly, and the disabled. Humans are, Kittay emphasizes, in need of others' care, to a greater or lesser extent, for a longer or shorter period of time, throughout the life span—during infancy; while growing up; when they experience failure, sadness, depression, sickness, or injury; in bereavement; and when elderly, for example. The failing of social contractarians and liberal individualism is that they disregard these human needs, often fundamentally and acutely manifested, and proceed to assume that we are all equally capable (physically and mentally, financially and culturally) of participating in social decision-making, presuming that everyone is independent and self-sufficient at all times. The reality is quite different—everyone needs to depend on others at some point in life, and it is this interdependence among humans as social beings that needs to be recognized when considering the greater social good.

From the above position, Kittay criticizes the way in which the current U.S. Family Medical Leave Act operates; while it allows a member of a family in need to take a leave of absence from work without risking loss of employment, it does not oblige the employer to continue payment of wages for the duration of the leave.[25] In my view, the FMLA has one more flaw: the way it grants leave assumes that medical emergencies are temporary or short-lived, with a limited duration of (typically) up to twelve workweeks of unpaid, job-protected leave. In this scheme, families containing members with disabilities or chronic medical conditions are not well served. They are forced to continue, business as usual, as there would be no particularly "good" weeks in which to take leave. Furthermore, as Kittay critiques, if such leave is not paid, the costs incurred in taking care of the family member with a disability and/or chronic health condition fall solely onto the shoulders of the family itself, basically meaning that unless the family is endowed with disposable income, there is no way the FMLA can work for the disabled and the chronically ill.

Such blind spots are clearly seen when one looks at the situation faced by the disabled in the U.S. Even after the (belated) proclamation of the 1990 Americans with Disabilities Act, the disabled and families with disabled members continue to suffer from discrimination, disadvantage, and disenfranchisement.[26] This is seen most acutely in the area of providing education and personal care for children with disabilities. Since a general revision of the tendency to institutionalize the disabled in the U.S., "family-centered care" has emerged during the last few decades as the central tenet of service provision for children with disabilities. The hitherto-numerous hospital schools have been closed, and the private home has come to be seen as the primary caregiving place for children, combined with schools that should, ideally, be *included* (i.e., integrated) rather than segregated.[27] The 1993 Individuals with Disabilities Education Act (IDEA) further stipulated that each child with disabilities is entitled to receive an Individualized Education Plan (IEP), which must be reevaluated every year and measured against the changing developmental needs of the child. Under the IDEA, the family's or guardian's involvement in the IEP became an important part of the education of a disabled child.

These family-centered measures, however, do not simply enhance the well-being of the family as a whole. They can, in fact, increase the family's burden, effectively compromising the family's efforts to care for their child with disabilities. For example, the guardian's right to participate in the child's IEP meeting does not have a federal mandate and is not guaranteed in reality. There is no legal obligation on the part of the employer to secure the pay of a parent who is absent from work in order to attend a child's IEP meeting, and for such a parent to skip work to exercise his or her right to be at the meeting could mean a loss of income or of paid leave time.[28] As the mother of a child with a disability, I can attest to this. When I missed one meeting at work due to my daughter's medical condition, my cumulative sick-leave time was reduced by eight hours, although the meeting itself did not last for eight hours. If I keep missing meetings at this pace—with my daughter's almost-daily appointments for therapy and clinical appraisal, and given her generally fragile health (requiring regular follow-up appointments in oncology, ophthalmology, autolaryngology, orthopedics, neurological developmental pediatrics, pediatric specialty dentistry, rehabilitation medicine, and gastroenterology, even setting aside frequent occurrences of flu and fever, and numerous ER visits)—before long I will have very little sick leave left for myself. It seems little accommodation is made for a faculty member like me who is the primary caregiver to a child with disabilities.

Many of us are also caregivers to elderly parents or at least, as in Yuki's case, are trying to fill this role; and, furthermore, many of us playing these multiple roles are women. I am aware that academic employment is much more privileged than other regular employment, where hours are more rigid and there is no flexibility for choosing on which days and at which times one wishes to work (or teach). In contrast to Yuki's long hours, her multiple responsibilities toward her parents and daughter, and other stressful factors, my caregiving situation with regard to my daughter might seem less difficult. But commitment to care for the disabled, for a person totally reliant on one's care, ultimately presupposes certain commonalities, with shared difficulties and obstacles. For one thing, care for the disabled is broad-ranging: it encompasses hygiene, transportation, education, socialization, physical and other therapies, medical appointments, feeding and nutrition, and toileting, to mention only a few components. In my case, I have virtually trained myself to be an advocate for my daughter's rights (requesting that certain goals be inserted in her IEP, for example), in addition to being an amateur technician regarding her wheelchair adjustment and positioning; a home medic, in order to manage her gastric tube, her night-long pump feeding every night, the occasional oxygen supply, and the administration of regular doses of her medications; an agent, in order to negotiate with the ever-difficult insurance company to obtain items and services that my daughter requires; an experienced laundry person, as required by my daughter's frequent reflux (my record being eight loads of laundry a day); and a watchperson, in order to ensure her general well-being—such as in relation to her health and education, but also as a provider of fun and joy, doing things like singing theme songs from PBS kids' programs or playing Beethoven's piano sonata in C minor, her all-time favorite. Indeed, Tronto's aforementioned four elements of care fit my situation amazingly well: I need to be first and foremost attentive, as my lack of attentiveness could easily compromise my daughter's well-being; I must be responsible, as my neglect of responsibility, even for one night of her pump-feeding, for example, would compromise her nutrition; I must be competent and disciplined, as my incompetence might result in serious consequences as far as my daughter's health was concerned; I need to be responsive, especially since my daughter is nonverbal and her ability to communicate is extremely limited—if I were lazy in responding to her vocalizations, even in the middle of my night's sleep, I could be missing important signs, such as an indication that her night tube was leaking all over her bed, for example.

These multitasking branches of the practice of care distance caregiving for a child with disabilities from the generically supposed mother-child relationship, in which child care is temporary—one day, the child will grow into an adult, alleviating the need for parents to provide the kind of care that small children require, although of course there will be other kinds of care to follow. Unlike (say) ordinary child care, caring for a child with a disability is, as Tronto states, ongoing.[29] It is this aspect of endlessness and constancy that makes care for the disabled inside the family not simply a matter of—I do not know how else to say it—love, but also of moral responsibility. What I mean is that the love that I have for my daughter cannot explain it all: I need to be able to perform and fulfill a vast range of duties and tasks, which love cannot always guarantee. A good society must be able to recognize the morality of this commitment and provide support so that the caregiver's labor does not go unrecognized as completely private work and, therefore, socially irrelevant and meaningless.

In Kittay's vision of *doulia,* my labor as a primary caregiver for my disabled child should be placed in an environment where I can both work and take care of my daughter, without having to worry about potentially losing my work due to the additional time off and extra work I need to do in order to provide for my daughter. Kittay herself is an acclaimed academic and also mother to a daughter with a disability.[30] But this should not mean that only those of us with firsthand experience of trying to combine motherhood (of a child with a disability) with the pursuit of an academic career can understand the importance of *doulia.* What about other caregivers, including people like Yuki's father, and Yuki herself? Without societal understanding and a support system which is legally guaranteed and customarily accepted, such a practice of care—*doulia*—that does not compromise the well-being of the caregiver herself will not be possible to attain.

Applying this to the situation faced by Koreans in Japan (or any other stateless peoples in the world), lack of access to membership in the nation-state again works to their detriment. A Japanese newspaper has reported that, as of 2006, 15 percent of the entire Korean population in Japan is classified as senior, or *kōreisha,* a term normally used to refer to those above the age of sixty-five.[31] Elderly Koreans in Japan in their sixties or early seventies mostly qualify for *kōreisha hoken,* or health insurance for the aged, which is issued by municipalities. As for social security and the national pension, the late opening up of this possibility for Koreans in Japan has meant that elderly Koreans face severe constraints. This is because as of 1982, when Japan ratified the United Nations Refugee Convention and, accordingly, opened up social security for non-Japanese permanent residents, non-Japanese applicants who were thirty-five years of age or above at that point did not qualify for the senior pension, or *rōreisha kiso nenkin.* In 1985, the national pension system in Japan was reformed, and it became mandatory for low- and no-income individuals such as housewives and full-time students to make social security contributions. But, again, non-Japanese persons aged thirty-five or above at that point were excluded, which left them with no safety net for their old age.[32] Elderly Koreans, such as Yuki's parents, who receive pensions have typically built their retirement funds by contributing to programs offered through their employers, which need to be distinguished from social security and the national pension. Some employer-based pension schemes (such as the dental surgeon's pension) exclude nonnationals, while others (such as the teacher's association pension) allow nonnationals to participate.

Local municipalities offer many subsidized services for elderly care, including home visits by helpers and therapists in the areas of rehabilitation, preventative medicine, and personal caregiving, in Japanese known as *kaigo*. Though subsidized, these require varying amounts in out-of-pocket payments and copayments. According to the Japanese Ministry of Health, Labor, and Welfare, in August 2006, the average monthly cost of home-visit personal care (excluding bathing care) was estimated at 53,200 yen (approximately $500), and the same service if bathing care was included went up to 57,000 yen. The cost of a nurse's home visit was estimated at 41,000 yen, and a home rehabilitation service, 24,300 yen. The Ministry also estimated that, nationally, the total number of persons who received multiple personal care services amounted to 3,332,700, and the combined cost for all of these services per person (for the month of August 2006) was 152,600 yen (approximately $1,400).[33] In other words, Japan's current system of long-term care provision presumes a substantial payment on the part of the recipient. This categorically excludes elderly persons who receive no social security or any kind of pension, including a vast number of elderly Koreans in Japan.

In dealing with local municipalities, moreover, elderly Koreans face multiple obstacles, including the consequences of a habit that they have acquired over decades of dealing with the Japanese bureaucracy. Older generations of Koreans display strong hesitation, repugnance, or indifference when approaching Japanese municipalities, due to their decades-long exclusion, self-detachment, and separation from Japanese local governance. They may or may not be aware of the fact that at least some of the caregiving services provided by the municipalities are available to them because of their low-income status or advanced age, coupled with their permanent resident status in Japan. However, because of their absence of meaningful interaction with the Japanese local municipalities over many decades, they do not have the proclivity or inclination to explore available resources through the municipal offices.

The only interaction that elderly Koreans have routinely had with the offices of Japanese local municipalities has been when reporting in person for Alien Registration. Historically, prior to the recent series of reforms, Alien Registration in Japan was a notoriously oppressive institution. The law used to stipulate that one had to carry the certificate (which used to be in a cumbersome book form) on one's person at all times, even when one went to the public bathhouse around the corner from one's dwelling. If one failed to report a change of address within two weeks, one risked imprisonment, and indeed, many were arrested on the grounds of not having carried the certificate in person or having failed to report a change of address on time. An unstable residential situation coupled with oppressive police detention is the image that older-generation Koreans in Japan associate with local municipalities. Understandably, avoidance and self-distancing are typical approaches that elderly Koreans in Japan adopt in relation to local municipality offices. We may sense the same reaction in Yuki's parents' reluctance to borrow a handicap-adapted toilet seat from the municipal office. Furthermore, one also needs to remember that many elderly Koreans do not speak (let alone read or write) Japanese with ease. The bureaucratic jargon, specialized terminology, and complicated and endless paperwork, in addition to the vast amount of information pertaining to applications for long-term care insurance, municipal subsidies, and other rebates and benefits, would be simply too overwhelming for an elderly Korean to handle.

As is well known, women have traditionally adopted a diverse range of caregiving roles in Japan. Among Koreans in Japan, this tendency is somewhat intensified, due to the lingering effects of Confucianism's three principles of obedience for women: when young, obey one's father; when married obey one's husband; and when old, obey one's eldest son. A consequence of this rule would be an increase in the caregiving burden of the mother or daughter-in-law. Especially if one were to marry a firstborn son, one would often live with one's parents-in-law, taking care of them on a daily basis, with increasing frequency. There is, of course, reciprocity of a kind. The mother-in-law may take care of the grandchildren to briefly alleviate the burden of her daughter-in-law in her daily chores. However, whereas such an act (even when motivated by the mother-in-law's own desire) is seen as beneficence, the daughter-in-law's service is mandatory.

This image is an ideal-typical image of the daughter-in-law; in reality, there is a great amount of diversity and deviation in terms of particular domestic arrangements, including residential arrangements. Today, families consider options such as nursing care or close-by, yet separate, living arrangements, in order to cater to the needs of aging parents. But such alternative arrangements are always costly. In the case of families with limited resources, the burden is to be taken up by women, in the form of unpaid domestic labor.

Many of the Korean women I know who are in the position of having to do the "caregiving relay" (that is, after having taken care of their children, they now have to take care of their elderly parents-in-law) are in their forties and above. Many do not have careers, often performing extra, unpaid work for small, family-run businesses or working part-time outside the home. They typically characterize themselves as housewives. I talked and interacted with a total of six women, each of whom is married to a firstborn son, specifically asking questions with regard to their caregiving situations. Upon my asking them what aspect of their lives vexed them most, the women claimed that the fact that they could not take care of their own parents, while they had to take care of somebody else's parents, no matter how personally close they were to them, bothered and saddened them most. A few of them also voiced the concern that no matter how well or sincerely they took care of their parents-in-law, they would always be suspected of neglecting their duties by their siblings-in-law, especially by their sisters-in-law.[34] Thus, some felt that the battle was already lost before it had begun. Others emphasized that they had been able to develop friendships with their mothers-in-law or fathers-in-law over close to two decades of interaction, and were now able to view the prospect of providing long-term care for their parents-in-law in a more positive light.

None of the women's living parents-in-law were currently incapacitated or required heavy-duty, round-the-clock personal care, although all of them had some medical conditions that needed to be monitored and regularly checked by a physician. One had survived a stroke, but was successfully rehabilitated. None of the women, at least for now, considered a nursing home to be an option, for both emotional and financial reasons. All of them either lived with their parents-in-law or one surviving parent, or lived very close to them. All said that sending their parents-in-law to a nursing home would be cruel, and, interestingly, all stated they would not trust Japanese nursing home employees and would be sorry for their parents-in-law to have to live amid Japanese old people. They would add that it would be too expensive in any case, if one were to opt for a reputable nursing home. O Mun-Ja, a Korean female literary activist in Japan who recently placed her ninety-year-old mother in a nursing care facility after an agonizing decision-making process, painfully describes how her mother is left out of recreational activities due to the awkwardness she feels in relation to joining Japanese peers.[35]

Here, we are brought back to the point made by Yuki's parents, that they did not want to have Japanese caregivers inside their home. Yuki, as we saw, is not in a position to have to take care of her in-laws, and was not able to help her own parents as much as she would have liked. In her perception of care and that of other women, being Korean, or, more specifically, being elderly and Korean in Japan, figures as an important factor. Why is receiving care from Japanese caregivers seen as something that elderly Koreans in Japan would dislike, and why is this dislike accepted with little contestation by younger women who, after all, will have to bear the burden of taking care of their elders by not accepting the help of Japanese professional caregivers? How should we understand this ethnic factor, in light of the moral prerogatives of care that I have explored in this section?

CARE AND GENERALIZED EXCHANGE

In their studies of the developmental psychology of boys and girls, both Kohlberg and Gilligan have used one particular hypothetical situation to observe and analyze their young subjects' moral reasoning, and its tendencies and emphases. It is referred to as "Heinz's dilemma," and it goes like this:

> In Europe, a woman was near death from cancer. One drug might save her, a rare form of radium that a druggist in the same town had discovered. The druggist was charging $2000, ten times what the drug cost him to make. The sick woman's husband, Heinz, went to everyone he knew to borrow the money, but he could only get together about half of what it cost. He told the druggist that his wife was dying, and asked him to sell it cheaper or let him pay later. But the druggist said, "No." The husband got desperate and broke into the man's store to steal the drug for his wife. Should the husband have done that? Why?[36]

I have already touched upon differences presented in the interpretations of moral reasoning and the development of boys and girls: that boys tend to think in terms of abstract principles and girls in terms of direct, personal relationships. Put differently, as discussed by Clement, from the justice perspective, Heinz's dilemma is understood to be a clear-cut conflict between "the right to life and the right to property"; while from the care perspective, the presentation of this dilemma itself is immensely frustrating, as it lacks details as to why and how Heinz could not possibly solicit more loans from other people or why Heinz and the druggist could not possibly talk it out in order to reach a mutually satisfactory agreement.[37]

If presented with Heinz's dilemma, the first thing that a Korean living in Japan might well ask is, "Is the druggist Japanese?" Whether the druggist is Japanese or Korean holds a key to this dilemma. Depending on the druggist's ethnicity and his relational positionality vis-à-vis Koreans in Japan who are in need (here Heinz is assumed to be a Korean), stealing from him can begin to hold a different meaning. If the druggist were Korean, and he still did not help a fellow Korean who was desperately in need of a drug that would enable his wife to live (and which the druggist himself did not need other than for the purpose of making a profit), the druggist would be labeled as immoral (ethnically rather than ethically speaking, that is) and deserving of the fate of being robbed.

I have earlier suggested that due to the lack of access to political life, stateless Koreans in Japan tend to emphasize personal and kinship (and, by extension, intra-ethnic) relations when interpreting moral prerogatives. In a situation where little public assistance is obtainable in any viable or dignified means from the state granary of the host society (or so it has been believed),

Koreans in Japan are resigned and accustomed to the reality that their safety net in life comes from their families and possibly their Korean friends and other members of their ethnic network, if they have any such ties—and not from Japanese public funds, the police, municipalities, or the government. Premised on this, moral judgment takes on a distinctly personal and ethnic twist.[38] Combining this element with the ethic of care, in Korean households in Japan, taking care of elderly parents or sickly children becomes a moral issue—just like in other societies, such as our own, where care is assumed to involve daily and hourly responsibility on an ongoing basis, as in the case of raising a child with disabilities or medical complications—but with the additional ethic of ethnic morality. Bearing this in mind, let us now return to Yuki's case.

As has been seen, what is prominent in her story is the tension or mutual betrayal between the desire or ideal of family support and solidarity, on one hand, and the reality of family discord, on the other. In theory, the morality of ethnic justice is inclined to suppose that, ideally, Koreans (both inside and beyond the immediate family) should take care of each other in situations where they cannot hope to expect a readily available public safety net to be provided by the Japanese nation-state. In reality, however, stories such as Yuki's are not uncommon. This is because life itself can be a struggle for Koreans in Japan, as resources are limited and virtually no public subsidies were available for (say) home loans or small-scale enterprises prior to their obtaining maximal permanent residence in the early 1990s. Often, competition for survival in the ethnic enclave might set one Korean against another in a more direct manner than among the wider Japanese mainstream population. The jealousy of Yuki's sisters-in-law, Yuki's marriage itself, and Yuki's parents' position vis-à-vis their affines all seem to speak to a strong undercurrent of tension flowing through the web of kinship under the surface of the diasporic community.

On the other hand, the lack of resources for caregiving (for the disabled, the young, the elderly, and the chronically ill) is not simply an ethnic issue among Koreans in Japan. The rising proportion of the population that requires in-home care or home visits (*kaigo*) is straining public resources as well as the private savings of all generations of Japanese. Nevertheless, it is worth noting that Koreans in need of care still find it difficult to solicit, and are hesitant and wary of soliciting, *kaigo* from Japanese helpers. This hesitation might well be a thin veil that financial constraints and the acuteness of their needs may soon strip off. Still, the hesitation is real, and it lingers on. What does this tell us about Koreans' expectations of their host society, and the moral structure of the host society itself? Can we not see here the reality that Koreans in Japan have been efficiently and effectively disciplined into law-abiding, undemanding, and docile diasporic sojourners within the Japanese state, who voluntarily exclude themselves from benefits and entitlements? Can we also not see here the clear workings of boundaries of humanity, within which only members of nation-states are included?

Yuki, according to her autobiography, discovered that as an elderly person with special permanent resident status, her mother was entitled to have providers of massage and other forms of therapy visit her home on a regular basis at subsidized cost. And, indeed, she was able to persuade her parents to accept some of these services. But her parents themselves were extremely unwilling to explore any such possibilities, or were perhaps simply uninterested, as if already resigned to the belief that Japanese state and local municipalities had very little to offer them. And such is the reality that Yuki's parents' generation has lived through.

Here, the logic is that Koreans in Japan have to be self-sufficient, but not in the way that Western liberal individualism envisions. Rather, such self-sufficiency assumes family or another kinship group (and not individuals) to be the smallest unit. The size and constituency of this unit are flexible — it can expand to include distant relatives, and it can shrink by sanctioning some of its members, as in the case of Yuki's husband. Justice, in this sense, is ofter subordinated to the survival and honor of the unit. This does not mean that members always care for each other, although failing to do so can lead to bitter emotional consequences. Relationships, rather than abstract principles, act as the measurement of justice — just as in the care orientation, in contradistinction to the justice orientation.

At the beginning of this chapter, I identified that, overtly or covertly, the characteristics attributed to the Japanese self, as opposed to the Western self, are feminine in the scheme of Western developmental psychology. I also identified above that the formation of the ethnic Korean self in diaspora follows the pattern of girls' developmental formation (in the West), notably, prioritizing close and personal relationships over a set of abstract principles of justice. But these are not the same, as I have also argued, when connected with ethnic and national-civic factors. For diasporic Koreans and, especially, elderly Koreans, Japanese are not included in personal relationships in the way Koreans are. Furthermore, as can be glimpsed from Yuki's autobiography, Korean personal relationships are enmeshed in kinship relations, not just within the nuclear family or bilaterally, but cross-generationally.

What comes to my mind in this connection is the logic of generalized exchange as portrayed by Marcel Mauss's work on the gift.[39] According to Mauss, the logic behind the exuberant, lavish, and self-destructive mutual gift-giving of the potlatch is found in the importance placed on the continuity of this institution itself, and its exponential expansion in scale as a result of its continuity, seen as representing the wealth and prosperity of the community at large in the long run. In my view, this resembles the investment logic to which we, as capitalist contemporaries, are accustomed: our retirement funds will grow over a long period of time, and it is important that we keep putting money in. In both cases, the returns are expected to be larger, and to not be procured quickly, but only after making numerous investments over an extended period of time. Ancient sacrifices also operated according to this logic: by offering a portion of the collectivity—be it a virgin, war booty, or crops—to the gods, the community deservingly demanded an eventual larger return in the form of rainfall, a good harvest, prosperity, or victory at war. In these cases, the participants in transactions are not engaged in direct exchange. Rather, they are engaged in what Mauss calls generalized exchange, whereby one's investment generates greater returns by way of being circulated among many parties over a long period of time encompassing multiple generations. One's sacrifice is rewarded, not by getting back what one has offered immediately and in a direct manner, but by the community at large receiving benefits at a later stage, even after the deaths of particular individuals. As such, the receiver does not reciprocate in an immediate and direct fashion for gifts that he or she has received. Rather, it is through repeated instances of gift-giving that the community at large insures the increase of the overall value of all the gifts both given and received inside that community, which in turn results in further thriving of that community.

The logic of generalized exchange fundamentally contradicts the core of liberal individualism, in that in the former, the individual as the sacrificed (or victim) is not seen as self-sufficient, autonomous, or independent; he is, rather, not himself, but part of the community, or a larger social unit. Furthermore, the nature of the gift itself is distinguished from the commodity. This can be seen most clearly in the case of the sacrificial animal in a ritual. The moment a sacrificial animal is segregated from the rest of the herd, for example, the sacredness of the animal supersedes its individuated existence, and it acquires a new ritual identity. Thus, gifts for the gods in sacrificial rituals become unlocatable in terms of possession, ownership, or alienability. According to Henri Hubert and Marcel Mauss, *"Sacrifice is a religious act which, through the consecration of a victim, modifies the condition of the moral person who accomplishes it or that of certain objects with which he is concerned."*[40] If we combine the logic of transformation of the moral person in sacrificial rituals and the logic of the gift, that is, that of generalized exchange, we begin to see the moral foundations of caregiving: that in caregiving, the one-on-one, individualized, give-and-take transactional morality (of liberal individualism) encounters difficulty; rather, the reward or return is transcendentally distributed in time and space. And, if so, caregiving is itself a fundamentally social endeavor, not an individual one, in spite of the fact that an individual person or object is selected for sacrifice and just as his/its moral transformation results from such a participation in the ritual individual caregivers may be personally and morally affected by the act of caring. For the care that the caregiver offers bears attributes of a sacrificial offering that has been estranged from its individualized existence during the ritual, thereby becoming a medium (or messenger) for bringing better return to the community at a later time. Seen in this way, it becomes wholly justifiable to support and protect the caregiving carried out in individuals' private homes with public funding and provisions.

The logic behind caregiving—as envisioned by Tronto, Kittay, and other feminists who connect *oikos* with *polis* by closely overlapping the personal good with the greater social good—is similar to the logic of the generalized exchange of the gift economy. The person who is sacrificed does not need to be directly reciprocated for his or her sacrifice; however, the community at large will receive a greater return. The direct exchange or reciprocity that we are accustomed to as individualist moderns demands a rapid, short-term achievement of equivalent or better returns: when we purchase something, we expect that the use value of the merchandise should match (or surpass) the price we pay. In the gift economy, direct exchange and the quick-fix equilibrium do not work. Likewise, the purpose of care is to enable generalized exchange to continue ad infinitum. It is, in other words, not person-to-person reciprocity, or the exchange of equivalent values, that concerns the ethic of care, but a mechanism that enables person-to-person care to undergo a metamorphosis and become part of the greater social good. My point here is to assert that in the diasporic community of denationalized Koreans in Japan, such an elevation of personal sacrifice to the level of the public good becomes imminently difficult, due mainly to their being deprived of public life. This deprivation reduces a personal sacrifice made inside the diasporic community into purely a private act with little impact on a larger sociopolitical life in the (host) national state.

Given human finitude and fragility, any one person can be at the same time a giver and receiver of care. As found in the case of Yuki, when one is keenly aware that one has to, ought to, and indeed wants to care for someone, obligations to third parties and other situational constraints may prevent one from being able to provide such care. On the other hand, as can be seen in Yuki's disappointment in her father, it is difficult to accept a situation where a person who has been assigned to care for the needy is not fulfilling his or her duty, even when it is understood that ongoing caregiving is extremely hard work, involving enormous self-sacrifice. If public assistance were to become available, even in partial form, the morality of caregiving inside the diasporic homes would take a different turn. I should be more precise: if the denationalized had access to public life, their caregiving and care-receiving would bear more public and socially meaningful worth.

The logic of generalized exchange, or care as gift, is a powerful barometer for measuring the moral integrity of the Japanese nation-state vis-à-vis its ethical responsibilities toward providing a safety net for Koreans and other non-nationals and long-term legal alien residents. Let me reinvoke the notion of *doulia* as proposed by Kittay. If society had been capable of providing adequate rest and recreation, rejuvenation, and respite to Yuki's father, the primary caregiver to her mother, he probably would not have had to (try to) abandon (if only temporarily) his caring duties for his wife in such an abrupt manner, leaving everything on the shoulders of Yuki. If society had been capable of providing Yuki with a safety net so that she could take care of both her mother and her business, while at the same time raising her daughter, Yuki's personal dilemma would have been eliminated. We do not have such a society, either in Japan or in the U.S. But the additional factor here is that Koreans in Japan, outsiders in relation to the beneficence of the nation-state of Japan, really have no recourse to apply for viable and dignified public assistance. Thus, it is not only the binary of public/private, but also national/non-national boundaries that need to be deconstructed and dissolved in order to enable persons who care for others to be cared for.

Commentators often criticize the Japanese government for its double standard: Koreans are, in the fullest sense, taxpayers of the Japanese state, incurring local municipal tax, business tax, income tax, and other miscellaneous taxes, yet they have neither electoral representation nor the other political rights usually given in exchange for payment of taxes.[41] While I am sympathetic toward such a stance, this argument, in my view, brings us back to the social contract: taxation without representation is immoral, in this view. The weakness of this view, as seen from the ethic of care, is that this still leaves out the most vulnerable (the unemployed, the poor, and the disenfranchised) in light of the taxation system, as it rests its proposition on the basis of individual-to-individual, value-equivalent exchange. This stance is still plagued by moral-logical weakness, omitting the fact that the different capacities (financial, intellectual, and physical, for example) of individuals will preserve, enhance, and reproduce the existing power hierarchy and the uneven distribution of wealth and benefits, leaving out those genuinely in need.

The moral obligation to help people in need, when placed in the Japanese context vis-à-vis Japan's formerly colonized people, is indissolubly connected to the issue of unresolved postcolonial compensation and the unfair (and unlawful, seen internationally) treatment and other injustices systematically meted out by the Japanese state on Koreans and other long-term non-Japanese residents in Japan from its former colonies—including, for example, its one-sided cancellation of Japanese nationality for Koreans in Japan in 1952.

Membership in a national community, or the loss thereof, here becomes an issue to be placed at the forefront of any debate on human rights—those who are not nationals do not even deserve to be considered for welfare, benefits, or beneficence, regardless, that is, of how very real their needs may be. According to this formula, basic human rights are envisioned and limited on the basis of individual capacities and the national or civic membership status. Put bluntly, in this thinking, individuals whose financial, intellectual, physical, or other capacities fall below a certain standard, as well as those who are not members of a national polity, are not deserving of being cared for in order that their basic needs be met, even when this might jeopardize their lives. Ironically, the taxation-based demand for rights and benefits reproduces the logic used by the Japanese government in order to exclude Koreans in Japan, implying that those not endowed with the required capacities or (national) status do not deserve to live. Rather, assistance and care should be envisioned on the specific basis of individual needs, in close engagement with the notion of greater social good, following the principle of the generalized exchange of the gift.

It is a curious practice of modern society that we establish a welfare system in order to benefit those in need, yet stigmatize and look down on those who receive the benefits of such a system. The existence of derogatory terms such as "welfare queen" attests to this. The stigma is intensified when one is not a full member of the nation-state. A spokesperson for "middle America" (whatever that might mean) would try to incite anger if a family of recent immigrants were receiving a disability benefit or social security. To begin with, immigrants lag behind in obtaining the necessary information related to the public welfare services to which they are entitled. Furthermore, due to the domination of employment-based health insurance policies in the U.S., immigrants have much lower rates of health insurance.[42]

The hurdle is multifold, including poverty or economic disenfranchisement, cultural exclusion, and the lack of national membership, among other components. How people in need—regardless of the severity of their disabilities, their financial capacities, or whether or not they are members of the national community—are taken care of and can take care of each other thus becomes a moral test for society. This is especially the case for stateless Koreans in Japan. Like the mainstream Japanese population, a large number of them are entering old age and, like Yuki's mother, may be suffering from chronic medical conditions or disabilities, with or without social security or pensions. This is the last surviving generation with a living memory of colonialism. These are the ones who were subjected to injustices on the basis of crude and direct forms of ethnic discrimination. These are the ones who sustained the bottom layer of the postwar Japanese economic boom, with minimal pay and long labor hours.

These are the ones who were deprived of opportunities, education, and freedoms as human beings. Their well-being, or lack thereof, will attest to the quality and viability of Japanese society as a moral human society.

NOTES

1. Gilligan (1982, 1986); Kohlberg (1969), for example. See also Chodorow (1978).

2. Grace Clement, *Care, Autonomy, and Justice: Feminism and the Ethic of Care* (Boulder, CO: Westview Press, 1996). See particularly Clement's argument for approximating the morality of justice and the ethic of care.

3. Nihon fujin dantai rengōkai, ed., *Joseihakusho 2004: sekai no nagare to nihon no josei* [White paper on women, 2004: Global trends and women in Japan] (Tokyo: Horupushuppan, 2004), 201; Ministry of Health, Labor, and Welfare, Japan, "Abridged Life Tables" (2004), www.mhlw.go.jp/ (accessed December 15, 2006).

4. See Shōya Reiko and Nakayama Tōru, *Kōrei zainichi kankoku chōsenjin* [Elderly Koreans in Japan] (Tokyo: Ochanomizushobō, 1997), for example, and also Koh's (2001) critique.

5. Nel Noddings, *Caring: A Feminist Approach to Ethics and Moral Education* (Berkeley: University of California Press, 1984); Joan Tronto, "Women and Caring: What Can Feminists Learn about Morality from Caring?" in *Gender/Body/Knowledge*, eds. A. Jaggar and S. Bordo (New Brunswick, NJ: Rutgers University Press, 1989).

6. For example, Martha Nussbaum's recent polemic against social contractarians will illuminate this. Nussbaum's critique is based on the latter's almost reckless assumption of the moral power of humans as beings with dignity and rationality. For such an assumption fails to see that equal citizens do not always possess equal capabilities to cooperate with each other and participate in society. People with disabilities are in the forefront of such a list. Many of them are not in a position to participate in social activities and decision-making as equal citizens, and they are often heavily dependent on others for care. Nussbaum points to the rights and entitlements of the disabled as citizens. Her alternative is "capabilities approach," by which she proposes to see humans as beings with multiple needs—physical, emotional, economic, personal, public, and cultural—each vulnerable to their needs as well as circumstantial changes such as illness or altered income status (Nussbaum 2006). But here, too, an uncanny restriction of the rights of the disabled to those of (disabled) *citizens* raises its head. This becomes clearer when Nussbaum goes on to discuss global inequality in terms of social justice. She compares, rightly by all accounts, how people with different nationalities under different national-state systems enjoy more or fewer privileges and are subjected to more or less misfortune and injustice, globally speaking. Conspicuously left out are those with no national home. The disabled; the poor; the starved population in the developing world; and women are included in her discussion, while their inclusion in her theory hinges upon their membership in a national-state order, and not in humanity at large—i.e., not being nothing more or less than human, not being a bare life. Here, the political identification as being a national bears primacy over being merely a human.

7. Eriko Aoki, "Korean Children, Textbooks, and Educational Practices in Japanese Primary Schools," in *Koreans in Japan: Critical Voices from the Margin*, ed. S. Ryang (London: Routledge, 2000b).

8. Kim Yeong-dal, "Hoshō: kaisetsu to tōkei no hosoku" [Supplement: Explanation and supplementation of statistics], in *Sūji ga kataru zainichi kankoku chōsenjin no rekishi* [History of Koreans in Japan seen from statistics], ed. Y. Morita (Tokyo: Akashishoten, 1996), 176.

9. Recently, some scholars have taken alternative approaches to the hitherto-deprived civil status of Koreans in Japan. Erin Chung invokes a series of terms such as "de facto citizenship (2000: 168)," "active citizenship 'from below' (2000: 163)," and "cosmopolitan citizenship (2000: 175)." Eika Tai suggests that, in light of the recent visibility of multicultural values in Japan, Korean ethnic identity now faces a possibility of opting for Korean Japanese in a more compounded and cooperative model (2004: 374). What underpins these views is the conviction that Koreans' cultural literacy in Japanese society is a valuable asset, and that it makes them eligible to be fully integrated as members of the civic community and local public and political affairs in Japan. Chung, for example, highlights the term *shimin*, taking it as "citizens," as opposed to *kokumin*, or nationals. In this thinking, Koreans can be *shimin* if not *kokumin*. This raises an important point about the term *citizen*, as we use it. At least in U.S. English, we use it to denote a broad range of capacities, including memberships in various corporations and organizations other than the national state. In this sense, I do not object to introducing the concept of citizenship, as we use it, to the understanding of the ontological reality of Koreans in Japan. Similarly, Tai's focus on the new Korean identity invokes the expanding Korean participation in Japan's civil society in ways more effective than those of the past, where Koreans tended to be oppositional and dissident. While not discrediting these new attempts, I would like to caution against the potentially deceptive effect of constructing the new, looser concept of citizenship and identity. At the outset, it needs to be pointed out that Japan has no significant tradition of a conceptual vision of "citizenship," as its use of *kokumin*, or nationals, often supercedes the concept of citizen. It is unrealistic to proceed much further with the *shimin-kokumin* distinction.

10. Jean Piaget, *The Moral Judgment of the Child* (1932; repr. New York: Free Press, 1997).

11. Clement (1996: 76–80); Carol Gilligan, *In a Different Voice: Psychological Theory and Women's Development* (Cambridge, MA: Harvard University Press, 1982); Carol Gilligan, "Moral Orientation and Moral Development," in *Woman and Moral Theory*, ed. E. Kittay and D. Meyers (Lanham, MD: Rowman and Littlefield, 1987).

12. Virginia Held, *The Ethics of Care: Personal, Political, and Global* (Oxford: Oxford University Press, 2006), 15. See also Held (2006: 62–66) for a brief overview.

13. See Chikako Kashiwazaki, "The Politics of Legal Status: The Equation of Nationality with Ethnonational Identity," in *Koreans in Japan*; but also see Lim (forthcoming). For a detailed discussion of the issue of name usage, see Ryang (forthcoming).

14. See for example, Kim (1980), a sequel to his first book, which covered the suicide of a twelve-year-old Korean student in a Japanese public elementary school, the cause of which was suspected to have been insidious, constant, and sinister bullying by his classmates on the basis of his ethnicity.

15. Hannah Arendt, *The Human Condition* (Chicago: University of Chicago Press, 1958b), 39.

16. Joan Tronto, *Moral Boundaries: A Political Argument for an Ethic of Care* (New York: Routledge, 1994), chap. 3.

17. Nakane (1970) is the major source for the dissemination of such a view in the Western discourse on Japan since the 1970s.

18. Noddings (1984) quoted in Virginia Held, ed., *Justice and Care: Essential Readings in Feminist Ethics* (Boulder, CO: Westview Press, 1995), 29. See also Ruddick (1980, 1989) for a take on maternal pacifism that presupposes women's natural endowment for peace and care.

19. Tronto (1994: 102–5).

20. Tronto (1994: 126–37).

21. Tronto (1987) quoted in Held (1995: 106–7).

22. See, for example, the now-classic Scheper-Hughes (1992).

23. Tronto (1994: 126).

24. Eva Feder Kittay, *Love's Labor: Essays on Women, Equality, and Dependency* (New York: Routledge, 1999), chaps. 4, 5.

25. Kittay (1999: 133–40).

26. Disability studies is a rich and fast-growing academic discipline. Its recent debate on transition from medical model to social model; its rapprochement with other disciplines, such as women's studies and anthropology; and its self-enrichment through incorporation of cultural studies, for example, are attracting a wide range of attention and participation from scholars. To cite only a few influential works: Corker and Shakespeare (2002); Ingstad and Whyte (1995); Snyder and Mitchell (2006); Smith and Hutchinson (2004). In the Japanese context, see Nakamura (2006), Tsuchiya (2002), and Yōda (1999).

27. There is a host of studies in the history of disability, including Byrom (2004) and Longmore and Umanski (2000). For "family centered approach," for example, see Turnbull and Turnbull (2002) and Wang, Turnbull, et al. (2004).

28. For parents' advocacy in relation to IEP, see Wang, Mannan, et al. (2004).

29. I have commented on this briefly. See Ryang (2006b). Also, here I wish to mention that I am aware that among disability activists and intellectuals, there is a debate over potentially and practically oppressive effects of care as well. See for example, Shakespeare (2006: chap. 9).

30. Kittay (1999: chap. 6) details her personal experience.

31. *Tōyō keizai nippō* (September 15, 2006), quoted in O Mun-Ja, "Zainichi issei no kaigo mondai—haha o hōmu ni takushite" [The question of care for the first generation Koreans in Japan—after having left my mother in the nursing home], in *Zainichi josei bungaku: Chi ni fune o koge*, vol. 1 (2006), 122.

32. O (2006: 114). Also, it needs to be emphasized that non-Japanese persons with disabilities aged twenty or above as of 1982 (that is, those individuals born as recently as 1962) were excluded from eligibility for the disability pension (*shōgaisha kiso nenkin*).

33. Ministry of Health, Labor, and Welfare, Japan, "Kaigo kyūfu jittai chōsa geppō" [Monthly survey on care cost], August 2006a, www.mhlw.go.jp/toukei/saikin/hw/kaigo/

kyufu/2006/08.html (accessed December 15, 2006); Ministry of Health, Labor, and Welfare, Japan , "Dai 7 hyō Kaigo sābisu jukyūsha hitori Atari hiyōgaku, yōkaigo jōtai kubun, sābisu shurui betsu" [Chart 7: Per capita cost for personal care service, relative to the degree of needs and services], August 2006b, www.mhlw.go.jp/toukei/saikin/hw /kaigo/kyufu/2006/08hyo7.html (accessed December 15, 2006); Ministry of Health, Labor, and Welfare, Japan, "Dai 2 hyō Kaigo sābisu jukyūsha sū, yōkaigo jōtai kubun, sābisu shurui betsu" [Chart 2: Number of personal care service receivers, relative to the degree of needs and services], August 2006c, www.mhlw.go.jp/toukei/saikin/hw/kaigo/ kyufu/2006/08hyo2.html (accessed December 15, 2006).

34. We are reminded of a case that Bernstein (1983) depicts through the eyes of the caregiver herself, Haruko.

35. O (2006: 112).

36. Kohlberg (1969) quoted in Clement (1996: 11–12).

37. Clement (1996: 12–13).

38. An unbiased reader will know that I'm not saying that Koreans in Japan disregard Japanese law or are willing to harm Japanese in order to protect Koreans. I'm simply suggesting moral prerogatives, and not the action.

39. Marcel Mauss, *Gift: Forms and Functions of Exchange in Archaic Societies* (Glencoe, IL: Free Press, 1954).

40. Henri Hubert and Marcel Mauss, *Sacrifice: Its Nature and Functions* (Chicago: University of Chicago Press, 1964), 13, emphasis in the original.

41. For example, see Lee's equation when describing the situation where no social security is available for elderly Koreans in Japan, despite their having been taxpayers throughout their working years (2002: 212).

42. According to the Iowa Governor's Developmental Disabilities Council report in 2003, Asians, African Americans, Hispanics/Latino(a)s, and Native Americans are unserved and underserved groups with regard to children's developmental disabilities, due to an absence of culturally competent information in native languages, and also regarding the native cultures of immigrants, in dealing with developmental disabilities (Governor's Developmental Disabilities Council, Iowa, 2003). A survey from the University of California, Los Angeles, on the other hand, shows that California's immigrant adult population is 36 percent uninsured, as opposed to 16 percent for native-born adults (Benjamin et al. 2000: 3).

Chapter Five

Terra Incognita

Family Maps of Diaspora

Terra incognita. An unknown land, a land that one does not know, a land that one will never know. Diasporic families travel from one such land to another. Before getting to know one land, they move to another unknown territory. Before learning the language of that land, and before their words have ceased sounding like strangers' babbling to native ears, they move on to expose themselves to a new language. This chapter is about these families.

In closing this book with this chapter, I shall first tell the stories of two families, those of Jacey and Ryjung, each characterized by complicated histories of movements across borders. By using their stories as background, I'd like to address one issue that concerns current studies of diaspora. Following Ian Hacking, I would characterize this as an *ecological niche*, that is to say, a condition that enables a certain cluster of discourses to emerge as dominant—in this case, the medicalized discourse that assumes diaspora (along with many other phenomena in modern lives) to cause trauma and suffering. I'd like to problematize this by arguing that while such an assumption may not be unwarranted, it needs to be treated with due caution, as it may well result in privileging medical or diagnostic discourse, thereby reducing sociohistorical issues to the status of psychosomatic issues and, in the final analysis, exalting the authority of science and medicine at the expense of the self and the agency of diasporic individuals. My aim is modest, yet I refuse to replace a sad face with a happy one by simplistically replacing diaspora as trauma with diaspora as empowerment. Rather, I shall strenuously remain faithful to the complexity and ambiguity of life in diaspora, focusing on being open, inconclusive, and inviting for the future debate on consequences of diaspora. So far in this book, I have explored ontological conditions faced by Korean women in diaspora. While I have not belittled their burden and the difficulties they face in life, I have consciously attempted to avoid overshadowing their lives with what have become fashionable keywords in academe—*pain* and *suffering*. In this chapter, I work closely with these concepts, yet at the same time resist the temptation to wholly succumb to their sway.

I shall first introduce the reader to the stories of two families—those of Jacey and Ryjung. Although not related or (as far as I know) acquainted with each other, through their histories, these two families manifest mutual synchrony in their articulation with the diachrony of Korea's history. Their stories are woven into the tapestry of the modern Korean diaspora, involving a mosaic of incrementally transnational, long-distance, and multiple displacements—first to parts of Japan and China, then to Hawaii and North and South America, and now, in increasing multicontinental moves. Tracing the family history of Korean diaspora, I question the relationship between diaspora and suffering, as this angle presents itself as particularly relevant in thinking about diaspora in today's world. First, I briefly look at how this concept can be problematical, depending on its deployment; then, in the final section, I directly and critically deal with the diagnostics of diaspora.

Appropriately for the final chapter of a book like this one, the reader will find that I raise more questions than answers; but I hope to have done so with some persuasion, and with allusions to possible future directions that research might take in relation to diaspora, both specifically within the Korean context and also within the broader, global context.

WAR AND DIASPORA

The world-renowned cartographer Arthur H. Robinson once remarked, "In the modern history of cartography, it is a fact that periods of war have generally led to developments in mapmaking." He continues by reflecting on the correlation between "the ultimate stupidity of man" and "cartographic innovation."[1] War has also been responsible for the birth of many diasporic communities in the world, including the Korean one, and, subsequently, for mapmaking by diasporic families, that is, a cartographic innovation of an alternative kind. The families of Jacey and Ryjung, whose histories I am going to present here, have been directly affected by war, by a war that is often remembered in the U.S. as (paradoxically) a forgotten war. But, if one is Korean, this war is far from forgotten—it is a war that has eternally touched, altered, and often torn apart the lives of every Korean—the Korean War.

"That our family had to leave," writes Jacey with resignation, "was unavoidable." Her grandfather was the son of a large landowner at the northern tip of the Korean peninsula, then under Japanese colonial rule. His favorite pastime was to go off for long rides on his beloved Harley-Davidson motor-cycle. After Japan's defeat, the fact that the family had been landowners dur-ing the colonial era became a life-threatening liability, northern Korea was placed under the control of Soviet occupation forces. While Korea's postlib-eration partition into North and South, respectively occupied and governed by the Soviets and the Americans, was widely regarded as temporary, a series of Sovietization reforms that took place in the North had very real effects on the everyday lives of residents. The landholding class was seen as doubly guilty—for having been pro-Japanese and for being an exploitative class. Jacey's grandfather's family gave up all its possessions and lived under tremendous pressure and uncertainty for the first three years following the liberation of Korea. In 1948, separate regimes were set up in the North and in the South, further advancing the Northern commitment to Soviet-style gov-ernment and the move toward socialism. This did not, however, precipitate the family's uprooting, at least not for the time being.

The South, for the family, was unknown territory, with very different cli-matic conditions, cultural traditions, and economic infrastructure. Unlike the North, which shares a long border with China, the South is sea-bound on three sides. It had been, ever since the establishment in 1392 of Korea's last dynasty, the Choseon, the center of politics, royalty, and high culture. The North, by way of contrast, was seen as somewhat backward, wild, and bar-baric. This was due to its proximity to the Manchus, which southern aristo-crats looked down upon. Of course, the historical fact that China's last empire had been established by the Manchus was conveniently forgotten. Northern aristocrats and landowners were always aware of the disdain with which the southern upper classes viewed them. The family's cultural unfamiliarity with the South, its lack of material means, and the unresolved, unstable nature of conditions prevailing around and beyond the thirty-eighth parallel cutting through the middle of the peninsula prevented the family from making a de-cisive move.

But when UN soldiers crossed the thirty-eighth parallel following MacArthur's amphibious landing at Incheon in the fall of 1950, cutting off the middle part of the western coastline of the peninsula and stranding hun-dreds of soldiers of the Korean People's Army (KPA)—which had almost uni-fied the entire peninsula under its domination by mid-September, that is, less than three months after the war's outbreak—the family faced the urgent need to make a decision.

It was not a simple decision of whether to remain in the North or to go over to the South. It was, moreover, never a simple matter of whether to support the Soviets or the Americans. In a way, the KPA's advance to the South at lightening speed had spared the family from the turmoil of war. But the news of the U.S. landing was disturbing, as it augmented an already heightened sense of confusion and uncertainty. Fall in northern Korea is short. Leaves were already changing color. Family members were made increasingly nervous about whether or not they could survive the coming winter under the chaos of a U.S. military invasion. Moving further up, into northeastern China, was a possibility, though a remote one: China was, after all, foreign territory, and had just entered a chaotic period following the establishment of Mao's government. As the conflict intensified, now with the presence of Chinese volunteers joining the KPA, the family decided to abandon their ancestral home and to move to the South.

It was exactly around the time that Jacey's grandfather's family began its arduous southbound journey that Ryjung's grandfather, a defector from the North, met her grandmother, now an acclaimed pianist in South Korea. They eventually got married, leaving Ryjung's grandfather in the South after the ceasefire agreement of July 1953. This seemingly unthinkable romance was actually not so difficult to imagine. Evidently, atrocities were committed in all corners of the Korean peninsula, and proof of massacres (including those committed by U.S. troops) continues to be revealed even to this day. At the same time, it is also true that the Korean War was a civil war that (ironically) enabled Koreans from the South to enter the North and vice-versa, something that had been impossible since the Allied partition of the peninsula in 1945 along the thirty-eighth parallel. Dispersion of families, accidental estrangement, loss of sick family members while moving, and other misfortunes and tragedies occurred, yet new unions and romances were also born between individuals amid the turmoil.

Ryjung's grandmother came from an extremely privileged background. She had studied piano at a music college in Tokyo during the colonial period, and was teaching as a professor in a newly established music college in postliberation Seoul. She had been married for some years and had a daughter when the war broke out. Within a couple of weeks, Seoul was under KPA occupation. One day, her husband, a nationally renowned tenor, failed to come home. It was rumored that he had been kidnapped and taken to the North, perhaps along with many other skilled and qualified persons from the South. Ryjung's grandmother waited for months, until the authorities pronounced her husband dead. Her grief and frustration were immeasurable. She was now a young widow and a single mother, and the country was in chaos and everything was in short supply.

In the middle of her despondence, she met a northerner who provided a considerable amount of help and became her companion. After the KPA's withdrawal to the North, Ryjung's grandfather, now married to her grandmother, stayed on in the South. Ryjung's grandmother soon had another daughter, Ryjung's mother. Once the ceasefire was reached in 1953 and the Demilitarized Zone was newly drawn, altering the straight partition following the thirty-eighth parallel into one that sloped by approximately sixty degrees to the northeast and southwest, the North and the South entered a new phase of détente. Ryjung's grandfather joined the South Korean army and became a major, and had advanced to the rank of general by his retirement.

Exhausted, Jacey's grandfather's family reached the South virtually empty-handed. The family was one among thousands of what would today be termed refugees. The difference was that Jacey's grandfather's family and thousands of other Korean War refugees were not even recognized as refugees, and hence did not benefit from assistance through the type of international relief operation that we are now familiar with. No such things were available to Koreans at that time. Thus, displaced and uprooted, they had to start rebuilding their lives on their own. Thanks to the family's hard work, Jacey's grandfather's family was eventually able to overcome the severe economic hardship it had faced, and younger children were born in the South, including Jacey's father.

More difficult to deal with, however, were the cultural and political feelings of uncertainty, and a persistent haunting caused by the family's lack of roots. The family was consistently made to feel excluded in southern society, and that feeling was more strongly registered by the older generation, that is, Jacey's grandparents. The elders knew that ultimately, in the eyes of the southerners, they were viewed with suspicion as nonorthodox, nonauthentic South Koreans. Thus, having failed to be fully embraced and accepted by the southerners, Jacey's grandparents, together with the family of her oldest uncle, migrated to the U.S. in the mid-1980s; while Jacey's father and mother and their two little girls (of whom Jacey was the younger) remained in South Korea, for reasons related to her father's business. It is at this point that Jacey's story of personal reclamation enters the map of her family's history:

I was born in Seoul, Korea in 1982. In 1985, the company my father worked for recruited him to oversee a new branch that was being built in Santiago, Chile. In one of the better parts of Chile, my older sister and I attended a Catholic private school and after-school Korean class on the side. My younger sister was born a year later in Santiago Hospital. Two years later, my parents became concerned about our education and future and felt that Chile offered few prospects. Instead of returning to Korea, they chose to join my uncle's family and grandparents in the U.S., and began a restaurant business. My sister and I were enrolled in public elementary schools, where we were placed in an English as a second language (ESL) program for a few years. We continued to attend very white-based public schools throughout middle school and high school.

I am accustomed to being asked the question: "where are you from?" I respond by inquiring if they want to know where I live or what nationality I am.

For most people, this question applies to both—your home implies your place of naturalization. In my case, however, the term "home" or "homeland" comes with no specific attachment to a geographic location. I have never returned to Korea since I left it at the age [of] three, and have very few, vague childhood memories of it. There is little reason for me to attach the word "home" to Korea, the country I was born in. I have lived in the U.S. for most of my life, but I do not have U.S. citizenship: I only have U.S. permanent residence and Korean citizenship. Although the U.S. is the home of my personal history, the analogy is that of being a guest, or the renter of an establishment. With no right to vote, I live under house rules where I have no say. On the other hand, although my Korean citizenship gives me political entitlement, my exercise of that right is seriously compromised due to my own lack of familiarity with that country's public debate.

In my parents' and grandparents' cases, it would be valid to say that there is a desire to return to Korea, which stems from an actual perception of Korea as their home and homeland, although my grandparents and parents have lived very different lives in Korea and thus have very different personal histories attached to it. Their recollection of home may very well differ from Korea today, as well. But my parents have never referred to the U.S. as "our land." Interestingly enough, I have never heard them use the English word "home" as opposed to "house" when referring to their current place of residence, granted that the distinction may not be as evident to them since the Korean word *jip* implies both. Nonetheless, there is a clear longing for Korea and a perception of the U.S. as a foreign land. As for myself, I have no particular desire to return to Korea permanently. I'd like to visit and see what it is like, but that desire does not go beyond one that any potential tourist could develop.

My parents have made a personal choice of not applying for U.S. citizenship after receiving permanent residence, attributing a symbolic meaning to holding onto their Korean citizenship. In the U.S., there is a clearer separation between ethnicity and nationality, unlike in a mono-ethnic society, such as Japan, where Japanese nationality also means Japanese ethnicity. But the existence of multiple cultures in the U.S. does not negate the pretence of cultural homogeneity or dominance that is distinctly American, granted that what this thing called "America" means is far from defined. My parents and I clearly identified ourselves as Korean while we lived in Chile. Considering only a handful of Koreans lived in that country, there were not enough Koreans attempting or desiring to obtain naturalization for there ever to be a conflict of national or ethnic identity. In Chile, my status as Korean was clearly recognized and any cultural differences were perceived as natural or to be expected. I celebrated my sixth birthday wearing *hanbok*, the traditional Korean dress, and offering my classmates Korean festival food.

The move to the U.S. from Chile was followed by a few years during which I rejected integration into American culture. Until the age of nine, I refused to speak in English and instead had a Korean friend communicate for me in school. Because I had received private tuition from an American while I lived in Chile, the language barrier shou_d have played a lesser role in my resistance. Rather, in my child's mind, I felt as if I was being forced to give up who I was because my teachers disliked that I was different from other students. My ESL teachers made a lot of effort to make me speak English. Hoping to give me a fresh start, my parents transferred me to a private school with an American first name. This was the last straw, and I scon gave in, speaking English fluently and with no particular psychological stumbling. Using an American name of my choice made me feel as if I had regained some control over my life, and I began to open up to my new peers.

My college life has immersed me deep within a Korean circle again. Korean and Korean American students on campus often label and stereotype each other as *yuhaksaeng*, or overseas students, and *kyopo*, or Korean immigrants. The former are seen by Korean Americans as being "fobbish" and artificial in that they speak Korean loudly in public, tend to come from wealthy families, and use their parents' credit cards to go drinking and shopping for designer clothes. *Kyopo*, on the other hand, are seen by international students as culturally ignorant, having forgotten Korean traditions, and [as] American-wannabes or "bananas" who dress like country bumpkins. A *yuhaksaeng* once told me that his intolerance toward Korean Americans came from the fact that there was no doubt in his mind that they were Korean, but that they were Koreans who had absolutely no understanding about what it meant to be Korean. I found it interesting, since he assumed that there was only one way of being Korean . . . Perhaps my parents might insist on a similar vision, although I am certain their version of being Korean and his version of it would be very different. And what about my grandparents? Would they even be considered Korean by a South Korean's standards today? From my grandparents' perspective, there was no other choice in the end but to leave their home. That our family had to leave was unavoidable. We have always moved around—from the north to the south, to another south, then to another north. Are we to leave again, I wonder? Sometimes I feel like a vagabond who belongs to neither place, being forced to migrate with the changes of season.

In-betweenness, the condition of being periodically torn between two extremes, though not even living in two different localities or societies, is also a characteristic that Ryjung attributes to herself. She has even experienced this sensitivity inside her home. "My parents had very different upbringings,' writes Ryjung, who had a complicated growing-up process, due to her parents' broken marriage on top of recurrent uprootings on both maternal and paternal sides, though each in very different ways. Both Ryjung's mother and her older sister (Ryjung's aunt) received music tuition from their mother (Ryjung's grandmother) from an early age, and attended the university in Seoul where their mother taught. After college, Ryjung's mother went to study in the U.S. at a time when it was very difficult for Koreans to do so because of the weakness of the Korean currency. In the U.S., she met Ryjung's father, who came from another diasporic family, but their family backgrounds could not have been more different.

My father is the third child (second son) of a large family. His family migrated to Brazil in the 1960s when he was in middle school. The family experienced many hardships in Brazil because they did not speak the language and his parents were not very educated. His older brother repeatedly got into trouble for petty crimes, and consequently, my father was treated as the oldest son. From a young age, my father assumed the role of household provider and took charge of the family finances. My father played a significant part in pulling his family out of poverty, and from these experiences my father has come to believe that a man has special responsibilities and rights inside the home. He is a devout Protestant, which validates my father's beliefs in the superiority of men, it seems. My mother was from a very wealthy family. Her mother was a university professor and her father was an army general. When my mother was in college, her mother divorced her husband, who had taken a mistress. For a woman to divorce her husband at that time in Korea was considered very brazen. It was one example of what an independent-minded woman my grandmother was and still is. My grandmother's virtue was transferred to my mother who taught me that, as a woman, I was no less than a man.

The difference between my mother and my father became increasingly prominent as I grew up. My mother firmly believed that I was an American—Korean, yes, but American in that I was not subject to Korean customs and traditions— assuring me that being a second generation Korean American female was not a disadvantage in any way. She was very much involved in my school life and extracurricular activities, despite the fact that she almost single-handedly ran the business that my parents jointly owned. My father was aloof: the only time I spent with my father was when we went to church, which mother refused to attend. We attended a Korean congregation where the idea that women were inferior to men was repeatedly emphasized in various guises. Whenever I engaged in an argument with my father, he often began scolding me, saying "A woman shouldn't talk that way."

My parents were very unhappy in their marriage and I rarely spent time with both parents at the same time. My behavior and speech changed drastically depending on which parent I was with, because each parent expected me to be a different person: for my father, conservative and polite, for my mother, spontaneous and liberating. When I received my first acceptance letter from a college, my mother was proud; my father said, "You don't have to go to college. You can live with me until you get married."

What was confusing to me was that my father held very traditional Korean beliefs, yet he did not care if I could speak Korean or not. For my mother, on the other hand, though very liberal in her beliefs, learning the Korean language and having knowledge of Korean culture were very important parts of her home education for me. So, for example, I spoke no English until I was six, when I learned it at school, since my mother always spoke to me only in Korean. I gather from this that my father represents a belief that "Koreanness" is retained, in some sense, naturally—possibly through blood—while mother's position culminated in the belief that one's identity was always acquired and earned. Separate filial piety became easier for me to maintain, as my parents formally divorced while I was in college.

When I began college, I had to reevaluate my bicultural identity. Although I grew up managing fairly well to maintain both my Korean and American selves, compared to my high school, where I was only one Asian American student, at college, 25 percent of the student population fell into the Asian and/or Asian American category. Furthermore, they seemed to socialize almost exclusively among themselves. More specifically, typically speaking, Korean students befriended other Koreans, rather than other non-Korean Asian students. Within this "Korean" grouping, a further sub-division existed, depending on whether one spoke Korean to one another or not. Korean American students referred to those Koreans who spoke in Korean to each other as FOBs, meaning "fresh off the boat."

I had a hard time relating to either the group of Koreans or the group of Korean American students on campus. Besides, many of them were pre-meds, which I was not. Many of them also went to church (each to different churches based on their group orientation, i.e., whether the church offered Korean services or not), but I did not. Honestly, I found myself not liking the Korean American community, and it bothered me that I could not like my fellow people or the people that were supposed to be closer to me than any other. At the same time, I increasingly became aware that whether I liked it or not, other non-Asian students assumed that I was one of them anyway.

As my family life spread in various directions after my parents' divorce—my father re-married and relocated to the West Coast, my mother moved to Korea, [then] came back to the U.S., to Hawaii, with her Korean boyfriend—my childhood home in the U.S. appeared to have been lost as well. I no longer had any location or, even more simply, a town that I could claim as my home—not in the U.S., not in Korea, not anywhere.

Looking back, I think that I compromised myself by believing that I could not create my own identity—ethnic or otherwise. Growing up, I tried hard to satisfy the different sets of beliefs that each of my parents held on to. In college, I tried to negate whatever came closer to me (Korean or Korean American), dissociating myself from either, yet not able to avoid the identification that the mainstream white population glued onto me: that is, Korean or Korean American, or, even more vaguely, Asian. As the years in college advanced, I made a conscious effort to expose myself to the possibility of becoming someone. I met a professor with a multicultural identity more complicated than my own, and she encouraged me to examine my Korean identity from an academic standpoint, which I did through independent research and through enrolling in courses that were related to my questions. I [did research on] Korea for my psychology and anthropology papers, and made a few research trips there by earning grants and scholarships. I now am able to say that I can be completely different from any Asian American person I know and still be entitled to an Asian American identity. Having graduated from college, I find myself evaluating how I have changed in the last four years: I think the most significant change has been that I am comfortable with myself—not with my certainty, but with my own uncertainty.

Whenever I go to Korea, I feel I am visiting my homeland, because this is how my mother views the experience. Korea is, somehow, no longer my father's homeland. Brazil never became his homeland, either. I wonder if the U.S. has finally given him one. As for my mother, due to the fact that she grew up into adulthood in Korea and has family connections there, she probably feels that she is going home whenever she goes to Korea, although my grandmother moved to the U.S. recently due to her old age and my grandfather passed away in 1985. When I'm in Korea, I stay with my maternal family. I don't know whether my father still has members of his extended family in Korea and I am not sure if I am interested in finding out about them. This is ironic, considering that my father was always the one that insisted on "Korean womanliness" when I was growing up. It is doubly ironic, since Korea is changing. My mother, who was born there and grew up there, felt she was rejected when she moved there as a return-divorcee from the U.S. Hence, she and her boyfriend decided to move out of Korea and are now living in Hawaii. Home, in this way, I realize, can sometimes reject you even though it is the only place you call home. Similarly, I am fully aware that the U.S. may refuse to offer me a home. But what else can I do? One can only try living somewhere, calling it home.

In the sagas of these two families, captured in the eyes of Jacey and Ryjung, what is notable is that at every important juncture of national history, they are leaving—they keep leaving, rather, without being able to settle in one place. Is it, however, correct to say "without being able to settle"? Should I, in fact, say "without having to settle"? Is diaspora, as it were, a curse or disease on one hand, and something else on the other, something different and possibly positive, or at least noncontradictory, nontormenting? Is it, more simply put, something that should not necessarily be seen as particularly problem-generating in and of itself, in terms of emotions and health? Or is it something that damages us very badly, possibly irreparably?

DIASPORA AND SUFFERING

The twentieth century was a century of violence, suffering, and pain. Atrocities, massacres, mass-rape, genocide, and destruction on an unprecedented scale were committed, including in Armenia, Nanjing, Hiroshima, Auschwitz, India, South Africa, Vietnam, Cambodia, Chile, Guatemala, Bosnia, Rwanda, and Darfur, to name only a few places. Suffering and pain—the placement of these concepts into the center of intellectual exchange, therefore, is understandable and, perhaps, justified. Yet at the same time, it is also the reality that twentieth-century suffering has been kind to a select few corporations and industries, including the international weapons trade and global pharmaceuticals. Particularly, the elevation of the medical establishment into a sacrosanct, commanding position vis-à-vis our everyday life on one hand, and the overarching ubiquity of medical news, drug commercials, and even medical dramas in our everyday lives on the other hand, is simply overwhelming. Our lives have come to be placed under the thorough scrutiny of medical knowledge and related authorities and, worse still, we are even made to willingly participate in this endeavor. Twentieth- and twenty-first-century selves are disciplined and trained into making themselves accountable in the eyes of the medical establishment. One simply needs to remember how thoroughly and earnestly people fill out patient-health-history forms at physicians' clinics.

Is this a sign that we are to understand our modern existence in terms of the psychosomatic configuration of pain and healing, wellness and illness? And how is this related to the modern diaspora? Today, a large part of our daily life is shaped and framed by medical, medicalizing, and psychosomatically diagnostic discourses. Often, for example, a nation's "health" is "diagnosed," and it seems that everyone is, at some point in life, supposedly traumatized. Unemployment can be associated with depression, rather than with the class struggle, industrial action, or protests against an incompetent government. Domestic violence can be explained in terms of a husband's pathology, such as alcoholism, rather than in terms of gender inequalities or the exploitation of women. A restless child may be evaluated by a psychiatrist in terms of the child's brain-chemical balance in order to prescribe medication for it, while little consideration or even assistance is given to the child's mother, who may be working three jobs and raising the child single-handedly. Phenomena that used to be explained in terms of ideology appear now to be explained in terms of mental health. Personal characteristics that used to be seen as simply unusual or nonconforming appear now to be understood in terms of mental illness. Socioeconomic exploitation can be ultimately, it seems, justified as a human psychological proclivity.

This is not to mock or deny the utility of health-oriented discourses. Indeed, in the twentieth century, a century of intense violence and destruction, the deployment of discourses of healing and recovery proved to be a salvation. Not everything, however, benefits from the deployment of health-related discourses. For the uncritical use of such discourses may well result in the privileging of medical science, handing over to it the authority to interpret our social lives and cultural world, thereby augmenting the voice and authority of the already-powerful dominators in our society, including pharmaceutical industries, health insurance companies, the medical establishment, or so-called life experts. Furthermore, the emphasis on psychosomatic causality results in the obfuscation of the socioeconomic causes of misfortune by replacing them with health-generated problems—be it a brain injury or a chemical imbalance—that is to say, hiding socially generated problems behind individual maladies.

In many cases of social-scientific study, symbiotic relations emerge between interpretive, culturalist language and medico-scientific language, and the use of medically referential terms may enhance the portrayal and understanding of everyday lives. Indeed, in chapter 1, I intentionally deployed several psychosomatic symptoms as analogies to my cases in order to further illustrate a discussion that is useful for understanding the formation of the self in diaspora. Metaphors of illness, it has been said, humanize the patient and his or her psychosomatic self-representation.[2] However, it is also true that too generous an application of medical and health-related concepts to sociohistorical phenomena at large might create some problems—especially in studies of diaspora, in which, more often than not, the traumatic experience of loss of home and the pain of forceful relocation are assumed to produce mental illness (see below).

In taking up this position, I am inspired by Thomas Szasz's works. The following passage criticizing psychiatry represents this position well:

> The nominal aim of psychiatry is the study and treatment of mental disorders. But what are mental disorders? To accept the existence of a class of phenomena called "mental disorders," rather than to inquire into the conditions under which some persons may designate others as "mentally ill," is the decisive step in the embracing of the mental-health ethic. If we take the dictionary definition of this discipline seriously, the study of a large part of human behavior is subtly transferred from ethics to psychiatry. For while the ethicist is supposedly concerned only with normal (moral) behavior, and the psychiatrist only with abnormal (emotionally disordered) behavior, the very distinction between the two rests on ethical grounds. In other words, the assertion that a person is mentally ill involves rendering a moral judgment about him. Moreover, because of the social consequences of such a judgment, both the "mental patient" and those who treat him as one become actors in a morality play, albeit one written in a medical-psychiatric jargon.[3]

As Szasz emphasizes, if mental health concerns the issue of morality, rather than the science of medicine, and, in fact, the way psychiatry is portrayed as a medical rather than moral profession itself creates an ethical problem, then we are also faced with an enormous obstacle in having to justify or carefully delineate our use of mental-health-inspired language in thinking about social reality. For the medicalization of social phenomena (as in the presupposition of mental-health issues behind moral deviance) encompasses both the metaphoric use of medical language and the actual application of diagnostic language to sociocultural phenomena, and separating the two becomes, at times, impossible. Yet these need to remain separate, insofar as morality is an individual commitment or position that is formed in relation to sociohistorical change, as opposed to medical science (including neuroscience), which purports itself to be universally scientific. There is no easy way out.

One good example of this conundrum can be seen in the way the term "suffering" is used. As stated, suffering, along with pain, has come to earn the status of common currency in certain circles of anthropologists, especially those who are inspired by medicine. While terms such as *suffering* and *pain* are not necessarily or exclusively medical terms, their diagnostic implication does not escape the reader. Furthermore, as can be seen in the following passage by Arthur Kleinman and Joan Kleinman, the authors' proclivity to use, depend on, or refer to illnesses and health-related issues when discussing a social phenomenon does much disservice. Let us see:

> We can speak of suffering as a social experience in at least two ways [. . .] 1) Collective modes of experience shape individual perceptions and expressions. Those collective modes are visible patterns of how to undergo troubles, and they are taught and learned, sometimes openly, often indirectly. 2) Social interactions enter into an illness experience (for example, a family dealing with the dementia of a member with Alzheimer's disease or a close network grieving for a member with terminal cancer). As these examples suggest relationships and interactions take part, sometimes a central part, in the experience of suffering.[4]

The authors are referring to media representations of pain and suffering. Read carefully: there are some inconsistencies. First of all, what do they mean by "collective experience"? How is an experience experienced collectively? Second, they state that social interactions "enter into an illness experience"; but social interactions indeed enter into almost any experience, since almost any experience, and not just an illness experience (whatever that may be), is socially created. Yet, at the same time, the person experiencing these experiences is an individual. And, going back to "collective experience," how is this different from or similar to "social experience," since society and collectivity are not exactly the same? Above all, what is "an illness experience"? Is this an experience of oneself being ill or of caring for the ill, being cared for in relation to one's illness or dealing with an illness as an object to understand? The authors then suggest that "relationships and interactions take part" in the "experience of suffering." But is there any suffering that is not social? Yet, at the same time, is there any suffering that is not individually experienced? The trajectory shifts rapidly, it seems: it is first a collective experience; then an illness experience; and, finally, the experience of suffering. Are all illnesses suffering? If so, in what way? Is a broken bone an example of suffering or, perhaps, losing one's child through illness? Is poverty or a lack of education suffering, or is having an incompetent national leader a kind of suffering? What is suffering, and how far, collectively that is, does it stretch? The Kleinmans' passage simply raises more questions, for their use of illness references is conflated—not paralleled or analogically juxtaposed—with social and cultural phenomena.

What I want to problematize in the above passage is, moreover, the morality of pain and suffering. Applying Szasz's words here, we may state that the distinction between suffering and nonsuffering is an ethical one. To some, recognizing oneself as suffering might be tantamount to admitting a moral defeat. To others, such recognition might be considered a form of spiritual salvation. To yet others, suffering may be a necessary precursor for achieving a higher goal and, as such, may pertain to the realm of the good. As long as the experience is a phenomenon that involves the individual's personal emotions, dedication, values, ideology, or vision, to which he or she is personally susceptible and for which he or she is personally responsible—which are, in effect, sociohistorically configured—then the distinction between suffering and nonsuffering "rests on ethical grounds."

While it is true that, as the Kleinmans assert, suffering is socially created and socially experienced, this does not cancel out the fact that the identification of suffering involves a moral-ethical judgment. One only needs to think about the fact that colonization is a benefit when seen from the colonizer's point of view, while it creates suffering when seen from the perspective of the colonized people. If so, how is it that the Kleinmans (and like-minded others) are able to present it as if it were a universally diagnosed consequence of social phenomena? While the legitimacy of studying pain and suffering as experience or representation is unquestionable, the legitimacy of guarding against medicalization or the overarching deployment of psychosomatic discourse as the key to understanding social phenomena is equally unquestionable.

If we remember how effective and captivating the discourse of eugenics was, and still is, in creating a structure where those deemed to be physically inferior, of feeble nerves, or mentally impaired and impure (seen from the authorities' point of view) are rejected, discriminated against, and exterminated, often on the basis of their *moral* inferiority, this admonition should be self-evident. Moreover, the implementation of radical eugenics policy, according to which certain people are selected as fit and superior and certain others as unhealthy and inferior, does not require the actual existence of extensive, precise, and tested medico-scientific knowledge, as can be seen in the recent histories of nations such as Japan, Germany, and the U.S. It is, rather, the use of the body of medico-scientific discourse and the resulting elevation and privileging of science that I am problematizing here.

According to Szasz, psychiatry ultimately promotes conformism: in totalitarian societies as well as in our own, if an individual, who has otherwise caused no harm to others, is seen as having different (or deviant) inclinations, he or she is segregated from the rest of the society and institutionalized, in order to be rehabilitated.[5] Seeing suffering everywhere in the world and being compassionate is one thing, and such an inclination is a moral-ethical one; while trying to establish a social scientific theory of suffering is quite another. This is because such an endeavor inherently contains the potential or aspiration of turning everyone into a suffering being, akin to what psychiatry attempts to do, that is to say, of turning everyone into a pathological being, in conformity with what modern scientific society sees as psychologically normal, which is, in its turn, constantly replaced with the morally normal. In this scheme, if one did not feel pain on hearing certain news, one would be having an emotional disorder; if one did not suffer with others (such as in the Kleinmans' "social" suffering), one would be suffering a mental problem and require psychiatric intervention. But—and I reiterate, following Szasz—these are not to be confused with each other; the overuse of medically inspired, psychosomatic language or a mental-health-oriented approach in social scientific research makes it all too easy for this confusion to happen. Furthermore, due to the socially accepted and enhanced (moral) authority of medicine in general, especially in the U.S., this confusion goes more often than not undetected.

In this framework, labeling violence as an epidemic or a public health problem can be misleading, since such an identification would call for solutions using health-oriented forms of intervention or the use of drugs, for example, as opposed to juridical, governmental, educational, and moral reforms, for example. Similarly, focusing only on a husband's alcoholism as pathology (calling it a disease and a disease only) would leave intact domestic gender relations, in addition to a situation where the powerless suffer from exploitation, yet lack societal protection. Of course, there are numerous cases where, due to the authorities' refusal to grant recognition of damage and disorder, individuals have not been fully compensated or given proper treatments (either medical or social), such as in cases of war veterans suffering from posttraumatic stress disorder or soldiers suffering from secondary radiation as a result of nuclear explosive experiments. Such cases obviously require an emphatic use of medical references for substantiation of damage and injuries. And there are the opposite cases as well, where the authorities' "one-size-fits-all" labeling of certain racial groups or immigrant populations under disease names results in augmenting racial and ethnic prejudices, ultimately leading to the possibility of persecution or even extermination of these groups. Such practices need to be monitored and criticized. It should be clear to the reader that I am not denying the value of medical research per se—I am merely disputing the approach adopted by social-scientific studies that excessively rely on the authority of medical discourse, since such a tendency comes with a cost when studying diaspora, as we shall see below.

DIASPORA AND MENTAL HEALTH

How does the foregoing detour help us think about diaspora? The concept or ethos of collective suffering is routinely envisioned in studies of diaspora. Longing for the homeland, a sense of eternal banishment, and ongoing wandering throughout the world are often captured as factors weighing upon one's self, consciousness, and psychic health. Histories of persecution, such as the pogrom of Alexandria in 68 C.E., or the Great Kanto Earthquake massacre of Koreans by the Japanese in 1923, all seem to encapsulate the reality of suffering—collective suffering, that is, according to the Kleinmans. How about the Armenian genocide in Turkey? The mass rape, burning, and massacre of Chinese Catholics in Indonesia? The mass slave trade out of Africa to Europe and to North and South America? In these instances, lives were taken as not being human, or at least not equivalent to those of the killers, but as something else, or as "killable" lives. Such cases of persecution mark diasporic outsiders as, say, unmarkable: a sacrificial animal is markable, in that it has a position in the ritual; unsacrificeable lives are not markable, because of their having no position in the ritual order. Compounded with the nation-state-centered view of humanity, as emphasized by Arendt, which emerged distinctly and became consolidated during the twentieth century, today, stateless, nationless diasporic peoples constitute unmarkable lives, for they are placed outside the existing, nation-state-centered international order. Does this make them vulnerable? Yes, it does. But, does this cause them to experience suffering, pain, or unique forms of illness?

There seems to be uncertainty, or a lack of clarity, within the vague and unexplained assumption of the collective suffering of diaspora, which corresponds with the frustration that the Kleinmans' above-quoted passage elicits in us. In both cases, the premise is that suffering needs attending to, collectively and socially, and that, furthermore, suffering, pain, and illnesses are out there, existent for us all. In the Kleinmans' passage, tautologously, suffering is supposed to be a social and collectively experienced phenomenon, and, therefore, social interactions and relationships are accorded a central place in suffering. In the presupposition of the collective suffering of diaspora, the original persecutory history is told and retold so as to become ingrained in the consciousness, affecting the formation of self and the identity of individuals in the group. In this way, the story of collective suffering is recycled as something that individuals inherit, and as something that individuals are supposed to recycle again inside the collectivity. Here, remotely but concretely, the tale of suffering provides a point of legitimation or identity for a certain social group.

Does this not point to the fact that what we call *suffering* here is redeemable, due precisely to its social identity and acceptability? In other words, this suffering is registered as *human* experience. The experience of one who has been dehumanized, on the other hand, has lost all social qualities and connections. Reflecting on Primo Levi's and other survivors' writings on dehumanized inmates, called the *muselmann*, in Auschwitz, Giorgio Agamben depicts the extreme situation in which a human could lose the last streak of self-esteem and dignity, the moment, that is, that turns the human into a nonalive, nondead being—due to his loss of will to live, his recognition of his own death becomes nullified.[6] Does a muselmann suffer from anything? Perhaps not, as he has lost all the attributes of social existence. In this picture, paradoxically, the extreme suffering in fact eliminates suffering. Here, we see clearly that when reflecting on a total dehumanization, references to pain or suffering simply fail our comprehension.

Writing critically on the currently existing conceptions of diaspora among the Jewish people, Erich Gruen notes two trends of envisionment: grim and gloomy on one hand, and advantageous on the other. For the sake of brevity, I shall refer to the first as the *curse* and the second as the *virtue*. In his study of the Jews in ancient Greece and Rome, Gruen writes, "The destruction of the [Second] Temple in 70 CE, of course, constitutes a principal watershed for the Jews of antiquity. Both of the analyses mentioned above [of the two diverging trends] apply primarily as constructs to comprehend *Jewish mentality in the generations, even centuries,* after that cataclysmic event."[7] If the first trend—deeming the diaspora to be a curse—was to endlessly visit and revisit the loss of the center, the dispersion that ensued, and the banishment far exceeding death in terms of penalty, then the second trend—deeming the diaspora to be a virtue—stems from the attitude regarding the Jewish origin or center as ubiquitous, regarding the Jews as "the people of the Book." This latter is slightly different from George Steiner's notion, which I mentioned in the introduction, of seeing the sacred papyri in Jerusalem as the Jewish origin, since in Steiner's view, the sacred text is immovably housed in Jerusalem, while in Gruen's interpretation, "the people of the Book" can find the sacred book in their mind—that is, their home is portable: "Diaspora [in this view] is no burden, indeed a virtue in the spread of the word. This justifies a primary attachment to the land of one's residence, rather than the home of the fathers."[8]

In the second view, diaspora is hard to associate with suffering or pain. But as Gruen renounces: "In modern interpretations, a dark picture prevails. Diaspora is something to be *overcome.*"[9] Something to be overcome—something that makes one weak, sick, poor, barren, and unhappy, for example. And only in the event that it has been overcome will one be strong, healthy, rich, fertile, and happy again. But how does one *overcome* diaspora? Or is it really something that needs to be overcome? The assumption that diaspora is something to be overcome, however, is readily visible. For example, James Clifford, arguing against limiting the application of the notion of diaspora to the classical Jewish case, points to the plural and discursive dimensions of diasporas. According to him, diaspora as a cultural form or discourse cannot remain fully and exclusively nationalist, no matter how much emphasis is sustained on ethnic purity. In other words, although diasporas are definitely the product of nation-state norms, the return to the mother nation or the creation of the group's own nation does not solve the dilemma of diasporas. But even Clifford acknowledges that: "Peoples whose sense of identity is centrally defined by collective histories of displacement and violent loss cannot be 'cured' by merging into a new national community,"[10] that is to say, diaspora is something that needs to be cured.

In a great number of cases, authors of research into immigrant illness find their *raison d'être* in the assumption that the experience of displacement must yield mental and physical health issues. This is not to discredit such research, but simply to attend to the premise that it stands on. For it is notable that in many examples of such research, the goals are preset, looking to see how the already established assumption that immigrants suffer from a higher occurrence of mental-health concerns can be reendorsed.[11] While their findings do not always agree with each other, their points of departure rest on a set of factors that they deem to be legitimately causing problems. These include the experience of cultural change, acculturation, language barriers, homesickness, alienation, and so forth—in a word, the consequences of diasporic existence. Refugee health bears even clearer witness. Let us read: "By definition, refugees have traumatic pre-migration and pre-settlement histories, and it is widely assumed that their experiences jeopardize mental health."[12] I do not doubt that these issues exist; I merely wish to emphasize that population categories such as "refugee" and "immigrant" are used in reference to bounded groups of bodies whose mental and physical health are already supposed to be at jeopardy and in grave danger of worsening.

A similar trend is found in the case studies of the Korean diasporic population in the U.S. We are told in recent studies that relatively higher incidences of mental-health concerns are reported among Korean American youth in comparison to Chinese and Japanese American youth groups; Korean American male college students' decrease in self-esteem and depression are associated with the difficulty of maintaining their cultural values; the problems of acculturation are closely related to manifestation of depressive symptoms among a total of 230 Korean American older adults in Florida; Korean immigrants require special attention in the area of mental-health care, due to their cultural beliefs and attitudes toward mental-health problems; immigrant children, including Korean-speaking children, are exposed to more violence and depression, and more frequently to cases of posttraumatic stress disorder; and self-expression of "depressed elderly Korean immigrants" is influenced by linguistic and "psycho-socio-cultural factors."[13] The authors of these studies come from a diverse range of disciplinary fields, including nursing, psychiatry, psychology, geriatrics, gerontology, public health, education, and social work. In many of these studies, a population group called "Korean Americans" is preselected to form the body from which data can be extracted or even expected. In some of the studies in depression among Korean Americans, the subjects are already labeled as "depressed" to begin with. In other words, the diagnosis of medical authorities precedes the research, the primary goal of which is to reconfirm and reendorse the existing medical verdict. How does this help us understand diaspora and the way it is currently studied in the United States?

It is here that I wish to draw on the concept of "the ecological niche" as deployed by Ian Hacking in his lectures on a form of transient mental illness that became widespread in France and Germany for a time during the nineteenth century, which is referred to as the *fugue* or "mad travel" (fuguers being understood to be "mad travelers"). The fugue is a mental illness that causes the sufferer to have to depart, be gone for a substantial duration of time, then come back, and repeat the entire process again and again against his will.[14] Hacking suggests an interesting answer to the riddle by asking questions such as these: why only in France and Germany, why more in Bordeaux than elsewhere in France, and why men? Cases of the fugue at the time were first and mainly recognized among this population—male residents of Bordeaux—but with one more characteristic, that of being either a draftee or a voluntarily enlisted soldier. They were not poor and neither were they vagabonds; they often had respectable jobs. When their fit for traveling started, they would cry, because they did not want to leave, yet their entire existence—body and mind—forced them to leave and keep leaving, beyond the town border, provincial border, and national border, to unknown countries, witnessing fascinating events and changes in their contemporaneous world.

Hacking suggests many possible explanations for the emergence (and eventual disappearance) of this illness. First, the reason that cases of the fugue were found in France and Germany but not in England was related to the institution of conscription in the former two countries, as opposed to in England. Fuguers may have been, therefore, in fact, deserters rather than mental patients. He also finds that, in some cases, childhood head injuries had been recorded, but that no serious attempt had been made to follow up by monitoring the condition of these individuals and treating any further complications. Furthermore, Hacking notes emphatically that it was the era of the beginning of large-scale continental tourism, and does not fail to draw the reader's attention to the boredom and stagnation of life in Bordeaux as a region. The fact that fuguers related their tales of great marvels during their travels to other countries only under hypnosis is another factor that Hacking notes as a sign of its status as a pathologically sustainable mental illness of the time. This is because hypnosis was a new method of treatment developed at the time, and it is important to consider the likely eagerness of medical practitioners to experiment with its application. Coincidences between multiple factors thus created what Hacking calls "the ecological niche" for the diagnosis of fugue to be born.

With this in mind, when we turn our eyes back to the ever-growing body of literature on immigration-related illnesses, especially that concerning mental illness (with a particular focus on depression), I wonder if we notice a parallel with the nineteenth-century ecological niche that produced the fugue: the ever-dominating and ever-expanding pharmaceutical intervention in relation to depression, with the pervasive availability and aggressive marketing of antidepressants continually invading our living rooms, may be playing a much larger role in creating an ecological niche for research on suffering, pain, and illness. Furthermore, the endless human flow (both legal and illegal, if you like) that challenges the twentieth-century ethos equating humanity and nationality (where, as in Arendt, only those who have nationality have humanity) may create a niche that enables researchers to assume that the denationalized cultural other, who is socially deviant and has a hard time conforming with the mainstream, must already carry or gradually develop mental illness. Is not such an assumption related to the birth and growth of immigrant cancers and diasporic depression?

Raising this type of question is relevant, considering that, although it is true today that more and more social scientists, especially medical anthropologists and public health studies practitioners, are writing about health and the healing of the community, it nevertheless remains the case that this endeavor has developed unevenly, prioritizing certain regions or areas of the globe while disregarding others. This is a problem that we are forced to acknowledge if, for example, we consider how difficult it has been, and continues to be, for the world to get hold of concrete information on the ongoing massacres in Darfur, due to the diversity of related interests, including those of multinational corporations and numerous nation-states. Some diseases are given urgent attention, while others are not, even though both can be equally detrimental and life-threatening. Similarly, certain diasporic groups are eagerly studied by medical researchers, while others are not, which itself reflects the uneven distribution of the ecological niche.

Am I, then, suggesting that immigration, refugeedom, and diaspora do not bring us pain? No, I am not. They do—they do so in the most insidious of ways, on an ongoing basis. The experience of being violently uprooted from home is a painful one—medically speaking or not—and undermines our abilities, strength, health, and wealth. What I hesitate to do, however, is establish a pre-supposed, unexamined, a priori correlation between certain forms of life (such as diaspora) and certain forms of mental illness (such as depression). For such an approach thwarts our critical thinking and turns us, as researchers, into parts of a larger machinery that, in the final analysis, benefits the global capital and its purveyors in various guises, including the ones clad in academic robes. Diaspora, precisely, is a form of life that resists global capital. Diaspora carries an ontology of nonfixture, incorrigibility, and antisedentalization. With more or less pain, with more or less trauma, with more or less suffering, diaspora can offer a form of life that is livable, manageable, and perhaps even healthy.

In the family sagas of Jacey and Ryjung, there is no self-reference related to being depressed or sad; neither, by way of contrast, is there any self-reference related to being overcompensatively positive about life because of the multiple cross-border displacements of their families. But, as can be seen in the constant meandering in the self-inquiry of both women, the dominant (host) society usually pressurizes members of the diasporic population into questioning themselves as to who they are, who they want to be, who they should be, why they cannot be like others, and why they cannot settle in one place and identify themselves in a singular manner (i.e. as American, rather than Asian American). School discipline (as in ESL classes) constantly shapes the consciousness that if one cannot do that, that is, if one cannot become like other Americans, then one is a failure, not right, and maybe ill.

As Korean Americans growing up in the U.S., Jacey, Ryjung, and their cohorts are the objects of surveys, interviews, and monitoring with regard to exposure to violence, acculturation stress, or depression, among other culprits of mental illness. Their parents and their cohorts, as the first generation of immigrants to the U.S., are subjected to the same types of studies. And their children will be monitored, surveyed, and studied in order to measure the degree of acculturation (conformity) or the lack thereof (deviance). Their diasporic life itself has been, and continues to be, one characterized by a hesitation to succumb to a singular identity, as Jacey and Ryjung both declare, that will continue to manifest itself until they become at home with their multiple identities. Medicalized labeling does not allow for such an option.

Jacey, Ryjung, and many others are part of the global dispersion of Koreans. As such, their family maps of diaspora, marking multiple stops and sojourns, some long and others short, some stable and others unsettling, cannot be depicted according to the cartographic conventions of regular mapmaking. The history that the two families share, a history of colonialism, the Korean War and the mass human flows that accompanied it, and the multiple border-crossings that followed, is not simply the history of the end of one chapter; it is also the history of a new beginning. Their equally multiple displacements and relocations—from the north to the south, then to the other south and to the other north, and from the east to the west and back and forth again and again—together constitute a form of life at large, not a cause of some autochthonous mental illness. Calling this form of life "social suffering," it seems, would be to belittle its complexity and potential, while also undermining individual resilience; calling it "trauma" would be forcing Jacey, Ryjung, and others like them to act as patients, or victims, subjecting them to healing and recovery and thereby discrediting their words until their completion of treatment or rehabilitation. Furthermore, in light of Szasz's words, if psychiatry involves moral values, pathologizing the other (diasporic or otherwise) is itself a moral act.

Terra incognita. An unknown land, a land that one does not know, a land that one will never know. Diasporic families travel from one such land to another. Before getting to know one land, they move to another unknown territory. Before learning the language of that land, and before their words have ceased sounding like strangers' babbling to native ears, they move on to expose themselves to a new language. Whether this form of life is a blessing or a curse, a form of doomed madness or a fortuitous advantage, a source of misery resulting from the loss of one's only home or a source of freedom gained from the acquisition of multiple homes, still awaits verification.

NOTES

1. Arthur H. Robinson, "Geography and Cartography Then and Now," *Annals of the Association of American Geographers* 69, no. 1 (1979): 97.

2. Nancy Scheper-Hughes and Margaret Lock, "Speaking 'Truth' to Illness: Metaphors, Reification, and a Pedagogy for Patients," *Medical Anthropology Quarterly* 17, no. 5 (1986): 137–38.

3. Thomas Szasz, *Ideology and Insanity: Essays on the Psychiatric Dehumanization of Man* (Syracuse, NY: Syracuse University Press, 1991), 26.

4. Arthur Kleinman and Joan Kleinman, "An Appeal of Experience; The Dismay of Images: Cultural Appropriations of Suffering in Our Times," in *Social Suffering*, ed. A. Kleinman, V. Das, and M. Lock (Berkeley: University of California Press, 1997), 2.

5. Szasz (1991: 28–30).

6. Giorgio Agamben, *Remnants of Auschwitz: The Witness and the Archive* (New York: Zone Books, 1999), chap. 2.

7. Erich Gruen, *Jews amidst Greeks and Romans* (Cambridge, MA: Harvard University Press, 2002), 232–33, emphasis added.

8. Gruen (2002: 232).

9. Gruen (2002: 233), emphasis in the original.

10. James Clifford, "Diasporas," in *Routes: Travel and Translation in the Late Twentieth Century* (Cambridge, MA: Harvard University Press, 1997), 250.

11. See, for example, Ortega et al. (2006) and Hickling (2005), to cite only two.

12. Morton Beiser, Laura Simich, and Nalini Pandalangat, "Community in Distress: Mental Health Needs and Help-Seeking in the Tamil Community in Toronto," *International Migration* 41, no. 5 (2003): 233.

13. Yeh (2003); Hovey, Kim, and Seligman (2006); Mui and Kang (2006); Jang, Kim, and Chiriboga (2005); Kim et al. (2002); Jaycox et al. (2002); Pang (1998: 93)

14. See Ian Hacking, *Mad Travellers: Reflections on the Reality of Transient Mental Illnesses* (London: Free Association Books, 1998).

References

Abelmann, Nancy (2003). *The Melodrama of Mobility: Women, Talk, and Class in Contemporary South Korea*. Honolulu: University of Hawaii Press.

Abelmann, Nancy, and Lie, John (1995). *Blue Dreams: Korean Americans and the Los Angeles Riots*. Cambridge, MA: Harvard University Press.

Abu-Lughod, Lila (1986). *Veiled Sentiments: Honor and Poetry in a Bedouin Society* Berkeley: University of California Press.

Agamben, Giorgio (1995). *Homo Sacer: Sovereign Power and Bare Life*. Stanford, CA: Stanford University Press.

―― (1999). *Remnants of Auschwitz: The Witness and the Archive*. New York: Zone Books.

―― (2000). *Means without End: Notes on Politics*. Minneapolis: University of Minnesota Press.

―― (2005). *State of Exception*. Chicago: University of Chicago Press.

Ahearn, Laura (2001). *Invitations to Love: Literacy, Love Letters, and Social Change in Nepal*. Ann Arbor: University of Michigan Press.

Allison, Anne (2006). *Millennial Monsters: Japanese Toys and Global Imagination*. Berkeley: University of California Press.

Anderson, Linda (2001). *Autobiography*. London: Routledge.

Aoki, Atsuko (2005). "Kikokukigyō ni okeru 'nihonjinzuma' o megutte" ["Japanese wives" that were involved in the repatriation cause]." In T. Sōji and C. Pak (eds.), *Kikokuundō towa nandattanoka* [What was the repatriation movement?]. Tokyo Heibonsha.

Aoki, Eriko (2000). "Korean Children, Textbooks, and Educational Practices in Japanese Primary Schools." In S. Ryang (ed.), *Koreans in Japan: Critical Voices from the Margin*. London: Routledge.

―― (1958a). *The Origins of Totalitarianism*. New York: Harcourt Brace.

―― (1958b). *The Human Condition*. Chicago: University of Chicago Press.

―― (1993). *Men in Dark Times*. New York: Harcourt Brace.

—— (2000). *The Portable Hannah Arendt*. New York: Penguin.

Arias, Arturo (2001). *The Rigoberta Menchú Controversy*. Minneapolis: University of Minnesota Press.

Barnouw, Victor (1963). *Culture and Personality*. Homewood, IL: Dorsey Press.

Bateson, Gregory, and Mead, Margaret (1942). *Balinese Character: A Photographic Analysis*. New York: New York Academy of Sciences.

Battaglia, Debbora, ed. (1995). *Rhetorics of Self-Making*. Berkeley: University of California Press.

Bauman, Zygmunt (2005). *Liquid Love*. Cambridge, England: Polity.

Behar, Ruth (1996). *The Vulnerable Observer*. Boston: Beacon Press.

Beiser, Morton, Simich, Laura, and Pandalangat, Nalini (2003). "Community in Distress: Mental Health Needs and Help-Seeking in the Tamil Community in Toronto," *International Migration* 41 (5): 233–45.

Benedict, Ruth (1934). *Patterns of Culture*. Boston: Houghton Mifflin.

—— (1946). *The Chrysanthemum and the Sword*. Boston: Houghton Mifflin.

Benjamin, A. E., Wallace, Steven, Villa, Valentine, and McCarthy, Kathy (2000). "California Immigrants Have Mostly Lower Rates of Disability and Use of Disability Services than State's US-Born Residents," *UCLA Center for Health Policy Research Policy Brief*, July 2000: 1–4.

Bernstein, Gail (1983). *Haruko's World: A Japanese Farm Woman and Her World*. Stanford, CA: Stanford University Press.

Bourdieu, Pierre (1990). *The Logic of Practice*. Cambridge, England: Polity Press.

—— (1991). *Language and Symbolic Power*. Cambridge, England: Polity Press.

Bruner, Jerome (1990). *Acts of Meaning*. Cambridge, MA: Harvard University Press.

Burgos-Debray, Elisabeth (1984). *I, Rigoberta Menchú: An Indian Woman in Guatemala*. London: Verso.

Byrom, Bradley (2004). "A Vision of Self Support: Disability and the Rehabilitation Movement in Progressive America." Ph.D. Dissertation, University of Iowa.

Campi, Alicia (2004). "The McCarran-Walter Act: A Contradictory Legacy on Race, Quotas, and Ideology," *Immigration Daily*, www.ilw.com/articles/2004,0708–Campi .shtm (accessed June 27, 2008).

Caprio, Mark, and Yu, Jia (forthcoming). "Occupations of Korea and Japan and the Origins of Korean Diaspora in Japan." In S. Ryang and J. Lie (eds.), *Diaspora without Homeland: Being Korean in Japan*. Berkeley: University of California Press.

Caudill, William (1961). "Around the Clock Patient Care in Japanese Psychiatric Hospitals: The Role of the Tsukisoi," *American Sociological Review* 26 (2): 204–14.

Caudill, William, and Doi, Takeo (1963). "Interrelations of Psychiatry, Culture and Emotion in Japan." In I. Galdston (ed.), *Man's Image in Medicine and Anthropology*. New York: International Universities Press.

Caudill, William, and Weinstein, Helen (1969). "Maternal Care and Infant Behavior in Japan and America," *Psychiatry* 32: 12–43.

Cavell, Stanley (1994). *A Pitch of Philosophy: Autobiographical Exercises*. Cambridge, MA: Harvard University Press.

Cha, Theresa Hak-Kyung (2001). *Dictee*. Berkeley: University of California Press.

Chan, Sucheng (1991). *Asian Americans: An Interpretive History*. Boston: Twayne.

Chang, Edward, and Leong, Russell, eds. (1994). *Los Angeles—Struggles Toward Multiethnic Community: Asian-American, African American, and Latino Perspectives*. Seattle: University of Washington Press.

Cheng, Ann Anlin (2001). *The Melancholy of Race: Psychoanalysis, Assimilation, and Hidden Grief*. New York: Oxford University Press.

Chodorow, Nancy (1978). *The Reproduction of Mothering*. Berkeley: University of California Press.

Choi, Chungmoo, ed. (1997). *The Comfort Women: Colonialism, War, and Sex, Positions*, special issue 5 (1), Spring 1997.

Chon, Wolson (2006). *Kaikyō no aria* [Aria over the strait]. Tokyo: Shōgakkan.

Chung, Erin (2000). "Korean Voluntary Associations in Japanese Civil Society," *JPRI Working Paper* No. 69, www.jpri.org/publications/workingpapers/wp69.html (accessed January 7, 2007).

—— (forthcoming). "The Politics of Contingent Citizenship: A Comparative Study of Korean Political Engagement in Japan and the United States." In S. Ryang and J. Lie (eds.), *Diaspora without Homeland: Being Korean in Japan*. Berkeley: University of California Press.

Clement, Grace (1996). *Care, Autonomy, and Justice: Feminism and the Ethic of Care*. Boulder, CO: Westview Press.

Clifford, James (1997). "Diasporas," in *Routes: Travel and Translation in the Late Twentieth Century*. Cambridge, MA: Harvard University Press.

Cole, David (2002). "Enemy Aliens and American Freedoms," *The Nation*, September 23, 2002, www.thenation.com/ (accessed February 21, 2006).

Constable, Nicole (2003). *Romance on a Global Stage: Pen Pals, Virtual Ethnography, and "Mail-Order" Marriages*. Berkeley: University of California Press.

Corker, Marian, and Shakespeare, Tom, eds. (2002). *Disability/Postmodernity: Embodying Disability Theory*. London: Continuum.

"Court Axes Tax Cuts for Chongryun Hall" (2006). *Japan Times*, February 3, 2006, search.japantimes.co.jp/print/nn20060203a2.html (accessed April 1, 2006).

Crapanzano, Vincent (1980). *Tuhami: A Portrait of a Moroccan*. Chicago: University of Chicago Press.

Cumings, Bruce (1980). *The Origins of the Korean War*, vol. 1. Princeton, NJ: Princeton University Press.

Dissanayake, Wimal, ed. (1996). *Narratives of Agency: Self-Making in China, India, and Japan*. Minneapolis: University of Minnesota Press.

Doi, Takeo (1962). "*Amae:* A Key Concept for Understanding Japanese Personality Structure." In R. Smith and R. Beardsley (eds.), *Japanese Culture: Its Development and Characteristics*. Chicago: Aldine.

—— (1973). *The Anatomy of Dependence*. Tokyo: Kodansha International.

—— (1988). *The Anatomy of Self*. Tokyo: Kodansha International.

Eakin, Paul J. (1999). *How Our Lives Become Stories: Making Selves*. Ithaca, NY: Cornell University Press.

Field, Norma (1993). "Beyond Envy, Boredom, and Suffering: Towards an Emancipatory Politics for Resident Koreans and Other Japanese," *Positions* 1 (3): 640–70.

Fisher, Helen (1992). *The Anatomy of Love: A Natural History of Mating, Marriage, and Why We Stray*. New York: Fawcett Columbine.

Fivush, R. (1988). "The Functions of Event Memory: Some Comments on Nelson and Barsalou." In U. Neisser and E. Winograd (eds.), *Remembering Reconsidered: Ecological and Traditional Approaches to the Study of Memory*. New York: Cambridge University Press.

Fivush, R., and Reese, E. (1992). "The Social Construction of Autobiographical Memory." In M. Conway, D. Rubin, H. Spinnler, and W. Wagenaar (eds.), *Theoretical Perspectives on Autobiographical Memory*. Dordrecht, Netherlands: Kluwer Academic.

Flaherty, Alice W. (2004). *The Midnight Disease: The Drive to Write, Writer's Block, and the Creative Brain*. Boston: Houghton Mifflin.

Foucault, Michel (1977). *The History of Sexuality*, vol. 1. Harmondsworth, England: Penguin.

Frank, Anne (1995). *The Diary of A Young Girl: The Definitive Edition*. New York: Doubleday.

Freud, Sigmund (1963). *Sexuality and the Psychology of Love*. New York: Touchstone.

Fromm, Erich (1956). *The Art of Loving: An Enquiry into the Nature of Love*. New York: Harper and Row.

Fujii, Kōnosuke (1980). "Kaihōgo nihon ni okeru chōsenjin gakkō no kokugo kyōkasho" [Korean textbooks in Korean schools in Japan after the liberation], *Zainichi Chōsenjinshi Kenkyū*, June 1980, 84–109.

Gaylin, Willard, and Person, Ethel, eds. (1988). *Passionate Attachments: Thinking about Love*. New York: Free Press.

Giddens, Anthony (1991). *Modernity and Self-Identity: Self and Society in the Late Modern Age*. Stanford, CA: Stanford University Press.

―――― (1992). *Transformation of Intimacy: Sexuality, Love and Eroticism in Modern Societies*. Cambridge, England: Polity.

Gilligan, Carol (1982). *In a Different Voice: Psychological Theory and Women's Development*. Cambridge, MA: Harvard University Press.

―――― (1986). "Remapping the Moral Domain: New Images of the Self in Relationship." In T. Heller et al. (eds.), *Reconstructing Individualism: Autonomy, Individuality, and the Self in Western Thought*. Stanford: Stanford University Press.

―――― (1987) "Moral Orientation and Moral Development," In E. Kittay and D. Meyers (eds.), *Woman and Moral Theory*. Lanham, MD: Rowman and Littlefield.

Gjerde, Per, and Onishi, M. (2000). "Selves, Cultures, and Nations: 'The Japanese' in the Era of Globalization," *Human Development* 43: 216–26.

Goffman, Erving (1962). *Asylums: Essays on the Social Situation of Mental Patients and Other Inmates*. Chicago: Aldine.

Goody, Jack (1998). "Love, Lust and Literacy." In *Food and Love: A Cultural History of East and West*. London: Verso.

Gorer, Geoffrey (1942). *Japanese Character Structure and Propaganda*. New Haven, CT: Institute of Human Relations, Yale University.

―――― (1948). *The American People: A Study in National Character*. New York: Norton.

―――― (1967). "English Character in the Twentieth Century," *Annals of the American Academy of Political and Social Science: National Character in the Perspective of the Social Sciences* 370: 74–81.

The Governor's Developmental Disabilities Council, Iowa (2003). *State Plan FFY 03*, www.state.ia.us/government/ddcouncil/state_plan.html (accessed April 24, 2007).

Gruen, Erich (2002). *Jews amidst Greeks and Romans*. Cambridge, MA: Harvard University Press.

Hacking, Ian (1998). *Mad Travellers: Reflections on the Reality of Transient Mental Illnesses*. London: Free Association Books.

Haring, David, ed. (1956). *Personal Character and Cultural Milieu*. Syracuse, NY: Syracuse University Press.

Harvey, David (2005). *A Brief History of Neoliberalism*. Oxford: Oxford University Press.

Hayes, Carol (2000). "Cultural Identity in the Work of Yi Yang-ji." In S. Ryang (ed.), *Koreans in Japan: Critical Voices from the Margin*. London: Routledge.

Held, Virginia, ed. (1995). *Justice and Care: Essential Readings in Feminist Ethics*. Boulder, CO: Westview Press.

Held, Virginia (2006). *The Ethics of Care: Personal, Political, and Global*. Oxford: Oxford University Press.

Hickling, Frederick (2005). "The Epidemiology of Schizophrenia and Other Common Mental Health Disorders in the English-Speaking Caribbean," *Pan American Journal of Public Health* 18 (4–5): 256–62.

Hinton, Leanne (1999). *Involuntary Language Loss among Immigrants: Asian-American Autobiographies* (SuDoc ED 1.310/2:436982). Washington, DC: ERIC Clearinghouse on Language and Linguistics.

Hiroyama, Shibaaki (1955). "Minsen no kaisan to chōsensōren no keisei ni tsuite" [On the dissolution of Minjeon and the emergence of Chongryun], *Kōanjōhō* 22: 5–11.

Hōmushō [Ministry of Justice, Japan] (1967). *Hōmunenkan* [Justice Ministry yearbook]. Tokyo: Hōmushō.

—— (1976). *Shutsunyūkoku kanri—sono genkyō to kadai* (Immigration control: Current situation and future tasks). Tokyo: Hōmushō.

Hovey, Joseph, Kim, Sheena, and Seligman, Laura (2006). "The Influences of Cultural Values, Ethnic Identity, and Language Use on the Mental Health of Korean American College Students," *Journal of Psychology* 149 (5): 499–511.

Hsu, Frances L. K., ed. (1961). *Psychological Anthropology: Approaches to Culture and Personality*. Homewood, IL: Dorsey Press.

—— (1972). *Psychological Anthropology*. Cambridge, MA: Schenkman.

Hubert, Henri, and Mauss, Marcel (1964). *Sacrifice: Its Nature and Functions*. Chicago: University of Chicago Press.

Hudson, Mark (1999). *Ruins of Identity: Ethnogenesis in the Japanese Islands*. Honolulu: University of Hawaii Press.

Hur, Won Moo (1988). *The Korean Americans*, Westport, CT: Greenwood Press.

Hurston, Zora Neale (1984). *Dust Tracks on the Road*. Urbana: University of Illinois Press.

Illouz, Eva (1997). *Consuming the Romantic Utopia*. Berkeley: University of California Press.

Ingstad, Benedicte, and Whyte, Susan Reynolds, eds. (1995). *Disability and Culture*. Berkeley: University of California Press.

Inokuchi, Hiromitsu (2000). "Korean Ethnic Schools in Occupied Japan, 1945–52." In S. Ryang (ed.), *Koreans in Japan: Critical Voices from the Margin*. London: Routledge.

Inoue, Teruko, Ueno, Chizuko, and Ehara, Yumiko, eds. (2004). *Ribu to feminizumu* [Lib and feminism], *Nihon no feminizumu* [Feminism in Japan] vol. 1. Tokyo: Iwanami.

International Crisis Group (2005). "Japan and North Korea: Bones of Contention," *Asia Report* 100, June 27, 2005, www.crisisgroup.org/home/index.cfm?l=1&id=3533 (accessed February 14, 2006).

Israel, Nico (2000). *Outlandish: Writing between Exile and Diaspora*. Stanford, CA: Stanford University Press.

Iwamura, Toshio (1972). *Zainichi chōsenjin to nihon rōdōsha kaikyū* [Koreans in Japan and the Japanese working class]. Tokyo: Azekurashobō.

Jakobson, Roman (1968). *Child Language: Aphasia and Phonological Universals*. The Hague: Mouton.

—— (1971). *Studies on Child Language and Aphasia*. The Hague: Mouton.

Jakobson, Roman, with Santilli, Kathy (1980). *Brain and Language: Cerebral Hemispheres and Linguistic Structure in Mutual Light*. Columbus, OH: Slavica.

Jang, H., Kim, G., and Chiriboga, D. (2005). "Acculturation and Manifestation of Depressive Symptoms among Korean-American Older Adults," *Aging and Mental Health* 9 (6): 500–507.

Jankowiak, William, ed. (1995). *Romantic Passion: A Universal Experience?* New York: Columbia University Press.

Jankowiak, William, and Fischer, Edward (1992). "A Cross-Cultural Perspective on Romantic Love," *Ethnology* 31 (2): 149–55.

Jaycox, Lisa, Stein, Bradley, Kataoka, Sheryl, Wong, Marleen, Fink, Arlene, Escudero, Pia, and Zaragoza, Catalina (2002). "Violence Exposure, Posttraumatic Stress Disorder, and Depressive Symptoms among Recent Immigrant Schoolchildren," *Journal of American Academy of Child and Adolescent Psychiatry* 41 (9): 1104–10.

Jordan, Lesley, and Kaiser, Wendy (1996). *Aphasia: A Social Approach*. London: Chapman and Hall.

Kang, Chol-hwan (2002). *The Aquariums of Pyongyang: Ten Years in the North Korean Gulag*. New York: Basic Books.

Kashiwazaki, Chikako (2000). "The Politics of Legal Status: The Equation of Nationality with Ethnonational Identity." In S. Ryang (ed.), *Koreans in Japan: Critical Voices from the Margin*. London: Routledge.

Kelly, William, ed. (2004). *Fanning the Flames: Fans and Consumer Culture in Contemporary Japan*. Albany, NY: SUNY Press.

Kendall, Laurel (1996). *Getting Married in Korea*. Berkeley: University of California Press.

Khosa, Jasvinder (2003). "Still Life of a Chameleon: Aphasia and Its Impact on Identity." In S. Parr, J. Duchan, and C. Pound (eds.), *Aphasia Inside Out: Reflections on Communication Disability*. Maidenhead, England: Open University Press.

Kim, Chan-Jeong (1980). *Zoku boku mō gaman dekinaiyo–"ijimerarekko" no jisatsu sonogo* [I cannot stand it any longer–suicide of a "bullied kid" and afterwards]. Tokyo: Ikkōsha.

Kim, Elaine, and Yu, Eui-Young, eds. (1996). *East to America: Korean American Life Stories*. New York: New Press.

Kim, Mi Ja, Cho, Hyang-In, Cheon-Klessig, Young Sun, Gerace, Laina, and Camilleri, Dorothy (2002). "Primary Health Care for Korean Immigrants: Sustaining a Culturally Sensitive Model," *Public Health Nursing* 19 (3): 191–200.

Kim, Tae-gyu (2005). "New Individual Identification System Sought," *Korea Times*, February 24, 2005, search.hankooki.com/times/times_view.php?term=new+individual+identification+system+sought++&path=hankooki3/times/lpage/tech/20050 2/kt2005022420180211800.htm&media=kt (accessed February 14, 2006).

Kim, Yeong-Dal (1989). *GHQ Bunsho kenkyū gaido: zainichi chōsenjin kyōiku mondai* [A research guide for documents on Korean ethnic education in Japan issued by the General Headquarters for Allied Occupation]. Kobe, Japan: Mukugeshobō.

—— (1996). "Hoshō: kaisetsu to tōkei no hosoku" [Supplement: Explanation and supplementation of statistics]. In Y. Morita, *Sūji ga kataru zainichi kankoku chōsenjin no rekishi* [History of Koreans in Japan seen from statistics]. Tokyo: Akashishoten.

Kitayama, Shinobu, Markus, Hazel, and Kurokawa, M. (2000). "Culture, Emotion, and Well-Being: Good Feelings in Japan and the United States," *Cognition and Emotion* 14 (1): 93–124.

Kitayama, Shinobu, Markus, Hazel, and Lieberman, C. (1995). "The Collective Construction of Self Esteem: Implications for Culture, Self, and Emotion." In J. A. Russell et al. (eds.), *Everyday Conceptions of Emotion: An Introduction to the Psychology, Anthropology and Linguistics of Emotion*. Leiden, Netherlands: Brill.

Kitayama, Shinobu, Markus, Hazel, Matsumoto, H., and Morasakkunkit, V. (1997). "Individual and Collective Processes in the Construction of the Self: Self-Enhancement in the United States and Self-Criticism in Japan," *Journal of Personality and Social Psychology* 72 (6): 1245–67.

Kittay, Eva Feder (1999). *Love's Labor: Essays on Women, Equality, and Dependency*. New York: Routledge.

Kleinman, Arthur, and Kleinman, Joan (1997). "An Appeal of Experience; The Dismay of Images: Cultural Appropriations of Suffering in Our Times." In A. Kleinman, V. Das, and M. Lock (eds.), *Social Suffering*. Berkeley: University of California Press.

Koh, Sun Hui (2001). "Two Japanese Treatments of Japan's Ethnic Korean Community," *Social Science Japan Journal* 4 (2): 275–79.

Kohlberg, Lawrence (1969). "Stage and Sequence: The Cognitive Developmental Approach to Socialization." In D. A. Goslin (ed.), *Handbook of Socialization Theory and Research*. Chicago: Rand McNally.

Kokot, Waltraud, Tölölyan, Khachig, and Alfonso, Carolin, eds. (2004). *Diaspora, Identity, and Religion: New Directions in Theory and Research*. London: Routledge.

Kondo, Dorinne (1985). "Gender, Self and Work in Japan: Some Issues in the Study of Self and Other," *Culture, Medicine and Psychiatry* 9: 319–28.

—— (1990). *Crafting Selves: Power, Gender, and Discourses of Identity in a Japanese Workplace*. Chicago: University of Chicago Press.

Koshiro, Yukiko (1999). *Trans-Pacific Racisms and the U.S. Occupation of Japan*. New York: Columbia University Press.

Kuper, Adam (1988). *The Invention of Primitive Society: Transformation of an Illusion*. London: Routledge.

Kusserow, Audrey (1999). "Crossing the Great Divide: Anthropological Theories of the Western Self," *Journal of Anthropological Research* 55: 541–63.

Kwon, Tai-Hwan (1997). "International Migration of Koreans and the Korean Community in China," *Korean Journal of Population and Development* 26 (1): 1–18.

Lebra, Takie (1973). "Compensative Justice and Moral Investment among Japanese, Chinese and Koreans," *Journal of Nervous and Mental Disease* 157 (4): 278–91.

—— (1976). *Japanese Patterns of Behavior*. Honolulu: University of Hawaii Press.

—— (1983). "Shame and Guilt: A Psychocultural View of Japanese Self," *Ethos* 11 (3): 192–209.

Lee, Sandra Soo-Jin (2000). "Dys-appearing Tongues and Bodily Memories: The Aging of First-Generation Resident Koreans in Japan," *Ethos* 28 (2): 198–223.

Lee, Yangji (1989a). "Yuhi," in *Yuhi*. Tokyo: Kōdansha.

Lee, Yangji (1989b). "Aoiro no kaze" [Blue breeze], in *Yuhi*. Tokyo: Kōdansha.

Lewis, C. S. (1960). *The Four Loves*. New York: Harcourt Brace.

Lie, John (1998). *Han Unbound: The Political Economy of South Korea*. Stanford, CA: Stanford University Press.

Liebowitz, Michael (1983). *The Chemistry of Love*. Boston: Little, Brown.

Lim, Youngmi (forthcoming). "Reinventing *Zainichi* Korean Roots and Routes: Invisible Diaspora among Naturalized Japanese of Korean Descent," in *Diaspora without Homeland: Being Korean in Japan*, eds. S. Ryang and J. Lie. Berkeley: University of California Press.

Lindholm, Charles (1997). "Does the Sociocentric Self Exist? Reflections on Markus and Kitayama's 'Culture and the Self,'" *Journal of Anthropological Research* 53: 405–22.

—— (1998). "The Future of Love." In V. C. De Munck (ed.). *Romantic Love and Sexual Behavior: Perspectives from the Social Sciences*. Westport, CT: Praeger.

—— (2007). *Culture and Identity*. Oxford, England: Oneworld Publications.

Lock, Margaret, and Sheper-Hughes, Nancy (1987). "The Mindful Body," *Medical Anthropology Quarterly* 1: 6–41.

Longmore, Paul, and Umansky, Lauri, eds. (2000). *The New Disability History: American Perspectives*. New York: New York University Press.

Lowe, Lisa (1996). "Unfaithful to the Original: The Subject of *Dictee*," in *Immigrant Acts: On Asian American Cultural Politics*. Durham, NC: Duke University Press.

Macfarlane, Alan (1986). *Marriage and Love in England: Modes of Reproduction, 1300–1840*. Oxford, England: Blackwell.

Malinowski, Bronislaw (1926). *The Sexual Life of Savages*. Boston: Beacon Press.

Mandelbaum, D. (1953). "On the Study of National Character," *American Anthropologist* 44: 147–87.

Marcuse, Herbert (1966). *Eros and Civilization*. Boston: Beacon Press.

Markus, Hazel, and Kitayama, Shinobu, eds. (1994). *Emotion and Culture: Empirical Studies of Mutual Influence*. Washington, DC: American Psychological Association.

Martindale, David (1968). "Sociologie de la notion de caractère national," *Revue de psychologie de peuples* 223 (1): 62–69.

Mathews, Gordon (1996). *What Makes Life Worth Living? How Japanese and Americans Make Sense of Their Worlds*. Berkeley: University of California Press.

Matsubara, Hiroshi (2007a). "Korean Residents in Anguish: Nuclear Fallout," *Asahi.com*, January 2, 2007, www.asahi.com/ (accessed January 4, 2007).

—— (2007b). "Cover Story: Money Game," *Asahi.com*, January 3, 2007, /www.asahi.com (accessed February 22, 2007).

—— (2007c). "Korean Residents in Anguish: Broken Dreams," *Asahi.com*, January 4, 2007, www.asahi.com/ (accessed January 4, 2007).

Mauss, Marcel (1954). *The Gift: Forms and Functions of Exchange in Archaic Societies*. Glencoe, IL: Free Press.

McCormack, Gavan (2002). "North Korea in the Vice," *New Left Review* 18, www.newleftreview.net/ (accessed February 14, 2006).

—— (2005). "Disputed Bones Fracture Japan–North Korea Relations," *OhmyNews*, April 20, 2005, english.ohmynews.com/articleview/article_view.asp?menu=c10400&no=221670&rel_no=1 (accessed February 14, 2006).

—— (2006). "North Korea and the US 'Strategic Decision,'" *Japan Focus*, article 498, www.japanfocus.org/ (accessed February 14, 2006).

Mead, Margaret (1953a). *Coming of Age in Samoa: A Psychological Study of Primitive Youth for Western Civilization*. New York: Modern Library.

—— (1953b). "National Character." In A. Kroeber (ed.), *Anthropology Today: International Symposium on Anthropology*. Chicago: University of Chicago Press.

Mead, Margaret, and Metreaux, Rhoda, eds. (1953). *The Study of Culture at a Distance*. Chicago: University of Chicago Press.

Miller, Laura and Bardsley, Jan, eds. (2005). *Bad Girls of Japan*. New York: Palgrave.

Ministry of Health, Labor, and Welfare, Japan, (2004). "Abridged Life Tables," www.mhlw.go.jp/ (accessed December 15, 2006).

—— (2006a). "Kaigo kyūfu jittai chōsa geppō" [Monthly survey on care cost], August 2006, www.mhlw.go.jp/toukei/saikin/hw/kaigo/kyufu/2006/08.html (accessed December 15, 2006).

—— (2006b). "Dai 7 hyō Kaigo sābisu jukyūsha hitori atari hiyōgaku, yōkaigo jōtai kubun, sābisu shurui betsu" [Chart 7: Per capita cost for personal care service, relative to the degree of needs and services], August 2006, www.mhlw.go.jp/toukei/saikin/hw/kaigo/kyufu/2006/08hyo7.html (accessed December 15, 2006).

—— (2006c). "Dai 2 hyō Kaigo sābisu jukyūsha sū, yōkaigo jōtai kubun, sābisu shurui betsu" [Chart 2: Number of personal care service receivers, relative to the degree of needs and services], August 2006, www.mhlw.go.jp/toukei/saikin/hw/kaigo/kyufu/2006/08hyo2.html (accessed December 15, 2006).

Ministry of Justice, Japan (2004). "Registration of Foreign Residents," *Immigration Bureau*, www.moj.gov.jp/ (accessed March 1, 2007).

Mintz, Sidney ([1960] 1974). *Worker in the Cane: A Puerto Rican Life History*. New York: Norton.

Morita, Yoshio (1996). *Sūjiga kataru zainichi kankoku chōsenjin no rekishi* [History of Koreans in Japan seen from statistics]. Tokyo: Akashishoten.

—— (2007). *Exodus to North Korea: Shadows of Japan's Cold War*. Lanham, MD: Rowman and Littlefield.

—— (forthcoming). "Freedom and Homecoming: Narratives of Migration in the Repatriation of *Zainichi* Koreans to North Korea." In S. Ryang and J. Lie (eds.), *Diaspora without Homeland: Being Korean in Japan*. Berkeley: University of California Press.

Mui, Ada, and Kang, Suk-Young (2006). "Acculturation Stress and Depression among Asian Immigrant Elders," *Social Work* 51 (3): 243–55.

Nakamura, Karen (2006). *Deaf in Japan: Signing and the Politics of Identity*. Ithaca, NY: Cornell University Press.

Nakane, Chie (1970). *Japanese Society*. Berkeley: University of California Press.

Neiburg, F., and Goldman, M. (1998). "Anthropology and Politics in Studies of National Character," *Cultural Anthropology* 13 (1): 56–81.

Nelson, Katherine, ed. (1989). *Narratives from the Crib*. Cambridge, MA: Harvard University Press.

Nicholi, Armand, Jr. (2002). *The Question of God: C. S. Lewis and Sigmund Freud Debate God, Love, Sex, and the Meaning of Life*. New York: Free Press.

Nihon fujin dantai rengōkai, ed. (2004). *Joseihakusho 2004: sekai no nagare to nihon no josei* [White paper on women, 2004: Global trends and women in Japan]. Tokyo: Horupushuppan.

Noddings, Nel (1984). *Caring: A Feminist Approach to Ethics and Moral Education*. Berkeley: University of California Press.

"North Korea Claims Nuclear Test" (2006). *BBC News*, October 9, 2006, news.bbc.co.uk/2/hi/asia-pacific/6032525.stm (accessed November 22, 2006).

Nussbaum, Martha (2006). *Frontiers of Justice: Disability, Nationality, Species Membership*. Cambridge, MA: Harvard University Press.

Nygren, Anders (1953). *Agape and Eros*. London: SPCK Press.

O, Mun-Ja (2006). "Zainichi issei no kaigo mondai—haha o hōmu ni takushite" [The question of care for the first generation Koreans in Japan—after having left my mother in the nursing home], in *Zainichi josei bungaku: chi ni fune o koge*, vol. 1:107–23.

Ohnuki-Tierney, Emiko (1993). *Rice as Self: Japanese Identities through Time*. Princeton, NJ: Princeton University Press.

Okely, Judith (1996). *Own of Other Culture*. London: Routledge.

Okely, Judith, and Callaway, Helen, eds. (1992). *Anthropology and Autobiography*. London: Routledge.

Ong, Aihwa (1999). "Introduction," in *Flexible Citizenship: The Cultural Logics of Transnationality*. Durham, NC: Duke University Press.

—— (2006). *Neoliberalism as Exception: Mutations in Citizenship and Sovereignty*. Durham, NC: Duke University Press.

Onishi, Norimitsu (2007). "Abe Rejects Japan's Files on War Sex," *New York Times*, March 2, 2007, www.nytimes.com/2007/03/02/world/asia/02japan.html?ex=13304 91600&en=46b8ee3c003bb079&ei=5088&partner=rssnyt&emc=rss (accessed May 5, 2007).

Ōnuma, Yasuaki (1980). "Zainichi chōsenjin no hōteki chii ni kansuru ichi kōsatsu" [An examination of the legal status of Koreans in Japan], part 4, *Hōgaku kyōkai zasshi* 97 (2): 192–268.

Ortega, Alexander, Feldman, Jonathan, Canino, Glorisa, Stenman, Kenneth, and Alegría, Margarita (2006). "Co-occurrence of Mental and Physical Illness in US Latinos," *Social Psychiatry & Psychiatric Epidemiology* 41: 927–34.

Orwell, George (1983). *Nineteen Eighty-four, A Novel.* New York: New American Library.

Pak, Cheong-Gong (1969). *Ōmura shūyōjo* [The Ōmura camp]. Kyoto: Kyotodaigaku shuppankai.

Pak, Kyeong-Sik (1989). *Kaihōgo zainichi chōsenjin undōshi* [History of Korean movement in Japan: After the liberation]. Tokyo: Sanichishobō.

—— (1992). *Zainichi chōsenjin, kyōseirenkō, minzokumondai* [Koreans in Japan, forced labor mobilization, national questions]. Tokyo: Sanichishobō.

Pang, Keum Young Chung (1998). "Symptoms of Depression in Elderly Korean Immigrants: Narration and the Healing Process," *Culture, Medicine and Psychiatry* 22: 93–122.

Paradis, Michel, ed. (1995). *Aspects of Bilingual Aphasia.* New York: Pergamon.

Park, Hyun Ok (2003). *Two Dreams in One Bed: Empire, Social Life, and the Origins of the North Korean Revolution in Manchuria.* Durham, NC: Duke University Press.

Park, Soon Jo (1983). *Kankoku, Nihon, Ōmura shūyōjo* [Korea, Japan, the Ōmura camp]. Osaka: JDC.

Person, Ethel (1988). *Dreams of Love and Fateful Encounters.* New York: Penguin.

Piaget, Jean ([1932] 1997). *The Moral Judgment of the Child.* New York: Free Press.

Plath, David (1980). *Long Engagements: Maturity in Modern Japan.* Stanford, CA: Stanford University Press.

"Police Raid N. Korea-Related Facilities" (2007). *Asahi.com*, April 26, 2007, www.asahi.com/ (accessed May 8, 2007).

"Police Search Chongryun Affiliate over '80 Abduction" (2006). *Japan Times*, March 24, 2006, search.japantimes.co.jp/print/nn20060324a4.html (accessed April 1, 2006).

Pratt, Mary Louise (2001). "*I, Rigoberta Menchú* and the 'Culture Wars.'" In A. Arias (ed.), *The Rigoberta Menchú Controversy.* Minneapolis: University of Minnesota Press.

"Pro-Pyongyang Group Searched" (2006). *Asahi.com*, March 23, 2006, www.asahi .com/ (accessed April 1, 2006).

Rebhun, Linda-Ann (1999). *The Heart Is Unknown Country: Love in the Changing Economy of Northeast Brazil.* Stanford, CA: Stanford University Press.

Reed-Danahay, Deborah, ed. (1997). *Auto/ethnography: Rewriting the Self and the Social.* Oxford, England: Berg.

Robinson, Arthur H. (1979). "Geography and Cartography Then and Now," *Annals of the Association of American Geographers* 69 (1): 97–102.

Rosenberger, Nancy, ed. (1992). *Japanese Sense of Self.* Cambridge: Cambridge University Press.

Ruddick, Sara (1980). "Maternal Thinking," *Feminist Studies* 6: 342–67.

Ruddick, Sara (1989). *Maternal Thinking: Towards a Politics of Peace*. Boston: Beacon Press.

Ryang, Sonia (1992). "Critical Synthesis on North Korea as Embodied Ideology," *Social Epistemology* 6 (1): 3–12.

Ryang, Sonia (1993). "Poverty of Language and the Reproduction of Ideology: Korean Language for Chongryun," *Journal of Asian and African Studies* 28 (3–4): 230–42.

Ryang, Sonia (1996). "Do Words Stand for Faith? Linguistic Life of North Korean Children in Japan," *Critique of Anthropology* 16 (3): 281–301.

Ryang, Sonia (1997). *North Koreans in Japan: Language, Ideology, and Identity*. Boulder, CO: Westview Press.

Ryang, Sonia (1998). "Nationalist Inclusion or Emancipatory Identity? North Korean Women in Japan," *Women's Studies International Forum* 21 (6): 581–97.

Ryang, Sonia (2000). *Koreans in Japan: Critical Voices from the Margin*. London: Routledge.

Ryang, Sonia (2000a). "Ethnography or Self-Cultural Anthropology? Reflections on 'Writing about Ourselves,'" *Dialectical Anthropology* 25 (3–4): 297–320.

Ryang, Sonia (2000b). "The North Korean Homeland of Koreans in Japan," in S. Ryang (ed.), *Koreans in Japan: Critical Voices from the Margin*. London: Routledge.

Ryang, Sonia (2000c). "Gender in Oblivion: Women in the Democratic People's Republic of Korea (North Korea)," *Journal of Asian and African Studies* 35 (3): 323–49.

Ryang, Sonia (2002). "Technologies of the Self: Reading North Korean Novels from the 1980s," *Acta Koreana* 5 (1): 21–32.

Ryang, Sonia (2003). "The Great Kanto Earthquake and the Massacre of Koreans in 1923: Notes on Japan's Modern National Sovereignty," *Anthropological Quarterly* 76 (4): 731–48.

Ryang, Sonia (2004). *Japan and National Anthropology: A Critique*. London: Routledge.

Ryang, Sonia (2005). "Dilemma of A Native: On Location, Authenticity, and Reflexivity," *Asia Pacific Journal of Anthropology* 6 (2): 143–57.

Ryang, Sonia (2006a). *Love in Modern Japan: Its Estrangement from Self, Sex, and Society*. London: Routledge.

Ryang, Sonia (2006b). "Does It Have to Be hESC? A Note on War, Embryo, and the Disabled," *Anthropological Quarterly* 79 (3): 509–29.

Ryang, Sonia (forthcoming). "Introduction: Between Life and Death; Diaspora and Koreans in Japan." In S. Ryang and J. Lie (eds.), *Diaspora without Homeland: Being Korean in Japan*. Berkeley: University of California Press.

Ryang, Sonia (in preparation). "North Korea: Ethnology of the Political."

Sacks, Oliver (1995). *An Anthropologist on Mars: Seven Paradoxical Tales*. New York: Vintage.

Safran, William (2004). "Deconstructing and Comparing Diasporas." In W. Kokot, K. Tölölyan, and C. Alfonso (eds.), *Diaspora, Identity and Religion: New Directions in Theory and Research*. London: Routledge.

Sahlins, Marshall (1985). *Islands of History*. Chicago: University of Chicago Press.

Said, Edward (1978). *Orientalism*. New York: Penguin.

Sasanuma, S., and Park, H. S. (1995). "Patterns of Language Deficits in Two Korean-Japanese Bilingual Aphasic Patients — A Clinical Report." In M. Paradis (ed.), *Aspects of Bilingual Aphasia*. New York: Pergamon.

Scalapino, Robert A., and Lee, Chong-sik (1972). *Communism in Korea*, 2 vols. Berkeley: University of California Press.

Scarf, Maggie (2004). *Secrets, Lies, Betrayals: The Body/Mind Connection*. New York: Random House.

Scheper-Hughes, Nancy (1992). *Death without Weeping: The Violence of Everyday Life in Brazil*. Berkeley: University of California Press.

Scheper-Hughes, Nancy, and Lock, Margaret (1986). "Speaking 'Truth' to Illness: Metaphors, Reification, and a Pedagogy for Patients," *Medical Anthropology Quarterly* 17 (5): 137–40.

Schmitt, Carl (1922). *Political Theology: Four Chapters on the Concept of Sovereignty*. Chicago: University of Chicago Press.

Scott, Joan (1992). "Experience." In J. Butler and J. Scott (eds.), *Feminists Theorize the Political*. New York: Routledge.

Shakespeare, Tom (2006). *Disability Rights and Wrongs*. London: Routledge.

Shall We Dance? (1996). Feature film, dir. Suo Masayuki.

Shall We Dance? (2004). Feature film, dir. Peter Chelson.

Shin, Gi-Wook, and Hwang, Hyung Moon, eds. (2003). *Contentious Kwangju: The May 18 Uprising in Korea's Past and Present*. Lanham, MD: Rowman and Littlefield.

Shostak, Marjorie (1981). *Nisa: The Life and Words of a !Kung Woman*. New York: Vintage.

Shōya, Reiko, and Nakayama, Tōru (1997). *Kōrei zainichi kankoku chōsenjin* [Elderly Koreans in Japan]. Tokyo: Ochanomizushobō.

Shweder, Richard (1979a). "Rethinking Culture and Personality Theory Part I," *Ethos* 7: 255–78.

——— (1979b). "Rethinking Culture and Personality Theory Part II," *Ethos* 7: 279–311.

"Sin Guang Su's North Korean Spy Ring under Investigation" (2006). *Asahi.com*, March 24, 2006, www.asahi.com/ (accessed April 1, 2006).

Smith, Bonnie, and Hutchinson, Beth, eds. (2004). *Gendering Disability*. Piscataway, NJ: Rutgers University Press.

Smith, Sidonie, and Watson, Julia (2001). *Reading Autobiography: A Guide for Interpreting Life Narratives*. Minneapolis: University of Minnesota Press.

Snow, Catherine (1990). "Building Memories: The Ontogeny of Autobiography." In D. Cichetti and M. Beeghly (eds.), *The Self in Transition: Infancy to Childhood*. Chicago: University of Chicago Press.

Snyder, Sharon, and Mitchell, David T. (2006). *Cultural Locations of Disability*. Chicago: University of Chicago Press.

Spiro, Melford (1993). "Is the Western Conception of the Self 'Peculiar' within the Context of the World Cultures?" *Ethos* 21: 107–53.

A State of Mind (2004). Documentary film, dir. Daniel Gordon.

Steiner, George (1985). "Our Homeland, the Text," *Salmagundi* 66: 4–25.

Sternberg, Robert (1998). *Love Is a Story: A New Theory of Relationships*. Oxford: Oxford University Press.

Stoll, David (1999). *Ribogerta Menchú and the Story of All Poor Guatemalans*. Boulder, CO: Westview Press.

Stone, Lawrence (1988). "Passionate Attachments in the West in Historical Perspective." In W. Gaylin and E. Person (eds.), *Passionate Attachments: Thinking about Love*. New York: Free Press.

Strathern, Marilyn (1988). *The Gender of the Gift: Problems with Women and Problems with Society in Melanesia*. Berkeley: University of California Press.

—— (2000). "Introduction: New Accountabilities." In M. Strathern (ed.), *Audit Cultures: Anthropological Studies in Accountability, Ethics, and the Academy*. London: Routledge.

—— (2004). *Commons and Borderlands: Working Papers on Interdisciplinarity, Accountability and the Flow of Knowledge*. Oxford, England: Sean Kingston.

Swidler, Ann (2001). *Talks of Love: How Culture Matters*. Chicago: University of Chicago Press.

Szasz, Thomas (1991). *Ideology and Insanity: Essays on the Psychiatric Dehumanization of Man*. Syracuse, NY: Syracuse University Press.

Tai, Eika (2004). "Korean Japanese: A New Identity Option for Resident Koreans in Japan," *Critical Asian Studies* 36 (3): 355–82.

Tennov, Dorothy (1979). *Love and Limmerence: The Experience of Being in Love*. New York: Stein and Day.

Tronto, Joan (1989). "Women and Caring: What Can Feminists Learn about Morality from Caring?" In A. Jaggar and S. Bordo (eds.), *Gender/Body/Knowledge*. New Brunswick, NJ: Rutgers University Press.

—— (1994). *Moral Boundaries: A Political Argument for an Ethic of Care*. New York: Routledge.

Tsuchiya, Yō (2002). *Shōgaishakazoku o ikiru* [Living the life of a family with the disabled]. Tokyo: Keisōshobō.

Turnbull, Ann P., and Turnbull, H. R. (2002). "From the Old to the New Paradigm of Disability and Families: Research to Enhance Family Quality of Life Outcomes." In J. Paul et al. (eds.), *Rethinking Professional Issues in Special Education*. Westport, CT: Ablex.

U.S. Census Bureau (2007a). "Population: Table 24; Resident Population by Region, Race, and Hispanic Origin 2000," *Statistical Abstract of the United States 2005*, www.census.gov/prod/2006pubs/07statab/pop.pdf (accessed March 1, 2007).

—— (2007b). "Population: Table 8; Immigrants by Country of Birth 1981 to 2005," *Statistical Abstract of the United States 2005*, www.census.gov/prod/2006pubs/07statab/pop.pdf (accessed March 1, 2007).

—— (2007c). *The American Community—Asians: 2004; American Community Survey Reports*, February 2007. Washington, DC: U.S. Department of Commerce.

U.S. Department of Commerce, Bureau of the Census (1993). *We the Americans: Asians*. Washington, DC: U.S. Government Printing Office.

Verhaeghe, Paul (1998). *Love in a Time of Loneliness: Three Essays on Drive and Desire*. New York: Other Press.

"Video Shows Execution, Life inside North Korea" (2005). *CNN.com*, November 14, 2005, www.cnn.com/2005/WORLD/asiapcf/11/13/nkorea.hiddenvideo/index.html (accessed November 22, 2006).

Wagner, Edward (1951). *The Korean Minority in Japan: 1904–1951*. New York: Institute of Pacific Relations.

Walker, Alice (1984). *In Search of Our Mother's Gardens*. London: Women's Press.

Walsh, Andrew (1991). *The Science of Love*. Buffalo, NY: Prometheus Books.

Wang, Mian, Mannan, Hasheem, Poston, Denise, Turnbull, Ann P., and Summers, Jean Ann (2004). "Parents' Perceptions of Advocacy Activities and Their Impact on Family Quality of Life," *Research and Practice for Persons with Severe Disabilities* 29 (2): 144–54.

Wang, Mian, Turnbull, Ann P., Summers, Jean Ann, Little, Todd D., Poston, Denise, Mannan, Hasheem, & Turnbull, Rud (2004). "Severity of Disability and Income as Predictors of Parents' Satisfaction with Their Family Quality of Life During Early Childhood Years," *Research and Practice for Persons with Severe Disabilities* 29 (2): 82–94.

Weil, Simone (1951). *Waiting for God*. New York: Putnam.

Weiner, Annette (1976). *Women of Value, Men of Renown: New Perspectives in Trobriand Exchange*. Austin: University of Texas Press.

Wender, Melissa (2000a). "Mothers Write Ikaino." In S. Ryang (ed.), *Koreans in Japan: Critical Voices from the Margin*. London: Routledge.

—— (2000b). "Fleshly Inscriptions of History: Yi Yang-ji's *Koku*," *Korean and Korean American Studies Bulletin* 11 (1): 27–47.

Wolf, Dennie (1990). "Being of Several Minds: Voices and Versions of the Self in Early Childhood." In D. Cichetti and M. Beeghly (eds.), *The Self in Transition: Infancy to Childhood*. Chicago: University of Chicago Press.

Xenos, Nicholas (1993). "Refugees: The Modern Political Condition," *Alternatives* 18: 419–30.

Yan, Yunxiang (2003). *Private Life under Socialism: Love, Intimacy, and Family Change in a Chinese Village, 1949–1999*. Berkeley: University of California Press.

Yau, Jennifer (2004). "The Foreign Born from Korea in the United States," *Migration Information Source*, www.migrationinformation.org/feature/display.cfm?ID=273 (accessed February 2006).

Yeh, Christine (2003). "Age, Acculturation, Cultural Adjustment, and Mental Health Symptoms of Chinese, Korean, and Japanese Immigrant Youths," *Cultural Diversity and Ethnic Minority Psychology* 9 (1): 34–48.

Yōda, Hiroe (1999). *Shōgaishasabetsu no shakaigaku: jendā, kazoku, kokka* [Sociology of disability discrimination: Gender, family, state]. Tokyo: Iwanamishoten.

Yoshimi, Yoshiaki (2000). *Comfort Women*. New York: Columbia University Press.

Yoshitome, Roju (1977). *Ōmura chōsenjin shūyōjo* [The Ōmura Korean camp]. Tokyo: Nigatsusha.

Yu, Eui-Young (1977). "Koreans in America: An Emerging Ethnic Minority," *Amerasia Journal* 4 (1): 117–29.

Yuh, Ji-yeon (2005). "Moved by War: Migration, Diaspora and the Korean War," *Journal of Asian American Studies*, October 2005, 277–91.

Index

About the Author

Sonia Ryang received a Ph.D. in Social Anthropology from Cambridge University, England. She was a Research Fellow in Anthropology at the Australian National University and Assistant Professor and Associate Professor of Anthropology at Johns Hopkins University. She is currently Associate Professor of Anthropology and International Studies, C. Maxwell and Elizabeth M. Stanley Family and Korea Foundation Scholar of Korean Studies, and the Director of the Center for Asian and Pacific Studies, University of Iowa. Her publications include: *North Koreans in Japan: Language, Identity, and Ideology* (1997), *Koreans in Japan: Critical Voices from the Margin* (2000, editor), *Japan and National Anthropology: A Critique* (2004), *Love in Modern Japan: Its Estrangement from Self, Sex, and Society* (2006), among others. She is the series editor for New Asian Anthropology from Lexington Books.

Praise for Rita A. Gordon

"Rita Gordon crafts masterful tales full of depth, romance and passion that always leave you desperate for more!"

— J.L. Seegars, USA Today Best-Selling Author

"Rita Gordon has proven to be a natural in the contemporary romance genre."

— Johanna McCloy, Editor, *Six Car Lengths Behind an Elephant* and *Dare to Be Fabulous*

London Calling

"Sweet marriage-of-convenience romance with touching depth."

— *BookLife by Publishers Weekly*

"The novel's focus on family, friends, love, and grief—and how early tragedy can shape life's trajectory—elevates this from a romance novel to a moving reflection on the power of human connection amid life's smaller moments."

— *BookLife Reviews, Editor's Pick*

"A slick and satisfying romance with plenty of heart and heat."

— *Kirkus Reviews*

30 Days in Belfast

***Publishers Weekly* Indie Spotlight February 2023 (Romance & Relationships)**

"An addictive, rollicking tale of friendship, love, and lust."

— *Kirkus Reviews*

"Gordon's debut offers readers a winning combination of intrigue and romance, revealed slowly through the lens of opulent travel and luxurious living."

— *BookLife Reviews*

"I loved the relationships between the characters, the storyline was heartwarming and after a while, I couldn't put it down. Would definitely recommend!"

— *LoveReading, Indie Books We Love (starred review)*

"A[n] easy, beautiful, knowledgeable read!"

— *Goodreads Reviewer (five-star review)*

Taming a King

LoveReading, November 2024 Indie Books We Love (Favorites)

"Taming a King is an eminently readable bodyguard romance for fans of the trope."

— *LoveReading, Indie Books We Love (starred review)*

Troy

"Troy is an intoxicating mixture of cerebral suspense and heart-pounding action nicely intertwined in a sweet love story."

— The Retired Reader

"This story is a masterclass in the art of the slow burn."

— A.L. Blanks, author of *Started with an Inconvenient Dream*

Seven Days in Seattle

BookLife's Best of 2024 Romance

"Swoon-worthy romance indulges fantasies of wealth and seduction in Seattle."

"Readers will connect with the realistic banter whose humor and subtlety is worthy of a Hollywood script."

"In Seven Days in Seattle, Rita Gordon weaves a swoon-worthy story that kept me riveted until the end."

"...intriguing story with a complex protagonist that flouts convention."

"Seven Days in Seattle is a riveting fusion of passion, sightseeing, and coincidence with twists and turns every reader will wish to experience firsthand. To Rita A. Gordon: more, more, more, please!"

"Rita Gordon has proven to be a natural in the contemporary romance genre. Beyond the hot and steamy romance, Gordon also takes you on a trip to Seattle (like a little travelogue) and beautifully weaves in references to African American literature, history, music, and art."

The Days with Rain

"The relationship between Rain and Parker was so deeply nuanced, packed with layers of frustration, annoyance, heartbreak, and sadness. When a book can evoke such a range of emotions, I know it's a winner."

The Fall of Us

"If you crave a billionaire romance that will leave you smiling from ear to ear, this is your book."

— A. Noelle Smith, author of *Shadows and Sunshine*

Other Titles by Rita A. Gordon

Standalones

30 Days in Belfast
Taming a King
Troy

Let It Rain Series

Seven Days in Seattle
The Days with Rain
The Fall of Us

Inspirational

The Book of Love

Subscribe to Rita's newsletter at:
https://www.ritaagordon.com/subscribe-page
Read more at ritaagordon.com

London
Calling

"Love is fire—consuming, relentless, impossible to ignore. It is the ache in your chest when they're gone, the breathless antic-ipation before a kiss, the undeniable certainty that you would risk everything for just one more moment."
— Rita A. Gordon, The Book of Love

London Calling

A Novel

RITA A. GORDON

12:56 a.m. | California, USA

London Calling

Copyright © 2025 Rita A. Gordon

www.ritaagordon.com

All rights reserved.

This is a work of fiction. Names, characters, places, and incidents are either a product of the author's imagination or are used fictitiously, and any resemblance to actual persons, living or dead, business establishments, events, or locales is entirely coincidental. All trademarks and trade names are used in a fictitious manner and are in no way endorsed by or an endorsement of their respective owners.

Includes sexual situations, potentially sensitive and offensive language, and mature themes. Recommended for ages 18 and older.

The publisher is not responsible for websites (or their content) that the publisher does not own.

Front cover illustration by Ksenia Onegina

Cover design & Interior design by Rita A. Gordon

Author's photo by Abigail Huller

First Edition October 2025

Library of Congress Control Number: 2025911751

ISBN: 979-8-9927196-1-1 (hardcover)

ISBN: 979-8-9927196-2-8 (paperback)

ISBN: 979-8-9927196-3-5 (ebook)

Published in the USA by 12:56 a.m. | www.twelvefiftysixam.com

Contents

Dedication

To all the wandering spirits, may you find love, peace, and happiness.

Author's Note

I'm excited to share the story of Aaron Adler and Jasmine Ross. I first introduced the Adler brothers, founders of Saola Technology, in the *Let It Rain* book series. Then, in *Taming a King*, I offered a closer look at Aaron as he becomes one-third of a love triangle.

Throughout these stories, I hinted at the Ross family's elusive sister, Jasmine. In *London Calling*, we gain an in-depth look at the complex life of the woman behind the mystery. As her story unfolds, we learn that, like her older sister in *Taming a King*, she is still grieving the loss of her mother, who died when she was young. Although I was an adult when I lost mine, I, too, understand the grief of losing parents. And even though some passages were difficult for me to write, this story contains many references to grief, which I strive to handle with care.

Still, this is a love story. Sometimes love comes to us in unexpected ways—which is the case with Aaron and Jasmine. I hope you enjoy reading about how fate brings them together. Fall in love with them, page by page. Experience their ups and downs as they navigate this thing we call...life.

As with all my books, this one comes with a trigger warning. Please be aware that some passages in this work allude to and describe acts of physical violence, both on and off the page. It discusses death, including the loss of a parent. Additionally, there are passages that allude to predatory behavior. As with everything I write, my intent is to *do no harm*. With that in mind, I advise you to consider your health and well-being before diving into this love story.

Prologue

Rolling Stone

Jasmine

IF YOU GOOGLE "A rolling stone gathers no moss," you'll probably find a picture of me next to it. That's my life in a sentence—always moving, never settling, no roots to weigh me down. After graduating from university at nineteen, I left home and never looked back. And now, I'm on the go again.

Wind whips through my hair as I grip the edge of my seat, rocking with the rhythm of the open-air Jeep. The air is thick with dust and the lingering scent of sunbaked earth. Across from me, past the professor, the land stretches endlessly—a canvas of golden fields, acacia trees, and clusters of plants I'll never know the names of. I scan the horizon, searching for the elusive Black Buck antelope, but instead, my gaze catches on something else—the stark, surreal beauty of Rajasthan.

I'm in India, deep in Jodhpur, Rajasthan, having just left the House of Rohet Garh with two men: my driver and a professor. I don't know them, but they know the way. We're heading into the heart of Bishnoi territory, a people who have lived in harmony with this land for centuries.

Harmony. People, earth, elements coming together to make something whole. All playing a part in making this thing we call life work.

The Jeep jolts, then slows, rolling to a stop before an arched gateway flanked by stone walls. The heat is punishing, wrapping around me like a second skin, but my beige linen scarf shields me from the worst of it.

I exhale slowly.

Okay, here we go.

Either this will be the best story I tell my family over drinks one day...or the last day of my life.

Beyond the gate, I follow the professor into the heart of the village. As we walk, he explains their way of life—no electricity, no running water, just an unshakable reverence for the land. But as I take in my surroundings, a quiet unease creeps in. There are almost no people. I catch a glimpse of a woman wearing a vibrant red Odhani just as she disappears into her house, the door closing behind her.

Where is everyone?

The cautious part of me wonders if they're avoiding me. A foreigner, yet one who looks like she could belong—skin just as golden but curls wild and untamed. Or maybe there's something more. Something I should be paying attention to.

The professor leads me to a pastel-blue mud-covered hut. Inside, it's dim, the only light spilling from the open doorway. The space is no bigger than a small New York apartment, but it feels smaller, heavier. No windows. No decorations. Just thick walls, a thatched roof, and silence. The floor, hardened, compacted cow dung, is covered by a worn woven rug. At its center, a brass contraption gleams dully.

I'm introduced to two men, elders of the Bishnoi community, supposedly priests. We exchange traditional pleasantries—pressed fingers form a steeple, a slight bow.

"Let's sit."

The four of us lower ourselves to the floor, forming a circle around the small device. The opium, they explain, is pressed with sugar and filtered through water. A ceremonial practice. A spiritual venture. Yet my mind flashes to headlines—women disappearing, terrible things happening to those who don't belong. My driver, my bodyguard, warned me just last night. "We can't be on the road after dark," he said. But he's not here now.

The same thought grips me now as when I descended into a dark cave alone in the Plitvice National Forest just before dusk—*What have I gotten myself into?* Back then, the air was damp, the walls closed in around me, and every step echoed with the possibility of the unknown. Now, instead of stone and shadows, I face three unfamiliar men and a ritual I barely understand.

I force a breath, shaking the thoughts away, allowing my internal struggles that have nothing to do with this place to dissipate. *This is safe. This is a ceremony.*

One priest pours the liquid into the other's hand and then drinks from it. Eventually, the filtered mixture is poured into the professor's cupped hands, and he holds them out to me. I take a slow, deliberate drink. The warmth unfurls inside me, and the world shifts, edges blurring. A weightlessness settles over my body, pulling me into something deeper, something older.

San Francisco.

Sunlight glints off the glass building. I'm five years old, swinging my father's hand on one side, my brother Jake's on the other. We just finished shopping, and now we're heading to meet Mom and my sister at her favorite Chinese restaurant. The scent of roasted duck and spices lingers in the air. I remember being so happy, so safe.

Then sirens. The wail cuts through the city's noise. People gather near the restaurant, voices rising. A feeling envelops me that I don't understand.

My father's grip tightens before he lets go. "Stay here," he commands, pushing my hand into Jake's. His face is unreadable as he pulls out his phone, pressing it to his ear.

"I need you to—." His voice disappears into the crowd.

Soon, I would learn he called Uncle Rick, the country's wealthiest and most powerful Black man. By day's end, I would understand that everything changed at that moment.

That was the day my mother died.

That was the day I stopped belonging anywhere.

Talk to Me

Aaron

One year ago.

Before I see her, I feel her. A shift in the air, a pulse of familiarity just beyond the glass wall. *June.* My best friend's sister. The woman I've loved for nearly half my life but am not in love with. *I wish I were.* It would be easier.

My heart still stutters when she's near. My eyes still search for her first in a crowded room. But it's never *that* kind of love. If it were, maybe I wouldn't feel like something was missing. I don't understand my tie to Jake and June, but I embrace it. Over the past few weeks, I've watched her with Aedan, my friend and her bodyguard. She thinks no one notices the stolen glances, the way her breath catches when he's nearby. But I do. So does he. And yet they pretend.

I smile, and she quickly disappears down the hall, heading toward my office.

Standing before my team, I wrap up the meeting. The fiscal year is on track. We have our competitive advantage. Bill nods as I mention expansion plans, but my mind is already outside this room, following June's retreating figure. "Great meeting, everyone." I don't wait for stragglers or side conversations. I'm already moving.

When I reach my office, she's already there, curled into the sofa like she belongs. Because she does. She's stunning as always. Gone are the long braids I love, replaced with her untamed afro that beautifully frames her face. A black off-the-shoulder dress hugs her curves, her elegance effortless. But tonight, something is different. I can see it in her eyes before she speaks.

A moment stretches between us, heavy with things unsaid. I cup her cheek, my touch familiar, steadying.

"Talk to me, beautiful."

"The board approved my proposal."

On instinct, I pull her into a hug. "Congratulations." I lean back to get a better look at her. A tear escapes and runs down her cheek. "That's not what you came to tell me." I brush the tears away with my thumb. More take their place.

She shakes her head. I already know the answer.

"I'm ready."

Ready. Ready to open her heart to a man. *But not to me.* The words coil tight in my chest, a slow, suffocating realization that steals my breath.

"But not for me."

"I promised you." She stands and walks to the wall of windows, the glow of the city spilling golden light over her frame. She looks so damn fragile at this moment, and yet, there's a quiet strength in the way she squares her shoulders. I follow her, stopping just behind. In the reflection, I catch her face, her trembling lips, the silent tears slipping down her cheeks. Something in my chest twists. An ache, deep and raw.

"You love him, don't you?"

She turns to face me, stepping closer until the heat of her body meets mine. Then she wraps her arms around me, pressing herself against my chest as if she can fold herself into me, as if I can somehow hold her together.

I don't return the embrace. I can't. She's not mine to want, not mine to keep. My hands clench at my sides, a war raging beneath my skin—one part of me desperate to gather her close, to claim her, to take whatever she's offering, and another part forcing me to hold the line.

I search her eyes, trying to find something...anything that explains why we weren't meant to be. Why she's here. Why she's doing *this*.

"I don't know," she whispers. "I don't even think he likes me. All I know is that I don't want to lose you."

Her words land like a blade between my ribs. I swallow the sharp, painful truth and push past it.

"You and I are tied at the hip—I doubt you could ever lose me. What do you need from me, beautiful?"

"To provide us the certainty we discussed."

Certainty. A promise I once made. But the certainty she wants and what I can give her aren't the same.

"We both know that you're not mine to take."

"I'm giving myself to you."

I exhale slowly, my fingers twitching with the need to touch her. To pull her back into the safety of my arms, even if only for one night. But she doesn't belong here.

"Where is Aedan?" My voice is rough, strained. "You should be with him."

I start to step away, but she grabs my hand, her grip tight, desperate. A shock of warmth spreads from her touch, unraveling my restraint thread by thread.

"I don't know where he is."

I frown, my jaw tightening. "What do you mean? How did you get here?"

"I left and took a taxi straight to you. My phone is in the suite. No one knows I'm here."

My pulse kicks up a notch. A sharp mix of protectiveness and frustration barrels through me.

"What are you doing, June?"

She lifts her chin, determination flickering in her eyes. "Following through on my promise. When you first asked me, it seemed strange at the time, but I get it now. You're right. We are linked, but I don't understand why. Maybe you're in my life to get me to this moment or perhaps to move past it. Whatever the reason, you're the only one who can put me on my path to forever."

I drag a hand down my face, my control slipping, fraying at the edges.

"Come on, beautiful. I'll take you back to Aedan."

"No, Aaron."

Her voice is soft, but it lands like a punch to my gut. She's never called me by my name like this—without the teasing, the usual warmth, the distance we've always kept between us.

It does something to me. It makes me feel possessive, like she's *mine*.

"You told me I could come to you. I don't know what's going to happen between Aedan and me. What I do know is that I want this moment...with you. You have to give me that."

She's right. We made a promise that day at a restaurant in Belfast. She would let me know when she was ready to start dating again.

"I'm asking you to give me a chance to know that the things you felt for me years ago are either still there or gone. Let me give you the kiss you denied yourself. If we aren't meant to be, you'll know at that moment. I'll accept that."

She hesitated a moment before saying, "Okay, I can commit to that. The first step, the first kiss, on my journey to find my forever begins with you. You get one shot, handsome, but it has to be organic. If it doesn't feel right, I'll tell you."

And now she's here.

My resolve cracks. My breath hitches as I snake an arm around her waist.

"I'm convinced you were once mine in another space and time."

Her lips tremble. "I feel the same. We can try."

I cup her face, my thumb tracing the damp path her tears have left. "Are you sure you want to do this?"

She nods, her voice breaking. "I do love you."

She combs her fingers through my beard, the light scrape of her nails sending a shiver down my spine. My restraint snaps. I dip my head and press my lips to hers, slow, *torn*. It's soft and loving, but I don't open her mouth. I don't deepen the kiss. I won't possess her. Because she's not mine to have.

I pull away, my breath unsteady, my forehead resting against hers. Her eyes shine with unshed tears.

"Kiss me like you want me."

My hands tighten on her waist. I want her. *God, I want her.*

"You're not mine to want."

Her gaze searches mine, pleading. "I need to know what it feels like to be yours. At least give me that."

A curse catches in my throat as I grip her chin, tilting her mouth open before crushing my lips to hers. This time, I take. I lick into her, swallowing her breathy gasp, savoring, claiming, memorizing. My body hardens against hers as my hands roam down, gripping her hips, pressing her closer, demanding her surrender.

She melts into me, giving in, giving herself.

And then it hits me. A slow, sinking certainty. I'm not the man for her. Someone else is.

The realization steals the air from my lungs. I break away, clenching my jaw, dragging in a deep breath to steady myself. I adjust my stance, adjust myself, willing my body back under control.

"We have to stop." My voice is hoarse, raw. "I'm five seconds away from stripping you naked." I pause, forcing myself to meet her eyes. "I'm taking you to someone who can finish this before I do. Because if I make love to you, I promise I'll never let you go."

CHAPTER I

Two Weeks

Jasmine

TWO WEEKS. THAT'S ALL I have to get through. Two weeks in London, and then I'm off again: Paris for the summer, Samoa after that, locking in another year of uninterrupted travel.

I shift my overnight bag higher on my shoulder as I step onto the damp London pavement, the familiar scent of rain and exhaust curling around me. London buzzes, sure. But it's a disciplined kind of chaos—polished, punctual, and buttoned-up, like everyone's got the memo to keep their emotions on a leash. Very different from what I've grown used to. Compared to the whirlwind of Delhi or Shanghai, London feels...muted. In India, the streets thrum with color, voices, and spice in the air. You feel life brushing past your skin. In China, the pace is sharp and relentless, as if everyone's chasing the future with fire in their lungs. But London? London moves, yes, but in straight lines. It's brilliant in its own way, just...a little too starched at the collar.

This time, I'm here because of Dr. Owusu.

He first reached out through my cousin Rose. He was consulting on her European art exhibition, unaware that she originally wanted me for the job. At the time, I was in a remote part of Sub-Saharan Africa, cut off from cell service, with no guarantee I'd even make it out. I did. And once

I resurfaced, I confirmed that Dr. Owusu was the real deal—a brilliant historian whose work on Black British history has changed the field.

Once again, I'm filling in for him.

A private three-hundred-person dinner at the British Museum, an institution drowning in stolen Black artifacts. The irony isn't lost on me. Dr. Owusu was supposed to deliver the keynote speech, but when he got an emergency call about his sister's health, I was the natural replacement. He'd anticipated a long recovery and had already sponsored my seven-month visa, of which I have forty-five days left—if I need it. This is my third time returning to London just to stand in for him.

I should be honored. Instead, I'm restless.

My sister, June, just had her first baby in Ireland, and I actually stayed put longer than usual—long enough to hold my nephew, long enough to feel something unsettling settle in my chest. Long enough to remember why I left...back then. Now, I'm back in London, where I seem to land when I need to pause but never plan to stay.

I exhale and hail a black cab. *Two weeks.* Then I'm gone again.

Settling into my London flat in Holborn doesn't take long. I drop my bag in the walk-in closet and pause at the mirror, running a finger through the soft coils of my shoulder-length hair, twisting a few strands for added definition. My reflection stares back—warm brown skin, sharp cheekbones, eyes that have seen more of the world than most people do in a lifetime. A beige cashmere sweater over a white T-shirt and jeans will do for a quick meal. Tomorrow, I'll stock up on groceries, but for tonight, the pub will suffice.

I exit my temporary home. The building belongs to Parker and Rain Page, old friends of my family. They live in the top level, but they're not in town. That leaves me as the only resident, a fact I don't mind. Being alone has never bothered me.

I take the longer route, opting for the winding alleys instead of shortcuts, stretching my legs after spending too many hours in an airplane seat and on taxi rides. London hums with life—crowded sidewalks, taxis flashing their occupied signs, wet pavement reflecting neon lights. I don't have to be here. I never have to work a day in my life...if I choose. But I accepted a job—not just anywhere...here. In doing so, I've traded lush, untamed landscapes for this—the pulse of a city that doesn't know me. Maybe that's why I chose it.

The pub is lively, warm with conversation and the rich scent of beer and grilled meat. Unlike the rowdy dives I've visited in other parts of the world, there's an air of quiet sophistication here—polished brass railings, lacquered bar tops, and a mirrored wall reflecting back the sea of dark suits and loosened ties.

I take a seat at the bar.

"Hey, you're back." Len, the bartender, wipes down the space in front of me, setting a coaster down with familiar ease.

I wonder if he remembers me because he's good at his job or because I'm the only curly-haired Black woman who regularly walks through that door. A quick glance around confirms it's probably the latter.

If my brother or sister walked in, people would recognize them instantly. *Ross.* A name synonymous with innovation and wealth. We're heirs of one of the most powerful tech companies in the world, founded by my uncle, Rick Ross. They thrive in the tech world. But me? No boardrooms, no press appearances, no family business. I vanished the day after college graduation, hopping on a first-class flight to Africa in search of something I couldn't name.

Peace. Roots. Maybe even a way back to...*her.*

I touch the gold peace-sign pendant at my neck, the only thing I have left of my mother. She died when I was five—too young to understand, old enough to remember. Some losses shape you more than you realize.

Len hands me a menu, but I don't need it. "Malbec and the chicken pie."

"Coming right up." He types in my order, then places a glass of water in front of me. Thoughtful. Or maybe it's just because I'm American.

I take a sip, scanning the room. Mostly professionals—lawyers, finance types, people who fit into this world in a way I never have. My life doesn't come with business cards or nine-to-five routines. My wardrobe consists of jeans, cargo pants, and sundresses, depending on what remote corner of the world I'm in—and for events—a fitted black dress.

Len returns with my wine, pouring the deep red liquid into a glass. I swirl it, inhale notes of dark fruit and spice, then take a sip. "Umm." Smooth.

"Cheers," a voice intrudes.

I glance over. A man wearing a navy suit tips his water glass toward me. Beady eyes, stubby fingers. The type who probably enjoys the tradition of a powdered legal wig.

I don't entertain him. Discreetly, I slide a delicate platinum band from my right hand to my left, letting the dim bar lights catch on the metal as it settles on my ring finger. A relationship is the last thing on my mind. I have no desire to settle—or to stumble into something fleeting. The first and only guy I ever let get that close was a mistake. Some days, I wonder if he ruined it for everyone else...or if I was just never built for staying.

"Chicken pie." Len sets a linen cloth down before placing the dish in front of me. Steam curls up from the golden crust, carrying the rich aroma of buttery pastry and roasted chicken.

I take a bite, savoring the warmth—until I feel it. A stare. Persistent. Uninvited.

God, not tonight.

I don't want to make a scene, but if this man doesn't take the hint, I might have to. The thought of someone as slight as me drop-kicking a guy in a tailored suit amuses me. I take another bite.

Len reappears, refilling my water. "Are you on the lecture circuit again?"

"Yeah. British Museum."

"I'll let my aunt know. She's into that sort of stuff."

Before I can respond, the man interrupts. "You're a professor?"

I turn to him, setting my fork down. "Do I know you?"

He grins, extending a hand. "Bane Roth."

I don't take it.

"Bane." As in the bane of my existence. I don't say it, but the temptation is there.

"You are?"

"Just here to eat, Bane." I mentally rewind my words, hoping Bane misses the unintended double entendre.

Len steps in. "Did you decide on a drink?"

"I'll have a Guinness."

As Len pulls the draft, I focus on my meal, willing Bane to lose interest.

"You're American," he presses. "If you're lecturing at the British Museum, you must be something special. That's good. I have unique tastes."

I set my fork down, patience unraveling. "Mr. Roth, I'd prefer to eat in peace."

"It's not a conversation I'm after."

"Then you're definitely barking up the wrong tree."

"Ah, come on. You're a pretty one. Have a drink with me."

I slide my plate forward. "Len, can you pack this to go?"

Bane huffs. "Well, that wasn't very nice."

"Quickly, please."

Len nods, prints my receipt, and hands it over. I scribble a note on it—*Hold his credit card until I'm long gone.* Sliding it back to Len, I catch his smirk of understanding.

A minute later, he hands me the bag. "Take care."

I grab it without another glance at Bane and walk out the door, disappearing into the London night.

This time, I take all the shortcuts. The alleys have different names, but otherwise, they're just like any I've walked through. Dark. Dingy. Devoid of anything good. I'm two blocks away from my building when I hear a woman scream.

"Get off me!"

CHAPTER 2

Charm and Calculation

Aaron

ANOTHER BIG YEAR FOR Saola technology—the company my brothers and I built from scratch, fueled by late nights, stubborn ambition, and a hell of a lot of risk. Now we're leaders in the AI space, with a suite of cloud-based products so sharp and scalable it feels like we're barely keeping up with our momentum.

And we're not slowing down.

If we land this acquisition in time for our annual conference, it'll be the headline that finally buries last year's scandals for good. All eyes will be on us, exactly where they should be.

I grab my jacket off the back of my chair. My phone buzzes just as I slide one arm through the sleeve.

"I want everything running smoothly," Alex, my older brother, says without preamble, his voice low and clipped over the line.

"Everything's under control." I check my watch. If I leave now, I'll be right on time. I always am.

I stride toward the elevator, the sharp tap of my shoes echoing in the quiet corridor. London's gray light filters through the floor-to-ceiling windows, casting long shadows across polished floors. Another meeting. Another move on the board. And I don't intend to miss a step.

"You said that last year," my brother reminds me, "and then the BDC printed that story about you and June."

"Which they retracted."

"After it nearly tanked client confidence."

"It won't happen again."

"See that it doesn't."

We both know the stakes. Saola Technology is on the verge of finalizing a multi-million-dollar acquisition of Mission AI. This is our biggest acquisition so far, which will grow our AI team and increase revenue exponentially. We cleared the initial phase of the Competition and Markets Authority's investigation, but scrutiny is far from over. One misstep. One headline. One rumor—and it could all fall apart. After last year's debacle, I expected the CMA to shut us down at first glance. But it wasn't just a scandal. It was a smokescreen. A rogue criminal trying to manipulate the press to hide his own crimes. A reminder that perception is everything in this business.

The article in the British Daily Corporation is a reminder of how quickly public perception can turn.

"Double Trouble. It appears American titan Ross Enterprises can't stay out of the news. Once again, they're on the wrong side of it. Known for its groundbreaking AI technology, Ross Enterprises is led by the mega genius Rose Ross. Ross Enterprises and Saola Technology appear to be in a legal conundrum here in the UK. Former Saola employee James Drummond alleges he was wrongfully terminated after applying for an open role vacated by their former COO, June Ross. He further states that Ross Enterprises' European operation discriminated against him after he applied and was rejected for a position there, subsequent to being terminated from Saola. He asserts, 'I believe Mr. Adler, President of the European offices, and Ms. Ross, Ross Enterprises' new COO, are in cahoots on recruiting and hiring practices in the UK.' He further cites seeing them together recently at a technology

event, wherein Mr. Adler was the keynote. As of the date of this article, we have not spoken with either Saola Technology or Ross Enterprises."

"I'm about to meet a potential client for dinner," I say.

Alex exhales sharply. "We have people for that."

"And I have a vested interest in securing this deal."

He doesn't argue, just sighs. "Fine. Call me after."

"I'm here now. I'll talk to you tomorrow." I end the call as the car pulls up to the restaurant.

The doorman nods as I step inside, and the hostess greets me with a practiced smile. "Mr. Adler, your table is ready."

I follow her. The rhythm of this place is as familiar as my own office. Even so, out of habit, I assess the layout, noting exits and points of entry. An old reflex from years spent with June. After what happened to her mother, she never sat with her back to the door. Eventually, it became second nature to me, too. Some may chalk it up to my need for control. But control isn't just something I like—it's something I live by. It's why I'm here tonight, handling this meeting myself instead of delegating it. Deals like this require precision, and I don't take risks.

But as I approach the table, something shifts. A feeling. A wrongness. The woman waiting for me isn't my potential client. It's Bridgette Bromley. She smiles, all charm and calculation, and suddenly, I know—I've just walked into a trap.

The last time I saw Bridgette was at the Biennial UK Tech Awards a little over a year ago. Saola was nominated for two awards: Tech CEO of the Year and Innovation for the Greater Good. Alex, Andrew, and I attended, and June was my guest.

Bromley Inc., founded by Bridgette's grandfather, wasn't nominated for anything, which left me wondering whether she was there to network or just for show. With her personality, I assumed it was the latter. She wore a sequined dress that shimmered every time she moved, as if she wanted the entire room to know she was there. Maybe she did.

And now, she's sitting with a cocktail in front of her, her perfectly manicured nails drumming against the table as if I've kept her waiting.

I pull out a chair and sit. She tracks my every movement; her eyes are bright with the kind of amusement that usually spells trouble.

"I suppose Fabien isn't working for Brixton?" I ask.

She smiles like I've asked the question out of genuine interest.

"No. He works for my Dad. How are you?"

"You didn't orchestrate this meeting out of concern for my health. What do you want, Bridgette?"

She pouts, exaggerated and theatrical. "Ah, London, that's not happiness to see me."

"My name is Aaron."

She smirks. "*She* calls you London."

"You're not her."

She laughs—a slow, practiced sound. "You always had a thing for_." She taps her lips, pretending to think. "What's her name again? It was something ridiculous—Sun? Moon?"

Heat creeps up my neck. The way she mocks June makes my patience thin fast. I don't know what she thinks this accomplishes. If anything, it makes her look worse—petty, spoiled, self-absorbed.

"Her name is June," I say flatly.

"Right, right. June." She drags out the name like it tastes bad. "She's married now, has a kid. Not yours, I hope? That could be interesting...little Moon beams."

I exhale slowly, gripping my patience like a frayed rope. "Her name is *June Ross King*."

I glance around. A few too many eyes flick in our direction. Coincidence? Maybe. But Bridgette doesn't do coincidences.

I catch the server's eye and motion with my fingers to bring the bill to pay for her drink. He nods.

Bridgette leans in, dropping her voice. "Don't go." She reaches out, fingers grazing the back of my hand. I pull away. Her lips part slightly, but her gaze scans past my shoulder. Briefly. Calculating.

Our server appears. "Anything else? Maybe something to go?"

"No, thank you," I say. He leaves. I stand.

Bridgette exhales sharply. "Stop. Okay. You're right. That's not what I came here to talk about." She flips her hair, as if resetting the conversation. "Well, partly. I do think we'd make a great-looking couple."

My patience is nearly gone. "You have one minute."

She sighs, tracing slow circles on the table with her finger. "Dad's been pressuring me to take on a bigger role at Bromley. You know, since he doesn't have a son to turn things over to." She lifts her gaze. "I wanted to get your advice."

I study her for a beat, searching for sincerity and finding none.

"I think you need to talk with your father."

I move to leave, but she stands, too.

"I thought you'd want to help me." She touches my arm and I step back.

"I'm not sure why you'd think that." I reach for the bill, sign it, and drop it back on the table. "You have friends. People on your payroll. I'm neither." Her smile falters for the first time. "If there's nothing else, I'm leaving. Good evening."

"Can we at least have drinks?"

"Goodnight, Bridgette."

I turn and walk away. I don't need to glance back to know she's still watching me.

CHAPTER 3

Flicker of Light

Jasmine

JUST A FEW STEPS from the main street, at the end of the alley, a large, burly man is pinning a woman against the wall. She's fighting—her arm jammed against his throat, straining to keep him at bay—but he's bigger, stronger, and she's losing.

I sprint down the alley, silent and swift. He doesn't notice me, but she does. *Good.*

"Help," she screams, her voice raw with panic.

I lift a finger to my lips, silently signaling that I'm here. That I've got her.

My body moves on instinct, the muscle memory drilled into me since I was ten. My brother, Jake, made sure I knew how to handle myself. I've got one shot. I don't hesitate. I drop my bag, coil my body, and swing my leg back before driving my foot straight between the bastard's legs. The impact is brutal.

A guttural groan escapes him—choked, pained, "Uh—." His grip loosens and he crumbles forward, collapsing to his knees and clutching himself.

"Get behind me," I command. The woman stumbles back as I deliver a sharp kick to the side of his head. He slumps, dazed. "SOS," I call out, the pre-programmed command that will activate the emergency alert on my phone. The piercing siren blares through the alley, bouncing off the brick walls.

Two men passing by stop in their tracks. Their eyes dart from the woman to me to the man on the ground.

"Did this bastard hurt you?"

"I need to get her out of here," I say.

One of them lunges, pinning the groaning attacker to the pavement. "Go."

I don't hesitate. I grab her hand, scoop up my things, and run.

We don't stop until we're around the corner, under the glow of a street-light. My pulse is still hammering, but I turn to her, cupping her chin gently, tilting her face up so I can check for bruises. Then I realize. She's not a woman. She's a girl—warm ecru skin, light brown spiral curls spilling past her shoulders, and wide, wary eyes. No bruises, but when I press along the back of her head, she flinches.

"Ouch."

My jaw tightens. That bastard slammed her too hard against the wall.

"Are you okay? Did he hurt you anywhere else?"

"I...I'm okay." Her voice is small but steady.

I exhale, trying to push down my anger. "Do you want me to go back? I can press charges."

The thought of it—going back there, kicking him again, making him pay—inches at me. But I feel confident the men I left behind will handle him.

"I want to go home," she whispers.

I nod. "I'll walk you," I say, squeezing her hand reassuringly. "I got you."

Her shoulders relax slightly. We walk in silence, the city's night rhythm humming around us—cars in the distance, the shuffle of footsteps. But this girl walks like she's always listening for danger. Like she knows what it means to be prey. She walks like me.

Not just the pace or posture—it's something in her eyes. That hyper-awareness. Like she's always scanning the edges of her world for danger.

At five six, I may be small in stature, but I can pack a punch. My siblings and I learned early that danger lurks where you least expect it. My sister doesn't worry about that anymore—her husband is her bodyguard. The rest of my family has security. Not me.

I have training in self-defense, martial arts, tactical skills, and kickboxing. I can handle myself.

After my mother died, my father kept me close—closer than he did my older siblings. Maybe because I was the smallest. Or the way I changed after losing her. Perhaps I reminded him of her. I don't know.

But it was my brother, Jake, who became our rock. He convinced my father to train me, recognizing what my dad didn't—my need for independence. I didn't have a mother to show me how to be. So Jake became that for me.

When we stop in front of an old building, my stomach twists. *I know this place.* It's been empty for months. Its owner, some foreign millionaire, went to jail for fraud. The property has been tied up in legal battles ever since. *She lives here?*

She hesitates before saying, "Thank you again...," then pauses, waiting for my name.

"Jasmine. Jasmine Ross."

"Thank you, Miss Ross."

I glance from her to the building, my chest tightening. "You live here?" She nods.

"Are your parents home?"

She presses her lips together. "No."

I swallow hard. "What's your name?"

"I should be going inside."

"Sweetie, look at me." I soften my tone. "I'm here to help. What's your name?"

A long pause. "Amara."

"Amara." I hold her gaze. "This place has been abandoned for months. How are you living here?" She doesn't answer. "Show me."

"It's fine. I'm okay now, I promise."

She's not. I see it. The way she wrings her hands, the exhaustion in her eyes.

"Amara," I say gently. "Let me see where you're living."

Reluctantly, she turns and leads me around the side of the building, slipping through the back entrance. The darkness swallows us whole, but she moves with familiarity, guiding us into a small, hollowed-out parlor. I listen attentively, ready to take action if needed. The glow of a candle flickers to life. The space is bare. A folding chair. A blanket on the floor serves as a bed. A small wooden table, scratched and worn, sits beside it. Probably left behind by the previous occupant or established by someone handling the last traces of business before shutting down this place. That's it. That's her home. My throat tightens.

"Amara, where are your parents?"

She doesn't flinch when she says, "Dead."

The way she says it—flat, emotionless—hits me hard. It's so different from how I responded at her age to questions about my mom. Questions no child should ever have to answer.

"How old are you?" The question comes out of my mouth before I realize.

"Sixteen. Almost seventeen."

There's a bundle in the corner. I nod toward it. "Are those your things?" She nods.

I inhale sharply. "Get them."

She blinks. "What?"

"You're coming with me."

"No." Her voice is thin, but there's something else beneath it—hope. She wants me to insist.

"Amara, trust me." I hold her gaze. "Let me get you somewhere safe. Somewhere with heat. Electricity. Food."

She hesitates. "I'm okay here."

"You're not okay here," I counter. "I know this isn't how you want to live."

Her breath shakes.

I step closer, my voice softer now, remembering the sound of my mom's voice when she used to talk to me. Her low tone, soft, soothing, making me feel safe. "It's just me. No one else. No judgments, no questions...just a safe place for you to stay."

She swallows hard. Then, finally says slightly above a whisper, "Okay. Just for the night."

As she turns to gather her things, I finally get a good look at her clothes. Worn denim pants—frayed at the seams, but not dirty. A knit sweater that's seen better days, the sleeves stretched and misshapen from wear, just enough to reveal she's making do with what she has for far too long. There's care in the way she's dressed, though—like she's trying. Not just to stay warm, but to hold onto some version of herself that still believes she's worth being seen. Her boots are scuffed, soles worn thin, but her laces are tied neat and tight. She's doing the best she can with what she has. That small detail guts me more than anything else.

I nod, relieved. She gathers her things, and together, we step into the night.

CHAPTER 4

Storms and Solutions

Aaron

WITH MY KNEES SLIGHTLY bent and palms braced against my thighs, I catch my breath, inhaling the cool, damp London air outside my Knightsbridge home. I had a good run—five miles at a solid pace. The morning is still wrapped in shadows, the sun teasing the horizon but not yet fully risen. I roll my shoulders, shake out my arms, and stretch my calves before heading inside.

It doesn't take long to get ready. Shower. Trim my beard. Suit up. Routine is control, and control is what I need.

As I fasten my cufflinks, my phone vibrates—once, twice—and then erupts in a series of buzzing notifications. I frown and pick it up, the sheer volume of messages sending a prickle of unease down my spine.

Then it rings. *Alex.*

I swipe to answer, putting him on speaker. "It's nearly ten there. Shouldn't you be getting some rest?"

His response is immediate, clipped. "I take it you haven't seen the news?"

I pull my phone away and tap into my notifications. The first image freezes me in place. Then the next. And the next. A slow burn of anger coils in my gut.

Bridgette.

"Fuck," I mutter.

"Yeah," Alex bites out.

"It's not what they think." I exhale sharply, jaw tightening.

"But it's what they saw. We talked about this, Aaron. You said you were meeting with a client."

I re-examine the photos, slower this time. There's one with Bridgette's hand grazing mine across the table. Another, timed to perfection, shows her touching my arm as I stand to leave, like some tender farewell caught mid-motion. Every frame is composed with surgical precision. Not candid. Not accidental. These aren't precious moments—they're setups. Carefully orchestrated shots that look less like two old acquaintances having lunch and more like a lifestyle ad for some luxury brand. I can almost hear the tagline: *elegance, power, connection.* It's absurd. Every gesture, every glance deliberately captured. It's like seeing an ad I never agreed to be in. All perfectly staged.

"I was blindsided," I admit, scanning the headlines. Speculations, assumptions—every single one wrong. "Bridgette had a photographer planted. She set me up."

"Explain."

"She heard about June's pregnancy and assumed I was back on the market—for her. Tricked me into meeting her under the pretense that her father was pressuring her to take on a bigger role at Bromley. I left the moment I realized what she was doing."

"Well, the damage is done." His tone sharpens. "This isn't just another tabloid headache, Aaron. The CMA is already scrutinizing us. A scandal, or even a hint of impropriety, gives them an excuse to stall the acquisition. Or worse, block it entirely."

Tension grips my shoulders. "I'll fix this."

"Do it fast," Alex says. "And don't let her pull this shit again."

He ends the call and I head out.

The rain has stopped. As I take the short walk to the office, I use the time to gather my thoughts on how to handle Bridgette. There's no point in wondering what she was thinking—I already know. Bridgette Bromley only thinks about one person: herself.

I joined the executive ranks at Saola after completing my master's degree at Oxford, but my journey with the company began long before that. Alex founded it right after his undergraduate degree, and eleven years later, I joined him upon finishing mine. By the time I earned my master's, I was second in command. Two years after that, as we expanded internationally, I took over as President of European operations. That's when I met Bridgette.

It was during the opening night of our annual *Tech Force* conference. I was the keynote speaker, and afterward, I sat at a reserved table with my guest, June, my brothers, and key Saola staff. The room buzzed with industry leaders, investors, and innovators. Then Bram Bromley arrived, his daughter in tow, making his rounds.

My brothers and I stood as they approached.

"This is quite the event you've put together. I'm impressed by the turnout." Bram said, his gaze sweeping the room.

"The AI tech community has really embraced the event," Alex replied smoothly.

"I take it this is your first time attending?" I asked.

"Yes. Word got back to me that this was the place to be." He paused before adding, *"I wanted to stop by to say hello and introduce my daughter, Bridgette."*

"Nice to meet you, Bridgette." I gestured to my right. *"This is my friend, June."*

Bridgette offered a half-hearted nod in June's direction. *"Nice to meet you."* Then she turned her attention back to me, a slow, deliberate smile curving her lips. *"I hope we see more of each other."*

Her meaning was clear.

They didn't linger long—just long enough for Bram Bromley to establish a presence and for Bridgette to make her intentions known.

When I arrive at the office, I head straight to the top floor. As soon as I step out of the elevator, my assistant, Kate, is on my heels.

"Morning, Aaron. Your brother is in your office." She holds her phone. "Have you seen this?"

"Morning, Kate." I walk past her without looking at the screen. "I've already seen it."

She studies me briefly. "You didn't stop for coffee. Would you like me to get you some?"

"That would be nice. Afterward, get Bridgette Bromley on the line."

"On it." She turns away, heels clicking down the hall.

When I step into my office, I find my younger brother, Andrew, lounging in my chair, feet propped on my desk, hands clasped behind his head.

"What are you doing?"

He grins. "Testing out my new office, since you seem determined to get yourself fired."

I drop into the chair opposite him. "I'm not getting fired."

Andrew cocks his head. "Then explain why Bridgette Bromley suddenly materialized on our side of town?"

"Your guess is as good as mine." I fill him in on the story Bridgette spun about needing my advice on stepping up in her father's company.

Andrew listens, unimpressed. "Right. Like that's ever going to happen."

"I didn't say I believed her."

"At least I know one thing—you didn't go see her willingly."

Andrew may be the youngest, but he's sharp. He's spent years watching Alex and me, absorbing what we do well and calling us out when we could do better. He has a knack for reading people, for seeing angles no one else notices. It's why we put him in charge of acclimating new executives. And he knows damn well I wouldn't voluntarily step within ten feet of Bridgette Bromley. She lives for headlines in *The Society Magazine*.

I take a slow breath. "I still need to talk to her, to get ahead of this media fiasco before it spirals further out of control."

"If you have to meet her in person, I can go with you."

"Kate's setting up a call for today."

I stand and move to the windows, looking out over the city. Andrew doesn't say anything, but I know he's watching. He knows I'm already piecing together how I plan to fix this. We built Saola Technology from nothing—our own legacy, something more than trust funds and a surname. We watched our parents climb the corporate ladder, sacrificing time supporting others' dreams for success. That wasn't going to be us.

Andrew's voice turns serious. "Aaron, after the BDC article, you need to start taking this perception problem seriously. We know you're not a playboy, but this thing with Bridgette? It's about to cement your reputation as one."

"I'll have her make a public statement."

"You need to do more than that." He leans forward. "Our reputation is built on the quality of our technology and the strength of our character. You know as well as I do that image matters." I exhale, my brain kicking into overdrive. He continues. "This isn't our last acquisition."

"Of course not. No one's questioning our product."

"But—."

"You don't have to say. The Character Diligence committee doesn't just look at code and revenue." I comb my fingers through my beard. "Things settled after the BDC retracted their story. They didn't raise an eyebrow when someone snapped a picture of me with June."

His eyebrow raises. "Don't make me state the obvious."

"I'm not thinking about getting with June."

"You couldn't if you wanted."

I shoot him a *no shit, Sherlock* look. "Maybe I'll just become celibate."

Andrew smirks. "Like you haven't been since you asked June out."

I narrow my eyes. "What do you know?"

"Only that I've watched you change since you two admitted you weren't soulmates." He tilts his head, studying me. "She might not have been, out it made you start looking for your person."

I stare at him, stunned. He's too damn perceptive for his own good. Because he just put words to something I wasn't ready to admit—not to him, not to myself.

Am I ready to settle down?

CHAPTER 5

Croissants and Conversations

Jasmine

IT'S EARLY. TOO EARLY. The only reason I get up before the crack of dawn is to catch a flight—not today. Today, I have to get a kid to class.

Amara.

God, she looked so helpless yet hopeful last night. I didn't want to push too hard, but I coaxed enough from her to know she's more like me than I expected. Strong-willed. Determined. Smart. And alone. Despite everything, she's still on track to finish her A-levels ahead of schedule. *Four months.* That's how long I have to get her into college. I don't know anything about raising a teenager. I barely know how to take care of myself. But when I looked in her eyes, I saw mine. And I knew I couldn't leave.

I take a deep breath. The flat is unusually quiet this morning, the kind of silence that makes a space feel untouched. The city hums beyond the glass windows, but inside, the warmth of soft lighting and the faint scent of fresh linen gives the illusion of serenity. It's a stark contrast to the chaos of yesterday. The idea of staying here longer than planned sits heavy on my chest. I glance at my overnight bag on the dresser in the closet before heading out of the room—a constant reminder that I'm supposed to be leaving soon. That I don't stay anywhere for too long. Settling down means attachments, expectations, and eventually, disappointments. The last time I thought about staying in one place, I was nineteen. I'd just graduated, my whole life ahead of me, and for a brief, fleeting moment, I considered staying in San Francisco with my family. Then my father, in his quiet yet firm way, encouraged me to chase the life I wanted. I did. I never looked back—until now.

In the kitchen, I begin preparing the croissants, absently spreading butter across the flaky layers while thinking about last night. When we returned home, I reheated the chicken pie from the restaurant and coupled it with a freshly made salad. That was our dinner. After dinner, I showed Amara around the building, making sure she knew who had access—just my family and the Pages. Even as large as this place is, it gives me peace knowing she's safer here than anywhere else in London. Before she went to bed, I gathered her clothes, washed them, and let her pick a few things from my wardrobe—a fresh start.

What am I doing? This girl may not want my help, yet she is still here. I'm still here. I have a few sessions to fill in for Dr. Owusu over the next two weeks, including the keynote at the museum, and I was supposed to be done with my time in London. But I'm not done.

It's seven. Abandoning the croissants, I head down the hall to wake her. A soft knock on the door gets no response. I push it open. The bed is empty, the covers are pulled back just slightly. When I press my palm against the mattress, it's warm.

I don't panic. If she had left, my phone would have alerted me. I walk through the flat, checking rooms, calling her name.

"Amara. Which room are you in?"

Silence.

Then I remember. Last night, when I asked how she managed to live alone for so long, she told me, "I pretend I'm the only one in the world, in a room with no walls and no windows."

I know where she is.

I step into the library, my gaze landing on the bookshelf that conceals the steel and Kevlar door to the safe room. I press my palm against it.

"Amara, are you in there?"

A pause. Then, softly, "I'm here."

I exhale. Pushing the door open, I find her curled up in a chair, cross-legged in pajamas, writing in a notebook. Her expression is calm, but there's a tightness in her posture, like she's bracing herself.

"Hey, sweetie. How are you?"

"I'm okay."

"You hungry? I made breakfast sandwiches."

"I don't usually eat breakfast."

Why would she? No one has been there to take care of her.

"What's that?" I nod towards her notebook.

She looks down, tracing a line with her finger as if she can feel the words. "A journal. I saw you have a few things here, and I thought..." Her voice trails off.

"You can keep your private things here, too. No one can get to it—just you and me. And I won't look, unless you tell me." I walk to a shelf and pull down a thick, leather-bound book. "Here." I hand it to her, pulling off tape securing a key to the back.

"A dictionary?"

"No, a fireproof lockbox. You can store your journal here. We can buy some more after school."

She takes it carefully, unlocking it and peering inside. "I can fit a few of these in here."

"Five, maybe six."

Her fingers tighten around the key. She looks up at me, her eyes flickering between gratitude and uncertainty. "Thank you."

"Ready for breakfast?" She nods. I gently touch her shoulder. "You can come in here anytime. But I promise, with me, you're just as safe in this building as you are in this room. I won't let anything happen to you."

She locks her things away, and together we exit the room. As we approach her bedroom, I say, "How about you get ready for school, then meet me in the kitchen? If you need anything, you know where my room is."

By the time she emerges from her room, showered and dressed in my oversized jeans and a hunter green sweater, I've almost finished my coffee. She hesitates at the counter, then sits. I slide a plate in front of her.

"You look good in green."

She runs a hand down the sleeve. "I like the feel of this."

"It's cashmere. Keep it. If you like the style, we can go shopping and pick it up in different colors." I lift my cup. "Coffee?" I laugh to myself, trying to remember whether I drank coffee at her age. I was already halfway through university.

"Do you have tea?"

"Yeah, in the cupboard." I move to get it.

"I can get it."

I watch as she moves with confidence in her steps. *Good.* Life hasn't beaten her down completely.

"Amara, did your parents know how advanced you were in school?"

She sets her cup under the coffee maker and presses the hot water button. "They were too caught up in their own mess. My dad was always gambling, and my mom...she kept trying to fix everything. Like, she spent all her energy covering for him and pretending things were okay. Eventually, she started drinking." There's a bitterness wrapped in bereavement in her tone.

I get it.

I hesitate. "Sometimes people do things to mask what they're feeling."

"Or they just have addictions."

She steeps her tea, adds milk, and rejoins me at the counter.

I change the topic to ease the conversation a little. "We didn't get to talk much last night. Are there things you'd like to know about me?"

"You're American. Why are you in London?"

Of course, she'd start with the tricky question. I can't sugarcoat my answer. Trust is built on honesty, even when it's hard to hear. I learned that when my father sat Jake, June, and me down and told us what had happened to Mom.

"I'm filling in for a professor who went back to Africa to care for a sick family member. I have multiple degrees, including one in art history. I'll be delivering a keynote next Monday night on his behalf."

"So, you won't be here long?"

I hold her gaze. "I had planned to leave in two weeks." I pause, watching her expression shift. "Then I met you." She blinks, startled. "You said you wanted to attend college out of the country once you graduated." I set my cup down. "You remind me of me. I was one of the youngest graduates at my university. I've decided to stay in London until you graduate and help you get into the university of your choosing."

Her fingers tighten around her cup. "What?"

"If you trust me." I exhale. "I know it's only been a day, but sometimes that's enough to know when something matters."

She takes a bite of her croissant, taking her time to respond. Her eyes shine and I can't tell if it's from gratitude or grief.

"My mom's parents came here from Nigeria, but eventually returned. She stayed in London, met my dad when she was twenty-one." I study her features. Her complexion is fair like mine, but her hair, although brown, is lighter and has a smoother curl pattern. She notices my scrutiny. "My dad was White British."

I nod. "Both my parents are Black Americans. My mom was Creole."

"Was?"

"She died when I was five."

A pause. Then, softly, "I'm sorry."

And there it is...the condolence.

They come often and unexpectedly when you lose a parent as a child. People ask about your mom, and they don't expect the answer you give. *She died when I was five.*

Then comes the pause. The widening of eyes. The quick intake of breath, as if they can inhale the shock away. And always, the soft, automatic response—*Oh, I'm sorry.*

I nod. I say thank you. I reassure them, as if it's my job to make *them* feel better about my loss. And then, just like that, I move on. But the moment lingers, the reminders settling into my bones. *She's gone.* She's been gone. And somehow, it's still a surprise to people. Amara has many more years of experiences like this to come.

When you're young, condolences follow you like a shadow. People whisper about how *sad* it is, how *hard* it must have been. Teachers, parents of friends, even strangers—always an expression of sympathy, an acknowledgment of absence, a reminder that my life isn't quite normal.

But then you grow up, and something shifts. People stop offering condolences when they learn you've lost a parent. Maybe they assume time has softened the edges of grief, that by now, it's simply a fact of life. But losing a mother at five isn't the same as losing her at fifty. There's no lifetime of memories, no decades of love to hold onto. Just fragments. A laugh I think I remember. A scent that fades a little more every year. A voice I can no longer quite hear in my head.

When you lose someone young, you spend the rest of your life *knowing* they should have been here for every milestone. Every birthday. Every achievement. Every quiet, ordinary day.

So yes, I know she's gone. I've known it for as long as I've known how to speak. But every unexpected condolence is a reminder that she *shouldn't* be.

I nod to her croissant. "Do you like those? I made extra for lunch."

She nods. "Thank you."

I sip my coffee. "Did you have any homework?" When the words come out of my mouth, I'm reminded of my father. He was so attentive to my education after my mom passed away. Mine more than the others. For good reasons. Jake spent more time taking June under his wing.

"I did it all before I left school yesterday."

"Yeah, I remember those days. I used to do the same thing. Well, what do you think? Do you think we can manage this until you're ready to head off to college?"

As I sip my coffee, waiting for her, I let my thoughts drift. Trying to forge a connection between my past and now. Maybe I was never meant to live a rootless life forever. Maybe, just maybe, I've been waiting for a reason to stay. And now, I might have found it.

She smiles teasingly at me. "Can we see how the week goes?"

"Yeah. I'm confident the week will go fine."

Now, I just need to contact Dr. Owusu to extend my visa.

CHAPTER 6

Reality Check

Aaron

DISCUSSING MY DILEMMA WITH Alex and Andrew solidified one thing: I need to do damage control—fast. Media storms like this don't just fizzle out; they build, spiral, and if unchecked, destroy. I've seen companies burn in days. I won't let Saola be one of them.

A knock at my door. I already know who it is. *Kate.*

"I have Bridgette Bromley on the line."

I exhale slowly, settling behind my desk. In front of me, a digital picture frame flashes photos—precious memories of the important people in my life. The most recent one was added only last week. In it, Aedan embraces June, and in her arms, their child.

"Thanks." Kate nods, shutting the door behind her. I pick up. "Why is my name linked to Bromley Inc. in the press?"

"No, hello? No 'Hi, how are you, Bridgette?'" Her voice is all faux sweetness.

"I'm not in the mood for games." My tone is clipped, controlled.

She sighs. "I told you: Dad wants me to take a bigger role."

"That wasn't my question." I lean back in my chair, fingers tapping the desk. "How did the press get those photos?"

"Oh, come on, London, you know how it is. The press follows me everywhere."

"My name is Aaron." My patience thins. "And let's be honest—the press isn't interested in you. They're interested in who you're with. Did you stage that meeting to create this narrative?"

"I may have had an idea they'd be around."

"So, yes." Silence. "What did you expect to gain from this fiasco?"

"I told you I have to take a bigger role."

"And what—your new job title is 'Professional Opportunist?'" My voice sharpens. "Are you trying to boost Bromley's stock price at my expense? Did you really think this would work?"

"Why would I try to harm Saola," she purrs, "when all I really want to do is get closer to you?"

There it is.

Desperation disguised as ambition. She's forcing a connection that doesn't exist. The last time the media speculated about my love life, it was with June Ross. But June was different. She was my best friend, my safe place. And when she fell in love—real love—with Aedan King, it didn't change what we had. The world could speculate all it wanted. June and I knew the truth.

Bridgette, on the other hand, is trying to craft a story that benefits no one but her.

I lean forward. "I'm not available. And I'm not interested in whatever 'offer' you think you're making."

She laughs softly. "Oh, come on, Aaron. Think of the power move. Two tech titans—."

"I'm a tech titan. You're playing with fire." My voice is steel now. "I expect a statement clearing this up."

"Why would I do that? According to the news, we're a couple."

I let out a sharp laugh. "Do you really want to play games with me, Bridgette?"

"No," she says smoothly. "I want to date."

The audacity.

I shake my head. "Not happening. And let me give you a reality check—when the press realizes those photos were a gimmick, they won't blame me. They'll blame you. And your father? He'll be thrilled to know his daughter is running PR stunts instead of fixing Bromley's problems." More silence. "Yeah," I murmur. "You didn't think this all the way through, did you?" I let that sink in before delivering the final blow. "You have twenty-four hours to clean up the story."

I hang up.

This thing with Bridgette is a headache I don't need. I lean back in my chair like I'm buckling in for the ride.

My phone buzzes. It better not be her. I glance at the screen and smile. *JR.*

My best friend and the one who introduced me to the second most important person in my life, June Ross. Jake and I teamed up on a class project our first year at Oxford, and we've been tight ever since. Everyone needs someone who believes in them, who hypes them up when things go sideways. That's us. He calls me his ride or die. I call him mine.

We've always pushed each other to do better—him with numbers, me with tech.

I swipe to answer. "Hey, mate. I suppose you saw the news."

"I was surprised to see you on the wrong side of it again. How you doing?"

"Besides trying to clean up this PR mess, I'm holding steady." I let out a breath. "Got to see your nephew, though."

"He's going to be a heartbreaker," he says, his voice filled with pride. "I heard you missed catching baby sis by a day."

"Yeah, I heard. Maybe one day our paths will cross. Perhaps when I'm old and settled."

Jake laughs. "Right."

"Speaking of, when are you settling down, mate?"

"I've been too focused on work for that."

"Same. The acquisition has been absorbing all my time. Now this...mess."

"You'll get through it. Let me know if you need my help."

"Just glad you called."

"I gotcha, man. I'll text you before I head out there again. Chin up."

"Thanks, mate."

CHAPTER 7

Change of Plans

Jasmine

I DON'T KNOW WHY I thought getting Amara off to school would be difficult or scary. Trekking through Africa, hoping rebel forces wouldn't stop me, was terrifying. Jumping out of a plane with just a parachute and a prayer was petrifying. But sitting in the back seat of a black taxi, talking with Amara, felt...natural. Easy, even. There's a rhythm to our conversations, an unspoken understanding that requires no effort. Maybe it's because we're close in age. Perhaps it's because we have so much in common. Or maybe it's something deeper—like I was meant to find her.

The thought lingers as I go about my morning. Filling in for Dr. Owusu gives me the variety I need. As a guest lecturer, I do what I do best: share my knowledge, not just from university studies but from real-world experience that no textbook can capture. I write on the whiteboard, then turn to my students.

"As we can see, researchers still haven't solved the mysteries of Giza. They hope to utilize advanced radar technology to gain further insights. I'll leave you with this question: What do you think they'll find?"

Murmurs ripple through the classroom, some students scribbling notes while others lean toward each other in quiet debate. I check my watch. Just enough time to go through my email, reach out to Dr. Owusu about the extension, grab a bite to eat, and do some grocery shopping before picking

47

up Amara. I wonder how her day is going, knowing that—for the first time in a long time—she isn't alone anymore.

Leaving the lecture hall, I make my way to the professor's lounge, the faint hum of academic chatter filling the corridor. I slip inside, find a quiet corner, and check my phone. Only a few emails: one from a student who couldn't make it to class today, and—.

My heart slows.

An email from Dr. Owusu, time-stamped ten minutes ago. I open it immediately.

"Greetings, Ms. Ross, I trust you are well. It is with a heavy heart that I inform you my dear sister has passed away. I will return within a few weeks. I would like to thank you for your flexibility and generosity over the past year in supporting my work. I am forever grateful. Dr. Owusu."

A slow exhale leaves my lips, but it doesn't release the pressure in my chest.

I blink at the words, reading them again to make sure I haven't misunderstood. My thumb hovers over the screen for a moment before I type a response, offering my condolences and gratitude for the opportunity to fill in for him.

I press send, then sit back, staring at nothing in particular.

I was banking on that extension. Now, I'm out of options. I'll have to leave when my visa expires and return on a standard six-month visitor visa. It's not ideal. At least I have some time to help Amara adjust before I go, but for the first time, the thought of leaving...of uprooting myself again—makes my stomach churn. I close my eyes, pressing my fingers against my temple.

***

"Never go grocery shopping on an empty stomach." That's what my father used to tell us on the rare occasions when he took us to the store. It

wasn't that he didn't want to take us—we had people for that. No, most of our outings with him were curated: art exhibitions, opening nights at the opera, fundraisers, and exclusive dinners. The places where the uber-rich bring their children to remind the world they're *present*.

But his point is valid. So here I am, back at my usual spot at the pub counter, curbing my appetite before I do something reckless like walk into Harrods and buy half the food hall.

Len wipes down the space in front of me, setting a coaster down with a friendly smile. "Sorry about last night."

"It's not your fault."

"You okay? Seems like something's bothering you."

"I'm good."

"Would you like a menu?"

I shake my head. "I'll have the beetroot and goat cheese salad."

"Bread and butter with that?"

"That sounds great. Thank you."

"Malbec?"

"Sparkling water."

He reaches under the bar, retrieves a cold bottle, and sets a glass in front of me. Holding up a scoop of ice, he quirks a brow. I shake my head.

"You got things to do today." He fills the glass and slides it toward me.

"Something like that." I take a sip, letting the fizz distract me.

"You sure you're okay?"

"I'm good. Just some unexpected travel is all—visa stuff. Nothing I can't handle."

"Got it. I'll be back with your order."

I exhale, my gaze drifting to the bar shelf mirror. Same setting, different suits. The lunch crowd filtering in. I should be relaxed here. I should be able to enjoy a meal in peace.

Then I see him.

A slow, deliberate approach. A smirk like he's already won something. Returning like a bad rash.

Bane.

Damn. He's determined to live up to his name.

"Well, what have we here?" He slides onto the stool beside me, too close for comfort. "Didn't think I'd see you again."

"Same."

"I think we got off on the wrong foot last night."

"On the contrary, we didn't get off on anything."

Len returns with my meal, setting the plate down with a knowing look. "Can I get you anything else?"

"No, thank you."

He turns to the bane of my existence. "What can I get you, Mr. Roth?"

"I'll have the soup of the day and a beer. And before she leaves this time, put her meal on my tab."

I hold Bane's gaze but address Len. "Don't."

"But I insist."

"I'm not sure what you're used to, Mr. Roth, but I pay my way in life. That's not up for debate."

Bane leans in slightly, voice dropping to something almost intimate. "How long did you say you were here for?"

"I didn't."

His smirk deepens. "You might want to rethink how you speak to me. I'm just trying to make friends."

"I don't need any more friends." I pick up my fork. "Now, if you'll excuse me, I'm going to eat my lunch."

Len busies himself at the other end of the bar, wisely staying out of it. I keep my focus on my salad, treating Bane's presence like background noise. He starts up again anyway, talking like we're long-lost friends.

Then he says the words that send ice through my veins.

"I'd be careful if I were you. People like me...we notice things. Who comes. Who stays. Who shouldn't be here at all."

My hand stills around my fork. He must have overheard my conversation with Len.

I turn to him, my face carefully neutral. "Is this your kink? Forcing yourself into conversations where you're not wanted? What part of 'I'm not available' are you struggling with?"

I fold my arms, ensuring the ring I placed on my left hand yesterday catches the light.

His gaze flickers to it. "A fiancé, huh?" He chuckles, slow and smug. "I could put an end to that with the swipe of a pen."

Fuck.

He's right. If I had a real fiancé, we'd have to give notice of our intent to marry. And if he's fishing for information, I've just given him a scent to follow.

I take a slow, deep breath, forcing my body to stay relaxed. But my mind is already spinning ahead.

Forty-four days. Four months. A problem I could have handled—until now.

I push my unfinished salad aside and slide off the stool, smoothing my shirt as I stand. "Len, close out my tab."

I don't wait for a response. I don't acknowledge the true bane of my existence sitting to my right. I shove my phone into my pocket and head for the door, the weight of his gaze pressing against my back.

I need to call my sister.

CHAPTER 8

The Favor

Jasmine

FIVE BAGS LATER, I realize I could have just skipped lunch altogether. Seeing Bane again knocked the appetite right out of me. Instead, I'd done what any rational person does when stress coils tight in their chest—I over-shopped. Not out of hunger, but out of sheer frustration, stuffing my cart with things I didn't need just to fill the empty space gnawing at me.

As I start unpacking, I hit call on my sister's name. June picks up before the first ring ends.

"Jas?" Her voice is soft, edged with the gentle exhaustion of new motherhood. In the background, I hear the faintest rustling—her newborn, probably shifting in sleep. "Are you okay?"

"Hey, how's baby King?"

"Just got him down."

"I can call back."

"No," she says, and I hear the warmth in her voice. "It's good to hear your voice again. Last week was...nice. It felt good having you home. Are you ready for another adventure?"

"I think I found one."

"Where to this time?"

"More like...what?"

A pause. "I don't understand. Do I need to come get you? Are you hurt?"

"No, nothing like that." I inhale sharply. The words don't come easily, but I say them anyway. "I need a favor."

June is silent for a second. I can practically hear her raising an eyebrow. "A favor. From me? You've never asked me for anything, Jas."

"June..."

"Okay, honey. Tell me—I promise, I got you."

So, I tell her. About Amara, the girl I pulled from an alleyway. About Bane, and my visa situation. June listens the way only she can—without judgment, without interrupting. Just absorbing every word.

When I finish, she exhales.

"So, you got any advice?"

"Just so we're clear—this girl, Amara. Are you absolutely sure she's not...taking advantage? You know, considering who you are?"

"She has no idea who I am."

"That doesn't mean others won't clue her in. And you said she's hesitant to stay with you long-term?"

"She doesn't know what she wants. But if she doesn't stay, she goes back to the streets. Or worse. And you and I both know that's no place for a young girl."

A quiet moment stretches between us. We don't have to say it aloud to know what we're both thinking—what it was like to grow up without a mother, how we had to figure out too much, too soon.

"She must be special," June finally says, voice softer. "For you to even consider changing your plans."

"She's like us," I admit softly. "No mother figure. And I know we turned out okay, but I wouldn't wish that kind of emptiness on anyone."

There's a pause on the other end, long enough that I wonder if June is replaying our childhood, too.

"We didn't exactly give Jeannette a chance," she says eventually.

I scoff, my throat tightening. "Be honest, June. She was the adult. We were kids, broken ones at that. She didn't try hard enough."

I take bagels out of the bag and set them on the counter, lightly tracing the edge of the pack, while inside, I'm tracing the outlines of memories I've tried to leave in the past.

She could have tried harder. That's what it really comes down to. There were so many moments when she could have stepped up. When silence between us stretched too long, when we cried ourselves to sleep, when we lashed out or shut down or just needed someone to say, *I see you. I know this hurts.*

Even if she didn't know how to fix it, she could have done something. Anything. Found us a therapist. Dragged Dad out of denial. Asked questions. Sat with us in the ache. But instead, she pulled away. Acted like love was a switch that only worked when it was easy.

We needed her. But she wanted him more.

June doesn't say anything at first, and I hear the faint rustling of her shifting. "Okay," she murmurs. "Give me a few hours to think on it. If you feel this is the right thing, we'll make it happen."

My heart beats heavier in my chest. Not with doubt, but with the weight of doing something different. Of choosing to be the kind of woman we once needed.

"Thanks, June."

"What about this Bane situation? You think he's going to be a problem?"

"The worst kind."

"Are you okay if I call in a favor from one of the elites?"

I let out a breath. "I don't see a way through this without it."

More rustling. Then another voice—deeper, steadier. *Aedan.*

"Hey, King," he whispers to his son.

June's voice is teasing. "Aedan, say hi to Jasmine."

A moment later, he's on the line. "Jasmine. How are you? Shall I send the jet for you?"

I laugh. "Not this time. Maybe next."

"Noted."

"Kiss baby for me."

"I will," he says before handing the phone back to June.

"My man worships the ground that baby walks on, and he can't even walk yet," she says.

I smile, then hesitate. My voice is quieter when I finally say, "Did I tell you how beautiful it was to see you two together?"

She's silent for a half beat, then I hear it—the thick emotion in her voice. "Yeah. And Jas... I miss you. I love that you're only a few hours away now."

If this works out, I'll be here longer. I surprise myself by thinking the words, then do the unthinkable by giving them life.

"If we can solve my problem, it'll be like that for a while." I swallow hard, not used to this weight in my chest. "I'll let you go. Just...know I miss you, too."

"K," she says softly, and the call ends.

I stare at the bags on my counter, at the ridiculous amount of food I bought, and blow out a breath.

If anyone can help me fix this, it's June.

CHAPTER 9

The Perfect Mate

Aaron

MY PHONE BUZZES, AND I smirk when I see the name. *June.* I'm surprised she even has time to call with young King running the household like a tiny dictator.

"Hey, handsome," she says, the video shaking as she settles into a chair.

I prop my phone up on the desk.

"Hey, beautiful. Please tell me this call has nothing to do with you running away from Aedan again."

"You're on speaker, mate." Aedan's voice rumbles in. "And the only person my wife will be running to is me." He appears over June's shoulder, pulling her onto his lap like some territorial beast.

"Hey, mate. Good—I see *you've* learned your lesson."

"It took a second."

"How's the little King?"

"Sleeping."

"You have that effect on people," I tease.

June rolls her eyes and shifts so her face fills the screen. "Anyway. I didn't call so that you and my man could puff your chests at each other. Although a wrestling match between you two could be interesting."

"Anything for you, beautiful," I reply smoothly.

"Alright, Sunshine, get on with it," Aedan presses, his arm locked around her.

"I really wish I was there so I could butter you up to ask this favor, but. ."

"I'll send the jet."

Aedan leans back in mock offense. "Mate, you're pushing it."

"Never mind. Listen, London—this is serious. Can you marry my sister?"

I cough. Hard. "What?"

"You heard her, mate. Jasmine needs a husband."

"Is this some elaborate scheme to make sure your wife doesn't run back to me?"

Aedan doesn't dignify that with a response.

"Hear her out," he says instead.

June continues. "I'll let Jasmine explain the details, but it's only for six months. Tops."

"What?" I blink. "This has to be a joke."

"It's not a joke," Aedan confirms.

"She needs a man."

I narrow my eyes. "Needs?"

"Not like *needs*, need," June clarifies quickly. "It's a temporary fix to a problem."

"That involves marriage," I state flatly. My brain is already conjuring Alex's face when he hears about this mess.

"Temporary marriage," she corrects.

"Right. So, naturally, you thought of me?"

"Well, have you met yourself? Who wouldn't want to marry you?"

"Flattery is suspicious at this stage."

She sighs. "Look, I *would* have asked Jake to help me find someone, but—"

"JR doesn't know, and you don't want him to," I finish for her.

"Exactly."

"He's going to know the second he sees her."

"Yeah, but he doesn't need to know the details."

"This is the elusive sister, right?" I ask. "The one I've never met."

"I only have *one* sister."

"You say that like I keep track."

She glares. "London."

"Get someone else."

"Only you can do this?"

"Why?"

"Babe," June says, turning to Aedan. "Can you step out while I answer him?"

"No."

She exhales, preparing for battle. "Fine. Don't complain when I say what I have to say."

I cross my arms. "June. Why me? Why not one of my brothers?"

"First, the person has to live in London. And—"

"Andrew lives in London."

She presses her lips together before finally letting out a breath. "Because you're the only person in this world I would have married if I hadn't married Aedan."

Aedan exhales through his nose. "Damn it, June."

I smirk. "Well, there goes our friendship. King will never let me in the house again."

They exchange a look that's a conversation in itself.

"He'll do whatever I ask," June says lightly.

"Within reason," Aedan mutters.

I lean back, rubbing my temple. "Alright. Last question—what do I get out of this?"

"My undying love and gratitude."

"You get to continue living," Aedan interjects.

"Mate, get over it. Your wife loves me, and that will never change."

June groans. "Will you two stop?"

I exhale. "So this has a definitive expiration date?"

"Yes."

I close my eyes. I already know I'm going to regret this.

Chapter 10

It Starts and Ends with Us

Aaron

THE RESTAURANT HUMS WITH low conversation, the clink of silverware against fine china, and the occasional burst of laughter from a nearby table. Sunlight filters through the tall windows, casting a warm glow over the pristine white tablecloths. It's an elegant space, but not pretentious—a place for business brunches and quiet indulgences, not grand romantic gestures. Perfect for this meeting.

I stand when she walks in. *Jasmine Ross.* Fair honey-brown skin, about five feet six at most, a striking mix of her siblings, June and Jake, whom I refer to as JR. Her presence commands attention, though she moves with an easy grace. A white blazer hangs off her shoulders, sleeves pushed up at the elbows, and underneath, a low-cut tank top that hints at defiance rather than provocation. Light blue jeans, heels that add a few inches but don't diminish our height difference when she stops in front of me.

She's stunning. More than the pictures. More than I expected.

I dip my head to brush a polite kiss against her cheek. She smells like spiced vanilla and something subtly floral—unexpected, intriguing. It's then that I notice it—the gold peace sign necklace, similar to the diamond-encrusted one I gave to June—a silent tribute.

"Jasmine. It's nice to finally meet you." I pull out a chair for her, the warmth of her skin briefly touching mine as she sits.

"Aaron. Or do I call you London?" Her voice is rich with amusement.

"I answer to both." I hand her a menu.

"My sister calls you London."

"Your brother calls me Aaron."

"Well, London. It's nice to meet you." She studies me, eyes sharp with curiosity. "I suppose I should come up with a special name for you."

"Besides honey?" I counter smoothly. A tease. Testing the waters.

She smirks. "Well, this isn't awkward at all."

The waiter approaches. "Are you ready to order, or would you like more time?"

I gesture to Jasmine. She doesn't look at the menu, just at me, as if I'm a puzzle she's considering whether to solve.

"Eggs Benedict, a side of berries, and Darjeeling tea," she says.

"First flush?" I ask. She nods.

I turn to the waiter. "My wife will have eggs Benedict with a side of berries. Heavy on blueberries. And first flush Darjeeling tea. I'll have two eggs over easy, bacon, and toast."

My wife. I like how that rolls off my tongue as if it were meant to be.

"And your drink, sir?"

"Coffee, black."

The server disappears into the back, and my eyes shift to Jasmine.

Jasmine arches a brow. "Your wife?"

"That's why you're here, isn't it?" I don't blink.

She tilts her head. "Why would you order extra berries?"

"You wouldn't have ordered a side if you didn't like them." I take a measured sip of water. "I'm making sure my wife gets what she wants."

"You're tall like Jake."

"You're the perfect height."

She watches me, lips curving slightly before she asks, "So, tell me. What's wrong with you?"

I bark out a laugh. "That's direct. I could ask the same."

"I asked you first."

I lean back, considering. "You tell me."

"I suspect you tick a lot of boxes for the right person. I want to know why my sister didn't marry you. Are you gay? You do know my brother likes women, right?"

I exhale sharply, surprised into amusement. "I don't suppose you have an inner voice?"

"I don't need one."

Of course, she doesn't. Jasmine Ross, the youngest of the Ross empire, was raised with the world at her fingertips. She graduated from university at nineteen, spent the past seven years traveling the globe alone. No one tells her what to do.

Still...she's looking for a husband.

"Do I tick any of your boxes?" I smirk.

"You didn't answer my question."

"There's nothing *wrong* with me."

The server returns with our meal. I watch as she delicately places a napkin on her lap. Her hands—small, elegant, unpolished nails—move with the kind of precision that comes from practice. Refined. Controlled. Yet I know from her family that she was trained in combat. She could likely dismantle someone twice her size if she wanted to. The contrast fascinates me.

I lift my fork. "Bon appétit."

We eat in silence, punctuated by quick glances, unspoken observations. Then, without hesitation, she reaches across the table with her fork and spears a strip of bacon from my plate.

"You still hungry?" I ask. "I can have them bring you something."

"What? Were you going to eat that?"

"I might have, given the chance."

She chews unimpressed. "I'll remember that for next time."

I shake my head. "You're nothing like your sister."

"Good."

"Good?"

"Yeah, I won't have to worry about you liking me." I pause, setting down my fork. She continues, "I heard you had a thing for her. Does my brother-in-law know you're still pining for his wife?"

I stiffen. *There it is.* Skepticism? Defensiveness? Maybe a bit of curiosity. Or perhaps something more—something even I refuse to admit.

"I'm not pining," I say evenly. "Like your brother, she's my best friend—I'd do anything for her. Including marrying you."

She snorts. "Gee, thanks. Don't worry. It won't be for long."

"You know, for someone who needs me to stay in the country, you could try to be nicer."

"This is all I got."

"You sure about that?"

"Positive."

I study her, something shifting beneath my ribs. She reminds me of June, but not in the way I expected. June was reckless, vibrant in a way that pulled people into her orbit. Jasmine is sharp edges and cool distance. I can't tell if she's keeping me at bay because she doesn't trust me—or if she doesn't trust herself.

"You met a lot of people during your travels," I say. "No one here you have an interest in?"

Her expression flickers, the playfulness gone. "Are you inquiring about my love life?"

"Trying to figure out why I'm here, instead of someone you know. An old fling, maybe."

A beat of silence. Her posture shifts, her gaze hardens.

"I'm not here to talk about that."

Right.

"I doubt anyone else would be willing to put up with you," I say, trying to nudge us back to something lighter.

"Same goes for you." She wipes her mouth and stands. "Thanks for breakfast, Mr. Adler." Her voice is smooth, impersonal. She reaches for her purse, pulls the strap over her shoulder, and walks out without another word.

Damn.

She leaves, and I let her go.

I don't chase after her. I should, but I don't. Instead, I sit here, fingers tapping against the table, replaying the conversation in my head. I'm not even sure where it went wrong. One moment, we were talking—if you can call it that—the next, she was standing, giving me one last look before disappearing through the door.

I exhale sharply, rubbing a hand over my jaw. This wasn't how it was supposed to go. June asked me for one favor—meet her sister, talk to her, and make this ridiculous arrangement work. It shouldn't have been difficult. But somehow, I managed to mess it up before we even started.

Jasmine Ross is...unexpected.

I don't know what I was expecting, but it wasn't her. It wasn't the sharp wit or the fire in her eyes when she called me out about June. It wasn't the way she looked at me—assessing, measuring, deciding. And it damn sure wasn't the way I reacted to her.

Attraction complicates things. I don't have the luxury of making reckless decisions. Not anymore. My brother's voice is already in my head, reminding me of my responsibilities, of the scandal that nearly cost me everything, of the fact that settling down isn't a choice but an obligation.

Maybe that's the problem.

Maybe I see this whole situation as another form of control, another forced decision, another way my life isn't my own. And instead of handling it like the competent, logical man I'm supposed to be, I let something in me...something stubborn, something reckless, sabotage it before it even begins.

But that doesn't explain her.

Jasmine walked away for her own reasons, and I don't understand them. Not yet. But I will. Because whether I like it or not, this starts and ends with us. And I'm not done yet.

CHAPTER 11

Rough Days

Jasmine

As I step outside, the sun is shining, and there's a slight breeze reminiscent of cool breezes on the Marina in San Francisco. It's a beautiful day—too beautiful to deal with Aaron's craziness. Thank God there's a taxi heading this way. I step to the curb and flag it down.

"Page building in Holborn," I tell the driver, then take my phone out.

I hesitate before tapping the screen.

This was supposed to be simple. A meeting, a proposal, an agreement—nothing more. But with Aaron, it doesn't end there. Piecing together what June's told me and my brief glimpse into the man, Aaron is so much more. He's complicated. Controlled. Annoyingly handsome. The kind of man who expects the world to fit into neat little boxes, and yet, when I was sitting across from him, I could feel the way I threw him off balance.

The way he threw *me* off balance.

And that's the problem.

I don't get thrown. I move, I shift, I leave before anyone can pin me down. But with Aaron, there's history. A past I wasn't part of but can't ignore. He thought he'd marry June. *My sister.* And now, here I am, entertaining a fake marriage with him like it's just another adventure.

But it isn't an adventure. It's a risk. A commitment to a man I never met before today.

If it works—if I can pull this off, what does that mean for me? For us? And if it doesn't...then what?

I sigh, gripping my phone tighter. I should just walk away, but this isn't just about me anymore. It's about Amara—the girl who suddenly crashed into my world, needing help in ways I understand all too well. She reminds me of myself, all sharp edges and survival instincts, except I had privilege to fall back on when I ran. She doesn't.

This isn't just a reckless choice—it's a sacrifice—a way to give her something steady when I've never had the patience to be steady myself.

So why does it feel like I'm the one standing on shaky ground?

I exhale sharply and finally tap the screen.

June answers immediately.

"Well, that was a colossal waste of my time," I say.

There's a pause, then, "What was a waste of time?" Aedan's deep, melodic Irish accent catches me off guard.

"Oh, hey, Aedan. I was trying to reach June. Is she there?"

"She's in the shower."

"And you're not? Damn. I guess the honeymoon is over."

He barks out a laugh. "So we're clear; I was headed there before you rang, little lady." I hear the faint sound of running water getting louder and louder.

"Honey, what are you waiting for?" my sister calls out in the background.

"Between you and your sister, apparently, I can't get to the shower fast enough," he tells June.

"My sister. What?"

"Sunshine, your sister is on the phone."

My cheeks warm, trying not to think about the private moment I'm interrupting. "Um, Aedan, don't bother. Tell her to call me after...*long* after whatever is taking place is done," I say, quickly ending the call.

It doesn't take long to get home. The moment I step inside the Holborn flat, I exhale, letting the weight of the morning settle over me. The meeting with Aaron had gone about as well as walking barefoot on broken glass. My chest still carries the sting of it, frustration and something unspoken caught in my throat.

I toss my purse onto the console table and sink into the couch, the plush cushions swallowing me whole. Silence blankets the space, save for the hum of the city outside. I tap my phone awake and scroll to the one person I know will answer without hesitation...Jake.

It takes a few rings, long enough for doubt to creep in, but then his groggy voice breaks through.

"Jas?" The background is dark, his voice thick with sleep. Guilt pricks at me. I've been so distracted, I didn't even check the time zone.

"Hey, Jake. Did I wake you?"

"It's okay," he says, a yawn stretching between us. "How are you? Where are you?"

"I'm good. Still in London." It's only a half-truth. My body is here, but my mind feels untethered, floating somewhere between past choices and uncertain futures. "I just wanted to hear your voice."

"That's nice," he says, warmth threading through his tone. "I'm assuming you couldn't get a hold of sis?"

He knows me too well. June is always my first call, my anchor.

"She and Aedan are in the shower."

"God, spare me the details."

"My sentiments exactly." A small smile tugs at my lips, the first real one all morning.

"So, talk to me."

I hesitate, pressing my palm against my temple. "How did you know so early on that joining the firm was the right thing to do?"

A soft chuckle. "I don't know if it was. Numbers come easy to me. RE needed someone with my skills, so I kept moving up the ranks."

"You're like a rockstar in the finance world," I say, and I mean it. He's built a name for himself—stable, respected, certain. Things I've never been.

"That means a lot coming from you." There's a pause, then, "I thought about becoming a professor once, but academia didn't feel like the right fit."

"Why not?"

"I wanted to be around innovative minds, people who push boundaries, not just theorized about them."

"You mean people outside of your area of expertise. Like June and the others."

"Exactly. Variety. Collaboration. I still don't know if I made the right decision, but I'm happy. I enjoy the people I work with." His voice softens. "I wish you were here."

My throat tightens. I want to tell him I miss him too, that I miss all of them. That there are moments when I wish I were more like them. But the words knot in my throat, tangled in uncertainty.

Instead, I murmur, "I'm still figuring things out."

"That's okay too," he says, his voice steady, reassuring. "Take your time, sis. Whatever is for you will come exactly when you need it. We got you—me, June, Dad. We love you."

I close my eyes, absorbing his words like warmth on a cold day.

"Thanks, Jake."

"I'm glad you called. Love you."

"Love you, too."

I hang up, the silence settling in again, but this time, it feels different. Less empty. Less...alone.

***

My discussion with Jake reminded me of what it means to be a Ross. Like the skyscraper towering over San Francisco, we may sway when the earth trembles, but we don't bend, and we sure as hell don't crumble. I didn't when a rogue thug stole my mom's life. I didn't when I stepped into the unknown, alone. And I won't crumble now.

During the cab ride home, Amara is quiet. I get it. Life dealt her a bad hand, and suddenly the flip of a card has offered her a chance at a new life—one with me. She's had most of the day to think about whether she wants to accept it or...what? Even for me, the alternative is too bleak to consider.

When we arrive back at the flat, Amara quietly slips out of her coat and hangs it in the foyer closet before heading straight down the hall past the bedrooms. I don't have to guess where she's going—straight to the safe room to write in her journal.

I let her be, knowing she needs time to process. This isn't just about school or a new home—it's a whole new life. And no matter how much better this one may be, it doesn't erase the weight of where she's been.

I think about how I was at her age, though I was already in university. Mentally, I was like her—a motherless child, lost, trying to find my place in the world. Searching for...*her*. The woman who could guide me, help me see who I was beyond expectations, beyond circumstances. I had to figure it out on my own. Amara doesn't have to.

By the time she emerges, it's almost dinner time. I've just finished plating our pizza and salad when she walks into the kitchen, her expression distant. I pull out a chair for her, and she drops into it with a sigh.

"Rough day?" I ask, setting a plate in front of her.

She shrugs, picking at the edge of her crust. "Kids looked at me differently today."

I settle into my chair and take a sip of water. "Because you got a ride?"

"Not just that. My clothes. My hair...stuff. People had things to say." She hesitates, then pushes her plate slightly away. "And...a boy noticed me for the first time."

I lift a brow. "Ah. And how do we feel about that?"

"I don't know," she admits. "I mean, I liked it. But it also felt weird."

I nod, understanding all too well. "Change does that. Makes you feel like you don't know where you fit."

Amara looks down, tracing patterns on the table with her finger. "I don't want to stop being me just because I have different clothes and better things now."

"You don't have to," I say. "You can still wear some of your favorite things. Mix them with the new. Make it your own."

She doesn't look convinced, so I pull my phone from my pocket. "Here, look at this." I scroll through my pictures until I find one of June with her full, natural afro, dressed in one of her signature modern seventies outfits—bold print top, mixed with muted skirts, and four-inch heels. She stands out everywhere she goes, not because she follows trends, but because she owns her look. "People notice June," I tell Amara. "Not because she's a wash-and-repeat of everyone else, but because she's bold enough to be herself, no matter what anyone thinks. That's how we were raised."

Amara studies the picture, then glances at me. "I wish I could wear my hair like that."

I smile. "There are times I wish I could, too. But I'd have to do too many things to get my hair to stand up like that."

"My hair won't do that either."

"And it doesn't have to," I say gently. "Do what works for you. Be you." I consider the advice someone once gave me. *Be you.* I hold Amara's gaze, giving weight to my words. "And anyone who can't accept that needs to step back."

She's quiet for a long moment, then finally picks up a slice of pizza. I watch as she takes a bite, a small smile creeping onto her face. It's then I realize, we'll be fine. *She'll* be fine.

One step at a time. One piece of herself reclaimed at a time. That's how we move forward.

Chapter 12

Brothers

Aaron

DAMN IT. JUNE IS going to kill me. That is if Aedan doesn't first.

The elevator dings, and I step onto the executive floor, adjusting my cufflinks out of habit. I consider calling June, but that thought quickly dies a sudden death. She has her hands full already. I can handle this.

As I stride toward my office, Kate intercepts me, her heels clicking in double time to keep up. "I think you should know—"

"Please don't say it's Bridgette again."

"No, it's—"

She doesn't get to finish. Because as soon as I push open my office door, I understand exactly what she meant.

Andrew is here again. But this time, he's not in my chair.

Alex is.

Kate exhales, hands on her hips. "I tried to tell you."

"It's fine, Kate. Reschedule my next meeting."

She nods, shooting me a look that says *good luck*, before slipping out and closing the door behind her.

Alex leans back in my chair, fingers templed beneath his chin like an ancient king surveying his domain. Andrew lounges nearby, arms crossed, waiting.

"Alex," I say, walking in. "When did you get in?"

"An hour ago. I expected you to be here."

"That's another story."

Both brothers track my movement as I cross the room and lean on the credenza. The weight of their scrutiny is palpable.

"I'm listening," Alex says, voice all business. Andrew just raises a brow—silent, expectant, *amused*.

I inhale. "Let me start with: I dealt with Bridgette."

Alex nods. "I read her statement. It's enough to keep the auditors at bay...for now. Your face tells me that won't last."

I exhale. "I'm getting married."

Silence. Then....

Andrew presses his lips together and shakes his head, slow and deliberate, like he's trying to ward off a migraine.

Alex's eyes burn so hot I almost want to look away. *Almost.*

"In five minutes, I'm going to order a drug test and a psych evaluation if the next two words out of your mouth aren't *I'm joking.*"

"It's not a joke."

Alex snaps his fingers. "Kate—."

"It's okay, Kate," I cut in as the door opens. "I'll let you know if we need you." She gives us a baffled glance before nodding and disappearing again. "I can explain."

Andrew rests his elbow on the desk and his chin between his thumb and forefinger like he's ready for the show.

"We're listening," Andrew says, finally speaking.

"June needs a favor."

Alex's expression sharpens. "We've had this discussion already. What part of *she's married* are you not getting?"

"I'm not marrying her." I glance between them. "I'm marrying her sister, Jasmine."

A beat.

"Fuck me," Alex mutters, running a hand down his face. He leans back in my chair like he needs the support. "Hell, I thought you'd never even met her. What is she, pregnant or something?"

Andrew closes his eyes briefly. *Jesus, give me strength* might as well be written on his forehead.

"No, she's not pregnant," I say, barely containing my irritation. "Her visa is expiring. She needs to be in London for six months, max. This solves her problem. And it helps me, too. The media will see me as stable. By the time the CMA wraps its investigation, the marriage will be over."

Andrew tilts his head. "How is this even possible? You never met her."

"That's where I was this morning."

"Getting married."

"Meeting her," I clarify.

Alex pushes off the chair and walks to the wall of windows, staring out at the city. "So let me get this straight. You're going to marry a woman you met this morning for six months...then what? Get divorced?"

"That about sums it up."

Alex turns his gaze, pinning me in place. "Aaron, I know you love June—"

"This is not about that."

He studies me, looking for cracks. I give him nothing.

"And not your heart?"

June and I figured out over a year ago that we weren't in love. Did I want to let our connection go? No. But I had to. And I thought I did when I took her to Aedan. Thought I'd severed the last thread when I watched her walk down the aisle. But they're all still there. Not just her. JR, too.

And then Jasmine walked in. And suddenly, I realized maybe *this is* about her. That somehow, my connection to them was leading me *to* her.

Why? I don't know yet.

I respond truthfully. "No," I say finally. "This is about helping my best friend and her brother's sister. That's it."

Alex exhales, rubbing his jaw. "Throwing the CMA off makes sense. But Aaron, this is risky. I can't have you damaging our reputation. Or the Ross family's. I want to be kept in the loop. If this goes sideways—"

"I'll keep it in check."

Andrew lets out a low laugh. "So what, he can just up and get married?"

Alex glances at him, then back at me. His expression shifts, something like reluctant acceptance settling.

"He's our brother," Alex finally says. Then to me: "So...when's the wedding?"

CHAPTER 13

Try Again

Jasmine

As the saying goes, "If at first you don't succeed, try, try again." That's the mantra on repeat in my head following my disastrous breakfast with Aaron.

After getting Amara settled for the night, I must have picked up my phone a thousand times. Fingers hovering over the screen, ready to call Aaron and...what? Talk? Apologize? I haven't quite figured that part out yet.

After my shower, I change into my PJs and plop onto the bed, settling cross-legged with my phone in hand to work on my keynote speech. Halfway through my edits, his name pops up on the screen. My breath catches.

Aaron.

I hesitate for a second, then tap the screen, my smile small and unsure. "Hey."

"Hey," he replies, his voice lower, softer than I expect.

His hair is slightly tousled like he's been running his hand through it but he's still handsome as ever.

"Video-call, huh?"

His response is immediate. His voice...velvet. "I wanted to see your face."

My pulse races. "What if I wasn't dressed?"

"You wouldn't have picked up."

I huff a quiet laugh. "You're right."

"You okay to talk?" he asks, studying me like he's trying to read between the lines.

I nod. "I shouldn't have walked out."

"I could have handled things better."

This is it. A breath. A beat. A second chance.

"Can we try again?" I ask.

His lips curve slightly. "Hi, I'm Aaron Adler. People call me Aaron, Adler, A-squared, but your sister calls me London."

I mirror his smirk. "Hi, London. I'm Jasmine Ross. I don't spend enough time around people for them to give me nicknames, but my family calls me Jas."

"Hi, Jas."

For a moment, the air between us lightens, but it's fragile, a thin layer of ice over deep waters. I exhale slowly. "Can I be honest?"

"Always."

"I don't know what I'm doing."

"Most times I do. In this situation, I don't either. But I promise, Jas, we'll figure it out...together." His voice is steady, his gaze unwavering. "Now, tell me why you need to be married."

I tell him everything—Dr. Owusu, my visa situation, the way my status in the UK is hanging by a thread. Then I mention Bane, explaining why leaving isn't an option. The second I say Bane's name, Aaron's silvery gray eyes darken, turning slate.

"Where is Bane Roth?"

"I don't know. I've only ever seen him at the pub."

"Don't go there again without me."

I roll my eyes. "I can handle him."

"That's not the point. I'm not the kind of man who would let my wife eat alone in a pub. I'd make time to be with her."

My heart stutters. "Your wife."

"You."

The word settles between us, heavier than it should be. For seven years, it's only been me. In less than a week, I've acquired an entire family.

Amara. He doesn't know...yet.

"London." His nickname rolls off my tongue with casual ease. It's the one my sister gave him when he first called her looking for Jake.

"Yeah?"

"Did my sister mention I have a kid?" Silence stretches, thick and unrelenting. I watch the range of emotions flicker across his face before I break the silence. "She's almost seventeen."

His brows furrow. "How is that possible? You would have been—"

"She's not my biological daughter." I exhale and tell him about Amara, how I found her, why I couldn't walk away. How this ties to my visa. He listens without judgment, only quiet consideration.

"How is Amara?" he asks.

"Adjusting."

"Does she know what you're doing? About *us*?"

"I plan to tell her soon. I've been slowly building her trust."

He nods, exhaling sharply. "So, I get a package deal."

"Temporarily." My voice wavers. "I didn't mean to upend your life with my issues."

"Temporarily," he repeats. But there's a hint of something like the word tastes bitter, as if he's testing its weight on his tongue. Or maybe I'm just imagining things.

"There's one more thing..." I hesitate.

He arches a brow. "What's that? You have a son?"

"No." A smirk tugs at my lips before I sober. "According to the laws, we have to give thirty days' notice to wed. That's putting my timeline close to my visa expiration."

His expression doesn't shift. "Getting one in twenty-four hours won't be a problem. Let's meet tomorrow to sign our documents."

My stomach twists. "You have that type of connection?"

"*We* have that type of connection," he corrects. "However, this escalates your timeline."

"For?"

"Having your conversation with Amara. You two should be moved in by the time we get married on Saturday."

My breath catches. I lean back into the headboard. Married. Saturday.

I don't respond. The words get lodged in my throat. He notices, tilting his head.

"Don't worry, Jasmine, I won't disrupt your life any more than it already has been. Our marriage is on paper only. You and Amara can continue as planned. But...this marriage also solves one of my problems."

"I don't understand."

"My public persona has taken a few hits lately."

"Bridgette. I saw that," I say, rolling my eyes. "She's notorious in social circles, even in the States, for her tabloid antics."

"But the business world doesn't know that. A marriage will give the appearance of stability. Clients like that."

"I get it. That's why my brother keeps his private life under lock and key."

"Yeah. He's a good guy. I just wanted you to know this marriage benefits both of us. We can talk more tomorrow about what our public life looks like."

I nod, but my chest tightens, and my finger hovers over the screen, ready to end the call. Marriage on paper only. It feels so...cheap. But what did I expect? I'm basically forcing my life onto him. But if he's right...maybe this helps him too. *Maybe.*

"Jasmine."

"Yeah."

"We'll be fine."

I swallow hard, offering him a tight nod before the screen goes dark.

CHAPTER 14

Showtime

Jasmine

TWO WEEKS. THAT'S HOW long I had planned to be here. Never imagining that in two days...I'll be married.

A yawn escapes as I lean against the kitchen counter, cup in hand, sipping my tea, waiting for Amara. The warmth seeps through my fingers, but it does nothing to ease the weight pressing on my chest. I didn't get much sleep after my call with Aaron last night. Even after I finished writing my keynote, my mind refused to rest. I spent most of the night up, thinking. Rationalizing. Debating.

How do I tell Amara about Aaron and what that means for *us*? How do I make her understand that this isn't a bad thing? That I'm not leaving, that *this*...this choice, this marriage, isn't about obligation or convenience. It's about *her*.

She's been let down too many times before. By systems. By people who should have fought for her. I refuse to be one more name on that list. But how do I convince her of that when I'm still figuring it out myself?

For years, my life has been movement—new places, new experiences, never staying long enough for roots to take hold. And now, in the span of days, I'm planting myself in the one place I never expected. A marriage. A home. A country that isn't my own.

Marriage. Getting married should scare me more than it does. I've stood on the edge of cliffs in remote jungles and maneuvered through the labyrinth of high society expectations with a practiced smile; however, *this*...the impending conversation with Amara, feels more daunting than any of it.

I exhale, tightening my grip on the cup.

Amara deserves to know the truth—not just the logistics, but the heart of it. That I'm not doing this because I have to. I'm doing this because I want to. Because for the first time in my life, staying, even if only for a while, feels like the right thing.

Footsteps echo in the hallway, pulling me from my thoughts. *Showtime.*

I take a slow sip of my tea as Amara enters the kitchen, watching her move with the quiet grace of someone who's learned not to take up too much space. She'll learn one day that it's okay to fill a room with her presence. And just like June, all eyes will land on her when she enters the room.

"Good morning." I greet her with a smile.

I study her as she goes to the fridge. She took my advice, wearing a pair of my jeans coupled with her sweater. She reminds me so much of myself at her age, navigating the world on her own, too self-sufficient for a child. I want to tell her she doesn't have to be.

"Morning," she replies, opening the door and taking out the orange juice.

I grab the plate of toasted bagels, fruit, and the assorted accoutrements: marmalade, cream cheese, ham, and butter—more than enough to make sweet and savory breakfast sandwiches. Figuring out what to make for breakfast for someone besides myself is a new adventure. I place everything on the counter and sit beside Amara.

"I love your outfit." I grab a bagel and drown it in cream cheese. "We should go shopping this weekend. Get the stuff you want. Clothes, products. Electronics."

"Shoes?"

"Those, too. How'd you sleep?"

"Good." She spreads strawberry marmalade over her bagel. Her voice is low, almost reflective when she says, "I didn't realize how much I missed sleeping in a real bed."

That's it. The little things, like a warm place to stay and the comfort of a bed. A clean, well-lit place. Waking up to fresh fruit and a delicious meal on your plate. This is why I'm doing this. It's also the reason why a large portion of my trust fund goes to organizations that support children in need.

I push the thought aside as I turn to her with a small smile.

"We can shop for different bed linens if you want."

"I like the ones I have."

I nod. "You spent some time writing yesterday. Do you write about your parents in your journal?" I ask.

"Sometimes."

"You said they didn't seem to pay much attention to you. Do you write about those things—the way they were or maybe how you wanted them to be?"

"I used to."

"And now?"

"I write about my days without them," she says simply.

"When they were alive, did you ever tell them what you thought? Like some of the things you write about?"

"No."

"Never said something like, 'Check this out, I crushed my last exam.'"

"No."

"I used to tell my dad he was boring," I admit.

Her unexpected laughter bursts into the room, bright and unrestrained. I blink in surprise, then laugh along with her.

"Why?" she asks, still smiling.

"Because one minute we'd be talking about school, and the next, he'd be checking his phone, answering email, taking a call. When I said it, he'd stop what he was doing. I wasn't mature enough to say what I really meant—that I wanted his attention. But in my own way, I got it."

She nods, thoughtful now.

"If you could have said something, what would it have been?" I ask.

After a long pause, she says softly, "Why can't we just be a normal family?"

My throat tightens. My heart stutters.

How do I break it all down for her? How do I express in a single day all the things I want to say? That I want to be the one she turns to when she has her first crush, the one who helps pick the perfect shade for her first lipstick and blush. I want to be there to tell her when her dress is too short, her heels are too high, that he's the wrong guy. That it's okay to cry. All the things my mother wasn't there to tell me. Things Jeannette didn't try.

How do I make her understand that I want to be the person she can rely on? That I want to *stay*?

"Amara, remember when I told you to trust me?" She nods. "You can absolutely. But I'm about to tell you something that I trust you will keep safe with you."

She gives me a pensive look. Then nods again.

I exhale, setting my tea aside. "My visa is expiring. If I don't do something, I will have to leave the country." I pause, watching her reaction, but she only listens, her face unreadable. "I don't want to leave you alone."

That part she understands. I don't tell her about Bane's threat—she shouldn't have to fear him. But I do tell her the hardest part.

"The timing of everything means that, in order to stay, I need to get married."

I give her a moment to absorb my words.

"You never mentioned a boyfriend," she says slowly.

"Because I don't have one. Not yet. I would be marrying a family friend—someone we trust. His name is Aaron. Aaron Adler."

Her eyes widen slightly. My stomach twists. I hate burdening her with this, hate making her feel like my life choices will affect her future. Because they will.

Then she surprises me. "I've heard of arranged marriages before."

"This isn't quite that. Our only agreement is my visa status. We'll end the marriage once you're in college."

She studies me for a long moment. "What if it turns out you really like him?"

I huff a small laugh. "I'm not the marrying type."

"But you don't know that."

My passport does. But I don't say that. Instead, I soften. "We'll see."

She tilts her head. "And what do I say about you at school?"

"What do you want to say?"

"That you're my parents."

A slow warmth spreads through me. "That's exactly who we'll be. I'm here because of you. No ifs, ands, or buts about it."

She hesitates, then asks, "What if I don't like this man?"

"Then we'll find another solution." My voice is steady, certain. "But I have a feeling this will work out. My two favorite people in the world love him dearly, and I trust them."

She holds my gaze for a moment longer, then nods.

I take another sip of my tea, but it doesn't soothe me.

I've just changed both our lives.

Now I just need to figure out how to keep this from...Dad.

CHAPTER 15

Terms and Conditions

Aaron

YESTERDAY I MET MY wife for the very first time.

Now, I sit at the conference table, pen in hand, signing my name to what feels like an endless stack of documents. Across from me, Jasmine bites her lips, scanning the fine print like she's memorizing every word. When she catches me watching, she gives me a small, knowing smile. I return it.

"Last one," Steve, our attorney, says, sliding the final document toward me.

Like all the others, I sign my name next to hers. All the terms are laid out in black and white. This isn't about dividing assets or merging households. It's about defining who we are on paper for the next six months.

How we got here—how we managed to pull this off—we don't discuss. We have powerful friends. But no matter how airtight the paperwork is, none of it will matter if the wrong person starts asking questions. Because in business, perception is everything. I learned that lesson.

I slide the document back to Steve.

"We'll have these on file. If you need anything, let me know." He places the papers in his briefcase, pats me on the back, and leaves, closing the door behind him.

Jasmine exhales. "Thank you."

"You don't have to thank me."

I let the words settle between us as I take her in. The tilt of her head as she studies me. The quiet strength in the way she carries herself, as if this is just another calculated move in her life. The warmth in her smile that acknowledges the adventure we're about to begin.

I observe her with a purpose. I want to be fully present for what comes next.

I place my hand, palm up, on the table. She glances down, then back at me before sliding her hand into mine. Her touch is warm. Steady. And for a split second, I feel something shift in my chest—something I ignore.

"Jasmine, I know this isn't the life you envisioned." My voice is quieter now, but firm. "For as long as I've known of your existence, I've understood who you are—an explorer, an educator, a spirit in the wind. If someone's lucky, they might catch a glimpse of you before you move on to the next adventure. Marriage, motherhood...that wasn't on your radar. But here we are. And what you're doing is honorable. I won't diminish it by simply placing a ring on your finger and calling it a day."

I reach into my pocket, pull out a small velvet box, and set it on the table between us.

Jasmine's eyes soften, but she shakes her head. "You don't have to do this."

"I know." I exhale slowly, steadying myself, then open the box.

"Jasmine Marie Ross, I've known of your existence for thirteen years. I never imagined the day I finally met you would also be the day I agreed to marry you. But I believe in what you're doing. I believe this is the best for the three of us. And as long as we're together, we'll be alright. I promise to protect you and Amara. As long as you're with me, you'll want for nothing." I hold her gaze. "All I ask in return is that you let me be that for you. So, will you marry me?"

For the first time, there's something unguarded in her expression—something vulnerable. Her fingers tighten around mine as her eyes glaze over, and for a brief moment, it feels real.

She blinks, then smirks. "Of course. Yes, Aaron Adler, I'll marry you."

There's a beat of silence. Then she arches a brow. "But you know you don't have to protect me, right? I can crush a man four times my size."

I study her with mock concern. "Four times your size? That's...concerning." She grins. I bark out a laugh, then slip the ring on her finger. "Yeah, I heard."

***

The distance from our attorney's office to the Page building isn't far, but traffic in London does what it does best—gives me time to catch up on email. I glance at Jasmine, who is staring out the window, lost in thought. Sensing my gaze, she turns to me.

"You have a bunch of meetings today?" she asks.

"Several. But I have time to come in...that's if you're okay with it. You know, just to talk."

"Yeah. It's fine." Her eyes flick past me to the street beyond the window. The car slows to a stop in front of the massive limestone Page building.

"What time does Amara get home?"

"I'll pick her up at three-thirty."

"Pick her up," I repeat, glancing outside. "In what?"

"A cab."

"Not anymore. Jeffrey will drive you."

"That's not necessary." The look she gives me is sharp, laced with defiance. I've seen it before, on June's face, when my need to control a situation clashes with her need for independence. I need to dial it back, get us on the same page.

"I prefer it, for your safety."

"I told you—"

"You can put down a man four times your size. That's not what this is about." I pause, shifting tactics. "Tell me. When you visit your dad, how do you get around?"

"One of his drivers."

"Why not use rideshare?"

"To protect my family," she admits. "Too many people in the States know our name. Someone could use me to get to them."

I lean forward. "Jeffrey, call Dean and have him meet me here. From now on, you go where Mrs. Adler goes."

"Yes, Mr. Adler."

I exit the vehicle and help Jasmine out. The Pages are good friends, and I've been to this building plenty of times, but I never spent time in her space. This section has always been reserved for her. Inside, I follow her down the hall into the kitchen.

"Would you like some tea? Water?" She exhales. "God, I don't even know what your favorite things are."

"I'll have water." She grabs a glass, fills it, and hands it to me. "I usually drink water if I'm not having coffee. In the evening, I have whiskey."

She pours herself a glass and sits beside me.

"So, how's this work, London?"

"Like this...one drink, one meal, one moment at a time. Then, at some point, we'll connect all the dots between what we thought we knew about each other and what we actually know." And by then, she'll be gone. But I don't say that part aloud.

She exhales. "I thought you were going to marry my sister."

Her voice is quiet, but the words land heavy. I knew this would come up. I just didn't know when.

"Jas, I thought I would, too." I run a hand through my hair. "But not anymore. I don't want you to think I'm harboring something for June. I'm not. I wish you were there that day we figured it out."

"What day?"

"I flew to SF to attend a rally with your sister. Later, we met up following her visit with your dad."

"They didn't always see eye to eye."

"No, but that day she and I talked. She said your dad admitted your mom was the love of his life. And I admitted to her I used to think she was mine."

Jasmine gasps.

"Yeah," I nod. "Your sister isn't my person. She's not my forever. When I look at you, I don't see her. I see you, Jas. And you're even more beautiful than any photo I've ever seen of you."

She blinks at me, then smirks. "You're good-looking, too."

"Thanks."

There's a beat of silence, then she says, "My evening drink is—"

I finish for her. "Malbec."

She nods.

"So, we're getting married on Saturday. I need to get a dress."

"Anything specific you want me to wear?" I ask.

She studies me, and the way she looks at me makes me feel like what we have is real.

"Wear gray," she says softly. "I saw a dress the other day; it's silvery gray, like your eyes."

"Then gray it is."

"June and Aedan are flying in with baby King."

"My brothers will be there."

"My father's going to kill me when he finds out."

"You need to tell him."

"Not now. I'll tell him and Jake in a few months."

"Your dad's a powerful man. I don't want him to find out second-hand."

My phone buzzes. I glance up at Jasmine. "I'll call you tonight. We can discuss it."

I stand. She stands, too.

"You have to go?"

91

"Yeah. But I can arrange dinner for the three of us tomorrow so I can meet Amara."

"She'd love that." Jasmine hesitates, then reaches up, tracing an invisible line down my cheek like she's trying to memorize my face. There's a softness in her touch, an unspoken understanding of who we're becoming. Her voice is barely above a whisper when she says, "I don't want our first kiss to be in front of strangers."

"It doesn't have to be. May I?"

She nods.

I pull her toward me, wrapping my arms around her. Her body molds to mine, like she was designed for me. I dip my head, searching her gaze, waiting for her to change her mind. She doesn't.

"Jas," I murmur, my voice low. "This arrangement doesn't come with conditions. Whatever happens between us will be on your terms. Always."

She nods. "I understand."

"This is what you want?"

"Yes. One gesture, one touch, one moment at a time."

I lower my lips to hers. The moment they meet, I feel it—the invisible thread binding us. Her lips are soft, warm, yielding. I deepen the kiss, tasting the sweetness that's all hers, like the delicate burst of ripe fruit. My eyes close as I savor her, savor this moment, savor...*my wife.*

And then it happens. The gold thread tethering us tightens, winding around us, pulling us closer. And I already know...I don't want to let go. Not now. Not in six months. Not ever.

Chapter 16

Grace

Jasmine

I'VE WALKED AMONGST THE lions in Botswana, stood beneath the brilliance of the Northern Lights in Iceland, and traced my fingers across the cool, ancient walls of the Alhambra in Spain. But none of that—none of it—compares to the wonder and thrill of kissing Aaron Adler.

The storm in his eyes. The quiet command in his touch. The way he kissed me—not just with desire, but with gravity that threatened to pull me under. I told myself I wouldn't be consumed. I *can't* be. He's only mine for six months.

And yet, when he whispered goodnight, I didn't want the night to end. But this isn't about us. This is for Amara.

I lean closer to Amara and tuck a stray curl behind her ear. "So. Exit plan?"

She rolls her eyes with theatrical flair. "I'm tired. We have to get up early tomorrow," she recites, her voice drenched in teenage boredom. Our secret code. If things go south at dinner, she uses it and we're gone. I just hope we won't need it.

"Perfectly delivered. You're ready."

The car slows in front of the restaurant. Aaron waits at the curb, devastatingly handsome in a black suit, white shirt, and a steel-blue tie that matches my dress like it was made for this very moment. Hands in his pockets, he's all polish and quiet confidence. When he spots us, a smile spreads across his face, slow and certain, and my chest does that annoying thing again, like it's trying to remember how to breathe.

Amara grabs my hand. "Is that him?"

"Yeah," I sigh, "That's him."

Aaron opens the car door and offers his hand. "Hi," he says, brushing a kiss against my cheek.

"Hi," I echo, too aware of how his nearness short-circuits my thoughts. "Give me a sec." I glance toward Jeffrey, who's opened the passenger door on the far side, but Amara slides across the seat to exit near me instead. I meet her on the sidewalk, straighten her coat, and whisper, "It's okay to let people help you." She gives a tiny nod.

With my arm wrapped around her shoulder, I turn to Aaron. "Aaron, this is Amara."

He shakes her hand. "Amara. Grace."

She lifts her chin. "You know what my name means?"

"You *are* the epitome of what your name means."

Her eyes widen slightly. "Thank you."

I offer my hand, palm up, and Aaron takes it in his. His touch is warm, grounding me. "I'm starving."

"Our table's ready," he says, guiding us past a sea of curious glances to a private booth with a perfect view of the restaurant but with none of the noise.

Once we're settled, Aaron turns to me with a quiet smile. "You look beautiful."

"Thank you. And thanks for wearing the tie. I just wanted to—"

"Coordinate." He finishes for me, amused. "Something you and..."

He trails off. I know where he's going.

"It's okay, Aaron," I say gently. "You don't have to walk on eggshells. It's a habit from when June and I were little. Our mom used to dress us in matching outfits."

Amara cocks her head. "Seriously?"

Aaron smirks. "Apparently, she hasn't quite let it go."

"Neither has June," I add.

Amara groans. "You two can leave me out of that trend."

Aaron chuckles. "You don't want to match Jasmine and me?"

"I'm too old for that," she deadpans.

The waiter arrives and takes our order. Amara and I can't decide between dishes, so we choose to share, and Aaron steps in, like he's always been part of the rhythm.

"I'll order the braised spareribs with polenta and a side of pasta," He says. "Let's eat family-style."

Amara gives an approving nod. "I like how you think, Aaron."

He smiles, pleased. "Bring extra plates," he tells the waiter. "We'll be sharing."

As the server leaves, conversation flows easily. Surprisingly so. The kind of ease that sneaks up on you—effortless, unforced. It feels like...*family*.

"So," Aaron says, "any thoughts on university?"

"I want to go to Sorbonne."

Aaron raises his brow. "Ambitious. Jasmine tells me you're brilliant. I don't doubt you'll get in."

"That's a great option, Amara," I say. "We'll build a list together. I'll help you with your application. Ever been to Paris?"

Amara shakes her head. "I've never been out of England. I've seen nearby cities, but..." She hesitates. "I want to go."

Her eyes shimmer with something I know too well—longing and quiet resilience.

She's like me, and yet not. I had the world at my fingertips before I could name the continents. My dad took me everywhere after my mom died—business trips disguised as family bonding. I was logging passport stamps before I lost my baby teeth. Learning on the road made the world my classroom.

But Amara's circumstances kept her here. Rooted. Waiting. Dreaming. The things she's wanted were out of reach...until now.

"Campus tours," Aaron suggests.

Amara brightens. "Can we?"

"Why not?" I ask. "We can start with local ones."

Her eyes flicker with hope. It's not the trips or the cities she wants—it's the attention. To be *seen*. Heard. Valued. To have the things her parents didn't provide.

I know that ache, too.

Amara tells us why she wants to go to Paris. We talk about art and fashion. In our short time together, I've noticed that she has taste and an eye for balance. Her style shows it too: thoughtful, layered. Creative.

Then, in the middle of it all, she looks at us, eyes sincere. "Thank you."

Aaron reaches under the table and touches my hand. I squeeze back, letting the moment relax between us.

"Another adventure," I say softly. My favorite word. My curse and comfort. *Will I ever be able to stay still?*

Dinner arrives. We share everything, passing dishes around like this is our tradition, not just a one-time performance. Aaron doesn't balk when I steal extra ribs from his plate. Just smiles and winks.

I share stories about my siblings and me. Aaron laughs as he tells stories about his brothers and their childhood mischief. Amara leans in, captivated by it all.

"They'll be there tomorrow," he says. "Excited to meet you. Ignore Andrew—he'll try to recruit you for a summer internship."

"Some of the best tech minds came out of their program," I add. "Like June. And Raven Nichols."

"Cool."

The evening slips by faster than I expect. When the plates are cleared, the only thing left is warmth.

Outside, the air is crisp and clear. Aaron's hand rests at my waist. Amara's fingers are tucked into mine.

Then a voice slices through the night.

"Is that you, Aaron?"

I turn toward the sound. And there she is.

Bridgette Bromley. Dressed like she's waiting for a camera crew, all high heels and hidden agendas.

"Bridgette." Aaron's voice is tight, barely polite.

She looks me over like I'm a handbag on sale. "I heard you *might* be here."

"Might be," Aaron says dryly. "Or *were* here?"

She shrugs. "Word travels fast when the Adler brothers make an appearance."

Aaron tightens his arm around me. "Bridgette, this is Jasmine Adler. My wife."

She blinks. Once. Then again. "Your *wife*?"

"Yes. And this is Amara."

"Hi," Amara says, blinking up at her.

Bridgette's perfectly glossed mouth opens, then closes. "I didn't know you had a wife. Or daughter."

Aaron doesn't dignify it with a response. I smile sweetly.

"She's mine," I say. "But we're a family."

Aaron gestures toward Bridgette. "Bridgette is Bram Bromley's daughter."

I pretend to search my memory. "Bromley...oh right. I remember now There was a piece in *The Society*—"

"That was blown out of proportion. It's been handled."

"Oh, not that one. A few years back. A video. Something about...you and that guy. Never mind." I flash her a sympathetic look. "Anyways, it's lovely to meet you." Then I turn to Aaron, snuggle into his side, and say in my most practiced tone, "Honey, I'm tired. We've got such an early morning."

"Yeah," he says, catching on immediately. "We do."

And as we walk away, Amara still clutching my hand, I realize something I hadn't fully understood until now. Aaron's helping me. But helping him gives me a thrill. And I love a good adventure.

All I Need

Aaron

FIVE DAYS AGO, I walked straight into a trap—a mess orchestrated by a woman so desperate for attention, she tried to dismantle my entire reputation with one staged photo and a headline. I should still be reeling from that. Maybe I am.

But today...today, I'm about to get married. To Jasmine Ross. And I can't tell if this is the most brilliant decision I've ever made—or the one that will completely wreck me.

What began as a temporary fix has started to feel like something else. Like something I want. But I don't know if she feels the same. She's impossible to read sometimes, laughing like the world can't touch her, disappearing into herself the next moment like she's already planning her next escape.

She says this is just for now. Six months.

But what if I want more? What if she doesn't?

I'm not used to feeling this unsteady. I like control. Certainty. And Jasmine is none of those things. She's an explorer wrapped in elegance, all fire and freedom—and I can't stop falling for her. Because that's exactly what's happening. Which means I might be walking into this marriage with my heart already exposed. And she might be walking into it with one foot out the door.

Stepping out of the elevator, I spot Alex as he exits the UN room we've reserved at the Four Seasons.

"Nervous?" he asks, smoothing the sleeves of his jacket like this is just another board meeting.

"Still questioning my sanity," I mutter, adjusting my cufflinks.

He smirks. "We're all on the same page. But this...this is the right thing."

Before I can respond, June emerges from the ballroom, a vision of grace in sky blue. Her presence, once complicated, now brings me calm.

"Hey, Aaron," she says warmly. "Thanks for everything you're doing."

"Don't thank me yet," I reply dryly. "Let's see if we can pull this off."

That's when it hits me—we didn't use nicknames. Not *Beautiful* and *Handsome*, not *J* and *London*. Just June and Aaron. The last thread of what we used to be...gently unraveling. Not out of loss. Just growth.

"Is everyone here?"

"Jasmine's still at the penthouse," June replies.

"Don't worry, mate," Aedan chimes in, stepping up beside her. "She's not running." He pulls June into a side hug. They exchange a glance—quiet, intimate. The look of people who've chosen each other with certainty.

"That's what I came out to tell you," June continues. "I went to get her, but...she wants to walk in with you."

"Amara came down with me," Aedan adds.

I nod slowly. "I'll go get her."

"Don't keep us waiting," Alex calls after me, his voice teasing, but his eyes full of pride.

I take the elevator to the seventh-floor penthouse. My heart's a war drum in my chest, steady and loud. The second I open the door, I call her name.

"Jas."

"I'm here."

She steps into view, and the air leaves my lungs. The liquid silver silk strapless dress clings to her like a second skin, light catching every curve. But it's her eyes that stop me—steady, warm, and focused solely on me.

"You okay?" I ask.

She nods, then shrugs one bare shoulder. "I just figured...we're in this together. We should go in together. One step, one moment at a time."

I close the distance between us. Spiced vanilla enveloping me. She's stunning, but it's the softness in her voice, the quiet resolve, that undoes me.

My thumb grazes her bottom lip. "You don't wear lipstick."

"No," she murmurs. "Just clear gloss. I don't keep up with color trends." Preoccupied with exploring the wonders of the world—why would she?

"May I?" I ask, my smile tugging crooked. "Practice."

She nods.

I dip my head and kiss her—not rushed or hesitant. It's a claiming and a promise. I kiss her like the breath between now and forever lives in this moment. When I pull back, I can't move, can't think. She feels like mine...but she's not mine until she tells me.

She rests her forehead against mine. "I think we're ready."

"Yeah," I whisper. "That."

I wipe a smudge of gloss from her lips. "You look beautiful, Mrs. Adler."

"You're handsome as ever."

We leave the penthouse hand-in-hand. I don't let go. Not in the elevator, not when we step off on the second floor, not even when my palms start to sweat.

The UN ballroom is breathtaking. Twenty-six-foot ceilings soar above us, lacquered wood gleaming in the soft, golden light. On one side, a long table draped in white linen overflows with flowers, candles, and gleaming fine china. On the other, a single row of chairs, each filled with a piece of our makeshift family—my brothers Alex and Andrew, our young cousin Demetrius, June and Aedan, and Amara sitting tall and proud.

Jasmine and I walk together toward the minister. I grip her tiny hand like it's my tether to our time ahead. The ceremony begins—first a prayer, then the vows—but all I can see is her. Her eyes, her stillness, her quiet bravery.

A reel of our future plays in my head: lazy mornings, whispered dreams, children's laughter, Amara's graduation. I can barely breathe.

The minister's voice fades beneath the pounding in my chest until his words slice through: "Do you take this woman to be your wedded wife, to have and to hold, in sickness and in health, till death do you part?"

I don't hesitate.

"I do." And I mean it with every cell in my body. "With this ring, I thee wed," I say, sliding the band onto her finger.

Then I pull her close and kiss her—not for show, not for ceremony—but because in this moment, she's everything I'll ever need.

CHAPTER 18

Assurance

Jasmine

AND JUST LIKE THAT, I'm married with a kid.

I should be running scared. This should feel like freefall, like the moment just before impact, but instead I feel...safe. Secure. My arm is wrapped around Amara, her head nestled on my shoulder as we step into Aaron's four-story Knightsbridge home. She's wiped out.

The ceremony was a gauntlet for her: smiling, shaking hands, remembering names. Everyone wanted a piece of her, and to her credit, she gave what she could. She and the youngest Adler, Demetrius, bonded over whatever teenagers bond over: music, memes, existential dread. And just like Aaron predicted, Andrew offered her a summer job.

Afterwards, we all returned to the penthouse for drinks. June's au pair brought in baby King, and everyone fell in love with him on sight. It felt...warm. Safe. Like family. Even if it's a temporary illusion, the feeling is real enough to cling to.

In the foyer, Aaron slips my coat from my shoulders with the kind of ease that makes me pause. I help Amara with hers.

"Your rooms are ready. I can give you a tour," Aaron offers.

I glance at Amara, who looks like she's one blink away from unconsciousness. "Maybe in the morning. Let me get her settled."

He nods and leads us through a home that feels like a glossy magazine spread come to life—modern minimalism softened by old-world elegance. Picture frame molding, clean black lines, marble, glass, and gold.

Just as we near the stairs, something crashes to the floor with a loud thud. Startled, I freeze.

"Don't worry," Aaron says casually. "That's just Elizabeth."

I blink at him. "I'm sorry—who?"

A beat of silence. Then a soft meow.

"Elizabeth's a cat," he adds, chuckling. "I promise there's no surprise girlfriend living upstairs."

A sleek gray cat slinks into view, tail high and completely unbothered.

"I didn't know you had a cat," I say, bending slightly as she brushes against my ankle.

"I didn't—until the cat distribution system picked me. She just wandered into my life. Same day I met you, actually."

"Well, hello Queen Elizabeth," I say as the cat sniffs Amara's shoe.

We ascend two floors, with Elizabeth walking ahead as if she owns the place.

"The main bedroom is one floor up," he says. "You're welcome to take that, or..." He gestures to a room across from Amara's. "This one. It's closer."

"This one is fine," I say. He gives me a warm smile that shouldn't affect me the way it does.

It's strange, this arrangement—married in name, but not in body or spirit. Yet here I am. Here *we* are.

"Good night, Amara," he says.

Her voice is barely above a whisper. "Good night."

We slip into her room and close the door. It's spacious and already feels like her. Her belongings are neatly arranged. I unzip her dress, then collapse into an oversized chair as she moves through her nighttime routine.

When she emerges, teeth brushed and bonnet on, she crawls into the bed with a satisfied sigh. I rise and join her, sitting on the edge.

"How are you feeling?" I ask.

"Sleepy."

"Did you have a good time?"

She nods. "Was it scary?"

"Marrying Aaron?" She nods again. The question surprises me. "No," I say, smiling. "I understand now why my brother and sister trust him. He's the kind of man who shows up. The kind you can lean on when it counts."

And that's the truth. Somehow, what should feel transactional feels...something else. Maybe it's the way he's carried all of this—steady, considerate. Or maybe it's me. Maybe for the first time, I'm considering how I live my life. Maybe I want something that lasts—even if it's only for now.

"You and your sister are so beautiful together," she says softly.

"You, me, and her—*we're* beautiful together." I gently tug her bonnet into place. "Now sleep." *We'll figure the rest out tomorrow.* I don't say the last part out loud, but I think it.

She yawns, turns over, and within moments, she's gone.

I linger at her bedside, replaying the day—the kiss in the penthouse that felt like a claim, the way he looked at me in front of the minister, like I was already his.

The soft sound of Amara snoring pulls me out of my head for a moment. Eventually, I leave her room and cross the hall to mine. Another beautiful masterpiece—white walls, black trim windows, luxurious silence. I step into the walk-in closet and catch my reflection. The silk dress, the makeup fading around the edges, the questions in my eyes.

"What am I doing?" I whisper, searching for clarity.

Am I doing this for her? Or is it about me? About longing for something I was too afraid to name?

I reach behind me, tugging at the zipper. Nothing. I twist and try again. Still nothing. A ridiculous frustration bubbles inside me. Sharp. Hot. My heart races. I slump to the floor, my back against the dresser, knees drawn up, tears rising uninvited.

I hate crying. It feels like losing control. But the tears don't care. They fall anyway.

Eventually, I give up, drag myself into bed, dress and all, and lie there in silk and sadness, listening to the quiet echo of my own doubts.

Time slips away, and sleep comes. I dream of the opium ceremony in Rohet Garh. I see my mother's face. But I wake myself up before it gets too real.

One thirty. I wasn't asleep long. I push off the covers, pad quietly out of the room and downstairs in search of water. As I pass a sitting room, I hear his voice.

"Jas?"

I stop. Follow it. He's there...*Aaron*. Shirt unbuttoned, sleeves rolled, glass of whiskey in hand, sitting on a low couch in a softly lit room. He's such a beautiful man.

"Hey," I say, standing in the doorway.

"You okay?"

"No," I say, voice barely above a whisper.

"Want to talk about it?"

I nod. He gestures, and I cross the room, sinking onto the couch beside him. He hands me the glass. I sip. Hand it back.

"I couldn't get this damn dress off," I say, tugging at the now wrinkled fabric.

"I can help you with that." His voice is gentle. "But that's not what's really bothering you." I curl into myself, knees to my chest, and he wraps his arm around me, pulling me close. "Talk to me."

I take a breath. Then another.

"I'm scared," I say finally. "I'm not used to taking care of anyone but myself. I don't want to ruin her life. Or yours."

"This is new to me, too," he says, setting the glass down. "We might mess up. But we'll figure this out. You're not alone in this."

"But Amara..."

"Seems to be adjusting better than we are." I nod, a quiet laugh escaping through my nose. "What's one thing weighing heavy on you?" he asks.

I hesitate. There's something about this moment—him, me, the night folding in around us like a secret. I let the words come. "For so long, I've wanted what we're about to give to Amara. A family. Stability. A place where she belongs and knows she's safe."

"You don't feel you had that?"

"Not after my mom passed. My stepmom didn't know what to do with us. I don't even think of her as part of my story."

"What was it like?"

"We didn't eat meals with her. Not unless we had to. We had a cook. We could grab something if we wanted, but we were rarely with them...together I mean—as a family. No family outings. No closeness. At least not with Jeannette. Not like...before."

"That's why I hadn't met you before now," he says softly. "You didn't want to be around her."

"I didn't want to be around anyone. Missing Mom hurt too much."

"But you showed up for Rose and June."

"I knew Jeannette wouldn't be there."

He nods, understanding more than he says.

"We both have events upcoming," he says after a moment. "We'll go together. As a family."

"My keynote's Monday."

"We'll be there." He tugs gently on my shoulder. "Do we need to coordinate?" he adds, teasing just enough to soften the moment.

I lay my hand across his thigh, palm up. He covers it with his.

"Maybe," I say.

And in this quiet moment—his arm around me, his body warm and steady beside mine—I feel something I haven't felt in a long time. Assurance. Maybe even hope.

We can do this.

CHAPTER 19

Chips for Breakfast

Aaron

I DIDN'T RUN THIS morning. Didn't even think about it. I want to stay in and let the day unfold with my newfound family.

Sleep barely touched me last night. Not when Jasmine curled up beside me, her head on my shoulder, like we'd done it a thousand times before. We talked until the small hours—quiet, unhurried, as if the world outside didn't exist. Filling in years of blanks. Laughing in low tones. Sitting in that peace where you feel like someone sees you...really grasps the heart of who you are.

There's something between us. Silent. Weightless and heavy at the same time. I suspect she's fighting it too, though for different reasons. I got a taste of why I'm holding back last night. After hours of having her near, I helped her out of that dress, and she finally slipped off to bed. Her absence hit me like a sharp inhale in an empty room. Like she took something with her when she left.

I don't like the feeling. I never missed someone the moment they left a room—not even with June. Yet it's a constant with Jas. And that scares me.

If I fall too hard...if I let myself want her the way I already do...I'm not sure I'll come out of this unscathed.

I put all that aside and head downstairs, catching a whiff of her scent mixed with...burnt toast? I laugh under my breath. *This should be interesting.*

When I walk into the kitchen, she's standing at the counter in an oversized sweatshirt I recognize, munching on a waffle. Barefoot. Hair a little wild. Sunlight catching the edge of her cheekbone just right.

I cross to her, dip my head, and steal a bite right from her hand. I pause mid-chew. Crunchy doesn't begin to cover it. "What in the world? Why does this taste like sweet drywall?"

"Excuse you," Amara pipes up from the table. "I *like* it. It's like eating sweet chips."

"Thank you, Amara." Jasmine gives her a mock toast with the waffle.

"We have a cook." I remind them, trying not to laugh. "I just gave Martha the day off. Thought we could go out for breakfast."

"We don't need a cook," Jasmine says. "Between the three of us, I'm sure we can figure it out."

"I wouldn't bet on that," Amara mutters, stabbing a blackened corner of a waffle.

"Hey, I thought you were on my side."

"I am. But I've also seen you try to boil water."

Jasmine raises a brow, playing offended. "Unbelievable. A house full of traitors."

I reach for a waffle. "Alright, alright. Amara's right. It *does* taste like chips."

Jasmine turns toward me, smirking. "You're impossible."

It's then I notice the oddly rounded puff under her sweatshirt.

I squint. "What's happening here? Are we...having a baby?"

"What? No." She shoots me a look. "You may look like a Greek god, but last time I checked, you weren't capable of immaculate conception."

My lips twitch as I place my finger under her chin, lifting gently. "*Greek god*, huh?" I murmur. "I like the sound of that."

"I can hear you two," Amara sing-songs.

I chuckle. Kids.

Jasmine shifts, and I get a better look. Lowering my hand toward the lump—*Ouch*. A gray paw swats me away.

"Why is Elizabeth living inside your sweatshirt?"

"Because someone hasn't house-trained her. And if she thinks she's going to walk across this kitchen counter—"

She doesn't get to finish. I lean in, laughing, and press a kiss to her cheek

If this is what my future mornings look like: burnt waffles, kids, stray cats, and Jasmine in my clothes—I'm all in.

I hold her gaze and say softly, "Morning, Jas."

Then I reach inside the sweatshirt and gently extract the cat, who shoots off with an indignant *meow*.

"Good morning," she says, eyes twinkling.

Jasmine and I join Amara at the table. It's easy between us, the kind of morning that feels soft around the edges. The kind that used to happen every weekend in my parents' home—my mother humming while she passed out pancakes, my father reading the paper, but still somehow engaged in every conversation.

Here, though, it's different—quieter in some ways and louder in others. Our conversation turns to upcoming events and how we'll tell Reed and JR about our marriage.

Amara stuns us when she says, "What do you think he's going to do? This is the person who trusted you'd be okay traveling the world at nineteen. If he loves you and respects Aaron, as you said, then the most he'll say is, *Why didn't you tell me?*"

I glance between Jasmine and Amara. "Out of the mouth of babes."

"You're right, Amara. I suppose I don't want him to be disappointed in me," Jasmine says softly.

I catch the flicker of emotion in her eyes. She's strong—stronger than most—but there are moments where I see the girl who lost her mother at five. I grew up with both my parents still showing up, still loving each other out loud. Jasmine learned to navigate the world with one missing. That kind of loss leaves shadows that don't always show in the light.

"I think he'll be understanding," I say. "He'll probably give me a hard time—making sure you're treated well."

"He's seen you around my siblings. I doubt that's his concern."

"But your heart's involved."

"Uh, is that about sex again?" Amara asks.

"No," we both say in unison.

I clear my throat and decide to change the subject. "How about we spend the day on the town?"

"I need an outfit for the museum," Amara says brightly.

"We can start the day shopping," Jasmine offers.

"Pick up whatever you need. Then we can grab a late lunch and catch the early show."

"A musical?" Amara asks, her eyes beaming with something that looks like wonder.

I blink. "Yeah, is there one you want to see?"

"I've never been. I always wanted to see *The Lion King*."

Never been? That stops me. I grew up on shows—matinees and standing ovations, arguing with my brothers over which was best on the ride home. To me, theatre is a part of childhood, of memory, of "remember whens." For Amara, it's a maybe someday. Her smile is wide, but it reaches somewhere deeper in me. This must be what Jasmine felt the day she met Amara.

I glance at Jasmine. She already knows what I'm thinking. We both nod.

"Then we'll see that."

***

The morning goes smoother than I expected. Sharing space with Jasmine and Amara feels…natural. Like we've been doing this for years. Like we're already something. But I don't take it for granted—not for a second. Jasmine says this setup is temporary, a fleeting arrangement to solve a practical problem.

And yet, this small taste of them in my life? It doesn't feel temporary. It feels like the beginning of something permanent. Something I'm already tethered to.

We enter Westfield—Amara's pick. The place is buzzing, sprawling across five glittering floors that stretch endlessly in every direction. Glass ceilings let in shafts of pale light, bouncing off polished tiles and storefront windows. The air carries that blend of fresh pretzels, espresso, perfume samples, and new leather. It's over-stimulating in the best way.

Amara's eyes are wide, shining with excitement. She spins slowly in place like she can't decide where to look first. I have a hunch it's been a while—if ever—since she's been able to browse freely without thinking twice about cost or consequence.

We take it in slowly, easing into the rhythm of the crowd. Window shopping, exploring the layout, letting the current of people guide us. Jasmine holds Amara's hand; I hold Jasmine's. We're a chain of three, anchored in the chaos. It would be easy to lose someone here. Easy to forget where you came from in a place this size.

The last time I was here, I was probably Amara's age. That lifetime feels sepia-toned now—simpler, easier, before Knightsbridge, before press scandals, before everything required calculation. These days, if I want something, I order it. Harrods delivers. My tailor delivers. I haven't had to "shop" in years.

But this? This is different.

Jasmine tugs my hand gently. "Let me check something," she murmurs, pulling out her phone. "The map shows the teen store we want is this way."

"Then that's where we're headed," I say, taking her hand back.

We find it without issue, thanks to Jasmine's internal compass—probably sharpened from years of navigating foreign cities alone. Inside, we go straight to the dress section. On the drive here, we agreed to coordinate for Monday's museum outing. Jasmine's tradition is becoming *ours*.

Amara moves through the racks with laser focus, plucking hangers and evaluating options with surgical precision. She's fast. Jasmine and I trail behind her, amused and mildly overwhelmed.

"Can I wear pants instead of a dress?" she asks, glancing over her shoulder.

I lift an eyebrow, then look at Jasmine. "If that's what you want. What did you have in mind?"

"I like the style where women wear tuxedo suits."

"We may not be able to find that here," Jasmine says, already scanning her mental list of alternatives. "But I know exactly where we can."

She leads us to a sleek, modern boutique two floors up, with mannequins in architectural silhouettes. Amara beelines for a black, double-breasted tuxedo-style pantsuit with a sleeveless top. She disappears into the fitting room and returns minutes later like a different person.

My breath catches. She looks...older. Sophisticated. Confident. She gives us a small twirl, and I realize the top is backless.

"You might have to wear a jacket over that," I say, trying to keep my tone light.

"Ah." Amara turns to Jasmine, eyes wide with hope. "Jasmine?"

Jasmine squeezes my hand before speaking. "I like it. It has a young adult look with a flair for fashion. Still formal. It's fine."

I sigh, lightly outvoted. "If you say so. But if any man even *thinks* of approaching you—"

"I'll beat them to a pulp," Jasmine cuts in, calm as ever.

"Not before I drag them out by the collar," I add.

"Like Rory from winter break?" I shoot her a knowing look layered in lost memories. "Don't give me that look. I heard about that," Jasmine says, throwing a smirk over her shoulder.

My jaw tightens. Rory. The drunk idiot who got too close to June was lucky all I did was toss him out of the party. By this throat. I'd do worse if someone ever tried anything with Amara.

The heat crawls up the back of my neck, instinctive and primal. Because this is my family now. Jasmine. Amara.

Amara finds a pair of shoes that complete the look—black patent wedge loafers with a sleek gold accent. We leave the boutique and stroll toward a larger department store next to a men's accessory shop. Jasmine pauses in front of the display

"I already have a fitted black dress," she says thoughtfully, "but I was thinking about accenting it with gold accessories."

"You'll look stunning," I say. "I don't have a gold tie, but I can pop next door while you two shop."

As I gesture toward the men's store, something flickers across Jasmine's face. She starts to reach for me, her hand lifting halfway, fingers curling slightly, but they stop midair. Her eyes lose focus, like she's staring at something I can't see. Something behind the glass. There's a tightness in her jaw, a flicker of panic or grief ghosting across her expression.

Amara has her hand on the door handle, ready to enter the store.

"Amara," I call out. She stops. "Hold a sec." Jasmine's trembling. I step close and cup her cheeks, trying to anchor her. "Jas, are you okay?"

She nods in quick, short succession, but it's not convincing. Her body tells the truth—tight, rigid, fighting for air.

"Look at me, honey. Take a deep breath." She inhales. Then exhales. "Another." She takes several more. "What's happening?" I ask gently.

"This is how—"

She doesn't finish, but she doesn't have to.

I know. I remember what June told me. That day, Jasmine went shopping with her dad and JR while her mom and June split off to shop somewhere else. They were supposed to meet at the Chinese restaurant. But when they got there, it wasn't a reunion—it was sirens. Police tape. Her mother was gone. Just like that.

"Okay," I say, pressing my forehead to hers. "I got you."

I pull her into a hug, solid and close, and after a beat, I reach for Amara. She steps in without hesitation. Her arms wrap around us, anchoring all three of us.

"We'll stay together."

There are many sides of Jasmine, and this is one—raw, vulnerable, unguarded. And I love her more for it.

Love? Is that what I'm feeling? Or maybe the start of it. In this moment, holding both of them, everything sharpens.

I didn't come here today expecting a memory to ambush her. I didn't think a tie and a dress would take us down this road. But this is what it means to love someone, *isn't it*? Not just showing up for the good days, but standing steady when the past knocks the wind out of them.

She carries so much. And Amara, too, quietly watching, learning what it means to feel safe, maybe for the first time in a long time. She's trying to understand this life where you can walk into a store and buy something because you *want* it—not because you need it, not because you've saved up for months. Just because it brings you joy.

And Jasmine—God, she's been carrying that day with her for years. I saw it hit her like it was happening all over again.

I don't want her to carry it alone anymore. Not her. Not Amara. Not for a single second longer.

This...right here...isn't pretend. It's not convenient. It's not temporary. This is my family. They don't have to say it back; I feel it in my bones. I've got them, and I'm not letting go.

116

We break from our hug. I open the door to the shop and gesture for them to enter. Jasmine places a hand on Amara's shoulder and calmly says, "Sweetie, whatever happens, don't leave Aaron's side."

Then she turns to me, and for a second, time stutters. Her eyes, usually so full of fire and light, are distant again, stormy like she's somewhere else entirely. Somewhere I can't reach. Lost in a memory, maybe. A moment I'm not part of.

Her lips part, but no sound comes. Just a look. A quiet, aching look that feels like a goodbye wrapped in guilt. Like she wants me to understand, to forgive her for what she hasn't done yet.

Then she mouths it—*I'm sorry.*

Before I can say a word, she's gone. Turning, rushing through the mall like the air in here is too thick to breathe. Like if she stays one second longer, she'll shatter.

For a second, I stand there stunned as she disappears in the crowd. On autopilot, my hand reaches for Amara's.

"What's happening?" she asks, her voice unsteady.

"It's okay, sweetie. Jas just needs a moment. Let's get to the car," I say, already walking. I take out my phone. "Jeffrey, Mrs. Adler's headed out. I need an ETA on her location to you."

There's a pause, then he says, "I have her. She's heading away from me."

"Keep track of Mrs. Adler. Amara and I are headed out."

"I'll be waiting."

"Where's she going? What's wrong?"

I place my arm around Amara's shoulder as we leave the mall. "Remember what Jasmine told you about her mom?"

"She's gone. Like mine."

"Sometimes old memories get overwhelming, and being around people is hard," I say, recalling how June would fall into moments of quiet when something triggered a memory. "Now is one of those times."

When we arrive at the car, Jeffrey is waiting beside the open door. I help Amara in, and then turn to Jeffrey. "Where's my wife?"

"Headed back. It's not clear which house yet."

When I get in the car, I pull out my phone and call Andrew. He picks up right away. "How's married life?" he says, his voice light, breezy.

"Meet me at the house."

"That doesn't sound good."

"I'll explain when I get there." I end the call without saying anything more. I don't want to distress Amara more than she already is.

"Will she be okay?"

"Yes, Amara. I promise she'll be okay."

"Sir," Jeffrey interrupts. "Mrs. Adler is headed to Holborn." I nod.

Turning to Amara, I say, "Uncle Andrew will meet us at the house and stay with you while I pick up Jasmine. While I'm gone, you're in charge of the house. Can you handle that?"

"What does that mean?"

"That means no one comes or goes unless you approve. Of course, you should discuss it with Andrew first, but..." I smile. "You can decide whether he calls Martha to make us a late lunch or have something delivered. And make sure he doesn't let the cat out."

"I can do that."

"Of course you can." I look out the window. I inhale and exhale slowly, calming myself. I'll find her. I'll help her get through this. Because we're a team. And sometimes one member of the team has to be the anchor. Some days it might be Jasmine, and other days it's me. Right now I'm on point.

I'm here for my family. Whatever they've been through, whatever old grief rises up—I'll hold the line. Because that's what you do for the people you love.

I've got you. Both of you. Now and always.

CHAPTER 20

Example

Jasmine

I SLAM THE BATHROOM door behind me, knees hitting the tile before I even realize I've dropped. My stomach twists again, violent and relentless. With sweaty hands, I clutch the rim of the toilet like it's the only thing anchoring me to the earth.

I can still hear Amara's soft voice. Still see her hand outstretched for mine. And I left her. I left *her*. No warning, no explanation. I just ran. What kind of person does that? What kind of mother would? Except I'm not her mother. I'm just the girl pretending to be someone strong enough to love and protect her.

But I want to be. I want to be like *my* mom.

She was soft-spoken but strong. Always listening. Always present. I still remember how safe her arms felt, how she smelled like vanilla and jasmine tea, how she made me believe nothing bad could ever happen—until it did. Until she was gone, and I was five, and the world suddenly felt it had no floor.

She didn't leave because she wanted to. She didn't run. She was *taken*. And somehow, even now, I'm trying to live up to someone who died too soon but left behind a legacy of love I can't seem to replicate.

Today, I did the opposite of what she would've done. I let fear win. I looked into Amara's eyes and saw the kind of trust that shouldn't be broken—and I broke it. I left Aaron standing there too, like a ghost of himself, holding my panic like it might explode in his hands. I could see it on his face. He *felt* it. Like he was trying to absorb my pain and couldn't understand why I wouldn't let him.

"Why didn't I let him?" I whisper.

What kind of woman runs from people who stay? What if I'm not the right person for this? For them?

And this marriage...this complicated arrangement—it suddenly feels fragile. Like if I breathe too hard, it'll crack. Aaron deserves someone with a clear head and a calm heart. Not a mess of memories and emotions barely stitched together. Certainly not someone temporary.

I want to believe I can do this. I *need* to believe it. I want to be someone Amara can count on. Someone Aaron doesn't regret marrying. But right now, I'm just that little girl again—lost, overwhelmed, and wondering how to keep breathing when grief fills the air like smoke in a sealed room.

"Jasmine," Aaron's voice cuts through the fog, low and warm, followed by the soft click of the bathroom door unlatching. "Jas, honey. Are you—"

"I'm okay," I say too quickly, my voice hoarse, raw.

He crosses the room in two strides and lifts me gently, easing me toward him. But I brace my hand against his chest, needing space, needing air. I turn away, lean over the sink, rinse my mouth, and splash cold water on my flushed face.

But Aaron's not turned away by my erratic behavior. He doesn't push. Doesn't press.

"Let me help you." His voice is soft. He takes a towel from the rack, runs it under cool water, and waits.

I look at him in the mirror. At the man who sees past the walls I try to build. I cling to the lie—*I'm fine*—like it might tether me to the version of myself I want to be. The one who doesn't fall apart in a department store. The one who knows how to hold it together when it matters.

"I told you, I'm okay."

He turns me gently and lifts my chin, his fingers warm against my damp skin. His eyes—those steady, unshakable eyes search mine. "It's okay to feel things."

The tenderness undoes me. I blink, trying not to cry. His touch is careful, deliberate, as he dabs the towel against my cheeks and jaw, wiping away everything I tried to wash down the drain. Everything I've been running from.

Then it hits me. I look past his shoulder toward the door. "Amara?"

"She's with Andrew," he says.

I swallow hard. "I shouldn't have left." I reach for his arm, curling my fingers around his wrist. "Give me a minute. Please."

He nods, backing away, the door clicking softly shut behind him.

Damn. I could have handled that so much better. If this is going to work—*really* work–if I'm going to be the example Amara needs, I have to get myself together. No more hiding. No more running.

I brush my teeth, clean up the space, and breathe deep until my heartbeat slows. I step out and head down the hall where the faint hum of conversation greets me. Aaron sits at the kitchen counter, phone to his ear.

"Yeah. She's fine," he says, his tone calm but grounded. "Did you want to talk to her?" He spots me and extends his hand. I slip mine into his and he gently pulls me to his side. "It's Amara," he whispers.

"Put her on speaker," I say. He sets the phone on the counter and taps the screen. "Hey, sweetie," I say, forcing brightness into my voice.

"Jasmine. You scared me."

The ache in my chest deepens. "Ah, honey. I didn't mean to. I'm okay now, promise."

"We'll be back shortly," Aaron adds. "What did you and Andrew decide on for lunch?"

"Burgers and chips." Her voice bubbles through the phone, full of light.

"Garlic chips," Andrews calls from the background.

I chuckle. "Can't wait. Keep Queen Elizabeth off the counters."

"I will. Bye," she says, and the call ends.

A quiet settles over us. I don't let go of Aaron's hand. He swivels on the stool, turning toward me. I move between his knees, one hand on his, the other absently brushing nonexistent lint from his sleeve.

"I'm making a mess of this, aren't I?"

He squeezes my hand. "No. You're grieving. You're trying. And that's what matters." His eyes lock on mine, firm and tender all at once. "When I married you, I married *everything* about you. So don't run from me. Don't hide your fears, your tears, your joy, your frustration. Let me see it all. Let me carry some of it with you."

My throat tightens. I nod, biting the corner of my lip.

"Back there," he continues, "you were scared. And overwhelmed. I saw it. If you need to get away, I'll go with you. If you need to cry, scream, shut down—I'll hold you through it. I want to be the place you go when you don't know what else to do."

I close my eyes and rest my forehead against his.

"But Amara—," I whisper.

"Needs to see that it's okay to *feel*. She needs to know that being strong doesn't mean being silent. And that she's safe with us, no matter what she's feeling. We're her safe place."

"You're right," I say. "I'll talk to her when I get back."

"We'll talk to her," he says gently. "Together."

"I think it's time I got help for this."

"And I'll be right there with you, too."

He wraps his arms around me and pulls me close, my face tucked against his chest. I breathe him in. Safety. Warmth. Home.

"Let's go home," he says quietly.

His phone buzzes on the counter. I lift my head, untangling from his embrace. My eyes drift to the screen.

Bromley.

CHAPTER 21

The Proposal

Aaron

YESTERDAY, I GOT A large slice of my new life. It took some finessing, but we got the day back on track. I was right—Amara is resilient. And as for Jasmine...she's something else entirely. Complex in a way I didn't expect. Being with her is like watching a time-lapse of a rose blooming—layers unfolding so quickly it leaves me breathless, yet somehow, I know I've only scratched the surface. Now I understand why I hadn't seen her until this week. She wasn't meant to enter my life until I was ready to recognize her.

I'm looking forward to seeing what today brings. First, I have to deal with Bromley.

Standing at the wall of windows, I stare out over the city, thoughts stuck on the Bromley scandal. The timing doesn't sit right. Bridgette arranging that meeting last Monday felt too calculated. Now, here I am—meeting with her father a week later.

"I see you've learned your lesson," Alex says, pulling me out of my thoughts.

I turn and take a seat across from him at the conference table. "We still have to be careful what we say."

When Bromley's call came through yesterday, I let it go straight to voicemail. The trust between Jasmine and me is still new. Fragile. No way I was risking that by taking a business call over the weekend, especially from someone who isn't even a client.

I have a family now. It wasn't until Jasmine and Amara came into my life that I understood what family really means. Before that, family and business were one and the same.

The conference room door opens and Kate steps inside. "Putting you through to Mr. Bromley now." She taps her phone, and Bram's face appears on the large monitor.

"Alex, Aaron. How are you?" he says, syrupy sweet. "I hear congratulations are in order. On your nuptials, Aaron."

"Thanks," I say evenly. "You mentioned in your voicemail that you wanted to discuss new client referrals."

"I like a man who gets straight to business."

"We have our own business development team," Alex cuts in. "Why do we need your help?"

"You've cornered the market in AI tech. We've got a thirty-five percent share of the banking institutions using our product."

He's right, their end-to-end platform is gaining traction, shortening financial transaction timelines from months to weeks. But Bromley lacks an AI division. If they had one, they could integrate it across their system, cut time even further, and earn their clients billions.

Building that capability would require human capital, and capital's not something Bromley has in excess. Not anymore.

"You've seen a ten percent increase. That's a good year," I say.

"We could do better."

I take a breath. "So what exactly are you asking for, Bromley?"

"A partnership."

"We don't do partnerships."

"This could move your product into the finance sector."

"We can enter finance on our own," Alex says. "That's not our target."

"You wouldn't even need to do the work. We incorporate your AI tech. We find the clients. You profit."

"If our name is on a product, it's one we built. A partnership makes us a footnote in a product powered by Bromley." I lean back. "That's not how we operate."

"If you're serious about this, you're going to have to do it the hard way." Alex adds. "We can't help you."

"If not you..."

He doesn't get to finish.

"You called us," I say. "If you had someone else lined up, you should have started with them."

Alex leans forward. "Like my brother said, we don't do partnerships. Our product. Our name. Our stamp of approval."

"I think you lads are missing out."

"We may be," Alex says. "And we're okay with that."

"Is that all you wanted to discuss, Bram?" I ask.

"I was surprised to hear you're suddenly married. Maybe I'll get to meet the wife one day."

Fishing. That's what this is. Fishing for information. Which means he may have had a hand in Bridgette reaching out to me last week.

"We're not here to discuss my wife," I say. "So, if that's all. We'll end here."

"I hope you reconsider. You never know what spin the media might put on things."

"Is that a threat?"

"Just an observation. Good day, mates." The screen goes black.

I glance at Alex.

"Keep an eye on him," he says. "I don't want anything messing with our acquisition."

"Don't worry. I'm on it."

"We'll need a formal press release. Which means you have to talk to Reed Ross."

I sigh. This gets messier by the day. Jasmine was hoping to wait before telling her father. But with Bram sniffing around, we're out of time.

"I'll talk to Jasmine. I'll let you know when we're ready."

"Make it soon. We still got the auditors breathing down our necks."

***

I don't know what this feeling is, exactly—just that it coils in my chest like anticipation and contentment all at once. I'm excited to be home, and I suspect it has everything to do with who's waiting for me. *Jasmine.*

The faint hint of spiced vanilla greets me before I even round the corner. Her perfume, soft and sweet, always lingers in the air like a whisper of something intimate. The light and relaxed sound of laughter comes from the kitchen, drawing me like gravity.

I drop my keys in the dish by the door and leave my bag in the foyer without a second thought. I don't even take off my coat.

In the kitchen, Jasmine is leaning casually against the counter in a pair of worn jeans and a fitted t-shirt, the kind of look that shouldn't look as good as it does on someone so effortlessly elegant. Amara is perched on a stool across from her, feet swinging as she slices cheese and arranges it onto crackers with the same focus she applies to everything.

"Seems like good options," Jasmine says.

They don't notice me right away—not until Jasmine lifts her eyes and finds mine.

Her face softens instantly. Her smile...quick but warm, lands somewhere between greeting and secret. It steals the air from my lungs.

Before I can say anything, Elizabeth comes tearing across the floor, her zoomies on full display. She zips past Amara's stool and the counter like she's being personally chased by fate.

"What seems like good options?" I ask, stepping into the room and toward the only place I want to be—next to *her*.

"I narrowed down a few schools," Amara replies, without turning around. She places a slice of cheddar on a cracker and takes a bite like this conversation is no big deal, like it hasn't been quietly lurking in the background for the past week.

I reach Jasmine and gently cup her face, my thumb brushing along the curve of her jaw. Her skin is warm beneath my touch. I want to kiss her—God, I want to kiss her—but I settle for a soft press to her cheek instead. Something about the presence of family demands restraint, even when every cell in my body is aching to taste her lips.

"How was your day?" I murmur, my voice low enough for only her.

"Good," she says, eyes dancing. "I'm ready for tonight."

"Can't wait," I reply, and I mean it. I've never seen her in this light—commanding a room, delivering a keynote in Dr. Owusu's place. It feels like I'm being handed another piece of her. A piece I didn't know I was missing.

I pull her into a hug, one that lasts longer than it should, but I don't care. I need this—her, here, grounding me. Her scent settles into my lungs like home.

"Do you need privacy?" Amara calls out with a smirk.

Jasmine laughs and gently pulls away, giving me a playful nudge. I chuckle and walk over to join Amara at the counter. I grab a plate and help myself to some of the spread she's curated: cheeses, cured meats, crackers, grapes.

"Maybe when we get back from the museum," I say, glancing at her thoughtfully, "you and I can talk about that list. See what's really calling to you."

"Yeah," she says, her tone softer now. "I'd like that."

Elizabeth returns, her frenzy forgotten. She climbs into Amara's lap and instantly steals her attention. At the counter, Jasmine joins me, her small hands moving with practiced precision as she builds a plate of crackers layered with cheese and a delicate drizzle of honey. Then she reaches into my plate, takes a grape, and pops it into her mouth. My eyes land on her lips as she chews.

"How did your call with Bromley go?" she asks without looking up.

I release a heavy sigh. "He was fishing for a partnership."

"But you don't want one."

"No. I politely declined." I dish a few more grapes onto her plate. "That wasn't enough for him. We should hop on a call with Reed."

"What? Why?" Her voice tightens. "I thought we agreed to wait until next month."

"Bram seemed suspicious of our marriage."

"You've always kept your personal life out of the spotlight. Why is this different now?"

I don't want to go down this path, but I can't avoid it. "I've tried to keep it private, Jas. But this...us—people aren't expecting it."

"This. Just say it. People aren't expecting *me*." She starts to stand, but I reach out, catching her hand.

"Jas, we're a team. But you're right. Up until last year, people only saw me with—"

"My sister."

I nod. "Our families are known. We should do a press release soon. It solves both our problems. The guy at the pub—"

"Bane Roth."

My jaw clenches just saying his name. "Yeah, Bane. I've got a feeling he's waiting for you to show up at the restaurant. Let's plan to have lunch there, put the rumors to bed."

She stands abruptly, pushing her stool back. "No. I'm not catering to his suspicions. I get it—you want to keep things quiet during your audit, but—"

"Jas—" I stand too, but I don't get to finish.

Amara bolts from the room.

Jasmine and I both freeze. I move to follow, but Jasmine gently touches my arm.

"I'll go," she says softly and disappears after her.

Fuck. Our first argument. And it didn't even come from a place of disagreement—just fear. I'm just trying to protect her. Amara. Protect our families. There are people out there who would destroy us for fun. I can't let that happen.

I sit at the counter, raking a hand through my hair. Am I being too controlling? Too cautious? Maybe. But some things have to happen to make this arrangement believable. Public appearances. A family narrative. The world doesn't know we're only a few days in—they'll assume we've been married for months, maybe longer. And we have to look the part.

When Jasmine returns, Amara is tucked under her arm, her expression a mix of confusion and hope. Jasmine's smile is tight, but she's calm.

"It's just a misunderstanding," she says gently. "She thought we were fighting."

My breath catches. "Amara," I say, bending slightly to bring myself eye level to her. "We're not fighting, sweetie. We're just figuring things out, that's all. I'm sorry. Can you forgive me?" I open my arms.

She crosses the room and hugs me.

"My parents fought all the time," she says, her voice barely above a whisper.

Jasmine stands beside us, wrapping her arms around us both. "You don't have to worry about that here. Aaron might be handsomely irritating sometimes, but there's no anger between us."

"Jas is right," I say, tugging lightly at a lock of her hair. "Now, Amara, go get ready. We've got to look our best for the museum event."

We slowly pull apart from our group hug.

"Will you help me with my hair before we leave?" Amara asks Jasmine.

Jasmine brushes a curl over her shoulder. "Of course. Now go on, do your thing."

Amara nods and trots off, the cat trailing loyally behind her.

"Handsomely irritating, huh?" I smirk, pulling Jasmine gently between my legs.

"It's a gift and a curse," she says, lips twitching into a smile. "But you're right. I'll talk to my dad."

"We'll talk to him," I say firmly.

She nods. "But you'll have to give me a day or two to think about the Bane thing."

"Fair enough." I take her in. This woman. My wife. "Didn't realize how much I missed you until I saw you standing there."

The words tumble out of my mouth before I can stop them.

She smooths her hands down my arms. "I missed you, too."

I hold her gaze. "What are we doing, Jas?"

Her eyes soften, glimmering with something that looks a lot like hope. "I've never really dated before. Maybe we can start there?"

That one sentence—it releases something in me. Like a gate flung open. There's a chance for this to be real. For *us* to be real.

"May I?"

She nods.

I tip her chin and cover her mouth with mine. I kiss her—not just a soft press of lips, but a promise. A claim. I deepen it, tasting her, letting her feel how much I want this. Her. All of it.

When I finally pull back, she whispers my name like a secret. "Aaron."

"I know, honey," I murmur. "I feel it, too."

CHAPTER 22

A Night at the Museum

Jasmine

WE ARRIVE AT THE British Museum early to give Amara, who hasn't been there since she was much younger, a chance to explore before the event begins. Stepping inside the Great Court, with its soaring glass roof and vast open space, always takes my breath away. Tonight, it's transformed.

In the center plaza, a sleek stage has been erected in front of the *Reading Room* where I'll give my keynote. A digital projection of the *A History of Black England* event invitation glows across the massive stone wall, nestled between the two iconic staircases. It features a powerful portrait, an important work of Black art, overlaid with bold, elegant typography. Around the perimeter, round dinner tables are arranged in a graceful arc. Each one is dressed in white linen with crisp black napkins folded precisely beside gleaming silverware. A tall, narrow vase holds white roses, their soft petals glowing under ambient lighting. Classical music plays over the speakers.

"Wow," Amara says, eyes wide as she slowly turns in place, taking it all in.

I squeeze her hand. "It's a lot, isn't it?"

"I've only ever been to birthday parties at friends' houses," she says, a little dazed.

Aaron's hand finds the small of my back, his presence grounding. "This is nice," he says, glancing around. "You'll have several more of these to attend, Amara, before you head off to university."

"Really?" she asks, still looking up.

"If you like," he replies.

She tugs at my hand, pulling us toward the Enlightenment Gallery. I follow, smiling at her excitement.

"You want me to be your docent?" I ask Amara, pausing in front of a terracotta portrait bust of a man in an elaborate curly wig.

"I know who this is—Sir Hans Sloane," she says confidently.

I grin. "That's right."

"He's Irish, like your sister's husband. He gave his collection to the British. That's how this place started." She steps closer to the bust, studying it. "Are you going to talk about the stolen art?"

I glance at Aaron and press my lips together, surprised but not entirely caught off guard by her question. "I'm going to talk about Black art—how we've been represented in it over time. Not necessarily how every artifact got here."

"One of my friends said Sloane invented chocolate milk," Amara says. "They got mad when I told them he just brought it back from Jamaica."

"Sometimes people prefer the version of history that makes them feel better. There are so many things that mainstream culture borrows from Black culture—food, clothing, art, music—and it's not hard to trace those things back to their roots. Sloane may have documented chocolate drinks in the eighteenth century, but Jamaicans were making similar versions long before that. Even the Mayans had their own, centuries earlier."

Aaron chimes in, his tone warm and affirming. "From what I've seen, you have a sharp eye for the truth. If you speak up and someone chooses to ignore it, that's their loss. Hold to what you know."

Amara nods, moving on to the next item, absorbing everything like a sponge. We only have enough time to view a few of the exhibits on the first floor because more guests arrive, pulling our attention away.

"Dr. Prescott is here," I say to Aaron, lifting my chin. "I'll introduce you."

Aaron pulls me close and cups my cheek. The marble halls fall away. The air thins, the crowd fades, and it's just us. That happens often now—he touches me and the world quiets. My cheeks warm.

"You ready for this?" he asks softly.

This—our first formal outing in a business setting as a couple. Not just a couple. Husband and wife.

I should be nervous. The kind of nervous that coils in your gut and tightens your spine. But all I feel is warmth. Certainty. Jake and June always had good things to say about Aaron, and now I understand why. His steadiness. His quiet confidence. His eyes that never look past me, but into me.

I lean into his palm. "Yeah. I'm ready."

A soft touch on my elbow pulls me back to earth.

"There's a man heading toward you," Amara says.

Aaron gives a knowing wink and takes my hand like we've always done this. Like we'll do it forever.

Dr. Prescott approaches wearing a black suit with a burgundy bowtie, looking every bit the part of vice-chancellor.

"Hi, Professor Ross, it's an honor to have you here tonight. Thank you for agreeing to speak." He shakes my hand and glances at Aaron.

"Dr. Prescott, it's good to see you. The topic is close to my heart—always happy to help out Dr. Owusu. Let me introduce you to my husband, Aaron Adler, and our daughter, Amara."

His eyebrows flicker with surprise. "Amara, what a beautiful name. Mr. Adler. Nice to meet you," he says, shaking Aaron's hand. "I've had the pleasure of meeting your brother on campus. Our students are highly competitive, trying to obtain one of the prestigious slots in your internship program."

"We're very proud of our program," Aaron replies, his voice smooth but grounded.

Dr. Prescott's eyes flit between us. "I apologize—I didn't realize you were married, Professor."

"We're both private people," Aaron says, all calm assurance. "I'm sure you can understand that."

"Oh, of course."

My eyes skim past Dr. Prescott to the crowd entering, then back.

"I'd like to say hi to a few more people before the program begins," I add.

"By all means."

We weave through the crowd, exchanging greetings and navigating polite curiosities. A few of Aaron's clients are here, giving us the same confused once-over. I can practically hear the questions forming behind their eyes.

We break away from the crowd, giving Amara a chance to use the restroom.

"We'll wait right here," I tell her.

As soon as she disappears behind the door, the noise of the museum fades.

Aaron turns to me, eyes already fixed on mine. "How'd we do, wife?"

The word still sounds foreign—strange in my mouth, but not in his. In his voice, it sounds like the truth. Like something that's already been settled.

I tilt my head, studying him. "It feels strange saying I have a husband."

He steps closer, erasing the small space between us. His hand slides around my waist—firm, warm, steady. "So...is this our first date?"

I give him a playful smirk. "Does bringing Amara on our first date count?"

His lips curve, but he's not laughing. His gaze drops to my mouth, then slowly lifts again, searching me. Like he's looking for something behind my eyes. "Yeah," he says softly. "It counts."

Then, with the quiet confidence that still catches me off guard, he lifts a hand and brushes his knuckles along my jaw. I lean in without thinking, drawn to the gentle pull of him. He tips my chin, holding me in that way of his—like he already knows I'll let him.

"Can I kiss you on our first date?" he asks. "I know it just started. But I've been thinking about it since we left the house."

My breath hitches. Not because of the words. But because of how he's looking at me—as if I'm not just a woman he's falling for, but one he's already chosen.

I nod, barely. "I'd like that."

His lips find mine, and the kiss is...everything. Warm. Intentional. Soft but certain. He doesn't rush, doesn't press for more than I offer. Still, it lights something in me. A kind of ache I forgot I was carrying. It's not just want. It's the terrifying feeling that I could...stay.

We break apart, my forehead rests against his, and I close my eyes for a moment too long.

"I'm lucky," he murmurs.

"Why's that?"

His hand moves to cradle my cheek. "Because my wife is stunning, brilliant, and feels amazing in my arms. Thank you...for the kiss."

I laugh, but it's breathy and uneven. "You don't have to ask. I'll never deny your kisses."

His smile turns slow and wicked, but the heat in his gaze softens when he presses his nose to mine. "You have no idea what you're getting yourself into."

"I guess I'll soon find out."

The restroom door creaks and Amara steps out, eyebrows raised like she's seen this coming all along. "You guys, you know we're in public, right?"

We both laugh—caught, but not sorry. Aaron grabs her hand with one of his, mine with the other, and we head back into the Great Court to find our seats near the front. The music fades. The museum director welcomes the crowd. Announcements are made—new patron donations, scholarship funds, exhibit expansions—and then comes my name.

I glance toward the audience. Dr. Owusu's students are present. Wide-eyed and hopeful. I envy their certainty, the straight lines of their lives. They're headed toward degrees, lectures, careers, a kind of rootedness I gave up long ago.

Would I be different if I'd stayed still? Chosen safety? Chosen home?

My name floats over the speakers, breaking the thought. The audience claps. I rise. Aaron places a finger under my chin and tilts it gently.

"You'll be great," he whispers, and plants a kiss that grounds me.

I walk onto the stage. The crowd stills. I take the podium and breathe deep. The light hits my face. My voice comes clear, measured, then rises.

"'Old folks love to seem wise—and if you are silly enough to correspond with grey hairs, take the consequence.'" Soft laughter ripples through the room.

I gesture behind me to the screen. A portrait appears.

"This is Charles Ignatius Sancho, painted by Thomas Gainsborough in 1768. A distinguished man in a gold-trimmed waistcoat. Eyes full of thought. Graceful. Poised. But beneath the brushstrokes? A story. Sancho was born on a slave ship. He became a composer. A writer. A grocer. A voter. A father. A man who dared to be more than what the world told him he could be.

"History was not etched in textbooks. It was hidden in letters. In music. In silence. Until someone listened. There are many more like him. Black stories preserved in art but muted by history. Trapped behind museum glass, waiting for someone...anyone, to lean in and say: *I see you. I hear you. You matter.*

"History doesn't belong only to those who wrote it in ink, but also to those who lived it in defiance. Tonight, we honor the unheard. We resurrect the whispered truths. We hold the past in our hands and refuse to look away."

A hush hangs in the air. I continue, naming other Black British artists, scientists, freedom fighters. Their legacies. Their truths. And as I speak, I find something opening in me...something steady. Rooted. Not just a wanderer passing through.

When I finish, applause roars through the room. I return to my seat, pulse still racing. Amara reaches out and gives me a high-five. Aaron helps me into my chair, never breaking eye contact.

He leans close and kisses my cheek. His voice is low, reverent. "You did amazing."

"Thanks," I whisper, heart still thundering in my chest.

The program wraps, and a wave of chatter rolls through the venue, rising over soft music as people shift into networking mode—drinks in hand, laughter rising.

"Can I have a pop?" Amara asks.

"Of course."

"I'll get it." Aaron stands smoothly. "Wine for you?"

I nod. "Please."

He gives me a subtle wink, then disappears into the mingling crowd.

I reach over and gently tuck a curl behind Amara's ear. "So, what'd you think?"

She beams, then her face goes serious. "I want people to listen to me like they did you."

"They will," I tell her. "Sooner than you think."

But she stiffens. I follow her gaze over my shoulder—and there he is.

"Well, I came looking for one pretty lady and found two," Bane Roth says, his voice as slick as his smirk.

I rise instantly, placing myself between him and Amara. My spine straightens on instinct. "Are you stalking me?"

He lifts a brow, oozing casual arrogance. "Let's call it a personal interest."

"There's nothing here that belongs to you." My words cut clean and sharp. "If you have something to say—say it to *me*."

Just then, Aaron returns, placing a glass of soda in front of Amara and wine in front of me. His arm curls smoothly, possessively, around my waist. Claiming. Clear.

Bane notices.

"Well, look at this," Bane says, tone shifting to mocking curiosity. "Didn't know you were so well connected. Aaron Adler. Small world."

"You don't hear so well, do you?" I say, not backing down. "Aaron, this is Bane Roth—the man I told you about."

Aaron's eyes don't leave Roth's face. "Bane," he says, the single syllable landing like a hammer. "If you're not here to congratulate my wife, you've overstayed."

"*Wife?*" Bane echoes, dragging the word out. His gaze slinks toward Amara. "She's got a pretty little friend with her, too."

Aaron moves fast but controlled, angling his body until I'm tucked behind him, Amara beside me.

He stares Bane down, voice low and lethal. "Mr. Roth. I don't like your tone. And I *really* don't like the way you're looking at my wife and daughter." The word hits like a strike. *Daughter.* "You have two options," Aaron continues. "You leave right now, or I'll make sure you do."

Bane laughs, though it's brittle now. "Huh. Seems I was misinformed. Didn't realize either of you were married."

Aaron steps closer—so close Roth has to tilt his head to maintain eye contact. "Now you know. Goodbye, Mr. Roth."

I don't notice the men in suits near the entrance until Aaron subtly tips his chin toward them. Silent. Stationary. Watching. But not anymore. They're moving in now, quietly but with purpose.

Bane catches it, too. His eyes flick to the suits, then back to Aaron.

"I see I'm not welcome here," he mutters.

"No," Aaron says. "You're not."

Bane lingers for half a second too long. His eyes dart to me, cold and calculating. A warning wrapped in silence.

But I hold his stare. And I don't flinch.

He turns and slips into the crowd, swallowed by it. He's not done. I can feel it in my bones. He's deterred but not defeated. Too bad for him. He's never gone head-to-head with an Adler. And clearly forgot...I'm a Ross

CHAPTER 23

Hard to Pretend

Aaron

JASMINE'S SUGGESTION THAT WE date was the best idea. For moments like now, I'm not walking into a meeting with her to discuss our arrangement, I'm walking toward her to a date, toward something real, and hope stitching in my chest feels heavier than any deal I've ever closed. And I'm taking it all in...taking her all in bit by bit.

Slowly, over time, I'm learning more about Jasmine. How she works, what she needs, what she'll fight for. There are things in our lives that just *have* to happen because of who we are. Security. Privacy. Structure. But keeping her safe was the easy part. Sharing life with her—that's entirely something different.

We've settled into a rhythm. I take Amara to school in the mornings; Jasmine picks her up in the afternoons. We have a house staff, but Jasmine still insists on doing small things herself.

One morning, I found her at the stove making breakfast again, this time in one of my old button-downs, barefoot and determined. I leaned against the doorway, watching her stir eggs like she was on a mission.

"You know we have a chef for this," I told her, rehashing our conversation about waffle chips.

She glanced over her shoulders, eyes soft. "I know."

I crossed the room, wrapped my arms around her waist, pulling her gently back into me. "You're not my cook," I whispered against the shell of her ear. "You're my wife. And I want time to get to know you."

She stilled. Then slowly, she turned in my arms and kissed me—slow and intentional, like she heard me.

That kiss...I still feel it. And that's when I knew I had to pull back.

She should never have said I didn't have to ask. Because if I kissed her the way I wanted...the way that made her legs tremble...there'd be no separate rooms. No distance. No pretending.

But she's not my wife in that way.

Not yet.

The restaurant is tucked on a side street in Belgravia, the kind of place with pressed linens, soft jazz humming under conversations, and a maître d' who greets everyone like royalty. It's our fourth official "date," part of our commitment to...this thing between us. Marriage by arrangement. Affection by choice.

She's already here when I arrive. I spot her instantly, seated by the window with light pouring through the glass like a spotlight designed for her. She's scrolling through her phone with one hand, the other wrapped around a water glass. A vintage graphic tee under a structured blazer, jeans, and pointed heels—polished, but entirely *her*. God, she's stunning.

I cross the room, noting the way heads turn—not toward me, but her. Always her.

"Hey," she greets softly, looking up with a smile that hits me in the chest.

I lean down and press a chaste kiss to her cheek. "Hey, beautiful." I slide into the seat beside her instead of across.

"You're early," I say, gesturing to the server for water.

"I had time on my hands. I ordered for us."

"Thanks." I look around the restaurant, eyes drifting across the softly lit interior. "It doesn't bother you, sitting in the front?"

She frowns for a second, then realizes what I mean. "You're talking about June, huh?"

I nod once. "She tends to prefer tables in the back. Less visibility."

Jasmine takes a breath, her fingers lightly tapping her thigh. "I'm not June."

"I know."

She gives me a tight smile. "I love my sister, but I don't want to talk about her today. How was your day?"

"Busy. I got a call from the auditor. Nothing serious yet, but their inquiries have ticked up lately."

"You think that has something to do with me?" she asks, voice steady but cautious. "Or...us?"

"I don't want to assume. Could be routine. Could be timing. Saola's gone through this before. I'm not worried."

She toys with her napkin. "You've got your tech event in a few weeks. Maybe your PR could spin up a new campaign? Give people something else to focus on. Something...positive."

I turn toward her, fully. "You *are* the most positive thing in my life, Jas. And the most important."

She looks past my shoulder, then back at me, her voice quiet. "Lately, it feels like you're pulling away. I don't know if you're rethinking this or..."

"What makes you say that?"

"I don't know. You feel...different. A little more distant. Like you're keeping part of yourself in check."

Before I can answer, our food arrives—perfect timing, or terrible, depending on how you see it.

"I'll let you know if we need anything else," I say, without breaking eye contact with Jasmine. I thank the server and wait until he walks off.

She needs my full attention. I take a slow breath, lean in, and reach for her chin, tilting it just enough so I can see every inch of her face. Every truth she's trying not to say aloud.

"I'm not rethinking anything," I say. "You are the highlight of my day. I feel I could conquer the world with you beside me."

"Then why does it feel like you're holding back?"

"Because I am." She freezes. "You asked about the change...it's not disinterest, Jas. It's control. Whenever I'm near you, I want to pull you into my arms. Every time I kiss you, I want more. And if I let myself go the way I want to...the way you make me feel...there won't be any room left for pretending."

I press my thumb to her lower lip, watching it part slightly. "I want to be respectful. But Jas...I want you. As my wife. Not just on paper. In every way."

My lips hover above hers. Her breath catches. The air between us grows taut, heavy. Then I kiss her. Deeply. Thoroughly. Like I need her to breathe. Like she's the only anchor I have left in the entire goddam world.

She melts into it, a soft moan slipping free as her hand grips the lapel of my jacket. We're not alone, but I don't care. The chatter of the lunch crowd fades. The clinking of silverware might as well be miles away.

When I finally pull back, her chest is rising and falling like she's been running.

"Jas," I say, cupping her cheek. "In. Every. Way."

I guide her hand to my lap, letting her feel the truth for herself.

Her fingers curl around my hand, securing us both.

"I didn't realize," she says softly. "I thought you were second-guessing. I didn't know you were...holding back for me."

"Every damn day."

A small smile plays at the edge of her lips, and she leans in just enough for our foreheads to touch.

"I understand now." Her voice is quiet, but sure.

And just like that, it gets harder to keep pretending.

Chapter 24

Hi

Jasmine

WHEN I LEFT HOME at nineteen, I didn't know what to expect. People always talked about homesickness, like it was this inevitable rite of passage. For weeks, I braced for it, like waiting for a storm. It never came. Not when I landed in Singapore. Not when I moved to Cape Town. Not even in Tokyo. I thought I was immune.

Turns out, I was just waiting for the right person to miss.

Today, it hits me like a punch to the chest—homesickness, not for a place, but for a person. For...*Aaron*.

I've been in London for a month now. Married. Not quite four weeks, but long enough to know this is the longest we've been apart since the day I stepped into that restaurant and met my husband for the first time. He's in Sweden on business, and I'm trying not to count the hours until he's home.

"Do you have your list?" I ask Amara as we step out of the car. The city hums with Bank Holiday energy: families crowding sidewalks, shopping bags swinging, buskers playing saxophones on corners. The air smells like roasted chestnuts and something sugary from the bakery across the street.

"On my phone," she says, holding it up like a badge of honor.

Amara's been a dream. Aaron was right, she adjusts like she's been doing it her whole life. She's super smart, observant, and has a dry sense of humor

I live for. But sometimes she drifts. Quiet. Reflective. That's when she disappears into the library or the study with her journal.

Some days after school, we head to Holborn so she can sit in the safe room. Aaron and I talked about counseling—getting her someone to talk to about the parts of her past she won't even whisper. The things she buries deep.

I wonder sometimes if she's mirroring me. Holding on to things I should let go. If my own reluctance to stop running is rubbing off on her. Maybe she's waiting, like Aaron, for me to choose something, anything, over ghosts of the life I left behind.

"This is the store," Amara says, nudging me out of my spiral.

"Lead the way."

The store is chaos—music blasting from speakers overhead, the soft clatter of hangers, a mess of limbs and laughter as girls sort through racks of clothes. I follow her to the teen section. She could wear women's sizes, but the fit is off—too baggy, too grown. We're after polish and confidence, not frumpy.

"Can I get a short dress, or does it have to touch the floor?" she asks, eyes wide at a sparkly silver dress.

"You can wear what you want as long as it's formal."

"Except for my party."

"That's right. You set the dress code for that one."

We promised to throw her a party when she finishes school. Something special at the house: friends, music, food, the works. A space to just *be*. She deserves that. A celebration that says *you made it*. I want her to feel like her life is unfolding, not like she's surviving.

I barely make it through one rack when she's already got a few options and a dressing room waiting.

"I'll wait right here for you."

"K," she says and disappears behind the door.

I pull out my phone and type before I second-guess it.

Me: Hey, handsome.

The reply is instant.

Aaron: Hey, beautiful.

Me: Are you in a meeting?

Aaron: Stepping out to call you.

My heart does this fluttery thing. My screen buzzes. Incoming video call. I answer. "You didn't have to step out."

"I *wanted* to." His voice is warm velvet. His background is all glass and chrome and the Stockholm skyline. "I miss you."

"I miss you, too." I shift my weight and turn slightly from the foot traffic. "You flying back tonight or in the morning?"

"Tonight, but it'll be late. You'll be asleep."

"Wake me."

He smiles. "Tempting. Where's Amara?"

"Trying on dresses. I just wanted to say hi."

"And I needed to hear your voice." He pauses, his gaze softening. "Jas, I—"

"Save it," I say gently. "Tell me everything when you're home."

He nods, and the pause between us hums with unspoken things.

"Tell Amara I said hi."

"I will. Hurry home."

"I will," he says, and the call ends.

"Okay, I'm ready," Amara calls, drawing me back. I look up and smile. "You talked to him," she says knowingly.

"Yeah, how'd you know?"

"Because you have that look."

"What look? Let's see that dress on you."

"The look of love," she teases, stepping closer.

I grab her by the waist and tickle her. "What do you know about love, little girl?"

"Hey, you're going to wrinkle my dress." She giggles, wriggling away. Then she sobers slightly. "I know my mother loved my father...even with the way he was."

She's so young yet so observant. I can only imagine the things she's seen over the years.

I pause, searching her eyes, but she's already retreating. I nod slowly. "Aaron says hi. Now...what about this dress?"

"I like it."

"Let's take a picture for him."

I lift my phone, wrap an arm around her, and press our cheeks together. The blue satin of her dress gleams under the lights. I snap a picture and hit send.

"Ah, don't you two look *adorable*," comes a voice so sugary it sours.

I turn. *Bridgette Bromley.*

I instinctively reach for Amara's hand. "Bridgette."

"Well, I didn't expect to see you here with..." Her voice trails off with a dramatic blink.

"My daughter."

"Daughter. Right." Her voice drips with sarcasm. "Mother-daughter moments. How...charming."

"Amara, you remember Bridgette."

"Hi," Amara says, flat and unimpressed.

Bridgette tilts her head, studying us, processing, calculating. "Well, I've seen it all now."

"I doubt that." I smile coolly. "But we've got errands to run."

"Oh, I'm sure. Seems Aaron's been living a *very* interesting double life. No wonder he rushed into marriage. Did your daddy *make* him marry you?"

Amara stiffen beside me.

"Sweetheart," I say, squeezing her hand, "go change and grab the dresses you like."

"Okay. What's wrong with that woman?" She mutters. "She doesn't seem very bright. And why does she have so much makeup on?"

"Go change, sweetie," I whisper.

She disappears behind the door.

I turn to Bridgette. "You know, it's really sad when even a child can spot desperation."

Her expression hardens. "You think he has *no* interest in me?"

"I know he doesn't."

She smirks. "That's where you're wrong. I see the way he looks at me. I know what he wants."

I let out a short laugh. "Delusion must be your comfort zone."

"You wait and see."

"Bridgette," I say, stepping closer. "You're a footnote in a book Aaron already returned to the library. You can try all the tired tactics you want, but the truth is—he married me. And you? You're just noise. This conversation is over."

I don't wait for a response. I pivot and walk toward the dressing rooms. Because Bridgette Bromley is certifiable. And I've got better things to do than entertain fairytales.

***

I'm in Chile, sitting in a field of daisies, the Andes stretching in the distance like the bones of the earth. The wind carries his laugh. I can't see him, but I feel him. And then, the scent of amber and fresh rain wraps around me like a second skin.

It's only a dream. But he feels so...real. My eyes flutter open, heavy with sleep and something softer—hope...maybe. He's here. *Aaron.*

Sitting on the couch across from the bed, a white bath towel low on his hips, hair damp and curling slightly at the ends. His arms stretched wide across the back of the couch like he owns the moment, like he belongs here—because he does. His eyes are on me, quiet and unreadable, but unmistakably his. Watching me.

"You're home," I whisper, my voice thick with sleep and emotion.

"I am," he says. His voice is like gravel smoothed by time. "What are you doing?"

"I knew you wouldn't wake me."

"So you fell asleep in…"

"Our room." I finish for him. The words lie between us like truth. Even if it's the first time I've slept here, this space feels like it's always belonged to both of us. "How long have you been here?" I ask, my heart already unraveling.

"Not long."

"You were just going to watch me sleep?"

His smile curves slowly, like he's unsure whether to admit the truth. "Something like that."

The quiet wraps around us, thick and warm. I can feel it in my fingertips. The ache of missing him hasn't dulled. It sharpens now that he's close.

He doesn't move, but I do.

I slide out of bed, the sheets whispering against my skin, and walk to him. I climb onto his lap, one knee on either side of him, heart trembling. He doesn't resist. His arms come around me instinctively, like they've been waiting for this. For *me*.

I loop an arm around his neck and press myself into him, burying my face into the curve of his shoulder. His skin is warm, damp, real.

"I missed you so much," I breathe into his ear. My voice breaking.

His hand finds my shoulder, gently pulling me back until our eyes meet. Something flickers in his gaze—pain, restraint, love.

He cups my cheek like I'm fragile. "I'll help you to your room," he murmurs. "We can talk in the morning."

"I *am* in my room," I say, holding his gaze. "*Our* room."

His brow furrows. "What are you saying, beautiful?"

I take a breath and let it fall away—the fear, the what-ifs, the waiting.

"I'm saying that I want you."

He closes his eyes like my words knock the air out of him. When he opens them, he looks at me like I'm a wish he's scared to believe in.

"And in five months?" he asks, voice barely above a whisper.

"I haven't worked it out yet," I admit. "But what I feel for you is real. I don't want to run anymore. Not from you. The ache from missing you...it's unbearable. I don't want to be with anyone else."

He exhales like he's been holding his breath for weeks.

"I missed you, too," he says. "But you need to understand—if we do this, there's no pretending. Everything I give you—every touch, every kiss—has *forever* written on it."

He pauses, and his next words crack me open. "Because somewhere between meeting you at that restaurant and now, I fell in love with you. And if you walk away...it'll hurt, but I'll wait a lifetime for you to stop running and return to me. That's how strongly I feel about us. I love you, Jasmine."

His voice doesn't shake, but I do.

Because I believe him.

Because I love him, too.

And I tell him.

CHAPTER 25

Consumed

Aaron

I'M IN LOVE WITH my wife.

It's not just a thought—it's a pulse in my veins. The mantra anchors me from the second her name lights up my phone. When I excuse myself from the boardroom. When I'm careering through the clouds back to her. When I open the door and find her body curled beneath my sheets like she's always belonged there.

I don't breathe for a moment. I just stare. Then I fall to my knees beside the bed, like gravity finally caught up with me.

My wife.

She's here. In my space. In my bed. In my life.

I don't know how long I watched her sleep, memorizing every soft breath and strand of hair out of place. I don't know how I peeled myself away long enough to take a shower. Or how I didn't lose control when she climbed into my lap like I was hers to claim. Maybe I always was.

But I'm glad I waited—because hearing Jasmine whisper how much she wants me, hearing her say she loves me? That's everything. That's the unraveling.

She presses her cheek into my palm, warmth anchoring me. "I don't have much experience being with someone. Nor what it's like to settle in one place for long. But I know what I feel for you is real. And I don't want to run from it." Her smile wrecks me. Then she says the words that undo every thread of restraint I have left. "I love you, Aaron. Make love to me."

Pulling her into me...I don't kiss her. I consume her.

Jasmine's moans echo through the room, wrapping around me like a spell. Her fingers tangle in my hair, hips grinding against my length, hot aching beneath the weight of her need. She wants me...desperately. As much as I want her.

But not here. Not like this. Not our first time.

I break the kiss, breathing hard against her lips, holding back every instinct that screams to bury myself in her right now. "Are you ready to be my wife?"

My hand slips between us, sliding beneath her silk slip. I find her heat, her wetness, and the way her body reacts to my touch steals the breath from my lungs. *God.* She's soaked for me. Her thighs tremble as I tease between her folds, her walls clenching greedily around my fingers like her body already knows I belong inside her.

She gasps, shuddering in my arms. But I won't let her come this way. Not tonight. Her first release will be with me buried deep inside her—claiming her in the most intimate way a man can. Showing her...I'm her man.

She nods, eyes glazed, lips parted like she's offering me a prayer. Then she removes her slip, dropping it on the floor.

I lift her into my arms, take her to our bed, and lie her down in the center like the gift she is. She watches me as I settle above her, caging her in with my arms on either side. Her chest rises and falls in shallow breaths, anticipation dancing in every line of her body.

I dip my head and press a soft kiss to her lips. Reverent. Gentle. Almost too restrained for what's coming next.

Then I whisper, low and rough, directly in her ear. "When you come, I want it to be with me inside you. I want to feel it. I want evidence of my love dripping down your thighs. Do you understand?" She swallows, then nods, her eyes wide, shining. "Say it, beautiful. I need to hear you."

Her voice trembles, but her words are clear. Certain. "Take me as your wife. In every way."

I trail kisses along the curve of her neck, lingering at the pulse that flutters beneath her skin. Her scent—spiced vanilla, warm, sweet, unmistakable—wraps around me like a drug I never want to quit. I trace my mouth down her shoulder, across the delicate slope of her collarbone, then lower still, tasting the dip between her breasts.

I cup one, firm and soft in my palm, while I take the other in my mouth, drawing her nipple against my tongue. She gasps, her back arching into me, and I smile against her skin, loving how her body responds to my touch. I continue caressing her other breast, thumb brushing across the stiff peak, and she moans, low, breathless, wanton.

I kiss my way down her stomach, slow and reverent, breathing her in like I need her to live. Her fingers thread through my hair, her hips already shifting beneath me, searching for more. My hands splay across her ribs, then I glide downward, thumbs flicking her nipples as I descend.

When I reach her center, I pause—not to tease, but to admire. To worship.

I lean in and lift her hips with care, like she's sacred. Because she is. And I taste her. God, I taste her—and I swear my heart forgets how to beat. She's wet, ready, every flick of my tongue drawing a cry from deep in her chest. I feast on her, lapping at everything she offers like it's salvation.

"I need you inside me," she whimpers, voice breaking.

She'll have me. But not yet. The way she coats my tongue tells me she's close, and I want to watch her fall apart around me. One more stroke, slow and deliberate, then I pull away, ignoring her protest. I crawl up her body, kissing her ribs, her sternum, the spot just below her ear that makes her shiver.

"Brace yourself," I murmur, voice ragged with need.

She reaches for me, fingers curling around my length, guiding me to her slick entrance. Her eyes lock with mine, dark and burning. And then...I push in.

My breath leaves my chest in one harsh exhale. She's tight. Wet. Fucking heaven.

I bury myself in her inch by inch, savoring the way her body opens for me like it's been waiting for this moment. *For me.* Her walls clutch me, draw me in, and it's all I can do not to lose it right then.

I move, slow at first, setting a rhythm we find together, her hips rising to meet mine, her fingers digging into my back. Each thrust deepens the connection, like I'm anchoring myself to her, heart and soul.

"Aaron," she breathes, voice breaking. "I'm..."

She can't finish. I don't let her. I drive into her harder, deeper, and her body pulses around me as she comes with a cry that sounds like my name wrapped in worship. Hot, slick, perfect.

But I'm not done. Her release only stokes the fire burning through me. I grip her tighter, thrust faster. Her eyes flutter shut, tears slipping down her cheeks from the intensity of it all.

"Open your eyes, beautiful," I whisper, brushing her hair from her face. "I want to see the look in your eyes when I come inside you."

Her lashes lift, and those eyes—God, those big beautiful brown eyes snare me. I kiss her mouth, slow and deep, and hold her as I move within her, chasing that edge.

"Come with me," I growl against her lips.

And she does.

Our bodies crash together as the wave overtakes us, as I spill into her with a groan torn from the deepest part of me. It's more than a release—it's surrender. My body, my heart, my everything belongs to her.

I stay inside her, holding her, our hearts thundering in tandem. My love leaks from between us, warm, raw, and real, as I shift onto my back and pull her over me.

Her head rests on my chest, breath still shaky, fingers curled against my skin.

"I love you, Jasmine. Completely."

And this time, I feel it settle in her—the truth of it, the weight of it. Because she is mine. And I'm hers. For real.

***

The light is soft when I wake, a pale golden hue slipping between the curtains and settling over her warm skin like a kiss. She's still asleep, sprawled across my chest, one leg thrown over mine, her breath slow and steady against my neck.

I stare at her. I can't stop.

The chaos of the world has no place here, in this room, in this moment. All I know is the weight of her body on mine, the faint scent of sex still clinging to our skin, and the rise and fall of her bare chest with each breath. She looks peaceful. Wrecked. Loved.

My wife.

I drag my fingers along the curve of her spine, slow and light, just to feel her. She shifts, sighs, but doesn't wake. Not yet.

My hand trails lower, smoothing over the dip of her back, the curve of her hip, and I pull her gently, gradually, until her body fits against me like it's made for it. Like she's meant to be nowhere else but here—pressed to me, skin to skin, heat to heat.

My dick is already hard, thick and aching with the memory of last night and the sight of her now.

I nuzzle into her neck, breathing her in, and kiss the spot below her ear. She stirs, murmuring something soft and unintelligible. My hand slides over her hip, then lower, lower still, pulling her up my body even more until I reach it—fingers gliding through the slickness already gathering between her thighs. Still wet. Still warm. Still mine.

I groan into her skin.

She gasps, eyelids fluttering open as I slide two fingers through her folds. She's swollen from the night before, sensitive, but when I circle her clit, she moans and arches into my touch like she's waiting for it.

"Good morning," I whisper, my voice thick with desire.

"Aaron...," she breathes, and that sound...my name on her lips in that sleepy, needy tone—undoes me.

I shift her onto her back, covering her body with mine, fitting myself between her legs. Her eyes are half-lidded, dark with lust, but soft with something deeper. I kiss her mouth, slow and deep, tasting the remnants of dreams and desire. Her arms wrap around my neck, legs parting wider as I line myself up at her entrance.

And then I press in.

She's still so damn tight, and so wet it feels like a promise.

Her mouth falls open as I sink into her inch by inch, filling her completely. Her nails dig into my back, her head tipping back against the pillow. I groan at the feel of her—hot, snug, wrapping around me like velvet heat—and I hold myself there, buried to the hilt, not moving. Just feeling.

"God, I missed this," I whisper against her jaw. "Missed *you*."

"But you just had me," she murmurs with a teasing smile, though her breath is already shaky.

"Still missed you."

I start to move, slow and deep strokes that make her tremble beneath me. She clings to me, her hips rising to meet every thrust, her mouth parted in soft moans that echo through the quiet room. My hand find her breast, cupping the weight of it, thumb brushing her nipple until she gasps.

I kiss her again, this time messier, hungrier, and she kisses me back like she needs me inside and out.

"You feel like heaven," I rasp. "You always do."

She whimpers, lifting her hips, urging me deeper.

"I want you to come like this," I tell her, my pace quickening just enough to build the friction. "Soft and slow. Wrapped around me. Looking me in the eyes."

Her fingers frame my face as I drive into her, our eyes locked. Her lips tremble, her thighs tightening around my waist.

"Come for me, Jas," I whisper, voice breaking.

And she does.

Her eyes flutter shut, then open again, wide and vulnerable as she shatters beneath me, crying out my name like it means something more than just a word. Her walls pulse around me, gripping me so tightly I see stars.

I lose control.

I thrust one, twice, then spill into her, filling her with everything I have. My head drops to her shoulder, my heart pounding against hers, and I stay inside her until the last wave passes.

We lie there tangled, spent, my body draped over hers like a shield. And even now—especially now—I don't want to let her go.

"I love waking up in you," I murmur against the curve of her neck.

She hums softly, a lazy smile tugging at her lips as she wraps her arms around me tighter, anchoring me to her. Like she never wants to let go. Like she never wants to wake up any other way. Honestly, I feel the same.

Waking up buried in my wife—*my wife*—is the best damn feeling in the world. She's soft and sweet and sinfully addictive, and I haven't had nearly enough of her. My body wants to stay wrapped around hers all morning, but my mind reminds me of the life we're building together. A household. A family. Responsibilities that don't pause just because I'm in love.

So I force myself to break away, pressing a kiss to her temple as I slide out of bed. Her sleepy protest is almost enough to drag me right back under the covers.

Almost.

Instead of tempting fate with a shower together—I know exactly how that ends—I take mine first. Fast. Cold. Necessary.

By the time I'm dressed, she's still getting ready. I leave her to it, heading downstairs, still riding the high of her touch and the quiet certainty that this...*she*...is home.

The scent of fresh-baked pastries and coffee drifts from the kitchen, warm and comforting. A sign that the Martha has already started breakfast. I'm halfway down the hall when Elizabeth darts out of nowhere, brushing against my ankle with a chirpy, offended *meow* before vanishing upstairs.

I smile, distracted, reaching for the coffee.

Ding-dong.

Then the doorbell slices through the silence like a blade.

I glance toward the foyer, brow furrowing. We're not expecting anyone. With cautious curiosity, I stride to the door and pull it open. And freeze.

Standing on the front step, shoulders squared like a general surveying his battlefield, is a man who looks like an older version of my best friend.

Same intense eyes. Same proud jawline. Same air of power. But this man isn't my friend.

This man is Reed Ross.

Jasmine's father. And from the unreadable look on his face, I already know—.

This visit isn't friendly.

Chapter 26

Past and Present

Jasmine

LAST NIGHT REWIRED ME.

I feel it in my thighs. In the slow burn of my smile. In the way I'm humming while I tame my wild hair. Like I'm starring in the third act of some forbidden London love story and the credits haven't rolled yet. Aaron Adler touched me like he knew me before this life. Like he'd been waiting *forever* to make me come undone in his arms.

And I *let* him.

No guards. No games. Just skin and softness and a fire I didn't know I had room for.

This wasn't about proving anything. It wasn't about convenience, or fake-married logistics, or making sure the tabloid narrative matched the script. This...last night...was a truth neither of us dared to speak out loud until we were both breathless and clinging to sheets. Sore. Satiated. Spent.

God. My husband.

My smile stretches again, involuntarily. I swipe gloss across my lips and adjust the hem of Aaron's shirt, which I've stolen as my morning armor. It's too big and impossibly soft. Smells like amber and trust.

The doorbell rings downstairs, slicing through the memory like a blade. I freeze.

"Was that the door?" I call out, already halfway to the top of the stairs. No answer. I descend a flight and pass Amara on the landing—she's on the floor, cross-legged, trying to coax Elizabeth into her cat carrier. The cat is not interested in being civilized.

"She's dramatic," Amara mutters, side-eyeing me. "Like someone else I know."

"She's a cat. She's allowed to be."

"So are you."

I give her a look. She shrugs and goes back to her negotiations with Elizabeth, who has decided claws are more persuasive than reason.

I pad barefoot down the stairs, still wrapped in this dizzy afterglow that makes the world look hazy and golden. My heart is soft. Open. Unarmed.

And that's when I hear it—Aaron's voice, firm but cautious. "Mr. Ross."

I round the corner, and I *see* him. Standing in the center of the foyer like he owns the deed to the entire continent—my father. Reed Ross.

A tall wall of tailored cashmere, dark eyes, and barely reined-in disappointment. My. High. Dies. Instantly.

Aaron gestures him forward into the house.

"Dad?"

He looks up. Takes me in—bare legs, messy curls, *Aaron's* shirt—and something in his expression shutters. Not quite judgment. Something quieter. Sadder.

"Nice shirt," he says flatly. "Your husband's?"

I blink. "You...how did you—?"

"Not from *you*, if that's what you're asking." His voice is calm. Too calm. "But I assume it's true. Or should I be concerned you're wearing another man's clothes in your husband's house?"

I'm still standing on the bottom step, one foot halfway between past and present. Between daughter and wife.

Aaron stands beside him, jeans and a dark Henley on, posture tense but steady. He says nothing, just watches me. Watches *us*.

"Dad," I start, stepping forward. "It's not what you think—"

"Really? Because I think my daughter got married and didn't tell her father." He raises a brow. "Which part am I misunderstanding?"

My chest tightens. "I was going to call—"

"When? After your honeymoon? After the baby announcement?" He scoffs softly. "Help me understand the timeline here, Jasmine."

Aaron finally speaks, his voice even. "Sir—"

Dad turns to him, eyes sharp. "Aaron. You've been friends with my son for fourteen years. Spent holidays at our house. We invited you into our family long before this. Hell, we all assumed you'd end up with June."

"I never made that promise," Aaron says gently. "And I never led her on. You know that."

Dad studies him for a long second. "You're not wrong." He exhales. "But that doesn't mean *this* doesn't feel...abrupt. You and Jasmine hadn't even *met* before last month."

"I know it looks fast," Aaron says, glancing at me. "But it isn't empty. I didn't marry your daughter to save face or stage a show. I married her because she matters. I fell in love with her before I even realized it was happening."

Dad looks back at me. "You think I wouldn't support you? That I'd say no?"

"I didn't know what you'd say," I admit, voice barely a whisper. God, I feel so small, but I press forward. "You always let me go."

My dad pauses. My words strike a chord.

He steps forward, his tone softening. "I let you go because I didn't know how to hold you without hurting you. You lost your mother, Jas. You were five. You stopped talking for a year, remember that?"

I swallow hard. I remember.

"And when you finally started again, you talked about clouds and cougars and computer codes. I thought—maybe if I let you be brilliant and wild, you'd find your way back to joy."

Tears burn behind my eyes.

"But this?" he says. "This isn't wild, baby. This is permanent. This is forever. I deserved a phone call."

"I was scared," I say, voice cracking. "I thought if I told you, it would make it real."

He tilts his head. "And now? Is it real?"

I glance at Aaron, who's watching me like I hung the damn moon.

I nod. "Yeah. It's real."

Dad exhales, shoulders relaxing for the first time. He looks around the house—at the clean lines, the faint smell of coffee, the echo of Elizabeth yowling upstairs.

"This is a nice place," he says quietly. "Good bones. Feels like someone lives here."

Aaron steps beside me, his hand brushing mine. "We do."

Amara appears then, arms full of writhing Elizabeth, and eyes my dad like she already knows everything about him.

"Reed Ross," she says dryly. "The legend himself. Would you like some coffee or a tranquilizer?"

Dad huffs a laugh. The tension in his jaw finally eases...just a little. "I'll take the coffee."

"Smart choice."

Elizabeth launches herself out of Amara's arms and tears off across the room like the little menace she is.

Dad watches her go, then looks back at me. "Are we just going to stand here?"

"We were...about to have breakfast," I say, my voice still shaky.

He's a powerful man. A commanding presence. Yet right now, despite his measured tone, the intensity in his eyes reveals he's still angry. Still processing. Still my dad—equal parts protector and hurricane.

I lead the way. Dad follows. Aaron trails close behind.

In the kitchen, Martha is already at work, holding a coffee pot like she's been eavesdropping from the hallway, which, honestly, she probably has. She's already set the table. Amara sits with a glass of juice in hand.

We all take our seats at the round table. Dad sits directly across from me, eyes locked. His gaze doesn't waver, and the crease between his brows remains firm, even as Martha sets down a dish of eggs, a platter of bacon, and a plate of perfectly flaky croissants—our family-style tradition.

The way Aaron, Amara, and I have been eating since that first night at the restaurant together reflects how my family used to eat before everything fell apart. Before Mom died. Before those hollow years when Jeannette was pretending to be someone she never was. Before I left and never truly came back. No, this moment, like Dad's gaze, isn't lost on me.

"How long are you in town, Reed?" Aaron asks, holding his cup while Martha walks around the table pouring coffee.

"Just this morning. I came as soon as I heard the news."

I hesitate for a moment. The twenty-four million dollar question burns on my tongue. I have an idea about the answer, but I ask anyway. "How did you find out?"

"Bram," he says, his name comes out sharp and final.

"I should have—" I start. Aaron touches my hand under the table.

"Reed, we could have handled this better. You deserve as much."

Dad sips his coffee. Everything slows: his hand, the cup, the sound of ceramic meeting wood. When he sets it down, the weight of what he's about to say lands in the silence.

"Clearly, by the way you're dressed, there's something between you now. So, how did we get here?" His eyes flick briefly toward Amara. "How is this child involved in any of it?"

"Maybe we can talk about it after breakfast. When Amara's—" I don't get to finish.

"This isn't news to her. It is to me. I want to know how my daughter became an Adler—without so much as a phone call."

"I love Jasmine."

"That's not my question."

I draw in a breath. This isn't how I wanted to do this. "I...was heading back to Holborn after dinner...when I heard a scream. I didn't know it was a child at first. I pulled a man off her—" I pause, my throat tight. "Dad, he was trying to hurt her. And when I found out she was living in an abandoned house, completely alone..." I glance at Aaron. "I couldn't walk away."

I tell him everything, about my visa and Bane. He listens, but his gaze doesn't change. If anything, the disappointment on his face deepens.

"You could have called me. I could have fixed this overnight."

"I never thought—"

"What? You never thought I could help? That your problems weren't my responsibility? That just because I gave you space, I didn't care?"

Elizabeth darts across the floor. Amara rises quietly and slips out. I don't know if she's going after the cat or just fleeing the room.

"You want me to go after her?" Aaron asks.

"No. Let her be."

"Which is it, Jas?" Dad presses. "Because marriage....marriage shouldn't have been your first solution."

"I thought I could handle it myself."

"And now the Adlers are involved."

"I knew what I was getting into, Reed. It wasn't just her problem. It became mine, too."

"Are you saying you took advantage of my daughter?"

"No. I don't even know how to explain it. From the day I met Jasmine, I knew...there was something there. When she told me everything, I didn't hesitate."

"You still could have called me. I could've bought the house, paid a staff—"

"You don't get it, Dad." The words come out sharp and fast. "I didn't want Amara to live like I did after Mom died. Having Jeannette was like being raised by a housekeeper with a spreadsheet."

"Jasmine," he barks out my name.

"It's true," I say, more softly now. "Everything changed after she came I lost my mom... then you, in your own way. And I refuse to let that happen to Amara. With Aaron and me, she gets a home. A real one. Not a mansion full of strangers on payroll."

"So you were willing to risk a fake marriage for that?"

"It may have started that way. But there's nothing fake about how I feel for her. I love her," Aaron says.

Both our phones buzz at the same time.

Aaron swipes his screen. "It's the Holborn house. Amara is there."

I stand immediately. "I'll go get her."

"I'm going with you," Aaron says.

"No. Let me talk to her alone."

Aaron nods. I glance at my father. His eyes are still fixed on me, still full of a thousand unsaid things.

"I gotta go," I say. Then turn and leave.

CHAPTER 27

Gentleman's Agreement

Aaron

WHEN I WOKE UP buried in my wife this morning, the last thing I expected was to end up sitting across the table in a conversation with Reed Ross.

I've known this man my entire adult life, and he's not wrong about what he said regarding June. Like the rest of the world, I always thought I'd marry her. But sometimes life creates a series of events to bring the right person into your life. For me, that person is Jasmine. The day I locked eyes with her was when all the stars aligned. Our first kiss confirmed it. Last night, I made her mine, and I'm not about to let anything ruin that...not even Reed Ross.

"Does this happen often?" Reed asks, pulling me back into the room.

"Amara has some things from her past she's dealing with," I say. "Usually, she goes off to a room alone, but she has never run away from home before."

"Home?"

"Yes, Reed. This is her home."

"That child needs help. You and Jas are playing house."

"Everything you see here is real," I admit. "Why did you come here today?"

"I came to see if my daughter was okay."

"I was the only man besides Jake you trusted around June—until that day at your party last year when you met Aedan. Up until then, you expected me to marry her." I hold his gaze. "You know Jasmine is safe with me. So what is this really about, Reed?"

"She should have told me."

"You know now. She's my wife in name and everything else. We're raising a sixteen-year-old."

"She doesn't know anything about that."

"Yet, she's been on her own since nineteen. Just say it, Reed. You don't want to miss out on any more of her life."

"I love my daughter. I've loved you like a son."

"Then love us together. Trust that we'll figure this thing out with Amara. Jas is trying so hard to mirror all the good things she experienced with you and her mother. And I'm doing the things I learned. We'll make mistakes—"

"I made mistakes," he says, cutting me off. "Too many to talk about."

"Then tell Jas. But trust, she and I will figure our lives out together. I know this came as a shock—I blame myself for that, but I don't regret one second with Jasmine."

"Amara...she's going to need more than just you two."

"We talked about it."

He looks over my shoulder, then back at me. "I should have gotten them help. Taken them to therapy...all of us."

"They're adults now. You got them to that point. It's their choice what happens next."

"I only want the best for my daughter."

"The second you heard she was with me, you knew she had it."

"I always knew you were self-assured."

"Tell me I'm wrong."

"Don't let my daughter go the door half-dressed again."

"I won't."

And just like that, over cold coffee and half-eaten croissants, we reach something resembling a gentleman's agreement. Am I back in his good graces? Maybe. Barely. I'll still have to prove myself. Men like Reed Ross don't hand out full approval easily. No man really thinks anyone is good enough for his daughter.

Even with me, someone he once thought would marry June.

But he saw the way she looked at Aedan at his birthday party, just like he sees the way Jasmine looks at me. You don't build an empire without knowing how to read a room. He knows this isn't a fling. It's real. And that means something. Still, I'll earn it. The trust. The title. My place in his family, not because I'm married to a Ross, but because I love her.

That's everything.

CHAPTER 28

Larger Than Life

Jasmine

I DON'T HAVE TO guess where Amara is; I head straight to the safe room.

I open the door. "Amara? You in here sweetie?" I ask before pulling it completely open.

"Yeah."

I step in. She's in her usual chair with a journal on her lap. "Want to talk about it?"

Silence.

We sit that way for a moment. I think about how my dad would sometimes drift...how I still drift. We're all grieving...still. We're processing our emotions the best way we can.

"When I ran away from the mall that day, I was terrified. All I could think about was the day I found out my mom died. I couldn't control what I was seeing or how I was feeling, and that loss, that grief, swallowed me whole. Missing her hit me like a wave, and I didn't know how to stay afloat. I shouldn't have left. I should have told Aaron what was happening. But he found me. He reminded me that as long as I have him, I'm never truly alone. It's okay to feel things deeply: pain, fear, sadness—but having someone there to hold you through it makes it easier to bear. You're not alone, Amara. Not ever. Not as long as you have us."

"They tried to put me with some people after my parents died. They didn't care about me. I was just someone they had to feed. When I had the chance...I left. No one ever came looking for me."

"Did Aaron and I do something to make you feel that way?"

She shakes her head. "Your dad is mad at me."

"My dad is mad at *me*." I pause for a second, looking for a reaction. "He and Aaron would be here now, but I asked to come alone."

"He said he could have fixed this for me. I didn't ask for this life."

"No, you didn't. I chose to help you because I know what it's like to try and make it alone. I know you're strong, but I didn't want you to have to go it alone. Aaron feels the same. We care about you, Amara."

"I read about Reed. He could take me away from you if he wanted."

"No, sweetie. My dad is many things, bigger than life...scary at times, he has a lot of power. But he would never do something like that. Not unless *you* say that's what you want." I pause, allowing my words to sink in. "Is that what you want, Amara? Do you want to go back to the house you used to live in?"

She shakes her head. "No."

"Do you think I want you to go back there?"

"You might make me to make him happy."

My heart clenches. "I would never give you up to make anyone happy...not even Aaron. He loves you, too, you know. As for my dad...I stopped trying to make him happy years ago."

"You were right about Aaron. He's really nice. Except when I can't wear the things I want. And the security stuff."

"He's protecting you. It's his way of showing he cares."

There's a beat of silence, then she says, "I don't want to leave. But I don't want your dad to think I want him to fix things for me."

"Then that settles it. How about you let me deal with Dad, while you focus on school?"

"He won't try to take me away?"

"Never. You made him laugh. I don't know many people who can do that. He may still be mad at me, but with you...with you, I sense he feels he has a second chance."

"A second chance?"

"He wasn't as present in my life as he could have been. But with you, there's a chance he can give you some of the things he didn't give us."

"Attention?"

"Yeah, like that. You grabbed his attention with your brilliance and wit the second you walked into the room...that's hard to do."

"I didn't have to tell him that he's boring."

I laugh. "No, you didn't. He has a weird way of showing it, but he has your best interests at heart. Now, I just have to convince him that Aaron and I are made for each other." And that we can raise a sixteen-year-old. But I don't say that part aloud.

She blows out a breath. "Good luck with that." She looks down at her journal and then back at me. "Jas."

"Yeah."

"I don't need all the things that you grew up with."

"I know, sweetie. Some things are necessary because you *are* with us."

"This is hard."

"It is. But we'll get through it...together."

***

When we arrive home, Amara heads straight to her room. It's understandable; my dad is larger than life, even for me. But that has also shaped us as kids; we learned how to claim our space. We shouldn't shrink ourselves to fit anyone, not even my father. It's a lesson Amara is learning.

I can tell by the voices that Dad and Aaron have moved to the family room, so I head straight there. My dad is sitting in an occasional chair and

Aaron is on the couch. When I step into the room, Aaron gets up to greet me.

"Is Amara okay?" He wraps an arm around me and kisses my forehead.

"Yeah." I press my lips together and look at Dad. "She thought you were going to take her away from me."

Aaron leads me to the couch, where we sit.

"I hope you explained to her I'd never do that," Dad says, his voice commanding.

"But you came in here all big and bold, Dad. Telling me what I've done wrong. How you would have handled it. How did you think that would make her feel? How do you think it makes me feel?" I say louder than I expected.

"You should be used to how I am by now."

"It doesn't make it okay. I made a mistake, Dad. I didn't tell you I was making a huge life decision that would impact our family. It's done, but even if I had told you, I wouldn't do anything differently. Amara needed someone, and I needed her. And, through some divine intervention, I found the love of my life. Yeah, it happened fast. I'll admit I don't know how to navigate this new life, but I know, like a world map, I can figure it out."

Aaron laces his finger through mine, raises them to his lips and kisses them.

"I made mistakes, too," Dad says, shocking me.

"Yeah." I laugh. "A whole freaking lot. So, don't act like I have to be perfect. And leave Amara out of this."

"I didn't intend to scare her off. That's part of this communication thing. You never told me about her. Clearly, we both have work to do."

Aaron squeezes my hand. "I talked to Reed about Amara."

"I could have handled things better...with you, Jake, June. I see that now. I don't want you to make the same mistakes."

"I'm trying not to, Dad."

"I see that now." He sighs. "I didn't come here to fight. But you need to know, the things you do matter to me. *You*...matter to me. I should have known you were getting married."

"I know I matter to you, Dad, or you probably would have locked me in the house instead of letting me globe-trot."

"I still don't know if that was a good decision," he says. And for the first time since he arrived, I feel a lot less defensive and more determined to make things work with him, Aaron...this new life.

He nods once—his signal that we're finished discussing the matter. In a moment, he shifts to a different topic. The subject of my marriage is set aside, but not forgotten.

Dad hadn't planned to be here all day, but our discussions ran well into lunch and beyond dinner. It's only when he confirms with his pilot that I realize he's serious about leaving.

"Listen, baby girl. I need to leave, but I'll call you later. I didn't mean to upset Amara earlier. If there's anything she needs—"

"We've got it covered, Reed. But thanks," Aaron says.

We all stand and head to the foyer. I take a deep breath, letting the emotions of today settle. After all these years, I've finally turned a corner with my dad. But this is just the beginning.

Dad turns to me and says, "You look happy."

I am. Even if I still don't know what tomorrow looks like. Even if we broke every rule in the family handbook.

I nod. "I am."

I walk forward and hug him—really hug him—for the first time in too long. He smells like spice and memory.

"I'm sorry, Daddy."

"I forgive you, baby girl," me murmurs. "But if you *ever* let a Bromley deliver family news again, I'm cutting off your inheritance."

I laugh through my tears. "Deal."

***

The silence after my father leaves is thicker than I expect. It wraps around the living room like fog, soft but heavy. Familiar, but not quite.

The moment the door shut behind him, my breath caught in my chest. Not from fear. Not even from guilt. But from this strange, fragile relief. Like I passed some test I didn't even know I was taking. Like my whole childhood was holding its breath and now, finally, it can exhale.

I curl deeper into the couch, tucking my legs beneath me and pulling a throw blanket around my shoulders. I didn't realize how cold I was until now. Emotional adrenaline will do that.

Dinner was...civil. Warm, even. Dad asked polite questions. Aaron answered them with equal grace. After Amara rejoined us, she was...herself—brilliant, witty, honest. I was right about what I told Amara back at Holborn. Dad took an instant liking to her, like she was his first grandchild. I suppose technically, she is. We talked about June's new baby, my first real reason to learn how to properly fold a swaddle, and laughed at a few memories of Jake being overbearing in a way only big brothers can be.

But the undercurrent hummed the entire time. The things unsaid. The choices I can't take back. The weight of growing up. The absence of *her*.

There's still a lot to say. Years' worth of feelings, experiences...life that happened that may take even more years to unpack. Today was a start. A good one at that.

"He really does love you, you know," Aaron says, breaking the quiet from across the room.

He's leaning against the entryway wall, still in the same jeans and Henley he wore all day, barefoot now, sleeves pushed up, with a glass of whiskey in hand. There's a softness around his mouth that didn't exist when he was standing in front of Dad this afternoon, holding the line like a man who meant every word he said.

"I know," I whisper. "It's never been that. He just...didn't know how to love us *out loud* after she died."

Aaron nods, pushing off the wall and walking toward me. He doesn't ask to join me. He just sits. He sets his glass on the table, one arm behind me on the couch, the other warm against my thigh. His presence makes space in me I didn't realize was cramped.

"He didn't yell," I add. "He didn't ask me to leave. That's...surprising."

"Because he knows you," Aaron says simply. "And because he's a smart man. He knows what we are."

I tilt my head toward him, heart hiccupping in my chest. "And what are we, Mr. Adler?"

He smirks. The same half-smile he wore the first time we met. "Real. Unlikely. And maybe...unbreakable."

Unbreakable. The word lingers in the space between us, heavy and warm like the desert air in Morocco just before sunset—still, golden, full of promise. I've seen temples weather centuries, winds carve stone into art, and I know: the strongest things aren't untouched by time, they're shaped by it. Maybe that'll be us...weathered, tested, and in the end...still standing.

My throat tightens. "Is it crazy that I didn't expect him to show up today, but now that he's gone, I feel like I've been through a ten-round sparring match with the entire ghost of my childhood?"

Aaron laughs softly. "Not crazy. Just honest."

I lean into him, my head resting on his shoulder. He smells like amber, like home, and the kind of safety I spent years pretending I didn't need.

"June's gonna kill me about how he found out," I mutter.

"She won't," he says softly.

"She will."

"She's holding a newborn. You're at least safe until the baby latches."

I laugh, but the sound is tired. "I still need to call Jake. Tell him before we go public."

Aaron shifts to face me, his hand brushing my hair away from my cheek. "Want me to sit with you while you do it?"

I consider it a moment. The old me, pre-this-marriage, pre-this-love, would have said no. She would have insisted on facing everything alone. Proving she didn't *need* anyone. But that girl's grip on me is loosening. Day by day.

"Yeah," I say. "I'd like that."

His hand lingers against my cheek, warm and steady. "You're not alone anymore, Jas. We do things together, now, remember? One day, one moment at a time. Even the hard calls."

I close my eyes, letting his words sink into the places that still flinch from softness.

"I'm glad you opened the door today," I whisper.

He smiles. "I always will."

CHAPTER 29

All in the Family

Aaron

GOD. THIS IS MY favorite time of the day. No. Every moment I share with her is my favorite.

I lie propped on my elbow, watching her in the quiet stillness of the morning. The soft rise and fall of her chest, the way the light peeks through the curtains and dances on her skin. It's perfect. I wonder what she's dreaming about. Faraway places. Family? Or is it me?

I can't help but reach out, my fingers grazing the edge of her bonnet, gently tugging it off her head. Her wild curls tumble free, a messy halo of beauty that always takes my breath away. She teases me about how much time I add to her hair routine. The truth is, I don't care. I get lost in every inch of her, in the way my hands always find their way to her and around her body when I'm deep inside her.

I love everything about her, but God, her wandering spirit? That's what scares me. It's not the shit I deal with at work, not the auditors or the rival companies. It's her. The thought of her slipping away...of losing her, cuts through me like a blade. She says she loves me, and I believe her. I do. But is it enough? Will she ever be fully satisfied with me?

I run my thumb across her cheek, my touch barely a whisper, before I lean down to kiss her. Soft. Gentle. But this moment...it's all mine, every second of it. "Honey, we have to get up soon," I murmur against her lips, my voice hoarse with the ache of needing her.

She stirs, just a little, her lips parting slightly, a quiet sigh slipping from her. Her hand moves to my face, her fingers tracing my jaw, before she pulls me to her. Her kiss, slow at first, becomes urgent, desperate, as if she's been waiting for this moment. Her tongue slides against mine, teasing, daring, and my body responds instantly, burning with need.

I slide my hand lower, down the curve of her waist, until I find the place that makes her gasp. She's already so warm, so ready. I slide my fingers over her soft folds, feeling her, knowing she's aching for me. And when she reaches for me, pulling me closer, I don't hesitate.

I roll on top of her, pressing her into the sheets, feeling the slick heat of her body welcoming mine. I fill her slowly, deeply, every part of me claiming her, as if I could burn my name into her skin. She moans, a sound so full of longing and surrender that it nearly breaks me.

Yeah. This is my favorite time of the day. But more than that...she's my favorite. And I'm terrified that someday I'll wake up, and she'll be gone.

Not today. Today we're flying.

"My God, woman. I love you."

"Yeah." She smiles lovingly, lost in a daze. "I feel it."

I ease off her reluctantly, pulling her close as I breathe her in. I could stay here all day, but we have a schedule. The sun's already climbing higher, and in this house, efficiency is a reflex.

When I was younger, mornings at the Adler house were a war zone. My brothers and I were chaos wrapped in noise: bickering, playing, dragging our feet to get dressed or grab breakfast. My parents were always scrambling, trying to herd us into some semblance of order. We weren't bad kids...we were just boys. But those mornings were anything but timely.

Now, everything is different.

Jasmine's already up, moving with a purpose, organizing herself and Amara like she was born to do this. There's no rush, no frantic energy.

Just a quiet rhythm. We know what's expected, we know what needs to be done, and we do it—without noise. Most of the time. Elizabeth's an exception. But Jasmine...the way she glides through the house, a calm that's both natural and learned...it works.

It's not just me, a businessman who's learned the art of calculating risk instead of chasing control; it's Jasmine, an explorer, and Amara, a girl who's built herself up one book at a time. It's *us*. Together, *we* make it work.

We're out the door in no time, sliding into the back of the car. It's almost too easy, how smoothly we operate now.

Before we know it, we're in the air. The whirling hum of the helicopter blades fills the air as we ascend, a steady rhythm in my chest. I lean forward, gazing out the window. The world below shrinks as we rise, the landscape unfurling like a map of my past and future.

"There it is," I say, tipping my chin to the right of the aircraft. Jasmine and Amara both turn in sync, their eyes wide.

"Wow," Amara breathes, her voice amplified by the headset.

"Wow is right." Jasmine laughs softly, but there's an awe in her tone, too. "I thought summer homes in the Hamptons were something, but this.... Are you sure this is a cottage?"

I chuckle under my breath. She isn't wrong. The estate below us is anything but a cottage. The sprawling grounds stretch out beneath the morning light, all green and white, the private drive winding through towering trees. Rhododendrons burst with color in the shadows, and the place is a snapshot of history. The house emerges slowly as we curve toward it, a grand, pale stone structure standing proudly in the midst of the land.

Even from up here, it's imposing. Regal.

My father always called it the heart of the Adler legacy. Back then, I thought he was just being dramatic. But now, looking at it from this angle, with the acres of land sprawling beneath it...I feel the weight. I feel the pull of history, of family, of everything that's come before me.

The gravel circle below still frames that ridiculous statue my mother hated. And the lavender is in bloom again. I can almost smell it, sharp and sweet.

The terrace wraps around the back like open arms. From there, you can see the Weald of Kent stretching out for miles. As a kid, I used to stand there, imagining I could see all the way to the sea.

Funny how everything looks smaller from up here. And yet, it feels like everything. Like I'm soaring straight into the past. But I'm not.

I have Jasmine and Amara beside me. They're my future. And we're heading there together.

The helicopter dips, and the cottage briefly disappears under us. A few moments later, we land, the blades slowing to a whisper. I look over at Jasmine, her hand already reaching for mine. I take it without hesitation, squeezing gently as we wait for clearance to exit.

"Are you ready for this?" I ask, my voice steady.

Jasmine smiles, and Amara's eyes are wide, full of wonder as we prepare to step into the next part of our lives. Together.

A staff member meets us at the craft and takes our bags. As we step into the massive foyer, light pours through the stained glass above, and a crystal chandelier glitters like it's trying to impress us. My mother stands beneath it, elegant as ever, with my father's arm slung protectively around her shoulder.

Alex, Andrew, and Demetrius drift in from different corners of the house, their familiar energy grounding me instantly.

"Hey, Mum. Dad." I wrap them both in a hug, heart thudding. "This is Jasmine, my wife, and Amara, our daughter."

"And here she is," Mum says. She opens her arms to Jasmine, eyes brimming with tears like she's been waiting for this moment her whole life. She pulls back slightly and cups Jasmine's cheek. "You take my breath away."

"Hi, Mrs. Adler. Thank you. It's nice to meet you finally."

"Please, call me Ava." Her smile is soft and reverent. "You have no idea how long I've waited for this moment. Your siblings have always felt like family, and I never knew why...until now. You're the missing piece. My daughter."

"Mum, don't scare her."

"It's true. Henry, tell her."

My father steps closer, grounding Mum with a gentle hand on her shoulder. "Jasmine, it's a pleasure. My wife...she has a sense about people. You'll get used to it."

"I'd like you to meet Amara, too," Jasmine says. "We all came together at the same time. Maybe there's something to what she's saying."

"Welcome to the family, Amara," Mum says, eyes twinkling. "You've got a big future ahead of you. I have a feeling you'll be running Saola soon enough."

Amara's voice is confident. "Hi, Mr. and Mrs. Adler. Nice to meet you."

Andrew pipes in. "Now that Mum's given away my job title and scared everyone, what's for brunch?"

Alex leans in toward Jasmine. "It's good to see you again. Let's carve out time to catch up."

"Sounds good," Jasmine says warmly.

My brothers each take turns giving Jasmine and Amara a hug before we all move into the formal dining room, where brunch is already waiting beneath silver-domed trays.

"Can Amara and I eat in the kitchen?" Demetrius asks. "We have an idea for a computer game we're working on?"

Amara glances at us for approval.

"Only if Ava agrees," Jasmine says.

Mum grins. "Rainey, please set them up in the morning room."

Amara's whole face lights up.

"Thanks," Demetrius says, and the two of them disappear, already deep in talk about world-building and coding mechanics.

"Looks like we'll be adding a gaming division to Saola," Andrew deadpans, sipping his drink.

I roll my eyes.

Andrew turns to Jasmine. "So, you didn't join your family company. Ever consider taking a role at Saola? The marketing advice you gave my brother was on point. And from what I've heard, you're the sharpest one out of the Ross siblings."

"I haven't thought about what comes next," Jasmine says, her tone careful. "I'm still figuring out what I'm most passionate about."

My stomach clenches. That pause—*what comes next*? She means after Amara goes to college. When the terms of our arrangement expire. But I already know—I don't want it to end. I knew at the altar. When I slid the ring onto her finger. When I made love to her for the first time. That sealed it.

"Think on it," Alex says gently.

Mum changes the subject. "Your sister sent me a photo of her baby. Young King is beautiful. Have you two thought about children of your own?"

I nearly choke on my drink. "Mum."

Alex and Andrew both shoot me matching smirks—clearly enjoying this way too much.

Jasmine laughs softly. "I've just been focused on getting Amara ready for college."

Dad steps in, thankfully. "Understandable. It's a big milestone. She's lucky to have you showing her how it's done."

"Thank you," Jasmine says, her voice soft with sincerity.

We somehow make it through the rest of brunch without any more emotionally loaded landmines. Later, I give Jasmine a tour of the house. We don't explore all twelve bedrooms, but we hit the highlights. Out back, Demetrius and Amara have taken a break from coding and are now splashing in the pool. Andrew lounges nearby, cocktail in hand, keeping a lazy eye on them.

I linger in the doorway, my eyes tracking Jasmine as she wanders the gardens arm-in-arm with Mum. The sight makes my chest ache in the best way.

"I never thought I'd see the day," Alex says, coming up beside me.

"What day?"

"You. In love. For real this time." He exhales slowly. "With June, you were loyal. You cared. But this—" He gestures toward the garden. "This is different. You breathe when she breathes. I can see it."

"Because she *is* my breath," I admit. "My lifeforce."

He nods, a rare glimmer of approval in his eyes. "I'm happy it's working out. And I can tell Amara matters just as much."

"She's ours," I say. "We love her like she's always been here."

"Have you two talked about what's next for her?"

"Like what?"

"Adoption. We're weeks away from finalizing the acquisition. If her name comes out publicly, and she's not legally protected, someone will try to exploit that."

I tense. "You think I'm using her for PR? I'm not doing that. I can't believe you'd—"

Alex steps in front of me, steady and calm. His quiet way of telling me to lower my voice.

"This isn't about optics. This is about protecting her. You and Jasmine are everything to that girl. And right now, legally, she has no claim to either of you."

He's right. Between the Adlers and the Rosses, we've had more than our share of media chaos. Jasmine's family has even faced kidnapping threats. The thought of Amara being vulnerable like that.... It guts me.

I exhale. "You're right. I'll talk to Jasmine."

"Good. I'll have our attorney start the paperwork. We can move fast."

CHAPTER 30

Jasmine Marie Ross Adler

Jasmine

IT's LATE WHEN WE finally make it home. The street outside is quiet, still holding the hush of night. Amara had way too much fun on the Kent trip. Her eyes are barely open as she trudges inside.

Aaron helps me off with my coat, his fingers brushing against the nape of my neck. I turn in his arms, draw a slow line along his jaw, and give him a soft kiss. Just a taste.

"I'll be up in a sec," I murmur.

He nods, but that heat in his eyes is already flickering, coiled and waiting.

Upstairs, I sit on the edge of Amara's bed while she sleepily goes through her nightly routine, slower than usual. When she finally climbs under the covers, I brush her hair from her forehead.

"Did you have a good time?"

"The best. Our game's gonna be a hit." Her voice is thick with sleep.

"I'm sure it will be." I tuck the blanket snug around her and kiss her gently. No lingering. She's out in seconds.

Elizabeth hops up like she owns the place and curls against her. I leave the door cracked, my heart full...and aching just a little with anticipation.

Upstairs, the low hum of running water pulls me in like gravity. Aaron's in the shower.

The glass is fogged, but I can still make him out—one arm pressed against the tiled wall, head bowed under the stream, the muscles of his back flexing with every breath. He looks like he's praying for strength.

He's going to need it.

I peel off my clothes and step inside. The steam wraps around me instantly, hot and thick, but it's nothing compared to the heat between us.

He turns when he senses me. Water glides down the hard lines of his chest, over abs I've traced in the dark a hundred times. His eyes drag over me, slow and hungry. And just like that, we're not waiting.

He steps forward and lifts me effortlessly. My legs lock around him, his mouth crashing against mine with a hunger that feels like it's been burning all week. We couldn't have this in Kent. Not properly. Not like I wanted.

Not like...*this*.

He deepens the kiss, rough and tender all at once. His hands roam memorizing me all over again, and I melt into him, my body already aching for more, with a wetness that has nothing to do with water.

"Lift me," I whisper against his mouth.

He does, one hand supporting my back, the other guiding me as I position him inside me. The moment we connect, a gasp leaves me—sharp, desperate, electric.

I brace one hand on the slick tile, the other buried in his wet hair as I move with him. He matches me thrust for thrust, slow at first, then harder, deeper, until there's nothing but the sound of water and skin and our cries tangled together.

I ride him like I've been starved for him—and I have. My hips grind into him as he groans into my neck, his grip bruising, grounding. I. Feel. Everything. Him. Us. The need. The love. The release building with every crashing wave.

And when we're both unraveling, lost in each other as the world narrows to this...our bodies, our love, our breathless, beautiful chaos.

We come together, and I don't care who hears. Because my man is inside me, and I'm right where I belong.

I never knew it could be like this.

We linger in the water, clinging to each other as the aftershocks fade, mouths brushing in soft kisses that don't need words. My legs slowly release their grip around his waist, and he lowers me gently to the tile like I'm something fragile and precious.

We clean each other in silence, hands moving slower now. It's not about lust anymore...it's about love. It's always been about love.

When we finally step out, he wraps me in a thick towel and leads me into the bedroom, where we climb into bed. I straddle his hips as he checks his messages, as I start towel-drying my hair, trying to focus on something simple, something small.

"London."

He sets his phone on the nightstand, eyes locking with mine. "You haven't called me that in a while." He loosens my towel, his touch both reverent and teasing. His hands glide up my stomach, thumbs circling over my nipples with practiced care, and I almost lose my focus. Almost.

"Did you ever..." I hesitate, unsure whether this question matters or if I'm just chasing ghosts.

He looks up at me, brows drawing together slightly. "Did I ever what?"

"Did you ever sleep with my sister?"

His answer is instant. "No." He brushes my cheek with his thumb, gentler than the question deserves. "What's this about Jas?"

"But you loved her."

"I told you, I was never in love with her." He slides his hand to the small of my back. "I'm in love with you."

"Would you have slept with me if you weren't in love with me?"

"No."

"Even if I asked?"

"I'm not that guy," he says quietly. "You know that."

I stare at him, into his beautiful gray eyes, trying to process the weight of all these answers. "When did you know? At what moment did you fall in love with me?"

He takes a breath. "When you walked out on me the day we met."

"What?"

"The feeling of watching you leave and knowing I might never see you again..." He swallows, and there's a vulnerability in his eyes that pierces straight through me. "I never want to feel that again. That's how I knew."

I lean down and kiss him, lingering. "I'm sorry."

"I told you, I was partially to blame for you walking out that day." He grins and tickles my side, breaking the heaviness for a moment. Then, his expression shifts. He's serious again. "I have a question for you."

"Okay."

"What do you think about us adopting Amara? For her protection. Once we go public, she could become a target. And right now, we have no legal rights—no way to help her if anything happens."

"Do it," I say without hesitation. "I'll talk to her. I won't let anything happen to her."

"Okay." He exhales, nodding. "I'll start the ball rolling tomorrow."

But something's still hanging in the air. I feel it.

"There's something else," I say.

He hesitates. "You seemed...uncomfortable when Mum brought up the idea of us having kids. Do you ever want them?"

My chest tightens, a familiar ache creeping in. I don't know how to answer. What if I let myself get too close and something happens, and I have to lose him too? I fight the rising panic, but it builds like a slow wave.

"I don't know how to answer that."

"There are only two ways, Jas. You do...or you don't."

I shift, moving to climb off him, but his hands hold me in place—gentle but firm.

"Jas, honey. Do you, or don't you want children?"

My heart stutters. My breath comes too fast. It's like I'm back there, at the restaurant, hearing sirens, feeling the hole where my mother used to be. That suffocating silence when my life turned upside down forever.

I can't do this.

"You don't plan to stay after Amara graduates." It's not a question. "That's it. Isn't it? You can't answer the question because you won't be around long enough for it to matter."

Three seconds. I can make it to the door in three seconds.

"Jas. Talk to me. I can see the panic."

Two seconds. I can just get away, out that door, and run like I always do.

"Baby—"

I bolt. The towel slips through his hands as I fly from the bed, completely naked, heart pounding like a drum.

"Jasmine Marie Ross Adler."

His voice, full and commanding, stops me in my tracks. His words cut through the fog.

"I'm your husband," he says, his voice trembling but sure. "And I love you."

I crumble. My legs give way, and I collapse onto the floor, the cold of the wood beneath me grounding me, but it's not enough. The panic still roars in my chest, drowning out everything else. I can't breathe.

But then, his arms are there, lifting me, pulling me back into him. His warmth, his steadiness, anchors me as he sits on the edge of the bed and pulls me into his lap.

"Breathe with me, honey." He murmurs, his hands gentle on my back.

I try. In. Out. In again. Out slower. The air is thick, but slowly, I start to catch my breath.

"That's it. Once more."

The fog lifts, piece by piece. My vision comes into focus.

"I'm okay," I whisper, the words shaky but true.

He cradles me closer, his touch steady as ever.

"No, baby. You're more than okay. You're here. And you're safe."

Chapter 31

Remembrance

Aaron

"In the midst of chaos, there is also opportunity." Sun Tzu said it, and nothing has ever been truer.

Last year, a fabricated headline in the BDC tried to shake client confidence. This year, it's the Bromleys stirring the pot. But while they whispered and schemed, I worked. I planned. And today, I rise stronger than ever. I didn't just survive the scandal; I reshaped the narrative. Now, I hold the key to their future.

I glance across the table. Andrew meets my gaze with a knowing look. He sees what I'm doing—even if he doesn't know the full extent yet.

I stand.

"Thank you again for your time, Mr. Davies, Ms. Leighton."

They rise with me, and I walk them toward the door. We shake hands.

"And thank you for the invitation," Ms. Leighton says. "People don't usually want us at their event."

I meet her eyes, my grip firm. "There'll be over ten thousand in attendance: clients, competitors, some of the best in the industry. It'll give you insight into more than just Saola."

Davies nods. "Well, thanks again. We'll be in touch if we need more information."

"My EA will walk you out."

As they disappear down the corridor, Andrew and I head to my office. Of course, he makes himself at home in my chair, feet up like he owns the place, while I move to the window and take in the city. My city.

"Man," he says, leaning back with that dry, amused smirk. "That was the smoothest play I've ever seen. Calm, controlling, calculating. I think I just witnessed a masterclass on how to be ruthless—and I say that with love. Honestly, thank you. I might take your job next."

I glance back at him, one brow raised. He's joking. Mostly. But he's not wrong.

He's never seen this side of me up close. The strategic dismantling. The patience it takes to set the trap, the precision it takes to spring it. The Bromleys won't even realize what's happened until the CMA comes knocking on *their* door. And by then, I'll already be three moves ahead.

There's a soft knock at the door. It opens gently.

Kate steps in. "Mrs. Adler is here."

Jasmine walks in behind her, a breath of calm in an otherwise stormy day. Her scent reaches me before her voice does. Sweet. Intimate.

I watch her, my heart racing the way it does whenever she enters a room. Andrew's still sitting across from me, arms folded, watching, too.

"Ah, here comes the real power move. I suppose that's my cue to surrender the throne before I'm forcibly removed," he says.

I give Jasmine a knowing wink.

"Hey, Andrew," she says softly.

Andrew rises, but the shift in his expression is quieter, weightier. He crosses the room to greet her, his tone subdued.

"Hey." He kisses her cheek and gently squeezes her hand. "What do you think about me picking up Amara and Demetrius after school? Pizza, movie, some game work at my place. Give you...some space."

She meets my gaze over his shoulder. I nod.

"Yeah," she says. "I think she'd like that. Let me call the school."

"We won't be out too late," he says, and quietly slips out.

I open my arms, and she doesn't hesitate to fill them. God, I love this woman. Jasmine fits perfectly against me, like she always does. I breathe her in, grounding myself.

"How are you?" I whisper, keeping her so close, refusing to let her carry this day alone.

She lets out a breath, half laugh, half sigh. "And I thought the K2 was hard."

"Ah, baby." I press my lips to the crown of her head. "We got this. Together, remember?"

She nods in my chest and I lead her toward the desk. I pull her onto my lap and adjust the phone on its stand.

"Wait," she says, hopping off me. "You start the conversation."

"You sure?" She nods. But her fingers tremble slightly as they fall to her sides.

I tap the screen. JR picks up right away, wiping his mouth with a napkin.

"Hey mate, did I catch you at a bad time?" I ask.

"Luckily for you, I'm New York. You back in London?"

"Yeah, just got back. Only in Sweden for a week this time."

"Is June on the line, or are you tying her in?"

"Thought I'd talk to you first. Been a while. We've both been on the road. And today..."

"You don't have to say it, man. It's been harder on my sisters."

"You always say that. You're a good brother." He shrugs. "You heading back this way soon?" I ask.

"Yeah, Jasmine's there. You should meet her. She's lovely. I think she'd appreciate this... the way you've captured these moments."

He doesn't elaborate, but his voice carries more weight than words allow. That's why I do it. The videos, the pictures, the moments—year after year. A quiet archive of love and loss. I never told her. Not yet.

I glance at Jasmine. She nods once, grounding herself.

"It's funny you should say that," I start. "That's what I wanted to talk to you about."

I roll back slightly. Jasmine leans into the frame.

"Jas?"

JR's expression shifts instantly. His eyes light up, but there's something else in them, too. A flicker of ache. Time never dulled how much he misses her.

"Hey," she says, voice delicate. "I finally met Aaron."

"How are you doing, baby sis?"

"I'm okay. I heard you asking about June. We can connect her in a moment."

His eyes search hers. "You sure you're okay?"

"I am. But...I don't know how to say this, so I'm just going to." She inhales deeply. "I met Aaron shortly after I got to London. And...we're married."

There it is.

JR doesn't speak. He leans back in his chair, lips pressed tight. Watching the screen. Watching us.

I haven't seen that look since the night I threw Rory out for going after June. This isn't confusion. This is calculation. He's trying to piece together truth, timeline, intention. He knows us both too well to think this is a joke.

I lift my hand. Jasmine slides hers into it, a subtle show of love and strength.

This is harder than the day I told him I wanted to date June. Even after fourteen years of friendship, this...this is different. None of us saw this coming. Not even me.

"I think Troy might be in the area," JR says quietly. "But I'm not going to let him touch you. He gets to stand by and watch—"

"Jake, stop." Jasmine's voice cuts through the tension. "I'm in love with Aaron. I didn't plan to be, but I am. Life happens. You know that. I learned it at five—you at ten. I can't pretend this isn't complicated. It is."

I pull her gently back onto my lap. "And I love Jasmine. It's complicated, yes. But if you're willing to listen, we'll explain."

Jake's face is unreadable. "Up until a moment ago, you were my best friend. Now you're telling me you're married to Jasmine, and I'm just hearing about it. Make this make sense."

"I realize it seems fast, abrupt even. I promise there's a good explanation if you just...listen."

"My God, Aaron—you of all people know today was not the day—"

"Jake, please," Jasmine says. "I've never asked much of you. Just...listen to me."

JR sighs. It's long. Weighted. But then, his expression softens, and I realize it's because of her. "I'm listening, sis."

So, we tell him. About Amara. About the visa. About timing. About the truth of it all.

He listens without skepticism, but with care—he's JR, after all. Besides, he loves her. And he loves me, too, in that best friend way that means this hurts and heals all at once. Somehow, Jasmine binds us together even more tightly now. She's the last thread. The puzzle piece I didn't even know was missing.

"I don't agree with what you two did," he says finally. "I should have been your first call, Aaron. And Jasmine, I'm..."

"Don't say it, Jake. I'm sorry."

"Does Dad know?"

"Showed up on our doorstep when he found out."

Jake briefly closes his eyes before opening them again. The weight of what we told him sinks in. "And June...what the hell was she thinking? Get her on the line," he says while still trying to control his tone.

I tap the screen and add her in.

June's face pops up. She scans our expressions and smirks.

"And I thought telling him about Aedan was hard," she says, laughing.

"There's nothing funny about what I just heard."

"Uhm, hey, Jake," June says, sobering.

"I hear you're the architect of the biggest ruse in our family history."

"Jake," Jasmine says, her tone admonishing.

"Seriously, Jake. Our sister's in love. You should be celebrating."

"I would have been celebrating had this been legitimate. Had I known a month ago."

"Mate—"

"Don't call me that."

"Mate, we made a mistake in not telling people sooner, but that's the only mistake we made. There's nothing wrong with falling in love. And not even you can say we should have left Amara to fend for herself."

"I'm not going to debate how poorly this was handled. I need time to digest it. Unlike my sisters, I didn't have the good fortune of knowing about this sooner."

"I hope you're still headed out this way, mate," I say. "You're a big part of our lives, despite how you feel."

"Don't patronize me."

"Stop, Jake," June says. "We've all apologized. That's all we can do. If you want to let a mistake keep you from the most important people in life, that's really sad. But I hope you don't."

"I married your best friend, and I love him. If you want to be upset, be upset with the person who took our mother. That's what today is about, isn't it? Don't be mad at the person who breathed life into me after all these years."

"You're pissed. I get it, mate. But I know you well enough to understand you need to see what Jas and I have for yourself. Our home is always open to you. We'll see you soon. We love you." I say, and end the call.

Jake's hurting, and for good reason. He'll consider everything we said before deciding whether or not to kill me. Maybe.

I pull Jasmine into me. "He loves us. I promise, he'll come around."

***

Today was hard. Complicated. Epic in some respects. But I got through it. I'm starting to realize, slowly, how living with Jasmine and Amara touches every part of my life. It's not bad, not at all. It's just different. Even something as simple as sorting through the mail now has a new weight to it. As I flip through the envelopes, I stop on the one with Amara's new school ID card tucked inside. Her face...her beautiful little face, smiles back at me. I trace my fingers across her name—*Amara Julisha Ross-Adler*. It's a mouthful, sure, but it's hers. It's us. For real.

She wants to go to Paris. The application's already been submitted. And that scares the hell out of me. Because if she leaves...*when* she leaves, it means there's a chance Jasmine could leave, too. And I don't know if I can survive that. I just don't.

"I want more kids." The words slip out before I even realize I've spoken them. I didn't mean to say them, not yet, maybe never. Not unless she's here, unless she stays. Unless she can really commit to forever.

We're still figuring it out, still working on it. But now that all the paperwork's in place, we can go to therapy as a family. And it feels like progress, but also like a tightrope walk. Everything's so fragile, and I don't know if she sees it the way I do.

I slide Amara's ID card back into the envelope. She'll be so excited to take it with her. Then I open my laptop, trying to focus, trying to push work into the empty spaces of my mind. But it's hard to think about spreadsheets and deals when my head's full of *this*. I need to be up there with her, with both of them.

"Hey."

I glance up, my pulse skipping. Jasmine is standing in the doorway, her silhouette framed by the soft glow of the hallway light. Her voice is low, soft, but there's something about the way she says it that makes me shut my laptop without a second thought. No hesitation. Just...*her*.

"Hey. Are you okay?" I ask, studying her expression.

"Yeah. I just wanted to talk. Do you have time?"

She steps further into the office, and that's when I notice she's carrying a black leather document holder. I lean back in my chair, rolling from the desk to give her my full attention.

"Of course. What you got there?" I gesture toward the case, my curiosity piqued.

Jasmine hesitates for a fraction of a second, then crosses the room. Instead of taking the chair across from me, she perches on the edge of my desk, right where my laptop had been. Close. Intentional.

She smooths her fingers over the supple leather, tracing its edges in slow, deliberate strokes. Her face is stunning as ever, but there's a weight in her expression, something silent pressing against the air between us. That hesitation isn't like her. Jasmine is bold, decisive. But right now, she's something else. Vulnerable.

"I—I never said thank you."

"For?" I prompt gently.

She exhales, a small smile ghosting across her lips before she opens the leather flap and pulls out several gold metallic envelopes. My stomach tightens the moment I see them. I know exactly what they are.

She picks one up, turning it between her fingers before opening it. The delicate paper catches the office light, shimmering as she unfolds it.

She clears her throat and begins to read aloud.

"Dear Jasmine,

I hope this letter finds you well. I know we've never met, and I never had the honor of knowing your mother, but your brother Jake, who speaks of you and June with such admiration, mentioned that today is an important day for your family. He's flying back to be with you both, to remember her.

I just wanted to send my thoughts and prayers your way. I can't pretend to know what this day feels like for you, but I do know that love never truly leaves us. I'm told your mother showed you, in countless ways, how deeply you were cherished. I hope you never forget that feeling, even as the years pass.

Wishing you comfort and peace,

Aaron"

"This was the first letter I received from you. I thought you were just being courteous. Then, the following year, I received this."

"Jasmine,

I don't think I've mentioned—your brother, Jake, is my best friend. I call him JR. I hope that's okay with you. Your sister, June, is a friend, too. I first met her when she stopped in London on her way to Paris for the holidays. Both of them, without hesitation, spoke of you with pride. Their brilliant younger sister. Their wanderer. Their heart.

But that's not why I'm writing.

When JR told me he was returning home for your family's remembrance of your mother, I asked if I could honor her in my own way—by calling, offering my condolences, and sending this letter back to you. He agreed. He said it's important for you three to remember you are part of something greater than life itself. I love that.

During these times, he's solemn. I imagine you feel the same. And though I cannot fully know your grief, I grieve with you.

I believe everything, good or bad, happens for a reason. Sometimes, we understand in a moment. Sometimes, it takes years. Sometimes, we never do, but the meaning lingers, shaping the world in ways we may never see.

Your mother mattered. She left her mark. She lives on—in you, in the love that surrounds you, in the way the world shifts when you step into it.

Be well. Be strong. Be you.

Aaron"

She slides the letter back into the envelope, her fingers lingering on the crease before she lifts her gaze to mine.

"You got them?"

"Twelve in all." Her voice is steady, but something flickers in her eyes—something fragile, something I've never seen before. "I suppose there's one waiting for me back in the States. My dad says they come like clockwork."

She's right. I've sent one every year, without fail, to the only address that's ever been constant in her life—her childhood home. Jasmine never put down roots, never bought a place of her own. She moves through the world like a rolling stone, untethered, impossible to catch. And yet, even though we'd never met, I've always known where to find her.

Every year on the anniversary of her mother's passing, I wrote to her in remembrance. I spoke to JR and June on that day too—sometimes through a quick text, sometimes over video. But Jasmine...I never expected a response from her. Never even knew if she read them. Never even knew if she got them. Still, I wrote.

Last year, I was with June here in London. I'd taken a selfie of us during a building tour, but the picture I sent Jasmine wasn't that one. Someone had snapped a photo of us at the keynote luncheon—mid-conversation, candid. Candid, like the truth you don't pose for—the kind that slips through when you think no one's watching. I'd sent that instead. A moment, a memory. A reminder. That's what our call was about today. Remembrance.

Jasmine's fingers tighten around the stack of letters. Then, as if drawn by an invisible force, she pulls out another one.

"Hi Jasmine,

It's Aaron.

You've always been a force to be reckoned with, but graduating university at nineteen? That's something else. JR says you're brilliant like your mom. I think he's right. She'd be so proud of you.

I saw JR earlier today. He mentioned you left for Africa. He tried to pretend he wasn't disappointed, but I could tell. It's different this year. Your absence is felt. But I understand. Some journeys require solitude, and I know you're out there searching for something only you can find.

Still, I didn't want this day to pass without honoring what's always been important to you. So, I'm sending you a picture—JR and June on a video call, remembering, laughing, holding space for her and for you. I hope it brings you comfort, wherever you are.

Be well. Be strong. Be you.

Aaron"

"You never met with them again on that day. Until now," I say.

"I couldn't. But then again, I didn't need to. I have these." She lifts the stack of envelopes, her fingers trailing over the edges as if they hold something sacred. "You sending me these letters became my lifeline to my family while I was far away. It eased the pain of a day that still haunts my dreams. But through these experiences, I found peace."

"Tell me," I say, my voice soft, low.

"At first, whenever my siblings and I got together, it felt suffocating—like I was trapped in an endless loop of the day my mom died, reliving the loss over and over. When I graduated, that was enough. I took control of my life and never looked back. But then, you sent me the pictures—Jake and June laughing, living, just...being. And I realized something. They weren't weighed down by the past. They weren't just surviving; they were celebrating life instead of mourning loss. You freed me from the guilt of not being there. Your letters showed me that love doesn't have to be tethered to presence, that remembering doesn't have to hurt. Thank you."

I rise from my chair and pull her into my arms, guiding her onto my lap, her knees bracketing my hips. The letters slide from her fingers and scatter across the desk, but she doesn't reach for them. Instead, she presses herself against me, arms locking around my neck, head burrowing into my shoulder.

I close my eyes and inhale the soft, warm scent of her. My hands roam, one pressing into the curve of her back, the other tangling in her curls. She fits against me like she was always meant to be here. Because she is. She's the one I never knew I'd been waiting for.

We sit like that, clinging to each other, breathing as one. The moment stretches, pulses, deepens—until it's no longer just comfort or gratitude, but something heavier. Something inevitable.

Something that feels like...*forever*.

CHAPTER 32

Making History

Aaron

IT'S EARLY. TOO EARLY to wake her. But I want Jasmine to be the first to see the media's response to our press release.

Jasmine's body partially covers mine; one arm resting across my chest, and her leg between mine. I should reach for my phone and read the article, but instead, I relax in the beauty this moment offers with the love of my life exactly where I want her...*in my arms*.

"Honey," I say, pulling Jasmine over my body. She lets out a barely audible moan, then buries her face in my neck, arms pinned to my sides. I smooth my hands gently down her back and over the curve of her hips, then retrace my tracks, enjoying the silkiness of her skin. Blood rushes to my center as I thicken beneath her. "Babe, time to wake up."

Her lips dust my ear. "No," she whispers.

A small smile teases on my lips, simply happy that she's safe in my arms, that she's content, that out of anywhere in the world she could be...she's *here*. I hold her tight, trailing a finger down her spine. The weight of her body rises and falls in time with my breath. Our hearts sync. Minutes pass before her soft lips press against my ear, my cheek. Then, she lifts her head, hooded eyes coming alive. I gently smooth my hand across her head, sliding her bonnet off in the process. She presses her lips to mine, placing soft, sweet kisses with just enough fire to let me know she wants me.

I break the kiss and hold her gaze. "Every morning I wake up with butterflies, just knowing I get to love you another day."

"I wish I'd met you sooner."

She smothers my face in more kisses. I've learned it's one of her signs; she wants to make love. And we will. Just not this second.

"Honey," I say, cupping her face. "We should check the news."

"Later," she breathes, her mouth hovering over mine, making me want to devour her.

I give in to more heated kisses, then roll her on her back.

Staring down at her, I say, "I promise it'll be worth the wait."

I kiss her pouty lips, sit up, and slowly pull her onto my lap astride me. She reaches for my phone and hands it to me. I don't bother scrolling; there's a notification already waiting for my attention. Jasmine leans into me, burying her head between my shoulder and neck.

"Ready?" I ask.

She nods against me.

I read from the screen. The headline states: "BDC EXCLUSIVE: A Modern Royal Union, Saola Technology's Aaron Adler Weds Heiress Jasmine Ross in Ultra-Private Ceremony." The article continues: "In a move that captivated both financial circles and high society, Aaron Adler, the enigmatic President of Saola Technology, has formally announced his marriage to Jasmine Ross, heiress to the Ross Enterprises empire and daughter of tech magnate Reed Ross.

"The couple, speculated to be romantically linked after a series of quiet appearances at tech summits and philanthropic events, stunned the world with confirmation of their marriage, kept secret until today's official press release from Saola's London office.

"Even more surprising? The newlyweds are now parents to a daughter, Amara Ross-Adler, marking what some are already calling the next generation of transatlantic tech royalty.

"While details of the wedding remain tightly under wraps (unsurprising given the pair's fiercely guarded privacy), sources close to both families confirm that the ceremony was held in an undisclosed location 'befitting their stature, taste, and discretion.' Those fortunate enough to attend were reportedly required to sign NDAs. A testament to the level of security surrounding the event."

The article goes on to say, "A Century-Defining Merger of Minds and Empires. The union between the Adler and Ross families is more than just a romantic milestone. It represents the fusion of two of the world's most powerful tech dynasties.

"Adler, known for transforming Saola Technology into a global force in AI and sustainable innovation, brings with him a reputation for unmatched precision, discretion, and business acumen. Ross, a prodigious innovator in her own right, is famed for her philanthropic ventures, globe-trotting intellect, and boundary-defying work in ethical technological development.

"Together, they represent the epitome of modern leadership: visionaries with the resources, reach, and heart to shape the future.

"Industry analysts are already referring to this as *'the most significant corporate-social alignment in the 21st century,'* with implications not only for future business mergers, but for global philanthropic efforts spearheaded by the couple's newly formed Ross-Adler Foundation, set to be announced in the coming months."

Jasmine kisses me behind the ear. It takes all my energy not to roll her on her back and sink into her.

"There's more, babe," I tell her.

"Let me see that." She takes my phone and reads the rest aloud. My hands roam her body as she reads.

"The World Watches," she starts. "Though the marriage itself was quiet, its reverberations are anything but. From Wall Street to Westminster, speculation abounds. Will Ross officially take on an executive role at Saola?"

Jasmine leans closer and smiles against my lips. "Ooo. Inquiring minds want to know," she teases.

She straightens, continuing. "Could this signal a forthcoming merger between Ross Enterprises and Saola Technology? And what does this mean for the future of ethical tech and global development? The question still remains, despite both companies having already stated that they will remain separate.

"For now, the couple has declined to comment further, allowing the world just a glimpse of their new life through a single, elegantly-worded statement. Yet one thing is clear: this is no ordinary love story. It's strategic, symbolic, and an emotional alliance—equal parts legacy and revolution. As one insider put it bluntly: '*This isn't just a wedding. This is history.*'"

"What do you think, honey?" I ask.

She closes her eyes briefly and exhales. "For years, I've avoided the spotlight. In silence, I observed my family as they graciously handled the media's fascination with them. I never wanted this, but now it's on my doorstep. But I know everything will be okay, because we're in this together. You've proven that. The day you proposed, you promised to protect me and Amara in every way. I see it in the care with which you handled this. Thank you."

"I also promised to love you," I say, pulling her into me.

"I feel it." She gently combs her fingers through my beard. "Now, can we get to the good part?"

I bark out a laugh and roll her onto her back. "Yeah, let's make some history."

CHAPTER 33

Under Examination

Jasmine

THE HARDEST DECISION I made was getting on that plane at nineteen, carrying memories, a carry-on bag, and credentials. I didn't know what I was getting into, but I knew what I was getting away from—everything.

Over the years, I gained new experiences, met new people, and racked up more air miles than the entire population of the many countries I visited. I knew I was running. I knew I was hurting. I knew eventually I had to return. I didn't know when. But I knew I missed my family, still, I tucked that fact in the back of my mind and kept going. Now that I've stopped moving long enough to think, it's at the forefront following my discussion with Dad. Definitely in my face after talking to Jake and now...he's on his way.

The doorbell rings.

Aaron pulls me into an embrace and gently tips my face up. "You ready for this?" I nod in his hand. He gives me a kiss that's a little more than chaste, but it centers me.

We enter the foyer together. Even though Jake's my brother, my heart pounds at the thought of seeing him.

Aaron opens the door.

Jake stands there, clean-cut and confident, a six-foot-five wall of warmth and familiarity. Dressed in slate-gray slacks and a crisp white button-down, he looks like a younger version of our dad: same strong jawline, same steady eyes, except Jake's smile is easier, his energy softer. He's handsome in that effortless way that turns heads without trying, and when his eyes land on me, they light up.

"Hey, Jake." I hold my arms open, and he steps into them, wrapping me up like I'm still his baby sister. He presses a kiss to my forehead.

Gone is the tense look on his face that tested me during our last video call with June. I couldn't let that be the last exchange between us before his visit. We don't do silence, not the cold kind, anyway. There's no deep-rooted hate wedged between us...just a misstep. A bad decision made out of fear, not malice.

So, I called him. After the article came out. After he had some time to cool off. After I could no longer carry the weight of being the one who caused him pain. After I realized there was a non-zero chance he might actually come here to kill Aaron today.

But the truth is—nothing could ever truly break the bond between my siblings and me. This isn't some dramatized mess designed for shock value and forced conflict. This is real life: messy, yes, but rooted in love. He's my brother. He's Aaron's best friend. We are all intertwined, and despite the hurt, we love each other.

So, I picked up the phone and said the only thing that mattered: *I love you, and I can't wait to see you.*

His response?

"*Same.*"

"I missed you, sis."

I linger in his embrace, his scent, clean and citrusy, flooding my senses. His love wraps around me like armor. I couldn't have asked for a better brother. He's the one who held us together after Mom passed. He made sure we always studied together. Even when I was too little to have any homework, I'd sit beside him as he explained what he was working on. The remembrance days, the martial arts, those were all his ideas. So much of who I am is because of him.

Jake leans back, getting a good look at me. He lifts my peace sign necklace and holds it in his hand. "Looks good on you."

"Thanks. I missed you, too," I tell him.

Aaron steps closer. "Hey, mate," he greets Jake.

Jake unlatches himself from me and gives Aaron a handshake, shoulder bump hug. *Good*. I exhale. No one's going to die today.

"Hey, man," Jake says. "Or should I say brother?"

"Come on in, mate," Aaron says.

We enter the family room, where Amara sits cross-legged on the floor, laptop open. Elizabeth, who was curled in a ball beside her, walks up to Aaron and brushes against his pant leg.

"Amara," I say, gesturing. "This is my brother, Jake."

She stands, setting her laptop aside, and shakes Jake's hand. "Hi, Uncle Jake."

Jake glances at me, and I smile knowingly. There's no avoiding that we've all been thrust into this built-in family.

"Amara, you're as beautiful as your name."

"Thank you." She bends down and picks up Elizabeth. "This is Elizabeth. She's fussy."

Jake strokes Elizabeth's head. "Hey, Elizabeth."

"Can I get you a drink?" Aaron asks. "It's not too early for a whiskey."

"Then that's what I'll have."

Aaron disappears down the hall, and for a moment, the energy in the room shifts. Jake crosses the space with the kind of ease that only comes from familiarity, like he knows this place, not just from memory but from muscle. He settles onto the couch, one arm stretched across the back as if it belongs to him, or maybe he belongs to it. I follow, lowering myself beside him, acutely aware that he's been here long before me. Before I even knew Aaron existed.

It's strange, realizing I'm the new one in this dynamic. That I walked into a story already in progress. And if Jake and Aaron hadn't become friends, where would that leave me? Who would I be? Would I even be here?

Amara shifts on the floor, refocusing on her laptop with the steady click of the keyboard filling the silence.

"Still mad at me?" I ask.

"I was never mad at you. Although I would have liked to have been there."

"I'm sorry. I was scared to tell you."

"You're not afraid of anything."

"He's your best friend. I was afraid of disappointing you."

"You're my sister. I love you." He holds my gaze. "You look happy."

"I am."

"That's all that matters. But I had to see it for myself."

"Ugh, I know this must be weird for you."

Aaron returns with a tray containing a glass of wine, the whiskey flask, two glasses, and flavored sparkling water. He sets the water in front of Amara, who's too focused on her screen to look up. Then, he hands me a glass of wine, and Jake, whiskey.

"What's weird?" Aaron asks.

"You marrying my sister."

"Get over it, mate. We're in love."

"So, I hear."

Aaron bends, gently cups my chin in his hand, and kisses me. I'm stunned and electrified.

"Uhm, you know we're still here," Amara says.

"That part," Jake says.

Aaron breaks the kiss, leaving me in a haze. "Are we clear on where I stand in this matter?" he asks Jake.

Jake sighs. "Spare me the dramatics. I can tell by the way you circle her like you're in orbit. I believe a toast is in order," he says, holding up his glass. "To kismet. The only thing that explains this thing between you two."

I clink my glass to his. "To kismet."

"To love," Aaron says. He settles into a chair across from us. Amara gets up, clearly having had enough of us. "What did you think of the article?" he asks Jake.

"It's a first for Jasmine," Jake says, looking at me. "But it's good. We need to discuss the foundation."

"Now?" I ask.

That's Jake. CFO of one of the largest companies in the world. A man who has a love affair with numbers. A permanent fixture in Forbes. And the world's most eligible bachelor. He's business all the time. I should have seen this coming, but I thought he'd at least wait until we met at the office.

"Now is a good time. Especially with the amount of money we estimate to give away each year."

Like him, I have a head for numbers. I don't need to pull up my spreadsheet. I rattle off the number Aaron and I discussed. Jake's already seen a list of entities that will benefit from our charitable giving.

"Even though we're not required to have a minimum distribution in the UK, we want to keep everything equal between what we give in the States and here," I say.

"Makes sense." Jake's brows furrow before he adds, "I wish you had joined us."

I look at Aaron, then back at Jake. "Working for the foundation, I don't have to choose."

"I trust your decision, but I need you both to know what's on my mind."

"I appreciate that, mate," Aaron chimes in.

"So does this mean you'll be spending most of your time here?" Jake asks.

I freeze. I haven't made any final decisions.

"I...I can manage the foundation from anywhere."

Jake looks at me, then at Aaron. "You're married. Explain this to me." he says, his voice taking on a clipped edge.

"I haven't—"

"Aaron," he says, cutting me off.

"You're right. We are married. Jasmine is the love of my life, and I believe her when she says I'm hers."

"But."

"She's not sure whether she's ready to build on what we have here and now...or over time."

Jake directs his attention to me. "Still chasing the rush," he says. "You don't want to be married?"

"I do...to Aaron. I just...I..."

"Marriage is a commitment. You love him or you don't. Which is it?"

My face is warm. My heart begins to race. I inhale through my nose and exhale out my mouth.

I can't lose it. Not today.

Focus. Focus.

Aaron looks at me. He senses what's happening. Jake knows, too. He's seen this before.

"Jas?" Jake calls my name, trying to pull me back in.

It sounds like he's in a tunnel. I can't look at him.

The door is only a few steps away from Aaron.

I stand.

Aaron's eyes lock on mine. He holds his hand out. I cross the room heading toward the door. I hesitate a second. His eyes soften and I instinctively place my hand in his. He pulls me onto his lap, wrapping one arm around my waist. With his other hand, he laces his fingers with mine, surrounding me with love, grounding me. I exhale. He promised to be my safe space, and he is.

I'm okay. He's got me. I'm safe.

"I love Aaron more than I could have imagined loving someone. This marriage...this marriage is real. I'm in therapy, Jake. I'm still trying to make sense of my life...trying to understand what the past seven years were about. If it weren't for Aaron, I'd be throwing up in the car halfway to your jet by now. On my way to God only knows where." Aaron squeezes my hand.

Jake presses his lips together. His eyes shift between me and Aaron. Throughout my life, he's been able to sum up my feelings by reading my face.

He nods once. "I understand. I don't want to see either of you hurt."

"I'd never hurt her, mate. You have to trust we're working through this together."

"I see that."

I sigh heavily. "So...are you done examining our life? I'm hungry."

"I am," he replies. "But, Jas, you need to remember this is not a first-class plane ticket. You can't just change your mind without consequences."

"I know, Jake. I know."

Jake's not wrong. He's just trying to help me, but I've been on this journey for years. Even before that, the unexpected death of my mom formed my life into something unrecognizable, and through therapy and support from Aaron, I'm just beginning to understand the woman shaped by grief and saved by love.

We go to the kitchen and have lunch. The conversation is much lighter.

Still...I have a lot to think about. How do I balance what I feel for Aaron with the pull of the road? How do I heal and not forget about her?

How do I stay?

CHAPTER 34

France

Jasmine

THE RIDE IS QUIET. Fast. Smooth. The scenery blurs past like brush-strokes on stretched canvas. Green fields, clusters of stone buildings, then the flickering of poles slicing the horizon as we speed through towns too small to name. We're on a train bound for Paris, and for the first time in weeks, I feel something settle in my bones. Not peace. Not quite that. But something close. Something comfortable.

It feels good to be moving again.

"Stop looking at me like that," I tell Aaron, catching a glimpse of the handsomely devilish curve of his mouth. "We're almost there."

I lift my chin, pretending to ignore the way he's staring at me like I hung the stars. He's far too smug after this morning. I took my time with him. Took care of him the way I like to. His reward for choosing the train over a private jet. Amara's dream—not mine. She was so set on taking the train. But that's the thing about dreams. They have a way of becoming contagious.

"I can't help myself," he murmurs. "My wife is beautiful. Amongst other things."

His leg brushes mine under the table, slow and deliberate. Electricity, soft and familiar, hums up my spine.

Amara sits beside me in a window seat with her oversized blue head-phones clamped on, glancing between us like a bored referee. She rolls her eyes and goes back to whatever teenage digital vortex she's in. I laugh under my breath. She's so over us. But she's not over this experience.

Here we are, living her dream. It's hers, yet I feel it in my bones, too. There's a quiet joy in watching her excitement bloom; her eyes wide at the station, cell phone bursting with selfies and blurry shots of us laughing. This, right here, is the kind of memory that sticks.

We'll play tourist for the next few days, ticking off landmarks and pas-tries before heading to the Sorbonne to walk the campus. She's already disappointed she can't live in the dorms. There are too many eyes. Too many risks. I get it. With Aaron's last name and mine, it's not safe. It wasn't for me, either. One of the few things Aaron and I never have to debate.

So much has shifted in just a week. We've started therapy, the three of us, trying to untangle what we've each carried in silence. Amara will join us until she leaves for university.

Leaves. The word lands heavy. Finite. A subtle kind of grief. That's when our agreement ends. The paper one, anyway. The one that brought us together, however falsely at first. After that, it's decision time.

Do I stay? Or do I follow the wind again—let it lift me away from this life, this man, this version of myself that terrifies me with how much she wants to root?

God, what do I do?

I look at Aaron. His eyes are already on me, like he knows. His smile softens, the teasing gone.

I turn away, eyes shifting to the window where the world slows. I don't want to picture a life without him. But I also don't know if I'm ready to surrender my freedom. I've spent so long moving, always moving, I'm not sure I know how to stay.

The train eases into Gare du Nord, metal on metal, the sound crisp and final.

We're here.
And maybe, just maybe, I want to be, too.

***

Like at home, settling into our Four Seasons suite is effortless. We have a plan, sure. Amara, however, calls the shots. Well, within reason, of course. When we arrive, I'm starving, so lunch is a priority. And the best way to eat lunch in Paris? At an outdoor table, with a view. With red wine and French bread...naturally.

Then it's off to the Eiffel Tower.

The Champ de Mars is thick with people: tourists snapping pictures of themselves with the Tower looming behind them, each person vying for that perfect shot. Aaron, with his effortless charm, manages to clear a path for us, ensuring we get our own perfect family photo.

Here we are, standing in a line, shoulder to shoulder: Aaron, me, and Amara. All of us arms around each other, connected.

"This was constructed for the 1889 World's Fair," Amara says, her voice a little breathless from excitement.

"One of many constructed for World Fairs," I add.

"I wish I could see some more of them," she says, her tone wistful.

The stranger who offered to take our photo hands Aaron back the phone. I glance at Aaron, then at Amara. My pulse picks up. This is it. The moment I've been dreading and anticipating all at once. Continuing what we have. Making plans like this might be permanent somehow.

"We can make that happen," I say, surprised by the words as they slip out.

My heart beats harder, faster, as the gravity of what I've just said hits me. *We.* That's a word I'm not used to. But it's real, isn't it? It's us. Amara wants to explore. I want to explore. Maybe we can do this together.

Our journey doesn't end here. We can make time to explore. There will be school breaks and holidays, family vacations, and now, Amara's list of sights she wants to see. This isn't just about getting her into school; it's about helping her thrive and creating a life for her as part of a family—our family.

Aaron holds out the phone, showing us the photo. Amara and I lean in, looking at the image of us...together.

"My mom always talked about us coming here as a family," Amara says, her voice quieter now.

The words hit me like a cold wave. I freeze, a rush of emotion flooding me. These are the things my mom would have taken me to do had she been here. And yet, I'm doing them now...*with Amara*. Not only am I experiencing Paris through a different lens, but I'm also giving Amara the things she's always wanted. And in doing that, I'm giving myself something, too. I can feel it—the connection. The closeness.

"You finally made it," Aaron says, his voice warm with a touch of pride in it.

"With my new family," Amara replies, a small smile tugging at her lips.

And just like that, I feel it—the shift. Like a magnet pulling me closer to them. I've been chasing something, some...undefined high for so long, but maybe this is it. Maybe I'm not chasing the rush of independence or excitement anymore. Maybe I'm chasing this—*them*. Maybe I'm finally trying to close the distance between us. Not just Aaron and Amara. Us.

CHAPTER 35

Minutes Away

Jasmine

I WAS ONLY SUPPOSED to be here for two weeks. Amara finishes school in two days—today, really. Tomorrow's just a technicality. Then we have two and a half months before we take her back to Paris.

She's so excited about the move. Excited for today. And I'm excited for her. I remember what it was like to be that young, stepping into the world with wide eyes. She has more experience being on her own than I did at her age. I've learned how terrifying that can be for her through therapy. It's an ongoing process, but I think we all learned a little more about each other. I learned that Aaron's need for control masks his fear of being vulnerable. I love him so much. I really do. He has me rethinking my life.

Now I'm headed to his office to bring him a special lunch.

The car slows as we pull up to the Adler building. It's not far from our little world. Minutes from home and school, depending on which direction I'm headed.

When we stop, I slip off my flats and switch into my spiked heels to match the pastel blue A-line dress I'm wearing. It's not too much for an office, more like something I'd wear for Sunday tea at the Ritz. There's plenty of material, but it moves when I do. I grab my purse and lunch bag before stepping out.

217

Inside, I take the elevator straight to the executive floor. I don't wait for Kate. I knock softly and step into his office.

Andrew's sitting in Aaron's chair. Aaron's lounging on the couch, one arm stretched across the back, looking so fine in his dark blue suit. Hair slightly tousled. His eyes light up when he sees me, and his lips curl at one corner.

"Well, well, looks like someone's delivering more than just food today," Andrew says.

I roll my eyes. "Hey, Andrew."

He stands and glances at Aaron with a grin.

"I'll leave you two to...digest," he says, winking at me before he slips out, closing the door behind him.

I set my purse and bag down on the desk, then walk over to Aaron, taking my time to straddle his lap.

"Hey," I murmur, smiling. "I just came by to bring lunch."

"My favorite," he says with a grin, then gently pulls my face to his and crashes his lips to mine. My man's kisses never fail to leave me breathless.

We finally come up for air, both of us panting. I don't waste any time. I reach between us, unbuckle his belt, and free his shaft. He groans as I wrap my fingers around proof of his desire and stroke him.

"Gonna need you to use your indoor voice, beautiful," he moans.

"My indoor voice is just my outdoor voice when it comes to this."

"Then I guess I'll be swallowing your cries."

He holds my hips. I lift and then lower myself onto him, slowly riding him as we move together, finding our rhythm. Savoring the feel of every solid inch of him thrusting into me. It's intense, beautiful, and thrilling all at once. And we reach the edge, it happens in sync—him sucking my tongue, swallowing my moans, fingers pressing into my hips locking me in place, while he pours into me in waves.

When it's over, he holds me for a while, savoring the moment...the closeness...the tie that only exists between us.

After we clean up, he kisses me again and says, "You can bring me lunch anytime you want."

I untangle myself from him, walk over to the desk, and pick up the lunch bag.

"This is food," I say.

He walks over, pulling me into him. "I prefer you. Are you eating with me?"

"No, I have a few errands to run before I pick up Amara."

"Errands," he echoes. Then reaches between us, slipping his hand under my dress and between my swollen folds. "Not like this."

My breath hitches as he caresses me. "Aaron." I breathe his name.

My body, still sensitive from earlier, still craving him, pulses under his touch. My mouth falls open. He covers it with his and kisses me hard while he works my body. He strokes me until I come on his hand, causing evidence of our lovemaking to run down my leg. Aaron doesn't remove his hands until the pulsing stops. Until my breathing comes under control. Until he's satisfied with his effect on me.

"Lunch is over," he whispers against my lips. He removes his handkerchief, dips it in his water glass, and cleans between my legs. "My wife wears underwear when she's not with me. I assume you have some."

I smirk. "I do."

***

I'm still riding the high from lunch with Aaron when my phone buzzes. It's a call from Amara. Her voice trembles through the line, tearing through the calm of my day like a knife.

"Jas."

My heart skips a beat. "Hey, Sweetie. You okay?"

"The dean...he asked me to come to the office," she says. "He said some-one's coming to pick me up. When I asked who, they wouldn't tell me. I called you."

My stomach sinks. "Where are you now?"

"Heading to the office," Amara replies.

"Okay. Walk slow. Everything's gonna be fine. I'm three minutes away, tops. I won't let anything happen to you. Do you understand?" I push out the words, trying to keep the edge of panic out of my voice.

"I understand," she says, the words shaky but obedient.

I lean towards Jeffrey, my driver. "Pull up Amara's location, and get Dean on the line. Have Aaron on standby. He needs to be at the school. Now."

"Got it," Jeffrey says without hesitation.

"Sweetie, do you have the earbuds I gave you? The ones that match mine?" I ask, my voice low and firm.

"Yes," Amara answers, voice barely above a whisper.

"Good. Take one out and put it in the other ear. I need you to hear me. Can you do that?" I keep my voice steady, despite the pounding in my chest.

"Yes," she confirms.

"Don't talk to anyone else. I'll know when it's done," I instruct her.

I slip one of my earbuds in, hearing a soft beep, then another. "Jeffrey, we're connected."

"Got her," he says. His voice is steady, but I know he's holding his breath, too.

"Okay, sweetie. I'm two minutes away. When you reach the office, slide your phone into your back pocket, but don't hang up. Say 'I understand.'"

"I understand," Amara repeats, like she's been drilled.

I reach for my shoes, kicking off my heels and slipping into my flats, my pulse hammering.

I'm almost there.

"I can see the school," I tell Amara, jumping out of the car. The sharp scent of asphalt fills my lungs. The cool rush of wind whips through my hair as I sprint toward the building. "Put your phone away. When it's in your pocket, say 'done.'"

"Done," Amara responds, her voice faint but steady.

"If you can hear me say, 'I think this is the right office,'" I say, my heart lodged in my throat.

"I think this is the right office," Amara confirms.

I exhale, the air tight in my chest. "Good. I'm here."

I rush in. I see her through the narrow glass window of the office. My heart drops. And then...there he is.

Bane Roth.

A cold shiver creeps down my spine. Every muscle in my body tightens.

"Hey, lovely. I've been looking for you," Bane's voice comes through my earbuds in a low, predatory drawl as he talks to Amara.

Then...Aaron's voice, calm and deliberate, crackles through my earbud, grounding me. "Jas, ETA one minute."

His voice is a lifeline, but I can't call out to him. Not yet. Not while Amara is in danger.

"I'll wait here for my mom," Amara says, her voice a quiet declaration of defiance.

"Your mom is dead. But don't worry, I'll be your daddy," Bane whispers, leaning in close enough for her to smell his putrid cologne. I remember how it lingered in the air like a vulture waiting to feast on the dead.

I push the door open with a force that sends it crashing against the wall. I step in and it shuts behind me. The room goes still. Amara locks eyes with me—her hand trembling, reaching for me as if the world itself is coming undone.

"Mom!" Her scream rips through the air, raw and desperate, and it sends a jagged blade of fear through me.

Bane doesn't even flinch. His attention is so consumed by his sick plans that he doesn't see me coming.

I grab his hand, tight, and twist, digging my nails into his skin until he releases Amara with a hiss of pain. Without thinking, I open my other hand and with the quickness of a viper, I strike, hitting him in the throat. His body crumples to the floor with a sickening thud.

"I'm here," I hiss through gritted teeth as I kneel over him. The pressure of my knee digs into his chest. My hand clamps around his throat. "Her name is Amara Ross Adler. And *I'm* her mother."

Aaron's voice crackles in my ear again. "Get Amara. I'm right behind you."

The door slams open behind me, and I hear the muffled shuffling of boots and the sound of security flooding the room. But my eyes never leave Amara. She's right there, her arms stretched out toward me, her face pale but resolute.

I stay on Bane, my knee pressing harder into his windpipe, but the strength of Aaron's presence surrounds me. Then, his hand are on my shoulder, pulling me up from Bane's crumpled form. His voice urgent, commanding. "Get Amara. We're leaving."

I don't need to be told twice. Amara launches herself into my arms, and I hold her tight, as if my very body can shield her from all the horrors in this world.

As we turn to leave, I glance behind me just in time to see Aaron, a wall of muscles and rage, lift Bane like he's nothing more than a ragdoll. His grip is around Bane's throat, fingers flexed like steel.

Then I hear it. A sickening crack.

I let out a small, satisfied smile, knowing that whatever happens next, something inside of Bane just shattered.

CHAPTER 36

Unfinished Business

Aaron

GETTING NEWS THAT MY family's in trouble sends a surge of rage through me. Breaking Bane's face helps. Just a little.

I exit the school with only one thing on my mind. My family.

Outside, it's chaos: students, teachers, reporters. I walk past it all, blocking it out. When I slide into the car beside Jasmine, Amara's in her lap, head pressed into her neck. Jasmine's fingers are tangled in her hair.

She finds my hand.

I turn to her, cupping her cheek. "You okay?" Jasmine nods. I lower my hand, wrapping it around Amara's. "You're safe now," I tell her.

Amara's slim fingers curl around the fabric of Jasmine's dress beneath my hand. *She's safe.* Thank God. I lean back, pulling out my phone to call Andrew.

"Are they with you?" he asks immediately.

"Yeah. Heading home. There'll be photos. Get Page on it, ASAP. Tell him to keep my family's name out of the media at all costs."

"On it."

I pause, my mind already on the next thing. "And Andrew...let them rip Bane Roth to shreds."

"Understood."

We ride home in silence. When we get there, I pause a moment, looking at my family standing before me in the foyer. Safe. Home. Together. I bend down and cup Amara's face in my hand.

"Are you okay?"

She nods in my palm. "Bane stinks," she says, her voice small.

I look up at Jasmine. Her brows are furrowed, her lips pressed tight. I pull Amara into a tight hug, feeling her arms wrap around me like a lifeline.

"Yeah, you're alright."

Jasmine's hand gently lands on Amara's shoulder. "Let's go upstairs and get cleaned up."

"Okay," Amara murmurs, and they disappear upstairs.

I rub my thumb across my knuckle, the remnants of Bane's blood still there. I head to the bathroom and wash my hands and face. Staring at my reflection in the mirror, I don't recognize the man looking back at me. This version of myself...the one who'd burn everything to protect his family, rarely surfaces.

I walk to the family room and pour myself a whiskey. I toss the first one back, feeling the burn as it goes down. I pour another and sit on the couch. I pull out my phone and set up a video call with my brothers.

Alex is the first to speak. "What's the fix?"

Andrew's reply is swift. Decisive. "I'm on it. This won't hit the media."

"That's not why I called," I say.

Alex's voice is layered in caution when he says, "Something tells me I'm not going to like the next words out of your mouth."

"I want everyone in the Home Office associated with Bane destroyed."

Alex is silent for a moment. "And..."

"Everyone who let that lizard slither into the school," I add, voice low.

I hold my brother's gaze. This is family we're talking about. It's mine. It's ours. It's personal.

Alex leans back, pinching the bridge of his nose. He exhales, and his voice hardens. "Do it."

I don't usually play this hand. But someone decided to mess with my family, and being the nice guy won't get me the justice I need. I'm about to send a message...don't fuck with my family.

"Anything else?" Alex asks, his tone softening.

"One more thing. Don't be late to the party this weekend." I let a smile tug at my lips.

"I'm bringing cupcakes," Andrew deadpans.

Alex rolls his eyes and ends the call.

I lean back on the couch, feeling the weight of everything settle on my shoulders. This won't be over until it's finished.

***

The house is quiet. Settled.

I peek in on Amara, who's sound asleep, Elizabeth curled in a ball at her feet. Quietly, I head upstairs.

Jasmine's already in bed, her tablet in hand. She looks up as I enter, setting it aside with that smile that makes my heart race.

I climb into bed beside her and pull her onto my lap so she straddles me, craving her closeness. She leans in, burying her head in my neck.

"Drop a man four times your size," I murmur, sliding my hands down her bare back to grip her hips, pulling them into me, needing the warmth of her skin against mine.

She straightens, a playful curve to her lips. "Told you."

I hold her gaze a moment, letting the silence between us speak for all the unspoken things today. Then I kiss her, slow and deep, letting my lips and tongue convey everything I can't put into words.

I break the kiss, my breath a little heavier. "Jas, I don't want you to leave."

"I'm trying to stay."

"What's holding you back?"

She hesitates, her fingers tracing the line of my jaw. "I'm afraid."

"Of me?"

She shakes her head. "No. Of losing you. Of...losing myself in you."

"You don't have to change to be with me. Let me create space for you to thrive. If it's adventures you're seeking, let's have them together. Let's find those precious moments in a day that bring us joy."

"Like earlier."

I laugh softly. "I'd like that to be more like a daily thing." I brush my lips against hers. "Adventures don't always have to be big. They could be as simple as a picnic in the park, stolen kisses in the hallway at the museum, *lunch*...in the office."

Her look turns serious.

"Amara called me Mom."

I nod. "I heard it. You are."

"I was scared. Then I heard your voice over the earpiece...I knew we'd be okay."

"I'd never let anything happen to my family."

She looks up at me, vulnerability in her eyes. "I love you, Aaron Adler."

I roll her on her back, kissing her deeply. She moans softly against my lips, and I move, positioning myself inside her. Pushing in, I claim my love...my life...my wife.

She's everything I can't control, and now she's the one thing I can't let go.

"Stay."

CHAPTER 37

Full House

Jasmine

OUR HOUSE IS FULL. Of adults. Of kids. Of mess. It smells of icing and hotdogs and pizza and fries. And I love every minute of it. The noise is comforting. For once, the chaos doesn't feel like something I need to run from. It feels like home.

"You really know how to throw a party," Andrew says.

"It's my first."

"I can't tell. You're a natural."

"It's likely my last."

I hear the words leave my mouth before I can stop them. I don't want this to be my last, but I can't stop thinking about how fleeting everything feels. It's not that I don't enjoy this—this being all of it: the house, the family, the stability. But I still feel that tug inside, that whisper telling me to pack a bag, grab my passport, and leave. It's who I've always been. Or at least who I thought I was.

Andrew turns to me, studying my face like it's a problem to solve. "It's not your last."

My brows furrow. "How do you know?"

"Because when you look at my brother..." He glances at Aaron across the room, his eyes softening for a split second. "I see your future. I see my unborn nieces and nephews. I see trips in private jets." He smirks. "I see myself being kicked out for more office lunches, and I see lots more parties...like this...the kind where I have to bring cupcakes."

"You're your mother's son," I say, the words slipping out as I half-laugh. *And I'm my mother's daughter*...I think. Or a product of her absence? Always running, always escaping. But I'm not sure I want that anymore.

"I am. And you're my sister-in-law, and we love you."

I should be happy. I should be soaking in this moment, letting it anchor me. But instead, I feel a pang of uncertainty, like I'm standing at the precipice of a dark cave and wondering whether I should venture in.

"Would your brother be mad if I said I love you, too?" I ask.

A familiar arm snakes around my waist. A gentle kiss behind my ear tells me everything I need to know. "Clarify, you love him as a brother," Aaron says, his voice warm and certain, the kind of certainty that I crave but sometimes fear.

Alex steps over to pipe in. "And only if I'm included."

My eyes burn with unshed tears threatening to fall. God, I don't deserve this. Not after everything. But here I am, feeling more loved than I ever have in a long time. Feeling like...I belong. "Thank you."

Aaron turns me around and pulls me into him. His arms around me are a security I relish and it feels as if everything I've ever wanted might actually be right here, right now. *But what if I'm not ready for it? What if I run again?*

What if I don't?

"Andrew, go make someone else cry," Aaron says, his voice half-playful, half-serious.

"I did."

"Is this business?" Alex asks, his voice is steady but stern.

I'm starting to understand how the Adler brothers operate, each one filling a distinct role in their quiet, powerful constellation. Andrew is the fixer. The one who notices the cracks before they spread, the one who smooths the sharp edges no one else sees. He's the seer, too, reading people like open books and always a step ahead of the fallout. Alex is the boss, the center of gravity, calm even when everything around him is chaos. He doesn't need to shout to be in charge. His presence alone steadies the room. And then...then there's Aaron—sharp, brilliant, impossibly precise. The brain, the strategist. A tech whiz on par with Rose, but with the meticulous control of someone who can't afford mistakes. He's the one who holds the line when the stakes are high, the one who keeps everything running, even if it means holding his breath to do it.

I turn in Aaron's arms to face them, my mind still swimming with thoughts of what I'm letting go of, what I'm choosing to stay for. "It's okay. What happened, Andrew?"

"There's an article about Bane set to be released Monday in the BDC. About his predatory behavior," Andrew says.

"Names?" Alex asks.

Andrew shakes his head. "Not ours. There were other victims. The Home Office knew about it. Buried the complaints."

"And the school?" I ask.

"The list of culprits reached higher on the roster than expected. You two need to set up that trust fund for Amara. The payout when our attorneys get done will be huge."

I gasp. Not because of the payout, though that's a shock in itself, but because of the weight of what this means for our lives. For Amara's future. For my future. This is no longer just about me and my old life on the move. It's about a family...my family, and what happens next. It's about a place in the world I've never truly had until now. These past few months, I've been building a new life with Aaron and Amara, and I can't see extracting myself from that.

Aaron places a hand on Andrew's shoulder. "Good work."

I watch them, still processing everything. *Is this my life now? A life I didn't expect but might actually want?* I didn't come here to settle down. I came to solve a problem, to be a temporary presence. But now...now I can't help but wonder if I've already found the place where I'm supposed to stay. The place I didn't even know I was searching for.

"Mom," Amara's voice pulls me back into the room. Aaron's arm tightens around my waist.

"Hey, sweetie, having fun?"

"Yeah, can I spend the night at Tina's? Sheila, Bev, and Adrina will be there."

"No." The words, reminiscent of my mother's, flow out of my mouth before I realize it. She always protected me. Like I'm protecting Amara.

"Sweetie, we don't know those families. If your friends want a sleepover, they can have it here," Aaron says, his voice gentle.

"I have around-the-clock security," Alex says. "I'll talk to Mum, I'm sure she won't mind watching them."

"Same," Andrew offers.

I look at Amara. "Sweetie, have a chat with your friends. You can have it here or at your uncle's. Let them know Ava will be hosting."

"Uncle Andrew has a movie room," she says.

Aaron rolls his eyes. Alex sighs.

"Seems I'm the chosen one." Andrew deadpans. "Come on, kiddo, let's go talk to Mum."

"Oh, Dad, Elizabeth got out again."

"I'll find her," Aaron assures Amara.

The brothers trail Amara in search of Ava.

I turn in Aaron's arms. "And you want more of these?"

He smirks. His lips hoovering above mine. "Yeah. A house full."

I nod. "Okay."

I'll stay.

CHAPTER 38

Peace

Aaron

A SECOND TO BREATHE. That's all we need right now. A chance to get away from it all: tabloids, acquisitions, auditors, all of it. Since the day we met, Jasmine and I have been swimming in the deep end, never coming up for air. Never seeing daylight. Never experiencing who we are outside of the part of us that's always on, always responding, always ready for the next threat, next issue, next day.

We don't know who we are as a couple that's not under pressure. But this week we'll find out. Because starting today, it's just us. My wife and me.

The house in the countryside is all set when we arrive. Nothing on the scale of our Kent home. That's where Amara and her friends are for the week. Mum is falling in love with the idea of having children around again. They're not far away. Enjoying their last bits of freedom before heading off to university in a month.

Jasmine's already inside while I'm wrapping up a call with Andrew.

"I can respond to Bromley," Andrews says.

I close my eyes, not wanting to think about it, but that side of me that needs to control the situation persists.

"I'll deal with him when I get back."

"If I can take down a government organization, I can handle this. Remember, you're on holiday. You need to let go."

I take a deep breath. He's not wrong. His quick work dealing with Bane is one for the books.

"Keep me posted," I say, and end the call.

Stepping into the cottage, the familiar scent of fresh pinewood fills my lungs as the door clicks shut behind me. The room is cozy but unmistakably refined.

"Jas."

"Upstairs."

When I get upstairs, Jasmine's standing in front of the mirror deciding which sundress to wear.

I already know which one I want to see her in. "The white with yellow flowers."

"Was that Andrew?"

"Yeah. Just working on something."

"Should I be concerned?"

I walk up behind her, my hands sliding around her waist. I look at our reflection in the mirror, my palm flattening against her bare stomach, my thoughts drifting to what it'll feel like when we have children. Because Jasmine says she's staying. *She's staying.* I let the thought wrap around me like a blanket. Warm. Comforting. I'm going to show her every day just how much she means to me.

"You've got that look again," she says.

"It's you. I'll never get tired of looking at you. *You* bring me a level of joy I never knew was possible. The look on my face...is the look of love." I slide my hands up her body, palm over her breast. "And I love every damn thing about you." I kiss her neck. "Now, put on that dress before I change my mind about what's waiting for you."

She turns in my arms, lowering her hand between us, finding me already rethinking our day. She squeezes the bulge in my pants. "Not even a little taste?"

I growl in her ear. "Jas. The yellow flowers, please."

"Fine."

I know I should leave and let her change, but I don't. I sit on the edge of the bed and watch as she slips into the dress. She removes her bra since it's a halter top, then sits on my lap so I can tie it. She stands, running her fingers through her hair, making her curls even wilder than before.

Everything about her steals my breath. She catches my reflection in the mirror. I gesture for her.

"Put your foot here."

She places her bare foot on the bed between my legs, her toe grazing my length. I slide my hand up her leg, past her calf, and cup her between the thighs. Her warmth sends a shiver up my spine.

"You won't need these," I say, tugging at her silk underwear.

"Then you need to take them off," she says, lowering her foot and heading for the door.

I laugh to myself because my wife is pushing every button I have. I catch her in the hall and pull her into me. "We're about to have lunch, beautiful." I drag my nose along her cheek. Her breath hitches.

I step back, holding out my hand. Not saying a word. Waiting. She slides her underwear off and hands them to me. I put them into my pocket.

"Happy?"

"No. Not until you are."

"I want you."

I gently tip her chin up with my finger. I dust my lips across hers. "Let me make the day special for you. I promise you'll feel every bit of my love today and every day." She nods, and I kiss her deeply.

When we break the kiss, I lace my fingers with hers and take her through the house and to the back door.

Standing in the threshold, I point. "We're going there." I gesture to the green field, where a white quilted blanket is spread out with a picnic spread worthy of Architectural Digest. In the distance, the view stretches for miles—rolling hills dotted with ancient oak trees, the soft green hues deepening under the afternoon sun. The fields stretch, looking like an impressionist painting, vibrant and alive, framed by a distant skyline that seems almost surreal.

She turns to me, eyes wide. "I've never had a picnic before."

"This'll be the first of many. Are you ready?"

She nods. I lead her out to the field, where our spread is set up under a tree. There are tiered serving trays filled with cakes, sandwiches, fruit—all the things that make this moment special.

We sit in the middle. I hand her a plate, and she fills it with whatever catches her eye. I pour us both a glass of champagne.

She lifts her glass. "May our days be filled with moments like these. To firsts."

I raise my glass and tap it to hers. "To firsts."

Jasmine's eyes wander over the fields as she eats, taking in the beauty, while I fall further in love with her. She's beautiful, delicate in a way. Her flowery dress spreads around her, the fabric catching the breeze, caressing her skin.

"This is so beautiful. We should have breakfast out here."

"If that's what you want."

She reaches into my plate for blueberries and pops one in her mouth. "Why do you have so many blueberries on your plate?"

"Because you like them."

Ever since that first day at the restaurant. I add extra to my plate, because I know that's her thing.

"Amara asked if she could move into her apartment sooner. I told her I'd discuss it with you."

"Any reason why we wouldn't let her?"

"No."

"Kate can update her itinerary."

"Do you think Amara will return to London after completing her degree?" she asks.

"I haven't thought about it. Oddly enough, she's a mixture of me and you in more ways than one." I pause, taking her in. "Would you be opposed if she stayed in Paris?"

"I want her to be happy."

"Are you happy?"

"I am. Really happy." Jasmine shifts closer to me, her legs tucked under her, knees pressed to my thigh.

I study the curve of her smile, the way the sun kisses her honey brown skin, the warmth in her eyes when she looks at me. And I remember the day she decided to stay. Something cracked open inside her, and light spilled out. I've been turning that moment over in my mind ever since.

I reach for her hand, needing the contact. "Something changed in you on the day of Amara's party," I say, my voice low. "I saw it in your eyes. When I told you I wanted a house full of kids...when you looked at me like that—what did you see?"

She doesn't answer right away, and I wait. I've learned to give her space when the words come slow. But her fingers tighten around mine, grounding us both.

"I realized in that moment," she says softly, "that, like me, you have dreams. Dreams of the future, of how you want your life to unfold. Family, kids, health, success..."

Her voice catches, and my chest pulls tight. God, she has no idea how much I admire her. How often I look at her and wonder how someone who has seen the kind of loss she has can still speak about life with this much hope.

She continues, "Looking around that room, I realized each person there has dreams. My parents had dreams, too. And they didn't find them by running. They found them by taking a chance. Risking it all for that one thing that makes them happy. That one person. Even if it doesn't last. Even if it's brief."

I watch her—really watch her. I know what she's thinking. Her father took a chance. He married the love of his life. Now she's gone. Jasmine looks up at me through her eyelashes. There's a soft glow in her eyes, something raw and unguarded. I've never seen anyone so exposed, so brave at once.

"What if it does last?" she asks, her voice trembling just enough to break me. "What if it transforms? What if sharing the moments given to us provides a lifetime of happiness?"

And just like that, my breath stutters in my chest. I swallow hard.

She's not just choosing me. She's choosing to believe in *forever*. *Our* forever.

"I have dreams, too," she whispers. "I dreamt of having what my parents had. And following the feeling of being free brought me to the one person I can have that with...who makes me want to stay. And that's you. I don't want to run anymore. I want to stay—and risk it all. Because you're worth it."

A lump forms in my throat. I don't care if this is the hundredth time she's said it or the first. I'll never get used to the sound of Jasmine Ross choosing me.

"This...this love between us is worth it," she says. "This feeling is worth chasing. Risking it all. Because I love you. I want to be part of your dream, because you're mine."

Something inside me shatters—in the best way.

I pull her onto my lap without thinking, wrapping my arms around her like I could fuse us together. Our heartbeats sync and I savor the moment.

God, I knew the day I met her.

I knew I'd never want to be apart from her. But hearing her say she wants to stay? That she's choosing *us*...me...after all she's endured. That's the kind of miracle you don't see coming. That's the kind of love that changes everything. That's the kind of love that lasts.

I press my face to her hair and close my eyes, holding her like our future is already here...warm, real, and alive in my arms.

CHAPTER 39

Rite of Passage

Jasmine

TIME IS FLYING, AND for the first time in my life, I just want it to slow down.

That's what our mini escape was about. Slowing down. Reconnecting. Experiencing each other in a way that isn't forced. And we did just that. But it was fast—so fast. Fast and full of laughter, full of discovery, full of us. Full of...love.

I had my first picnic. I made love under the stars.

I talked about mom—for real this time. The pieces I still carry: silver dollar pancakes, the scent of vanilla and jasmine tea on her clothes, the sound of her laughter. The way she made me feel safe. The ways she showed...love.

I want more days like those. But I also want more days like these. When Aaron, Amara, and I are out as a family. It's bittersweet. This is her last major outing with us before she heads to university. The biggest one yet—Saola's annual conference.

Her biggest, but not her last. When she comes home for the holidays, there will be Saola Technology and Ross Enterprises charity events, the galas, the year-end holiday parties. She's part of both families now, and that means showing up. There will be speeches to give, presentations to deliver, moments where she's standing on stage representing us all.

So no, this may be the biggest one so far, but it's not the last. Not by a long shot. This is the beginning of it all. This is where she learns the weight of her name.

I smooth my hands down my pink lace dress and tuck a curl behind Amara's ear.

"I still can't believe you made Dad wear a pink tie," she says flatly.

Aaron smooths his hand down his tie. "I have to admit, my tie collection is more colorful."

"You love it," I say.

"I love you," he says, pulling me close. "Let's find our table."

We move through the crowd, weaving past soft conversations and the occasional burst of laughter as we search for our table. The lighting inside E-Hall has completely transformed. This morning, it was all sharp angles and sterile brilliance. Bright panels lighting every corner, screens flickering with graphs and code, and voices overlapping.

Now it feels almost intimate, the massive space dimmed to a warm glow, shadows softening the sharp lines of steel and glass. Spotlights wash the tables in amber while the vaulted ceilings above fade into a deep indigo, like a sky just past sunset. The transformation is subtle but deliberate. Tonight isn't about innovation. It's about influence.

Amara walks beside me, silent but wide-eyed, soaking it all in. This is her life now, too. Her legacy. She handled herself well this morning, even when the panel drifted into dense territory. I brought her to one of the technical sessions early, just to let her see what it's like when you're surrounded by people throwing around breakthrough ideas like casual conversation. She didn't say much then, but I saw the way she leaned in when they started talking about predictive algorithms for social infrastructure. She's paying attention. That's all I need.

Along the way, people stop us for quick greetings. As president, it's not unusual for others to vie for Aaron's attention. This is all part of Amara's initiation—a rite of passage. She's learning how to read a room full of power, how to move with purpose, how to feel the weight behind her name. How swiftly her life is changing. Why she can't live in the dorms. Why she'll have a security team in Paris. After today, I'm sure she understands.

"I see our table," Aaron says, guiding us forward.

When we reach the table, Andrew's already there, chatting it up with someone.

"Speaking of...," Andrew says. "Aaron, Bill and I were just talking about you."

"I'm excited to put pen to paper and close the deal next week," Bill says.

"It's been a long time coming," Aaron replies. "Bill, this is my wife, Jasmine, and our daughter, Amara. Jasmine, this is Bill Kaylor, CEO of Mission AI. They'll be joining us soon."

I extend a hand. "Mr. Kaylor, I've heard good things. It's nice to finally meet you."

"The pleasure is mine," he says, shaking my hand, then Amara's. "I feel like I'm meeting royalty."

"You'll have to get used to that. We'll be seeing a lot more of each other," Aaron says.

"Well, I'll let you get settled. Our table's just to your right," Bill says, then leaves.

Aaron pulls out my chair. His hand brushes against my lower back, warm and grounding. Amara sits between me and Andrew, already engaged in lively chatter about the game she's developing.

"One day, Amara will be keynoting here," Aaron says, looking past me in her direction.

I hold his gaze, taking a second to admire the man I married. Handsome. Smart. Strong. Loving. "I have a call with Rose next week."

"You've decided?" He leans in close.

"I'm going to see if she convinces me otherwise."

His lips dust mine. "I can be persuasive myself."

"We're in public." Amara's sing-songy voice brings me out of my haze.

Then her hand nudges my knee. I look up. Headed toward our table is Bridgette Bromley. I squeeze Aaron's hand.

"I see her."

"Well, if it isn't the table everyone's pretending not to watch—power, pretty faces, and a picture-perfect marriage. You always did like keeping things...interesting."

"And yet, somehow you found your way here, anyway. Must've missed the spotlight," Andrew deadpans.

I bite my lip, stifling a laugh. She's so full of herself. "Bridgette. If you're lost, I can have someone show you to your table," Aaron says.

"I was hoping you would."

"We have people for that," Amara says, shocking me and making me proud at the same time.

"Well," Bridgette huffs. "Seems the apple didn't fall too far from the tree."

"That's a good thing," Aaron says. "She's a great example of brilliance and grace." Aaron lifts his hand, and within seconds, a staff member appears at the table. "Ms. Bromley needs assistance finding her table."

"I'll take care of her, sir."

Amara gives Andrew a subtle high five as he places his palm on the table. "Good job," he says with a quiet smile. "You definitely live up to your name."

The lights dim slightly. The program begins. Andrew steps onto the stage to welcome everyone. He speaks with the calm confidence of someone who knows exactly what's at stake and exactly what he's doing. Afterward, the head of product development steps up to highlight what's ahead for Saola in the new year—ambitious, exciting, and forward-thinking.

Then comes the announcement we've all been waiting for: the keynote speaker, Aaron.

He kisses me before standing, quick, warm, anchoring, and I absorb every ounce of love he offers in that fleeting moment. As he walks to the stage, all I can think about is how incredibly handsome he looks under the lights and how natural he is in front of a crowd. This is his element. He commands the room with quiet charisma, and every eye is on him.

He speaks about Saola's journey, its triumphs, its challenges, and the vision that carries it forward. I listen with pride swelling in my chest.

"I couldn't have done it without the work of our amazing team and the support of my beautiful family," he says, gesturing to our table.

The spotlight shifts to us for a beat. I smile. He catches it and gives one back. Beside me, Amara lifts her chin slightly, her gaze drifting to the audience—steady, composed, aware. This is her moment, too. After tonight, people will seek her out. They'll want to talk to her, shake her hand, pitch ideas, curry favor. Because now they know...she's someone to watch.

The crowd rises in a standing ovation. I rise, too. Aaron deserves it.

When he returns to the table, he pulls Amara and me into a hug, pride and affection written all over his face.

"Yep, Amara's definitely vying for my job," Andrew says.

We all laugh.

The program wraps up, and the social hour begins. Dancing, drinks, conversation. Small clusters of people are scattered around the venue. Our little team is spread out, too, but I can still see everyone.

Kate, who's always on, gives me a quick rundown of our upcoming travel schedule. She's a stickler for details and wants Amara's move-in day to go perfectly.

"I'm making sure you're all set for the trip," she says, tapping her phone.

"We're good," I assure her. "Except for one piece Amara wanted shipped from the house, everything else we brought in Paris. We're only traveling with luggage."

Across the room, I spot Amara chatting with Andrew and one of Saola's newest recruits from the Sorbonne. Knowing Amara, she's peppering the poor girl with a million questions about campus life.

Aaron is just beyond her, near the bar, surrounded by a small crowd of executives.

"You should be enjoying yourself," I tell Kate, nudging my chin toward the guy who's been sneaking glances at her. He gives her a small smile when she turns. "Go dance. Give the man a chance."

"Mrs. Adler—," she starts.

"I'll be back." I smirk, already moving toward the hallway.

The restroom's occupied when I walk in. After handling my business, I linger at the sink washing my hands, catching my reflection in the mirror.

Five months ago, I came here to deliver a keynote. A few lectures. I never imagined I'd end up with a husband, a daughter about to start college, and roots deeper than I ever thought I could grow.

For years, I chased something across cities and countries, believing I was chasing her. But all along, I was chasing the version of me *she* would have helped me become had she lived: a woman who loves fiercely, who builds a family, who shares her knowledge instead of running from it.

I was always chasing...me.

The bathroom door creaks open, snapping me out of my thoughts. I catch her reflection in the mirror behind me.

"Bridgette Bromley," I say dryly. "Can't seem to shake you."

She leans against the wall, arms crossed. "Neither can your husband. You might want to keep him on a tighter leash. You never know... more photos of him and me might accidentally slip out. Could cause quite a panic at Saola. Bromley's just waiting to scoop up your IP if the stock dips. All I have to do is light the match."

I dry my hands slowly.

"You really are your father's daughter," I say. "Betting everything on lies and hoping no one notices the fire started inside your own house. Thing is—" I turn to face her fully, "Aaron and I? We're fireproof."

A toilet flushes behind us. A woman in a blue dress steps out, washes her hands quickly, and with a polite, knowing smile, murmurs, "Excuse me," before slipping out.

I look back at Bridgette. "I'll send someone to help you find your way back to your table," I say cooly, and leave.

When I find Aaron, he's standing with Andrew, Amara, and...the woman in the blue dress. Aaron wraps an arm around my waist and kisses my cheek.

"Honey, this is Ms. Leighton. She's with the Competition and Markets Authority."

Ms. Leighton smiles warmly. "Mrs. Adler, it's an honor to meet you. You have a lovely family. You must be so proud of your daughter heading to the Sorbonne."

"Nice to meet you, Ms. Leighton. We are proud," I say. "Andrew thinks she'll be running Saola in no time."

Aaron chuckles. "Ms. Leighton, I hope the conference gave you some good insights."

She meets my gaze, smiling. "Very enlightening. It's clear why other companies are turning to Saola for guidance. You've set a new standard for innovation in the industry. Thank you for the invite. And congratulations on the acquisition."

Aaron looks down at me. "Ready to go home?"

I squeeze his hand. "Yeah," I say, "I think I've seen everything I needed."

CHAPTER 40

Roll the Dice

Aaron

FOR THE FIRST TIME in my life, it feels like everything is falling into place. Since Jasmine walked into my life, all fiery eyes and restless energy, the pieces have been clicking together like they were always meant to. Home, family, career...everything I've worked for. It may not have been a straight path, but we're there.

I lean back in my chair as the chatter from the conference room fades into the background. The room smells like fresh coffee and quiet ambition. I glance at my phone, idly scrolling, until a headline grabs my attention.

"It's shaping up to be a banner year for Saola Technology. Over 10,000 innovators from across Europe gathered for Saola's annual tech conference, a three-day showcase of the company's latest advancements. Aaron Adler, President of European Operations, delivered an impressive keynote outlining Saola's bold vision for the coming year. The company also celebrated the successful $100 million acquisition of Mission AI, a defense-focused tech firm, a move that positions Saola to become an unstoppable force in the evolving world of artificial intelligence."

Not bad.

I glance to where my brothers are still gathered near the end of the table.

"They make it sound easy," I say, holding up my phone.

Andrew smirks. "That's the media for you. Wrap up a year of blood, sweat, and strategy in one neat paragraph." He slow claps. "Bravo, by the way. Inviting the CMA to the conference? Brilliant."

I nod. "Bromley left me no choice. Something felt off. They were way too quiet in the press. When Jasmine told me what happened in the restroom...I thought Bridgette would cause a scene in public, not...*that*."

"Bridgette has been dying to make headlines," Alex says, leaning against the table. "She got her wish."

"Yeah, just not the kind she wanted," Andrew mutters.

Alex glances at him. "What about Roth? The younger one's headed to university soon. We don't need any surprises there."

Andrew leans back, folding his arms. "Handled. He's looking at jail time. No mention of Amara in the news. Any future headlines about her will be about some award-winning game she designed. She's sharp. So is Demetrius."

"The next generation of Adlers," I say with a faint smile.

And there'll be more to come. But I keep that to myself as I stand and go to my next meeting.

It's been a solid day on every front. And now, I'm ready for one more thing to make it perfect: Jasmine.

I'm just standing to leave when Andrew pops his head into my office.

"Alex and I are grabbing a drink. You in?"

Six months ago, I'd have been the first to say yes. Tonight, everything in me is pulling me home.

"Not tonight," I say, grabbing my jacket. "But I'll walk out with you."

We head down the hall, passing Alex's office. He falls in step with us. When the elevator doors close, Andrew glances my way.

"Jasmine's been good for you."

"In more ways than one."

"I finally feel like I've got a real shot at your job," Andrew jokes.

"You've actually been delegating," Alex adds, nudging me.

I smile but say nothing. They're not wrong. Jasmine taught me that letting things go doesn't mean losing control. That vulnerability doesn't weaken me—it makes things real. With her, I learned that telling the truth about what I need, what I feel, what I love...that's the power.

"Yeah," I say quietly. "I see things more clearly with Jas in my life."

The elevator dings. We cross the lobby to where our drivers wait. Dean opens my door just as the car ahead opens.

And out steps Bridgette Bromley. *Of course.*

I freeze. Not out of fear, but out of pure irritation.

Andrew sees her, too. "Looks like someone didn't get the message," he says loud enough for her to hear.

Bridgette walks up, stopping short of us. "I was coming to see Aaron. But since I have all three of you..."

"If this is about doing business," I cut in, "you know exactly where we stand, and after that stunt you pulled—"

"That's what I wanted to discuss," she says, her voice softening. "It was a misunderstanding."

Andrew snorts. "Tell it to the CMA."

"You can help me," she says, trying to recover. "Just tell them—"

"You told them enough," I say. "This conversation is over."

"You rolled the dice and lost," Andrew adds flatly.

Alex steps forward. "If you have anything else to say, talk to our attorney."

I move toward the car. "I'm going home. To my wife." I glance at Andrew. "Handle this."

He purses his lips. "Gladly."

I get in the car, close the door, and don't look back.

I'm heading home.

***

Every day, my love for them deepens. It roots itself in places I didn't even know were hollow. Knowing they're here...*my family*—fills me with a kind of joy I didn't realize I was missing until I found it.

I want to see my wife. I want to hold her, hear her voice, share the quiet pieces of our day like a sacred offering.

As I step into the house, I move through the foyer, searching.

"Where's my family?" I call out, heading down the hall.

"Back here," Jasmine replies, her voice warm, nearing. "I was just in the garden."

She reaches me in a few steps and melts into my arms, her hands gliding up my back. We hold each other like time stopped just for us. Like we've been waiting all day for this very moment. Waiting for the second our hearts sync.

"Hey, beautiful," I murmur. "Did I interrupt something?"

She tips her head up. "The movers accidentally let Elizabeth out. Amara's out back looking for her."

"That cat's got a wandering spirit...reminds me of someone else I know."

She swats me lightly. "I've settled...somewhat. Anyway, where's my kiss?"

I lift her chin and press my lips to her. The kiss is deep, anchoring. It says all the things we don't have to say out loud and promises of things to come.

"This is always the best part of my day."

"I missed you, too." She traces her thumb across my mouth, erasing the evidence. "I saw the article. Congratulations."

"The media got it right this time."

"They didn't stand a chance to spin it," she says, pulling away gently. "But we've got to find Elizabeth. Amara's beside herself."

"She eat yet?"

"Not yet."

We step into the library and exit through the back door to the patio. Amara is near the hedges, calling softly.

"Hey, kitty kitty...Elizabeth?"

"Hey, sweetie," I say gently. "I'll find her. How about you and Jas have some dinner?"

"Okay," Amara replies, giving me a hug before heading inside.

"You should eat first," Jasmine says.

"I won't be long."

She walks with me to the front door, then rises on her toes, waiting. I don't make her wait long. I kiss her, slow and sure, until she exhales like she's letting go of the day. Then I step outside.

The street is quiet. Faint sunlight filters through the trees as I walk the sidewalk, imagining the path a curious cat might take.

The first time I saw Elizabeth, I'd just finished my morning run. I was cooling down near the steps, catching my breath, when she appeared—silent and graceful, winding around my ankles like she'd always belonged here.

"Hey kitty," I said.

She purred. Her fur was smoky grey, but her eyes...God, her eyes were the color of sea glass. I'd never seen a cat with eyes like that. She followed me inside, and I gave her water. She drank like she hadn't had any in days.

I thought about putting her back outside. I opened the door, but she stayed. So, I showered, got dressed, ready to meet Jasmine for the first time. I figured the cat would be gone by the time I returned. She wasn't.

Even after Jasmine walked out on me that day, something told me to try again. Something about her stayed with me. Just like the cat.

Elizabeth never left.

Later, I brought her a collar—silver with an aquamarine jewel, the exact shade of her eyes.

"Elizabeth?" I call out, scanning yards, bushes, and curbs. "Come on, girl..."

And then...I see her.

She's stretched out near the curb, like she's sunbathing. But the sun is almost gone...storm clouds slowly gather.

My pace quickens. "Elizabeth!"

She doesn't move. I jog closer. Something inside me tightens.

I stop.

She's still.

Too still.

Her body's turned toward the house. Toward home.

No. No, no, no.

"Fuck." The word tears out of me. "Fuck."

I gather her gently in my arms, her fur still warm from the sun.

She was on her way home.

God.

So was I.

CHAPTER 41

Wandering Spirits

Jasmine

WHEN AARON WALKS THROUGH the door, his voice is low, almost hollow. "I found her."

"Where was she?"

I step into the foyer and stop cold. Elizabeth is stretched out in his arms the way she does when she's lounging in the sun-drenched hallway. But she's not lounging.

"She got hit by a car." His voice is steady—but barely. There's something tight about it. Frayed.

I don't even try to stop the tears. "Oh my god." I rush to him, but the moment I get close, my feet falter. I can't look.

"I have to make a call," he murmurs, turning away, his jaw clenched against the emotion he's too controlled to show.

Amara comes running in, her energy unchanged. "Where in the world was Elizabeth—?" She freezes. A sharp breath catches in her throat. "What—?"

I pull her into my arms, swallowing the knot in my throat. "She's gone, honey."

She buries her face in my shoulder, her small frame trembling.

There are things in life so final, they feel unbearable. Death is one of them. Elizabeth hadn't been with us long, but she'd already become part of the family. She did what animals do so well—she loved without condition. Without question. That kind of love settles into your bones.

And now she's gone.

Like me, she was a wanderer. She showed up on Aaron's doorstep the same day I did—uninvited, unexpected. Like me, she had a spirit that resisted confinement. Even when she had a home, she craved the open door.

I know craving well. I've lived most of my life wandering: city to city, country to country—trying to outrun something I couldn't name. It's taken years, along with the strength of my husband holding me through crisis, and ongoing therapy. But I see it clearly now. I was living in grief. Not just grieving my mother, but the version of myself that died with her.

No one prepares you to lose your mother at five. No one tells you that grief steals more than just the person. It takes your sense of self. It rewrites your world. When she died, it was as if I stopped existing, too. My memories became echoes. Her touch, her laugh, the warmth of her presence—gone. And with them, the girl I used to be. The girl who was part of something...a family.

No. What they don't tell you is that when someone you love dies, you lose two people: them and the version of you who knew life with them in it. I had to grieve my mother, but I also had to grieve my old self.

For years, I thought I was searching for her. But really, I was trying to find the pieces of myself that shattered the day she left. I thought if I wandered far enough, stayed in motion long enough, I could stitch together the old reality. But the truth is that version of me is gone. She's not coming back.

What I didn't know then was that healing doesn't come from finding who you were—it comes from allowing yourself to become someone new. I only began to feel whole again when I stopped running and started letting people in. I still have a lot of healing to do, but I'll get there...slowly.

Elizabeth wandered, too. And now her journey's over. Mine isn't. Not yet. But I understand her. I honor her. She found her way into Aaron's life. Into Amara's. Into mine. She belonged—just for a moment.

And maybe that's the lesson. That belonging isn't always about time. It's about presence. About impact. Some souls brush against ours for only a heartbeat, and still, they manage to leave paw prints that never fade. Elizabeth didn't stay long, but she didn't need to. She reminded us that even the briefest connections can root themselves deep. That love—quiet, unexpected, fiercely felt—can arrive without warning and still change everything.

She was here. And that mattered.

***

It's raining. The kind of steady, quiet rain that makes the whole world feel hushed. Dark storm clouds crawl across the sky, thick and unyielding. The mood in the house mirrors the weather: heavy, still, gray.

Dinner passed in silence. Amara barely touched her food before excusing herself to write in her journal. That was hours ago.

I knock gently and ease the door open.

"Hey," I say softly. "You wanna talk?"

She doesn't answer right away. Just closes her notebook and lets her legs slip from the couch to the floor. I cross the room and sit beside her.

I glance toward the journal. "If I were writing tonight, I'd say I've never seen a fluffier, more beautiful gray cat than Elizabeth."

Her fur was the exact shade of the sky outside. But I don't say that part.

"I drew her," Amara whispers.

"Can I see?"

She opens the journal to the page with a carefully drawn portrait. Elizabeth is curled up at the foot of her bed, just like she was every night, marking our time together like the second hand on a clock.

My chest tightens.

"She looks peaceful," I say.

"Why does this hurt so much?" Amara asks, resting her head against my shoulder.

I wrap my arms around her. "Because we love with our whole hearts."

She pauses, then quietly says, "Are you going to stay?"

"Yes, sweetie. Aaron's stuck with me."

"And we'll always be a family?"

I nod, stroking her hair. "Yes. We're your family. And if you ever want to explore where you come from—either side—I'll be with you every step of the way."

She hesitates. "If they wanted me...they would've come for me."

My throat tightens. "I'm glad you found me."

She turns her face toward me. "You saved me."

"Oh, Amara...you are my saving grace. Amara. *Grace*."

And it's true. I don't know if I would've stopped moving...stopped searching. But she entered my life and everything changed. She anchored me—without even knowing it.

There's a soft knock. Aaron steps into the room.

"Any room for me in here?" he asks.

I pat the space on my other side. He sits and takes my hand, lacing our fingers together.

"How are you two holding up?" he asks gently.

"Reflecting," I say.

Amara surprises me by lifting her notebook toward him. "I drew this."

He leans in to look. "It looks just like her." His voice is thick with emotion. "We should frame it."

"Really?" she asks.

"Yeah," he breathes. "I miss her already."

"Me, too," Amara says.

"So do I," I whisper.

"When I was little," I say after a beat. "I used to believe it rained whenever someone felt sad."

Amara tilts her head. "Like the clouds are holding our tears?"

"Exactly."

"I think they released mine today," Aaron murmurs.

"Mine, too," I say.

Amara leans against me again. "They have mine, too. It might rain tomorrow."

Yeah. It might just rain again.

CHAPTER 42

Amara

Jasmine

MANY MEMORIES OF MY mom have blurred over time, softened by years and distance. But one remains sharp, etched in perfect clarity—my first day at school.

I must have been five. Mom had laid out several outfits on my bed the night before, each one ironed and folded with care. The fabric smelled like lavender and starch. She held each dress up with a hopeful smile, asking, *"What about this one, Jas?"* I chose the pleated blue one, not just because it was my favorite color, but because I knew she liked how it brought out the warmth in my skin. She told me once that she liked seeing me in clothes the color of jewels because I was precious. Even then, I wanted to make her proud.

That morning, both she and Dad took me. I walked between them, my tiny fingers wrapped around their hands, swinging gently with each step. I felt safe. Like nothing in the world could touch me as long as I was tethered to them.

When we reached the classroom, she knelt beside me, her hands shaking slightly as she adjusted my backpack straps. Her eyes brimmed with tears she couldn't hide, no matter how hard she tried to smile. *"Baby," she whispered, smoothing down my braids one last time, "we'll be back in a few hours." Her voice cracked.*

Dad was silent, his face calm but tight around the edges. He rested a steady hand on her shoulder, grounding her. It wasn't until I was older that I realized he was being brave for her—that his strength was something she could lean on in that moment, something I didn't understand at the time, but felt.

And now, all these years later, I find myself in her place.

Amara is leaving for university, and I'm the one trying not to fall apart. I've helped her pack, folded her clothes with quiet reverence, lingered too long on the little things: her favorite hoodie, her notebooks, the framed photo of the three of us on our first trip to Paris. I've triple-checked her documents, made a list of emergency contacts as if she doesn't have it all saved on her phone.

I keep telling myself she's ready. She's brilliant. She's steady. She's so much more prepared than I was at her age. But even with all that knowing, my heart is clenching in my chest like it's bracing for impact.

Maybe this is what my mom felt, kneeling beside me on that kindergarten floor. Watching someone you love begin their own story, knowing that your role in it is about to shift.

We're going to Paris. I'll help her settle in, stock her fridge, and fluff her pillows. I'll do everything I can to make it easier for her. But I know the hardest part will be walking away.

And I don't have to wonder who will steady me the way my father steadied my mom, because I have Aaron.

We know we'll see her during breaks and holidays. Still, it's a lot to process. We didn't have years to prepare for this like most parents—only a few months. Now, we're standing on the edge of a moment that feels like a new kind of beginning. Going out on her own is a big deal. Letting her go is even bigger. She'll be a freshman, then a sophomore, then a junior, and we'll be there every step of the way, watching her grow and carve out a future for herself. We'll support her in ways my mother couldn't support me.

The doorbell rings. I abandon my last-minute packing and head down to answer it, passing Martha, who's busily getting our house in order and ready to shut down until our return. After Aaron and I get Amara settled in Paris, we'll take a month-long vacation. Our first stop is the private hideaway owned by the Pages in the Netherlands. We're thinking of building something nearby.

When I answer the door, it's the courier. We're expecting the final documents for the foundation. I'm learning what it's like to work with my brother, what it's like to have a job where it's not just about me and getting things done in my own time. No, Jake is all business, all the time. I smile thinking about him.

Wow. I'm beginning the next phase of my life, and stepping into it is more exhilarating than any solo trip I've taken. I get butterflies just thinking about my future with Aaron.

"Thank you," I say to the courier, then close the door. I leave the documents in the foyer and head back upstairs.

I need to check on Amara; she's been in her room for a while. She found a few extra things of mine she wanted to take with her. She's grown up before my eyes, in the short time we've been together. I lean against the door frame and peek in.

"Knock, knock," I say. "Are you almost done?"

Amara steps out of the closet. "That's all for my clothes, but I can't find one of my journals."

I enter her bedroom and look around, searching in places where a secret journal might be. Her room is just as neat as it was the day we moved in. "I thought we packed them all. Did you check the library?"

"Yeah," she says, placing a finger to her lip. "I think I left it at Holborn. Can we check?"

"Sure. We can grab lunch while we're out."

"Can we eat at The Wolseley? I've never been."

"Sounds like a date." I pull out my phone and make a reservation. "Let's try their afternoon tea. If you're up to it, we can walk to the Holborn House from there."

She tilts her head. "You're being sentimental."

"How can you tell?"

"Because you want to walk."

I gently pull her into me. "Okay, Miss Know-it-all."

"I'm not gone forever. I'll be back home in a few months."

"I know, sweetie. I just...this will be the longest we've been apart."

"You keep saying you're a call away."

I laugh. She never fails to make me smile. "That's right."

It doesn't take us long to get ready.

Martha helps take down the luggage and store it in the foyer closet.

"Can you make sure Mr. Adler gets these? The courier dropped them off."

"Yes, Mrs. Adler."

Amara and I exit and head to the car. I ask Jeffrey to drop us at Wolseley. It's not far enough to put us off schedule, but far enough that we have to drive.

"We plan to do some walking in the area. You can head back to the house. I'll call in a few hours."

"Yes, Mrs. Adler. Let me know when you're ready."

The moment we step into The Wolseley, it feels like the city has dressed up for us.

The buzz hits first, a soft swell of conversation layered with the clatter of cutlery and the occasional burst of laughter. It's the kind of place that doesn't try to impress you. It just is. Grand without being gaudy. Confident without showing off.

My eyes sweep over the scene: the gleaming black and white marble floor, the towering columns like something out of a Viennese palace, and the chandeliers—opulent but not overdone—casting a soft golden glow that makes everyone look like they belong in an old film.

It reminds me of Paris, a little. Vienna, maybe. Places I'd run to when the world felt too heavy. But there is something unmistakably *London* about it too—sleek, reserved, quietly proud. A place that knows its worth.

Amara and I step up to the reception stand. A hostess approaches with a polite, quiet smile. I smooth a hand over my shirt, knowing that although we don't look like the people here, we *do* belong here. I may not be in the States, but I have a way of matching the energy in a room, and this one pulses with history, money, and secrets told over champagne. A vibe I know all too well.

"Reservation for two. Ross-Adler," I say.

"Of course."

Amara and I move past sharp-suited businessmen, discreet power lunches, and the occasional flash of diamonds on wrists lifting bone china cups.

This is the world I was born into. The world I spent years running from. Now it's the world I've introduced Amara to.

We take our seats on the elevated level with a view of the entire restaurant. The waiter leaves us with menus before disappearing.

"Are you nervous about school?" I ask.

"A little."

"You'll be fine. Like you said, we're only a call away."

"And a flight away, per Dad. He loves traveling by jet."

"Yeah, the train was a bit much for him. But he did good."

"Is that how you traveled before meeting him? By jet?"

"No. I traveled commercially. Of course, when I was in remote regions of foreign countries, I had a driver who knew the way, but nothing fancy, and certainly nothing my father would have approved of. Mostly mud-covered cars or Jeeps. The only time I flew private was with my family."

"Were you scared?"

"Sometimes. But that's part of the thrill. Constantly braving the unknown, never knowing what each moment would reveal, or whether I'd survive."

The waiter brings water to our table as we make our afternoon tea selection, then he disappears again into the kitchen.

"Do you miss it?" Amara asks. "Traveling."

"Sometimes. But every day since I returned to London has been an experience, and I'm excited to continue this journey. Honestly, being a wife and mother is a thrill in the best way."

"I was scared the day you found me."

"I know, sweetie. You'll never have to go through that again."

"What about people like Bane?"

I take a deep breath. There's no subtle way to say what I have to say. "Sweetie, remember what we talked about—about Jeffery and his role?"

"Yeah, he's not just a driver. He's our protector."

"It's the same with the people assigned to you. They've been given strict instructions. Anyone who tries to get to you won't have the chance to explain themselves. There'll never be another Bane."

She gasps. "What about—?"

"This is part of our life...*your life* now. We can't take chances."

"What if a guy likes me?"

"Dating?"

"Yeah."

"You're too young for that," I say, hearing my dad's voice in my head.

"I'm not saying now."

I soften my tone. "When it's time...when you're ready, your team will do a background check. Your dad and I have to clear them first. And we'll meet them, of course."

"Ugh. Seriously?"

"I know. It sucks. But I promise...it's not as bad as it seems. If you ever want to talk...call me. No matter what time it is."

She nods. She's smart. She may not want to hear it, but she gets it.

We've been on an accelerated learning curve these past few months. Me figuring out how to be a parent, a wife, a lover. Amara trying to figure out how to be the daughter of two parents the world knows. Trying to figure out how to transition from the shadow to the spotlight. If the conference was any indication of how she'll do—she'll be fine.

The tiered trays of colorful goodies arrive and our eyes widen at the decadent spread. The Wolseley definitely knows how to impress. Silver stands gleam under the soft lighting, each layer adorned with delicate finger sandwiches: smoked salmon on rye, egg mayonnaise with cress, and cucumber with mint, cut into perfect little rectangles. Fluffy scones, still warm, sit in the middle tier beside dishes of clotted cream and tart strawberry jam. At the top, an assortment of miniature cakes and pastries dazzle like jewels: rose-petal macarons, glassy fruit tarts, lavender shortbread, and the smallest eclairs I've ever seen. Every bit looks like it was crafted to be savored and admired. We don't hesitate to fill our plates.

As Amara and I enjoy our afternoon tea, we continue our conversation between sips of Darjeeling and bites of pastry. I savor everything: the food, these precious moments with her. I savor them the way I imagine my mom cherished each moment with us. And wonder if Amara sees it—the sparkle in my eye when I look at her. I remember the way my mom's sparkle made me feel seen. How just being around her made me feel safe. This is what I want for Amara.

When we finish brunch, we walk to Holborn, burning off some of the calories we'd eaten. Some.

"I'm going to check the bedroom one last time," I tell Amara, as she heads to the safe room.

I wonder how it feels for her to return here for the last time before she leaves. This is where our life together began. She hadn't been here long before we moved in with Aaron. I'm glad she has both of us.

I walk down the hall and enter the bedroom. I scan the room and double-check the storage. It is as clean as I left it. I don't know what leads me to the kitchen, but I go there. I look around, hand dusting the marble counter as I walk. This is where I had my first kiss with Aaron. The way he looked at me, with the promise of a lifetime in his eyes. I knew it then. When he kissed me, I had my first taste of forever. *He* is my forever.

I take a deep breath, holding back the tears of love I never thought I'd experience.

We're gonna have a good life. I can feel it in my bones.

I explore a few more rooms, then head back up the hall to the library. When I enter the safe room, Amara is flipping through the pages of one of her notebooks. I sit beside her.

"This is a picture I drew of my parents," she says, extending her hand, showing me the page.

As I examine the drawing, I see that she clearly has her father's eyes and her mother's full lips. I stare at the drawings, absorbing the moment. These are the people who gave her to me. It's as if my mom and her parents are somewhere sharing a secret. It's hard to grasp that it was through our losses that we found each other.

She gazes at me in a silent moment of understanding. She closes the book and bites her bottom lip. I open my arms and she fills them. I embrace her, rocking her, holding onto this moment—the one before we begin a new chapter in our lives.

My mom wasn't there to take me to first grade. But I'll be there to watch Amara graduate. Aaron and I...together.

CHAPTER 43

Feels Like War

Aaron

THE AIR FEELS HEAVIER this morning. Not unpleasant, just tinged with that quiet melancholy that comes with change. Soon, Jasmine and I will be empty nesters. It's ridiculous, really, considering it's temporary. We've agreed to have children in a few years, once we've wrung every last drop of adventure and intimacy from these early years of marriage. Not that we haven't already started. This morning was...conclusive proof.

But it's more than physical. We want the full stretch of each other. We want the slow mornings, the inside jokes that span continents, the arguments in foreign supermarkets over which pasta to buy. We want life, wide and unfiltered. Outside the predictable orbit of our London bubble.

Now, I'm at Andrew's house, perched at his kitchen island, sipping coffee and pretending this visit is necessary. He invited me over with some vague excuse about having something for me. But I know him. He's deflecting. Keeping me out of Jasmine and Amara's way while they get ready. He's entirely too cheerful about it, which makes sense—he's stepping into my shoes while I'm gone and it suits him more than he'll admit.

"Send this with our kiddo," he says, sliding a plastic container across the counter like it's a handoff in some covert operation.

"What's this?" I ask, lifting the lid.

"Just send it."

I inspect the contents. "Marshmallow Krispie squares. With chocolate chips." I smirk. "Since when did you become a homemaker?"

"Since I became an uncle," he replies, all smug and satisfied.

I won't say it aloud, he'll never let me live it down, but he'd make a phenomenal dad. I've seen how he is with Amara and Demetrius. Patient. Principled. A steady voice without being overbearing. They come to him with real questions, real worries, especially about heading to university younger than most. He listens. He challenges them. And when Amara clapped back at Bridgette, he was quietly impressed, though he later suggested a more strategic approach. Jasmine agreed.

Jasmine. God, I miss her already, and I left the house less than an hour ago.

She and Amara were still getting ready when I stepped out. I fish out my phone from my pocket, half-hoping to see a message from her. Nothing.

"So, when are you settling down?" I ask, trying to keep things light.

"No time soon. I have a big job ahead of me."

I laugh. "Don't get too comfortable. I'll be back."

He grabs two bottles of water from the fridge and tosses me one. "How's Jasmine holding up?"

"She's good. Mostly. Amara's leaving is hard. And...Elizabeth."

His expression softens. "Sorry to hear about that."

"Feels like I'm getting a crash course in family life: grief, pride, all of it at once."

"Anything I can do?"

"You're already doing it. And I know you joke about taking my job—"

"I'm not joking," he says flatly.

I laugh, hard. Shake my head. He lifts an eyebrow, dead serious. And maybe he is.

"I just wanted to say when the time comes...you're ready."

That shuts him up. For once. He nods slightly, and we let the silence stretch for a moment—not awkward, just full of things we aren't saying.

I check my phone again. Still nothing from Jasmine or Amara.

"You waiting for a call?"

"Just thought she'd have texted by now."

His eyes narrow. "What's wrong with your fingers?" I blink. "Text your wife," he says, grinning.

I have no comeback. I just do it.

Me: Hey. Just checking in. I love you.

I stare at the screen.

"Give her a minute."

"So, what's happening with this game the kids are working on?"

"You mean our interns."

"I like how you switch it up."

"We've got a prototype and development roadmap."

"You think this could go into production?"

"I recommend we give it some time. Let's see how Amara and Demetrius handle this over the next year. They've got to focus on school. If they demonstrate they can balance both, I'll talk to finance."

"Amara's been through so much in such a short time."

"She's getting help, right?" I nod. "And she has you and Jasmine. She's in good hands."

"Yeah, it's wild how kids bounce back."

I check my phone again. Nothing.

Andrew raises an eyebrow. "Man, call your wife. I'll give you some space."

Andrew disappears into some other part of his house. I tap the screen to call Jasmine. The call goes to voicemail.

Damn it. Where's my wife?

I call Jeffrey. He answers immediately.

"Boss."

"Where's Mrs. Adler?"

"I drove her and Amara to The Wolseley."

"Is the still there?"

"Checking now."

"What do you mean, checking? You should be outside waiting."

"Mrs. Adler asked to be dropped off with instructions that she was walking to her next destination and would call me when she's ready for pickup."

"Drop me her location."

I look at the screen, waiting for the GPS to signal her location.

"Mr. Adler...she's not tracking."

"What?"

"She's offline."

"That's impossible. Pull up Amara."

"Same."

"God damn it, Jeffrey, find my wife."

Andrew enters the room. "By your tone, I take it you're heading out."

"Jasmine's offline. So is Amara. I don't know what to think."

"If their phones are off, I'm sure there's a good explanation."

"What if she left?" My chest constricts just thinking about it.

"What are you talking about?"

"Our agreement has expired. Maybe she changed her mind."

Andrew puts his hand on my shoulder. "You give each other life. She's not gone. Go home, get your wife," he says with certainty. "And, Aaron, call me before you fly out." I nod.

He doesn't have to say it twice.

In the car, I attempt to reach her several more times with no success, then I call Jeffrey again.

"Any word?"

"None. Wolseley says she left thirty minutes ago."

Fuck. Where is she?

***

When I walk into the house, I'm a man on a mission. My chest is tight, my jaw locked.

"Jas," I call out, louder than I mean to. "Jas, you here?"

Silence answers me. I move through the living room, past the family room, into the hallway like a man chasing a ghost. My voice bounces off the walls and falls flat. My heart is pounding now, faster with every step.

Martha appears from the library, dust rag in hand. Calm, composed as always.

"Good afternoon," she says with a polite nod.

"Martha, have you seen Mrs. Adler?"

"She left earlier with Amara. Jeffrey drove them."

"Did she...did she say anything when she left?"

"Yes," she says, stepping back into the library. A moment later, she returns with a large envelope and places it carefully in my hands. "She said to make sure you got this."

My breath leaves my lungs. I stare at the envelope, thick and official, stamped with the logo from our attorney's office.

No.

No, no, no.

This is it. The ending I've been dreading since the beginning.

Our agreement was always temporary. Just until Amara was in college. That was the deal. Six months. Half a year to play house, to pretend, to lie to everyone—myself most of all—that this could ever last.

But I believed her. God, I believed her. She told me she loved me. She whispered into my mouth, into my skin. She looked at me like I was hers. Said she'd stay. And I let myself hope—like a fool.

My heart sinks. My throat closes. I feel like I'm drifting, like the floor beneath me is shifting, and I can't get my balance.

She's leaving. She's really leaving.

She can't be. *We're in love.* My heart tells me as I let the mantra play in the back of my mind, seemingly against odds with reality.

I grip the envelope like it might bite me, like opening it would tear the ground from beneath my feet. I can't do this. I can't watch her walk away. Not her. Anyone but *her*.

Then the sharp click of the front door latch grabs my attention.

It opens, and in walk Jasmine and Amara—windblown, flushed, whole.

Relief hits me like a freight train. I'm moving before I even realize it, crossing the room in long, desperate strides.

"Jas," I say, voice rough. "Honey...what happened? I—I thought."

I pull her into my arms, clutching her like she's air and I've been drowning.

She pulls back slightly, brows drawn. "What happened? I just got your texts. They all came through at once. We rushed home."

I glance at the envelope still clutched in my hand. "I thought—God, I thought you were gone."

She frowns, then gently takes the envelope from my hand. "We can deal with this later."

"What?" My brain is still in pieces. "I don't understand."

"I don't want to deal with the foundation stuff right now," she says, tossing the envelope onto the console table. "Let's get Amara settled."

I blink. "Foundation?"

She smiles softly and leans in closer, dragging her fingers through my beard like she's grounding me. "You thought I was leaving?"

I don't respond. I can't. My throat is still too tight. My chest feels cracked open.

She huffs a low laugh. "You're everything to me, Aaron. I'm not going anywhere that you aren't." Then she leans in, her voice a wicked promise against my ear. "And you owe me tonight for thinking differently. I don't want to be able to walk tomorrow."

A groan escapes my throat as I drag her into me and kiss her hard. I don't care that Amara's here. I don't care that the staff is here. I kiss her like I've just returned from war. Because that's what it felt like...losing her, even for a moment.

She came home.

She's still mine.

CHAPTER 44

Hello, My Life

Jasmine

TODAY HAS BEEN ABOUT Amara. Getting her here, getting her settled, and watching the first bricks of her new life fall into place. She's standing at the edge of something entirely her own. A blank canvas full of firsts: new city, new school, new rhythm. The days ahead will be dense with learning—academic, emotional, social. She'll dive into theories and practice, make friends, lose some, and find herself toeing the line between being part of an elite world and simply existing as one face in the crowd. *If she wants.*

That's the part that matters most. She gets to choose.

When I was her age, I already knew how to navigate my father's world. I'd perfected the smile, mastered the pleasantries, learned the codes that opened doors and silenced questions. But I walked away from that. Not in rebellion. In clarity. I wanted to be known for something other than my last name—or not known at all. I wanted to get away from who I was and run toward who I could become. Even if I didn't know what that was.

So, I left, taking only my first name with me to places where it meant nothing to anyone. I didn't need a legacy there. I needed freedom.

Amara's coming from the opposite direction. Her name is beginning to carry weight—thanks to recent headlines, family revelations, and the whisper of expectations that follow privilege. People will start to know her. Or think they do. But she's not running. She's arriving.

She knows I can help her navigate both sides of the coin because I've lived on both. And she has Aaron, too—seasoned in the subtleties of high society, fluent in the language and its silence. Between the two of us, she's not alone as she sketches the outline of her future.

She's the architect now. She gets to decide what kind of life she wants to build. Whether the ceiling needs to be higher, the doors fewer, the windows wider. Whether the floors are wood or stone or something entirely new. No one gets to choose that for her. Not the family name. Not the headlines. Not society.

Only her.

Now, as we stand at the threshold of her Latin Quarter apartment, holding her close...I step back, releasing her. It's symbolic in more ways than she can ever understand. Aaron's hand is on my shoulder just as my dad's was on my mom's that day in kindergarten. It hurts...real bad. But still...I'm clinging to this feeling with everything I have because being this close to Amara is the closest I've been to my Mom since she left. This is how she must have felt then. I feel it in my bones like I know it's going to rain. This is how she felt right before she closed her eyes and took her last breath.

I try to hold it together, to no avail. Hot tears stream down my face. I blow out a breath.

"Okay, baby, I love you. Call us if you need *anything*."

Aaron pulls Amara into a hug, kissing her forehead. "We'll be here through the end of the week."

Amara smiles, trying to be strong for me. "Okay, Mom, Dad, I will. I'll be fine. I can't help but be. Randy's going to kill anyone who comes near me...remember?" she says flatly.

I laugh through the tears. She's right. Our security team assigned the hottest-head but most well-trained person to her.

"You're right, baby. I'm going for real this time."

We turn, exiting the apartment, and I listen as the door latches behind us. Aaron laces his fingers with mine and leads me to the car in silence. For the entire fifteen-minute ride to the Four Seasons, I rest my head on his shoulder, never looking up until he helps me from the car.

It's late. I want to drink and push out the feeling of loss, but I also want to savor it. This is my life. This is my choice. I chose to get her to this moment...this...this is the price.

I still haven't said anything when we arrive at the penthouse. The second the door closes, Aaron pulls me into him, gently tips my chin, and searches my eyes. I don't know what he's searching for, but I know what he finds Love.

"How can I help you through this?" he asks. He dips his head and dusts his lips against mine.

"You already are. You love me."

He presses his lips to mine and kisses me, deeply, fully. He literally takes my breath away. When he breaks the kiss, he smiles against my lips.

"Get ready for bed. I'll order us something."

I take a shower, and by the time I'm done, there's fruit, treats, champagne, and an assortment of tasty distractions waiting. I eat a few berries and a cute little French cake. Aaron's sitting on the couch, one arm stretched across the back, the other with his phone pressed to his face on a call being debriefed by security, no less. Making sure they are on top of everything. They are.

I fill a small plate with treats, then cross the room and sit on his lap, a knee on either side of him. I feed him a strawberry.

"I want daily reports." He cups my cheek and rubs his thumb across it "Yes, my daughter knows," he says, staring at me. Then he ends the call.

"You're a good dad. Sometimes controlling in—"

"You want me any other way?"

"Not at all. I was going to say in a good way. You're controlling when it matters. I fell in love with you. Amara needs a father like you. *We* need you."

He may be controlling, but he's not controlling us, he's protecting us. Controlling the things that might break us. Clearing the way of obstacles, of danger, of things...of people that would destroy us. In doing so, he's making space for me to be wild and free. Allowing me to just be...me.

As for Amara...he's opening a clear path for her to flourish.

I set the plate on the side table and rest my head in the space between his shoulder and his ear. My favorite spot. It's warm. His scent envelops me. I can just eat him, and I do; I gently bite his neck, sucking his skin in the process. His body responds beneath me, and I smile against his skin. He's mine.

"Today was hard," I whisper in his ear.

"For me, too. We made it through."

I kiss his ear, cheek, his eyes, his forehead. He laughs. He's happy. He knows me. He knows I want him.

"I'm sorry about today. Amara and I were in the safe room. We got lost in memories. I should have told you before we went in."

"You're here now."

"I hurt you."

"No. I need to trust our love. I knew deep down you wouldn't leave, but..."

"It was confusing. I can see how it looked...from your perspective."

"I love you, honey, since the day I met you."

"You called me your wife. That day and every day since."

"Something inside me knew. Walking in with those fiery eyes and restless energy, you couldn't be anything else but *my* wife."

Aaron holds my gaze for a moment. He gently presses his thumb to my bottom lip, opening my mouth, then covers it with his and licks into me.

Our kiss is wet and messy, and I swear my insides are already pulsing with need for him.

When he breaks the kiss, we're panting.

"Marry me," he breathes.

I nod in succession, tears streaming down my face. "If my husband's okay with it. I will."

The gray storm clouds in his eyes are glazed with unshed tears. His love for me is always unmistakable. Always on the surface.

"Yeah, I'll have you as my wife, again and again, for as long as you'll have me."

"Yes. I'll marry you, Aaron Adler."

I lean in and kiss my husband, savoring every bit of him, his touch, his scent, the way his beard grazes my skin. The way his need rises against me.

Without breaking the kiss, he stands, carrying me with him to the bed. He breaks the kiss and lays me down in the center of it. Slowly, he takes off everything, his shirt, shoes, pants, all of it, and I watch all six-foot-five of my man as he gets ready to take me. Because I want to be taken. I want him to claim me as his wife. Over and over again. I want to be full of him...full of his love. I want to remember the feel of him between my thighs for weeks to come.

My body pulses at the sight of his length...I'm ready for it all.

He crawls up my body, and I widen my legs.

"Ready?" he asks, lowering his hand between my thighs, slipping it between my folds, and stroking me. "Perfection." He licks my lips. My body clenches around his fingers.

He removes his hand, and like he did on our first night together, he positions himself at my entrance. Slowly, deliberately, he pushes in...and claims me. All of me. Not just my body, but the fragments I once scattered across continents, the pieces I thought no one would ever bother to gather.

I. Feel. Everything.

Every nerve ending ignites. Every breath is a sacred prayer. Every movement is a memory etched into my skin.

Seven years ago, I left home...searching. For freedom. For meaning. For something unnamed and intangible. But I didn't know then that I was searching for *me*. Not the version shaped by legacy or expectations, not the girl molded by grief and privilege, but the woman I'd become only when I saw myself reflected in his eyes. Clear. Unwavering. True.

Love does that. It strips us bare. Tears away the blinders and the walls we build brick by shaky brick. It dismantles the façade we wear like couture, tailored to impress and deflect, hiding all the vulnerable, tender truths beneath. Love exposes. It demands. It heals.

And with him—this man, my husband—it's not just skin against skin. It's soul meeting soul in the quiet, sacred space where fear used to live.

Aaron is exactly what I needed. Somehow, through divine intervention, we found each other.

He's everything.

He's my friend, my protector, the love of my life...*my husband*.

Forever.

For always.

For real.

Epilogue

Family

Jasmine

Six months later

"We don't have time, honey. We need to get ready." Aaron says, stepping into the closet and tugging off his charcoal Henley.

I trail behind him, not ready to let go of the moment.

Since we touched down in San Francisco, it's been one social obligation after another: dinner last night with the Blumbergs at a hilltop villa with far too many forks, breakfast this morning with Dad and Jeannette at a rooftop restaurant, and drinks this afternoon on the Pages' balcony overlooking the bay. Tonight, the final stop on our family tour—Dad's house. June and Aedan are hosting a birthday party for baby King, who somehow is already one. It'll be the first time we're all in the same place.

The first time *I've* been in the same place.

Years of chasing freedom meant missing out on milestones. I was always somewhere else, collecting stamps in my passport while trying to make sense of who I was. I didn't know that finding myself would look like this—his shirt crumpled on the floor, his jeans half undone, and our life braided together so seamlessly that adventure doesn't feel like escape anymore. It feels good. Freeing.

The only person missing from the mix is Amara. She's deep in the thick of her coursework, practically buried in books and lectures and whatever else they throw at university freshmen these days. In between...she works on game development. I get it. She's focused, determined, trying to build something for herself. We still do our weekly video calls, though. Sometimes we even manage to loop in the rest of our siblings, turning it into a loud, chaotic mess of overlapping conversations, inside jokes, and screen freezes. But I know they miss her, too. We all do.

That said, we definitely got our Amara fix back in December when we hosted the Ross-Adler family Christmas. She was home for the holidays, full of stories and her unmistakable humor, but there was something different about her, too. She seemed calmer, more thoughtful, and maybe even a little wiser. It's wild how just a few months away at school can do that. She's still Amara, but she's growing up right in front of us, and I feel this strange, proud ache watching it happen from a distance.

Aaron tosses a fresh t-shirt onto the dresser beside me, pulling me out of my thoughts and back into the closet. Back to focusing on how handsome my man is.

"You said that this morning before we met Dad for breakfast," I say, shimmying out of my jeans and tugging my sweater over my head. "We had time."

Aaron takes off his jeans, one brow cocked. "Did June say we had to wear all purple or just something purple?"

"Something purple." I grin. "I was thinking that short paisley wrap dress."

His eyes flick down my body, his mouth twitching. "That'll do nicely."

I step into his space, curling my arms around his neck and rising on my toes. He lifts me easily—God, I love how strong he is—and sets me down on the edge of the dresser. Cool wood meets the backs of my thighs.

"The wrap dress," I murmur. "You get handsy with me in that one. Honestly, that might be the *best* reason to wear it."

He plants one hand beside me on the dresser, trapping me, his mouth hovering near mine. His voice is low and wicked. "Aedan's going to kill us if we're late. Well, me. You could show up two hours in and still get hugs and compliments."

"He's your friend. He wouldn't dare." I run a finger down his chest. "Fifteen minutes max."

He barks out a laugh. "One hour. Minimum. You know better."

Aaron cups my chin, and the kiss he gives me is slow and deliberate, the kind that builds and builds until I feel weightless. Breathless. My eyes flutter closed. I sigh into his mouth as he deepens it—his hand sliding to the small of my back, pulling me closer until there's no space between us. Then he lowers his hand down the curve of my hip, beneath the edge of my panties, and slides them down and off in a single motion. His fingers find my center, testing me.

The way he touches me, possessive yet caring—it sends a thrill through me. He knows my body, honors it, and still explores it like it's new every time.

"God, woman," he mutters, voice rough. "One hour. I take my time. Paisley dress. No underwear. And if the mood strikes you while we're out...you have to use your indoor voice."

Yes. I bite back a smile. He's learned to speak fluent Jas.

We've made something between us that feels as wild as it does steady. I've drawn him out of his button-down shell just enough to keep things interesting—and in return, he's shown me that home isn't a place. It's a person.

My life is slightly different now, but in a good way. He bans skydiving. Says I have too much to live for. No more death-defying ski trips or impulse base-jumping invitations. But I still get my thrills.

Like the Seven Stars Kyushu train in Japan.

That night was silk and steam and moonlight gliding across lacquered windows. The train was a palace on wheels: dark wood paneling, gold trim, and velvet armchairs that rocked gently with the tracks. I wore nothing but a silk robe and the glow from the paper lantern beside our bed. The scent of cedar mingled with the faint trace of vanilla oil on my skin.

He made love to me as the train carved through mist-laced mountains, cherry blossoms swirling past like confetti. The rhythm of the wheels echoed his name under my breath. The world blurred outside, but inside, time slowed. Just us. Just this. Just our love.

"We *had* this discussion," I say now, breathless from his touch, drunk on the memory, body craving him. "My outdoor voice *is* my indoor voice when it comes to this."

"You don't really want your dad to hear you scream my name, do you?"

"Okay, library first floor. You're gonna have to kiss me through it." I whisper, breath catching.

"Deal."

Before the word even settles in the air, he lifts me, his hands sure, his mouth already back on mine like he's starving. And he carries me to bed like he owns every second of the next hour. Which, technically, he does. It's part of the bargain. An hour before the party. Just one. He intends to spend every minute of it thoroughly, devoutly, and without apology.

And he does.

Every touch is deliberate, every caress laced with intent. He makes good on his promise, mapping me with his hands and mouth like he's afraid to leave any inch untouched. I lose track of time, of breath, of everything but the feel of him. *Oh my God*, when he enters me.... His skin, his voice, the way he says my name like it's the only word he knows. He doesn't just take his hour—he consumes it, devouring me and leaving me trembling and entirely undone.

When we're finally spent, we shower, steamy and quiet, like we're trying to pretend we haven't torn each other apart. I towel off, put on my lotion, and slip into the paisley dress he likes. No underwear. That part isn't for him. That part's for me. For the delicious, reckless thrill I know will follow.

Before we walk out the door, he pulls me into him. "You good?"

"So good."

We get in the car. As expected, he can't keep his hands to himself the entire ride across town. His palm skims up my bare thigh like it's drawn there by instinct, like he's checking to make sure I kept my promise. I did. Of course I did.

And I love it. Every teasing graze, every stolen touch. I love how he can't help himself around me.

"Is it possible to love my wife too much?" he murmurs, fingers still exploring, eyes fixed on me like I'm both the question and the answer.

God help me, I hope not.

***

Aaron

The last time I was here seems like a lifetime ago. It wasn't. It's been a little over a year...not quite two. Reed's birthday party. That was the day June told Jake she was in love with Aedan—not me. We didn't have to tell Reed...he guessed it. Something about the look in her eyes gives her away.

Now, walking into the courtyard of the Ross home, filled with family and friends...I know they see it. The way Jasmine and I look at each other...cling to one another, like we're each other's everything—because we are.

"Baby girl, Aaron. Come on over here." It's uncanny how easily I can distinguish who he's referring to when using the term of endearment. There's a different ring to it when he's talking to Jasmine. Quieter.

With my hand resting on the small of her back, I guide her toward him. "Hey, Dad. Did Uncle Rick make it?"

"Yeah, baby girl...He's here. Make sure you talk to him. He's still a little sensitive because you're not joining the firm, but he gets it." He pats me on the shoulder. "I have something for you," he says, pulling something from his pocket.

He hands me a gold envelope. Jasmine's envelope. The last one I sent.

"Is that mine?" she asks.

"He's your husband now. Let him do the honor."

"Thank you, sir. I will." I take the envelope and slide it into my pocket. The significance of his gesture isn't lost on me.

June and Aedan walk over and join us. "Hey, you two," June greets.

"Jasmine, mate...it's about time you two made an appearance."

Jasmine gives me a knowing look that makes me want to take her upstairs, lay her out, and feast on her. I hold the thought.

"Hey, King. June." I give June a kiss on the cheek.

"Baby girl," Reed directs his attention to June. "Where's my young King?"

"Inside with Rick and Rose swooning over him."

"As well they should be. I'm going to get the little King." He announces before disappearing inside.

"Come on, Jas. Let's go see what they're up to." June grabs her sister by the waist, following the path Reed just took.

"It's good to see you finally settled, mate," Aedan says.

"Feels good. Different."

"I'm happy I don't have to kill you."

I bark out a laugh. "Like you could. Anyway. I see June is happy, which means *you* get to live to see another day."

"It's strange how our lives intertwine. I never pictured this."

"Neither did I, but I'm happy. Jasmine's happy," I say.

"I have one claim over her that you don't," he says with a wry grin.

"Don't make me kill you at your kid's party."

He laughs. "It's not that serious, mate. I met her before you."

282

He's not wrong. I may have loved his wife long before he did, but he met mine long before me...he was one of the lucky ones, like catching a glimpse of the elusive gazelle.

"Yeah, but I married her."

"Have you started planning?"

"Family?"

"Yeah. More kids. You have a little experience under your belt with Amara. That's no small feat."

"We talked about it. Right now, we're enjoying ourselves."

"I get it, mate. Take your time."

"Well, well." JR's voice rings bold yet breezy. "The Adler and King dynasty...hopefully not clashing."

"It's all good, mate." I pull JR into a shoulder bump hug. "Talking about dynasties. When are you starting your own?"

"Not even thinking about it," he says.

"The way June's best friend keeps eyeing you—," Aedan chimes in.

"I think we have enough of siblings' best friend scenarios happening here to last me a lifetime...literally."

I laugh hard. "Hey, I make no apologies for falling in love with your sister."

"Same," Aedan says.

JR shakes his head. "Let's talk about something else."

"Like the baby June and I made." Aedan smirks.

"See, this is the problem. I can't disown you two."

"Okay, okay. We're done. Let's go celebrate, baby King." I say, cutting him some slack.

I love my friends, and I especially love the camaraderie. Does it make it a little strange that we're all part of the same family now? A little. Does it strengthen our bond? A lot. It feels good...right. We belong together. We are a dynasty. Adler. King. Ross. And there's no stopping us.

My friends who've become my newfound family and I head inside. Jasmine joins me at my side as soon as I enter...and I'm home. Wherever we are together is home.

***

Aaron

We've had a long day hanging out with our family and friends. All brought together by a one-year-old. The way our life has unfolded is short of a miracle. Kismet, JR calls it. Whatever it is, I'm happy.

Now it's our time alone. I'm lounging on the couch, whiskey in hand, when she walks in like sunshine on a rainy London day.

"What you got there?" I lift my chin.

"Cake."

"Beneath the plate."

"Your letter. Can you read it to me?"

She strides across the room and takes her usual position on my lap. I love my woman. Every soft, curvy, beautiful inch of her. I lean past her, setting my whiskey on the table. I hold her hips, helping her settle in. I feel her heat through my silk pajama pants, tempting me to toss her on her back and dive in. But I don't. Not right now.

She eats a forkful of cake.

"Are you sharing?" I ask. She nods. Then she dips her head and kisses me. I don't hesitate to lick right into her, savoring the taste of my wife mixed with butter cream frosting. When I have my fill, I break the kiss. "You want me to read it now or after?"

"Now. I want to hear a letter in your voice. The way you meant it to be read."

Gently, I take the gold envelope from her hand and slide the letter out. She sets her plate on the table and leans against me, chest to chest.

I take a moment, allowing her heart to sync with mine. Then, I read it out loud, channeling memories of the day I wrote it.

"Hi Jasmine,

"I hope wherever you are, the sun warms your face during the day, and the stars light your path at night, because beyond all that, I believe she's still with you. Watching. Protecting. Loving you in ways words can't quite hold.

"Your sister is with me in London today. She came as my plus one for a keynote I delivered this afternoon. Someone snapped a photo of us. It looks like we're deep in conversation, all serious and reflective. But the truth? We're plotting our escape from dry chicken and watered-down cocktails.

"I'm sure you've already seen the other picture. Me and JR on a video call. He misses you. They both do.

"We've never met, you and I, but your absence has a weight to it. It lives in the quiet spaces between moments with them. Sometimes, being around the two of them feels like standing at a table missing a leg. Still functional, still standing, but a little off balance. A little less steady than it could be. Maybe one day, the fourth leg will find its way back, and everything will feel whole.

"Until then, be well. Be strong. Be you.

"Wherever you are, don't forget—you're still deeply loved.

Aaron"

Today I stood at that table. It was strong and steady. Because of her. *Jasmine.* She's here. With me. Today. Tomorrow. Forever.

***

Jasmine

Five years later

Somewhere in the background, my phone is buzzing. I don't care. My only focus is—

"Oh, God. I'm..."

I don't get to finish. Aaron thrusts once...twice, and I splinter beneath him.

"Aaron," his name falls from my lips like I'm worshipping him. My back arches from the pressure and pleasure of it all. My walls pulse around him.

"I got you, babe."

He continues pumping in me, drowning out the buzz...chasing his own release, and sending me over the edge again. We come together in a cacophony of grunts, screams, and bodies clashing in sweat.

"Jas."

He rolls on his back, pulling me onto him. Holding my hips in place, keeping his precious seeds from slipping out. I told him I wanted one more kid. Including Amara...that'll make four. Together, we'll be a family of six.

My body holds on to his thick length within me like my life depends on it. The texture of his skin pressing against my walls reactivates me. I place a hand on his chest and another holding his length in place, not wanting him to slip out. Not wanting to stop. Chasing more of him. I begin to move...rocking against his shaft.

"Babe," he pants, holding my hips in place, thrusting up.

I smile down at him. We can't help ourselves.

Then the buzzing starts again.

"Who the hell is calling?" He grunts.

He rolls me on my back and pumps into me hard, fast, deliberate.

It doesn't take long for us to come together again.

This time, he doesn't pull me over him. He lies on top of me. I'm so full of him and his love that the evidence runs down my thighs between us.

When our breathing comes under control, he sits up, pulling me onto his lap.

"You'll be having our baby in nine months. We might have twins this time."

I laugh. When I do, a little more of our love spills. "Okay, handsome. But I'm gonna need you to do that four more times today."

"Five."

"Fine. Five."

I reach over to pick up the phone to see what's happening. Between our family businesses and the foundation, there's always something. My screen lights up with several messages. The only one I'm interested in? *Andrew.* He's the pulse of our families.

Andrew: Have you two seen this?

There's a link to an article. I don't bother to read the entire thing before I hand the phone to Aaron, who, like me, only reads the headline.

"An unlikely pair. Amara Ross Adler and Beau Bromley."

"Amara," Aaron screams her name so loud that I almost fall off his lap.

"Babe, don't wake the kids," I whisper-shout.

I lift my hand to cover his lips, but he gently grabs my wrist, laying my hand flat on his chest.

"Amara Julisha Ross Adler. Get. In. Here. Right. Now."

I slide off and next to him, pulling the sheets over us. I should be upset, but I just shake my head and laugh. This is *our* lives. Forever. For always. Real.

THE END.

Thank you

Thank you for reading *London Calling*! If you enjoyed this story, I'd love for you to share your thoughts by leaving a review on Amazon, Goodreads, or your favorite book platform. Your support means the world and helps other readers discover the book.

If you'd like to see more of Aaron Adler, you can revisit where his story began in *Taming a King* or catch a glimpse of him in *The Days with Rain*, book 2 of the *Let It Rain* book series.

Thank you again for your support and for being part of this journey!

END NOTE: While London Calling is a work of fiction, student homelessness is a very real issue across the globe. The glimpse you see in this story only scratches the surface—reality is often far more dire. As a world traveler, I once found myself in a similar situation as the main character, moved by an overwhelming desire to help a homeless student I'd just met. If you'd like to learn more about the challenges students face both in the U.S. and the UK, here are a few resources/articles to read:

'Invisible' crisis: Student homelessness in CT hits record-high, advocates fear more are at risk

California's hidden homeless children: living in garages, doubled-up and unseen

Private landlords and hotels 'cashing in' on England's hidden homelessness crisis

Want to help in your local area in the USA? Contact your school district's local homeless education liaison, your national state level organizations, or dial 211 or visit 211.org to find local services and shelters in your community, including those that specifically help homeless youth.

Synopsis: London Calling

What started as a favor might be my forever.

I've built my life around control—my reputation, my career, my heart. But when a scandal threatens Saola Technology, the company my brothers and I built from the ground up, I need a clean slate to keep the vultures at bay.

Enter Jasmine Ross, the little sister of my two best friends and the last person I ever expected to marry. She's everything I'm not—wild, untamed, impossible to pin down. She's spent her life running from attachments, but now, she needs me just as much as I need her.

A fake marriage solves both our problems: I get my redemption story and she gets to stay in London to be the guardian of a teenager who's captured her fierce, wandering heart. It's perfect on paper.

But from the moment Jasmine walks into that London café, all fiery eyes and restless energy, I know I'm in trouble. Because this isn't just about saving face anymore—it's about her.

The more time we spend under the same roof, the harder it is to remind myself that this is pretend. And when the lines between what's real and what isn't blur, I start to wonder: will we survive the fallout if this all comes crashing down?

Because Jasmine isn't just my fake wife. She's the one thing I never saw coming. And now, I don't know if I can let her go.

Excerpt

Taming a King

She was born to rule his heart. He was sworn to protect hers.

In a world where fairy tales are nothing but broken promises, June Ross has learned to trust no one but herself. Scarred by a traumatic childhood event, she's built her life on the ironclad belief that love is a dangerous illusion and guards her heart with walls so high that even she can't see over them. But when a deadly threat from the past resurfaces, she finds herself under the protection of Aedan King, a hardened bodyguard with his own battle-worn past. Trained to take a bullet without flinching, Aedan never expected to be blindsided by the one mission he can't walk away from: breaking through June's defenses and convincing her that true love isn't a fairy tale—it's the most perilous adventure of all. With danger closing in, June must decide whether she's willing to trust someone else to protect her for the first time in her life, or if she'll let fear keep her from the only man willing to risk everything—even his life—for her.

"Taming a King" is a standalone, bodyguard, contemporary romance.

Excerpt

Taming a King

PROLOGUE

Fairy Tales

"We delight in the beauty of the butterfly, but rarely admit the changes it has gone through to achieve that beauty."
– Maya Angelou

June

I stopped believing in fairytales years ago. Long before my first kiss, I learned there is no such thing as a knight in shining armor. Before my first sexual encounter, I realized real princes don't exist. Years before my first heartbreak, I concluded that I'd never sit beside a king. Staring down the barrel of a gun, I learned that the only person coming to my rescue...was me.

Exhausted, I close my eyes.

The sun streams brightly through the shop windows, warming my face. I'm seduced by the soft lull of diners' voices surrounding me. Briefly, I glance at my watch and then turn to observe the patrons. Smiling faces, chopsticks in hand, conversations between bites—it all feels surreal. Though I'm in a restaurant, there is no scent hovering in the air hint-ing at the deliciousness awaiting me. That's how it is in Japanese restaurants—clean, calm, aesthetically pleasing, unsurprisingly good.

The warmth from the sun is suddenly gone, replaced by a shadow suspended above me. I turn, expecting familiar faces, but find the devil cloaked in a black hoodie instead. Before I can scream, a heavily tattooed hand clasps my neck and the touch of a cold steel blade converges with my cheek.

"Don't say a word," the deep raspy voice says.

I don't know if he actually says the words or whether they are a figment of my mind, forged from fear. Just as quickly as he appears, he's gone. The sound of a pop followed by the clunk of something collapsing captures my attention. I turn toward the sound; the walls are splattered with what I pray is sauce and the sound of a siren in my head overtakes me. *What's happening?* I can't stop the noise that sounds like the scream of electricity cutting through the silence when you're trying to sleep, only louder.

"No," I scream.

Mom?

Taming a King

Copyright © 2024 Rita A. Gordon

Playlist

Something in the Way // Jorja Smith
Butterflies (Demo Version) // Floetry
Lucky // H.E.R.
The One // PJ Morton
Midnight Love Affair // October London
Don't Let Me Fall // Cleo Sol
Hi (feat. India Arie) // Robert Gasper
The Call (407) // Devin Morrison & We Are KING
Trade It All // PJ Morton
Anything For You (The Duet) // Ledisi & PJ Morton
Sweetness (feat. Leon Thomas) // Elmiene
Through the Fire // Chaka Khan
Best Part (feat. H.E.R.) // Daniel Caesar
Like You'll Never See Me Again // Alicia Keys
Hey ! // We Are KING
I Found You // PJ Morton
Pandora: https://bit.ly/londoncallingpl
Apple Music: https://music.apple.com/us/playlist/london-calling/pl.u
-55D6XvlSJW84a

Acknowledgments

Writing Jasmine and Aaron's story was a true delight, though not without its challenges. Weaving in Amara's narrative while simultaneously exploring Jasmine's journey as a woman who lost her mother added layers of depth and complexity that at times were difficult to navigate. Although this story is entirely fictional, the themes and emotions it touches on resonated with me in ways I didn't expect.

A heartfelt thank you to Cassandra—your sharp editing skills and insightful feedback continue to push me to grow as a writer. I learn something new from you with every project, and your guidance means the world to me.

To my readers, your unwavering enthusiasm, support, and love for my characters fuel my passion. Thank you for joining me on this journey and for allowing these stories to become part of your lives.

To my ARC team, thank you for your continuous support and for being part of my writing journey. You assist new readers in discovering my work, and I am eternally grateful.

A special thank you to Janil and the incredible members of The Smut Peddler Collective. Your consistent support in promoting my work has meant more than I can express. We are bound by community, sustained by love.

And finally, to my friends and family who continue to cheer me on—thank you. Your encouragement is everything.

Love you all, Rita

About The Author

Rita Gordon is a romance novelist and former corporate baddie who writes Black and interracial romance stories where love triumphs. As an emerging voice in the contemporary romance genre, she brings an emotionally rich perspective to storytelling. Inspired by the power of love and the beauty of cultural exploration, her writing captures the complexities of the human heart, leaving readers spellbound with each page turn. When she's not busy tackling her TBRs and writing, she creates intricate floral illustrations for her coloring books, combining her love for detail and storytelling, travels the world, drawing inspiration from diverse cultures, and volunteers in her community.

To learn more about the author, visit **ritaagordon.com**.

Connect With Rita

Stay in touch! You can find Rita here:
SUBSCRIBE TO RITA'S:
Newsletter: https://www.ritaagordon.com/subscribe-page
Patreon: https://patreon.com/AuthorRitaAGordon
FOLLOW RITA ON:
Facebook: authorritagordon
YouTube: @AuthorRitaGordon
Bluesky: @authorritagordon.bsky.social
Instagram | Threads | Pinterest | X: @rgordonshaw
TikTok: @authorritagordon (ritagordonwrites)
Goodreads:
https://www.goodreads.com/author/show/21524163.Rita_A_Gordon

ritaagordon.com